MW01532053

COVERT Loves

COVERT Loves

A Novel

William Bowles

iUniverse, Inc.
Bloomington

Covert Loves
A Novel

iUniverse books may be ordered through booksellers or by contacting:

iUniverse
1663 Liberty Drive
Bloomington, IN 47403
www.iuniverse.com
1-800-Authors (1-800-288-4677)

ISBN: 978-1-4620-6360-4 (sc)
ISBN: 978-1-4620-5339-1 (hc)
ISBN: 978-1-4620-6361-1 (ebk)

Library of Congress Control Number: 2011960051

Printed in the United States of America

iUniverse rev. date: 11/04/2011

CONTENTS

Acknowledgement:

I would like to express my sincere appreciation to Colonel William Grace III USA (Ret) for his unswerving support and advice during the writing of this novel.

I would also like to thank Colonel Jim Morris USA (Ret) and Mrs. CJ Morris for all their assistance in the editing and formation of the novel. Their advice and encouragement was invaluable.

Glossary:

GERMAN:
Aldershorst: Eagles Nest
Auf Weidersehen: Goodbye
Bahn Hof: Train station
Bestimmt: For sure
Bemerkenswert Ahnlichkeit: Remarkable resemblance
Danke Schon: Thank you
Deustch: German
Du bist ein junger soldat: You are a young soldier
Estaunlich: Amazing
Du bist mein leipling fur immer: You are my darling forever
Frohliche Weihnachen: Merry Christmas
Fraulein: Single girl
Gasthaus: Inn
Ja: Yes
Kaserne: Military Post
Kommen sie heir: Come here
Leibling: Darling
Mach Nicht: It makes no difference
Mutter: Mother
Panzer: Tank
Prosit: Cheers
Sprechen sie Deutsch?: Do you speak German?
Strasse: Street
Verboden: Forbidden
Willkomen: Welcome
Wondershon: Wonderful
Zugspitz: The highest German peak in the Alps Mountains

Other:
AFN: Armed Forces Network

Ao Dai: Dress for Vietnamese women
Bacsi: Vietnamese for Medical Corpsman
BEQ: Bachelor Enlisted Quarters
Boonies: The swamps, jungle or forested areas
CID: Criminal Investigative Department
CPL: Corporal
CQ: Charge of Quarters
CSM: Command Sergeant Major
DOJO: Japanese gym
DMZ: Demilitarized zone
DZ: Drop zone for parachutist
EM: Enlisted man
EUCOM: European Command
Flying Twenty: Temporary pay of twenty dollars
Gig: Deficiency
Ground Pounder: Slang term for Infantry troops
KIA; Killed in action
LT: Lieutenant
LTC: Lieutenant Colonel
Land of the big PX: Army slang for the USA
Land of the Morning Calm: Historical name for Korea
Leg: Derisive term for non-airborne qualified soldiers
MAAG: Military Assistance Advisory Group
Maggie Drawers: Signal for missing the firing range target
MOS: Military Occupational Specialty
Nam: Short title for South Vietnam
NCO: Non commissioned officer
NCS: Net control station
NVA: North Vietnam Army
PFC: Private First Class
Punjii stake: Sharpened bamboo stake
Puzzle Palace: The Pentagon
PX: Post Exchange
Recon: Reconnaissance
SFC: Sergeant First Class
SFG: Special Forces Group
SF: Special Forces
SGM: Sergeant Major

The old Man: Affectionate term for a
Commander of any size unit
To Streamer in: When a jumper's parachute fails to open
XO: Executive Officer

CHAPTER 1

Welcome to Germany

"When she was sixteen, she was raped! She had twins, half-white and half-black they are what you called half-breeds." The grinding, grating, gravel voice of the First Sergeant echoed and reechoed in my mind. "She was raped, she had twins, and they are half-breeds." Over and over the voice droned on. I rolled over on my bunk. Finally, it eased up. How in the hell did I wind up in this situation? I'm ready to return home, and all I have to show for almost four years of service is three broken hearts. Still suffering the effects of last night's drinking, I recalled my arrival to Germany.

December 1948, I was a young soldier on guard duty. Standing alone beside the rail of the troopship I stared intently at the oily, gray seawater of the harbor as it splashed against the ship in the dim, dawn light. Slowly, shifting my weight from one leg to the other, I removed my hat. I wiped the accumulated pockets of snow from my hat and brushed it from my face. It was the first time I had ever experienced such heavy snow. Removing my gloves, I blew lustily on my hands rubbing them together quickly to restore circulation, and get some warmth back into my fingers. Just a few days ago I was drinking beer with a couple of other guys during my two week stay at Camp Kilmer, New Jersey, now here we are docked at a harbor in Germany.

They berthed the ship at the dock very late in the afternoon yesterday, but we were not permitted to disembark. I glanced down at my watch, four-fifteen in the morning. In two more long hours I'll be off guard duty, and off this miserable troopship, the USS General Rose.

It'll be great to get away from troops vomiting, vomit on the stairwells, in the latrines, or as the crewmen called it the head. To get away from the stench of unwashed bodies, and to walk on a solid surface that wasn't continually shifting and moving will be a pleasure.

In the growing light the buildings on the dock began to take shape, and through the swirl of snow and fog, I could see a huge dimly lit sign: "*Willkommen in Bremerhaven,*" then a second sign in English, "Welcome to Bremerhaven." So this is Hitler's Germany, and my first overseas tour of duty. I felt a growing sense of excitement. I'm cold and tired of this ship, but at least Hitler's dead, and his Third Reich just history. Thanks to the hundreds of thousands of Americans who came here before me, I didn't have to fear getting shot at, wounded or killed while in Germany.

I volunteered for the Army, but I would have been drafted if I hadn't. I want to travel to as many countries as possible. I want to see and experience everything that I can during these three years. If combat happens, then I want to experience that also. Most of all, when I return home I want to know exactly where I'm going with my life.

Glancing around the deck and seeing no one, I stepped behind the huge vent funnel and quickly lit a cigarette. I inhaled deep puffs, the smoke and cold air burned my lungs. This cigarette taste good. Screw the Corporal, he won't be up here he's probably sleeping. Besides, I owe it to myself for doing a great job on guard duty, even though I don't know what in the hell I'm guarding.

A couple more quick puffs and I dropped it on the deck, and grinding it out beneath my boot, No use taking unnecessary chances. Well Ken me boy, you got away with that one.

I walked over to the opposite rail where I could see men cranking up the huge cranes. MP's and other soldiers were on the dock talking to some of the civilians who seemed to be everywhere. Something was finally beginning to happen, for me not soon enough. I walked across to the far rail and stared again over the ocean towards home, watching the white caps and the rise and fall of disappearing waves.

I recalled leaving home, everyone kissing me, and I can still hear my aunt saying, "Bless your little heart, take care of yourself, you hear."

Out loud I spoke to myself, "Let's see what Germany and Europe is all about, and what this country and the Army has in store for me."

Glancing up towards the bridge, I saw the Corporal of the Guard heading in my direction. Pulling my collar on the old horse blanket overcoat higher around my neck I waited.

The Corporal stopped a couple of feet away, and with a silly grin on his face he asked, "How're you doing old soldier?"

I thought why you silly bastard, I'm freezing my ass off. Instead I said, "I'm okay, just glad to be getting off the ship today, and back on to some solid ground for a change."

He laughed, "We'll be disembarking shortly. You're released from guard duty. You can take off."

I immediately headed for the dining area, then changed my mind and went downstairs. The idea of getting off this floating toilet made Germany seem better with each step I took.

Quickly, I went down the stairwell and through the various troop compartments until I reached my compartment. My friend Kelly Grady, who was from my hometown, and had enlisted when I did was talking with some guys that I didn't know.

"Grady, have you eaten breakfast yet?" I asked

"Yeah, but it's not worth the trip."

"All I want is some hot coffee, some warm air, a couple of eggs and that'll do the trick," I said.

I left him standing there and walked to the mess area. It was crowded, but I finally got two eggs, a couple strips of bacon, and two pieces of toast. I placed my tray on the table and ate very quickly. At least the trays weren't sliding off the table. I quickly drank my warm coffee and lit one of my last two cigarettes. My feet began to thaw, and in short order I felt much better. I listened to a couple of guys on the other side of the table arguing about which subway to catch to go someplace. I had never seen a subway, there are none in Alabama. I really didn't give a damn which one they had to catch. I finished eating and returned to my compartment.

Grady asked, "Seen any Krauts?"

"Yeah, there're all over the docks. We should be getting off shortly," I replied. I checked my duffle bag to make sure all my clothing, shaving kit and boots were inside.

The compartment Sergeant hollered, "At ease!" All the talking ceased.

He said, "You will be disembarking in about thirty minutes. You are to get your bags and line up in the order I call your name."

He called a name and the guy would answer, "Here Sergeant." I listened closely to the roll call. "Rizzuto, Slymanski, Mullins, Roberts, Hodes, Amato," the names rolled on. My feet began to tingle the same way they used to when I was on the roof of a house, or barn, and when that happened I intuitively knew I should be on the ground

"Fisher, Kenneth Fisher," the Sergeant called, and looked around the area.

I don't know why I didn't answer, I just didn't. Then I called out "Here Sergeant." He looked at me with a look of sheer disgust. Sarcasm dripping from his voice, he said, "Don't you know your own frigging name? Get the hell out of here!"

I didn't reply, I lifted my heavy duffle bag, slung it over my shoulder and moved out smartly. On the top deck, the cold wet snow hit my face with a vengeance. I pulled my collar tighter, my service cap lower on my head, and moved slowly towards the gangplank. A Corporal called out the names and checked them off as we answered. I quickly went down the gangplank chute.

I glanced at my watch as I stepped onto the dock and into Germany for the first time. It was seven o'clock in the morning, December 2, 1948. I felt a little lightheaded but happy. I was young, eighteen years old, and the world and all it had to offer belonged to indestructible me.

After much milling around, lining up, roll calls and bitching, we finally loaded onto the big two-and-a-half-ton trucks, and began to convoy out of the dock area. We were informed we were going to the replacement center located in the town of Marburg, Germany. We arrived at the local train station, and after unbelievable shuffling around, roll calls and lining up again, we were directed to rail cars. The cars were much smaller than our American rail cars. The seats were little wooden benches, the windows small, soot streaked and dirty. Worse yet, the cars were cold, very cold. It had taken almost five hours to unload all the troops from the ship, and get them ready for further movement. I estimated there were about a thousand of us.

Finally, with a bellow of whistles, amid swirling steam, the train slowly pulled away from the station. We passed through dozens of small villages and towns without stopping. The countryside looked much the same, all snow covered. From the houses seen here and there, smoke curled out of the chimneys and was then whipped away by the wind. A few people could be seen out in the fields. Many others were following wagons that were pulled by oxen. We pulled into a station, and the train stopped for several minutes. Grady was hanging out the window talking with some young boys who were selling something. He didn't speak German, so he had to be using hand signals, or something similar.

He hollered back, "They're selling beer."

I gave him a thumbs-up. He gave one of the boys a pack of cigarettes and got two beers. Despite the noise and commotion I tried to read the local German signs. Something was V*erboten,* not sure what. That's all I could understand. Grady leaned back from the window as the MP's began chasing the boys away from the train. He handed the two beers to me, and I hid them inside my overcoat.

With a series of jerks, the train moved away from the station. We had been issued box lunches, so I checked mine out, two pieces of cold chicken, two slices of bread and an apple. Yuck! I shoved the box beneath my seat. I pulled the beer from beneath my overcoat. What a funny looking bottle, it had a hinged top with a rubber cap stopper. I popped it off and took a small drink. Not bad, not stateside beer, but not too bad.

Grady watched me and then asked, "How do you like the kraut beer?"

"Not bad," I replied, handing the bottle to him. Actually, I didn't like it, but guessed I was supposed to drink beer like everyone else. Grady took a big drink from the bottle, and then put the cap back on. Apparently, he has more experience in drinking than I do.

He and I talked for a while about the many things we had in common. Both being from the same home town, Lynell, Alabama, there was a lot we could talk about.

His family was a lot like mine, mill workers in the local textile factory and had lived in our town all their lives. It's a beautiful picturesque town situated on the state border between Alabama and Georgia. Alongside the town the broad, muddy Chattahoochee River meanders its way slowly south toward Columbus, then on to Florida. I thought, at least I'm away from there for a few years.

The train clattered along. I stared out the window and studied the countryside. It looked peaceful enough. But only three years and some few months ago, World War II was raging across Europe. Now here we are with no weapons, but no one's shooting at us. It seems sort of unreal to be here in what had been Hitler's Germany. I really wished I'd been old enough to get in on the fighting. I watched out the window as the snow continued to fall making everything appear uniformly white. In the late afternoon the temperature was sinking rapidly. The sky appeared more gloomy, grayer, and the snow thicker. I dozed off for a few minutes.

Grady woke me up.

"Here, take a drink of this." Grady handed me a bottle then introduced me to Sam Amato, a slim, young, nice looking Italian guy. Grady said, "Amato bought it from a conductor for a half-pack of cigarettes."

"What is it?"

"It's vodka," Amato replied.

I had a bad taste in my mouth, so what the hell, this should eliminate that. I'd had moonshine before, and this couldn't be any worse. I twisted the cap off turned up the bottle and had a drink. That crap hit my stomach like a punch from Joe Louis! Tears came into my eyes, and I could hardly speak. Grady and Amato both laughed as they each took a big drink to show me it wasn't that bad. I really didn't want any more of that stuff.

I borrowed a pack of cigarettes from Grady. A few of us stood in the doorway and talked about our home towns. We lied about the number of girls we'd screwed, and how easy basic training had been. In general, we talked and lied like hell about everything. It was fun and helped pass away the hours.

We stopped in a couple more towns and the same thing happened. Young boys on both sides of the train selling booze, and the MP's chasing them away. The kids must think the American Army is a bunch of alcoholics. I drank a couple of beers, felt rather silly and slightly drunk. That damn German beer packed a punch.

It was dark now, and the car was as cold as a whore's heart. The rickety train kept clattering along, the wooden bench becoming harder and harder.

The Sergeant came through our car and said, "Get your gear together; we'll be in Marburg shortly."

I was tired, hungry and cold. I figured a hot meal and a warm stationary bed would solve all my problems.

The train slowed down gradually, stopping at the station. Looking out the window I could see soldiers everywhere. We all stood up and slowly moved toward the exit doors. Grady was behind me, his face flushed, and talking a mile a minute. I knew he'd had too much booze for his own good.

The troops began to exit the train. I stepped out into about eight inches of snow. My duffle bag with all my earthly belongings seemed to weigh a ton. We were told to line up in platoon fashion. Our names were called off, then we loaded onto two-and-a-half—ton trucks.

After about twenty-five minutes of driving through winding city streets and up a long hill, we rode through an open double gate into a large quadrangle area. The trucks stopped. We unloaded and stood by the trucks. Our names were called off again, and we were told which building we were assigned to. Grady and I along with Amato were in the same group, so we entered the building.

Once inside a Corporal told us, "Go to the supply room, draw your bedding and find a bunk up on the second floor. Chow will be served in thirty minutes."

We went to the supply room, drew two sheets, one blanket, and one pillow and pillow case. We signed for it all and left for the upstairs bay area. Selecting a bunk in the open bay area I quickly made up my bed. A voice announced on the public address system, "Chow is being served in the mess hall on the other side of the quadrangle."

Grady put his sheets and pillow on the bed, and not even undressing lay down covering up with his blanket. In less than five minutes he was sound asleep.

Amato and I left Grady and walked to the mess hall where we had a good meal and some hot coffee. After eating we lit cigarettes and talked about our experiences on the ship.

"What's your first name again?"

Amato replied, "My first name is Salvatore, but people call me Sam."

"My first name's Ken, and I'm from Alabama."

"I hail from Buffalo, New York." Taking a puff on his cigarette he continued. "Before I enlisted I worked in a General Motors plant making cars for several months. After enlisting I took basic training at Fort Dix, New Jersey."

His friend joined our table, and Sam introduced us.

"John Roberts, I'd like you to meet Ken Fisher, Ken's from Alabama."

We shook hands and John said, "I'm from Saratoga, New York, Sam and I took basic training together."

Roberts was about five foot ten, slender with blonde hair and blue eyes.

A voice came over the loudspeaker, "No one has a pass. Anyone caught outside the post will be court-martialed, and sent back to Bremerhaven."

That threat alone ensured that I would remain on the post. We picked up our trays and emptied the food scraps.

Back out in the cold night air Amato said, "Roberts and I are going to the PX."

"Roberts, here's a couple of dollars, will you pick me up a carton of cigarettes?"

"Sure, what type do you smoke?"

"Camels," I replied."

It wasn't very late, but I could feel fatigue setting in. The ten day boat trip, the extra night on the boat, the long train ride, plus the booze coupled with the excitement of arriving in Germany began catching up with me. I wanted to sleep in a warm stationary bed.

Entering the building where I was assigned, a voice stopped me with, "Goot Evening."

I glanced around. The man who had spoken to me was small with light hair, middle aged and shabbily dressed, obviously a German

He stared at me for a couple of seconds, then said in heavily accented English, "Velcome to Deustchland."

"Thank you, I'm glad to be here." I moved on up the stairs. The next day I found out he was the building janitor.

Undressing quickly and selecting a towel out of my duffle bag from among my three GI towels, all dirty, I went to the latrine. I washed up, brushed my teeth, then headed back to my bunk. The bunk felt wonderful after the boat's canvas hammock. Somewhere on the outer edge of consciousness, I heard the faint mournful sounds of a bugler blowing taps. My last thought was of the little man who welcomed me to Germany. I smiled, and the day was no more. It faded into memory.

I heard the bugler playing again, but this time it was Reveille. I sat up and glanced over for Grady. He wasn't there. I picked up my towel, my last clean set of underwear and dashed for the latrine.

The loudspeaker came on, "All new arrivals are to be in the quadrangle in twenty minutes."

Damn, not enough time to take a shower.

I rushed shaving and cut my chin. I wet a small piece of toilet tissue and paste it over the cut. I drew on my dirty uniform, buckled my boots and headed out into the bitter cold morning air. A light wind lifted and shifted the snow around the assembly area.

We formed into a platoon formation. The Sergeant said, "You men will be staying here for two or three days until you receive your unit assignments. You will be assigned to the Big Red One, the 1st Infantry Division, or the Circle C Cowboys, the Constabulary, or to a EUCOM unit."

Some guy spoke up and asked, "What's a Eucom unit?"

The Sergeant laughed and said, "That's the European Command."

Personally, I didn't care which one I went to as it was still all new to me. I just hoped Grady would be assigned to my unit. He was someone from home, likeable and easy going. Besides, we both had a distinctive southern drawl much to the delight of Amato and Roberts.

We were marched to an office and told we could exchange our American money for script. Military script they informed us is the American money the army uses in Germany. I exchanged mine and counted it. I had twenty-four dollars and thirty cents. With most of the month still to go, I knew I would be hurting before January and payday rolled around again.

After the formation the Sergeant said, "Report back to your barracks and clean up the place."

My assignment was to sweep the floor which only took a few minutes with a big broom. Someone was playing a small radio. I heard the announcer say, "This is AFN, the Armed Forces Network." The station played Eddy Arnold singing "*Cattle Call.*" Country music is my favorite type of music. I guess that comes naturally being from the South. I finished polishing my boots and lay back on the bed. Sleep came easily. I woke up with the PA system blaring, "Fall out for Chow." I put on my overcoat and gloves and dashed outside for the formation.

At the mess hall I had a few bites and some coffee. I left and looked for Grady. I ran into Roberts.

"Have you seen Grady?" I asked.

Roberts replied in his distinctive northern accent, "Grady is in the beer garden up at the Post Exchange."

Roberts looked tired to me, his tall frame slumping as if his overcoat weighed too much. He needed a haircut as his blonde hair was curling over his ears beneath his two sizes too small service hat.

"Here is your two dollars back," he said.

"What happened?" I asked.

"I couldn't buy any cigarettes, I didn't have a ration card."

"Why in hell do we need a ration card in the PX?" I asked.

"I don't know, but that's what they told me."

I left and wandered over to the PX. It was crowded and the jukebox was blaring. I bought a 3.2% beer at the bar, and pulled up a chair at Grady's table. We spent the afternoon talking and drinking with several other GI's. I had at least two beers, I wasn't into heavy drinking.

One guy said, "Last night some guys went down the hill to the fence around the post where they met some whores who will put out for a pack of cigarettes."

Another guy spoke up and said, "There are holes in the fence, the women know where they are. It was as easy as falling off a log."

I had no cigarettes, but I could borrow a pack from Grady. Grady and I decided later to slip out that night, and dip our wicks in *Deustchland.*

After the evening meal we just hung around the building. A fog began rolling in becoming ever thicker, but the snowing had stopped. I figured in weather like this the trip is going to be a total failure.

"Grady, no decent whore will be out on a snow covered hillside at night in this snow and fog," I said.

"Who said whores are decent," he replied.

It was such an excellent response; I just shrugged my shoulders, "Then let's go."

Four of us left through the back door. Going down the steep hill we began to slip, slide, stumble and fall in the heavy snow. The fog was now as thick as red Georgia clay. When we finally reached the fence there were a few dim lights strung out alongside the fence which weren't much help. No women were in sight or hearing.

One of the guys moved several yards up and down the fence calling out, "*Fraulein, Fraulein,*" but no one showed up.

I quickly grew tired of this stupid escapade. "Grady, I'm heading back, this is dumb."

With each step back up the hill, grabbing bushes, sinking and sliding in the snow, I felt increasingly foolish. Finally, reaching the top I walked back into the barracks, took off my uniform, and then slipped into my bunk to warm up. I wasn't sleepy but it was after lights out, so I lay there wanting to smoke a cigarette. Then it occurred to me that I didn't have any cigarettes, so I couldn't have gotten laid anyway. I had never experienced oral sex either. I don't think the girls back in Alabama do such things. But the guys returning from the war had told me all about it; I felt it was part of being here, and my patriotic duty to participate in such activity. With the disgusting thought of no cigarettes, and not getting laid, I finally went to sleep.

Reveille began playing. Fully rested I jumped up, bright-eyed and bushy-tailed. I went to the latrine, shaved, showered, brushed my teeth, combed my hair and got dressed. Back in the bay I kicked Grady's bunk.

He moaned, "What time is it?"

"It's twenty after six."

He jumped up and raced to the latrine to get ready for the formation.

The PA came on, "Fall outside for formation."

After roll call the Sergeant said, "Some of you will be leaving today."

I ate more that morning than I had the day before, if I was going to catch another cold ass train, I didn't want to be hungry. After eating, we went back to the building and just hung around. I watched a couple of card games and wished we could leave.

The PA system came on, "Everyone fall outside with all your bags and baggage."

Excitement rippled through the group as we stuffed clothes and shaving kits back into our duffel bags. We fell outside in formation lining up in the quadrangle, and putting our duffle bags down.

The Sergeant began calling out names. About sixty-five names were called. He told them, "You men are going to the Circle C Cowboys." Then another eighty or so names were called. "You gentlemen are going to the Big Red One Division." He then called another hundred or so names, "You boys are going to EUCOM." He looked around, "The rest of you fall back into the barracks and clean it all up."

Grady looked at me, "I'll be dipped in shit, we have another day here."

Laughing I replied, "They're looking for the sorriest outfit in Europe to send us."

"You're probably right, that's just our luck," he muttered.

Moaning, groaning and bitching every step, we carried our duffle bags back up the stairs. Some PFC came into the bay area and assigned us specific work details. We had to strip the beds, turn in the sheets, and clean up two floors of the building. We also had to count the sheets and pillow cases and tie them into bundles. That wasn't too hard to do. Another guy and I went to the basement to count the sheets again as they were brought downstairs. Fifty to a pile, tying them up then the same procedure with the pillow cases.

We shook hands introducing ourselves. "Hi, I'm Ken Fisher."

He said, "I'm Jack Taylor."

Jack was a PFC, so I knew he had been in the army longer than I had. He was well over six feet tall, skinny, pale skin, and a very deep voice with a southern accent.

"I'm from Alabama, what's your home state?"

"I'm from Neon, Kentucky. I was in the army the last year of the war. I got discharged after the war and returned home. I went to work in the coal mines, and then I got into some trouble. The judge told me, 'Son, you have two choices, join the army or go to jail.' So here I am back in the army, and on my second trip to Germany."

After a short pause, he went on to tell me, "I was working in twelve inch coal."

The way he said it I think I was supposed to be impressed, or at least surprised. I had never seen any kind of a mine much less a coal mine. I tried to give an intelligent unintelligible answer such as "Wow, damn, no kidding," and other such noncommittal replies. At any rate we got along well. I especially enjoyed talking with him since he had been in the war and I hadn't. Finally, after all the sheets and pillow cases were counted and piled up we left and went over to the PX. He bought some writing paper, and a pack of chewing gum.

It had stopped snowing, so we returned to the barracks. Everyone was finished with their jobs, so card games, letter writing and bullshit sessions were the order of the day. We all went to lunch in a group, then back to the barracks to sweat out the next formation. I lay down on my bunk and drifted off in a light sleep.

I woke up with Grady kicking me on the sole of my boot. I sat up.

"Let's go outside, we have another formation," he said.

"I hope this time our names get called. I'm ready to leave this place," I replied. I put on my overcoat, cap and gloves, and dashed down the stairs.

The Sergeant said, "We have more assignment orders so listen up and sound off 'Present' when I call your name: Grady, Amato, Fisher, Taylor, Watanabe, Winters, Laney, Hodes," and about forty other names

We all answered, "Present," when our names were called.

He said, "All the men's names I called are assigned to EUCOM. You're going to Wurzburg Military Post to the 6087 SCU."

I asked him, "What's a SCU?"

He replied, "It's a Station Complement Unit."

I really didn't know any more after he answered me than before I asked. I didn't care, at least I would be out of here and assigned to a unit on a permanent basis.

"You'll all be leaving in about four hours," he said.

We marched off to dinner. In the mess hall I finally got around to asking Grady, "Did you get laid or not last night out in that ice and snow?" Since he hadn't volunteered any information I had to ask.

He hem hawed around and tried to play it up big, but then he came clean and told me, "No, there were no women anywhere around the fence, it was a total bust."

It was about what I figured. I was right, no decent whore would be out getting laid on a night like last night, it was too icy and snowy for such action.

We left the mess hall and went to the beer garden where we both had a couple of beers. A fight broke out between some guys I didn't know. The MP's showed up quickly and ordered everyone back to the barracks.

Many of the men were sleeping, but I wasn't sleepy, so I found a novel and read it for a while. It was dull and unexciting. I put it aside and walked over to Taylor's bunk where he was writing a letter. Another guy walked up and introduced himself as PFC Pop Warner.

He said," I have a bottle of Schnapps. Do you guys want a drink?"

We both quickly said yes. I had no idea what Schnapps was, I'd never heard of it. From his duffle bag he brought out a bottle, uncorked it, took a big drink, and passed it to me. I had a small swallow and almost threw up. I quickly passed it to Jack. He took a big drink and handed it back to Pop who capped the bottle.

Pop was a little shorter than me. He was thin, his eyes sunken in and his teeth were nicotine stained. He also had a nervous twitch that I found irritating. We sat on the bunk and began talking. Pop and Jack began swapping war stories. I just listened, fascinated to hear war stories from the guys who had lived them.

Pop told us, "I was hit in the head by a shell fragment in Holland and left for dead as my unit moved forward. When I recovered consciousness, I walked to the aid station by myself."

I noticed that he had a big mostly bald shiny spot on the side of his head. To me, that was another world they were discussing. I knew some of the weapons they mentioned, and some of the terminology, but the idea of getting shot or hit with shell fragments just didn't register. Pop or Jack could get shot but not me. I thought, boy, would I love to have been with these guys during the war.

The PA voice said, "Personnel leaving today be in the quadrangle with bag and baggage at twenty hundred hours. Strip your bunks and pile the sheets and pillow cases in the middle of the floor."

We all moved our bags out to the formation area and lined them up.

The PA blared, "Fall out for roll call."

After roll call we were told to get our bags loaded on the trucks that were waiting. That didn't take long. Our convoy moved out through the big gate and down the cobble stone streets arriving at the train station. We unloaded and had another roll call. We were assigned to specific train cars for boarding.

After boarding, like all good soldiers we lowered the windows and looked out to see what the hell was going on. With nothing but soldiers in sight, I closed my window to block out the cold air, and then sat down on the narrow hard bench seat.

Everyone was talking and calling out names, the usual type conversations I had learned to expect. We had been told we would arrive in Wurzburg the next morning, so another cold night loomed ahead. Finally, with a jerk, a blast of the whistle, through clouds of swirling steam, the locomotive slowly began to move away from the station. With the snow it was almost impossible to see anything except a few buildings now and then. It was mostly open country. It was now after one o'clock in the morning. I thought I'll catch a quick nap. I tried to sleep but I couldn't, so I began looking for and found Grady. He was sound asleep.

Roberts was awake and motioned me over. "I have some Cognac want to try it?"

"Sure."

He pulled a bottle from his duffle bag and took a swallow. I had never heard of Cognac, but figured what the hell. I had a swallow. The taste wasn't bad. Not as harsh as moonshine, but smoother than schnapps. We walked over to the doorway stood looking outside, and had another drink. We began talking. He told me that he joined the army to get away from home, and to show his folks he could make it on his own.

I told him I joined because the doctor told me I had to eat or die. We had another drink to my long life, and another to him making it on his own.

I was a little loaded and I knew it. I'd never been drunk before, but I knew I was getting close. Amato showed up with a couple of bottles of beer. I immediately switched to the beer. Taylor joined us, and then a couple of other guys showed up. We were having a ball when an MP walked up.

"Who's got the frigging bottle?" he asked.

Roberts spoke up, "I left mine at home when I got out of diapers."

We thought that humorous and laughed. The MP grabbed Roberts by the necktie jerking him up and snarled, "I'll bust your head wise ass."

Taylor, straightened up to his six feet plus height and reaching over grabbing the MP, then threw him against the wall. Then without saying a word slapped him on the helmet liner he was wearing. I was stunned.

Jack snarled at the MP, "Get the hell out of here, or I'll throw you out the frigging window, do you understand?"

The MP merely nodded, he realized that Jack was older and meaner than us, and had an air of authority about him. He mumbled, "Hold the noise down." He then left the compartment.

That was the last we saw of the MP. Roberts thanked Jack for his help. The fun had now gone out of our group, so we drifted back to our seats. I pulled my collar up around my neck and tried to sleep. I was hot on the inside, and freezing on the outside, finally I dozed off.

A couple of hours later I woke up, it was beginning to get daylight. My mouth taste like a Calvary Troop had camped out all night with all the horses taking a healthy dump in my mouth. I looked for my box lunch, but it was gone. Grady had his, so he gave me his apple to eat which helped a little. I bummed a couple of aspirins, and swallowed them with no water. I figured the booze in my stomach would dissolve them.

It was full daylight now, and more and more buildings were coming into view. Someone yelled out, "We're coming into Frankfurt." We had to change trains here for Wurzburg. Frankfurt was a large city and a major target for our Air Force during the war. I remembered listening with my grandfather to Gabriel Heater, a news commentator during the war on our Philco radio announcing the news about bombing Frankfurt and other major German cities.

The train slowed down, more tracks appeared alongside ours. Most of them were all torn up, many rails twisted and missing railroad ties. It was a big train station, and this would be my first look at a major German city. A Sergeant came into our compartment to tell us we would be changing trains in Frankfurt, and he would guide us to our next train.

Slowly, the train pulled into the huge station, it was absolutely stunning. The entire roof of the huge building was missing. Jagged sheets of metal and tin were hanging grotesquely from twisted girders. All the glass was missing. What few walls remained was full of shell holes. Piles of concrete rubble were everywhere. This was my first real exposure to the absolute destruction of war. Seared into my memory is the sight of the train station. What a contrast to Penn Station in New York.

The train finally drew to a stop. We gathered our duffle bags and shuffled towards the compartment doors. When I stepped off the train, a corporal told us to move it out. We moved across another track under a guard rail, and into a waiting car. It was identical to the first one, hard wooden seats and cold as hell. Like me, the train was ready to move out. Grady was beside me talking a mile a minute, full of nervous energy. I didn't feel too good, but I knew I would live. Amato came over, and we talked for a while. The train sped along, soon we slowed down and came to a full stop in a town that the railroad sign indicated was Aschaffenburg. Troops getting off here were assigned to the 18th Infantry Regiment of the Big Red One, lst Division.

We pulled away from the station and the Sergeant said, "We'll be in Wurzburg very soon, so all you guys look alive."

My head no longer hurting, I knew the world was going to be all right. The train whistle blew a couple of times, and the train began slowing. We had to be nearing Wurzburg. Grady opened a window and we both looked outside. When a sign appeared with the word Wurzburg on it, I knew we had arrived. The train came to a complete stop and we unloaded. It was not a very large station. It was very much like the small station in my home town.

A Corporal began to tell us what to do next. "Line up in a single line. Sound off with your first and last names. Go through the gate and get aboard the trucks."

As I stood in line I looked at the station walls. They were completely covered with letter and pictures of people. I couldn't of course read the letters.

While waiting in line to move forward, someone said, "These are all missing people. The letters and photos were posted by relatives or friends looking for family or someone."

I noticed most of the pictures appeared to be of German soldiers in their uniforms. Hundreds and hundreds of them lined both walls. The fact that WWII had ended just three years earlier was once more forcefully driven home to me. Finally, we moved forward through the gate and loaded about the trucks.

Our truck filled quickly. The driver started the truck and drove away from the station. We crossed a large intersection. I was sitting at the end of the truck bench so I could see out the rear. We moved alongside a river, and across the river on a hill I could see what looked to be an old castle and some homes. We reached the end of the street and the driver made a right turn, and slowed down.

We moved slowly through the city, I had yet to see a complete house. Block after block after block of homes lay in complete ruin. What a beating Wurzburg had suffered. Buildings everywhere were totally destroyed. Roofs and walls were nonexistent, rafters hanging grotesquely, piles of rubble everywhere. Chimney's standing stark-naked attached to nothing. A slight unfamiliar stench was in the air. We turned another corner, passed through yet another major intersection, and there were blocks of two and three story office buildings with no damage whatsoever. Homes appeared that had suffered no damage. I suppose carpet bombing isn't very selective in it targets.

I looked out to the right and saw a building with a sign on it that read, "Wurzburg Rod and Gun Club." I wondered what in the hell is that? On the left side of the street there was a sign with an arrow indicating the location of the 57th Field Hospital.

On the opposite corner were the ruins of what might have been a very lovely home. There were still rusted segments of an iron fence that encircled the house. The front gate on the fence was twisted, rungs missing; even so it swung back and forth in the light breeze. On the opposite corner stood a house without the slightest bit of damage, it also had an iron fence around it. Though rusty it appeared to be intact.

We went up a long hill as I continued to study the houses and landscape. I saw a sign on a building in German lettering. I had no idea what it said. I did note that beside it was a second sign in English in bold black letters, "Off Limits."

The guy sitting next to me punched me on the arm, and pointed out the off-limits sign to me and said, "Look at that place."

Nodding I replied, "Well, at least we know one place that we won't be going."

I saw a big gate with MP guards on it, and above the gate was a sign, "Wurzburg Military Post, Leighton Barracks." Well, I know where I will be stationed for a couple of years. This is going to be my home, so I hope the years will be good for and to me.

Looking at the young military police on the gate I thought, just a shade over three years ago there were German soldiers on that gate. I'll be sleeping in barracks where those soldiers slept, working in buildings where they once worked. I'm very glad that we won the war.

We pulled through the gate. On my right I saw a huge office building with the American flag flying out front, next to it a smaller red flag with a white star in the center. A sign read Headquarters Wurzburg Military Post, BG Arthur Belcher, Commanding General.

A little further on the right was a small German airfield with a large damaged hanger, but I saw no planes there. A large German Cross was painted on the side of the building. We made a left turn then a right turn and were in a large quadrangle. Our truck stopped, the second truck pulled up behind us and stopped. The driver of our truck turned off the engine and came around the back, unhooking the strap across the rear and lowered the tailgate. With a word of caution he told us to dismount. I was the first one off the truck.

A Corporal shouted, "Fall into platoon formation."

We all grabbed our bags and shuffled into a formation.

"Sound off here when your name is called. After roll call, the First Sergeant will be out to talk to you."

Shortly thereafter the Corporal called, "Attention." He turned around and saluted the First Sergeant and reported, "All present and accounted for sir."

CHAPTER 2

Ironjaws and my new unit

The First Sergeant returned the salute, and the Corporal moved over to the side of our formation. We looked at our new First Sergeant. He was a huge man, about seventy-six inches tall. Several prominent scars left a ragged roadmap on his bronzed face. He was impeccably dressed, standing ramrod straight with black penetrating eyes. Taking his time, the First Sergeant stared at us as if we were weird exhibits in a zoo. Several rows of ribbons and badges were lined up on his Ike jacket, so I knew he had seen lots of combat. He was without question the most impressive soldier I'd ever seen. He was also one mean looking bastard. All eyes were riveted on him, not a noise was heard. He began to speak,

"Welcome to the 6087 SCU. This will be your home for the next three years. My name is First Sergeant Ironjaws Baker. I got the name 'Ironjaws' from the fact that once I take a bite out of your ass, I don't let go, and Baker because my Mama didn't always stay on the reservation."

"This is a Station Complement Unit. We man all the major functions of this post. You will be assigned to different sections within the company. Some of you will go to finance, signal, supply, and personnel. Some of you will go to military government and others to the sub-posts. No matter where you work, or where you're assigned, you still belong to me. Never forget that! My name is First Sergeant, pointing to the stripes on his sleeve. He had three up and three down with a diamond insignia in the middle. Diamonds are trumps, I run this outfit. Major Sullivan commands it, but I run it. You fuck up around here, and your ass is grass, and I'm the lawnmower."

"My office is in the building back of me on the first floor. Unless I invite you, I don't ever want to see you in my office. I've been in this army since 1928, I know everything about the army, I am the army. Once you realize that, we'll get along fine. These are my rules: One, do your job, two, soldier in the company, and three, stay out of trouble. If you do these three things, I'll be happy, and when I'm happy you have to be. Your next formation is here in two hours." He turned and walked away.

We were still at the position of attention, and we stayed that way for about three minutes. Moans and groans could be heard. Men shifted from one foot to the other. Finally, the First Sergeant came back in front of the formation.

Scowling, he looked around and said, "The last order you received was 'Attention' that's the order you carry out. Nothing else matters in your life except obeying that order. If you forget that you've got big troubles." He turned and left.

The young Corporal appeared and gave us, "At ease." He then called off our names and our room assignments. "Go into the building and locate your rooms. Leave your baggage then go to the supply room, draw sheets, pillows, pillow cases, and blankets. Make up your bunks and change into fatigues."

I was assigned to room 12 on the second floor. I groaned and lifted my duffel bag. It seemed to weigh a ton. I moved into my designated building. I could see the First Sergeant's office and the Commander's office on the bottom floor as I moved up the stairs. I found my room. Two name tags were on the door. One read Corporal Ed Clarkston, and the other name slot was empty, so I went inside.

Someone was asleep in one of the bunks. The other had to be mine. I dropped my duffle bag to the floor. He rolled over and opened one eye. Then he sat up and yawned.

I spoke to him first, "Hi, I'm Private Ken Fisher, I just got to Germany. Now I'm assigned here. I guess I'm your new roommate."

He was still yawning. I stuck out my hand, he shook hands with me. Finally, he got up scratched his ass and said, "Copacetic man. Welcome to Germany and the 6087. My name's Ed Clarkston. I knew you guys were coming as I work in the communications message center. We received the message yesterday morning that your group would be here today. Call me Ed. Put your bag in the corner."

He walked over to his wall locker where his fatigues were stacked neatly in the bottom of the locker. Reaching behind them, he pulled out a full fifth of cognac.

"Want a drink?"

"You first," I answered.

He took a large swallow and passed the bottle to me. I didn't want to piss off the Corporal with him being my new roommate, so I took a small sip and banded it back to him.

"Where's the supply room?" I asked. "I have to draw some sheets, blankets and stuff."

"It's downstairs, you can't miss it," he replied.

"Thanks." I then left for the supply room.

There was a long line of men waiting to draw their equipment at the supply room.

The supply sergeant came out of the supply room and shouted, "Form one line, one single line. I know your rank, so just sound off with your first and last names."

Finally, I reached the counter and signed for my blankets, pillow, sheets, wall locker, footlocker and left with no problem. I went back upstairs, made up my bunk then emptied my duffle bag on top of it. I filled up my laundry bag with dirty clothes. All my fatigues were dirty, and my two OD uniforms were dirty and needed dry cleaning. I pulled my boots off and lined them up underneath my bunk along with my low quarter shoes, then pulled on my ankle top boots. I had one pair of shorts, one undershirt and one pair of wool socks left that were clean. That's because I had hand washed them in Marburg. I put on a dirty pair of fatigues.

While I waited for Ed to return, I looked around our small room. Ed had a large picture hung beside his wall locker. The picture was of a beautiful girl in a small white bathing suit, in a sexy Hollywood pose, a very beautiful young girl indeed.

Ed returned from taking a shower and said, "Let's go eat."

"That's a good idea, I've developed quite an appetite. My fatigues are dirty, but what the hell, nothing I can do about that."

Before we left the room, Ed walked over and kissed the picture of the girl then said, "Good morning beautiful."

"Ed, who's that a picture of?"

"That's Bettie Page, the great love of my life," he replied.

"Well, she is very beautiful," I said.

Grunting he said, "The world's most beautiful woman."

As we walked out of the building, a light snow was falling. We walked down the street and turned left. I could see about a hundred yards ahead. Soon we could see and smell several garbage cans outside a building, so I knew the building had to be the mess hall. A sign read 6087 SCU Consolidated Mess. We went inside picked up trays and went through the serving line. I observed that the mess hall had GI cooks and German KP's that made me happy, they would do the KP instead of me. We had lunch, and the food was very good.

"Ed, tell me about yourself, our unit, and the town."

"Everything's copacetic. I drive a courier Jeep between here and the sub-posts of Kitzingen, Bad Kitzingen, and Aschaffenberg every day. I deliver military correspondence, some mail and other official materials. I'm sure many of your group will be assigned to the sub-posts, as the communicators are all our people," he replied.

I thought about that for a few minutes and said, "I sure hope I stay here, I'm tired of traveling for a while."

Fanning away the cigarette smoke, I studied Ed. He was a little taller than me. He had thinning blonde hair and green eyes. Ed was skinny with an engaging personality, and possessed a truly infectious smile. I figured he was one or two years older than me.

"Ken, tell me where you're from, how long you've been in the army, and what do you expect to get out of your tour in the army here in Germany?"

"Well Ed, I'm from a small town in Alabama. I grew up on a farm and plowed big assed mules. I've picked cotton and corn. I've worked in a cotton mill and in a saw mill, I dropped out of high school and joined the army. I want to see as much of Europe as I can. I want to grow up some, and for sure I want to set some personal goals, and know where I'm going when I do get out of the army."

Ed said, "Well, I'm from Ohio, and I've been here since early 47. I made a couple of stripes and then lost them, and made them back again. I don't smoke, but I do like to drink, and I do love women. I also have a German girlfriend that I may marry before I go back to the states. Germany and the army are lots of fun if you don't buck the system. I'll help you out until you get your feet on the ground, and learn your way around."

He leaned over extending his hand, we shook hands. I felt I had at least one new friend in my new outfit.

On our way back to the barracks, Ed pointed out the Enlisted Men's Club and said, "The post telephone switchboard is located at the rear of the building. In the building basement is the dry cleaners, the barber shop, and the Troop Information and Education office. Across the quadrangle is the Gym, at the end of the gym building is the EES snack bar and PX, the Service Club is upstairs at the rear of the building."

I asked, "What's an EES snack bar?"

Ed laughed and replied, "EES stands for European Exchange Service. They operate the snack bars and post exchanges."

Back in the barracks Grady came by. "We have a formation at three o'clock out in the quadrangle, they cancelled the first formation."

"Thanks," I replied, as he went on down the hallway.

I lay down on my bunk and tried to collect my thoughts. I wondered what in the hell does the word copacetic mean? Ed had used it twice. I gazed around our room. Ed had a couple of rods and reels leaning against his wall locker. He must be a fisherman. I don't know much about rods and reels. My fishing is limited to cane poles or trot lines along the banks of the Chattahoochee River, and smaller creeks near my home. I had definitely caught my share of bass, crappie and catfish I remembered proudly. Sharecropper Bob and I were probably the two best fishermen in our county.

Ed had his boots, low quarters and shower shoes lined up under his bunk. Mine were lined up too, but not as highly polished as his. I would save polishing shoes for tonight. I picked up the army's newspaper, "*The Stars and Stripes*" from Ed's bunk. I read an article about a political situation here in Germany, and another about the Berlin airlift. I also read an article about the Russians at the United Nations, and another about President Truman. In the sports pages the 18th Infantry Regiment was playing the 26th Infantry Regiment in a football game in Augsburg. General Clay, the European Commander, had given a briefing in Heidelberg to some visiting congressmen. The Constabulary was conducting maneuvers up on the border at the Fulda Pass. Then I read the comics, and drooled over the paper's beautiful pinup girl on the center page.

At three o'clock that afternoon we assembled in the street and were told to go over to the bleachers in the gym. Everyone was talking and asking questions, the problem was no one had any answers. I sat in the second row of the bleachers, we had been told earlier to leave the first row empty.

Someone hollered, "Attention!"

We all jumped up. When we did, the guy behind me a tall over anxious bastard bumped me in the back with his knees, and I went sprawling across the first row seats landing on the gym floor. When I looked up First Sergeant Ironjaws Baker was glaring down at me. I felt my face turn beet red, I was so damn embarrassed.

"Get on your feet soldier," he snapped.

I jumped to my feet and stood at attention.

"What's your name soldier?"

"Private Fisher, Sir."

"Well, Private Fisher, get your clumsy, uncoordinated ass back in the bleachers, and stand at attention until I tell you otherwise."

I spun around stepping back up in my row and stood at attention. I glanced at Grady, he had a big shit eating grin on his face.

Ironjaws, said, "Take your seats."

Everyone sat down except me. I remembered what he'd said about your last order. Ironjaws turned around, saluted some Major, and then moved over to the side of the formation.

The Major spoke next. "My name is Major Tom Sullivan. I am the Commander of the 6087 SCU. On behalf of the Post Commander, General Belcher, I welcome you all to the European Theater of Operations, and to Wurzburg Military Post. On my left is Captain Joe Tolliver. He is the Executive Officer of the unit, and you have already met the First Sergeant."

Being at attention I was able to get a good look at the Major. He seemed to be in his late thirties, well decorated, a flushed face, not much taller than me. The Captain was younger, fewer rows of ribbons, wore glasses and much taller.

The Major continued. "The mission of this unit is to support the Wurzburg military post, and all its sub-posts. Some of you will be assigned to sections within the unit here. Many of you will be assigned to sub-posts and will be leaving for your new assignments shortly. I expect you all to do your jobs, soldier hard, and stay out of trouble. Any questions?" No one said anything. He called out, "First Sergeant."

The First Sergeant exchanged salutes with the Major, did an about face and said "Seats. Private Fisher you may be seated."

Glaring at Grady as I sat down, he still had his shit eating grin on his face.

Ironjaws began to tell us what we could and couldn't do. "Most of the downtown bars called *Gashaus* are off limits to you. Most of the hotels are off limits. All of the parks are off limits. The Displaced Person's camp is off limits. Dealing on the black market is a court martial offense."

When we thought he couldn't say more, he went on to discuss the VD rate, money changers, prostitutes, prophylactic kits, appropriate use of our ID cars, our ration cards, passes, leaves and just about everything else. He then introduced the section sergeants. Sergeant First Class Perry from the communications center, James from finance, Bromwell from personnel, Slaughter from supply, and others.

"Be aware that if you get one Article 104, and one dose of clap, you very possibly will be sent home and discharged. Two doses of clap and your military career is finished."

After he finished we lined up in three rows to go to three tables and get our pictures taken, receive our rations cards, and to fill out personnel papers. That wrapped it up for the afternoon.

Sam Amato and I headed to the snack bar. We ordered two cups of coffee and lit our cigarettes. Grady came in and joined us.

"What's a DR?" Grady asked Amato.

Amato explained, "It's a delinquent report the MP's give you when you screw up, such as being caught off limits."

We discussed everything that had been explained to us, and then we talked about our First Sergeant.

I said, "I figure him to be mean, strict, fair, and won't take any shit off anyone. Hell, he's been in the army longer than I've been alive, so I have no plans to cross him."

I had found out earlier from Corporal Clarkston that Ironjaw's first name was Howard, First Sergeant Howard Baker.

It was near dinner time so we three went to the mess hall. Later in the barracks we gathered in Grady's room and speculated about who would be leaving in the next few days. I surely hoped I didn't have to move again. I went back to my room. Ed was there talking with two guys I didn't know.

Ed said, "Ken, let me introduce you to PFC Ray Washington. Ray, this is Ken Fisher, he's one of the new guys."

I extended my hand and we shook. "Glad to meet you."

"Same here, welcome to the outfit," he replied.

Ray was about my size, five foot eight, blonde hair, and a natural easy going way about him. He turned and said," Ken, this is Corporal Chuck Skinner."

"I'm glad to meet you Corporal," as we shook hands. Skinner was also about my size, light brown hair, and brown eyes, he also had a Midwestern twang in his voice.

Ray said, "I work in the crypto room in the message center, and Chuck is a radio operator in the radio room."

"What is a crypto room?" I asked Ray.

He replied, "We encode and decode all classified messages coming into or leaving the message center."

Chuck said," I'm a high speed radio operator, and I work two nets, the intra-command net between Wurzburg and all the sub-posts, and the inter-command net between Wurzburg and several other posts to include EUCOM headquarters in Heidelberg."

"I understand radio nets, but I don't know the difference between intra and inter nets," I replied

Chuck laughed, "Maybe you'll get a chance to learn."

Ed brought out his cognac, so I figured they weren't worried about the First Sergeant, or any of the officers coming up the stairs. They all had a drink, but I only took a small sip.

"Everything's copacetic, I'm going downtown, do you guys wanna go?" Ed asked.

Ray said, "No, Chuck and I are going to the Club."

Another guy walked into the room. "Hello Ed, where're you headed?"

Ed turned to me and said, "This is Jose Nunez, he's a teletype operator in the message center."

He turned back to Nunez, "I'm going downtown, do you want to go?"

"Yeah, let's go," Nunez replied.

Ed walked over and kissed his picture of Bettie and said, "I'll be back darling." He and Nunez left.

I assumed I would get to meet Nunez later at work.

Skinner walked out of the room, so I turned to Ray and said, "Ray tell me about the people here, and how things operate around here."

We sat on the footlockers and Ray said, "All the communications center personnel sleep on this one floor."

We continued to talk, and I asked him a million questions.

Ray said, "Ed has his own Jeep. Many of the older soldiers have their own vehicles. Ed's Jeep is still around from WWII. Jeeps are authorized 100 gallons of gasoline a month which seems to be enough. Ed doesn't smoke, so he sells his cigarettes on the black market. He shacks up with a girl named Ericka downtown, and will probably marry her. Ed told me he's had the clap twice, one article 104, and has been busted back to Private twice. He's been in the outfit since early 1947."

"Isn't Ed afraid of getting caught dealing on the black market?" I asked.

"Nah, I guess not."

"Does Ironjaws know about Ed having the clap?"

"I'm not sure, anyway Ed's still here, so I guess not. Do you want to go to the club with me and Chuck?"

"I guess I'll stay here. I might be shipping out tomorrow. I want to have my head on straight. Besides, I don't have a pass anyway. The First Sergeant told us we are restricted to the post for three days."

Ray left for his room, then immediately came back and said, "The hell with tomorrow, let's go to the club for a couple of hours. You guys won't be leaving for a couple of days. You haven't finished your in-processing yet, and that takes some time."

CHAPTER 3

The fight

I was dog tired, it had been a long day, or was it a long night and short day? I weakened, "Okay, but just for a little while," I replied.

"You have to wear your OD uniform."

"Mine are so damn dirty and wrinkled they stink," I replied.

"You can wear one of mine. They're all cleaned and pressed. I'm in room 14."

I borrowed a pair of pants and a shirt. He had PFC stripes on his Ike jacket, so I figured I had better wear my own no matter its condition. I used my shoe brush to hit my low quarters a few licks and a promise, then we left for the club.

A quick glance out my window revealed it was still snowing, but the club was just twenty-five steps away. We ran across the street and up the steps into the building. There was a large lobby, and a short hallway into the main bar and ballroom. I estimated about forty plus tables in the place, and half of them were filled with soldiers and their girls. Ray waved to several of them. We sat down at a table next to the dance floor. Skinner had gone on downtown.

A waitress came by our table and Ray ordered two Wurzburger beers. She returned shortly with two bottles and two glasses.

Ray filled his glass and raised it in toast. "Well Ken me boy, welcome to Wurzburg, here's to a good tour of duty."

Raising my bottle, I didn't use the glass I said, "I'll drink to that for sure."

We both had healthy swallows. We watched the people dancing and soon both bottles were empty. I motioned to the waitress and ordered two more beers. They only cost fifteen cents per beer, so I could handle that. I needed some cheap prices as I was almost broke, and wasn't sure when we would be paid.

Ray began explaining downtown to me. He said, "The main local bars are The Leopold, Boars Head, the Ring Hotel and The Golden Ram. They are all on limits and most of the troops go there. There are a couple of others but they are not as popular."

"Are there any prostitutes in those bars?"

He laughed, "Oh yeah, there are a whole bunch of local prostitutes, and they normally charge whatever you're willing to pay."

"How many marks do you get for a dollar?"

"The current exchange rate is somewhere between fifteen and eighteen marks per dollar, it continues to fluctuate. The cost of booze downtown is also very cheap."

The more he described a place so unlike my hometown the more anxious I became to get a pass and head downtown, and find it out for myself. We both had another beer, and ordered still another. I was getting woozy, I was inexperienced, and drinking was never my strong suit.

A big Corporal staggered up to our table, talking loudly, and spilling beer out of his glass. He came up to Ray, and draped his arm around his neck.

"Ray, would you believe I just got away from the MP's down town?"

From his voice I could tell he was really proud of himself, and he was also drunk.

He looked over at me, staring me up and down and asked Ray, "Is this one of the punk-assed kids that came in today?"

A look of pure agony crossed Ray's face.

"Yes, I 'm one of the soldiers that came in today asshole," I replied boldly. "Why do you call us names? You don't know me, you've never seen me before, so why don't you go find your own frigging table?"

"I don't like your punk-ass face, he snarled. I'll whip your skinny little ass, fall out in the quadrangle."

I was stunned at the truculence, and violence in his voice.

Snarling again he said, "Either come outside punk, or I'll drag your ass outside."

Standing up I drained my bottle and turned towards the door. He rushed ahead of me. He was much taller, bigger and outweighed me by at least fifty or sixty pounds. I thought, how in the hell can this be happening to me? My first night in the unit, and my first night in the club, and some idiot wants to whip my ass.

He swung open the door and rushed down the stairs. The snow was still falling as I followed him out. Reaching the bottom I stepped to his left. As I did my left foot slipped on some ice, and I went down on one knee. The bastard hit me on the side of my face. I fell back in the snow. As I struggled to get up on my feet, he hit me again between my eyes, and the lights went out.

When I regained consciousness, Ray was rubbing snow on my face.

"What happened?" I asked.

Ray helped me to my feet and said, "He hit you when you slipped on the ice."

I had blood all over my Ike jacket as well as Ray's shirt and tie. I was sick to my stomach.

"Who the hell was that Corporal?'

"That was Corporal Neil Sherron from the message center, he's a real asshole," he replied.

Ray half carried and helped me into our upstairs latrine. I took off my Ike jacket, tie and shirt. They had blood all over them. My face was a mess. Hell, I didn't ever recognize myself. My right eye was already closed, a cut over the other eye, and my nose felt broken.

Ray brought me a towel,

"Thanks Ray, go ahead to bed, I'll be fine." I washed my face several times and rinsed out my mouth. I finished cleaning up, and walked up the hallway to my room. Ed was asleep in his bunk, a bottle of cognac sitting upright in his boot. I picked it up and had a big swallow. I couldn't believe it, here just one day, and I'd gotten half-drunk, and got my ass whipped. If this is any indication of my future, it's going to be a really rough tour of duty.

It was eleven o'clock in the evening when I heard "Taps." People leaving the club were singing or talking. Jeeps cranked up and were driven off. People came up the stairs. I heard doors open and close, latrine facets running, commodes flushing, loud talk, laughter then gradually silence.

Ed had not moved since I'd come in. I had another swallow from his bottle and lit a cigarette. When I took the cigarette out of my mouth my lip stuck to the end. Damn, nothing is going right for me tonight. My face hurt so bad sleep seemed impossible. When I lay down the bed began spinning. I sat back up. I walked down the hallway to look out the end window. Though the dim lights around the quadrangle nothing was moving. I could see snowflakes floating across the beams of light. I returned to my room and took another drink from Ed's bottle. I recreated the fight in my mind trying to figure out what actually happened, I knew when I slipped on the ice he hit me. I didn't get to land even one punch. For sure I'd got my ass whipped. I lay down again but couldn't sleep. All I could think of was how badly my face hurt, and of that big bastard sucker punching me.

Then a light came on, *Get even*! Get that bastard while he's sleeping. I could feel the energy flowing back into my tired-ass body. The more I thought about it, the better I liked the idea. I pictured the bastard sleeping, me waking him up, and quickly punching him in his big foul mouth.

Ray had said he was in the message center platoon, so that means he has to be in this building on this floor. He was drunk, so that probably means he didn't have to work tonight. He's a pretty big guy, I might not be able to punch him out. Doubt crept into my mind, this calls for a strategy.

Then it hit me, use my combat boot. The heel is hard and heavy, and the buckled top I could use like a handle. The more I thought about it the better it sound. I picked up my boot, it was still wet and heavy. I swung it a couple of times, yeah, this'll work. I walked out the door. No one was in the hall, and no one was in the latrine. I passed each door and checked the name tags on it. At the end of the hall, the last room on the right, the door showed only Corporal Sherrons's name tag, it was his room.

What luck, the bastard sleeps in a room by himself. I eased the door open. The hall light offered scant light to see into the room. He was asleep. His bunk was pushed up against the wall. A small night light was still on. He must have been too drunk to turn it off. He snored slightly as I entered the room. I closed the door softly behind me, and walked across the room. He hadn't moved a muscle. I had a death grip on my boot. I reached down and shook him on the shoulder. He moaned a little then I shook him harder.

"Wake up Corporal."

I felt the sweat bead on my face and hands. Gripping the boot tighter I shook him again. He turned over and started to set up, "What's up?" he mumbled, opening his eyes.

"The jigs up for you tough guy."

Swinging the boot as hard as I could I hit him on the side of his head knocking him back into the wall. When he snapped back forward, I hit him again. He fell off the bed onto the floor. I grabbed him by his hair with my left hand, he was out cold. I rolled him over, his face was a bloody mess. He was definitely finished for tonight.

I eased the door open, no one was in the hallway, so I walked to the latrine and washed his blood off my boot and hands. Then I went back to my room and locked the door.

Exhausted, I sat down, I was shaking. I drank a quick swallow of Ed's cognac, and then smoked a cigarette. I felt good, I had gotten revenge on the bully. That bastard will think twice before he jumps me again. Lying down I passed out.

The next thing I knew someone was shaking me, it was Ed.

"What the hell happened to you?" he asked.

I sat up and replied, "Some big bastard whipped my ass outside the club last night." My right eye was totally closed, my lip swollen and my nose was crooked.

Ed began to laugh, "Welcome to *Deustchland*," he said.

I looked at my pillow, blood was all over the pillow case.

Ed said, "It's copacetic, get cleaned up we have an eight o'clock formation."

Slowly, I pulled myself out of bed. I ached all over. I hope like hell that the Corporal hurts as badly as I do this morning. I glanced at my watch, it was 6 o'clock in the morning. Damn, I hadn't slept but five hours. When I stood up the room began to sway. My stomach churned, I hung on to my wall locker until it stopped. Then I picked up my shaving kit and a towel, and went to the latrine. Only a couple of guys were in there. They left as I found an open sink and mirror and examined my face. One eye closed, both blackened. My lip cut, a smaller cut over my eye. What a hell of a sight I am. I filled the sink and slowly began to clean my face. I shaved carefully then brushed my teeth.

Grady came into the latrine and seeing me his eyes opened wide and mouth dropped open. "What in the hell happened to you?"

"Some big bastard sucker punched me outside the club last night and whipped my ass. We'll talk later, we have a formation to make shortly." I glanced into the mirror again, what a sad looking sight.

As I stared in the mirror, I saw Cpl Sherron walk into the latrine. My heart began pounding. I tried to will it to slow down. He hadn't seen me as he headed to the opposite end of the row of sinks.

Grady looked him then looked at me, he said nothing and left the room.

Sherron had dried blood all over his head and face. He looked worse than I did. I decided to bluff the son of a bitch. I picked up my shaving kit and swung it by the handle, turning I walked towards him.

"Good morning Corporal Sherron, how are you today?" I said.

He turned towards me and dropped his shaving kit, I heard a bottle inside it break. He stared at me through one half open eye, the other swollen shut. His top lip was badly split and swollen worse than mine.

"Thanks for beating me up last night, you're really tough. It looks like someone must have gotten to you also."

He balled up his fist. I stepped back one step, and swung my shaving kit behind me.

He stopped and snarled, "I'll have your ass court-martialed for hitting a Non-Commissioned Officer."

I saw that he had two front teeth missing. With all the sarcasm I could muster I answered him.

"That's rather disingenuous isn't it? You, an NCO beating up a Private, I don't think so! Let me tell you this, and this isn't a threat, this is a promise. I promise you rotten son of a bitch, if you ever screw with me again, I'll beat your head in again only worse. Whether you're asleep or drunk either way it doesn't matter to me, but I will do it!"

I didn't really mean it, but he didn't know that. I turned my back to him and walked out of the latrine as fast as self respect would permit, which was damn fast. We had the reveille formation and afterwards Sam, Grady and I went to the mess hall. I told them what had happened to me and by whom. I didn't tell that I'd gotten a full measure of revenge. That would remain my secret. I managed to eat a couple of soft scrambled eggs and coffee. I felt a little better. We walked back up the hill to our barracks and on upstairs.

Ed was telling some guys in the hall about someone beating up Corporal Sherron several hours after the Corporal had beaten me up at the club.

Joining them, I said, "Whoever did it gets a word of thanks from me."

I told Ed that I had drank some of his cognac, and then passed out in bed. Next thing I know you woke me up. I wasn't really sure whose side Corporal Clarkston would be on, after all they were both Corporals.

Ed replied, "That's copacetic, the sorry bastard deserved it. Whoever did it also has my thanks."

Ray verified that I had gone to bed right after the fight, which reinforced my explanation of what happened.

We fell out in the quadrangle for our first work formation, or whatever we were going to do. The First Sergeant called out names, and our assignments to different sections. I was assigned to the communications section in the message center. Almost all of my new friends were also assigned to the message center section.

"Corporal Clarkston, march these greenhorns to the headquarters building message center," the First Sergeant said, then he left.

We were to meet with the Signal officer and get our new initial job assignments. As we marched my head began pounding, and each step I took hurt. With one eye closed I had problems seeing. I felt uneasy about meeting my new boss the Signal officer looking so damn beat up, but there's nothing I can do about that.

Ed stopped the formation in front of the headquarters building and told us to move inside and downstairs into the film library. We did, and there were enough seats for everyone. My friend Jack Taylor sat down next to me, and we began to talk softly about what had happened to me.

"I'll fix that bastard for you, I'll; punch his lights out," he said.

"Someone got to him last night. He's in as bad or worse shape than I am," I replied.

Then Ed called Attention.

We all sprang up to the position. A Lieutenant Colonel entered the room and strode front and center, stopping in the middle of the room.

He said, "Take your seats. Good morning men, I'm Lieutenant Colonel Morris, I'm the Post Signal Officer. I welcome you to the post, and to the communications section. We have the best communications section in EUCOM, and I intend for it to stay that way. With all your help, it will."

The Colonel then noticed me, a look of disbelief crossing his face. "What in the hell happened to you son?"

I jumped up to the position of attention.

"You only arrived yesterday, and already you're in a fight? Or did that happen before you arrived here?"

"Well sir, it's a long story, but to make it about as short as the fight was, I lost."

He laughed. "I hope you are a better communicator that you are a fighter, better luck next time."

I quickly sat back down.

After telling us the history of the unit, and its role since WWII, he spoke about the unit's mission, and his expectations of us as soldiers. He introduced the section sergeant, Sergeant First Class Joe Perry as the man in charge of the message center and all signal operations. SFC Perry was a young man very big in statute, with a very round face. He weighed about two-hundred pounds, and had a pleasant demeanor. I immediately felt I could work for him and things would be fine. The introduction over, the Colonel turned the meeting over to SFC Perry.

Perry began to make work assignments. Roberts, Amato, Grady and I were assigned to the message center section. Others were assigned to the teletype section, the courier sections, radio repair section, signal supply and the photographic section. My head was pounding. I wanted a shot of Ed's cognac, or else a dozen aspirins. Most of my new friends were assigned to the same section I was, and that was good news to me, and I was happy about that. After last night I could stand having friends around for a long time. SFC Perry led us upstairs and introduced us to the personnel on duty in the section. I met two radio operators plus Corporal Skinner whom I had met earlier, and a tall Corporal named Terry Merlin. I met again the Spanish fellow, Jose Nunez in the message center section. After touring the sections, SFC Perry told us most of us would be going to the Army Signal School in the town of Ansbach. All communications MOS's were taught at the Ansbach School I later learned.

It was close to noon time, so a Corporal was told to march us back to the company and release us for lunch.

Perry instructed us, "After lunch spend the afternoon getting your laundry and uniforms in the cleaners, and your field gear in shape. Get your foot and wall lockers ready for inspection."

Before we left the message center I located and picked up a Webster's Collegiate Dictionary. I thumbed through the pages quickly until I found the word "Copacetic," according to the dictionary its slang and means, "Completely Satisfactory."

At the mess hall as we moved through the serving line, I could hear the KP's and cooks ooh's and ah's. I knew my face was a mess, but hell no big deal, nothing I can do about it.

I spotted Corporal Sherron at a table in the dining room. He looked terrible, I immediately felt better. He was eating very slowly, and only on one side of his mouth. My satisfaction increased each time I saw him wince. I moved to a table by the wall and took a seat with my back to the wall. Grady and Roberts came in and joined me at the table. We had a lively animated conversation about our new assignments. I finished eating first, so I left and wandered up the hill to the barracks. I walked upstairs to my room and lay down on my bunk falling asleep in less than five minutes.

About two o'clock Roberts came in and woke me up. He said, "Ken, you better get your stuff squared away."

I got up and went to the latrine, rinsed my mouth out with mouth wash, and hoped like hell my teeth would tighten. I returned to my room, sat down on my footlocker and began shining my boots and shoes. I did my boots, high tops and finally my low quarters. I used mahogany shoe polish on them all, and they turned out great. I checked out my field gear again. The mess kit and the utensils were clean. The canteen cup needed some elbow grease on it, but the canteen was in good shape. I spread out my shelter half, tent poles and pins, and rolled them into a horseshoe roll. I packed my backpack and placed the horseshoe roll on top of it lashing it down. I attached the entrenching tool, a small shovel. Placing it all on top of my wall locker, I stood back and admired my handiwork. It looked military and regulation.

It all looked pretty good and ready for inspection in my opinion. I hung up what few clothes I had left that were clean, and placed a couple pair of socks in my foot locker. I then took my two OD uniforms over to the cleaners located beneath the club. The German man who operated the cleaning shop complained about all the blood on my Ike jacket. I didn't really understand anything he said, so I simply said, "Okay," and left. I could get them back in one day, so that was a good deal. It would cost me thirty-five cents per uniform to get them cleaned and pressed. I returned to the barracks.

As I entered the building a PFC stopped me. He said, "The First Sergeant wants to see you right away in his office."

My heart fell to my feet. I was scared. All I could think of was that bastard Corporal Sherron had turned me in, and had preferred charges against me. Why else would the big Indian Chief want to see me?

"I'll be down right away," I replied.

Returning to my room I took several deep breaths, then I opened Ed's locker and took out his bottle of cognac. I immediately rejected the idea, figuring that would be a huge mistake. I placed his bottle back into his locker.

I walked downstairs slowly, as I was scared of Ironjaws. I reached the bottom of the stairs, turned right and slowly entered the orderly room. The company clerk, a Corporal, was typing something. He motioned me on into the office and told me to wait. He then went into an adjoining office. Upon returning he said, "Report to the First Sergeant."

I walked across the office and knocked on the door. I heard that unmistakable deep voice say, "Come in."

I stepped into the office and saw the First Sergeant sitting at his desk. I moved smartly across the room towards the front of his desk where he had positioned a small throw rug. I stepped on it preparing to snap to attention and render an impressive terrific salute. Instead, when I stepped on it with my one eye closed, I'd stepped on the corner. It slid forward and I fell backwards flat on my ass.

Damn, damn, can't I do anything frigging right? I picked myself up off the floor, and felt the blood rushing to my face. I was confused and pissed off at myself all at the same time. I snapped to attention and saluted the First Sergeant.

"Private Fisher reporting to the First Sergeant, Sir."

Ironjaws smiling, looked me up and down, returned my salute and said, "Stand at parade rest Private Fisher."

I assumed the parade rest position and glanced at him; both my hands were wet with sweat. Ironjaws continued to study my face. I couldn't look at his. I looked over his head, around his head, anyplace except in his eyes.

Finally, he spoke again, "Fisher, I've always said that if a man won't stand up for his rights, he won't fight, and if he won't fight he isn't worth a continental damn to this army. But nobody fights someone almost twice his size, unless they're stupid, or a hell of a lot better fighter than you are. Sherron outweighs you by more than fifty pounds. I heard about last night and you got the raw end of that deal. I've already seen Sherron earlier today. I want to tell you now plain and simple that I won't tolerate fighting in this outfit. I know there are times when you can't escape from doing so, and that may be your case. I've been in similar situations where a man is left with no choice. But this is the end of it. No more! It's over, totally fucking over. Do you understand?"

I meekly answered, "Yes Sir First Sergeant."

He said, "Every unit has its bully, until he gets his ass whipped. I've also been told that Sherron was drunk and fell down the stairs last night face first knocking out a couple of front teeth. Do you know anything about that?"

Then for the first time, I looked him straight in the eyes, he seemed to have a faint smile on his face.

"No sir, First Sergeant. Whenever that happened I was already in bed. I was out of it and didn't hear a thing. After the fight, PFC Washington helped me to my room, and that's the last thing I remember. Whatever happened to him I'm damn glad, but I had nothing to do with it," I replied.

He stared at me for another five seconds, the faint smile lingering on his face, and then said, "It's over. Forget it. Learn your job, do your job, soldier hard, and remember what I told you yesterday, fuck up and your ass is mine, and I'll nail you to the wall."

"Yes Sir First Sergeant."

"You need a haircut, your gig line is screwed up, and your belt buckle is covered with moss and slime. Get the hell out of here. I don't want to ever see you again in this office!"

"Yes sir First Sergeant." I snapped to attention and saluted him. I then did a very careful about face and moved out as quickly as I could. I walked up the stairs and met Amato. We went to my room and sat down on the footlockers. I told him I had just been in Ironjaw's office. He'd chewed my ass out, locked my heels and read me the full riot act. I skipped the part about me falling on my ass.

Sam had a million questions, but I felt out of breath and needed to relax a bit. Finally, I related most of the conversation and advised him never to go see Ironjaws, he'll scare the hell out of you. It was about chow time, so we left for the mess hall.

I felt a sense of relief now that the fight escapade was over. The First Sergeant hadn't killed me, or put me in the stockade, so nothing else should come out of it. I planned to steer clear of Sherron, let my face heal up, and learn whatever new job I get. I expect to go to the Signal School to learn my job, and that will get me and my problems out of everyone's sight and mind.

Just assigned to the outfit and most everyone now knew me on sight, or had heard about me getting my ass whipped, that was definitely not good. I have almost three years to do here, and I don't want to stay a notorious Private for three full years. I'd best shape up, try to make a stripe or two, and get off the First Sergeant's shit list. At the mess hall we had sauerkraut and wieners. I could eat that, and I was hungry. After eating and drinking two cups of coffee I began to feel right with the world again.

Sam and I walked back up the hill, it was snowing and the temperature was falling rapidly. The cold air felt refreshing on my battered face and neck. Flakes of snow fell down my collar and melted immediately. They helped to wash away my troubles, or so it seemed. In spite of my face, I felt good. I felt energetic, ambitious and ready to learn my new job and move on.

That night I shined my boots and shoes again until they really looked good. I checked my clothes in my wall locker, and my footlocker with its meager belongings. I didn't have enough clothes to fail an inspection, so no worry there. I felt like doing things right since nothing had really gone my way since I arrived here. I picked up a towel, my shaving kit and headed for the latrine to shower and brush my teeth. I met a couple of guys in there that I didn't know, so we introduced ourselves. One was Corporal Joe Carlton from Boston. The other guy was Corporal Bobby Ingram from New Hampshire. Both were assigned to and worked in the message center section. Corporal Ingram told me he was assigned to the sub-post in Bad Kissingen, and had come to town for some fun and excitement.

Carlton spoke up and said, "We're going downtown and strafe the *Strasse*."

"What the hell is that?" I asked.

Carlton replied," That simply means we're going to patrol the streets until we find some good looking women for the evening."

I laughed, "That I can understand no matter which language you use."

After a good hot shower I felt refreshed, and brushed my teeth. Back to my room I went straight to bed. My head no longer hurt, however my face was still out of shape. I could squint a little out of my left eye, and I had trouble breathing through my nose, but overall I was improving.

I woke up with the bugle playing reveille. I got up and cleaned up. I put on my fatigues, sweater, and field jacket. When I stepped out into the hallway Sherron was just a couple of steps away. He stopped and glared at me. I ignored him and walked on down the stairs. Neither of us spoke. As far as I was concerned the incident was over, and I hoped he felt the same way. Time would tell.

In the mess hall Grady, Amato, and Roberts were already at a table. After filling my tray, I joined them at their table. When I saw that Ray was by himself over at another table, I picked up my tray and moved over to sit with him.

He said, "I've been on the night standby shift and they called me in to decode a message. Although that took a couple of hours I still have to be back at work at eight o'clock. The other guy who works in the crypto room with me is Corporal Bill Pitts. You haven't met him yet."

Ray began to tell me about himself before he enlisted in the Army. He said, "I worked in a tool making plant. I graduated from high school and had been a fairly good athlete. I joined the army for excitement and the travel I expect to do." He stopped and went to the coffee urn and refilled his cup. Returning he said, "I just want to see the world, have fun, and maybe learn a decent trade before I get back to Seattle."

I didn't tell him too much about my own background as I had nothing to brag about, or anything exciting to relate. "Well Ray, that's pretty much the same reason I joined the Army."

We finished eating had another cup of coffee, smoked a cigarette, and then returned to the barracks.

Ed was in his bunk sound asleep. I went to see Grady. We talked about what we wanted to do. I mentioned radio repair would be a fine job, a good trade after I get out of the Army. He wanted to be a radio operator. The only thing I knew about radios was how to turn them on and off, and how to get the 'Grand old Opry' on Saturday nights. I figured if they teach me a job, any job, I could learn as easily as anyone else.

"Grady, why did you really join the Army?"

"Well, I was working in the cotton mill, and I started running around with this guy's wife. He found out about it, so I figured the smartest thing I could do was leave town until it all blows over, and he cools down."

"What if the guy is waiting for you when you get back home?"

He laughed, "Screw him, I'll worry about that when I get back home."

At eight o'clock we formed up in the quadrangle. PFC Taylor marched us to the headquarters building. There they took our manning board photographs placing them alongside all the other pictures of the message center personnel, issued us our new ID cards, and told to report to our sections.

We were authorized a carton and a half of cigarettes per week at ten cents a pack. I didn't smoke nearly that much, but figured I could use them some other way. I also found out from Skinner that the post was called a *Kaserne* and that *Mach Nichts* in German meant it makes no difference. The language didn't seem to be too hard to learn if someone would teach you.

After lunch that afternoon we had to report to our sections. I was happy; I was anxious to get the in-processing completed, find out my job assignment, and get to work. We arrived back at the headquarters building and went to the message center.

SFC Perry said, "You guys just hang around awhile the Colonel wants to interview each of you individually."

I went into the radio room, and none of it made sense to me. I had only heard Morse code in the movies. It did sound highly technical, and appeared to be a demanding job to master. The idea of being responsible for all this expensive sophisticated communications equipment, and operating it was rather intimidating.

CHAPTER 4

My new job

A Corporal came up to me and said, "Go across the hall and see Sergeant Perry."

I left the message center walked across the hall and knocked on the door which had a sign reading 'Signal Officer.'

"Come in," a voice answered my knock.

I opened the door and Sergeant Perry was waiting for me.

"Let's go into the Colonel's office. Report to Colonel Morris."

I followed Sergeant Perry into the office where the Colonel was seated behind his desk. Stepping briskly up to the front of his desk I saluted and said, "Private Fisher reporting to the Signal Officer as directed Sir."

He returned my salute, "Take a seat Private Fisher."

I sat in the chair opposite his desk, Sergeant Perry sat alongside the Colonel.

Smiling, the Colonel asked me, "How do you feel? You look a little better than when I first saw you."

Smiling I replied, "I think I'll live sir."

He then became official and said, "Fighting in the section is not permitted. That must stop, and you Fisher should stay the hell away from trouble. You're going to be here for almost three years, so learn to enjoy the army. Enjoy Germany, see the country, see Europe, and broaden your experience, you'll always be glad you did."

After a short pause, the Colonel asked, "What would you like to do in the section?"

"I think I would like to be a radio repairman," I answered.

Have you ever taken a typewriter apart?" he asked.

"No Sir."

"Have you ever taken a clock apart and put it back together?"

"No Sir."

Sergeant Perry asked, "Have you ever taken a radio apart?"

Again, I had to say "No."

The Colonel said, "I think you would make a good radio operator."

"Sir, I just left the radio room and none of it made any sense to me, but I'll do whatever you decide."

The Colonel said, "I'll let you know what my final decision is. Meanwhile, you're assigned to work with Corporal Skinner."

I knew the interview was over, so standing up I saluted the Colonel, did an about face and left his office.

Crossing the hallway, I rang the door bell and was let back into the message center. In the radio room I saw Cpl Skinner reading a magazine.

"Corporal Skinner, I've been assigned to work with you until a decision is made on what my final job will be."

Skinner looked up at me and a pained expression crossed his face. "Well, horseshit," he responded. "What in the hell am I supposed to do with you?"

"I don't know, I guess Sergeant Perry will tell you." I felt uneasy; I knew Skinner didn't want to teach me radio operations. I had no choice, but neither did he.

"What do I do first?" I asked.

"I guess the first thing you need to learn is the Morse code, or else none of this will mean anything to you."

Skinner walked over to a closet and pulled out a small machine and tapes of some type. He placed them on the counter where a small sign read Intra-post net. He then sat down and wrote on a legal size sheet of paper the alphabet, and alongside each letter he wrote down the dots and dashes that made up the letter, plus the numbers zero through nine.

"Memorize these and learn the Morse code." He then handed me a headset saying, "Use these earphone when you're on the machine. Sit here, it is the Intra Post Command net. It is a voice radio net we use to communicate with the sub-posts. We often use Morse code on it also."

I followed his instructions, and after about forty-five minutes of studying the alphabet, I was becoming bored. I lit a cigarette and watched Skinner as he was operating a device again. His finger and thumb moved so fast that I had no idea which one was sending dots or dashes. He finally finished and stopped.

"Corporal, how fast can you send and receive the code?"

"I guess around thirty-five words a minute."

I learned later just how damn fast that is. He showed me the telegraph key, and how it worked. It was obviously much slower than the speed key which he called a 'Bug.' He was apparently an expert on both devices.

He sat down at the radio desk, and I returned to my study of the Morse code.

After about an hour, Skinner said, "That's enough for today. Take the paper home with you and study it tonight. We'll start again tomorrow."

"What if I'm not assigned as a radio operator? If I am, shouldn't I be going to the signal school to learn all this?" I asked.

"I'll check with Perry and let you know what's up as soon as I can," he replied.

Carlton came into the room. "Hello guys." He sat down at the typewriter and typed in the station log that he came on duty as of seventeen hundred hours.

He and Skinner talked for a few minutes, and then Skinner and I left together. We walked out of the building into the snow. He pointed out the location of the radio repair shop, the signal supply office, and the post fire station. He explained, "The fire station siren is the post signal for alerts." When we arrived back at the company he asked, "Do you want to go have a couple of beers at the club tonight?"

"Sure, if you promise I won't get beaten up again."

He laughed, "Sherron is an asshole. He's always getting into a fight, and always with someone smaller than he is."

I replied, "Well, someone got to him, and I'm damn glad they did."

Skinner looked at me for a few seconds but said nothing. He went into the barracks and I went to the dining hall. When I saw they had liver I left and headed for the snack bar. The place was crowded, and the jukebox was blaring away. I guess not too many troops like liver. I ordered a cheeseburger, French fries, and a cup of coffee all for under a dollar. Ed was sitting by himself, so I joined him. I assumed he didn't like liver either. While we were eating I noticed a good looking young woman a few tables away. She and the woman she was with were both wearing blue uniforms.

"Ed, who and what are they?" I asked.

"They're Special Service women. They operate the Service Club. They try and keep the off duty troops occupied. They have different programs like ski trips, pinochle tournaments, billiard contest, bowling leagues and such. They try to keep the troops out of trouble. They don't have much luck, but entertainment is their job, and they do work at it." He had a swallow of his coffee.

"The black haired one is named Dotty. She's been here about four months, I don't know the other one."

I continued to glance at the young woman as I ate. Finally, she glanced my way I smiled, and winked at her with my good eye.

She smiled and looked away. She never looked back at me. Finally, Ed and I finished and left. Ed however, had noticed me looking at the woman and said, "Ken, enlisted swine like us don't rate with good looking American women, so forget it."

We walked on towards the barracks, then he added, "Why would you want to screw an American woman in Germany? You can do that back in the states. Over here you should screw European women."

I digested his remark, and by damn it made a lot of sense. We arrived at the barracks. Once back in our room Ed walked over and kissed his picture of Bettie saying, "I'm back beautiful."

After taking my uniform off I picked up a towel and left for the showers. I slowly washed my face and brushed my teeth. I wondered what the hell the service club woman thought of me, winking at her with my battered face, black eyes, and busted lip. I'm surprised she didn't call the military police and report me or something.

At least I'm getting better and feeling better each day. I returned to my room, put on clean shorts and undershirt and lay down on my bunk. I picked up the alphabet to study it some more. The numbers were the easiest, they had more dots and dashes to them. I memorized them rather quickly. I recited the alphabet and their Morse code equivalents. I said them out loud without looking at the sheet. Damn, that was hard to do, very hard to do.

Chuck came by the room, "I'll be ready to leave in about ten minutes," he said.

I got up, put on my shirt and tie then my freshly cleaned and pressed uniform. I checked the Ike jacket for blood stains and they were almost nonexistent. I was soon ready to go.

I checked Skinners room and Merlin and Ray were there talking about some girl they knew downtown. They referred to her as Combat Annie. Merlin had picked her up last night, and had sex with her for only five cigarettes.

"Why do you call her such an odd name as Combat Annie?"

Merlin answered, "Her name is Annie, and she wears combat boots."

Laughing I said, "Well, that makes sense to me. For five cigarettes, I'll be looking for her soon, she can have all my business."

While Skinner was dressing I checked Grady's room and asked him and his roommate to go to the club with us. They dressed in nothing flat. We linked up with Skinner, he was ready so we left for the club. We ran across the street and into the club. It wasn't crowded. We found an empty table and pulled up chairs. Skinner ordered us all a bottle of beer. The conversations began with everyone sharing what was going on with them and their jobs.

Ed came into the club and joined us at the table. After he drank a beer he said, "Everything's copacetic, I'm going to town, anyone want to go with me?"

Skinner said, "I'll go with you." I didn't have a pass, so I declined the offer. I didn't want and didn't need any more trouble with the company, or my section. Just we new guys were left, so I ordered another round of beers. That cost me seventy-five cents.

"Has anyone heard when we will get paid?" I asked.

Roberts spoke up and said, "I heard we'll get paid in full on the thirty-first."

I had about eleven dollars left in script and payday couldn't come soon enough for me. "We can't get paid on the thirty-first that's New Year's Eve," I said.

Roberts replied, "We better get paid, I'm almost flat broke."

Jack Taylor came in the club and joined us at the table. He looked tired. He ordered everyone another beer. It was developing into another regular army evening, drinking beer, bullshitting, lying and dumb-ass discussions about the army, our jobs, and naturally women.

First Sergeant Ironjaws came in with a woman who looked to be about his age. I assumed she must be his wife. She was a very lovely woman. That really surprised me. I just couldn't picture a soldier as tough as I figured him to be as married. I knew he didn't live in the barracks, but I had no idea where he did live. The image he had created for me was just pure army. He was ubiquity personified. He was always in his office, always on the quadrangle, dwelling always in the back of your mind. When I glanced at him, he was having some type of drink, talking to his wife, and then he was actually laughing. Hell, he's a man just like us. I guess I have an awful lot to learn about army people, and human nature in general. I had an unexplainable feeling, sort of a disappointment to realize that he was as fallible as we are. His introductory speech to us, and the ass chewing he had given me had created an unreal person in my mind. It's nice however to know that like us Privates, we puny mortals, he puts his pants on one leg at the time.

Someone ordered another round of beer, and the bullshit got deeper and louder. Ray came in and pulled up a chair next to me and had a glass of beer.

"Ray, tell me about the R and R places we've heard so much about."

Ray replied, "Garmish is the best place to go on leave or three day pass. The Casa Carioca nightclub in Garmisch has a huge ballroom with an ice show each night. Then a wooden dance floor is brought out to cover over the ice so you can dance. The food is great, drinks are cheap, and women are everywhere. They come from all over Germany, they know the GI's are there to have fun, and will spend lots of money."

"That's my kind of place. It sounds great. It sounds different and more exciting than anything I've ever known. Let's go there when I have some money, and can get a three day pass."

He nodded in agreement.

I added, "Back home in Alabama, moonshine and a Saturday night slow dance, or a little jitterbugging is the norm, but nothing like Garmisch."

He said, "Another great place to go is Bertchesgaden. It's a small town way up in the Alp Mountains. That's where Hitler's Eagle Nest is located."

I knew about the Eagle's Nest. I had seen it in the Movietone news in the theater.

Ray described how beautiful it was, and like Garmisch plenty of things to do and see. We agreed to go there also after our trip to Garmisch.

I guess we were getting a little loud. I didn't see him but I felt someone behind me. Then I felt a huge hand on my shoulder. Everyone stopped talking. I glanced over at Ironjaw's table he wasn't there, so I knew it had to be his hand.

I heard his now familiar voice say, "You men are getting rough and loud with your language. Hold it down!"

His hand left my shoulder. I turned my head and watched him walk back to his table. We quieted down after that. No one wanted to tangle with the First Sergeant. I heard him laughing later, but by then I was getting sort of tipsy, we all were. I suggested we call it a night and get ready for tomorrow. No one else wanted to stop, so I had another swallow of beer, then left the club and returned to my room.

After reaching my room I undressed and hung up my uniform in my wall locker. My head hurt, my one eye felt tired, so sleep came easily. I barely heard the faint mournful sound of Taps. What a sad melancholy tune late in the evening, actually its heart breaking at any time.

By Friday, I had most of the letters and numbers memorized. I knew exactly how many dots and dashes made them up. Chuck Skinner would send the characters to me on the telegraph key. I would try and copy them down. I barely recognized any of them by sound alone. I would recognize one, and then miss four or five. Chuck stopped sending and made me play the tape machine again, starting me at five words per minute.

"Ken, stay on the tape machine until you can recognize all of the numbers and alphabet. Believe me it'll come to you, it just takes time."

I practiced for about three hours and felt I was finally beginning to understand the code a little bit. I knew that practice, and practice alone would make me proficient. By the next week or so, I figured I should have pretty well memorized the alphabet and the numbers by their sound.

Chuck said, "Joe Carlton is going on a three day pass to Garmisch, so I'm going to work his evening shift. You can leave whenever you are ready."

I left the message center with Merlin. We walked up the street to the barracks. The wind was blowing; the snow swirling, and the wind chill had to be around zero. It wasn't snowing, but the fallen snow was lifted and flying around from the wind. We never had much snow in Alabama. Merlin went to the barracks, and I went to the mess hall. They had fish. I guess it must be a worldwide menu item for the entire army to have fish on Friday's. Every Friday since I'd been in the army we'd had fish. I had macaroni and cheese and a large piece of unidentifiable fish. It wasn't bad at all, and the coffee was good and hot.

After going through the serving line Sergeant Perry joined me at my table. He asked, "How do you like the radio operators job?"

"I suppose it's alright, I'm having some difficulty memorizing the Morse code and connecting it with the right letters of the alphabet and numbers," I replied.

He laughed, "It just takes time to get it all right, but it'll happen. I'm also a high-speed operator, and I learned the code just as you're doing. I operate a ham radio station, and I talk to people around the world."

"That sounds interesting and exciting, what's a ham radio station?" I replied.

He said, "It's a radio set operating on certain radio bands and frequencies. It permits you to communicate with other people on that same frequency around the world."

He paused for a sip of his coffee then continued, "The post has received nine space allocations for people to attend the signal school in Ansbach. That includes teletype operators and crypto personnel. But you won't be going as I have to get enough people trained to fill positions in the sub-posts first. You're assigned as a radio operator here, all the operators including me will work with you to get you fully trained."

I was a little stunned. What happened to my radio repair job request I wondered.

"You'll get the best possible on-the-job training, that's the best way anyway, you can do it," he said.

Was my fight with Corporal Sherron the real reason? Maybe they figured that I 'm a loser, and they don't want to waste a school allocation on me, I cursed Sherron to hell and back under my breath.

"Sergeant Perry, is it because of the fight with Corporal Sherron?" I asked.

"No, that had nothing to do with the selections. We just have to train the sub-post operators first."

"Well, I 'm really disappointed that I'm not going to school, but I accept the OJT, and I'll become a radio operator. I'll be the best operator I can be, that I promise you."

He stood up, shook my hand and said, "I believe you." He turned and walked away then turning back said, "Don't forget you have a barracks inspection tomorrow morning."

So my new job is now definite. I will be a Morse code radio operator. Well, I will do my best to learn the job, and keep my bold promise to Perry. I hate like hell to have to learn a new technical job by on-the-job-training, but I know I can do it.

I got another cup of coffee and lit a cigarette. Sgt Little from the message center came into the mess hall and joined me at my table. He was in his late thirties or early forties, slender of built, graying, and seemingly a nice guy. Sergeant Little I'd been told, had been in the army all during the war, had gotten out for a few months, and then reenlisted. He was from some place in Illinois.

We talked for a while and I said, "Sergeant Little, I'm not going to radio school, Perry said I was going to be a radio operator, and would have to learn by OJT in the radio room."

He replied, "No sweat Ken, I have full confidence in you and your ability, you'll do it easily."

"I wish I had your confidence, I don't have too much right now."

"Are you married Sgt Little?"

"No, I was, but I received a 'Dear John' letter from my wife. She divorced me during the war. I'm going with a wonderful German lady who lives downtown, and I probably will marry her before my tour here is up."

Corporal Merlin joined us. He asked Sgt Little if he was going to play bingo at the club this evening. Little told him yes, and he was bringing the *Frau.*

I assumed they both enjoyed bingo. Bingo is not too much fun to me, just dumb-ass luck if you win.

Little said, "Ken, why don't you join us for bingo this evening."

"I will for a little while anyway." I knew that I would as there was nothing else to do in the barracks except sit there, read or sleep. Hell, all my clothing and equipment was ready for inspection, so no sweat there.

"Sergeant Little, who conducts the Saturday morning inspections?"

He replied, "It changes, sometimes the CO, sometimes the XO and the First Sergeant, sometimes it's just the First Sergeant. We very seldom have Saturday inspections. We haven't had one in weeks."

I figured that since the unit has so many new personnel they have to have one, so I'll be ready. I had so few clothes, there wasn't too much to inspect. Then I remembered I had laundry to pick up in the supply room.

Leaving them I dashed for the barracks, then downstairs to the supply room. Damn, it was closed and locked. I went upstairs to the company clerk's office, the Charge of Quarters was already on duty. I asked him to let me in the laundry room.

He said, "I can't leave the orderly room, and I won't open the supply room."

So I was out of luck. I was flatly disgusted, nothing seemed to be going right for me. First the fight, no school, now no clean clothes for my lockers, very little money and my first inspection tomorrow morning. Army life isn't all that it's cracked up to be, or so it seems to me.

I went upstairs to my room. Ed was there and had had a couple of drinks. I mentioned to him, "I drank a little of your cognac. I should get paid at the end of the month, so I'll buy you another bottle of cognac."

"It's all copacetic" he answered. He reached into his locker pulling out his bottle and offered me a drink. I accepted, but took only a small sip.

"I'm supposed to meet Sgt Little and his girlfriend at the club tonight, are you going over?"

"Yeah, bingo starts at eight o'clock. I'll see you there." Ed then left to take a shower.

I checked my boots and shoes, dusted the top of my locker off, and checked my footlocker once more, which had almost nothing in it. I wished like hell I some money and a pass. I'd love to go downtown and see for myself what it's like. I want to check out the girls, drink some real German beer, and have some real German food. I'll be eligible for a pass tomorrow, so maybe all those things will happen.

I walked down the hallway to Ray's room but he wasn't there. John Hodes was in his room. I knew Hodes was about as broke as I am. "Wanna, go to the club with me for a little while?" I asked.

Having nothing else to do, he agreed. Grady walked by the room and I called to him, "Where the hell have you been?" The dumb ass looked to be half loaded. I hadn't seen him since earlier in the morning.

"I've been down at the German snack bar," he replied.

Hodes spoke up and said, "That's the snack bar where all the post workers go for lunch. All the dry cleaning people, janitors, drivers and such go there. It's down by the signal supply office."

Grady remarked, "They also serve real German beer. Me and Jim Osborne are going downtown tonight."

I cautioned him, "You don't have a pass, you'll get your ass in trouble."

Grady laughed and said, "Jim has a surefire method for getting on and off the post."

"Okay, I'll be in the EM club if you get back before it closes," I said.

I went back to my room and picked up the code sheet and tried to study it, but my heart wasn't in it. I undressed, grabbed a towel and headed for the shower. The hot shower felt great. I brushed my teeth and examined my face. Both eyes were still dark but getting much lighter. The cuts over my eye and my lip were almost healed. I surely wouldn't win any beauty contest, but that's nothing new. My main idea is to get completely well.

About a quarter to eight, Hodes and I went to the club. It was foggy, and the snow was piling up in drifts. The warm lights in the club, and the music were morale boosters. Our spirits rose just knowing that some people were having a ball. I spotted Little and his girlfriend, plus another younger girl at a table, so I steered our way over to them. He had saved a couple of chairs for us, and he immediately ordered two beers.

Sergeant Little was drinking straight shots of whiskey. The ladies were sipping some type red wine. He introduced his girlfriend to me and Hodes as Gisela, and the younger girl was Gisela's daughter Frieda. Gisela looked to be about the same age as Sergeant Little, and her daughter might be around twenty or so. Gisela to me was sort of mousy, but Little must see her differently. Sergeant Little had been through the war, and looked it, but so had she in a different role. So maybe they were good for each other.

Freida wasn't bad looking actually. She had blonde hair, grey eyes, and a nice smile. I talked with her for a few minutes. She spoke surprisingly good English, as did her mother. Since American soldiers had been here for over three years maybe they had to learn English to survive. Who knows, maybe they spent time in England before the war, or went to great schools.

I gave Hodes a dollar and he bought us each a bingo card. At exactly eight o'clock they began to call the first bingo game. They called one straight game, then the four corners then an X, then another straight game. I didn't win, so I wasn't very interested in playing. Finally, the caller took a break. Everyone reordered drinks and additional cards went on sale for half price. Little bought three more cards for the three of them. They all seemed to be happy and enjoyed playing the game. I wondered if the ladies had played bingo when it was still Nazi Germany.

Hodes spoke to the waitress, and ordered another round of drinks for the table. During the second half of bingo Sergeant Little won a bottle of Three Star cognac, then the daughter won a woman's wrist watch. They were all happy. Little opened the bottle of cognac and passed it around. He took a drink, John had a drink, and I merely took a sip. I began to feel silly, but it was a pleasant feeling, so I wasn't too concerned.

Finally, they called the game for the biggest prize which was twenty-five dollars. At the current exchange rate that equaled about three hundred seventy-five German marks. The game was called "Cover All" after several minutes someone shouted "Bingo" at another table, and the game was over.

Ray came in and pulled another table up to join ours. Then Ed and his girlfriend showed up. The cognac was passed around again, and the beer continued to flow. I was getting more than just tipsy, and so was Hodes. He, like me, was too young and inexperienced to drink this heavily. The band played popular American music. They played, '*Sentimental Journey*, and then *Little Brown Jug*.'

I asked Frieda to dance. No sooner had we gotten in the dance floor when the band began playing '*Boogie Woogie*' a fast dance tune. I had danced the jitterbug to this tune in the beer joints and honkytonks back in Columbus, Georgia, and Phoenix City, Alabama.

I danced a few steps with Freida, and she followed me perfectly. I thought she's much better at this than I am. We danced another couple of tunes then returned to our table. The band then played another slower tune I had never heard before, but it was beautiful.

"Gisela, What's that tune? It's beautiful."

"It's called 'Lili Marlene,' It's a German song that was very popular during the war."

Ed ordered another round of drinks for the table, and our crowd grew louder and without a doubt a little drunker. I knew I'd had enough. I glanced over at Sergeant Little, he was just staring into space.

"Gisela, What's wrong with Sergeant Little?"

She replied, "He's had too much to drink. "

Gisela said, "We have to go home now." They said good night and left. She and Frieda each took one of his arms and slowly led him out of the club.

Ed was laughing about something he had said. His girl friend Ericka seemed bored with the entire affair. She was a nice looking woman, blonde, somewhat heavier than Ed. She had a pleasant smile, and spoke very decent English. Everyone continued to laugh, drink and make merry. I knew I had reached my limit, so I just passed the beers along the table. A couple of soldiers that I didn't know joined our table. From their appearance they were having a ball and enjoyed themselves.

Finally, the band began to play, '*Goodnight Sweetheart*.'

Ray said, "That's the signal the club is closing. We have to leave."

The club manager came by our table and said, "You men don't have to go home, but you can't stay here."

Everyone downed their drinks. I noticed that Sergeant Little's cognac bottle was laying empty on the table. Lots of people are going to have headaches tomorrow I figured.

We put on our jackets and hats, and slowly headed toward the big exit doors. Outside the snow was still falling. The wind was whipping around, and the cold air seemed to aid in clearing my head.

From around the corner an MP jeep pulled up and stopped by the barracks. The MP got out and lifted up the seat. Out stepped Grady and his friend Jim. The MP led them both into the company orderly room and turned them over to the CQ.

We waited until the MP's left then we walked into the building. Upstairs I saw them both standing in the hallway talking. I walked up to Grady and asked, "What the hell are you into now?"

With a sheepish shit eating grin he said, "We got caught coming through a hole in the fence down by the main gate. The MP didn't write us up, just chewed our asses out and brought us back to the company."

"You are one lucky duck," I told him, then headed for my room. I thought Grady is a little wild. I hope he doesn't get screwed up over here. In my opinion he drinks too much. Then I thought that really isn't fair, after all I'm drinking too much myself, even if it is just beer.

I went to the latrine inspected my face for the umpteenth time, slowly washed up, and brushed my teeth. Returning to my room, I undressed and hit the sack. In five minutes or less I was half asleep.

Once in bed all the things that has happened to me since my arrival to Germany began crowding to the front of my mind. In spite of the fight, and the ass chewing from the First Sergeant, I was still excited to be here in Germany.

Learning my new job won't be easy. Sometimes I think nothing ever comes easy to me. But that's okay. When I learn the job, I will appreciate my route and efforts to success. Sergeant Perry seems to have quite a bit of confidence in me and my ability to learn, and I certainly will try my best not to let him down.

Funny, but all of a sudden Sergeant Little with his blank stare came to mind. I have no idea what he went through during the war, but obviously it had affected him tremendously. I have seen a couple of movies and read a couple of books where a man goes through too much combat and it changes him and his personality forever. Maybe the effects of too much combat, coupled with the sudden and perhaps unexpected 'Dear John' letter from his wife was too much for him to handle at one time. It doesn't matter, either way I wish him the very best of everything.

I'm happy that I have been able so far to make so many new friends. They all seem to be nice guys, mostly new to the army and new to Germany, so it will be a learning growing experience for all of us.

With such thoughts fading away, I sank into the eagerly waiting arms of Morpheus.

CHAPTER 5

Two Inspections

I woke up with someone jabbing me in my shoulder, and a flashlight shining in my face. I thought, oh shit that damn Sherron is going to punch me out again. In self protection I covered my face and head with my arms.

Then I heard the unmistakable voice of Ironjaws, "Get out of bed Fisher!"

I opened my eyes. The First Sergeant and the Executive Officer were standing there with the flashlight in my face. I couldn't figure out what the hell was going on.

The XO said, "This is a *short arm inspection.* Get up, drop your shorts and milk it down."

Dumb ass me, I asked, "What do you mean sir?"

The XO replied, "This is an inspection for venereal disease. Drop your shorts and milk your cock down."

Still feeling a little woozy none of this made any sense to me. I got up, unbuttoned and dropped my shorts, and wouldn't you know it, I had a terrific hard on, a blue-steel hard on. It was so hard even a cat couldn't scratch it. I was so damn embarrassed.

Ironjaws said, "Milk it down."

I did as instructed and nothing appeared, so the XO said, "Okay, go back to bed."

He switched off his flashlight and they left the room. I heard the XO tell Ironjaws. "This must be the hardest dick platoon in the army."

I felt so damn stupid, trying to put my shorts back on. I looked at my watch it was 4:15 in the morning. I jumped back into bed and was soon half asleep once more.

I thought, well at least I have passed my first inspection for today. I'll worry about the second one later. I laughed thinking about my hard cock with Ironjaws and the XO standing there. What a way to spend half the night, inspecting cocks.

Ed woke me up at six-thirty. I got up went to the latrine and cleaned up. I inspected my face. My eyes were less black, my eyeball less red, and the cuts almost healed. My teeth felt tight and normal. I returned to my room and dressed.

Ed walked over and kissed his picture of Bettie, and then we went to the mess hall for a breakfast of French toast. I was starving and ate like a horse. I didn't have the slightest hangover, not even a mild headache. I felt great. I finished my meal, but skinny Ed was still putting the food away like it was his last meal. He went back for a second helping returning with his tray fully loaded again. I swear he could eat more than anyone I'd ever known. It must be a gift to be able to eat so much at one time. I smoked a cigarette while I waited for Ed to finish. The inspection was scheduled for nine o'clock, so there was no hurry.

Finally, he finished, and then he said to me, "I shacked up last night with Ericka."

I told him about the short arm inspection last night, and that it was all new and strange to me.

He laughed, "I hope that you passed."

"Not getting laid lately, I had to pass," I replied. Finished, we left the mess hall and returned to the barracks and our room.

I went down to the supply room and got my laundry, rushing back upstairs to put it all away before the inspection. Ed helped me roll my socks and fold my towels placing them in my footlocker in the proper manner. We finished and had it all done correctly.

I walked down the hall to Grady's room, he was ready for the inspection. He said, "Me and Jim have to report to the First Sergeant right after the inspection."

"Don't worry too much maybe he'll go easy on you if you didn't get a Delinquent Report. He'll probably just chew your asses out, and let you go," I said.

Grady looked worried, "No way, he'll make an example out of us for sure."

"You dumb ass, I told you not to go off post without a pass." With that remark I returned to my room to wait for the inspection.

At nine o'clock I heard someone call, "Attention." I snapped to. I saw the Co and the First Sergeant pass by my room. I relaxed and peeked out the door and saw them go into the first room up the hall. Someone called, "Attention," again then silence.

Then another voice gave the command then silence once more. I heard Cpl Carlton call "Attention", he was in the room next to ours. I was by my bunk and Ed was standing in the doorway. He called, "Attention" and I snapped to. The CO and Ironjaws strode into our room.

The CO inspected me up and down and asked, "What's your name soldier?"

"Private Fisher," I replied

He looked into my wall locker then my foot locker, then at my boots and high tops. He told Ironjaws, "The boots and high tops are marked incorrectly."

Ironjaws wrote something down on his clip board.

A thin film of sweat beaded on my forehead. I knew I had been gigged. I wondered what the penalty was for that.

Finally, they left. I was happy to complete my first room inspection.

Ed said, "You'll be on some shit detail this afternoon."

What the hell, I had passed one inspection today, and failed the second. The first one was the more important to be sure. Passing one out of two inspections, and receiving just one gig isn't bad for a new Private.

Ed reached into his locker and pulled his bottle out. We both had a short sip of cognac. That cognac was beginning to taste pretty good.

After the inspection was completed we had a formation outside. The First Sergeant called out the names of those of us who had been gigged. "The names and your assigned details will be posted on the bulletin board in the hall way," he said.

After the formation, Merlin, Corporal Bill Pitts and I went to the snack bar for coffee. Pitts was the crypto guy who worked with Ray. He was married, and hailed from Maryland. I had been in his room once before and noted a large picture of his lovely wife on the wall. He said he wrote to her almost daily. I think he had been here well over a year or more. He was serious in his demeanor and very intelligent. He was stocky built, about six feet tall, and blonde hair.

Pitts said, "I went out with Betty last night, we spent the night at the Ring Hotel. The place was jumping and we had a great evening."

"What does it cost for a room at the Ring Hotel for all night, and who is Betty?"

He replied, "About three dollars or forty-five marks. Betty is my sometimes girlfriend, she works over in the switchboard."

"That sounds like a reasonable price to me," I said.

Betty was one of two switchboard operators working on post. So far I have yet to meet either one of the two operators.

Merlin had to work the evening shift. I offered to pull the shift with him, but he declined. I guess he didn't want to be bothered with a neophyte operator. I left and returned to my room and changed back into fatigues and boots. Having some spare time I stretched out on my bed and closed my eyes.

I tried to put the past couple of weeks into some perspective. So much had happened to me since arriving in Germany. Grady and I looking for prostitutes in the snow at Marburg, then the fight and my revenge, plus falling in front of the First Sergeant not once, but twice. I didn't get the job I wanted, or the school, and I have to learn my job the hard way. Finally, I had passed the short arm inspection only to fail my first barracks inspection, and now assigned to a shit detail. New friends, new faces, and a new job all at once. Wow!

I needed some normal average duty for a change. I also realized that I was drinking more than I ever had, I've drank more since getting to this unit than I have in my entire life. I have a fear of alcoholism. I've heard all my life about the evils of alcohol. But it seems around here it was part of the fabric of life. But I was beginning to glimpse that it could be my un-doing. Then I dozed off.

Pop Warner came by and woke me and said, "Let's go eat lunch."

We went to the mess hall. I ate very little as I wasn't really hungry.

Pop said, "Ken, I've been off post every night but one since we arrived here. I've already found a girl friend, and I'm moving in with her once I have a legal pass."

"Where does she live?" I asked.

"She lives in a couple of rooms of a bombed out apartment building, but its not too bad. It's across the river," he replied.

"Well, enjoy yourself, and good luck," I said.

Pop looked bad to me, his eyes were bloodshot and sunken in, his hands shaky and his breath was horrible. I forgave it all, as he was an old WWII veteran, and for me that made all the difference. We finished lunch and walked back up the hill and into the barracks.

I checked the bulletin board, I was gigged on my boots and one set of underwear. I thought it was both my boots. I was also detailed to clean M-1 rifles in the supply room.

A couple of other guys were assigned with me to clean the rifles. They were both new to me. At one o'clock that afternoon we reported to the CQ who took us to the supply room and opened up the rifle racks, issued us some cleaning patches, rifle rods, gun oil and told us to let him know when we finished, he would inspect the rifles. We had forty-eight rifles to clean.

We introduced ourselves and began to clean the rifles. We talked about our first impressions of Germany, and of our unit. Somehow the conversation shifted to the short arm inspection. Neither of us had ever heard of such an inspection before. It turned out we all three had erections when we got out of our bunks. The more we discussed it the more hilarious it became.

Peter, the taller of the two new guys said, "When I got out of bed, the XO said, 'Private, where are your shorts, why aren't you wearing underwear?'"

"Sir, I don't wear shorts when I sleep," I replied

"Well damn it Private, the army issued you shorts, and by god you will wear them, get some on right now," the XO said

Peter laughed, I said, "Yes Sir." Still laughing he continued, "I found a pair of shorts in my footlocker and put them on. My dick stood out like a flashlight with a red light bulb on the end."

The XO said, "Milk'er down."

Peter said, Well, I was still about half drunk, so I said to the XO, "Sir, I got laid earlier tonight, and I ain't touching that thing until I wash it off."

Jim, the other guy doubled over in laughter. I was laughing also as I could visualize the scene.

Peter continued, "Well at four-thirty this morning I had to take a shower, then the First Sergeant pulled my pass for seven days, and I'm on detail."

After I stopped laughing, I asked him, "Peter, what did you get gigged for?"

Laughing he replied, "You won't believe this, but I was gigged for "Failure to maintain personal hygiene."

We all three had a good laugh at such a dumb ass reason to get gigged. We discussed the proper way to mark boots and clothing. Finally, we finished the rifles. I went upstairs and got the CQ.

He came downstairs and inspected the rifles. He gave the rifles only a cursory glance and said, "They're clean, you guys are released from detail."

I strolled over to the snack bar and had a cup of coffee. I saw the Special Service hostess again. I smiled at her and winked. She smiled back but offered no further encouragement. She got up and left the snack bar. I watched as she walked away. She had a fantastic body, built like a brick shit house. I mused, what a terrific piece of ass that would be. Then I remembered what Ed had told me: "Enlisted swine don't make out with beautiful American women." I figured he's probably right. A low ass Private with a busted up face, against all the officers and NCO's around doesn't stand a chance.

That night I stayed in the barracks. I washed a couple pair of socks and underwear in the stationary sink in the latrine. Then I carefully re-marked my clothes and boots. I need to get a rubber stamp with the initial of my last name and the last four numbers of my serial number to really do it right. Around eleven o'clock I went to bed, heard Taps, and tried to go to sleep. Unfortunately, recent events kept tumbling around in my mind making me restless and unsettled. What will be my future in this outfit? Will I be able to master my new job? Will the fight keep me from being promoted? Such thoughts raced through my mind, gradually they subsided, and my breathing slowed, I fell asleep.

Sometimes later, I faintly heard our room door open, and the hall light streamed into our room. When I heard voices and laughter I sat up. Ed walked into the room with two women, and he was obviously high as a Georgia pine.

"Hey Ken, everything's copacetic," he shouted. "Look what I brought you. You can get your first piece of German nookie right in the comfort and privacy of your own bedroom."

Shocked and scared I said, "Ed you crazy bastard, what's wrong with you? Do you want to get us both thrown in the stockade?"

He laughed, "Don't worry the inspection is over. No one checks the barracks on the weekend other than the CQ. We can close the door and lock the room, have a few drinks and screw all night. I'll get them out of here before daylight." He walked over and kissed Bettie Page and said, "I apologize darling."

He turned her picture to the wall. He had a full bottle of Five Star Cognac, which he opened, took a drink then passed it over to me.

Before I took a drink, I asked him again, "Ed, are you sure we won't get caught? You know how damn much trouble I've been in already."

"Don't worry, don't worry, nothing will go wrong I promise you," he replied.

He turned on the small lamp between our two bunks, then closed and latched the room door. I then took my first look at the two girls. The girl he had his arm around was about five foot-four, blonde hair, a nice smile and had less than white teeth.

Ed said, "Her name's Margaret, and she speaks some English."

The other girl was no raving beauty, but appeared to be the better looking of the two. She had dark hair, brown eyes, and looked maybe eighteen years old. I smiled at her, and she returned my smile.

She then spoke to me, "*Sprechen sie deutsch*?"

I looked at Ed, "What the hell did she say?".

"She asked you if you speak German." He then spoke to her in German, and she said simply "Okay."

"Ed, what did you say to her?"

He began laughing and said, "I told her you're a hillbilly redneck, and can hardly speak English, much less German." Ed almost doubled over in laughter.

Hell, even I had to laugh at his Yankee brand of humor. I asked her, "Do you speak English?"

She replied, "Ja a little."

"What's your name?"

She replied, "Imgard."

"Well, hello Imgard, sit down here." I indicated a place on my bunk. I swung my legs over the side of the bunk. I was in my shorts, no point in putting my pants on now. I tilted up the cognac bottle and had a small sip. I thought to get through this night I might need a couple of swallows. Ed had been to the Leopold, then the Ring Hotel where he said he had picked the two girls up. I reached over and turned on Ed's radio. It was tuned to AFN, nice easy big band music was playing. The two girls took off their coats then their sweaters and lay them across the footlockers.

In English Margaret asked me, "How long have you been in Germany?"

I made a quick calculation and said, "About fourteen days."

She smiled and said in German, "*Du bist ine junger soldaten ja*?"

"Ja," I had no idea what she had said.

Ed spoke up and said, "She said you are a young soldier."

I offered Imgard a drink from the bottle. She accepted and had a small swallow. Then Margaret had a swallow. Ed was sitting on his bunk grinning like crazy, and then he reached over and pulled Margaret onto his bunk and began unbuttoning her blouse. She stood up and began to undress. I indicated to Imgard that she too should undress. I observed that neither of the girls shaved their armpits.

I asked Ed, "How much is this going to cost me?"

"Thirty marks."

"Ed, I don't have any marks."

"Everything's copacetic, I'll pay, and you can pay me back when you get paid."

"Okay."

Imgard undressed and then eased down onto my bunk. I moved over to make room for her. I cradled her head in my arm leaned over and gave her a light kiss, she returned it.

Ed spoke up and said, "No screwing until the lights are out, this is a military organization you know. We have rules and regulations."

"How old are you?" I asked.

She said, "I'm twenty-four and you?"

"I'm eighteen," I replied.

Then she kissed me again. I slid my hand up to cup her breast, they were full, warm and inviting. I could feel an immediate twitch in my cock, and a small burning in my stomach from the cognac. Margaret spoke up and asked for the money. Ed grabbed his pants from the floor and fumbled through his pockets, then handed her three twenty mark notes. The finances were settled for the evening. I had another small swallow of cognac.

Ed was in rare form and talking to Margaret in German, he obviously knew quite a bit of the language. I guess having a German girlfriend helps tremendously in learning the language. I reached over and turned off the night lamp. A faint sliver of hall light shone into the room from beneath the door. I slipped off my shorts and then assisted her in taking off her panties. I kissed her again, our tongues playing their own games. Ed and his girl were giggling then silence. The entire building was quiet.

A crazy thought flashed through my mind. "Ed, what if they have another short arm inspection tonight or tomorrow morning," I asked.

He laughed and replied, "Execute Plan B."

"What in the hell is that?"

He laughed again and said, "Commit suicide."

"I won't have to, Ironjaws will kill me for sure," I replied.

I moved over on top of her and we made love. We rested for a short while then made love again. Ed and Margaret were moaning and groaning, whispering in German. Then they became quiet.

I reached over and got the bottle and had a small sip of cognac. Imgard also had a small swallow. Ed turned the lamp on. Margaret was sitting on the edge of his bunk. She pulled the sheet up to cover herself. I think she actually blushed.

Ed said, "Let's go wash up a bit."

We both got our towels and headed for the latrine.

"Here use this prophylactic soap and wash up with it."

"Thanks." I followed his instructions to the letter. The very last thing I needed was a dose of gonorrhea.

"I'll give the girls to someone else. Go back to the room and bring them one at a time to the latrine. Let'em wash up a bit then tell'em to get dressed,"

"Let's hope we don't get caught in the hallway," I replied. Then I did as he requested.

Both girls agreed with no problem whatsoever. I took Margaret to the latrine first. She ran some hot water and with one of my towels and soap wet the towel and entered one of the commode stalls and closed the door. In a couple of minutes, she came out and quickly washed out the towel handing it to me. I escorted her back to the room and accompanied Imgard to the latrine where she performed the same procedures. We both returned to my room and the ladies both dressed.

Ed returned with a big shit eating grin on his face and said, "Everything's copacetic. I found two hard dicks that will take them out of here and home in the morning."

He said something to Margaret in German, and the women both got up and left the room with him. He returned shortly and said, "They're with Nunez and Nelson. Nunez has to go to work early in the morning, so he'll leave and drop them off downtown before he goes to work." He closed and latched the door, then walked over turning Bettie's picture around and kissing it said, "I'm sorry darling," then sat down on his bunk.

I had a sip of cognac and passed the bottle to Ed. He had a small swallow. I was feeling the effects of the cognac. I did feel better now that I had gotten laid. The girls were gone and Germany was beginning to look good once again.

"Ed, are all the German girls whores like these two?"

Ed was silent for a few seconds and then said, "Let me explain something Ken, and I hope you absorb and understand what I 'm saying. It's been three years and seven months since the war ended. Germany is in shambles and ruins. There is very little industry, and over half their cities are destroyed, many of their young men are dead. Husbands, fathers, brothers, sons, all killed in the war. The women, especially the young women have to make a living any way they can. If you are a woman and you have a family to feed, hungry children, starving babies, old parents, all with no money, then you'll do whatever you have to do to ensure their and your own survival. If that means prostituting yourself to get money, then that's what you do. Women have only one thing to sell that men want, so they sell it. These two girls may have been very well off before the war, but now they must sell their bodies just to survive. So don't be too harsh or judgmental. If what happened here in Germany happened in the United States, the women there would do exactly the same thing as they are doing here."

Ed's remarks and logic sunk in deep, the way he explained their plight made total sense. He opened up a new moral window for me to look at situations and people. I never forgot his remarks, and the basic underlying truth supporting them. Never again could I look at a prostitute without—perhaps subconsciously—remembering his remarks.

I smoked a cigarette, refused another drink, then turned off the light and called it a good night. I pulled the sheet and blanket up around my neck. What a beginning this had been. If I don't get the clap, and if we get that flying twenty dollars on Monday, the world will look much brighter.

I woke up Sunday morning about seven o'clock. Ed was still sleeping. I called his name and he grunted. I called his name again and told him to wake up. He groaned, rolled over and sat up on his bunk.

"Let's get cleaned up and go for breakfast."

I went to the latrine, washed up and returned to the room. Ed washed up and got dressed. Following his normal routine, Ed walked over and kissed Bettie with his customary, "Good Morning, beautiful."

"Ed, after last night you really need to apologize to Miss Page."

"Why? She didn't see anything."

We walked down to the mess hall and went through the chow line. I had toast, ham and eggs, and coffee. Merlin and Ray were at a table so we joined them.

Ray had bacon and eggs on his plate; he sprinkled his eggs with a large splash of ketchup.

I asked, "Ray, what in the hell are you doing ruining your eggs?"

"I'm putting ketchup on my eggs dumb ass, haven't you ever tried it?"

"No, but I'll try it tomorrow when I have eggs again," I replied.

Ed told Ray and Merlin about our social activities of last night. He was laughing telling them how scared I was, how the girls and the cognac worked, and that now I was truly initiated to Germany. The remainder of the day was uneventful.

Monday, all we new guys went to the XO's office and were given a flying twenty dollar bill which had to last over Christmas, and the remainder of the month. That would be a hard thing to accomplish. I knew without question that my activities would be limited to the EM club, the snack bar, and the service club.

All that week I worked in the radio room, studying the alphabet and then trying to identify the letters and numbers on the tape machine. By the end of the week, I had memorized the entire alphabet and all the numbers, but identifying them by sound was something entirely different. Skinner became frustrated, and kept me working on the tape machine.

Grady and his friend Jim had gone to see Ironjaws. He had chewed their asses out, and told them they were being reassigned to the sub-post at Aschaffenburg. They were leaving this week. Boy, I hated that. I had hoped that Grady and I would stay together. But the army does what it wants to do. I talked with Grady for a little while. I told him he could always come back to Wurzburg, just catch the courier Jeep. Several other troops were also being assigned to the various sub-posts at the same time.

I assumed that I too would be reassigned shortly also. I then reasoned that since I wasn't trained, and there were no training facilities at the sub-posts, maybe I won't have to go. It's best I try harder to learn my job here. I kept at the code, picking up a few more letters and recognizing more of the numbers by their sound.

I stayed out of the club all week, and just concentrated on my job, and staying straight in the company. I was ready to let the code go for a few days, and have some fun. But with limited funds I knew that my activities were severely curtailed. A couple of days before Christmas they had decorated the mess hall and the club. This will be my first Christmas away from home, and I don't have too much to be happy about. I recalled how we celebrated Christmas when I was a boy. It was always a wonderful time of the year to me. My folks could never afford lots of gifts, but the few I did get were given and received with loads of love and happiness.

I got off work at five o'clock and walked up to the mess hall. They had fish naturally. Once back in the barracks, I cleaned my boots and high tops, and then straightened up the room.

Ray came by my room and we talked for awhile. He was off until Sunday, so we decided to go to the club. It was Bingo night, but I didn't plan to play. We were sitting talking when Ed came in. He had just finished his courier run to Kissingen. He had his omni-present bottle of cognac with him, and had obviously been tapping it. He offered us a swig of it which we accepted, and that set the tone for the evening. He decided to go with us, so while he was showering we sipped from his bottle. No chasers except cigarettes. If you can hold the first swallow down, the others go down more easily.

"Ken, don't mention this, but Ed sells his cigarettes on the black market and gives most of the money to a local orphanage. He has done that ever since he arrived in the unit. His brother was killed in the war, and left a wife and three kids. Believe me underneath that devil may care exterior he presents, there is a heart of gold. That's his secret, let's keep it that way."

I nodded my head in agreement. I now understood my roommate much better.

By the time Ed was ready to go we had both drank several swallows from his bottle. He capped the bottle and hid it back of the uniforms in his wall locker, kissed Bettie and then we left.

The club was packed with people. The tables were filled with couples or groups of soldiers. We found one empty table and ordered a round of beer. I saw Ironjaws and his wife at a table with SFC Perry and his girlfriend. Ironjaws wasn't playing bingo but they were. I couldn't tell what he was drinking, but it was in a high ball glass. It appeared to be whiskey. Finally, bingo was over and some of couples left. The orchestra began to play and couples drifted to the dance floor. The women looked good, and I was as horny as a jack rabbit.

I saw the waitress take Ironjaws a drink, and it was straight whiskey. As big as he is, and as straight as I figure him to be, he fascinates me. To know he was in the army before I was even born is amazing. I've been in the army just over six months. He had his Class A uniform on as did everyone. Civilian clothes weren't permitted in Europe for military personnel. He had six rows of ribbons and numerous badges. I knew he was a well decorated war veteran and had seen lots of combat. I envied him, the idea of combat was stimulating, and I deeply regretted not being old enough to fight in WWII. Ironjaw's in his OD uniform was still the most impressive soldier I'd ever seen.

Ed suggested we go downtown for a while. I had a pass, but very little money. Against my better judgment I agreed to go. We left the club, piled into Ed's Jeep and drove towards the main gate. The MP waved us through without checking. I looked around the area, this was my first time off the post since arriving here.

CHAPTER 6

My very first one

Ed drove slowly, and I saw again all the bombed out houses and buildings. I had again a whiff of that unpleasant smell. I wondered how many people had died in the houses that were now reduced to twisted metal, splintered wood, and shattered concrete.

The wind was blowing about 15 or 20 miles per hour making things somewhat uncomfortable for us. We turned a corner and about halfway down the block through the dim headlights we saw something falling into the street. Ed drove closer, and we discovered it was a chimney that had blown over from the force of the wind. The bricks were strewn across the sidewalk and into the street. We quickly stopped and picked them up throwing them back into the rubble pile, which was all that was left of what was once a large house.

I wondered who had lived in the house? What memories they would have, how would they feel if they once again could see what was perhaps their happy home now just dust and rubble? War is far more than just destroyed buildings, it destroys families equally as efficiently and completely.

Ray wanted to go to the Leopold, and Ed wanted to go to the Ring Hotel. They flipped a coin and Ed won, so we went to the hotel. We drove around a big park, and Ed pulled up in front of the hotel and parked. After we climbed out we closed the plastic and canvas doors of the Jeep. I was excited about my first visit to a real German bar and hotel.

In spite of the freezing temperatures, I felt warm all over. Without a doubt the cognac and beer were responsible for that. We entered the front door and I noted a small counter to our left where a man sat on a stool. He spoke to Ed, and Ed answered back in German. Ed led the way down a long carpeted hallway that had numbered rooms on either side. At the end of the hallway were double doors. Ed opened one, and we walked into the bar and restaurant part of the hotel. There were mostly GI's with their girls, and two German couples. We sat at a table and Ed ordered us all cognac and cola. I sipped the cognac, and then sipped the cola, it tastes pretty good.

Ed said, "Pour your cognac in the cola and stir it up, it'll taste much better."

I did as he suggested, and it was much better. Ed paid for the round.

"Ed, where can I get some marks? I want to pay for the next round."

"Give me five dollars, and I'll get some marks for you," he replied.

I handed him the money and he left, returning in about five minutes and gave me seventy-five marks.

I ordered us another round of cognac and cola paying for them with my new marks. A couple of women came into the bar and sat down several tables away from us. They were both young and fairly good looking.

Ed said, "I think I know one of those girls, I'll check it out, you guys stay here." He walked over to their table, spoke to them and then sat down at their table. They began a conversation. He turned around and called the waitress who brought them two glasses of wine, and Ed another cognac and cola. About ten minutes later he returned to our table.

Ray asked, "Did you score, or is it a Maggies Drawers?"

Ed laughed and said, "No, Maggies drawers mean you totally missed your target, I didn't miss. One girl says she has the rag on, and the other one is waiting for her boy friend."

"Ed, what do you mean she has the rag on?" I asked.

Ed laughed, and then looked at me to be sure I was serious. "Ken, you really are a dumb-ass hillbilly. I mean she's flying the red flag, or in more polite terms she's having her monthly period. The one dressed in black will give you some loving for twenty marks if you get a room."

I jumped at the chance and said, "I'll go for that, Ray do you want to get some loving also?"

"Sure, I never pass up the chance."

We each gave Ed thirty marks, he left and went up the hallway. He returned shortly with a room key handing it to me. "Go up to room 10 and wait there." He then walked over and said something to the girl.

I went up the hall and reached room 10. I unlocked the door and stepped inside. Room 10 had a small table covered with numerous cigarette burns, a badly patched carpet, one chair, a double bed, and a stained sink with a cracked mirror, plus a small bathroom. Nothing fancy to be sure. I lit a cigarette and looked for an ashtray, but there wasn't one available.

A couple of minutes passed, and then I heard a light knock on the door. I opened the door and the young girl dressed in black was standing there, a smile crossed her face.

I smiled back and said, "Please come in."

She entered the room and said, "Hello."

"Hello."

She had a drink in her hand, "Your friend sent you this."

I took the drink, smelled it and recognized the odor of cognac and cola. I took a sip. She sat down on the bed, and I sat down besides her placing my drink on the small table.

Speaking fairly decent English she said, "You want to make love to me?"

"Yes," I replied.

Reaching over me she pulled the zipper down on my Ike jacket taking it off my shoulders. Gently, she pushed me back onto the bed. She unfastened my belt buckle, opened my pants pulling my shirt and undershirt out pushing them up on my stomach. Standing up, she opened her blouse, she wore no brassiere. She reached over and turned off the light, and sat down on the bed again. In the dim light I could see and feel her hands unbuttoning my shorts. I felt her hand stroking my stomach running lightly through my pubic hair barely touching my dick. It immediately sprang to life, and began to harden. In nanoseconds, I had a hard as railroad steel erection.

She grasped my left hand placing it on her right breast. I began to massage and caress it gently. Her nipple grew in size, and became very firm. She leaned over and kissed my stomach. She continued to kiss my stomach and ran her tongue lightly across, going lower and lower, I thought I would faint the feeling was so exciting. About three or four minutes later I lost it, the feeling ineffable. Shortly thereafter she reached over and turned on the light. She rose from the bed and spit into the small sink, ran the water and rinsed out her mouth.

Turning, she smiled and asked, "Did you like that?"

Weakly, I returned her smile and whispered, "Yes!"

She tucked in and buttoned her blouse, and then smiling at me left the room.

I got up and washed off a bit in the sink and dried off. I drank the remainder of my drink, adjusted my uniform, and I left the room locking the door behind me. I thought about the guys who had come back from the war and told me about this type of sex, and how it felt. Now I knew exactly what they were talking about. They didn't lie!

Reentering the bar area I joined Ray and Ed at the table.

Ed laughed and asked, "How did you like that, was that money well spent?"

"That was the best twenty marks a man could possibly spend, I said."

The girl in black was already at her table drinking wine. I gave the room key to Ray. He gave me his drink and waved to the girl. She smiled and nodded her head in agreement. Ray left, in a couple of minutes she also left.

I asked Ed, "What about you, are you going with her tonight, or what are you going to do?"

"I have an overnight pass, so I'll take you and Ray back to the *Kaserne* and then come back downtown."

About ten minutes or so later Ray came back into the bar area. I had already ordered him another cognac and cola.

He smiled and said, "That was terrific."

I nodded my head in complete agreement.

We finished our drinks and decided to return to the barracks. Ed drove us back, and let us off in front of the EM club.

It was just nine-thirty in the evening, so there was an hour and a half to go before the club closed. As usual on Saturday nights the club was crowded. I spotted Roberts and Hodes at a table, so we joined them. They had a pitcher of beer. The waitress brought over two glasses, so

I poured us a glass of beer and ordered another pitcher. The band was playing some American tune and several couples were dancing.

Sam Amato came in and joined out table. He leaned over and told me, "I got my orders this morning to leave for Ansbach Signal School on Monday morning, and then go from there to Bad Kissengen to be the radio operator."

That was bad news to me, Sam and I had become close friends. "Sam, I hate to hear that, I wish you good luck at the school, and in your new assignment. "We drank a toast to his new assignment.

We watched the couples dancing. I noticed one woman who was dancing with a Sergeant. I didn't recognize him or her. She was beautiful, about five foot three or four, with long dark flowing hair, slender, beautiful legs and a gorgeous ass. Her eyes were dark brown matching her hair perfectly. She appeared to be better dressed than most of the other women present. I assumed the Sergeant must take pretty good care of her. I watched as she smiled at her partner while carrying on some type of conversation. She had an extraordinary face. The guy she was dancing with appeared to be a little drunk. She glanced in my direction and I smiled and winked at her, she smiled back. I watched as she and her dance partner joined other couples at a table across the dance floor. The troops at our table continued to drink beer and discuss current events, especially those that directly affected us.

Finally, the band began to play 'Goodnight Sweetheart,' it was time to call it an evening. Slowly, we drank our beers. Donning our hats we headed for the exit.

As we entered the front lobby, the beautiful dark-haired girl and the Sergeant were close to us in the crowd. I edged over closer to her. She noticed me and smiled. He was in front of her leading the way out to the doors. Everyone was trying to exit the doors at the same time. As we drew closer to the door, I slid my arm around her waist and gently pulled her towards me. She smiled at me and made no attempt to remove my arm, or to move away from me.

I whispered, "My name's Kenny."

She whispered back, "My name's Rachel."

I removed my arm from around her waist, and thought what in the hell am I doing? I must be crazy! Her boyfriend will punch my lights out if he catches me with my arm around his girlfriend or his wife. She followed the Sergeant out the door disappearing in the crowd, the fog, and the night.

Ray, Sam and I walked across the street and into our barracks.

I remarked, "I'm beat, I'm going to bed." Ray and Sam agreed, so we each headed for our rooms.

Once in my room I removed my jacket, shirt and tie. I picked up a towel from the end of my bunk, my shaving kit and went to the latrine. I washed up with hot water and soap, finally brushing my teeth. Returning to my room, I hung up my towel and replaced all the items in their proper places. I went to bed as I was really tired.

I lay there thinking about the oral sex I had gotten, a man sure could learn to love such method of love making. Then I thought about the beautiful girl I'd briefly met in the club. I wondered who she was, and what her relationship with the Sergeant is? Are they married? Is she an American, German, possibly even English? I guess the answer to all those questions will have to wait for another day.

Sunday morning I woke up early. After showering and shaving I put on a fresh clean set of fatigues. I pulled on my polished high tops and left for the mess hall. Taylor was at a table by himself, so I went through the serving line then joined him. We talked about things going on in our lives, and I told him I had gotten my first ever oral sex last night.

"Congratulations," Taylor said, and shook my hand. "Every man owes it to himself, and deserves to get one of those on his first trip to a new town."

That seemed logical to me. Other men began to drift into the mess hall. Merlin and SFC Perry joined us then Bill Pitts arrived. I just sat and listened to them talk. I knew I could learn more by listening than talking. Bill told Perry about an especially difficult message he had received earlier in the morning. After a couple of hours of telephoning, and exchanging teletype messages with Heidleberg, he'd figured out what they were communicating.

SFC Perry turned to Taylor and asked him, "How do you like message center work?"

Taylor answered, "It's rather easy and its fine with me, I don't mind it at all."

Perry said, "How would you like to take over the message center operations in Hammelburg? You'll be in charge of the courier service, radio and teletype operations and the 6087 personnel for the sub-post. If you take the job, it would really help out the section." He paused before saying, "I have no one else with experience that I can place in the job." He paused again then added the kicker, "If you take it, I guarantee you'll make Corporal by the first of February."

That was the major selling point. Without hesitation Jack said, "I'll take it."

I was glad that he did, and hoped he would make Corporal as promised by Perry.

"Okay Jack, pack your stuff up today, you'll be leaving tomorrow morning with the courier." That sort of dampened our conversation, so we all finished breakfast and went back to the barracks.

Picking up my radio notes I began studying the alphabet codes and numbers once more. After about an hour of that, I opened up the Q signal book and studied the Q codes again that Chuck had checked in red for me to learn. I knew about fifteen of them which were sufficient for communications over the radio.

Tiring of this, I walked down to the radio center to see what was going on. The snow continued falling, and the temperature hovering just above freezing. I arrived at the headquarters building and rang the bell. Nunez opened the door for me. Skinner was operating the set today.

"What the hell are you doing here today?" Skinner asked.

"There's nothing to do in the barracks, so I thought I would come down here and maybe work on the tape machine."

"Be my guest," he replied.

I sat at the counter put on the headphone and turned on the tape machine. It was still set at five words a minute. I could get maybe three of five characters in a five letter group. I was getting better, and I knew it. After an hour I switched to the telegraph key and tried to send the code. I tapped out the code slowly on top of the key. Trying to hold the key wasn't going to be my style. I practiced with the key for about another hour. The afternoon wore on, and finally I returned to the barracks. Even doing absolutely nothing, I had developed an appetite.

Pitts was there. "I'm going to the mess hall and get a bite to eat, want to go with me?" I asked him.

"Sure, I'll go to chow with you, but first I have to take some cigarettes over to Betty at the switchboard. If you want to, I'll introduce you to the two operators."

I liked that idea, I had heard one of the girls was really good looking, and very well built.

"The girl I date sometimes is named Betty, and Carlton is going with the other girl who's named Wilma."

We walked across the quadrangle and up the stairs at the end of the building. Bill rang a doorbell outside the steel door which protected the wooden door to the switchboard room. A young girl about twenty or so opened the door and invited us in to the room.

Pitts introduced me to both Betty and Wilma. Betty was a lovely girl, dark hair, tall and a great figure. She was I guessed, in her early twenties. Wilma was a nice looking blonde, a little heavier than Betty. Betty it turned out was the best looking one of the two.

He gave Betty three packs of cigarettes. She hugged his neck and expressed her thanks. He and I then left for the mess hall.

While we were eating, I asked Bill, "Where are all the colored soldiers located? I seldom ever see them." I knew they were stationed someplace as I would see one every now and then. Mostly I had seen them driving by in big semi-tractor trucks and trailers.

"They're mostly stationed in Kissingen. They are in a big transportation outfit there. I think it's the 444th Battalion or something like that." Pausing for a second he said, "I have heard that the VD rate is very high in Kissingen, so you best stay out of that town. Going there is just asking for trouble."

I absorbed all the offered information and filed it away. Later that evening seeking something to do I walked over to the Service Club. Several GI's were involved in card games, and two guys were shooting pool. Several others were reading books or magazines. I picked up a magazine and found a nice comfortable chair, and settled down to read it. Just as I began to read the magazine, I heard a voice say, "Well hello!"

I looked up to see the Service Club hostess. I stood up and said, "Hello," and smiled my friendliest smile at her.

She said, "Is this your first time in the service club? I don't recall seeing you here before."

"Yes, this is my first time here," I replied.

I extended my hand and said, "I'm Private Ken Fisher. What's your name?"

She shook my hand. "Welcome, I hope to see you here more often, we do have fun. My name's Dolores Gomez, but my friends call me Dotty."

"Well Dotty, may I buy you a cup of coffee?"

"Why buy it, we have it here for you for free." She led the way to a coffee pot. I poured two cups of coffee, while she found a vacant card table.

After we sat at the table she said, "I'm from Miami, Florida, I've been in the Special Service club system about ten months, and here for four months. This is my first overseas assignment."

"Well, I'm from Alabama, and have been in the army about six months, and like you this is also my first overseas assignment. So we seem to have a lot in common." She smiled my remark off, but made no response.

"How did you get your face so bruised up and why?"

I briefly explained the fight with Corporal Sherron to her without too many graphic details.

She remarked, "Your face seems to be getting better, you should be completely recovered soon."

"I certainly hope so, but I don't expect to win many beauty contests." She just laughed.

Finally, I stood up and told her I had to return to the barracks. We shook hands and I said, "I'll be back for sure."

"Please do, I look forward to seeing you again," she replied.

Christmas came and went. Nothing exciting really happened. The GI's with families who lived downtown were all at home, and the men with shack jobs were all shacked up. We new guys and a few of the older ones managed to support the EM club during the period. I found out the club manager was planning a big party and dance for New Year's Eve. I really looked forward to that. Roberts, Hodes, Ray and I planned to make it together. Came the big night, I had my low quarters sparkling, my brass glistening, my uniform freshly cleaned and pressed. I looked sharp and I felt great, I was ready to party all night.

The club was going to stay open until one o'clock in the morning so we could really celebrate the New Year's arrival. We arrived at the club about eight o'clock in the evening, most of the tables had been taken already. Finally, we found an empty table down towards the back of the dance floor. The lights were dimmer in this section as they were all slanted back to shine on the dance floor and the dancers. The band was already playing and several couples were up dancing. The band played a couple of fast tunes then a couple of slow dances. For sure, some of the guys dancing were a hellava lot worse that I am. We ordered two pitchers of beer and glasses. I settled in to watch the couples dance. Some couples were really good and some were lousy. I noticed one couple who was obviously married. I recognized him as the manager of the post bowling alley. She was a blonde with a nice figure and large breast. She wore a white evening gown and looked outstanding in it. They were whirling around the floor laughing and talking, a very impressive couple. The guys began to compare the couples, but mostly we just watched. A couple of other guys joined our table, finding chairs and bringing them over. More pitchers of beer were ordered and began to flow freely. As the evening wore on I knew I was getting a glow on. With that thought, I just relaxed and really began to enjoy the activities.

New Year's Eve, 1948, was speeding along. With the New Year tomorrow I look forward to mastering my job on the radio, and maybe getting promoted to Private First Class.

Suddenly, I saw Rachel dancing with her Sergeant friend. She saw me at about the same time. She smiled at me, and I smiled and winked at her. I watched her as they completed the dance and returned to their table. They were seated several tables from us, more toward the middle of the ballroom. Damn, I thought, she is one good looking, beautiful woman. She turned and smiled at me again before disappearing from my view.

In a flash a fight started somewhere up near the front of the club. It was broken up quickly, and a couple of hotheads were escorted out of the club. That's a great way to spoil your New Year's Eve party I thought. Me, I intend to be the most peaceful person in this place. I saw Corporal Sherron sitting at another table some distance from ours. He appeared to be having a good time. Like mine, his cuts had healed, he even had two new front teeth. I experienced a feeling of pleasure knowing that I was responsible for his two missing front teeth. Hopefully, that will be a continuing reminder to him that punching people and starting a fight even with someone smaller, is not the best way to go, or the smartest.

Sherron's girlfriend wasn't very good looking, actually she was definitely unattractive. That gave me a perversely good feeling. I didn't like anything about the bastard. He was a bad event I'd experienced, a bad dream. I dismissed him from my thoughts.

We continued to sip our drinks, the conversation animated and enjoyable. I saw Rachel dancing with several men other than her boyfriend. She continued to glance my way, always with that intriguing smile. I pointed a finger at myself then pointed at her, then to the dance floor, and twirled my finger signaling that I wanted to dance with her. She nodded her head in agreement.

The band took a fifteen minute break. After their break, I walked up to her table where there were four couples sitting together. I asked the Sergeant if I might dance with his girlfriend. He appeared to be somewhat drunk, but he turned and asked if she wanted to dance with me. She said, "Sure."

CHAPTER 7

Rachel, the DP Camp, and STD

I led the way out to the dance floor as the band began playing one of my favorite melodies, "*Sentimental Journey*" I turned and she stepped smoothly into my arms.

"Hello Rachel, how are you tonight?"

With a dazzling smile, and her dark eyes looking into mine, she replied, "Hello Kenny, I'm fine, how are you?"

"I'm great now that you and I are dancing together, and you remembered my name," I pulled her closer to me and we began to dance slowly to the rhythm of the music.

"Is that Sergeant your husband?"

She shook her head. "No, we are supposed to get married next year. He's turned all the papers in to your headquarters. When they're approved and returned to him, I guess we'll get married."

I was pleasantly surprised that she had a barely noticeable accent.

"Do you want to marry the Sergeant?".

A rather pained expression crossed her face as she looked at me. Speaking softly she replied, "I don't know, I guess so."

"Rachel, you must make sure, absolutely sure before you marry him. Don't make a horrible mistake. How long have you been going with him?"

"Almost a year and a half."

"Where does he work? What outfit is he assigned to? Is he stationed here in Wurzburg?"

"He's a doctor's assistant in the hospital downtown," she softly replied.

"With the 57th Field Hospital?' I asked.

She nodded yes.

We continued to dance as a new tune began. I pressed her closer to me, and kissed her softly alongside her neck and ear several times. She tightened her arm around my shoulder.

She whispered in my ear, "Kenny, be very careful, or we'll both get into big trouble. The Sergeant is very jealous. He's always getting mad if men pay too much attention to me."

I whispered back, "I'll be very careful. The last thing I want to do is get you or me into trouble with your boyfriend."

We were facing the rear of the dance floor, and several couples were between us and the tables. Gently, she tilted my head down slightly and kissed me lightly on my lips. Being with her and her kissing me seemed as natural as anything I'd ever done. In spite of myself, I could feel a rapidly growing erection.

She felt it also, leaning back laughing she said, "*Leibling*, you're bad."

I laughed and replied, "It's your fault, I can't help it. You're beautiful, desirable, and it's impossible not to want to make love to and with you."

The music ended, and she hugged me tightly. When we returned to her table, I kept my left hand in my pocket holding my erection down. I thanked her and then the Sergeant. I glanced at my watch, it was ten-thirty. I knew that I had to slow down on the beer if I wanted to see the New Year arrive. I rejoined my table.

Sergeant Perry and his girlfriend were there, I greeted them both. They had a glass of beer with us. I poured myself a fresh glass of beer and watched the dancers.

The midnight hour rapidly approached. Several people were obviously drinking too much. People at a couple of tables began singing, "*Auld Lang Syne*."

The club manager walked up to the bandstand and announced over the microphone that he would count down the final thirty seconds of 1948. He had a drink in his hand and said that we all should have a toast to the United States Army, and to the New Year when it arrives. He glanced at his watch and began counting, thirty, twenty-nine, twenty-eight and down to the last second. Finally, he shouted, "Happy New Year!"

Everyone stood up and had a toast to the New Year, and another to the United States Army. I glanced up at Rachel's table, I raised my glass to her, and blew her a kiss. She reached out her hand catching the imaginary kiss then pressed her hand to her lips.

I felt both a little tipsy and somewhat sad. I hated to see the old year end. It had been such a meaningful year of change for me, joining the army, leaving home for the first time, basic training, and all the crazy things since then. I sat down and watched the others drink, whoop it up and have a ball. I poured another glass of beer, it had gotten warm in the pitcher.

Perry was telling Ray about a field training exercise we had coming up in two weeks. I thought, I'll get paid in two more days, I'm learning my job, my face is almost healed, I've made many new friends, so I have no reason absolutely no reason not to be happy and optimistic. After the pep talk to myself my morale began to rise, and I felt great once again.

At one o'clock, I told Ray that I had to go home, I was drinking too much. He agreed, and so we said our good nights to the crowd, and with shouts of Happy New Year ringing in our ears we headed for the big exit doors. I glanced toward Rachel's table but they had apparently left already. Ray opened the door and snow came swirling in, we walked across the street and entered our barracks. In a few minutes he joined me in the latrine. We brushed our teeth, washed up a bit then bid each other a Happy New Year, and good night.

New Year's Day was just a normal day. I joined several of the guys for breakfast, and then returned to the barracks. I had a copy of the '*Stars and Stripes*' so I read the paper, that didn't take very long. Next I turned on Ed's little radio and listened to AFN. They were talking about the Berlin Airlift, and the number of tons of food and supplies the Air Force had flown in over the holidays. Those guys didn't get a holiday from their mercy missions.

I then shined my low quarter shoes. I opened my wall locker and inspected my face in the small shaving mirror. My lip and the cut over my eye had completely healed. Both my eyes were normal, and my nose was straight again, so the New Year was starting off great. I sat down at the small table and decided to write a letter to my family, and another to my high school girl friend Megan. After completing the letters, I stretched out on my bunk and drifted off to sleep.

Ed came into the room and woke me up, "Ken, everything's copacetic, let's go eat."

I had missed lunch so I was really hungry. We walked down to the mess hall and had a great meal.

While eating, I asked Ed, "What does the German word '*Leibling*' mean?"

"That's the German word for darling," he said.

"Are you sure?" I asked.

"Yes, of course I am! Don't you think I speak frigging German?" he growled.

"My apology, of course you do Herr Professor," I replied.

Skinner came into the mess hall and joined us at the table. "Chuck, do you know we have a field training exercise coming up in two weeks?"

"Yeah, I know about it, it's for about three days. I don't know where we are going exactly. Tomorrow I'll give you a class on the mobile radio set. It's mounted on a two and a half-ton truck out back of the headquarters."

"Who all is going out?" I asked.

"I will be, Merlin, Ray, you and Roberts will go."

He had a drink of coffee then continued, "The field is where you'll learn to communicate. I'll teach you how to erect and orient antennas, it'll be a great learning experience for you."

Back at the barracks, we all gathered in Ed's and my room. I learned that we had pay call scheduled for nine o'clock in the XO's office. I was happy to hear that as my money had just about disappeared. Roberts come in the room with a bottle of cognac. He took the cap off had a swallow, and then passed it around the room. It was empty within a very short time. I didn't have a drink, I just didn't feel up to it.

Merlin said, "I'm going downtown to see my girl, I've got to go to work at midnight."

Ed remarked, "I'm going to the Leopold." He then walked over and kissed Bettie and said, "Good night beautiful."

Hodes and Roberts decided to go with Ed. Skinner asked Ed to drop him off at the Ring hotel, so I decided with my few funds to stay in for the evening. They all left on their different pursuits. I was up early the next morning, and had an early breakfast.

Back in the barracks the PA came on and announced all personnel should report to the first floor for pay call.

I joined Skinner in the hallway where the pay line was forming. Perry came along and told Skinner that he and I should go to the head of the line then after getting paid, go relieve Merlin on the radio. We moved up to the head of the line. Everyone we passed started bitching about us bucking the line, we ignored them.

I was told to report to the pay officer and sound off with my last name and my first name. I reported to the pay officer and was cautioned to sign my name exactly as it appeared on the payroll. It was typed out, 'Fisher Kenneth'. I signed the payroll exactly as told. The pay officer counted exactly sixty dollars and ninety cents in script, and said "Your pay is eighty-two dollars, seventy-five dollars base pay and seven dollars overseas pay. Your deductions are, the flying twenty dollars you received earlier, one dollar for laundry, and ten cents for the Old Soldier's Home."

Pocketing the money, I saluted the officer, did an about face and moved back out into the hallway. Skinner was paid next. He joined me and we left for the message center.

We arrived at the radio room and Merlin left for the barracks to get paid and go to bed. I sat down at the intra-command net and turned on the tape machine. With the earphones snuggled tightly on my head, I began to copy the code. To my pleasant surprise, I was able to copy four out of the five characters at five words a minute. With a big smile, I told Skinner that I could copy the characters. He came over, listened to the tape and watched what I wrote down.

He smiled and said, "You're getting it mostly right, missing a few but improving. Keep it up."

SFC Perry came into the radio room and told Skinner he'd take over. He said, "Take Kenny out back and explain the SCR-399 to him."

I turned off the tape machine, put on my field jacket, cap and gloves and walked out of the message center. Skinner led me to the mobile radio set. Outside he completely explained the radio set to me. It was really no different from the one inside other than being on a truck, and the set configuration, plus the PE-95 generator for electric power.

For the remainder of the afternoon, I made several voice calls to all the sub-stations and sent four test messages to other station in the net. Merlin came in told us to close down. He was taking over from back inside the radio room. We closed it all down and locked up the hut. Skinner and I walked to the mess hall for dinner. It had been a good day for me.

For the next several weeks, I worked daily on improving my code proficiency and ability to transmit and receive messages. By the end of January I had worked my way up to about eight or nine words a minute, it was now beginning to be fun.

Often Perry would come into the radio room and change the transmitter to the Ham frequencies. Sometimes he would get responses from operators in the states, and other times from France, Spain and other countries located around the world. It appeared to be a great hobby, and he surely loved it.

Outside the radio room in front of the headquarters building Perry had erected a telephone pole. On top of the pole he'd installed what he called a tuned array antenna. The pole was about thirty-five feet high and had several of what looked to be aluminum poles of various lengths all spread across a frame. At the bottom of the pole he had a gear with a handle attached which allowed him to rotate the antenna towards any direction he wanted. This permitted him to beam his signals to a specific section of the world. An antenna cable ran from the transmitter in the radio room up to the top of the pole where it was connected to the antenna. All that technical sophistication was way beyond my neophyte capabilities.

On the first day of February 1949, I was promoted to E-6 Private First Class. Boy, was I happy. Of course everyone who had come to the unit with me made PFC the same day, about forty or so of us. My pay immediately jumped about seven dollars a month with no change in the overseas pay. In view of my shaky start in the unit, I was proud to get promoted. I took both my Ike jackets to the tailor to sew on my PFC stripes.

That evening Ray, Roberts and I went to the club so Roberts and I could celebrate our promotions. It was Friday, so I knew there would be bingo games. While the crowd played the game, we just sat at our table and drank a couple pitchers of beer. Eventually, the game was over, and the band began to play. Couples drifted onto the floor and danced. It seemed life had more or less settled into a routine.

Then I saw Rachel and the Sergeant dancing. It had been about a month since I had last seen her. She remained as mysterious and beautiful as ever. She saw me about the same time and her eyes lit up. She gave me that beautiful smile, and over the shoulder of the Sergeant blew me a kiss. Just as she had earlier, I reached out plucking it out of the air, and brought my hand to my lips. Before I had an opportunity to dance with her the band began to play that sad song "*Goodnight Sweetheart*" signaling the evening was over. We finished our last swallows of beer and left the club. I looked for her, but they had left a few minutes earlier.

Later that month Perry announced, "All you guys have to take classes on telephone pole climbing." He had an instructor from a Signal Wire Company teach us the proper techniques of pole climbing. He arranged for two fifteen foot poles to be placed out back. "All you radio operators have to take the training," he reiterated. I strapped on the belt and spikes and began climbing. I went up and down the pole easily. By the end of the day I felt very comfortable in climbing up and down the poles. Toward the end of the month we scheduled and conducted another field training exercise.

We left Wurzburg and traveled toward Schweinfurt. In a pre-selected field location we erected the antennas, cranked up the generator, and established communications with all the stations in our net. There for the first time I had K-Rations. They were left over from WWII. Inside the box there were small dried crackers, a small round can of cheese, and a can of potted meat. There was also a narrow box of five Chesterfield cigarettes. I smoked the entire little pack before we returned to base. I discovered a small block of chocolate in the crackerjack sized box, I ate that also. The box was supposed to represent a complete meal, but to me it was more of a snack than anything else. I could understand how all the guys returning home after WWII were so thin. I thought my uncle and some cousins had been smart to go into the Navy, at least there you had a regular mess hall aboard each ship, and had regular food.

Skinner spent a lot of time explaining and demonstrating how the antennas were erected, and how to measure the footage of the wire that made up the antenna. He had his own formula which was different from the one in the instruction book. I had faith in Skinner and his operational ability and skills, but I simply felt much more comfortable in using the book formula. It seemed obvious that if one failed to match the wire to the frequency the output would be reduced, or non-existent and chances of establishing communications lessened

We stayed in the location for one day then we dismantled the entire set and moved to a new location. There we had to go through all the same procedures and set it all back up. We did this for three more days then we packed up and headed back to Wurzburg. Skinner had been right, operating out in the field and setting up, operating and dismantling the equipment is the best way to learn to communicate.

Arriving back at the *Kaserne*, we drove down to the motor pool and washed the truck and trailer and cleaned all the equipment. We also had to replenish all the supplies we had used, ensuring full gas cans, water and rations. All standard operating procedures were followed.

In early March, Ray and I were downtown one afternoon for a few cold beers when he suggested we go to the displaced persons (DP) camp, check out the women there and drink a few. I had never been there so I agreed. I reminded him that it was off-limits to us. "The MP's never check in the day time," he said.

We caught a taxi outside the Leopold bar. Ray instructed the driver to take us to the DP camp. It wasn't too far. The driver dropped us off at what turned out to be the camp canteen. We walked into the building and found an empty table. The place reeked with foul tobacco odors. Mud covered planks made up the flooring. Strange and unpleasant odors continuously assaulted our nostrils. We ordered two beers and paid for them. I heard two or three different languages being spoken. I didn't recognize any of them, but I could tell that people at one table weren't speaking the same language as people at other tables.

Ray said, "The camp is full of people from all over Europe who at the end of the war wound up here in Germany. The International Refuge Organization established this camp while they try to get things organized, and send families and individuals back to their native countries."

I had noticed when riding in that they were living in shacks, huts, and some even in ragged tents. Muddy dirt roads and pathways ran all around and through the camp. I really felt sorry for all these people, I also realized the terrible cost of war.

The devastating effects of the war and again its aftermath remained long after the firing guns and falling bombs fell silent.

Shortly thereafter two young girls came into the bar, they came straight to our table.

"Would you like to have some company?" the younger of the two girls asked me.

"Sure have a seat," I answered.

They sat down and Ray asked them, "Would you like something to drink?"

The one who had spoken to me replied, "Yes, two glasses of wine please."

Ray ordered two glasses of wine, and two more beers for us.

They both spoke limited broken English, so we spent a couple of hour's just talking and sipping beer and wine. We learned they were both from Romania.

I asked, "When are you two going to go home again?"

The girl seated next to Ray replied, "We're Gypsies. I don't know, the Russians now control my country, and the communists are very strict about whom they will allow back into the country." Sadly, she then added, "We may never get home again."

Ray ordered four sausages and rolls, we all ate and drank another drink.

The girl next to me asked, "Would you like to go to our room?"

"Yes," I answered.

We left the bar and walked down a narrow dirt path crossing gullies with double plank bridges across them. Finally, she entered a small shack.

We went inside and she said, "Me and my friend both live here."

I looked around, there was a small stove with the stove pipe running out through a hole in the thin wall. To say it was sparsely furnished would be too generous a statement. She tossed some sticks into the stove and added some old newspaper, struck a match to it, and it caught fire immediately. There was a small wash basin with a bottle filled with water above it. The drain pipe extended out through a hole in the side of the building discharging the brackish water into a ditch alongside the building. The plank floor was covered with some type of mud tracked canvas. It was a bleak, totally depressing place to live to be sure.

Ray's girl friend left and returned shortly with two bottles of beer. She gave us each one. The little shack had heated up and was becoming quite warm. I sat down on the small bed with the girl I had selected, and Ray sat on the other bed with his new girl friend.

One thing led to another, and soon we were all naked and in the two beds. Both of the girls I observed had armpit hair. I had learned earlier that European women didn't shave their armpits or their legs, so it really didn't surprise me too much.

We made love for an hour or so, then Ray's girl dressed and left to get us another beer.

"Ray, it'll soon get dark, so we'd better find our way back out of the camp and grab a taxi." He agreed, so we both got dressed.

Now came the hard part, how much did we owe the two girls? I asked my girlfriend, "How much do we owe you?"

She answered, "Twenty marks each, and two marks for the beer."

I gave her thirty marks. She smiled and hugged my neck. Ray gave his girl friend thirty marks also. They were both very happy. We finished the second beer, and then said our goodbyes.

Ray and I left, working our way back across the plank bridges, gullies and mud puddles to the main gate of the camp. Our shoes were covered with mud. A couple of taxis were available, so we caught one and returned to Wurzburg and the *Kaserne,* then to the club.

About ten o'clock in the evening I'd had about enough for one day, so I told Ray I was going to the barracks which I did. Back in my room I undressed and went to the latrine, turned on the hot water and took a good shower, brushed my teeth and returned to my room. At total peace with myself, I quickly went to sleep.

Two days later, I was in the radio room when I felt a burning sensation in my dick. I told Chuck I was going to take a leak. I left the message center and walked up the hall to the latrine. At the urinal I unbuttoned my fly and pulled out my cock. It burned, so I milked it down and a large drop of yellowish fluid oozed out. I almost fainted, I knew I had gonorrhea!

Panic set in. Holy shit, what in the hell do I do now? How do I get this stuff cured? Who can I tell that can help me without the hospital knowing, or the First Sergeant finding out? I felt sick to my stomach and threw up in a commode. I knew I should have stayed the hell away from that DP camp. Another drop oozed out, I was really scared. By now the fluid had stained my shorts. That created another problem. I'd best wash them out myself. Who knows, the laundry people might report such things. I certainly didn't know. I returned to the radio room.

We were near the end of our shift when SFC Perry came into the room and said, "I'm going to ham it up for a while, so you guys can leave."

Chuck and I left and went to the mess hall. I had very little to eat as my mind was frantically searching for ideas to get myself cured. I left the mess hall and returned to the barracks. I knew that I had to tell someone, hopefully someone who could help me. I thought of Pitts. He was older, and seemed more responsible than most of us.

I went to Pitt's room, he was sitting at his night table with his boots off writing a letter.

"Bill, can I talk to you for a couple of minutes?" I asked.

"Sure Ken, come on in."

Entering his room I sat down on the opposite bunk. Bill was a year or so older than the rest of us, and had been here longer than everyone except Ed and Perry. I figured he would maybe have an answer, or could give me some good advice.

Speaking slowly I said, "Bill, I think I have the clap. Ray and I went over to the DP camp, and we both got laid two days ago. I just found out my dick is dripping, and I don't know what to do about it."

"Well, stand up and drop your drawers, and milk it down. Let me take a look. If it's dripping I'll know it"

Hesitantly, I stood up and then stepped over and closed his door, latching it. I walked back and stood in front of him. I undid my fatigue pants and unbuttoned my shorts. I took out my dick and milked it down, sure enough another yellow drop oozed out. I took out my handkerchief and wiped the drop off.

Bill looked up at me and said, "Ken, you damn well do have the clap."

I felt rather faint, he had just confirmed what I truly knew. "What the hell can I do about it? You know I can't go to the hospital, and I don't dare let Ironjaws find out about it."

"Let me get dressed, and we'll see what can be done."

He pulled his boots on and got his field jacket. "Get a couple of packs of cigarettes and let's go see Betty."

I wondered what in the hell Betty could do about me having the clap. I got the cigarettes and followed him out of the building and across the quadrangle. We went up the back stairs to the switchboard room and he rang the bell.

A female voice shouted out, "Who is it?"

Bill answered, "It's Bill and Ken."

The door opened and Betty said, "Come in."

Bill asked her if she could come out for a couple of minutes, he wanted to talk to her privately. She reached back into the room, and retrieved her coat then stepped outside. He led her away several steps from me and they began to talk. After several minutes, they came back to the area where I was standing.

Betty spoke first, "Ken, meet me tomorrow afternoon at the front gate at five o'clock. I know a doctor who'll give you a shot of medicine that will cure what you have. It'll cost you fifty marks."

"No problem," I said.

"I'll meet you at the front gate at five. I'll be there in a taxi, so have enough money for the taxi also," she said.

"Okay, I'll be there and have the money we need."

Bill said, "Ken, give Betty the cigarettes."

I did, and she thanked me for them. She then went back into the switchboard room. Bill and I left for the barracks. I thanked Bill several times for his assistance with my problem.

He said, "No big deal, if you stay here long enough it happens to almost everyone. Maybe you can do me a favor one of these days."

"Just let me know," I replied.

We walked back into our barracks, Bill went to his room and I went to mine. Ed was there with a bottle of cognac. He offered me a drink, but I declined.

"Ed, do you have a pack of rubbers?"

"You mean a pack of condoms don't you?"

I nodded yes. He raised the lid on his footlocker, reached inside and then handed me a package of condoms with three individual condoms.

"They'll cost you twenty-five cents."

I reached for my billfold when he laughed and said, "Forget it, I was joking, it's all copacetic."

"Well I'm going to take a shower." I undressed and went to the latrine taking one condom with me. I took a quick hot shower then after drying off I walked into one of the commode stalls. I opened the small package and took out one condom. I unrolled it and pulled it over my dick. I had also brought a rubber band with me. I eased it over my dick and felt that it would stay in place and keep the condom on. Without an erection the condom probably wouldn't stay on. The band wasn't too tight, so I didn't worry about blood circulation. I then returned to my room. Ed was in bed and asleep. I lay down on my bunk, and then I really began to worry. What if they have a short arm inspection tonight? Ironjaws will do what he said and nail my ass to the wall.

I got off my bunk and quietly locked our room door. My instant emergency plan was simple, if they knock on our door, I'll hide in my wall locker and let Ed explain where I am. That turned out to be an almost sleepless night, I kept waiting for a knock on the door, but it never came.

The next day I asked Chuck, "Can I have the afternoon off?"

"Yeah, have you got a hot date?"

"Yeah, I have to meet her at five and need to change into my Class A's."

"Okay, have a ball."

"Thanks, I owe you a favor one of these days."

I left the radio room at noon and went to the mess hall. I had a quick meal and headed for the barracks. I took off the condom, flushing it down the toilet, and then washed my dick. I put on clean shorts and slowly got dressed. Trying to pass time I turned on the radio and listened to AFN. They were playing country music, and Hank Williams was singing "*Lovesick Blues*" I thought that guy can really sing, and I've got the lovesick part big time. That's not exactly what he's singing about though.

At four-thirty that afternoon, I left the barracks and walked down to the main gate. I saw a taxi parked outside the gate, so I walked toward it. Betty was sitting in the back seat. I opened the door and stepped inside.

"Hello Betty, thanks again for helping me out. When this is over I'll take you out to dinner and a nice evening."

'Is that a promise?"

"Yes."

She leaned forward giving instructions to the driver. He drove downtown taking several streets that I wasn't familiar with. Eventually, he pulled up to a house and stopped.

Betty said, "This is where we are going."

I opened the door on her side and we both exited the taxi. I paid the driver five marks as she told me the amount to pay. We walked up to the door and she knocked a couple of times. A voice responded saying something in German. She opened the door and we both stepped inside. A man in a white hospital type coat was standing there. Betty spoke a few words to him in German.

He approached me and said, "I'm Doctor Schungle, come into my office."

I followed him into the back part of the house. Betty sat down on a chair in the front room. He opened a door and went into a smaller room, I followed him. He stopped and turned around.

"Slide your pants and underwear down, and let me look at you."

I did as he requested. He had on thin rubber gloves, grasping my dick he milked it down, and sure enough a drop of yellowish fluid oozed out.

"You have gonorrhea, turn around."

I did as he instructed. He had a huge needle with a syringe filled almost full with a white liquid. He swabbed a small section of the cheek of my ass with alcohol, and then slapped me rather hard on the cheek with his hand. He immediately stuck me with the needle, squeezing the entire amount of liquid into my cheek. He then massaged the area, and wiped it off with a cotton swab and alcohol.

"Get dressed."

I got dressed as he requested.

He then said, "I gave you two million units of penicillin. That's more than enough to cure what you have. However, you cannot drink any alcohol for at least ten days. If you do you'll have a relapse."

I assured him I wouldn't drink for the prescribed period of time. I reached for my wallet, took out fifty marks and handed it to him. I asked, "How long will it take for the drip to stop?"

"By this time tomorrow," he replied.

"Thank you Doctor for your treatment, and your advice."

We walked back to the front of the house. Betty thanked the Doctor, and we walked outside.

"Are you alright?" Betty asked.

"Yes, he gave me a huge shot of penicillin in the ass."

She laughed and said, "Let's walk down to that corner where we can catch a taxi."

We walked to the corner and a taxi came by in just under five minutes. I whistled him down. I asked, "Betty, are you hungry?"

"Yes, I'm starved, we are past our normal dinner hour."

"Do you know a good restaurant?"

She did, so she then told the driver where to go. He drove a few blocks and stopped in front of a place named, "The Golden Swan." We exited the taxi and entered the restaurant. It was clean, and had a pleasant hunger inducing odor. We sat down at a table which had a small lit candle on it. She ordered a glass of wine, and I asked for a glass of water.

"What would you like to eat?" Betty asked.

"Anything is okay with me, why don't you order for the two of us."

She ordered two veal cutlets with potatoes. The meal turned out to be very good, and I ate all of mine. She managed to eat about half of hers.

After eating, we both smoked cigarettes and talked. "Betty, how old are you, if I might ask?"

"I'm twenty-one years old. I was born and have lived all my life here in Wurzburg." After taking a sip of her wine she continued. "Our home was destroyed during the war in one of the bombing raids. Now I live in a small apartment by myself. My mom died right after the war, and my father was killed several years ago somewhere in Russia."

"Betty, I'm so sorry."

She reached over and took my hand in hers. She smiled a sad smile and said, "Life goes on, and we do what we have to do to survive. Someday things will be better."

Continuing our conversation I asked, "Betty have you ever been married?"

Shaking her head, she said, "No, I've never been married, and I don't have any children." Pausing for a sip of wine she then said, "I learned switchboard operations working for the German army during the last year of the war, I was very young."

We finished our cigarettes. I paid the bill and we left the restaurant. After a few minutes wait I hailed and caught a taxi.

"Take me home, and then the driver can take you back to the *Kaserne,*" she said.

She gave the driver instructions to her house. We went through a section of town I knew slightly. The driver stopped in front of a house that showed some minor bomb damage but had been repaired. I opened the cab door and she stepped out. I immediately followed her out of the taxi. As she turned to go into the house I stopped her, and asked, "Betty, may I kiss you good night?"

"Do you really want to?"

"Yes!"

She leaned back toward me, and I placed my arms around her and kissed her gently on the lips. She put her arms around me and kissed me.

I said, "Betty, you are taking my breath away."

She laughed, "I'll see you tomorrow back in the *Kaserne*, Good night."

"Good night Betty, thanks again for your help, I won't forget it."

The driver then drove me to the post. I paid him six marks as Betty had told me what to pay him.

Entering the headquarters building, I went to the message center. Carlton was on duty in the radio room.

I walked in and said, "Hi, how're you doing tonight are you busy?"

"Nah, there's very little traffic, nothing is going on."

"Well, I'll see you later." I left and walked back to the barracks. I checked in with Bill Pitts and told him that Betty had taken me to see a doctor, and I had gotten a shot of penicillin. I thanked him again for his assistance, and expressed my desire that no one else find out about it.

Before falling asleep that evening, I swore to myself that I'd never sleep with another European woman without using a condom. The next day the drip had stopped, and disappeared completely. I felt cured.

For the next two weeks I stayed away from the club, and didn't go downtown. I knew if I did, I might weaken and have a relapse. It wasn't worth the risk.

On my next shift I went to the radio room with Skinner and signed us in on the radio log as operating the net as of five p.m. SFC Perry walked into the radio room and said, "Ken, you're being assigned a regular rotational shift, you'll operate the radios by yourself."

I looked at him in disbelief, "Are you sure that I can do this? Am I trained well enough to handle the nets and this equipment by myself?"

"I think so, and it's time we found out. Besides, I'll be here in and out all day, so if you have major problems I'll help. You can take off for the evening, report back here tomorrow morning at eight o'clock. By the way start learning and practicing your typing."

Returning to the barracks I ran into Roberts. "Guess what, I'm assigned a regular shift by myself beginning tomorrow morning," I told him.

"Great, I expect to be on by myself any day now."

I suggested we get cleaned up and go to the club for a few beers. I had stayed away from any drinking much longer than ten days, so I wasn't concerned about drinking and a relapse. He agreed, so after cleaning up and changing into Class A's we walked over to the club. He found us a good table, and I ordered us a pitcher of beer. Few people were there as it was still early in the evening.

We discussed our ability to send and receive Morse code. He could send and receive around ten or so words a minute, and I could maybe do fourteen words or so. I confessed I still made mistakes but they were becoming fewer in number.

Around eight o'clock in the evening couples began to arrive in the club. The band was tuning up, and was scheduled to begin around nine in the evening. I looked around and hoped that Rachel would show up tonight. Lucky me! Around eight-thirty she and the Sergeant with another couple entered the club. They sat down about three tables away from us. She saw me right away and flashed that brilliant smile. I smiled and winked at her. I then left for the latrine.

While I was at the latrine, Ed and Carlton had joined the table. Ed was saying he planned to go rabbit hunting this weekend. He stated he was a member of the Rod and Gun Club, and used their guns and ammunition. I had yet to see him go fishing or hunting, but I said, "Good luck,"

I glanced over at Rachel and made my little hand motion to dance. She nodded yes. I walked over to their table and asked the Sergeant if I could dance with his girlfriend. He looked up at me, and just waved his hand.

Rachel said, "Yes," and stood up. Together we moved out to the dance floor.

I said, "Hello beautiful. How are you tonight? It's been a long time."

She smiled, "I'm fine, and it has been too long."

I gently pulled her closer to me as her body molded itself to mine. We were near the back of the crowded dance floor. I kissed her as I had before, gently on the side of her neck. She uttered a small moan and tightened her arms around my shoulder.

I said, "I think your Sergeant friend is a little drunk."

"Yes he is, he started drinking early this afternoon, and just keeps drinking."

I replied, "That's too bad, you deserve better than that."

We were on the dark side of the dance floor, I turned so she was facing me. I bent slightly and kissed her on the lips, a passionate kiss. She responded, opening her lips her tongue slipped easily into mine. The music ended and immediately another melody began. I asked, "Shall we dance again?"

"Yes, of course."

During the second dance I asked, "Rachel, will you meet me downtown for a drink?"

Looking at me intently she asked, "Are you sure you want me to do that?"

"Yes, I wouldn't ask you if I didn't want you to. Will you meet me Tuesday night in the bar area at the Ring Hotel at six-thirty?"

CHAPTER 8

The Ring Hotel

"Yes, I'll be there," she whispered softly.

I kissed her again. We finished the dance and I escorted her back to her table. I then decided that I'd better leave and have a clear head tomorrow morning for my first solo tour on the radios. Bidding goodnight to the troops, I left and passed by her table. She looked up, I smiled at her and mouthed, "Good Night." Delightful images of she and I danced through my mind as I walked back over to the barracks.

Reporting for duty the next morning, I arrived at the radio room about seven-thirty. Merlin was on duty, and reported nothing unusual had happened.

I sent a short test message to the station in Nurnberg, tapping it out very slowly on the top of the telegraph key. The operator there received the message and signed off. Things seemed to be going very well. I studied the Q codes for a little while, and then read the manual on antennas and radio wave propagation. I still didn't understand radio theory very well. I pulled over the typewriter and began to practice my typing. That turned out to be a disaster. My fingers just wouldn't hit the right keys, but I kept trying. I sent and received several messages that first shift. A few carried different priorities. A couple of them were encoded so I turned them over to the crypto room for decoding and dissemination. At four forty-five that afternoon Carlton relieved me. I left for a bite to eat and then the barracks. Walking home I felt rather proud of myself. I had completed a full shift on the radio with no screw-ups. I can really do this stuff.

A bunch of the guys were in our room with Ed. Everyone wanted to go to the club, and I agreed. I took a quick shower and put on my Class A uniform and we left for the club. Much to my surprise, there sat Corporal Taylor. He was by himself, so we all joined him pulling two tables together, and ordering pitchers of beer. I sat down next to Jack as we shook hands. I had a million questions I wanted to ask him. But there was no chance to do so with all the jaw-jacking going on. He was able to tell me that he was fine, things were going well, and he had gotten his promotion just as Perry promised. I offered him my best congratulations.

I drank a couple of beers, it was such a pleasant environment and with friends it's always so easy to drink too much. That was a very disturbing thought. It seems when all your close friends are drinking and you're there, you feel almost obligated to drink with them.

I didn't have to go back on duty until Monday night, the five to midnight shift. That meant Tuesday, I would have the midnight to eight o'clock shift. That fit perfectly with my plan to meet Rachel. Around ten-thirty I'd had enough of the club, so I told Taylor I would see him later, and left for the barracks. It wasn't as cold outside now, spring in Germany seemed to be on the way. I surely hoped so.

I remembered springtime back in Alabama, to me that is the most pleasant time of the year. Things come alive and renew themselves. Birds sing, insects arrive, fields are plowed and crops are planted, flowers bloom, the bees buzzing, and life is wonderful.

Monday I reported in for duty at five in the afternoon, signed in and checked into the net. Nothing was going on, so I read a magazine. Then I opened up the intra-net and established communications with all of the sub-posts. I recognized Grady's voice as his southern drawl was unmistakable. I suspect my southern drawl is just as distinguishable as his. I wondered if he recognized my voice or not.

Closing the net I practiced my typing, but I couldn't see very much improvement. During the shift, I received a message from Heidleberg with a 'high priority' assigned to it. I had the sending operator slow down in his delivery. I wanted to be sure I was receiving it correctly. After I had the message, I placed it in the slit on the crypto door, and then I called the company and had the CQ wake up Pitts. He was the stand-by crypto man for the night. Shortly thereafter he showed up in the message center. After that the night was slow and boring with nothing of importance happening.

At midnight I was replaced on duty. I returned to the barracks and went to bed. The following morning I varied my routine, and goofed off all day. Later that afternoon I found Ed and bought some marks from him.

He had more than enough. I bought five dollars worth from him which amounted to seventy-five marks. I put on my uniform, checked to make sure my shoes were glistening, and my tie on straight, I left for my date with Rachel.

At the main gate I caught a taxi to the Ring Hotel. There, I spoke to the clerk and rented a room for the evening. The key indicated I had room number seven. I hope that is a sign of good luck. I checked out the room before I went to the restaurant bar.

A small table covered with cigarette burns, the room was musty, and didn't have an ashtray. The floor rug had been patched with different colored material. The bed was made, and the small lamp worked. I went to the bar area and selected a table against the far wall and ordered a beer. I placed my cigarettes and lighter on the table, and sipped at my beer. It was ten after six. I wondered if she would really show up. Could she get away from the Sergeant? What would I first say to her? What should I say? I told myself to stop worrying, events will take care of themselves, just act natural, just be yourself. The minutes ticked by, and I became increasingly nervous.

At twenty-five after six the door to the restaurant swung open and she walked in. She saw me immediately and walked over to my table. I rose to my feet and we shook hands.

I said, "Hello sweetheart, I was getting worried, I'm so glad that you came."

"I promised you I would, and I keep my promises."

"What would you like to drink?"

"Just a small glass of red wine."

I spoke to the waitress and ordered the wine.

"Did you have any difficulty in getting away for a few hours?"

"No, my friend is working tonight at the hospital, and he doesn't get off until one o'clock in the morning."

"That's great, I have to work the midnight shift tonight. I have to beat the curfew and leave here a little before eleven o'clock to get to work on time."

She cupped my face in her hand and said, "*Leibling*, five hours is enough time, sometimes for a lifetime."

I kissed her hand, "I hope that we may have much more than five hours together, but you may be right." I lit a cigarette and offered her one. She refused and said, "I don't smoke."

We continued to make small talk, and the evening became enchanting. The rest of the world disappeared except for the two of us. I thought, am I just in heat, or am I falling in love with this gorgeous woman. Am I already in love with her so much so that I don't give a damn about her sergeant friend or anyone else? I had no quick ready answer

"Let's go to my room, I rented one for the evening."

She smiled and said, "Yes, let's do that."

I paid the bar bill, and we left the restaurant. I put my arm around her waist as we walked down the hallway together. Stopping at room seven I inserted the key and opened the door. Rachel smiled and stepped into the room. I followed her, then closed and locked the door. She had on a light jacket, so I took it from her and placed it across the small table. She sat down in the chair and watched as I took off my jacket and placed it on top of hers. I then removed my tie and placed it on the table.

Facing her, I held out my hands and she stood up. I pulled her to me and gently kissed her. My kisses became more urgent as she moaned slightly. I held her as tightly as I could without hurting her. I released her and sat down in the chair pulling her onto my lap. We kissed again as I had an insatiable desire to taste the sweetness of her lips. The sexual passion and desire began building, the urge for satisfaction enveloping our bodies in its lustful searing, blazing heat.

I pulled back slightly and asked, "Rachel, what's happening to us, is this real or is it a dream?"

She kissed me softly above my eye and replied, "Kenny, whatever it is, it belongs to us. Many people live a lifetime and never have a moment like this. It's ours, its *wunderschon*, it will always be ours no matter what happens to us in the future."

I looked into her face, tears had welled up in her eyes. I kissed them away and said, "Sweetheart, please don't do that, tonight is a time for love and happiness, not tears."

Rachel smiled, and said, "Of course, you're right."

I slowly unbuttoned her blouse, removing it and placing it on top of our other clothes. Then I removed her brassiere laying it aside. She had full beautiful breasts, the nipples prominent, begging to be kissed, which I immediately did. She moaned softly holding my head tightly. I undid the button and the catch on her skirt and let it slide to the floor. I removed her panties placing them on the table. She stared intently at my face as I completed each movement, her beautiful dark eyes sparkling, alive with anticipation and desire.

I pulled her to me and kissed her deeply. She unbuttoned my shirt and pulled it free of my pants then took it off. I knelt and removed my shoes. I then undid my belt letting my pants drop to the floor. She reached over and unbuttoned my shorts which dropped to the floor. I stepped out of them as she moved into my arms. Holding her tightly I could feel her heart pounding—or perhaps—it was my own.

Stepping over I pulled back the heavy covers and invited her into the bed. We folded the heavy cover back to the foot of the bed, and just kept the light sheet to cover us. She moved closer to me her head on my arm. I was determined that this would not, could not, be a 'Wham, bam, thank you ma'am' session. I kissed her and caressed her breasts, caressed her stomach, and moved my hand softly over her mound of Venus. I kissed her deeply as my hand continued to explore her taunt body. She was ready, and I was explosively ready. I moved on top of her as her arms went around my neck. Slowly, I entered her. In a few minutes she arched her back moaning as she held me tightly. I gave up trying to restraint myself and exploded in an orgasm. I laughed and kissed her as the flush of orgasmic tremors subsided.

"Leibling, mein leibling," she said laughingly, and hugged me tightly. I rolled over to the side of her as she snuggled on my arm.

She said, "Kenny that was everything I dreamed it would be." I just hugged her tightly, and kissed her on the side of the face. With our initial passions temporarily sated we began to talk about other things.

"Are you German?"

"Yes, I was born in what is now East Berlin. I lived there almost to the end of the war."

"How did you become so fluent in English?"

"My father was a University Professor, and my mother was a school teacher, they taught me English."

"Where are they now?"

"They're both dead. They were killed when Russian artillery destroyed our house as they came through Berlin in 1945. I'm the only person in my family to survive their assault into Berlin." She began to tremble a little and I held her, reaching down I pulled up the sheet to cover us both.

"How old are you sweetheart?"

"I'm twenty years old."

"How old is your Sergeant friend?"

Softly she replied, "The Sergeant is thirty-eight years old."

"How did you get from Berlin to here in Wurzburg?"

She answered, "After we buried my family, I had no one left, no brothers no sisters, so I began walking and hiding from the Russian soldiers. The Russians were raping every woman and girl they found. For weeks I walked, begging for food, begging rides, sleeping in hay stacks, open fields, barns, and sometimes in ditches. I just wanted to get as far away from Berlin and the Russians as I could."

I kissed her on the brow.

She continued, "I had no destination. I just finally reached Wurzburg. I was sick, destitute, no decent clothes, no money, nothing. A farm family took me in and offered me a place to live, food, and clean clothes to wear. Finally, the war was over. I found a job and was able to support myself. I moved out and found a small room for rent in an old shattered building. It wasn't much, but it was mine."

"How did you meet the Sergeant?"

"I was working as a waitress in the Golden Goose *Gasthaus.* He was part of the hospital unit, several of them came in one night, and he seemed to be very nice. He had lots of money and didn't mind spending it. We talked and he came back several times. We went out and one thing led to another. He helped me move into a better place which he pays for, we now live together."

"Do you want to marry him, Rachel?"

She hesitated before replying, and then said, "I promised him I would."

"But you don't love him, if you loved him you wouldn't be here with me right now."

A long moment of silence followed my remark, I waited.

She then said, "I don't know, I just don't know."

I held her tightly, and kissed her on the top of her head.

"*Mein leibling*, the first night I saw you in the club, that night you put your arm around my waist, the first time we danced, the night we first kissed, I knew that I couldn't resist this feeling for you. When I first saw you I knew that you were who I really wanted. Our being together had to happen, I wanted it to happen, I made it happen, I can't explain things I don't really understand."

She then said, "Our marriage papers are in. When they are approved we'll get married. I'm sick of death, destruction, desolation, of funerals, of Germany, and poverty. I'm tired of having no family, nothing. If I marry him at best I will leave Germany behind forever. At worse, it could be a bad marriage, but I can get to America and hopefully have a home, children, and a family. There I'll never be frightened again. I'll never lose people to bombs. I can learn to live again. If I don't marry him, he'll leave, and I'll be back again somewhere in a room in some old building with nothing, no one and no future."

"Hush sweetheart, don't talk anymore. I understand what you're saying. I think I understand your feelings."

I knew she had faced and experienced horrors that I'd never known. I didn't know what else to say to her. I realized that when she was a teenager, only four years ago, she was dodging bombs, hiding from raping soldiers, trying to survive, while I had been picking cotton and plowing big-ass mules in the peaceful state of Alabama.

She placed her fingers on my lips and said, "*Leibling*, don't talk. Love me, love me tonight as I've never been loved before. Hold me tonight as no one has ever held me. Tomorrow is tomorrow. Tonight is ours, and I love you. We're together and you're mine and I'm yours."

I kissed her tenderly and then with increased passion. The sexual fires rekindled. I caressed her body and kissed her breast, nibbling on her nipples, kissing and caressing her entire body. I moved over and entered her again. The second time around I was able to exercise more control and timing. Our passions grew, her head turned, her back arching as she moaned and grasped me. Finally, we both reached a climax. Our muscles relaxing, our heart beats slowing to normal, and my breathing now normal I rolled over to the side. I lay there for a few moments holding her in my arm. I then got up and walked over to the small sink and found a small glass. I filled it with water and drank it. I offered her a glass of water, but she refused. I then sat down in the chair. Reaching over to my clothes I found my cigarettes and lighter. I lit one and used the glass as an ashtray.

She lay there watching me, saying nothing.

I put out my cigarette as she got out of bed; she entered the small toilet then returned. She stepped over straddled my legs and sat down. I held her close to me and tenderly kissed her lips then her eyes, all over her face.

I released her. She leaned back and flashed that smile I had grown to love so much and said, "*Du bist mein leibling fur immer.*"

I didn't understand what she had said, but it sounded nice, and that was enough for me.

"Rachel, please don't worry, things will work themselves out for us. I don't know the Sergeant, and I don't want to know him, not even his name. You promised to marry him, but you can break that promise and stay with me."

Softly she replied, "Yes, that's true. But what if you and I live together and we argue, or you get mad and leave me? What if you meet someone else younger and beautiful and leave me? What then? Don't you see my position? Don't you think that I lie awake at night asking myself these same questions?" She paused for a minute then continued, "You're young like me, and you have been in Germany only a few months. They may not approve our getting married for years, if ever." Tears welled up in her eyes.

I wiped the tears away and said, "Sweetheart, please don't cry. We have lots of time we can work all these things out." I pulled her closer to me.

She kissed me and said, "I do love you, I'll always love you, nothing can ever change that."

She wiggled around on my lap, smiling she said, "Tonight is ours. Let's not waste it on such serious matters. We must fill our memory books with what we say and do tonight."

Her wiggling around automatically had my attention. In short order I was erect once again. But making love while seated in an easy chair is neither the most practical, nor the most advantageous location for a great performance.

I picked her up, her legs circled my waist. I slowly moved to the side of the bed easing her down and lowering myself on top of her. He legs circled my thighs as we slowly and effortlessly made love, climaxing almost simultaneously.

As we relaxed she giggled and said, "*Du bists erstaunlich.*"

"What does that mean?" I asked.

"It means you my lover are amazing."

"No, you're the amazing one. With someone as beautiful and sexy as you, it's easy to make love over and over again." I rolled over and looked at my watch it was ten p.m.

"I guess we had better stop for tonight. We need to get dressed and ready to go. We have to catch a taxi as I have to report to work in another hour."

She nodded in agreement. I picked up my shorts and pants and put them on. I sat down in the chair and put on my shoes tying them. I put on my shirt and tie and slipped into my Ike jacket. She went to the bathroom and then quickly dressed. I glanced at my watch again, dressing had taken us both all of ten minutes. I sat back down in the chair and lit a cigarette. She came over and sat down on my lap.

"Rachel, when can I see you again? When can we meet again? I don't want to just see you now and then in the club with the Sergeant."

"Do you know Gertie, the blonde-haired woman who works in your snack bar?"

"No, I don't know her, but I do know who she is."

"She's a friend of mine, I'll let her know when we can be together again."

"I'll check with her every day," I said.

She leaned forward and kissed me passionately, then said, "*Leibling*, tonight, our first night is sealed in our memory books. It will not end here. We'll have many more nights, this I promise."

I returned her kiss and said, "Here, take these marks for your taxi. You catch one first and I'll take a separate one."

We walked out to the lobby together. Three taxis were parked outside. She walked out and got into a taxi and left. I lit another cigarette and walked outside and caught the second taxi, and told him to take me to the *Kaserne*.

I walked through the gate, turned right to our building and rang the doorbell at the main entrance. Nelson let me in. We went to the message center and I entered the radio room. Joe Carlton was on duty.

Joe spoke, "Hi, you're early and in Class A's no less. Been out on the town?"

"Yeah, I was downtown screwing around then headed back early to beat the curfew. You can take off if you want to, there's no use both of us hanging around."

He left as I removed my jacket and rolled up my sleeves, then signed in the log as the operator on duty.

Heidleberg came up on the net with a radio check, they had no traffic for me so I signed off. I walked out to the message center and made a cup of coffee, then returned and lit a cigarette. A million thoughts and emotions raced through my mind as I relived the evening activities. I recalled Rachel's expressions of fear, love and hope, and the depth of her emotions as she spoke wistfully of the future.

I recalled the sweetness of her kisses, the firm smooth slopes and contours of her young beautiful body. It had indeed been a magical evening. I shook my head struggling to control my thoughts and feelings, not sure that I understood what had occurred. I was amazed at how natural it all seemed.

In order to curtail the thinking I turned on the tape machine and adjusted the speed to fifteen words per minute. I put on the headphones, and pulled the typewriter over. I began to copy the code, typing it. I kept screwing up hitting the wrong keys, but I was determined to learn the keyboard. The code was a mite too fast for me, but I had to master it, and the typewriter. I did this until three in the morning. I sent out a couple of test messages to Augsburg and Munich then Frankfurt. I received a couple of messages back, and then my shift ended as Roberts showed up to relieve me.

At the club the next night I sipped a beer as the band began to play, couples danced and the mating ritual went on. I didn't dance as I felt that would be cheating on Rachel. Strange how one evening of love can change one's thoughts, emotions and life forever.

I returned to the barracks and went to bed. Sometimes later, I felt someone punching me on the shoulder and a voice saying get up. I woke up staring into a flashlight. I looked up and it was the Old Man and Sergeant Perry. I got out of bed and Perry told me to milk it down.

Damn, it's another short arm inspection. I followed his instructions, nothing appeared, so he told me to go back to bed. I glanced at my watch it was five-fifteen in the morning.

I slept another hour and a half. After getting up I performed my normal wash up routine, dressed, and left for a cup of coffee. I was off all day, so I read the *"Stars and Stripes"* and wrote a couple of letters. I wrote one to the family, and another to my girlfriend back home. I thought about her. She was a lovely girl, blonde hair, blue eyes, intelligent, and had sworn she loved me. I assume she is still a virgin as I had never made love to her. I knew in my heart that I would never marry her. I didn't say so in my letter, as it would be insensitive to do so, and serve no real purpose at this point in time. I knew also that I would never be able to settle down in my hometown, and spend my life working in the cotton mill. It wasn't because I'd become so worldly, but because of the experiences I've had, and more importantly the places and things I still wanted to see and do. This old world is a big place, and I still have a lot of it to see and experience.

Finally, I concluded it was also because of this undeniable bond that now existed between Rachel and I. I was smitten with Rachel, and I intend to marry her, screw that idiot Sergeant. I continued to try and write a nice letter to my girlfriend, one that would convey what I wanted it to, and nothing more. In the letter I explained that I would be over here for over two more years, and that she should date other men and enjoy herself. I explained that we had no firm commitment to each other, and she should do as she wished. I didn't think I was writing her a 'Dear John' type letter, to me it was being realistic, truthful and what I anticipated for both of us. It would be grossly unfair to ask her to sit at home not date anyone, not have any fun—I wouldn't. My letters finished I went downstairs and dropped them into the company mailbox. I checked the mailbox for the F's and had no mail, so I returned upstairs.

Roberts came by the room, sat down at the table and asked, "Do you want to go bowling with me?"

I didn't have much bowling experience, but having nothing else to do I said, "Yeah, let's go."

While he bowled, I kept score for him and he was a damn good bowler. He was bowling his second game when the manager's wife began bowling in the next lane. She was a good looking blonde with large breasts and an ass that everyone would appreciate. I watched her with normal male interests. She became aware of my observation, and really began to play it up big. She danced around showing off her physical attributes to their best advantage. It was a nice way to spend a dull afternoon. Roberts finished his game and we returned to the barracks.

Skinner came by the room and we went to eat. After we sat down at the table he said, "I'm coming up for reenlistment soon, and I'm thinking about transferring to the Air Force."

"Damn Chuck, I'm stunned that you're considering such a move. Aren't you happy with your job here?"

"Sure, I also have some friends here that I'll never forget, but I want to get promoted, and I can't do it here."

I knew he had a few years in the Army, how many I wasn't sure. I could surely understand him wanting to get promoted, but the idea of changing branches of service seemed too extreme to me.

"Well, Chuck let me know what you finally decide to do."

"You'll be the first one that I tell," he replied.

A little later on I walked over to the snack bar. I saw Gertie and walked over and asked her if she knew Rachel.

"Yes," she replied. "She's a friend of mine. Do you know her?"

"Yes I do, she is also a friend of mine. Did you see her today?"

"No, I didn't."

"Thanks, when you do see her, tell her Kenny asked about her."

She shook her head in agreement and said, "Okay."

I went upstairs to the Service Club. Dotty was playing cards with three other people. I walked over to the coffee pot and poured a cup of coffee, then found a magazine and a nice easy chair. I opened the magazine after noting that the cover had long since been ripped off. It had to be a couple of months old as I previewed the contents, even so it was mostly new to me. I found one interesting and appealing article.

It was a long article on the military government of Japan under General of the Army Douglas MacArthur. He was my all time favorite military hero. It wasn't too many years ago that he gave his famous, "I shall return," speech upon reaching Australia from Bataan.

About halfway through the article I heard, "Well hello again. I see you have come back to the club."

I looked up, it was Dotty. Standing up I said, "Hello." I extended my hand, she accepted it and we shook hands.

"How are you?" she asked.

"I'm fine, things are getting better."

She looked closely at my face and said, "Your face is normal, no scars, you're looking much better. Do you want another cup of coffee?"

"Sure."

She picked up my cup and said, "I'll get it."

Leaving the magazine in the chair I found a small game table. She joined me there with two cups of coffee.

"What have you been doing lately? I haven't seen you here in a few weeks."

I explained, "I've been working hard to learn my new job, and trying to stay out of trouble." We continued to make small talk for about half of an hour.

She said, "We're organizing an ice skating trip to Frankfurt. Would you like to go along with us?"

"When are you going?"

"This coming weekend."

I knew my schedule would permit me to make a day trip, but I hoped to be able to see Rachel.

"I don't know how to ice skate, and I have to work this weekend, so I can't make it this time, maybe the next time."

"Okay, I'll let you know when we have the next one scheduled, "she replied.

With that I bid her good night and left for the barracks.

I had to work the midnight shift on the weekend, so I had lots of free time. I put on my Class A's and walked over to the club. I sat with Sergeant Little and his girlfriend Gisela. Two hours into the evening and Little was up to his old tricks, staring vacantly into space.

"Gisela, When are you two going to get married?"

She replied, "All the marriage paperwork has been turned in, we expect it back any day now. We'll get married after the approval is given."

Wishing her and Sergeant Little well I left the club. I went to the gate and caught a taxi downtown to the Leopold club. I had a few beers and decided to return to the *Kaserne*. While drinking my beer I noticed a young black Private First Class sitting with a young German girl. That was unusual especially in this part of town, and in this club. Two young white soldiers were making remarks to him and the young girl. They appeared to be drunk, and he was trying to ignore them. He appeared to be totally sober. The young black soldier apparently had enough, so he and his girlfriend got up and left the bar. Shortly thereafter the two young drunks got up and left the bar.

I also left and walked outside and down the street. When I reached the corner I saw the young black soldier and his girlfriend. They were being harassed by the young white soldiers. I walked closer, and listened to their remarks. They were cursing them both, and threatening to beat the young black soldier up.

Walking over in their direction I said, "Let's make this a fair fight, two on one is not a fair fight."

The larger of the two, about my size, turned around and swung at me. I ducked his swing and decked him with a solid left. I think even Joe Louis would have been proud of that left hook. The black soldier hit the other guy and decked him. About that time I heard a MP siren. I told the black soldier to take his girl and run down the nearby alley. He grabbed her arm, and they disappeared down the dark alley.

The Jeep pulled up to me and two MP's jumped out. "What's going on the MP Corporal asked me?"

"These two guys are drunk and wanted to fight, so they got more than they asked for," I replied.

The two young soldiers were now up on their feet. The one I had hit was bleeding from a cut over his eye, and the other from a busted lip.

The other MP said, "We're writing you all up a DR for street fighting."

I handed him my identification card, and he wrote me up on a DR, at the same time the other MP wrote DR's for the two soldiers. I was told to get into their Jeep. The other two were told to report to their units.

The two MP's drove me back to my company area and released me to the charge of quarters. I went upstairs and went to bed. What a disgusting evening this has been.

The next morning I was told by Sergeant Perry to report to the First Sergeant. I knew an ass-chewing was coming. I was worried and a little scared.

I walked slowly downstairs, I knocked on his door, and I heard that terrifying voice tell me to come in.

I walked smartly across his office, stepped carefully on his rug and rendered a great hand salute, "PFC Fisher reporting as ordered sir."

The First Sergeant returned my salute and just stared at me. Finally, he spoke, "PFC Fisher, fighting is a mark of a good soldier. But street fighting is dumb. I told you once before I wouldn't tolerate fighting in this outfit. You must have won this time, you have no marks on your face. You are hereby reduced to the grade of Private. Get those stripes off your arms, and get your dumb ass to work. You're dismissed!"

I saluted him did an about face and left his office. I was pissed. I helped out a young black soldier, and I get busted. Damn, another mark against me, nothing seems to be going right for me these days. That seven dollar loss in pay will hurt.

Each day I checked with Gertie for almost a week. Finally, she told me, "Rachel wants to see you on Wednesday afternoon if possible, at the same place at one p.m."

Mentally checking my work schedule I replied, "Tell her I'll be there."

I was off on Wednesday, so I lay around the barracks all morning, that afternoon I put on my Class A's and had Ed drop me off at the gate. I had an overnight pass so I was prepared for whatever might happen. I caught a taxi at the gate and arrived at the Ring Hotel about twenty minutes before one. I walked into the lobby and stopped at the front desk, I paid for and obtained a key to room seven, and after checking it out I went to the bar area.

I sat at a small table in the corner and ordered a cold beer, a glass of red wine, and requested an ashtray. The waiter quickly brought it all to me.

Rachel came in and after spotting me she quickly walked over to my table. I stood up and we shook hands. Her smile was as always breathtakingly beautiful.

"Why don't we go to our room with our drinks?"

She shook her head in agreement and said, "Yes, let's do that."

I picked up my bottle of beer and she took her glass of wine. Reaching the room I unlocked and opened the door. She stepped inside, turning she took the beer bottle from me and placed both her wine and my beer on the table. Ithen locked the door.

She looked at me as I held out my hands, in two short steps she came in my arms. We kissed passionately, our tongues engaged in their own dance of love.

I drew back and said, “Sweetheart, I’ve missed you so much.”

She said, “I couldn’t get away from the Sergeant. He was on furlough for a week, and stayed in the house with me all that time. *Leibling, mein Leibling*, I’ve missed you so very much also.” Tears glistened in her eyes, and I kissed them away.

“Sweetheart, it’s no big deal. We’re together again and that’s all that matters. Put last week out of your mind. We belong together and to each other, nothing else matters.” She hugged me tightly.

CHAPTER 9

Our beautiful Affair

I put my Ike jacket and tie over on the table. Then I moved over to the chair and sat down. She followed me and sat on my lap. Holding her seemed to be the most natural thing in the world. I stroked her hair, kissed her face and lips, and held her tightly. She returned my kisses, murmuring words in German that I didn't understand. She slipped off my lap, stooped down and untied and removed my shoes. I watched her every move.

Softly she said, "Stand up *Leibling*."

I did as she requested. She removed my shirt, undershirt, and then undid my belt buckle, my pants dropping to the floor. I was left with just my shorts on. She smiled and unbuttoned my shorts, they also dropped to the floor. She then undressed quickly.

Drawing her to me I kissed her enjoying the feel of her warm and full breasts pressing against my chest, her arms came around me one hand holding me by the back of my neck. She whispered, "*Leibling*, with you I am truly a woman, when I'm not with you, I'm just a dry empty person."

I lifted her up in my arms, turning I placed her gently on the bed. By now I was fully erect. I moved over her then slowly we made love to each other. Our passions temporarily sated, I rolled over to her side.

"Sweetheart, each time I make love to you is a new and more wonderful experience. Sex with you is God's gift to me."

She giggled and replied, "I never knew a woman could feel this way, or sex could be so much pleasure and beautiful until you and I made love."

I got up from the bed and found my cigarettes and lighter and lit one. I sat down in the chair and had a drink of beer as she relaxed on the bed.

"Rachel, would you like your wine, or a drink of water or beer?"

"No thank you, I'm fine."

"Rachel, do you and your Sergeant friend make love like you and I do?"

She reared up on one elbow and looked at me, a look of annoyance crossed her face. "No, when he does have sex with me, it's over in two minutes, and then he just goes to sleep. I get no satisfaction or real pleasure. We don't make love, we just satisfy his desire. He's so mechanical about it all, and it makes me feel used and insignificant."

"Does he have sex with you often?"

"No, he does it sometimes once a week, usually once every two weeks. We have gone for three weeks many times without him touching me at all."

"What's wrong with him?" I asked.

She lifted her hands and then letting them drop said, "I don't know, he loves to drink. He doesn't care very much for sex, or love, or my feelings."

Stunned by this information I said, "Come here sweetheart."

She came around the bed and sat on my lap. I handed her the wine glass, she took a small sip and placed it on the table.

"I don't understand him at all. You're beautiful, sexy, desirable and lovable. You're young and have a young woman's desires. You obviously love sex and enjoy it. How can you stand to be with someone like him? Someone who ignores your needs and desires."

She shrugged her shoulders and replied, "I do what I have to do."

I began to speak again when she placed her fingers over my lips. Softly, she said, "No, *Mein leibling*, we must not waste our time together talking about him. Our time together is too precious to waste."

"Sweetheart you're right, forget that dumb ass. The few hours we manage to have together are truly too important to worry about other people." I kissed the side of her neck and asked, "Are you hungry?"

"A little bit."

"Good, let's get dressed and go to the restaurant, get new drinks and something to eat." She nodded in agreement.

I tasted my beer, it was warm, so I emptied the contents into the sink, and placed the bottle in the trash container. I poured her wine into the sink and put the glass inside the sink. We dressed and finally we were ready to go. I opened the door and we walked down the hallway to the restaurant. To my surprise there sat Ray drinking a beer. He waved to me and we walked over to his table. I introduced Rachel to him and told her, "Ray's my best friend. We work together in the message center." I requested she order us both something to eat.

Ray and I made small talk about things back on the *Kaserne* and work. Rachel ordered some kind of roast and gravy with rolls. The waiter brought over two plates and silverware. I ate most of my meal, but she ate only a partial amount. I continued to make small talk with Ray, as I lit a cigarette and had a drink of beer.

Ray said, "Rachel, I don't think I've ever seen you before, not even at the club on the Kaserne."

I broke in and said, "Ray, we can talk about that tomorrow."

He replied, "Sure, I'm supposed to meet Hodes at the Leopold, so I better shove off."

"Okay, I'll see you back on post."

He bid Rachel goodnight and expressed his pleasure in meeting her. "I'll see you later Ken."

"Okay, be careful, or at least be good," I replied.

I ordered another beer and another glass of red wine. We left the restaurant and walked back up to our room. I unlocked the door and we both stepped inside. I took off my jacket and removed my tie laying them on the table. I sat down in the soft easy chair and took a small drink of my beer. She came over and sat on my lap, taking a small sip of wine. I tilted her head up and kissed her. Holding her face I gazed into her warm dark eyes, they were twin pools of mesmerizing magic reflecting a sense of love and desire. She returned my kiss and laid her head on my chest.

"How long can you stay with me tonight?"

"Until about midnight, he'll come home a little after one in the morning, so we have lots of time."

"Wonderful," I said.

"Kenny, it seems that I've been running all my life. I guess I'm still running. At night I have bad dreams. I stop running and find peace and fulfillment only when I'm sitting on your lap with your arms around me, or on the bed with you holding me close."

Slowly stroking her hair I replied, "Sweetheart, I'm happy and satisfied when I'm with you, and I love you so much." I slowly began to unbutton her blouse.

She giggled, and leaning forward, kissed me lightly and said, "Yes *mein leibling*."

I removed her blouse and brassiere, her firm beautiful breasts so full inviting me to kiss them which I did. She moved forward and kissed my nipples and ran her tongue teasingly across my chest sending shivers down my back. I stood up and undressed her then myself. I turned the big cover back to the end of the bed as she moved to the far side and lay down. I lay down beside her.

She laid her head on my arm as I stoked her arm and shoulder. We cuddled saying nothing. Unlike earlier, I was in no rush so I lovingly caressed her. I shifted my attention and hand to her breasts gently rubbing and massaging each of them, the nipples firming up, and standing out in proud relief. She softly cooed as I continued. I caressed her stomach then running my hand across her mound of Venus playing with her soft pubic hair. She turned over on her back, and I moved on top of her. She moaned and threw back her head, her legs tightening on my thighs. In just a few moments of slow gently love making I climaxed.

Laughing I said, "Sweetheart, if that doesn't satisfy you, then I've wasted your time."

She pulled my head down kissing me then said, "I've never felt so complete, so satisfied, so much a woman as I do right now."

We lay quietly just holding each other. Eventually, I got up found a cigarette and lit it. I took a couple of swallows of beer, and just enjoyed watching her. I glanced at my watch, it was eleven o'clock. I thought the old saying is right, "Time flies when you're having fun."

"Rachel, I have an overnight pass, but I'll leave when you do. Without you here with me, I don't care to spend the night alone."

"Let's get dressed then," she replied.

We both dressed, I left my jacket off and she reached over and positioned my tie correctly beneath my shirt collar. I sat down in the chair as she once again sat on my lap.

She asked, "Are you really happy *leibling*?"

"Yes, you have made me a very happy man. Are you also happy?"

"Yes, my old life ended when I escaped from Berlin. I began to truly live again when I found you. I just hope it never ends."

I kissed her on the cheek and said, "Don't worry, things will work themselves out for us." I smoked another cigarette and finished the remainder of my beer.

She sipped her wine and said, "I guess we had better go." I agreed and gave her some marks for a taxi. We then left the hotel in separate taxis.

Back in my bunk, once again my mind was swirling from the events of the evening. I knew that I loved Rachel more than I ever thought possible to love someone. When I was with her I had a complete feeling of calmness. I knew that my love and emotions lay totally bare and exposed with her.

The idea of not having her was inconceivable. The idea of her marrying that drunken Sergeant was absolutely revolting. I also realized that she was emotionally insecure. She believed that he might be her only chance to leave Germany and find happiness in the United States. It did make sense. She was right, the army might not approve of us getting married. They could send me to someplace else in Germany, or to Austria, or for that matter they could send me anyplace in the world. I shuttered thinking about it. Finally, I fell asleep.

At breakfast Ray said, "So who was that beautiful woman you introduced me to last evening?"

I looked around the mess hall, it was almost empty. The KP's were busy washing off the tables and mopping floors. "Ray, you're my best friend. The woman you met last night has promised to marry some sergeant from the 57th Field Hospital. We met a few months ago in the club. I danced with her and saw her several times. I asked her to go out with me and she accepted. One thing led to another and now we're in love with each other. We meet every chance we get. "

I told Ray the whole story about her escape from Berlin, also about her worries and insecurity. I also told him that she keeps her promises. When I finished, I swore him to keep it a secret.

"My lips are zipped," he said

We left the mess hall and returned to the barracks. Later on the company clerk came in my room to tell me I had a phone call. I went downstairs and answered the phone. Sergeant Perry was on the line. After exchanging greetings, he said, "My radio antenna is stuck, and I can't get it to turn. No one else here at the office will climb the pole and fix it. Will you climb the pole and check out the antenna at the top for me?"

Sucker me, I said, "Sure, I'll be right down."

I went back upstairs to get my cap, when I went back downstairs I met Ironjaws.

"Good morning First Sergeant."

He grunted and asked, "Where are you going?"

"I'm going down to the message center."

"Come on, I'm heading that way, I'll give you a ride."

We boarded his jeep, and he drove us down to the headquarters building. I said, "Thanks," as I got out of the jeep and went into the building. I talked with a couple of guys who had taken pole climbing with me, but they wouldn't climb the tall antenna pole in front of the building.

I met Perry who explained to me what he thought the problem was, and what he wanted me to do. I went outside the building, then strapped on the climbing spikes and fastened the tool belt. Perry and a couple of guys were there watching me. With a show of bravado and a smile, I began to climb up the pole. For the first twenty feet or so I experienced no trouble whatsoever. However, as I climbed higher I became a bit nervous. Looking down, I thought this pole is a lot higher than I figured. I continued to climb planting the spikes deeply into the pole and slipping the belt up each time I moved up a step. Finally, I reached the top and found that the antenna gears were not meshing properly. I pulled the two gears together and hammered in the small spikes holding the gears in place. Finished, I replaced the hammer on my belt and hollered down to Perry that it's fixed.

I took my first step down, stepping first with my left leg sinking the spike deep into the wood then the right leg. When I moved to place my left spike again it broke out of the pole and I slipped. My belt now a restraining device was the only thing keeping me on the pole. My right spike was deeply embedded in the pole at a level with my stomach. I struggled to regain my balance and reinsert my left spike, but it kept slipping out of the pole. I quickly realized I was in a world of deep shit.

Perry began hollering up instructions to me as I began to swing involuntarily from side to side oscillating. I was afraid that my right spike would break loose. If that happened, and I slid down the pole the gouges and splinters from previous climbers would tear me apart. It would be as bad as sliding down a pole ringed with barbed wire. I dared not release my belt because I would fall and break my neck. My position was precarious, and becoming more so by the second. I grabbed the pole and hugged it with all my strength. Frantically, I tried to get my left spike back into the pole.

I glanced down, Perry was yelling up instructions. Then other people began to shout to me. Not a damn one of them really had any helpful advice. By this time I knew I was really getting in a bad fix.

Glancing down again, there was the First Sergeant watching me, saying nothing just watching me. The Signal Officer came out of the front door. Then I saw the General peek out the door. Damn, I thought, is the whole frigging post going to come out to see me hanging on to this damn pole, or do they want to just watch me fall to my death splattering all over the ground.

My right leg was beginning to tire, and my arms weakening. I knew what was happening, I was frozen to the pole. Even if my spike caught and dug in, I probably couldn't have moved. I thought, I'll be dipped in shit, this is so damn embarrassing. I saw Ironjaws go back into the building. He came back out, and about a minute later I heard the fire truck horns. What the hell, I wondered are we having a dumb ass alert?"

Looking up the street, I saw the fire engine heading our way. The driver pulled into the circular driveway and backed the truck up to about five feet away from the pole. The man on the back unlocked his ladder and extended it upwards toward me.

A great sense of relief washed over me. The operator extended the ladder to just below where I was located then he climbed up. He reached me then grasped my left leg and placed it on the top ladder rung. Now I could stand on one leg. That enabled me to break my right spike away from the pole, and stand on the rung with both feet. I slid my belt down and unhooked it. He and I slowly descended the ladder one step at the time. When I reached the bottom, I thanked the operator and jumped down from the truck.

Perry rushed over and asked, "Are you alright?"

"Yeah, just embarrassed as hell, but I'm fine."

I looked over at the First Sergeant and nodded. I knew he was the one who had called the fire truck for me. I mouthed the word "Thanks." He just smiled and walked away.

That pole episode cured me of any and all climbing desires I might have, or will ever have. I went into the message center. My hands were shaky, and my legs were weak. I had a cup of coffee and smoked a cigarette.

Hodes came over and said, "Me and Merlin are going to take a three day pass to Berchtesgaden. Do you want to go with us?"

Without thinking too much about it I said, "Sure."

They planned to go the first of May, which was about a week away.

I kept checking with Gertie in the snack bar, but she had no messages from Rachel. I told her that I was taking a three day pass and to let Rachel know that I'd be back in town on the fourth of the month. She assured me she would.

We got paid on the first and left immediately in Merlin's Jeep. We drove on secondary roads and on the Autobahn towards Munich and Salzburg. The countryside was beautiful. Spring had arrived and the meadows and valleys were coming alive with new grass and wild flowers. We stopped at several *gashauses* along the way and checked out the local beer. It was all good.

CHAPTER 10

The Aldershorst and Pop

The Alp Mountains came into view. It was my very first time to see real mountains. The snow covered peaks seemed to reach almost endlessly into the sky, they had to be several thousands of feet in elevation. Finally, we reached the town of Berchtesgaden. Merlin who had been here before knew where we could stay. We checked into a hotel and rented two rooms, placing our bags in the rooms. It had been a long day so far.

We went to a local restaurant and had a typical German meal of bratwurst and sauerkraut. One thing I will give the Germans, they know how to cook a great meal. After eating we strolled over to a beer garden. They had a band and people were sitting around drinking steins of bee,r and singing songs. I recognized the beautiful tune of "*Lili Marlene*'"

We ordered beer, smoked, and just watched the people dancing and singing. The waitress brought us each a large stein filled with foaming beer. I tasted it, and it was good, rather strong, but good,

The most popular band instrument was the accordion. The player strolled around through the crowd and played whatever tune they requested. We stayed there for about three hours, and I was getting to the point of feeling my beer. I enjoyed the pleasant feeling, but I didn't want to drink too much as I really wanted to see and experience all this historic town had to offer. I remembered movie news about the 'Eagle's Nest.' I recalled the movie tone news showing Hitler and his Generals as they walked around the place. From where we were in the valley the buildings looked tiny, and so darn high up on the peaks.

I ordered one more beer and sipped it slowly. I watched the local civilians as they danced to a waltz. Most of them were pretty good at it, but I simply can't waltz.

A little later, I told Merlin that I thought we should call it a night and get some shuteye. Both he and Hodes agreed, and finished drinking their beers. We returned to our hotel. I was in the one room alone, and they shared the other room with twin beds. I washed up a bit and brushed my teeth. I sat on the side of the bed and smoked a final cigarette for the day. I undressed and slid into the soft bed. It certainly wasn't like an army bunk, this mattress was really soft, and seemed to solicit and encourage sleep.

My room window was open, and a cool breeze swept down from the mountains. I snuggled deeper into the bed, pulling the heavy quilts tighter around my neck. The heavy goose down pillows and covers felt great.

All the recent events in my life began to tumble through my mind. My love affair with Rachel was wonderful. My episode on the antenna pole now that it's over is funny, and something that I will remember for a very long time. It's funny now, but it really wasn't funny when it was happening. I quickly fell into the willing waiting, welcome arms of my favorite night time goddess, Morpheus.

The next morning we had a quick breakfast and while eating Merlin said, "We're going to go to the '*Aldershorst*' today. "

"What the hell is that? I thought we were going to the Eagles Nest."

Merlin replied, "That is the Eagle's Nest, Hitler's mountain retreat."

I recalled a movie news short showing Hitler and his mistress Eva Braun on the terrace at the mountain top retreat.

Outside, I could see a building up on the very top of one of the mountain peaks. We loaded into the Jeep and Merlin roared off. The road was good as we kept climbing higher and higher. We passed through some tunnels and continued up the mountain. It was about eight-thousand feet to the top. Merlin parked the Jeep and we dismounted. I gazed around wide-eyed trying to absorb everything around me. From the peak the scenery was almost unbelievable, it was absolutely beautiful. I pointed out to Hodes the clouds drifting lazily through the valley hundreds of feet below us. The snow line extended down the mountain side then disappeared into the tree line far below. Looking across the peaks you could see for untold miles as peak after peak unfolded in a magnificent parade of mountain tops. We entered the compound, it had almost been totally destroyed. Smaller buildings around the main building were totally destroyed. Bomb craters, bullet and shell holes pockmarked everything the eye could see.

We stepped into the main room. The huge picture window was empty of all glass, and a cold wind blew briskly through the building as if conducting a cleansing of the place. I recalled films showing Hitler and his Generals holding a conference in this exact room, his dog Blondi beside him as they poured over maps, and devised their destructive death-dealing battles.

Writing was everywhere in the room. It covered the walls, and even the ceiling. I think every soldier or unit who had ever been here had scrawled his name and or unit identification someplace in the room. I walked over to the huge glassless window. On the window frame carved into the wood were the letter and numbers E/2/506/101-5/10/45.

"Merlin, do you know what these letters represent?"

Merlin after a quick glance said, "Yeah, that's Easy Company of the 2nd Battalion, 506th Infantry Regiment of the 101st Airborne Division. They were here in this room on May 10th, 1945," he replied.

On one wall was the big Circle C of the Constabulary scrawled in paint, and then some company from the Big Red One Division was scribbled. There were too many names and units to try and read them all.

Sloppily written on the rear wall was the ever present, "Kilroy was here, 5/45." Kilroy was the fictional humorous icon born in WWII. Everywhere I'd been in the army, from the rifle ranges at Fort Jackson, SC, to the latrines in Camp Kilmer, NJ, and now to Hitler's Eagle Nest in Berchtesgaden, Germany, Kilroy had been here before me.

We toured the entire compound for about two hours. We sat on the wall at the edge of the terrace overlooking the valleys and peaks where Hitler and his girlfriend Eva Braun had sat and talked. We smoked our cigarettes, and drank a couple of beers we had brought with us. We talked about a multitude of things, and watched the ever changing panorama of nature unfold far below us. Finally, we loaded up the jeep and headed back down the mountain.

That evening after dinner we went to a different *Gasthaus.* We ordered beer and observed the crowd. Some girls were in the bar area, and were obviously available for entertainment. Merlin and Hodes made a play for a couple of them, dancing and plying them with drinks. A third girl joined us at the table. I bought her a beer, and we talked for a while. Surprisingly she spoke very good English. I guess that should no longer surprise me. The US Army has been here for over four years now.

Hodes and the girl he had left for our hotel. Merlin was in rare form and continued to drink and dance. I bought the girl with me another beer. She drank slowly and didn't appear to be affected at all. I asked her, "Do you want to spend the night with me?"

Instead of answering me yes or no, she said, "Do you want me to stay with you tonight?"

I didn't answer immediately, and then I replied, "No, I'll pay you for your time, but no, we don't have to spend the night together." I couldn't cheat on Rachel. I ordered another beer.

About thirty minutes later she said, "I have to go now."

I gave her forty marks and said, "This is for your time with me."

She smiled, "*Danke Schon*, enjoy your holiday in Berchtesgaden."

I told Merlin I was going back to the hotel.

"Where's your girlfriend?"

"She had to leave." I walked away and returned to the hotel.

Waking up the next morning I heard laughter in the next room. The guys and girls were dressed and talking. I got up washed up a bit and dressed. I walked across the hall and told Merlin, "I'm going to breakfast."

We'll join you there, we have to leave later this morning," he replied.

They joined me at the table, but their girls had already left. We finished breakfast, loaded our bags in the Jeep and headed back to the autobahn, and the other roads that would takes us back to Wurzburg. We arrived at Leighton Barracks late that night, and I had to work the next morning. I dreaded that, but duty requires you to do whatever you are instructed to do.

I got up and conducted my normal routine then went to breakfast. Ray was working the day shift, so we walked to the message center together. On the way I told him all about our trip to the Eagle's Nest.

He interrupted me saying, "Ken, I've been there. It's a beautiful little corner of the world, but wait until we go to Garmisch."

I replied, "I can't wait."

While I was on pass both Ray and Pitts had received promotions. Ray made Corporal, and Bill Pitts made Sergeant.

At the radio room, I signed in on the log and checked into the net. Nothing was going on, so I pulled up some old messages, and practiced with the high speed key. The more I played around with it, the simpler it became. I reached the point I could actually send about fifteen words a minute with the characters clear and sharp. I was really proud of myself.

Perry came into the room and said, "Ken, the First Sergeant wants to see you when you get off duty."

"What's it about do you know?"

"No, I'm not really sure."

"I'm not in any trouble am I?"

"Nah, not that I know of."

"Okay, I'll be there."

I knew that I hadn't screwed up, so no sweat there. At about a quarter to five, Roberts relieved me, and I walked up to the barracks. I went into the building and straight to the clerk's office and told him, "I'm here to see the First Sergeant."

He went into Ironjaws office then came out and said, "The First Sergeant will see you now."

I knocked on the office door and heard him say, "Come in."

I walked smartly across his office floor, stepping gingerly on his small rug, and snapped to attention in front of his desk and reported.

He said, "Stand at ease Private Fisher. How well do you know Corporal Pop Warner?"

"We came over on the boat together, and have been assigned together since we arrived. I think he's a good man and a good soldier," I replied

Ironjaws stared at me and said, "Warner has been absent without leave for five fucking days now. Do you know where he's shacking up?"

"I think so," I replied.

"Warner is an old soldier. He was badly wounded in the head during the war, and he drinks too damn much, but I don't want anything bad to happen to him. I want you to go get him, and bring his shaky ass back here."

I was stunned at the information.

"Take my Jeep, and go get the dumb ass. No one goes fucking AWOL in my outfit. How long will it take you?"

"I'll have to change into Class A's. If I leave now I should be back in an hour or so at the most."

Handing me his Jeep keys he said, "Get changed and go. I'm going to the mess hall, and then I'll be here waiting for you in my office."

I saluted him and left his office. I quickly changed into my uniform and went downstairs. His Jeep was in its customary parking spot at the curb. It was dark already. I started his Jeep then left the post and drove down pass the Rod and Gun Club, pass the Ring Hotel, and then across the Main River. Pop had brought me to his place once before. I finally found the right street. I parked the Jeep and walked up to the door.

When I knocked I saw someone pull the window curtain aside to peek out. The door opened, and his girlfriend motioned me to come in.

"Freida, I want to see Pop."

Anxiety and worry was etched all over her face. She took my hand and led me into the back of the building to a bedroom. Pop was on the bed sleeping, passed out, or dead. I wasn't sure which. Several empty vodka bottles were on the floor beside his bed.

I asked her, "Is Pop drunk?"

"*Ja*, he has been this way for five days," she replied.

"I have to take him back to the *Kaserne*, help me get him dressed."

Together we sat him up, and I put his shirt and pants on while she put his socks and shoes on. I tucked his cap and tie in my back pocket, and then put his jacket on,

"Hold the door open while I carry him out."

I picked him up and slung him across my shoulders. Pop didn't weigh more than a hundred and twenty-five pounds. He was down to skin and bones which shocked the hell out of me. Outside she opened the Jeep door for me, and I placed him into the passenger seat. After I closed the door, he fell over against the other seat.

"Thanks Freida, I'll take care of him for you."

With her face a mass of worry, I pulled away from the apartment building. I drove rapidly back across the bridge and through the town. I finally reached the *Kaserne* gates and drove through with no problem, the guards recognized the First Sergeant's Jeep. I reached our barracks and parked the Jeep in Ironjaw's spot. Looking up I saw that the light was still on in his office. I went around the Jeep, and lifted Pop out again placing him across my left shoulder. I quickly moved up the sidewalk and stairs and into the building. I walked through the clerk's office into the First Sergeant's office, he was seated at his desk.

I crossed the room, saluted him and said, "Mission accomplished, I've got him First Sergeant."

He stood up and said, "What in the hell is wrong with him?"

"His girlfriend said he's been drunk for the past five days."

"Set him down in that chair," he growled.

I lowered Pop into a large chair in the corner of the office. Pop stunk. He smelled of booze, vomit, urine and perspiration. He had at least a five day growth of beard on his face, his uniform wrinkled, stained, and soiled.

Ironjaw's checked Pop over, even his pulse. He turned to me and said, "Let's get him upstairs and into his bunk. He's in no shape to talk to anyone tonight."

I reached for Pop when Ironjaw's growled, "You did your part, I'll take him upstairs." With that he picked Pop up like a small bag of cotton seeds and tossed him across his shoulder. At Pop's room I opened the door and flipped on the light.

The first Sergeant entered and laid Pop on his bunk. He took a blanket and spread it over Pop.

"Leave him there for tonight, maybe he'll sleep it off by morning. Thanks Fisher for your help."

"He's my friend First Sergeant, I'm glad to help. Your Jeep is parked outside with the keys in it."

I left for my room thinking damn, I missed supper tonight, and I'm hungry as a damn bear. What the hell, that's one way to stay slim and trim.

I walked over to the snack bar and had a cheeseburger and French fries. I walked down to the bowling alley and watched them for a little while. I returned to my room, took a shower, brushed my teeth and went to bed.

Waking up about eight-thirty the next morning, I got my shaving kit and left for the latrine. Our barracks was very quite since all the troops had gone to work. I pushed open the door to the latrine and walked inside. I immediately saw blood all over the floor. What in the hell is going on I wondered. A trail of blood led around the wall and floor into the shower room. I cautiously peeked around the wall, and then walked into the shower room. I saw Pop still in his uniform, unconscious, sitting on the little bench against the far wall, blood dripping down to the floor from both wrists. Little pools had formed on the floor beneath each wrist, a single edge razor blade lay at his feet in a pool of blood. It scared the hell out of me.

Dropping my shaving kit I raced out of the latrine. Forgetting I was in my underwear, I ran down the stairs and straight into Ironjaw's office. He was seated at his desk.

I shouted, "Pop's killed himself. He's upstairs in the shower room, he slashed both his wrists."

Ironjaws jumped up and raced upstairs with me right behind him. The CO must have heard me as he was right behind me. We raced into the shower room, and I slipped on the bloody floor and fell to one knee. I quickly got up but I had Pop's blood all over my one leg and hand.

The First Sergeant first checked Pop for a pulse on the artery in his neck. "He still has a heartbeat." He then pulled out his handkerchief tying it as a tourniquet around Pop's left wrist. The CO then did the same to his right wrist.

Ironjaw's said to me, "Go downstairs and call the hospital, get an ambulance here fast."

I raced back downstairs and grabbed the little phone sheet with its emergency numbers listed and called the hospital. I explained the situation to the clerk who answered the phone. He assured me an ambulance would be here in fifteen minutes or less.

Dashing back upstairs, I walked into the shower room. The Major and Ironjaws was standing over Pop talking. I noted that the blood had stopped dripping. I told the First Sergeant that the ambulance would be here within minutes.

Locating my shaving kit having dropped it earlier, I wet my towel and washed Pop's blood from my leg, hand and from my shaving kit. I then went back to my room and obtained another towel. I returned to the latrine washed up and shaved, that took all of about ten minutes. I combed my hair and stepped back around the wall to the shower room. Ironjaw's was smoking a cigarette and staring at Pop.

I said to the First Sergeant, "I guess we got here just in time to save his life, otherwise he would have bled to death." Ironjaw's just grunted.

A siren began wailing louder and closer. When the ambulance arrived at our building the siren stopped. Three men rushed into the latrine. One had a medical bag, and the other was carrying a folded gurney. The third man was a medic Sergeant in white. I looked at him, and I'll be damned, it was Rachel's friend. He immediately took charge of the situation, checking Pop's heartbeat. He then removed the handkerchief's replacing them with professional tourniquets. He instructed the two other men to place Pop on the gurney which had now been extended and sat upright.

He said to the CO, "The guy's heartbeat is very weak, and he has lost an awful lot of blood. We'll do the very best we can."

The two men had picked Pop up and placed him on the gurney, they then lifted up the gurney and left.

Returning to my room I dressed and walked over to the snack bar. I looked for Gertie, but she wasn't there. I had a cup of coffee and two doughnuts, I didn't have the stomach for a bigger breakfast.

While I was drinking my coffee, Dottie came into the snack bar. She went through the serving area picking up a cup of coffee and a slice of toast. She saw me, and walked over joining me at my table.

I stood up as she approached my table, "Good morning Dottie."

She returned my greeting and asked, "What's going on with the ambulance?"

I said, "A soldier had an accident in the latrine, and needed to go to the hospital."

She accepted my remarks, and asked no further questions. She then asked me, "Why haven't you been back to the Service Club?"

"I have been working at my job, and I went on a three day pass to Berchtesgaden. The mountains, the town and the area are really beautiful. I toured Hitler's Eagle Nest Retreat, saw the destruction inflicted on it, and read half the graffiti that's written on the walls. You have to go there while you're here in Germany."

She replied, "I'm looking forward to making the trip, especially seeing the Alp Mountains." Laughing she added, "There are no mountains in Florida." She continued, "I also want to visit Switzerland,

Austria, and Italy while I'm here. Maybe even Holland, Denmark and Spain."

"I think you certainly should do so. You never know how many chances you'll have to visit those countries. It's an opportunity of a lifetime that you don't want to miss. Dottie, you'll have to excuse me as I have to go get ready to go to work. I'll see you again a little later."

With that we said our goodbyes and I left for the barracks. Arriving back at the barracks I went to the latrine. It was cleaned up. I guessed that Ironjaw's had drafted someone to wash the blood off the walls and the floor. I returned to my room laid down on my bunk, and tried to digest all the recent events. I had thoroughly enjoyed the trip to Berchtesgaden and the Eagle's Nest. It is a historical site well worth seeing and will remain as one of the major sites connected with World War Two. I probably will not ever go again, but that place Hitler and his Generals cost a lot of American blood and lives.

Then I thought about Pop Warner. I'd seen him several days ago when he seemed well and in decent shape. I have no idea what made him go AWOL, go on a drinking binge, and then try to commit suicide. Who can tell what thoughts and emotions were running through his mind? I wonder did his head wound cause this. I hope he makes a full recovery and nothing bad happens to him, maybe at the worst they'll just bust him back to PFC.

I then thought about Rachel. I haven't seen her in several days. Somehow we must get that Sergeant out of our lives. She loves me, but she considers her promises sacrosanct. An admirable trait, but in her case she should forget it and break up with him, and live with me until we can get married, Perhaps someone, somewhere, had broken a promise to her, and she is over-compensating for that.

My thoughts turned to Dotty. She was no longer so standoffish, and seemed to like me. I had seen her and the other hostess out with a couple of senior Sergeants downtown, but it appeared to be nothing serious. More like just to have something to do. I had been told that the service club women were under almost as many restrictions in their activities and conduct as we soldiers are in ours, maybe even more so.

Getting up from my bunk I decided to shine all my boots and shoes keeping them ready for inspection. I wet my polish cloth and gave them all a spit shine until they glistened. It was time to eat, so I went down the street and had a hamburger steak and mashed potatoes. I also drank a couple of cups of coffee to help keep me awake. On my way to work I stopped by the snack bar to see if Gertie was working, but she wasn't. The evening was pleasant, so I strolled down to the headquarters in no big hurry.

After relieving Skinner he told me, "I've made the decision to reenlist in the Air Force, so I don't have too much longer here in the radio room."

"Well, good luck Chuck. I'm really sorry to see you go. Maybe we all can have a big going-away party for you in the club before you go."

"That's a damn fine idea, you know I love to party," he said laughing.

After he left I checked in with the Net Control station in Heidleberg. Then I checked the sub-post net. No one had anything to report. It was obviously going to be a long and dull evening. I turned on the tape machine and set the volume low without the headphone I began to copy the code. I could now accurately copy somewhere between eighteen and twenty-two words a minutes. For about an hour I practiced sending code on the telegraph key then the speed key. I was becoming increasingly proficient in using them both. Around eleven in the evening Roberts came in and relieved me. He had been to the club, and had what I considered to be a slight buzz on. There were no special instructions for him, so I left and headed back to the barracks.

It was a clear night, the stars shining brightly, and a half moon high in the sky. The temperature was cool but not cold. Walking up the street I thought of home. Back in Alabama this time of year the weather would be summer warm.

I thought of the many times in mid-May when my two closest friends and I would sneak off and go swimming in the local creek. They were both colored boys, and their mother was very strict with them, so we had to sneak off. One time we had gone fishing with their dad down on a big creek, I was walking across a log looking for the best fishing hole, when I slipped off the log and fell into the deep water.

I couldn't swim back then. Their dad jumped into the cold water and grabbed me just as I was about to go under for the second time. He pulled me out of the creek. I was scared and started coughing and crying. He held me close to him drying my face and comforting me, and assured me that I was going to be fine. He surely saved my life that morning.

I hugged his neck and tried to thank him, as my two friends stood wide-eyed watching their dad make my world right again. We remained best friends until they moved away. But, I never forgot them and the great times we'd had together.

I thought about the fact that I hadn't seen a dozen colored soldiers since I'd been in Wurzburg. I know that they are in the Army, and are over here in Germany. I'll have to ask Ed about it. I supposed he will just confirm what Pitts had told me. Finally, I reached the barracks, went upstairs and went to bed.

Early the next morning I located Ray and we had breakfast together. Several other guys were also at our table. I asked, "Have you guys heard that Skinner is reenlisting in the Air Force and leaves in a few weeks? I think we should have a going away party for him at the club."

They all agreed, so we decided that a Monday night would be the best time for the party. I left them eating and walked over to the Troop Information and Education Center located beneath the club.

I read several pamphlets and a couple of recent magazines to bring me up to date on current events. I found one very interesting article on a new communications media called television. I'd never seen television, but I had heard about it from couple of the newer guys in the company. Boy, this world is really moving along faster and faster.

Leaving the TI&E room I walked over to the snack bar. Gertie was working the tables, I got a cup of coffee and walked over to her.

She greeted me with, "Hello Ken, how are you?"

"I'm fine, hope you're well also. Have you seen Rachel?"

"Yes, she wants to meet you tomorrow evening about six at your usual place."

"Great." With a big smile I said, "Tell her that I'll be there."

She moved away and I finished my coffee, smoked a couple of cigarettes and went back to the barracks. I sat at my table and wrote my family a letter, and then I walked over to the gym and threw some basketballs around for a while. I then went up to the service club but Dotty wasn't there, so I read a couple of magazines, shot a game of eight ball pool with some guy I didn't know and won the game. I'm a pretty good pool player even if I do say so.

I returned to the barracks and most everyone was there, so we sat around and just talked, I mostly listened. With the exception of Pitts they all planned to go down town and hit the bars. Their goals remained the same, have fun, drink a little booze, get laid, don't spend too much money, and beat the curfew. Those goals are not always easy to do.

I went to eat then, back to my room. I turned on the radio to listen to country music, which I enjoy very much. There was a new song out by Hank Snow, entitled, "*I'm moving on.*" I thought that is a great song, and by one of my favorite artist.

The song made the top of AFN's country music chart in Europe the next week. Within days after the song became such a big hit, it seemed that everyone began using the phrase, "I'm pulling a Hank Snow," as a metaphor for they were leaving. No one ever simply said, "I'm leaving," they would instead say, "I'm Hank Snowing" or use a phrase such as "Let's Hank Snow." It was amazing how quickly the metaphor caught on, and everyone understood it perfectly.

About nine o'clock I figured I would go by the service club and improve my pool game before work. I went up the stairs to the service club. Dotty was there, so I invited her to a cup of coffee with me. We sat at one of the card tables and drank our coffee exchanging small idle talk. I then invited her to join me in a game of pool.

"Okay, but I've never played the game before. You'll have to help me," she said.

I racked the balls and explained we would play eight ball. I quickly explained the rules of the game, and how to chalk the tip of her stick. I then shot first and broke. I had the high numbers and she the low. We ran a couple of balls off the table, and then she had a hard shot to make. She held her hand awkwardly forming the bridge for the shot, so I told her to hold her hand a different way and walked up behind her.

She said, "Show me the correct way to hold my hand please."

She was leaning over the table rail. I leaned against her and reached around to reposition her hand for a better bridge and shot. Then I got the wild idea just to see what would happen, I slowly, and gently thrust against her buttocks once, then again.

She took her shot but missed the target ball. I slowly pressed against her again.

I stepped away, and she exclaimed, "Darn, I missed."

"Dotty, it takes practice, lots of practice, and I'm not the best of teachers."

Dotty looked at me, smiled and said, "You do very well as a teacher, and I like the way you teach."

Giving her a long look I replied, "We'll play again I promise you."

We quit the game and talked a little while longer. Finally, I told her I had to leave for work. We shook hands. I walked out of the club, and on down to the message center replacing Merlin on the radio.

After a dull evening my shift was finally over. I left for breakfast with Perry and Pitts. Perry said, "We have another field exercise coming up very soon."

After eating I went up to my room washed up and went to bed. Ed woke me up about three in the afternoon. I got ready for my rendezvous. I splashed on my favorite after shave lotion, and then walked down to the gate and caught a taxi.

At the Ring Hotel following my normal routine, I got the room key for number seven then found an empty table in the restaurant to wait for Rachel. I took out my cigarettes and lighter and lit one up. The beer was cold and good, glancing at my watch it was exactly six in the evening.

Rachel walked in and joined me at the table. I bought us both a drink and we left for our room. I hugged her around the waist as we went up the hallway, kissing her lightly on the top of her head. We stopped and I unlocked and opened the door, she stepped inside and I followed then turning and locking the door.

I opened my arms and said, "*Kommen sie heir, mein Liebling.*"

Laughing she stepped into my arms hugging me tightly.

"You're surprised that I speak German, Yes?" I raised her head and kissed her lips gently then more urgently. Finally, I just held her close to me.

"Being away from you is like being in a torture chamber, it's terrible."

She whispered, "Don't talk, just hold me and kiss me."

She said, "*Leibling*, I hate it when we can't see each other, I hate it us not being together, I hate it."

"We must do as you said, and fill our memory books with beautiful memories of nights like these," I replied.

She hugged me. We talked about my trip to Berchtesgaden. I told her how much I had enjoyed it, how beautiful the area and how impressed I was with the snow covered Alps. I described the Eagle's Nest with its destruction, desolation and devastation.

She said, "When I was a little girl my parents took me to Berchtesgaden for a holiday, but I can't remember much about it."

"Maybe you and I can go there one of these days. The mountain top retreat is just like it was at the end of the war minus any shells, vehicles or articles of war. It is no longer such a beautiful place with all the destruction that was inflicted upon it.

CHAPTER 11

Six unforgettable weeks

She squirmed on my lap, I got the hint and slowly kissed her, the passion fires were now lit and blazing. She slowly unbuttoned her blouse removing it. We both undressed, I pulled her close to me as we moved to the bed.

She moved to the far side, and then laid her head on my arm. I turned and kissed her face. She drew her leg up laying it across mine. I caressed it feeling the firm contours and silky smoothness of her thighs. I moved over on top of her as she opened her legs to me.

"Let me," she whispered, reaching down she grasped me and guided me as I made my insertion. We made tender gentle love. I climaxed in less than five minutes depositing my semen deep within her.

Rachel held me tightly and murmured a few words in German then kissed my face. I rolled over to my side as she snuggled close to me.

"Kenny, I have something to tell you."

I looked inquiringly at her and replied, "Darling, you can tell me anything except *Auf Wiedershen*. What is it?"

"My friend is leaving tomorrow evening to go to an army hospital in Austria for some type of special hospital training, he'll be gone for six weeks."

"That's wonderful." I hugged her close to me and kissed her. I reached for my beer. "Let's drink a toast to us being together for the next six weeks."

Laughing, she picked up her wine glass, "To us, always to us being together forever." She had a sip of wine and then said, "I had my period while you were gone, and he hasn't touched me in three weeks. I'm so happy and glad of that."

We began discussing the things we could do while he was away. It sounded like a beautiful dream. We laughed and giggled as we drank our beer and wine. We sat on the chair, and then she changed her position and straddled my lap. She kissed my chest, my face and eyes and lightly ran her tongue over my entire face. Rearing up a little she reached down grasping and repositioning me to eliminate any possible discomfort on my part. We stayed in that position for about five minutes saying very little. We were perfectly in tune with each other, our very beings in agreement, enjoying the pleasure of each other, and of our bodies.

She rose off my lap, and then taking my hand led me back to the bed. "You first," she said. I lay down on the bed on my back. She moved over on top of me. I watched her face as she made the insertion. She began moving very slowly, rhythmically. I groaned as her full breasts swayed slowly above me. I moved my hands to her waist, her eyes were alive with desire and passion. I aided her as she stared at me intently.

I could only moan, "I'm ready!" I surged upward as the orgasm gripped me. She sank down slowly, and leaning forward lay on my chest gasping. I held her to me. Has two people ever been as much in love as we are I wondered.

She lay there until I began to soften, she then moved off me and lay down snuggling in my arms. I held her close saying nothing, just holding her.

She said, "*Leibling*, we had better get dressed."

"Yes, I agree. It's been another beautiful night for us."

After we were dressed, she said, "I'll tell Gertie when we can meet again."

"I'll check with her every day," I replied.

Pulling her close to me I kissed her, and then gave her twenty marks for the taxi and to use for the next one. We walked out to the lobby, she kissed me and left. I walked back to the bar and bought another beer to take with me to the post.

The next six weeks were absolutely marvelous and unforgettable. Rachel and I spent some part of almost every day together. I traded work shifts constantly to have more time with her. We went on picnics, visited several old castles, went to good restaurants, stayed in different hotels, and we made love at every possible opportunity.

I was also promoted back to Private First Class and did that make me happy. My pay immediately jumped back up by seven dollars.

Her friend the Sergeant, returned at the end of the sixth week. Our wonderful vacation was over. I didn't see her for the next four days. I went by the snack bar and checked with Gertie. She told me Rachel wanted to see me the next evening, at our usual place at six o'clock. Gertie had a noticeably strained look on her face.

"Gertie, is there something wrong?"

"No, but do be there," she replied.

I assured her that I would, and to let Rachel know.

The next evening I arrived at the hotel about twenty minutes to six. I obtained the room key then went to the bar and bought a beer. I drank it quickly and ordered another. I felt nervous and jumpy for some strange reason. Maybe it was because of the strange way that Gertie had looked, or maybe it's just my imagination running wild, either way I'll find out soon enough.

A few minutes after six Rachel came into the bar area, I stood up. She stopped in front of me and said, "Kenny, please get me a large glass of wine, and another beer for yourself, let's go to our room."

"Of course sweetheart." I went to the bar and ordered a glass of red wine and another bottle of beer for myself. I intuitively knew something was wrong. Once we were in our room she stepped into my arms and began crying. I was stunned.

"Sweetheart, what's the matter? What in the world is wrong?"

She continued sobbing. Alarmed, I begged her to stop crying and to tell me what was wrong. Eventually, I got her to calm down a bit. She sat on the bed her hands in her face. I sat on the bed next to her as she continued sobbing in deep gasps. I hugged her and kissed her face, whispering soft words of encouragement.

"Rachel, please tell me what the problem is. What's happened to make you cry like this?"

She lifted her head, and looking into my eyes said, "Kenny, we are going to have a baby."

Shocked, I said, "Are you sure? Are you really sure that it's ours, and not the Sergeants?" She nodded her head affirmatively.

I hugged her and kissed her again and said, "That's wonderful! It's the best news possible, it'll be a beautiful baby. Rachel, it will be a baby boy, at least that's what I want it to be."

"Do you remember several weeks ago when I told you that I'd had my period when you were in Berchtesgaden, and that he hadn't touched me at all for three weeks before he left for his training?"

"Yes, I remember."

"You and I have spent most of the last seven weeks making love. I should have had my period over a week or ten days ago at the latest, it hasn't happened. I haven't ever been late, and this time I'm very late. I've had morning sickness, and I know that I am pregnant."

I took a drink of my beer, and offered her glass to her. She accepted and drank a tiny sip from the glass. "Sweetheart, this is good news, not bad, it changes nothing."

I had another drink of beer and lit a cigarette. My thoughts raced as I contemplated our future with a baby. But questions began jerking me back to cold reality. What about the Sergeant? How does he fit into this problem? Does he even know or suspect she's pregnant? Multiple questions for which I had no immediate answers, but answers had to be found.

She raised her head and kissed me deeply then said, "My dearest darling there's more that I have to tell you." Large tears flooded down her cheeks.

"Rachel, please don't cry, I'm very happy, I'm thrilled about the baby, things will work out for us. I'll do whatever it takes to make sure they do."

She placed her fingers on my lips and said, "*Mein Leibling,* please just listen to what I have to say. I have to tell you, and I have to tell you now tonight."

I lit another cigarette and had another sip of beer, she waited until I did that.

Tears streaming down her face she said, "The Sergeant has made all the arrangements, we're to be married at the hospital chapel Sunday afternoon."

I looked at her in horror, my heart began pounding. I said, "No, that can't be, it can't happen, I won't let it happen!"

Rachel placed her fingers on my lips. "We're leaving for America Tuesday morning. He told me this the day after he returned from

Austria. I had no idea this was going to happen. He lied to me, he told me we would go to America next year." She buried her face on my chest, deep sobs racking her body. The full force of what she had just told me began to sink in. I held her tightly as I tried to understand all that it truly meant. I was shaken and somewhat confused.

Rachel began to quiver and shake in my arms. I held her even tighter and said, "Be still sweetheart, calm down. Stop crying, let's think this thing through. Here take a drink of wine." I held the glass for her as she took a small sip. She raised her head and said, "I have to leave early tonight. He'll be home before nine o'clock."

I glanced at my watch it was seven thirty. My mind raced trying to formulate some ideas, some way out for us from this crazy impossible situation.

"Rachel, don't marry him. Don't leave with him. Stay here with me, we'll get married."

Crying, she said, "I can't do that, it's too late. I have to think of the baby. It must be born in America to be an American. If it's born here, and we aren't married then it will be a German." Choking back a sob she continued, "You and I talked of this before. I said then that the Army could send you away, or they might never give us permission to marry. You might not like me, or you could meet someone else. Then what would I do? What could I do alone with our baby?"

Her response was entirely logical, but logic plays no role when you are young and crazy in love. I raised her to her feet and hugged her to me. She kissed me and hugged me to her. I was at a total loss for words. Holding her I took another drink of my beer. She sat down on the side of the bed holding her face. I removed her hands from her face and stood her up again.

"Rachel, sweetheart crying doesn't help us in this. You may be right, it may be too late to stop this. A day and a half and you're to be married. Three and a half days and you'll be gone. I don't know that I can accept that. I know you keep your promises, but I wish you didn't. Stay here with me in Germany, marry me and refuse to marry and leave with him."

She kissed me tenderly and said, "*Mein Leibling*, remember our first night together here in this room? Remember the many other nights we have made love here, and those many other places, the happiness and joy we've shared together?"

Hoarsely I whispered, "Yes, I remember it all."

She continued, "Remember I told you then we must fill our memory books with memories of the love we have shared, the joy we have experienced together. I told you then and I tell you again, I love you, I will love you always."

She wiped tears from her eyes and continued, "For as long as I live there will be a special place in my heart and memory that belongs only to you. A place where no one can touch or remove. I will love and rear our baby, and he will be a good man like you, if it's a boy. I'm doing this because I have to. Time has run out for me. You my love must also do those things that you must do. Reserve a place in your heart for me and our baby. Love us always."

Although young, I recognized the finality of the moment. I could not muster an argument against her. My eyes misted over.

She held my face, kissed my tears and said, "My darling we have created life together. We have loved and laughed together, our love is like no other. Let us not cry together, for I shall surely cry the remainder of my life. The tag you wear around your neck, you have two, your dog tags, give me one of them to keep."

I opened my shirt reached in for the small chain that held my dog tags, I removed the one tag and handed it to her.

She read my name and serial number on it out loud. She kissed it then held it to my lips and said, "Kiss it my darling."

I kissed the small tag and then she kissed it again, and put it into her purse.

She said, "I must go now my love."

She reached for me and holding me around the neck kissed me passionately. I returned her kiss, my eyes now filled with tears.

She softly said, "*Auf Wiedersehen mein leibling*, my love, my life!" With tears flooding down her face she turned and walked out the door, and out of my life.

I sank slowly into the chair shocked in disbelief that she was gone, gone forever. Tears blocked my eyesight. I picked up the one full bottle of beer I still had, and drank it down without stopping. I kissed the spot on the glass where her lips had touched and drank the remainder of the wine. I then walked over to the sink and washed off my face. I dried my face and hands and automatically combed my hair. I put on my jacket and left the room locking the door behind me.

I went down to the bar area. Like someone in a trance, I sat at a table and ordered a beer from the waiter. I drank it slowly and smoked a couple of cigarettes. I then ordered six bottles of beer to go. The waiter was reluctant to sell me that many, but I offered him ten marks extra and he gave them to me in a small bag. I took them back to my room, sat down in the chair and opened up the first one. I slowly drank it. I felt like I was in a fog, I couldn't think straight. So many feelings and emotions rushing through my mind I couldn't separate them into an orderly process. One after the other I drank the six beers. I was totally drunk and I knew it. I went into the small bathroom and threw up in the commode. I had never been this drunk before. Stumbling, I collapsed onto the bed and passed out.

CHAPTER 12

The First Sergeant

I woke up, bleary-eyed, I glanced at my watch it was six-thirty in the morning, Saturday morning. I had a rotten, nasty taste in my mouth. I went to the sink and splashed water on my face, and swished water around inside my mouth and spat it out. After I put my jacket on I checked myself in the mirror, I looked like hell. I adjusted my tie and the cap on my head, lit a cigarette, unlocked the door and walked out of the room. I turned in the room key, and vowed never to return to the Ring Hotel.

Catching a taxi I instructed the driver to take me to Leighton Barracks. Arriving at the gate I paid the driver and walked up the street to the barracks.

When I arrived at our room, Ed was sleeping. Heavy odors of cognac and stale smoke hung in the air. I opened the windows to let in some fresh air, and then took off and hung up my uniform. I took a quick shower then returned to my room. I woke Ed up and asked if he wanted to go eat. He responded with less than decent civil remarks, telling me where and to what part of hell I should go.

Ray and I met in the hallway, so we went to the mess hall together. It was early and not many troops were there. We had bacon and eggs with a generous helping of catsup and coffee. Ray finished before me and lit a cigarette. Through a cloud of smoke he said, "Ken you look like hell. You look sick are you alright?"

I looked at him, I knew my eyes were red and sunken in a little. Last night and the beer did that to me. I really wasn't too sure of what to tell him or how.

"I guess I'm all right. Let me tell you what's happened." I told him about last night's activities, and about the baby. I told him how the Sergeant had set up the wedding for tomorrow afternoon, and they were leaving Germany Tuesday morning. I told him that she and I said our last goodbyes last night at the Ring Hotel. My telling him of the events had me half choked up.

He patted me on the shoulder and said, "What a rotten frigging break, let's get the hell out of here."

Back in the barracks I felt beaten, sick to my stomach, and I wanted to run away, but to where? I had no answers to the dozens of why questions that wouldn't leave me alone. My head swirling, my emotions drained and feeling physically exhausted I fell asleep. I had to go on duty on the early evening shift. Around three in the afternoon John Hodes came by the room and woke me up. I relieved Skinner from duty, and signed in on the log.

"Don't forget my farewell party this coming Monday night," he shouted as he walked out the office door.

"I'll be there for sure," I hollowed back. His departure was six weeks later than planned due to some screw up in transferring branches of service, and keeping his rank in the Air Force. I pulled the shift with nothing special or exciting happening. Then I went back to the barracks and went to bed.

Sunday morning I woke up and followed my normal routine. After eating I went back to the barracks and read the *Stars and Stripes*, listened to AFN, and just stared at the ceiling asking myself what could I have done differently? I heard a distant church bell tolling twelve noon from somewhere off post. I knew that shortly Rachel would be married to a man she didn't love, and pregnant with a child that wasn't his. What strange twists and turns life seems to deal us.

I got off the bed about two-thirty in the afternoon, dressed in my OD's and walked over to the club. I joined Roberts, Pitts and Ray at their table. I drank very slowly as I knew that I had to work the midnight shift. I was deep into my own thoughts, and I didn't give a rat's ass what they were talking about. I sat there for about two hours, and then left to get something to eat.

Sunday evening in the Army is always cold cuts, so I had the usual. I ate a baloney sandwich with cheese and some potato salad. I really wasn't hungry. I drank my coffee and walked back to the barracks. Later I went to the snack bar. I walked out of the snack bar and met Betty as she was getting off work. We had a good conversation as we walked down the street together. I gave her half of my cigarettes. She went on out the gate and caught a taxi home. I went into the headquarters building and to the message center. I relieved Merlin, checked into the net, and had no message traffic to send or receive. It was going to be a long night, so I put on the earphones and turned on the tape machine. I attempted to copy the code on the typewriter, but I just wasn't into copying code tonight, I turned off the machine and hung up the earphones.

Finding a couple of old magazines I read every article in them. Finally, I had a couple of calls on the radio. I received several messages, none of them classified or encrypted. I copied them all on the typewriter with good accuracy. I figured it was faster than twenty words a minutes, so I was improving. Finally, my shift ended.

SFC Perry came into the message center then into the radio room. We greeted each other with normal salutations. I asked Perry "May I have a three day pass beginning on Tuesday?" He checked the schedule and said, "Yeah, no problem."

"Don't forget that we finally will have the farewell party for Skinner tonight in the club," I said.

"I'll be there at least for a little while," he replied.

I left for breakfast, then went to the barracks, washed up a bit and went to bed. Sleep was abnormally slow in coming as all my thoughts centered on and around Rachel. I knew that by now she was surely married, and tomorrow morning she would leave Germany. I hope that they will fly to the states as I recalled how rough the ocean could be. A small troop ship in the North Sea and the Atlantic Ocean is not the best place for a pregnant woman, especially since that child is mine. The thought of never seeing, never holding my child was rough to accept. I will probably never know if it's a boy or a girl. With those distressing thoughts lingering in my mind, I finally fell asleep.

Skinner came by my room and woke me up around three in the afternoon. Getting up I showered, shaved put on my OD uniform and headed out to eat. I had a good meal, eating quite a bit for I knew I would be drinking beer that evening. My fear of excessive alcohol seemed to be disappearing, it was becoming too much a normal part of my life. I thought if my relatives or my grandfather knew how much I was drinking, they would faint. My grandfather might try to knock the habit out of me, as he was a tough old bird to be sure.

Ray and I went over to the club about six-thirty. They had three tables placed together along one side of the dance floor. We sat down and ordered beer. Sergeant Little and his girlfriend joined us, then Roberts, Nunez and Carlton came in. Merlin and his girlfriend drifted in followed by Ed and Ericka. Merlin told me he was working the midnight shift, so he would be leaving early. Finally, Skinner, the guest of honor showed up. His eyes sparkling and his face a bright shade of red. I knew he must have been drinking quite a bit already. We wound up with about fourteen people at the tables. Perry and his girlfriend came in a little later. For a Monday night there were quite a few people in the club. Our table was covered with beer bottles and glasses, plus full ashtrays. Cigarette smoke hung like a light fog in the stale air. The band began to play at nine o'clock. They began their repertoire with "*Smoke gets in your eyes.*" My thoughts immediately turned back to the last time Rachel and I had danced to that tune. I had kissed her on the neck, and she had returned my kiss and hugged me.

My spirit and morale sank lower than whale shit. I walked around the table and asked Ed, "Are you going out later tonight?"

"Yeah, but I'll be back around seven in the morning. I have to make the run to Hammelburg tomorrow."

I gave him thirty marks and asked him to pick me up two fifths of Cognac. He promised to do so.

We drank several toasts to Skinner. Perry and Merlin with their girlfriends left after the first toast. Eventually, the band began their goodnight tune, and we knew we all would have to leave the club. Everyone who had their girlfriends with them also began to leave. Those of us who lived in the barracks returned to the barracks, and we all went to Robert's room. He opened his new bottle of cognac, passed it around the group and I had several swallows. I got drunk all over again. We sat around and talked about just anything anyone wanted to talk about. Skinner, finally gave it up and went to bed. I sat there and listened to their conversations with no interest whatsoever, I continued to sip on the cognac. My mind was filled with dark brooding thoughts about Rachel and the baby.

Finally, the party broke up since most of the men had to work the next morning. I was on my three day pass after midnight, so I had no reason to rush. I walked up the hall to my room, removed my uniform and went to bed. Sleep came immediately.

Ed woke me up a little after seven o'clock the next morning. He said, "Everything's copacetic, here's your two bottles of cognac. Don't start on them until I get back this afternoon."

I mumbled something in return, and rolled over as I heard him give Bettie his good morning kiss. I dozed off for another hour or so. I slowly began to wake up, as thoughts of Rachel and my situation began pressing to the front. I got up cleaned up, and then returned to my room and got dressed.

My stomach was too upset to eat, so I made the decision not to go to the mess hall. I turned on the radio and listened to AFN news of the day, then to the country music program. I walked over to the window, and just stared out at the trees and grounds. I thought today Rachel and the Sergeant will leave, or have left all ready. I felt a sob choking in my throat.

Tears came into my eyes. I thought what a screwed up situation this has turned out to be. No love affair should ever end with two broken hearts. That's not the way love is supposed to be.

I reached under my bunk and picked up one of my bottles of cognac. Maybe this will make me feel better. I opened the bottle and took a big drink. It landed in my stomach with a jolt. I lay down on my bunk and listened to the radio. I had several more drinks and fell asleep. I woke up later that afternoon; I knew I couldn't eat so I had another big swallow of cognac. AFN was still playing, but now they had popular music on. I listened to Benny Goodman, Artie Shaw, The Dorsey Brothers and Glenn Miller, plus several other big bands. I continued to sip from my bottle, dinner time came and passed.

Ed came in. He cleaned up and said, "I'm going to town, and I'll probably spend the night with the *Frau*, I'll see you tomorrow morning."

"Okay, have a good time, say hello to her for me."

He left and I had another drink. Our room door was closed so no one came by. I realized that I was once again totally drunk. My last night with Rachel at the hotel wouldn't fade from my thoughts. Those memories so fresh, and so deeply embedded were overwhelming.

Finally, I drifted off to sleep. I woke up the next morning too sick to move. Ed came in the room and tried to get me up. I told him what section of hell he should visit, so he left me alone.

After everyone had gone to work I got up still dressed in my fatigues, and stumbled down to the latrine. I washed my face, brushed my teeth and returned to my room. My stomach was burning. I forgot the last time I had eaten, but the idea of eating made me want to throw up. My hands were shaking. I thought it must be Tuesday or Wednesday, either way I don't give a rat's ass, I'm on pass. I had a big drink from my second bottle. I didn't remember opening it up. I was surprised to see the other bottle empty setting by the end of my bunk. I glanced at my watch; it was about ten-thirty in the morning. I lay back down and dozed off again.

My door opened, and I heard someone enter my room, I was too tired to lift my head or open my eyes. Then I heard a voice that I had come to know so well, it was the First Sergeant.

In that inimitable voice he said, "Get up Fisher!"

I opened one eye and looked at him. "First Sergeant, I'm on a three day pass, and I don't have to get up."

His voice rising he bellowed, "Get out of that frigging bunk Fisher!"

"No, I'm not getting up until my pass is over."

He grabbed me by the front of my shirt and jerked me off my bunk. He threw me around and up against the door of Ed's locker almost knocking it over. My head was spinning.

Ironjaw's snarled, "You're not going to be another Pop Warner. You're going to straighten your ass out, stop your stupid drinking, sober up, and you're going to do it now!"

He twisted my left arm behind my back and shoved me out of the door into the hall. He pushed me toward the latrine, and kicked open the latrine door. He then shoved me against the wall and pushed my head into the stationary tub, forcing my head under the facet, and turned on the cold water.

I spit, sputtered, choked and got water up my nose and down my throat swallowing some of it. I thought the big Indian is going to frigging drown me. He finally jerked my heard up by my hair and released my arm. He then grabbed the front of my shirt.

"Fisher, you're going to take a shower, and you're going to shave. Then you're going to put on a clean uniform, and report to me. You're going to do it all in exactly thirty minutes. Do you fucking well understand?"

I didn't answer quick enough to suit him.

Grabbing me again, he snarled, "Go ahead, say no to me again and I'll beat your frigging ass right here, right now! It's best you believe me."

He drew back his arm to hit me, and I knew he would.

"Yes Sir First Sergeant, I'll do it."

He released my shirt, "In exactly thirty minutes you better have your drunken ass cleaned up and in front of my desk." He released me and left the latrine.

I shook the water from my face as I tried to half-ass sober up fast. I went back to my room, took off my fatigues, grabbed my shaving kit and rushed back to the latrine. I took a quick whore's bath, brushed my teeth, shaved then rushed back to my room. I put on a clean uniform and checked my watch, I had seven minutes to go. I lit a cigarette and sat down my footlocker. I picked up the empty cognac bottle, and the overflowing ashtray and threw them both in the trash container. I put the less than half full bottle of cognac in my wall locker and closed the door.

With two minutes to go I went down the stairs walked through the clerk's office and knocked on Ironjaw's door.

He answered, "Come in."

Stepping through the doorway I walked towards his desk, stepping carefully on his throw rug. I came to attention, saluted and said, "PFC Fisher reporting to the First Sergeant as ordered sir."

He returned my salute, looked at his watch and said, "Go close the frigging office doors."

Turning around I closed the door to the clerk's office, then crossed the room and closed the door to the Commander's office. I then returned to the front of his desk and stood at attention.

He just stared at me without saying a word. Finally, he said, "Stand at ease."

I relaxed a little and looked at him.

Then almost snarling he said, "Fisher, you're fucking up big time, and I won't allow you to do that. You have the potential to be a damn good soldier, and what you're doing now will end all of that. Pop Warner is back in the states, and not expected to make it. Are you headed down that same path? He was wounded, hurt and sick, but you have no damn excuse for your actions. My sources tell me that you've been going with some woman who married a Sergeant and went to the states." His voice began rising as he continued, "You're a soldier, but your actions are an absolute disgrace to the uniform, to the unit, the army and to yourself. If I have to I'll beat your ass every day, but you are not going to lie around your room staying drunk, moaning over some lost love, not now, not ever!" He pounded the desk top with his fist and said, "Do I make myself perfectly fucking clear?"

My head swimming, my stomach churning, thinking I might vomit at any time, I said, "Yes Sir First Sergeant."

He then said, "Before I got married I must have been in love a dozen times, or thought I was, and so will you. She's gone, so it's over. You probably will never see her again. That might hurt, but you and I both know it's true. Am I not right?"

"Yes, First Sergeant."

He glanced at his watch and said, "It's lunch time, let's you and I go have some chow."

He rose from his desk, walked over and opened the door to the clerk's office. I followed behind him. He told the company clerk, "We're going to chow."

We left and walked down the street together. After entering the mess hall we went through the serving line, and he selected our table. I sat down opposite him. Several of my buddies came into the mess hall, but none of them joined us.

He had a plate of pork and sauerkraut, and I had selected pork and mashed potatoes. I didn't think my stomach could take much else. He didn't speak at all as we ate our lunch. I ate a roll with butter which was the best thing on my plate. Finishing our lunch he sat back and lit a cigarette. I did the same and I drank a cup of coffee. My hands were shaking so badly the coffee almost spilled. I had delirium tremens (DT's) big time.

Finishing his cigarette he said, "I have to go back to my office."

Standing up and leaning forward his face inches from mine, his black eyes boring holes in mine he said, "Fisher, I meant every god damn word I said to you in my office, It's best you believe me."

I looked him square in the eyes and said, "Yes Sir First Sergeant."

"I'll see you around," he said as he turned and left the mess hall. I watched as he left, and I was relieved that he had taken it a little easy on me.

Summer had long since passed, September was here. Cool winds swept across the compound, leaves fell and the trees mostly bare now. The evenings and nights were cold. I knew here in Germany the snow was not far behind. I don't think I'll ever get acclimated to such cold weather. But for now the climate matched my thoughts and emotions. I felt stripped bare, and robbed of the person that I loved so much. The traumatic loss of Rachel gnawed at me, she was never far from my thoughts. For me life had lost much of its joy and glamour.

I wasn't bitter, just deeply hurt and disappointed at how things had ended for us. I no longer enjoyed many of the things that earlier had been so much fun. I continued to do my job, becoming proficient in almost every facet of it. I could now send and receive Morse code between twenty and twenty-five words a minute, and type it all accurately on the typewriter.

I wondered about the baby that was yet to be born. Would the Sergeant figure out that it couldn't possibly be his? Would he even care? Would it be a boy or a girl, and what will she name it, what will it look like? I would really like for it to be a boy, and I would like to be a part of his life, but that just isn't meant to be.

CHAPTER 13

My Conference with the Chaplain

I knew deep inside I had to get out of this mental slump, this emotional chaotic quagmire in which I found myself. I wasn't really sure of what to do. The loss of Rachel ate at me constantly. One day at work I called the Post Chaplain and requested a conference with him. He was available, and scheduled me for one morning of the following week.

While speaking with him over the phone I didn't tell him the reason for my request, that could wait until I was face to face with him. I cleaned up that morning and wore my best uniform. I walked into the chapel, I hadn't been here in months.

Normally, I'm not a church going person, I remembered that we had a group talk from the Chaplain, but for the life of me I couldn't remember his name. At the front of the chapel I saw an office marked, Chaplain Hodges. I knocked on the door and heard someone say, "Come in."

I stepped into the office and a Lieutenant Colonel was seated behind a desk. He rose to his feet and said, "I'm Chaplain Hodges, you must be PFC Fisher."

"Yes sir, I'm PFC Fisher."

He shook my hand and invited me to have a seat. I sat down in a nice comfortable leather chair opposite his desk. I began the conversation by saying, "Colonel, I have this, he interrupted me and said, "In this office I prefer to be called Father if you would please."

"Yes, Father." I began again. "I have a problem that I need to talk to you about, one that I don't know how to handle."

He leaned forward and said, "Son, please start at the beginning, tell me what your problem is, what caused it, how long it's been going on, and does it still exist."

I told him about my love affair with Rachel. I left nothing out. I explained how it all started, and how it ended. I told him of her pregnancy, and how and why we knew I was the baby's father. He listened intently, saying nothing.

He stood up and stared out the window in his office, listening to me as I poured out my heart to him. I explained to him Rachel's fears and emotions, and her desperate longing for security and stability. I ended my explanation by saying that I no longer knew how to handle it by myself.

He sat back down in his chair. Speaking softly, he pointed out that I had been wrong for initiating a relationship with Rachel while she was living with another man. He said, "You were in a covert love affair."

He asked, "What's the name of the Sergeant?"

"I don't know, I never asked, and I never wanted to know," I replied.

"Regardless of names, you both were in a loving caring relationship." He spoke of our ages being so close, and said, "I'm sorry to see such a relationship end so disastrously for both of you. In the final analysis, there is really nothing you or I can do to bring back that which you both shared. She's gone to the states, and the United States is a big country. The chances of finding each other are slim—if not impossible—certainly most improbable. If the Sergeant remains in the army maybe, just maybe, someday you might see her again. But where or when is pure speculation and totally unpredictable. What if you did find her, what then? She's now legally married. Would you commit adultery, would she? These are the type questions you must ask and answer yourself." He stopped and lit a small black pipe.

He continued, "You must remember my son the big gamble that she has taken. She married a man much older than herself, has gone to a new country with different customs and cultures, all on a gamble that the marriage will be a good one. She's gambling that the baby will be born well and healthy. Gambling that she at last will find the peace, security and stability she so desperately seeks." He puffed on his pipe.

"I have no doubt that she loved you as you have described, and you obviously loved her as much. Son, recognize you were the wild card in her deck. You don't know what your future holds, neither do I, and certainly neither did she. You wanted her to throw away her hand, and play the wild card which might have been a losing hand. I suggest you think about that." He puffed his pipe again, and took a deep breath.

He looked at me and said, "Son, let me tell you this. Your heart, the human heart, is different from all other parts of your body. It and it alone, has an infinite capacity for love. For example, you love your brothers and sisters, your aunts and uncles, friends and other people who enter into your life. But all those people you love differently from the love you have for your parents. To you they are always special people, and you love them.

When you love a woman it too is different. You will learn that you love your wife and your children differently from that of your parents. Nevertheless, for all these people it is still this wonderful concept and emotion we call love." He paused for a long moment.

He continued, "One day you'll find another woman, and you'll love again. Maybe many times for the heart maintains this unlimited capacity to love over and over again, and more than just one person. I highly suggest and recommend you try and ease Rachel and the baby out of your mind. Cherish the memories that you have of her and of you two together, but let them be what they truly are, just memories. Time will dim but never erase the memories, but it will lessen the hurt, and that will aid you as you go on with your life." He paused and puffed on his pipe again.

"PFC Fisher, is there anything else that you want to discuss? I hope that I have responded to your problem in an understandable and acceptable way."

I replied, "No Father, there is no other problem that I cannot handle by myself. This particular problem was one that I did not know how to handle, and I could not find a solution."

"PFC Fisher you are a very young man, you're not even twenty years old yet. You will find as you grow older that life will offer you many choices. Some choices you make will benefit you. You might make others that will be detrimental for you. All men and women are given choices as they move through their lives. I am neither saying, nor suggesting that you made a bad choice by falling in love with Rachel.

But in your case and hers there were too many factors that worked against you both, the deck was stacked.

Now you two have created a new life together, and for you that might present a problem of conscience as you move forward. You might never know if it is a boy or a girl, you may never know what it looks like, or the type person he or she will become. But, you will always know that somewhere there is a person that you fathered.

It is my belief that most of known covert love affairs do not in the end work out as they are hoped to. It is but one of the myriad of events that occur in our lives that we all must learn to deal, and to live with. You have a good head on your shoulders, you are bright and conscientious. I have faith in you and your ability to learn to live and deal with your problems. Finally, I urge you to believe in yourself, and look to the future positively. Good things will come your way for sure."

He appeared to be finished. I stood up and saluted him.

"Thank you Father for listening to my problem. I know that you are busy and probably have more pressing problems to deal with than mine. But to me, my problem was such that I had to have someone to talk to, someone who could understand my problem, and understand the mental chaos that it has created for me. I sincerely appreciate your time, your understanding and advice."

We shook hands, I saluted him again, and then I left his office.

CHAPTER 14

Musings of an old Chaplain

PFC Fisher left, and I watched as the door slowly closed. After watching the young soldier walk away I sat back down. For an old Chaplain, I still get surprised. After he left my office I considered all the things that he had told me. It was indeed a most unusual story, a tragedy to be sure, nonetheless a beautiful heartwarming love story. A question which had been bothering me for several weeks had now been answered. I know who Rachel is, and I know Sergeant Sanders the medic she married down at the hospital chapel, I performed their marriage ceremony. I recall how extraordinarily beautiful a young woman she was. I also recall being surprised at the big difference in their ages. I had asked myself a question then as to why she was crying and looking so distraught when marriage is supposed to be such a happy event. Now I have my answer. I said a prayer for them all, and a special one for the baby yet to be born.

I've been here two years now, and have married dozens of soldiers and their German War brides. While I'm certainly no expert, I feel that I know enough about human nature to think I can almost tell which marriages will work and those that may not. I would hesitate to predict if Sergeant Sander's marriage with his new wife will survive. She showed no obvious signs of pregnancy, but if PFC Fisher is correct, it won't be much longer before it shows. I sincerely hope that the Sergeant will accept the child as his, rear and care for it, take care of his young wife, and become a family for all to be proud of.

PFC Fisher is a young soldier. His manner of speaking and accent easily identified him as being from the southern United States. He was so serious, and so sincere that I had to accept and believe his entire story. He was not like the many other young soldiers I have married to young German girls. Many of them seemed too young for marriage, childish in their behavior, and unsure of their future plans, if any.

Covert love affairs almost never end the way the participants want them to.

Fisher's presentation of his love affair with Rachel was captivating. His serious demeanor, his delicate choice of words and the passion with which he spoke tells volumes about his character.

I sincerely hope and believe that one day he will once again fall in love, and with the right woman. I'm positive that he will. He's young and his life is still in front of him. The pain he feels now will inevitably fade away and pass. I hope that he will take my advice to heart, and forget the young woman. Most likely he will never see her again, and I think he realizes it. For him right now it truly is a huge problem, but I believe that he will handle it well. I will say another prayer for him.

Just four years or so ago, I was here in this country saying prayers over young wounded and dying boys just like him. Now I'm on my first tour here after the war, and our young men are marrying these women by the dozens. That is a good thing. War's end, animosities fade away, and life does and must go on.

That soft, southern accented voice of PFC Fisher however, will stay with me for a long time. I wish them all well.

CHAPTER 15

After the Conference

I felt better for having talked with the Chaplain. I'm sure that he really does have more pressing problems. But hell, that's what he is here for to listen to problems, and try to find solutions. I certainly wouldn't want his job. He probably gave me good advice, but I'm not sure that I accept and can follow it all. Time will tell I suppose. I'm sure that the Chaplain has heard similar type problems, but to me mine is a special one. Any problem that results in two broken hearts can't be an easy one.

I had listened with care to every word that the Chaplain had said. I have the feeling however that he thinks I'm young and immature, just another kid who thinks he is in love.

I recall reading somewhere a remark made by a young oriental man applying for admission into an American University. When told that his age and immaturity was a barrier to his entrance, he had responded by saying: "*To judge maturity by one's age, is an immature thought in itself.*" He was admitted to the university.

In my heart I knew just as Rachel knew that the love we had for each other was real, undeniable and unforgettable.

I walked slowly away from his office toward my barracks. I thought about and needed time to digest all his remarks. I thought about Rachel. I wondered was I really the wild card in the deck? I sat down on the top step by the bowling alley, lit a cigarette and continued to think about the situation. There were so many imponderables all with nebulous answers. I realize that I'm a PFC and make only eighty-two dollars a month. Could I have realistically supported a family of three on that amount? Had I been fair to ask her to give up a sure thing, and gamble that our cards would be dealt perfectly? Could our love survive and manage all the hardships that are placed on families in the military? I guess I'll never really know for sure. I now became determined to subdue and suppress the memories of me and Rachel. I simply had to if I was to retain my sanity. I would do it by spending more time with other women, and let all the chips fall wherever they may.

A few of us decided to go to the club that evening. Roberts, Ray, Hodes and I found a table near the dance floor, and ordered pitchers of beer. We watched couples dancing and talked about current events. I saw a young lady sitting with another couple who was very pretty. I walked over and asked her to dance. She agreed and we danced several dances before I returned her to her table. I didn't ask her name, and I didn't offer her mine.

Sitting down at the table after dancing I felt better. Somehow the feeling of guilt and total frustration had eased a little. We all had a few glasses of beer, and returned to the barracks without any mishaps. Several mornings later I was off duty, had slept late and missed breakfast, so I walked over to the snack bar and had a cheeseburger and coffee.

I then walked upstairs to the service club. Dotty was there doing some office work. I said, "Hello and good morning Dotty."

She rose from her chair and said, "Well hello stranger, where have you been so long?"

"I've been busy. We lost one operator and I had to work more shifts. I never seem to have enough time. It's good to see you again."

"It's good to see you again also." She poured two cups of coffee and we sat at a card table and chatted for about an hour. I mentioned that I was off work today. She invited me to drop by in the evening, and I promised her I would.

I managed to kill the remainder of the day. I took a nap, then showered and got dressed again. I walked over to the service club around nine-thirty. I chatted with Dotty and she said, "Why don't you stay while I close and lock up the club."

"Sure, I have no place I need to go."

I sat down on the large leather couch by the wall. She went around the large room picking up magazines and placing them back in the racks, turned off a couple of the larger lights, and placed the cover over the pool table. She then locked the front door entrance to the club then came over and sat down by me on the couch.

Lighting a cigarette I asked, "How has your evening been?"

"It's been slow and rather boring," she replied.

I put my cigarette out in the ashtray stand by the end of the couch so I could move closer to her. I put my arm around her shoulder and turned her face towards mine. I knew I was going to kiss her and thought well, she'll either accept my kiss, or slap the hell out of me.

I drew her face closer. As I bent to meet her I kissed her gently on the lips. Slowly she responded. Her arms encircled my neck as she returned my kiss, her tongue sought out mine. We kissed a couple more times and true to the laws of human nature, my cock became hard as a diamond. The old saying that, *"a stiff dick has no conscience"* is absolutely true.

Slowly, I cupped her breast and gently caressed it. I continued to tease, excite and motivate her breasts as I slowly undressed her. We lay back on the couch and I made love to her. That I didn't have a condom on didn't enter my mind, and apparently neither did it bother her.

After several short minutes of passionate love making I climaxed. She grasped me tightly as she had an orgasm. We both relaxed, but I didn't move from on top of her. Retaining my rigidity I kissed her passionately, she returned my kisses with equal fervor.

Breathing deeply she murmured, "That was wonderful!"

"It was for me also, let's don't stop so quickly." I slowly began my thrusting movements once more.

As I continued, she coordinated her movements with mine. The tension began building up and I whispered to her, "I'm ready." She grasped me tightly, and kissed me as I once again climaxed. I lay on her spent but happy and satisfied. Slowly relaxing, I sat up. She sat her and kissed me again.

She said, "Ken, I wanted you to do that, I've waited a long time."

"I've wanted to do that since the day I first saw you, so I have waited a long time also," I replied.

I kissed her again gently, rose from the couch and buttoned on my shorts. She and I both dressed, and I lit us cigarettes. She buttoned her blouse and sat down beside me.

"Let's have a cup of coffee, it should still be hot."

"Sure, that will be great, I can use a cup of coffee."

Getting two cups I filled them and returned to the couch. I put an arm around her as we sipped the coffee and relaxed from our first intimate consummation.

.Stroking her long black silky hair I said, "I want to do this again and again."

She laughed and replied, "Well, I certainly hope you do. But for tonight we had better go."

Agreeing with her I placed the two cups in a receptacle, and we left through the back door down the stairs to her Jeep. She got into the Jeep, then leaned out and kissed me good night. I closed the side door as she started the engine and slowly drove away.

Walking back to the barracks I felt totally at ease with myself. My self-selected physical and emotional therapy was beginning to work. Laughing, I said to myself, "Ed Clarkston, you were wrong. We enlisted swine do make out with beautiful American women once in a while."

I went upstairs to my room, undressed and hung up my uniform. It was still early so I reached into my wall locker and found my half finished bottle of cognac. I had a small sip and it went down easily. I turned on the radio and listened to AFN. The announcer spoke about the Berlin Airlift.

He said, "It began in June of 1948, and ended in September of 1949. Over two million Berliners had been fed by provisions from over a quarter million individual flights which had delivered over two million tons of food and supplies."

That was indeed an impressive record the Air Force, and the United States could be proud of for its humanitarian efforts.

My thoughts turned to Rachel, she had been gone since July and here it is approaching November. I counted the months up on my fingers. She had become pregnant in late May or early June, that means the baby is due in March or April. Will I ever know I wondered?

The music resumed playing after the Berlin announcement. Then I thought about Dotty. I think she wanted and needed sex as much as I did. She had an itch, and I scratched it.

I heard Ray and Ed coming in the building and on up the stairs. They came into the room and Ray grabbed my bottle and had a big swallow.

Ed said, "Everything's copacetic." He walked over and gave Bettie a kiss saying, "I'm home again darling."

Ed was pretty high, laughing and telling me how they had almost gotten a DR for being in an off-limits bar. They had jumped over a barbed wire fence and gotten away. I lit another cigarette, and just listened to the rehash of their evening activities. We sat there bullshitting for about a half an hour until my bottle was almost empty. Ed opened his locker and pulled out his bottle which was also about empty. Roberts had just gotten off work so he joined us in our room. We continued to talk, and just shoot the bull until both bottles were drained. Eventually, with both bottles empty we decided to call it a night and get some sleep. I glanced at my watch it was two-thirty in the morning. I went to bed and slept like a baby.

I think it was about the second week of November when I dropped by the snack bar and had coffee. Gertie was there and came over and sat at my table.

We exchanged greetings then she said, "I have a letter from Rachel. She told me that Sergeant Sanders is getting out of the army at the end of this month. He has a job with a big hospital in Chicago. She said to tell you she is well and getting bigger and she has no problems with her friend. You would understand that."

"Is that all?" I asked.

She nodded her head yes.

"Do you have an address for her?"

"*Nein*, this letter came from some town called Manhattan, near Fort Riley, Kansas. She said that it's a temporary address, and she'll write to me once she gets a new address in Chicago."

"Thanks Gertie, I really appreciate you telling me this."

She walked away from my table and returned behind the serving counter. I thought about what she had relayed to me. So the guy's name is Sanders. At least I know where Rachel is and will be, and where the baby will be born. Interpreting what she had said it appears that the Sergeant doesn't know, or doesn't care who the biological father of the baby is. Hopefully, he'll be happy to just have a baby in his family. I surely hope he will be. Knowing that I have an unseen son will haunt me for the remainder of my life, but I can see no avenue to correct the situation.

I'm very thankful that Gertie is still working at our snack bar, and in contact with Rachel. Otherwise, I would never have known what happened to Rachel and to our child. I keep thinking son, but it just might be girl. If it is a boy, I hope she names him Douglas, I like that name. I certainly hope she doesn't select a common name like Joe, Sam or Bill. Maybe Dennis, Sean, or even Vincent would be good.

Oh well, only time is going to furnish me the answer to the name of the baby, and whether it's a boy or a girl, and I have no choice in the matter whatsoever.

In early December we had another three-day field exercise. I was placed in charge, and we conducted the exercise without a hitch. While in the field we ate mostly the new C-rations. I had two of the team pile the empty cans into an empty ration box for ease of handling and disposal. I stepped out of the radio hut early in the morning to check out the area when I noticed an elderly woman and a young girl about twelve years old over by the box of cans. They were picking over the empty cans. The lady reminded me of my own grandmother with her snow white hair. As I watched her pick through the cans, tears welled up in my eyes. I walked over to the trailer and picked up a case of C-rations and gave it to her. The box had a wire band around it, so I found a long stick and pushed it beneath the wire, so both she and the girl could carry it. The old woman grasped my hand and kissed it. I pulled her to me, and hugging her I said," *Frohliche Weihnachten,* grandma."

Christmas was rapidly approaching and the club manager decorated the club. Dotty and the other woman decorated the service club. I bought and mailed home Christmas cards to the family. My first year anniversary in Germany came and passed. Sitting in the radio room on the evening shift, I reminisced about the past year. So many things had happened in my life, my arrival here, the fight with Corporal Sherron, and then my revenge. Climbing the antenna pole and having to have the fire truck get me down. Falling in love with Rachel, and the devastating loss of her. Now I have this on-going affair with Dotty. It has indeed been an eventful year. I'm over nineteen-years-old now, and I still have almost two more years to spend over here.

A few days later I was going downtown for an afternoon of beer and entertainment, I was pursuing my determination to go out with other women and put Rachel out of my mind. I didn't know what else to do to lessen the pain. As I walked to the gate, Betty came out of the headquarters building and shouted to me. I stopped, and she walked quickly over to me and we exchanged greetings.

We walked through the gate together and I asked, "Where are you going?"

"I'm going home, where are you going?"

"I'm guess I'm going downtown and have a few cold beers. I'm off until tomorrow evening, so I might as well have a little fun tonight."

She laughed and replied, "I have some cold beer would you like to have a beer with me at my place?"

"Sure, let's catch a taxi."

We caught the first taxi and Betty gave him directions to her house. Arriving there, she told me to give the driver five marks, which I did.

We walked inside her place, it was nice and warm. She had a small living room, one bedroom, eating area in the kitchen, plus a bathroom.

Looking around I said, "Betty you have a very nice place here."

She smiled, "Its home, but hopefully not forever."

I removed my overcoat and cap placing them both back of the door on a coat hangar.

Betty said, "Make yourself comfortable, take off your jacket and tie."

"That's a great idea."

Betty went to the small refrigerator and brought out two beers. I sat on the couch in the living area and spotting an ashtray on the table I lit two cigarettes. Betty sat down on the couch and gave me one of the beers. It was nice and cold. I gave her the cigarette. I slipped off my shoes and placed my feet on the coffee table, and had a drink of the beer.

"*Prosit*," we touched our bottles together, and I had another drink of beer.

Betty asked, "What have you been doing lately?"

"Nothing really, going out in the field, working a shift, and trying to stay out of trouble."

She rose from the couch and turned on the radio and tuned in AFN. Soft music emanated from the speaker, filling the room with soft romantic sounds.

We talked about her job, how she was getting along and other generalities. She rose from the couch and returned with two more beers. I offered her a cigarette which she accepted and I lit it, and another one for myself.

"Betty, come on over here and sit closer to me, let's not be strangers."

She moved closer leaning her head against my shoulder. We drank our beer and smoked without speaking. I took the bottle out of her hand and placed it alongside my own on the table. I then took her face in my hands and kissed her on the lips. I drew back and looked at her. She smiled, so I kissed her again. She responded as our tongues danced their lustful dance of passion and desire.

One thing led to another, and we walked into her bedroom. We were in no hurry so we undressed, lay on the bed, and slowly made love to each other. Temporarily satisfied we got up and returned to the couch. There we talked a little while and finished our beers.

"Would you like another beer?"

"Sure."

She went to the refrigerator and returned saying, "I only have one beer left. I know a little store just a few houses from here, I'll run over and get some more."

Locating my pants and taking out twenty marks from my wallet I gave them to her. She went to the bathroom, then quickly dressed and left.

In about ten minutes she returned with more beer. She handed two to me and placed the others in the refrigerator. She then removed her coat and hung it up. She turned and looked at me.

"Betty, I can't sit here naked all by myself."

She laughed and removed her blouse, skirt and shoes then joined me on the couch. I placed my arm around her shoulders and gently pulled her closer to me.

"What are your plans for the future sweetheart?"

She was silent and thoughtful for a minute then said, "I want to find someone, a good man who will love me for just being me. I hope to get married, I want to have children. I want to have my own home someday. I want to get a good job, and I want my country to do well. The war's over, and now it's time for me, and all the girls like me to make their hopes and dreams come true. I want to live without fear, without war."

Kissing her on the cheek I whispered, "You're beautiful, and you will get what you want."

We finished our beer in silence until I asked, "Are you hungry?"

"Yes, let's get dressed and go to a restaurant and eat."

"That sounds good to me, I'm hungry also."

We both dressed and left the house. She hailed a taxi and gave him instructions to wherever we were going. It took about ten minutes and the driver pulled up to a place called the Alpen Haus. I paid the driver what she told me to.

It was nice inside, a clean place with a very pleasant aroma drifting out from the kitchen. Betty led us to a table and ordered us two beers. She placed our order for beef steak and potatoes. We smoked, drank our beer and indulged in quiet conversation. The waiter brought us a large steak and home-fried potatoes. The meal was delicious. After we finished eating we talked some more then I suggested we return to her house. I paid the bill. It was only thirty-seven marks which was very cheap for a meal for two. We left and caught a taxi back to her house. Once there we partially undressed and sat back on the couch. She got up and turned on the radio, AFN was once again playing beautiful ballroom music. She lay on the couch with her head on my thigh. I smoothed her hair and gently stroked her face. As I continued to gently caress her she took my hand and kissed it. I lit two cigarettes and gave her one.

She rose from the couch and got two beers from the refrigerator, opening them she returned and gave one to me. She sat back down on the couch. We sipped the beer had another cigarette and made small talk. I suggested that we go to bed as I had a slight buzz on. She readily agreed, so I made sure all the cigarettes were extinguished. We undressed and holding hands we walked into the bedroom. I kissed her goodnight, and held her as she snuggled in my arms. We both were asleep in minutes.

Around six-thirty the next morning, I carefully got out of bed and wandered into the kitchen. I spotted a small coffee pot and a bag of ground coffee. Seeing that she had an electric hot plate, I filled the coffee pot with cold water and placed a couple of scoops of coffee into the pot. The water quickly boiled, I then turned off the hot plate and found two coffee cups filling them both. I placed one on a saucer and walked into the bedroom. Betty was awake and sitting up in bed.

"Good morning beautiful, here's a fresh cup of coffee for you."

She laughed and replied, "Thank you Ken. No one has ever served me coffee in bed before."

I lit a cigarette and handed it to her, then sat down in a chair by the bed. We drank our coffee and smoked the cigarettes. She rose and went into the bath room. I could hear her brushing her teeth and apparently splashing water on her face. She returned and sat on my lap. I kissed her and tenderly caressed her breasts. She took me by the hand as we went back to the bed. We lay across the bed both nude. I kissed and caressed her body as the sexual tension and desire mounted. I moved over on top of her, and slowly began that ultimate act of intimacy. She held me tightly, kissing my face and softly whispering words in German which I didn't understand. After a few minutes of slow coordinated deliberate movements we completed our act or love.

As we got up from the bed I asked, "Do you have to work today?"

"Yes, I have to be there at the regular time, eight o'clock."

"I'll get dressed and you do whatever you have to do, and we'll go to the *Kaserne* together." She nodded her head in agreement.

While she was in the bathtub, I refilled our cups draining the last drop from the pot. She returned and sat on the couch, brushed her hair and slowly drank her cup of coffee. I gave her a lit cigarette which she smoked. I turned on the radio and listened to the morning news. The world appeared to be still at peace, so I turned it off.

Betty said, "Ken, we had better go." We walked out of her house, turning she locked her door just as a taxi pulled up in front.

"The driver picks me up each morning, so he knew what time to be here." We both entered the taxi. We held hands as we traveled back to the post. Arriving back at the gate I gave the driver ten marks. We walked through the gate and on up the street. As we rounded the gym I stopped her. "Here's an extra pack of cigarettes I always carry with me." She kissed me on the cheek and told me goodbye.

Christmas week I offered to work for any of the operators who had girlfriends and wanted to be off with them. I wound up pulling three extra shifts, it was no big deal. I met Dotty several times in the service club, and we managed to find some time to be alone and be intimate. She really was a beautiful Spanish woman, flashing dark eyes, a brilliant smile with snow white teeth and long black hair. She would be so easy to love. Someday, someone is going to get very lucky and marry her.

New Year's Eve several of the guys and I went to the club. The place was crowded just like it had been the previous year. Couples were dancing, and the band was knocking itself out. I recalled last New

Year's Eve when Rachel and I danced and she had kissed me for the first time, and of the love that had grown out of that first dance and first kiss. I shook my head, I just couldn't believe that an entire year has passed since that happened, and all that has happened since then.

Finally, the club manager counted the last thirty seconds of 1949. He then announced the New Year. Everyone stood and toasted the army and the New Year. In memories eye I saw myself blowing Rachel a kiss, she reaching out catching it and bringing it to her lips. I coughed unexpectedly.

Ray turned and asked me, "Are you alright?"

"Yeah, I just had a swallow of beer go down the wrong pipe," I replied.

Wherever she is tonight I hope she remembers last year. I reached over and filled my glass with beer and chug-a-lugged it. We stayed until the club closed at one o'clock in the morning.

Ray said, "Let's get out of here." So we left everyone singing and headed back to the barracks. New Year's Day 1950, began with everyone in the barracks a little hung over. I hauled my ass out of bed and cleaned up, after a shower I felt much better.

When I returned to my room several guys were up and around. A few of us left for the mess hall and had breakfast. The cooks were up to the task as we ate heartily. The only people around not hung over were the guys who had worked the night before. I was off today, and that made me happy. I felt sorry for Hodes and Ray who both were on duty today. Listening to Morse code I think would warp my mind, and it's the last thing I need to listen to.

The next day we were paid and that boosted my morale, my funds had sunk dangerously low. I went to the snack bar, but Gertie wasn't working, so I had coffee and a doughnut. As I sat there smoking Dotty walked in and wished me a Happy New Year. I returned the salutations and we had coffee and engaged in small talk. I asked her if I could drop by that evening.

She grasped my hand and replied, "Yes, it's about time you came to see me." We talked for another half hour then she had to leave.

Back at the barracks I ran into Ironjaws and wished him a Happy New Year. He returned my greeting and asked, "How the hell are you?"

"I'm doing fine, staying out of trouble, and working hard," I answered.

"Good, this will be a good year for all of us," he said.

"I certainly hope so, last year was a rough one," I replied.

I was off until tomorrow morning, so I had to kill the whole day doing something. I went bowling for a couple of hours, and then I dropped by the TI&E room and read all of the latest magazines. At lunch time I walked down to the mess hall and had lunch.

To my surprise Grady was there, he'd come in on the courier run and had to go back later in the afternoon. We sat in the mess hall and talked about everything that was going on in our lives. Leaving there we went up to my room and continued talking about things back home. He brought me up to date on the latest happenings and gossip in our hometown of Lynell, Alabama.

He told me about his town, and how much he enjoyed being assigned there. He had also made PFC the same day we all had. I studied him closely, he had aged a little, and his southern accent was not quite as pronounced as I remembered it.

A Jeep horn sounded outside and he said, "That's for me."

We shook hands and I wished him good luck as he left to return to the sub-post.

After dinner I wrote a couple of letters to my family. I put a stamp on them and put them in the mailbox in the company clerk's office. About nine-thirty in the evening I walked over to the snack bar for a cup of coffee, and then I went upstairs to the service club. A few guys were there, a couple was playing pool, and some were reading. I found an easy chair and sat down to read a magazine. It had an article about all the new television shows that were now on the air back in the states. I found the description of various shows fascinating as I still hadn't seen television.

The troops began to leave the service club as the closing hour approached. Finally, I was the only one left. Dotty came out of her office locked the front entrance, circled the room turning off most of the lights and covered up the pool table. I poured two cups of coffee and turned off the coffee pot. I placed them on a table in front of our favorite couch. I placed an ashtray at one end of the table. She walked toward me, and into my open outstretched arms. I kissed her passionately and hungrily.

She returned my kiss with equal passion, embraced me tightly around the shoulders and said, "My, you're the wild one tonight."

"It's your fault, I haven't seen you for several days, no loving, no nothing would make you wild also."

She giggled, kissed me again she said, "That goes for the two of us. I've missed you also, and I've missed your loving."

We sat down on the couch. She lit a cigarette handing it to me, and then lit one for herself. We talked for a little while as we slowly drank our coffee. With our cigarettes and coffee both finished, I pulled her closer to me and kissed her again. She laid her head on my shoulder as I slowly caressed her arm, and then moved my hand to caress her breast. She lifted her head and kissed me, our tongues playing their own games of passion. I stood up and removed my clothing she then leaned over and kissed my stomach, her tongue creating havoc with my nerves. She stood up and I unbuttoned her skirt, she then removed the remainder of her clothing. We lay on the couch as I caressed and kissed her breasts, the nipples swelling and firming as I continued my manipulations. I kissed her stomach and ran my fingers through her pubic hair, she moaned softly and pulled me over on top of her. Without any hesitation we made love for several minutes before reaching mutual climaxes. I held her tightly, kissing her. Slowly softening, I rolled to one side.

We sat up and smoked a cigarette. She said, "By the way, I'm going to Switzerland in a couple of weeks for a week."

"I'd like to go with you, we could have a ball," I replied.

"I'm going with a group of Special Service women, so you wouldn't have any fun with that group."

"You're right, with a group of women fun and love would be out of the question."

Still horny, I began to caress and play with her breast again. She kissed me and whispered, "Sweetheart, I'm ready if you are." She then laughed and said, "My, you are really a wild man tonight."

"With you any man would be wild, making love to you is a man's wildest dreams come true."

Taking our time we were intimate for the second time. After resting for a couple of minutes I poured two cups of coffee, it was still warm. We sat quietly on the couch and drank the coffee and smoked a cigarette.

"Don't you think we should get dressed and leave now?" she asked.

I turned to her and placed my hand upon her smooth thigh and replied, "No, tonight I want to love you all night long, or at least as long as I can."

She placed her hand alongside my face, "All right lover, if that's what you want we can do that," she whispered.

Finishing my cup of coffee I said, "Dotty, please sit on my lap." She rose from the couch, and then sat down on my lap. I kissed her and caressed her breast. I rubbed her stomach rotating my hand from there to her breast. I kissed her face and lips, I rubbed her smooth silky legs and told her how beautiful she was. She said nothing just ran her fingers through my short hair.

She kissed me on the neck then grasping me she said, "You're ready!"

Gently, I lay her back on the couch, and in slow deliberate movements we made love once again. She held me tightly whispering soft words in Spanish.

With the act now finished I moved and sat up on the couch. She lay there still and quiet. I lit a cigarette and exhaled the smoke slowly.

"Ken, I've never been made love to like you have to me tonight, this is a night I will always remember."

I smiled at her, "Yes sweetheart, I too will remember this night always. A night like this with you is truly unforgettable. I suppose we can get dressed now and call it a night if you want to."

She rose from the couch and we both got dressed. She locked her office door and then we let ourselves out the back exit. At the foot of the stairs next to her Jeep, Dotty kissed me with a passion that surprised me after our just completed acts. I returned her kiss.

She whispered, "*Hasta Manana, mi amor.*"

CHAPTER 16

Garmisch and the Zugspitz Zombies

I got up late the next morning and missed breakfast. Ray had slept late also, so we had doughnuts and coffee together at the snack bar. When we finished, Ray looked over his cigarette and said, "Corporal Sherron is rotating back to the states. He wants to sell his Jeep."

"How much does he want for it?" I asked, knowing it was an old Jeep that had dodged and bounced its way across Europe in WWII.

"Three hundred dollars."

I grunted, "I don't have that kind of money."

"Neither do I," he replied.

We wanted the Jeep though, so we devised a plan. We had nine days, Sherron was due in Bremmerhaven on the 17th. Between the two of us we could come up with fifty bucks each. We also knew we could "borrow" fifty gallons of gas from Ed, which we could sell on the black market to bring us close to two hundred dollars total.

"If we wait until the 14th and offer him two hundred dollars he'll take it," I said. "What other choice will he have?"

Ray nodded in agreement.

"One thing though, you deal with that rotten bastard, I don't want anything to do with him," I said.

Ray agreed, we shook hands and returned to the barracks.

I had to work that evening, so I missed seeing Ed until the next morning when I told him what Ray and I wanted to do.

"That's copacetic," he said. Ed agreed to loan us the gas, so our deal was cooking.

We monitored Sherron's sale of the Jeep, he was having no luck. On the 14th Ray arranged to sit at the same table with him in the mess hall. I was seated several tables away observing them. They appeared to have an animated conversation as Ray made his sales pitch. Finally, they shook hands and Sherron handed a paper over to Ray.

Ray left their table and walked up to the counter to get a cup of coffee then came over to my table with it. He sat down and lit a cigarette. I watched as Sherron took his tray to the counter turned it in and left the mess hall.

"We have a deal, he was ready to accept any offer we made," Ray said laughing.

Smiling, "Our plan worked perfectly, what about his gas coupons?" I asked.

Ray reached into his shirt pocket and pulled out a gasoline coupon book passing it to me. There were coupons for sixty gallons of gas.

"I told him it was no deal unless he kicked in his gas ration book. He wanted to sell me that also," Ray said.

I laughed, "Ray, I finally got that bastard."

Smiling he replied, "You whipped his ass financially this time for sure."

So now we owned a Jeep. We got the gas from Ed and sold it downtown on the black market. We gave Sherron one thousand marks. At the current rate of exchange that was about sixty-six US dollars. Satisfied, I thought it serves the bastard right for sucker punching me. Sherron had sold us the Jeep for roughly two hundred dollars. We kicked in another seventeen dollars each, and used his coupons to repay Ed his fifty gallons of gas.

We decided to go to Garmisch in March on a three-day pass. We needed the extra month to save up a few more dollars. I'd been here over a year and had yet to visit EUCOM's fabulous Rest and Relaxation Center and playground.

We both figured it was too far to drive on a three-day pass, so we decided to the take the train. Right after payday in March we both had money, our passes, and our bags packed. I had to work until midnight, but I arranged for Roberts to relieve me four hours early. After he arrived I returned to the barracks and changed into my Class A's, and walked over to the club to get Ray. I found him with a couple of other guys, laughing, drinking, talking bullshit and the bastard was flat out drunk.

I had a quick drink of cognac and cola. “Let’s get our asses out of here Ray, we have to catch a train shortly,” I said forcefully.

He got up from the table, and could hardly stand much less walk.

Bill Pitts was there. I said,” Bill, will you help me with Ray?” Bill had volunteered earlier to drive us to the *Bahn Hof* and keep the Jeep while we were gone. He got up to help me.

We helped Ray out the door, down the stairs and into the Jeep. I dashed upstairs in our barracks got our two overnight bags and loaded them into the Jeep. It was a frigid night and I hoped that the cold air would sober Ray up, or at least help a little bit.

Pitts got us to the station just in time as the train was boarding. He helped me get Ray out of the Jeep then said, “Get aboard the train and find a seat, open the window and I’ll pass his drunken ass in through the window.”

I boarded and found two seats that were empty. I pulled the window down and shouted to Pitts. He had Ray over his shoulder and came up to the window with him. I knew this would be a problem. He literally shoved Ray through the window. I grabbed him by the shoulders protecting his head, and pulled him in the rest of the way while Bill lifted and shoved his legs. Ray folded into the wooden seat passed out. I waved to Bill, “Everything’s okay.” Pitts waved, and then walked away.

I sat down, reached into my bag and pulled out a half bottle of cognac. I had a couple of sips then placed it back into my overnight bag.

The other passengers in the car stared at us as if we were freaks. Screw them I thought, we won the frigging war. The train belched a cloud of smoke, and with whistles screaming the train slowly began moving and rapidly picked up speed. I continued to watch over Ray and smoked a couple of cigarettes. Eventually, I pulled my overcoat collar up around my neck and dozed off. The train clattered on through the night eating up the miles as it sped along. Each time the train stopped at a station I woke up.

Ray continued to sleep. Around six in the morning, I ‘d had enough jerking and jolting, so I got up stretched and lit a cigarette, then walked around a bit. All the other passengers were still sleeping. Glancing out the windows it was still dark as pitch outside. I went to the small bathroom at the end of the car, then returned to my seat.

I glanced at Ray, he had spittle drooling from the corner of his mouth. I thought to myself that serves him right, getting drunk on me when he knew we had to catch this train last night. I had a bad taste, so I pulled out my bottle of cognac and had a small sip to rinse out my mouth. I thought, am I becoming an alcoholic? I enjoy drinking just as much as everyone else in the outfit does. As Robert's always says, "A little toddy for the body never hurts anyone."

Pulling out a copy of the "*Stars and Stripes*" newspaper, I read about General Eisenhower and the establishment of the North Atlanta Treaty Organization (NATO).

I glanced at my watch it was a little before seven in the morning. Daylight was beginning to make its welcome appearance. I reached over and shook Ray. After a couple of vigorous shakes he began to come alive.

Finally, he had both eyes open staring at me, he asked, "Where in the hell am I?"

"You dumb ass, we're on the train to Garmisch. We're maybe an hour or less away," I replied.

He looked around the coach, "How in hell did I get here?"

"Pitts and I loaded you aboard the train last night. You passed out and slept all the frigging way here."

"Holy shit," he groaned. "The last thing I remember I was over in the club drinking with some of the guys."

"No sweat, we'll be getting into Garmisch soon. Let's find a place to eat then check into that hotel you told me about."

"Do you have anything to drink?"

"Yeah, do you want a shot of cognac?"

"Maybe that will help my head," he moaned.

"A hair of the dog that bit you always helps," I said.

"It certainly can't make me feel any worse," he muttered.

I pulled out my bottle and handed it to him. He took a big swallow and passed it back to me. I returned it to my bag.

The train whistle began to howl, I could feel the train slowing down. I looked out the window and saw for the second time the Alp Mountains. They were absolutely beautiful. Snow capped with light fragile clouds slowly swirling around their peaks. Like a spotlight the early morning sun lit up the mountain peaks. The train stopped, and Ray and I grabbed our bags and made for the exit. It was a clear sunny morning, but cold as a whore's heart. It had snowed during the night, and the ground was covered with a fresh pristine white coat. We walked down the sidewalk to a street that was already filled with soldiers and civilians. Ray spotted a restaurant, so we both entered and found a table. We both ordered steak and eggs, coffee and rolls. That was one of the best meals I'd had lately. After eating breakfast, smoking a cigarette and finished the last of our coffee, we paid the bill, walked out to the street and caught a taxi.

"Ray said, "Take us to the White Horse Hotel."

The driver drove a few blocks then crossed a bridge, the hotel was right there on our right. We paid him and then checked into the hotel.

It was German owned and operated, and cost us four dollars a night. We paid for two nights. Upstairs we inspected our room and put our bags away. I showered and shaved and put on a fresh shirt. Ray did the same, and his appearance and attitude improved considerably. We caught a taxi in front of the hotel and asked the driver to drive us around town. He drove around for half an hour, pointing out the nightclub Casa Carioca, the Army's R&R center. He then pointed out Lake Eibsee, several *Gashauses,* the Army Finance Center and the PX, finally returning to our hotel.

In the hotel bar there were a few other soldiers all with nice looking girls. We found an empty table and ordered two beers. We remained in the bar for a couple of hours just sipping beer and talking.

I told Ray, "Pitts had to shove you onto the train through the window while I pulled you in, you were passed out completely." He didn't believe me so I said, "Check with Pitts when we get back to the barracks."

We left the hotel bar and went to the hotel restaurant. I knew we had a long night ahead of us, so we ordered a good meal of delicious Bavarian cooking. It lived up to its reputation.

After dinner we caught a taxi to the Casa Carioca nightclub where we headed straight to the bar and ordered our standard two beers. The place was jumping even through it was still a little early. The band was playing and couples were on the dance floor dancing. I thought this is the nicest nightclub that I've been to in Germany, actually it was the nicest nightclub that I had ever been to. Several women appeared to be unattached so we directed our attention to them. We quickly found out they were the entertainment people who performed in the ice skating show, so that was a dead end for us.

Women were an absolute necessity if we were to enjoy our stay, so we left the club. We went to a nearby *Gasthaus.* There were several women there most of them young, nicely dressed and many of them very attractive. We bought a couple of beers. Trying to be suave and sophisticated we casually looked them over. I spotted one I thought to be the best looking of the women and had the nicest body. Ray also selected one he liked, so we sent them over two drinks, which they accepted. I then requested the waiter to invite them to join our table. They did, and the evening fun and festivities began.

We had another beer and Ray suggested we all go back to the nightclub. At the Casa Carioca we found a table for four and again ordered two beers, and two glasses of wine for the ladies. The band seemed to be playing all the popular American tunes of the past decade. We began dancing, slow dances then a jitterbug, Every now and then they would play a waltz, and I had to sit those out as I can't waltz worth a damn—if at all.

The band stopped playing and all the dancers were requested to leave the dance floor. The floor then retracted under a wall. Beneath the dance floor was an ice skating rink. The ice show began and the skaters were really good. There were also jugglers who performed their art on skates, and couples who appeared to me to be Olympic material. The show last about an hour. After the ice show the dance floor reappeared and the dancing resumed.

Feeling a bit tipsy, I suggested to Ray, "Let's get out of here with the girls, and head back to our hotel."

He quickly agreed. I talked with the girls and they agreed to go, I then negotiated prices. Their price was quite a bit higher than in Wurzburg, but what the hell we're on vacation. We left the club and caught a taxi to the hotel where the four of us went into the bar for a last drink of the evening. I realized as I sipped my beer that if I keep this damn drinking up, I'll have a lousy night and lousy vacation.

I had about two more sips of my beer then I took my girlfriend up to our room. After we made love a couple of times she said she had to leave. I gave her the amount I'd promised, and added ten extra marks for the taxi. She freshened up, dressed and left. Quickly cleaning up, I washed up brushed my teeth and went to bed. Before I fell asleep Ray and his girlfriend came into the room. I pretended to be asleep. I could hear them whispering and then the bed springs creaking. I fell gently into the waiting arms of the sleep goddess.

About six-thirty the next morning I woke up. In spite of having several beers I felt great. Putting on my pants shoes, socks and shirt I went downstairs to the small restaurant and purchased two large cups of black coffee and took them up to our room. Ray was still asleep alone in his bed. His girlfriend like mine had left sometimes during the night. I figure they probably worked a double shift last night. I woke Ray up. Groggily he sat up and accepted the coffee. "Ray, we're going up to the Zugspitz today, so we have to get an early start."

Groaning he rolled over, but didn't reply.

"If you can't drink with us big dogs, don't drink," I said.

"Screw you," he muttered. Holding his head he went into the bathroom. He filled the tub and took a bath. After he completed everything, I went into the bathroom, emptied the tub and took a shower, shaved and then we both got dressed. We went downstairs to the restaurant and had breakfast.

Ray paid his part of the bill, checked his wallet and said, "I'm out of marks."

"No sweat, we'll go by the finance office. It's near here, and we can buy some marks on our way to the ski lift."

Walking outside we caught a taxi to the finance office. I instructed the driver to wait. As we entered the office I saw a large carved eagle over the cashier's cage with a sign that stated, "The Eagle shits here." I thought that was so damn funny, I laughed and pointed it out to Ray. We then exchanged thirty dollars for marks.

Fully armed once again, we went back to the taxi. He drove us to the area to catch the cable lift up to the top of the mountain. The area was truly lovely. The town of Garmisch is situated in a valley; the mountains towering over and around the town like huge snow covered giant guards. We caught the cable car and ever so slowly the car moved up one level to the next. Looking down from the car you could watch people skiing far below. We rode the cable car on up the side of the mountain, the car was crowded, people standing in the aisle holding on to their ski poles.

It seemed to take forever to get to the mountain top. At the peak we joined the crowd in the sightseeing activities. Fantastic views greeted us on all sides of the area. Ray pointed out the snow covered peaks, the clouds moving slowly across the valley below, and Lake Eibsee off to one side of the mountain. The blend of mountain peaks, forest, snow, and lake has to be unmatched. There was a First Lieutenant welcoming us who appeared to be in charge of the bar and restaurant. I suppose he actually was in charge of all operations on the mountain top.

After spending some time viewing the magnificent panorama, we headed inside to the bar. They had a big sign over the bar which read, "Zugspitz Zombies, drink one and the second one is free.Cost two dollars.

Ray asked, "Do you think we can handle one?"

"Ray, I don't think so. If the army is going to give us free drinks for just drinking one, then the first one has to be absolute dynamite."

"Look around it seems several people are drinking them," he replied.

I glanced around the tables in the bar area and sure enough several people were drinking what appeared to be the same type drink.

"Okay, let's do it," I said, and then I ordered two Zombies.

The waiter brought us over two drinks, one apiece. They weren't the same as what the other people were drinking. Our drinks were larger and in large glass steins. There was a dark color to the liquid contents which also appeared to be foamy.

I turned to Ray and said, "Ray, I think we just screwed up."

He lifted his stein and replied, "Well, here's to our vacation."

I lifted my stein, touching it against his and took a drink. That shit hit my stomach like molten iron. I could feel the heat generating and building up as it settled down. Whew! My eyes watered as I tried to inhale some fresh air.

Ray took a smaller swallow of his drink and exclaimed, "Hell, that's not too bad we can handle these."

"Ray, let's go out on the terrace and get some fresh air. This drink is pure dynamite," I replied.

Taking our steins we walked out onto the terrace. The mountain air was chilly and was truly a breath of fresh air. The surrounding mountain tops were breathtaking in their natural beauty. Being from the flatlands of central Alabama, mountains were fascinating to me. We leaned against the guard rails and watched people as they skied down the slopes. All the soldiers were in their olive drab uniforms, and the women all in multi-colored civilian ski outfits, what a contrast. It was quite a sight. We continued to sip on our drinks. After the first swallow the others seemed to go down easier.

We bought a couple of hot dogs from a restaurant cart and ate them. About half of our drinks were consumed when we went back into the bar area and found seats near the far end of the bar. The waiter came over and asked if we were ready for another drink. We both still had portions left in our steins, although Ray had almost drank all of his. I declined to reorder us a refill at that time. We sat there sipping our drinks and watching the crowd for about fifteen minutes.

Ray got off his stool to go to the latrine, and collapsed on the floor. I jumped off my stool and grabbed him, lifting him up on his feet. He was embarrassed, but not hurt.

"What happened?" I asked.

"My legs just gave way."

"It's those frigging drinks, I told you we would get screwed up."

"What in the hell do you think they put in those drinks?" he asked.

I helped him on into the latrine. By the time he finished, he could hardly stand up. He leaned over a commode and threw up. I helped him back to his bar stool and we both sat down for a while. My head was also beginning to spin. I pushed his stein and mine away and said, "No more, its better we stick to stuff we can handle."

Ray grunted, looking sort of yellow he said, "*There ought to be a law against serving such rotgut crap to two innocent boys like us.*"

I just nodded my head in agreement. The bar tender took my placing of our steins on the counter as a request for refills. He walked over and asked, "You guys ready for another one?"

I shook my head no. "Keep your rotgut booze and my four dollars," I replied. He just laughed and walked away.

We walked outside. I looked over the rail and saw the little cable car coming up the sidet and suggested to Ray, "Let's take this car and get back down the mountain."

The car arrived and all its passengers unloaded. We entered the car and with me holding on to Ray we traveled back down the side. Getting to the bottom we left the lift area and caught a taxi back to the

White Horse Hotel. Ray went upstairs to our room, and I went to the bar. I found a small table and ordered a glass of beer. Sitting down I lit a cigarette and tried to unwind a bit, letting my stomach recover and settle down.

A little later I went up to our room. I heard Ray in our bathroom throwing up. I peeked in and he was on his knees hanging over the commode with his finger down his throat making himself throw up.

I laughed and said to him, "You never should have ordered that damn zombie crap." He grunted and continued to retch. I stretched out on my bed and fell asleep almost immediately.

I felt someone poking me on the shoulder, half asleep I thought, oh hell, another short arm inspection. I rolled over, it was Ray. I sat up and asked him, "How are you feeling?"

Ray replied, "I'm better, much better."

He had taken a shower, and changed uniforms. He looked halfway decent. I took off my uniform and took a quick shower. I redressed and stopped to shine my shoes and polish my brass insignia. I felt great.

Ray said, "Let's get something to eat, and then figure out what we want to do tonight."

"That sounds like a great plan to me," I replied.

We found a nice restaurant and after dinner we visited about four local bars before we selected one that seemed to have to most available women. We danced with several of them and eventually I selected one that to me was the most attractive. Competition was very keen as soldiers filled the bar, all seeking women for the evening's entertainment. Ray found one that he liked, so we invited them over to our table. We talked and bought each of them a drink and convinced them they needed to go to the hotel with us. They didn't need too much convincing. We caught a taxi to the hotel, and then had a couple of beers in the bar before we negotiated their price. Once the finances were successfully completed we went up to our room.

I turned on the radio and tuned into AFN. Beautiful big band music was playing adding to the romantic air of the evening. I turned off the overhead room light and just left the bathroom light on with the door mostly closed. I undressed while my girlfriend undressed then we got into the bed. Ray and his girlfriend did the same. For a long while all you could hear was giggles, bedsprings creaking and low whispers.

I reached over and tuned on the light on the nightstand. I found my pack of cigarettes and lighter and lit one up. I sat up on the side of the bed with the sheet covering my legs and lower torso. Ray sat up on the side of his bed and I gave him a cigarette. I looked at my watch, it was two-thirty in the morning. I turned off the light and walked over to my overnight bag and pulled out my bottle of cognac. Sitting down again on the bed I turned the light back on and had a sip of cognac, then passed the bottle to Ray. He had a drink and offered one to his girlfriend, she declined. He gave the bottle to me and I offered my girlfriend a drink, she accepted and had a small swallow.

Ray and I talked for a couple of minutes when he said, "Let's swap girlfriends."

I thought, damn that's a wild idea! I asked my girlfriend if she wanted to get in bed with Ray, and her friend could come over and get in bed with me. The two girls began talking to each other rapidly in German.

Finally, Ray's girlfriend said, "J*a*, we do it for twenty more marks each."

We quickly agreed, and I handed my girlfriend a twenty mark note. She asked me to turn off the light which I did. I could barely see her getting out of my bed and crossing the room. Through the dim light, I saw the other girl cross over and get into my bed. I turned the light back on, and Ray and I had another small drink.

I capped the bottle, and turned off the light. I slid back down in the bed and pulled my new girlfriend over close to me. I began to caress her breast and kissing her. I then reached over on the night table and found one of several condoms I had placed their earlier, I quickly slipped it on. I reminded Ray to use one of the condoms. I heard him get one and the package being torn open. Things quieted down and soon the earlier sounds could be heard again. I slowly made love to the young girl, and she responded with great passion. She obviously enjoyed the sex act even with a total stranger.

About three-thirty or so in the morning, my new girlfriend bid me goodnight and turning over she went to sleep. I soon fell asleep also. I woke up about seven in the morning. I got up and went to the bathroom, took a quick hot shower, shaved and went back into the bedroom. I woke all three of them up. My girlfriend got up first and disappeared into the bathroom for about a half hour. Then my former girlfriend got up and went to the bathroom. Finally, Ray had his turn in the bathroom.

I went downstairs and bought four cups of coffee and brought them back up to the room. We sat around drank the coffee and smoked. I suggested we go down to the restaurant and have breakfast. We had ham and eggs with several more cups of coffee. I told the girls we had to leave that afternoon, our train was scheduled to depart around one-thirty for Wurzburg.

After breakfast my first girlfriend said they had to go. So with a great show of remorse and reluctance we kissed them goodbye. We quickly packed our bags and checked out of the hotel. We walked around the town for a couple of hours soaking up the scenery before stopping in a bar and having a beer. I heard the whistle of the train, we paid for the beers, walked out to the station and caught the train home.

We arrived back in Wurzburg later that night. Pitts met us at the station in our Jeep. We told him all about our trip with all the details of the mountains, ski lift, Zugspitz Zombies and the girls. Arriving back in the barracks Ed was in our room with a half full bottle of cognac. We sat around on the bunks and footlockers and caught up on local events, and told them about our trip. With most of his bottle gone, we all went to bed. I had passed on the cognac, so I felt great.

I got up early the next morning. After showering and cleaning up I went to the mess hall for breakfast joining Roberts and Hodes at their table. We discussed the normal things, and of course my trip to Garmisch. They had to work the day shift, so I walked back up to the barracks with them. I then cleaned up my boots and shoes, and then took one uniform over to cleaners. I then read the paper, listened to AFN radio, and read half of a small paperback book. It was a detective mystery and a darn good one.

After having lunch I walked over to the service club. Dotty wasn't there so I returned to the barracks. I had to go to work at five that evening, so I grabbed a quick nap. Waking up I went to the mess hall and had a bite to eat.

Our little Jeep started immediately, so I drove down to the message center. That Jeep beat the hell out of walking everyplace. I relieved Carlton, signed in on the radio log, then checked in with all the stations and substations. No one had any traffic, so I knew it would be a long evening. I pulled out my little paperback book and read it for about half an hour and finished it. I placed it in the magazine rack for the next person to read.

I called Betty on the phone and talked with her for an hour. I made a date to meet her on Wednesday evening after she finished her day shift. Finally, my shift ended and Merlin replaced me. I encouraged him to read the mystery novel. I left, got the Jeep and drove up to the barracks. I was tired, so I went straight to bed.

I woke up with a flashlight shining in my face and heard that oh so familiar voice telling me, "Get up and milk it down." I threw my blanket off and stood up. The First Sergeant and the XO were conducting another short arm inspection. Naturally, I had another rock hard erection, it was so hard a tiger couldn't scratch it. This had now happened so many times I was no longer embarrassed. I looked at my watch it was three o'clock in the morning. I jumped back in bed and was soon sound asleep again.

On Wednesday I was off. I took Ray to work and then hung around all day goofing off. I picked him up at five o'clock that evening and took him to the mess hall. He knew that I was picking up Betty later at six. I had coffee in the mess hall with him, and then I left and drove over by the switchboard. Betty came down the stairs and got in the Jeep.

I suggested we go to a restaurant and have dinner and drink a few beers, she readily agreed and suggested we go to a different one than before. She gave me directions to a place called the Brown Bear. We went inside, and I found us a corner table and ordered two beers. I leaned over and gave her a quick kiss on the lips, she blushed and I laughed at her.

We talked for a little while then I requested she order us dinner. She ordered for the two of us and it turned out to be delicious roast beef. After eating we went by the store next to her place, and I went inside and bought a dozen beers. After parking and locking up the Jeep we went inside her place.

I placed several of the beers in her small refrigerator, then opened two and gave one to her. I took off my jacket and tie and hung them up. She kicked off her shoes and we both sat down on her couch, she leaned her head over on my shoulder, I put my arm around her, and slowly and gently rubbed her arm.

"What have you been doing lately?" I asked.

"Nothing really, just working," she replied.

"Ray and I just got back from a three day pass to Garmisch."

"That's great, I bet you both had a great time. It's a fun place. My family and I went there several times when I was a little girl. My father was an excellent skier and won several skiing contests before the war. I haven't been there since the war began back in 1939."

I said, "Maybe you and I can go there together one of these days."

She laughed, pushed my head and said, "Sure we will."

I protested, "I really mean it. What's to keep us from going?"

She looked at me and said, "There's nothing to stop us from going if you really mean it and want to."

"I'll work on it and make it happen." I pulled her closer to me and had a drink of beer. I leaned over and kissed her. She responded her arms going around my neck. I then stood up and she got up with me. I pulled her close and kissed her again. Silently, in mutual consent we both undressed, and sat back down on the couch. I gave her several kisses, not urgent lustful ones, but kisses of affection and desire.

Her head lying on my shoulder she said, "Ken, you're different from any man I have ever met. You seem to care about me, my feelings and my desires. You're not just hurry, hurry, bang bang."

I rubbed her back and did not reply. I leaned her back slightly and lightly rubbed her stomach, it was firm, solid with no fat whatsoever. I gently caressed her legs and moved to kiss her. She moaned and turning kissed me with a growing passion.

The passion fires now lit began to burn brightly, the hot lustful haze overtaking us both. I picked her up and carried her into the bedroom placing her gently on the bed. She moved to the side giving me room to lie down. I lay on the bed and pulled her towards me, we exchanged caresses, and then we consummated what we had begun.

I kissed her face and said, "Thanks sweetheart." I rolled off her and went to the bathroom then sat down on the couch. With her bathrobe on she stretched out on the couch with her head on my thigh. I drank some of my beer, softly stroked her temples as we sat there and just talked about nothing of consequence.

"Betty, do you have to go to work in the morning?"

"Yes."

I glanced at my watch, it was close to midnight. "Do you want to go to bed?"

"Yes, I am tired it was a hard day today," she replied.

I was a little tired also, even though I had no specific reason to be. "Let me finish my beer, and I'll be ready to go to bed."

She kissed my hand and said, "Take your time, there's no reason to hurry."

"Sweet thing, I never get in a hurry when I'm with you," I replied.

She laughed and said, "Only when you're undressing then you hurry."

I smiled, finished my beer, then picked her up and took her back into the bed room. I placed her on the bed and she moved over making room for me. I turned out the light and she put her head on my arm. I held her around the shoulder, and in short order we both were asleep.

Waking up at six the next morning I quietly got out of bed, found the coffee and coffee pot and made the coffee. I smoked a cigarette as the coffee pot boiled and bubbled and completed its task. When it was finished, I filled two cups and placed one on a saucer and took it into the bedroom, Betty was lying there awake.

She smiled at me and said, "Good morning lover. I love it when you stay with me you always serve me coffee in bed."

"It's because of what you do to me when I'm in your bed," I replied.

She sipped her coffee, and I sat down on the side of the bed. I lit a cigarette and gave it to her. I then went into the other room and returned with an ashtray. We talked for several minutes mostly about unimportant things. She finished her coffee and then extinguished her cigarette. She moved to get out of bed, I walked back into the other room and turned on her radio, tuning to AFN.

I listened to the news which was mostly about events in Berlin and the obstinacy of the Russians. Meanwhile, Betty took a bath and began dressing. I washed my face and we prepared to leave. We walked outside got into the jeep, and I drove us back to the *Kaserne*. I dropped Betty off by the stairs at the switchboard, and then I drove over to the company area and parked the Jeep.

Back in my room I got my shaving kit and went to the shower. The hot water felt great as it cascaded down over my head. Dark thoughts seemed to crowd to the front of my mind as my thoughts turned to Rachel. I realized that I had initially tried to drown my heartbreaking loss of her with booze, but that didn't work. Now, I was trying to occupy my time with other women and sex sessions to help forget about her.

I thought about Dotty and Betty, both beautiful, desirable women. I cared for them both, not love, but a feeling of respect and genuine affection. I felt perfectly safe with them. We had sex without worrying about other distractions. With their unknowing efforts, I was getting back to being my original happy carefree self.

Ray and I continued to travel all over with our Jeep. We drove to Kissingen, and Schweinfurt, we went to all the sub-posts and even up to Frankfurt, Stuttgart and Heidleberg. We had a ball. A hundred gallons of gas a month was more than enough for us. Our Jeep was a great investment.

In late April spring was definitely in the air, the grass was greening, and a teasing hint of flowers still unborn could be seen everywhere. While we were sitting at a table at lunch time, SFC Perry came in, and after going through the serving line came over to our table and sat down.

"I have some big news for you guys," he said.

We came alive and were immediately all ears.

"Perhaps you guys know that President Truman has signed a bill integrating all the Armed Forces."

Hodes asked, "What the hell does that mean Sergeant?"

Perry answered, "That means that from now on black soldiers and white soldiers will be assigned to a unit based on the unit needs, and the individual's military occupational specialty (MOS). You'll share the same barracks, and the same mess halls. You'll share work, and do all the same jobs without regards to your skin color."

We all tried to let the information sink in, and to digest what it all meant.

Perry spoke up again and said, "We had three new people report in this morning to the company. All three of them are black. One's a Corporal he's assigned to the finance section, one Private who is assigned to the photographic section and one PFC who is a radio operator and assigned to our section."

I asked, "What's the radio operator's name?"

Perry replied, "His name is Bell, Booker T. Bell."

Roberts spoke up and said, "I don't give a damn what color he is, if he can do his job then I have no problems." We all echoed the same sentiments.

Perry said, "Good! Gentlemen this action by the President is irreversible. No matter your personal feelings or prejudices, we have to live with it and adjust. I expect your full cooperation. Anything less is not acceptable. Bell will be on shift with you Roberts tomorrow on the evening shift at five o'clock." Perry drained his coffee cup and then left the table and mess hall.

Ed spoke up saying in a singsong manner, "This ain't copacetic, the army is a changing, the army is a changing."

Breakfast over, we all drifted back up to the barracks congregating in Ray's room. We sat around and discussed what this integration meant if anything. I think by consensus we agreed it would have little effect on our lives. No use worrying about things that may never mean too much.

About that time a black soldier walked down the hallway carrying his duffle bag. Stopping in front of Ray's room he asked, "Is this room number fourteen?"

Ray answered, "Yes, this is room fourteen, it's my room."

The soldier said, "I've been assigned to this room, I guess with you."

We all just stood there wondering what the hell would happen next.

Ray said, "There's an empty bunk in here, so I guess that will be yours as well as that empty foot and wall locker."

The soldier entered the room, and put his duffle bag down on the bunk. We all more or less watched him like he was some sort of strange outer space creature visiting us. I left and returned to my room. One by one everyone left and went to their rooms.

Later, I walked over to the service club and saw Dotty. I convinced her we should get together that night after closing time. It didn't take too much convincing as she was happy to see me. I genuinely liked her and she liked me, we had a good relationship. I think she felt safe with me. I was three years younger than her, and my cock was almost perpetually hard. I enjoyed being with her for sure. She was young, beautiful and had the obvious sexual desires of all young women. I think we appreciated the sheer pleasure of each other's company. We had all that together, but for me I didn't think it extended too much further than respect, affection and great sex. Love for me at this point in my life wasn't possible, but I did thoroughly enjoy being with her.

That evening about ten o'clock, I walked over to the service club. Four guys were sitting around a table talking, and Dotty was typing something in her office. I got a cup of coffee and found a small table with several magazines on it. I found one magazine that appeared to be interesting, and began to review the articles. The four guys got up and left calling out goodnight to Dotty. She followed them to the door closing and locking it. She then performed her nightly chores going around the room and straightening up the books, pillows, covering the pool table, and turning out lights. I rose from the table and got her a hot cup of coffee.

Her chores completed she joined me at the table, before she sat down she gave me a kiss and said, "I'm glad that you came."

I kissed her and replied, "I had no choice, you're like an irresistible magnet pulling me here."

She giggled and sat down. We discussed current events, and what was happening in our worlds. She told me that she had her first black soldier visit the club earlier in the evening. I mentioned that we now had three of them assigned in our unit, and one was in my section in the radio room. I reached across the table and softly pulled her arm upwards, she got up and anticipating my desire came around the table, and sat on my lap. I hugged her closer and gave her a kiss. She responded, our tongues dancing their own magical, lustful dance. She held my head and stroked my face for a few minutes, neither of us speaking. Finally, she kissed me again and slowly began unbuttoning her blouse. Without saying a word we both rose and went over to the couch.

There I undressed her then myself. We lay on the couch caressing each other for a few minutes fanning the flames of passion to a raging peak. Still without speaking a word we engaged in that most wonderful and thrilling of all physical actions. Our passions temporarily sated I rose and got us another cup of coffee while she lit us cigarettes. We both drank the coffee and smoked. I lay back on the couch with her head on my arm.

"Dotty, I enjoy being with you more than you know." It wasn't a lie, I gently caressed her and told her how beautiful she is. She listened quietly as I continued to tell her sweet things. She rose up and pulling my head down kissed me deeply, lovingly, I returned her kiss, the hot passion fires reignited. We made love again. Then we dressed, walked to the back exit and down the stairs. I kissed her goodnight. She started her Jeep and left. I walked slowly back to my barracks, thinking how damn lucky I am.

I worked the next few days pulling my shift with nothing eventful happening. PFC Bell came on duty with me for the daytime shift. He seemed extremely reluctant to operate the radio set, why I didn't know. I offered him all the encouragement I could. Eventually I insisted he send some pending traffic to the sub-posts. I was pleasantly surprised that he was a half decent radio operator. I had him operate both of our nets and he did well. I told him so. Then I closed both nets down, and told him to initiate the stations and set them up on the correct frequencies. He did it without prompting. I told Perry that Bell could operate the sets, and to include him in the rotation schedule. Our radio section became racially integrated overnight.

CHAPTER 17

Italy, Korea and Dotty

Later that month Roberts and I were promoted to Corporal as well as Hodes, Amato and Grady. That increased my total pay to about one hundred twenty-two dollars a month. We went to the club that evening, and had a small but lively promotion party. By closing time we were all about half lit. Joking with each other, we walked back across the street and into our barracks.

Merlin married his girlfriend, and received rotation orders to the states. He planned to get out of the army, and go to work someplace in California his home state. We held a great going away party for him.

The next day I walked over to the snack bar, Gertie was working. We greeted each other. Since I was the only person in the snack bar she sat with me at my table. I had a cheeseburger with coffee. I was anxious to hear what she had to say, hopefully with news about Rachel.

Gertie said, "I had a letter from Rachel, and she asked me to tell you that you're the father of a baby boy. He weighed seven pounds and three ounces at birth. She named him Kenneth, and she calls him Kenny. She said he has dark hair like yours, and looks exactly like you even big brown eyes. She also said she thanks you with all her heart for this beautiful child."

Thrilled and speechless, I just stared at Gertie, my mind racing trying to develop a mental picture of the baby. "Did she send a picture of the baby?"

She shook her head, no.

"Do you have an address for her?"

Again, she shook her head no.

"Damn, why won't she send an address?"

Gertie replied, "Rachel said they were living in a temporary apartment in Chicago, and they would be moving to another place in the near future. She'll write and let me know when she has a permanent address."

A couple of soldiers entered the snack bar, so she had to leave. I shook her hand and said, "Thanks Gertie, I really appreciate you telling me all this."

The idea I was the father of a boy was thrilling in spite of the situation. I knew this was going to happen. I shouldn't be so surprised. A feeling of helplessness swept over me. I just sat there and drank my coffee, my mind almost going blank. I shook myself trying to make reality out of this information. I knew she was going to have our baby back in the states. I know also that she is now married. I should do as Rachel told me, "*Do the things I have to do*." I got up and left the snack bar.

I was working the day shift when I received a call from Sam Amato. He wanted me to go to Sicily with him to visit his grandparents. I asked him when, and how much money I would need to go. He wanted to go the first of June, and estimated that maybe we could get by on two-hundred and fifty dollars.

I had more than enough leave time, so I said, "Sure, let's go, we'll have a ball. It should be a great trip, and I've always wanted to see Italy."

I saved most of my pay in May, and all my pay in June. We obtained the necessary Visas, our round-trip train tickets, and left the morning of June first.

We traveled through Stuttgart, then to Zurich, Switzerland, and on to Italy. Naturally, we sampled beer on our way, that was a given. The Swiss Alps were breathtakingly beautiful, and the countryside post card perfect. Finally, we arrived in Rome. We located a downtown hotel that was reasonable in price, the Hotel Florida. I thought what an unusual name for a hotel in Rome, Italy.

For two nights we hit the night clubs having fun with the local Roman beauties. We bought them wine or phony cocktails, which for us American soldiers had been inflated to two or three times the local price.

Italian women didn't shave beneath their arms either. I was careful and cautious in having sex, no use in taking unnecessary chances. The third morning Sam and I went to Vatican City and viewed the Sistine Chapel. I studied Michelangelo's fresco, "Creation of Adam." I was deeply impressed as I recalled reading about it all in history books in high school. There were statues and fountains all over the city. Rome has to be one of the most impressive cities in the world. We even had a chance to visit the Coliseum. I recalled from my history studies that it had been dedicated by a Roman named Titus in the year 80 A.D. It is a powerful impressive place. Standing at the top looking down, I could easily visualize the early Christians being fed to the lions, and gladiators fighting for their lives. History has to be the most fascinating of all subjects of study.

We caught the train again and headed south passing through Naples and on down to the southern tip. There we went by ferry over to Sicily. Arriving there we headed for the province of Agrigento, and then to the little town where his grandparents lived. His mom and dad had emigrated from there to America around 1920.

Upon our arrival all his relatives were there to meet and greet us. In addition to his grandparents, all his uncles and aunts, cousins and anyone who ever knew his mom and dad turned out to meet us. Sam could speak and understand decent Sicilian, but I couldn't speak or understand one damn word. Sam played the role of interpreter as much as possible, but it was a losing game for me. The second morning we were there after having some vile tasting coffee, we were to tour the town. The streets were all sand and dirt, and the sand was blindingly white. My eyes watered and closed almost automatically. I just couldn't open them in the sunlight, with the sun blazing and the sand so white, it became impossible for me to see. One of his cousins led me to a small shop where I bought a pair of dark sun glasses which solved my problem immediately.

We had two meals a day, and the evening meal, the major meal was a sight to see. It consisted of several courses of pasta, different meats, breads, various vegetables, fruit and glasses of wine. I ate some of everything more out of courtesy than actual hunger. Much to my disgust I became constipated. My stomach grew tight, hot and swollen, and hurt like hell. Try as I might I couldn't go to the bathroom. The tighter my constipation became the less I could eat. It became a nightmare of a situation. I told Sam to ask his cousins if I could buy some Milk of Magnesia, or some local remedy in the village. His cousin left and returned in about fifteen minutes with a large bottle of black liquid.

I immediately drank about half of the bottle's nasty tasting contents and followed that with several glasses of water. In about twenty minutes or less I had to go to the bathroom. I went to their outdoor bathroom, and without too much graphic detail I emptied my bowels to my immense relief. There was no toilet tissue, so I slipped off my undershirt and used it instead. The shirt was unimportant, relief was the major thing.

We stayed four days in their town. They must have taken dozens of photographs of us. Both of us on donkeys, at their church, and almost every other place we went. They gave us copies before we departed. I was happy to leave because of the physical problems I'd encountered.

We returned to Italy, and caught the train back to Rome. There we spent two more days and nights. Our money was getting low, so we stayed in a less expensive hotel, played around with less costly girls, and drank cheaper drinks. I continued to protect myself by using the proper prophylactics.

Leaving Rome we returned through Switzerland into Germany, and on to Wurzburg, arriving there early in the morning. As we got off the train at the *Bahn Hof,* Army MP's met us and told us we had to go directly to our barracks. This was confusing until one MP explained the European Command had changed the military script overnight, and no soldier was allowed off their post. Millions of American script dollars on the black market became useless, as the money changers couldn't cash it in or exchange it for the new script. We both had a few German marks so we caught a taxi to the post and walked into my barracks. The company clerk told me we could exchange our script in the XO's office. Sam and I went in and exchanged our script for the new script. The old one had been red and green the new one was blue and red. I exchanged about thirty dollars and some cents. Sam had about twenty dollars left.

We went upstairs and Ed was in the room. He had a bottle of cognac, so we had a drink of that. We got the word the script exchange was over. I still had two days leave left. That night after we cleaned up, Sam and I walked down to the gate and caught a taxi downtown to the café Leopold. We drank a few beers and made out with a couple of local girls, doing what all good soldiers do in such cases.

The next morning we caught a taxi back to the *Kaserne*. That evening we went to the club, had a few beers and just watched the dancers. I thanked him for inviting me to go with him to Italy to visit his grandparents, and of how much I enjoyed the trip. He caught the courier Jeep early the next morning to Bad Kissingen. Our leaves and trip had been very good ones.

I slept in the next morning catching up on some much needed rest. Too late for breakfast I walked over to the snack bar for two bacon and egg sandwiches and coffee. A new girl was working in the snack bar.

I called her over and asked, "Where's Gertie?"

She replied, "Gertie got married last week and left."

Dumbfounded I asked, "Is she coming back?"

She shook her head, "No, she quit and moved to Munich with her new husband."

Stunned, I let out a long slow breath and simply said, "Thanks." She walked away from my table.

Deep dark, despair settled over me like a blanket. I realized that I had lost my last link with Rachel. Without Gertie, I had no possible way to know anything about Rachel, where she was, how she was, how our baby was, no nothing. I was absolutely devastated. I got up and got another cup of coffee. I sat back down. I knew that I had to face reality. I had to analyze this situation and my future. I knew it would be stupid of me to think that somehow, someway, she and I could get back together. I only knew she and my baby boy, and that ass she married were some place in or around Chicago.

I remembered her telling me that I should reserve a special spot in my heart and memory for her as she would for me. That our book of memories should be filled with the days and nights we had spent together, remembering the love we had and the things we said and did, all those wonderful moments when the world was ours. Silently, I spoke to her and said, "Yes *Leibling*, that's what I'll do. I'll reserve a very special place in my heart and memory book for you and for our baby boy whom I will never see or know, but you two will always be there. You and I enjoyed a love for a brief moment in our life together that too few people experience. I'll close this Chapter of us. My book of memories filled as you suggested with pictures of wondrous beauty of you and I. *Auf Wiedersehen* my love." I finished my coffee and left the snack bar.

Two days later, I was on duty in the radio room when I and all the stations on the net received a call from the net control station in Heidleberg that we had incoming 'Flash' priority traffic. 'Flash' priority is the highest priority given to emergency messages. I quickly replied, "Ready."

All the other stations in turn responded similarly. I called out to the clerk to find Perry "ASAP" and bring him to the radio room. In about two minutes Perry came charging into the room and asked me, "What's up?"

"I'm standing by to receive a Flash message." I said.

He turned and told the clerk to get the Signal Officer over here. In another minute or so Heidleberg began sending the message, it was encoded. Both Perry and I copied it with him on the typewriter, and I wrote it down on a blank sheet of paper. There were sixty-five encoded five letter groups. I acknowledged receipt to Heidleberg as did all the other stations. Perry turned and gave the message to Pitts who was already in the radio room. The Signal Officer went into the crypto room with Pitts. There was definitely an air of excitement racing through the message center. No one here had ever received a flash priority message before.

About ten minutes later, the Signal Officer stepped out of the crypto room with a manila envelope and raced out of the room. A few minutes later the fire station siren began screaming out the post signal for an 'Alert.'

Perry came back into the radio room, and calling all the people in the message center to gather around then he said, "On June twenty-fifth, North Korea had invaded South Korea, and all US Forces in Europe are now on alert status. You're to go to the company get your field equipment, draw your M-1 rifles, and report back here to the message center."

He took over the radio station. Two clerks and I raced out to my Jeep and drove to the company. Arriving at the company, I went upstairs to my room. I picked up my field pack, helmet, and rifle belt; I then locked my wall locker and foot locker. I went down stairs and drew my individual rifle. I waited for the two clerks, and then we loaded back onto the Jeep and returned to the message center.

In the radio room, Perry told me to get the mobile radio station up and running and take control of our station. I took all my gear out to the radio truck. I removed the tarp from the generator and cranked it. It started immediately and ran smoothly. I disconnected the power cord to the headquarters building, and connected the internal power cable. In less than five minutes I had taken over the base radio station, and was operating. Roberts, Carlton, and Bell showed up.

I had Bell check the gas in the truck and make sure that all our five gallon gas cans were full. He also checked for cases of K-rations, and the new C-rations in the event we moved out into the field. Standard operating procedures required the trucks and cans to be filled at all times. All our rations and water were stored inside the generator trailer. We were in great shape and could move out when ordered.

We sat around inside the hut waiting for any additional traffic, or further orders from Perry. Little traffic was being passed. I began to wonder where in the hell North and South Korea are located. I don't think that I had ever heard of the two countries.

"Carlton, Do you know where these two countries are?"

He shook his head no, and replied, "I think they are someplace out in the Pacific Ocean."

"Well Joe, if I might opine, that is a mighty damn big ocean, you're not very much help," I replied.

He said, "We have a big world map in the message center, I'll get it and we can find out for sure."

He left and in a few minutes returned with the big world map folded over. We opened it and began searching for Korea. Finally, we found it not very far from Japan. It was a large peninsula jutting out into the ocean. North of it was China and Manchuria. The big map had the two countries divided by a red line on the 38th parallel.

"Well, that's a hell of a long ways from Wurzburg. The North Koreans can't shoot at us. I guess we are on alert because of what the Russians here in Germany might do. What they might do is worth thinking about."

I went back into the message center and asked Perry, "How long will we be operating the mobile van?"

He replied, "I don't really know. You should keep the operators present schedule and rotate the troops for chow. Hook the van back up to the commercial power cable, and save the gas and generator."

I went outside and carried out his instructions. We operated in our normal shifts in the van for the next three days. Lots of high priority classified traffic was sent and received over the next several days. Several days later we came off the alert status. AFN radio was filled with news of the fighting in Korea.

Troops were being rushed to Korea from Japan and Okinawa, and my military hero, General of the Army Douglas MacArthur, was named the first Commander of the United Nation forces. President Truman immediately issued an order that extended the enlistments of all military personnel for the duration of the war. I wasn't sure what effect that would have on me, or my personal enlistment date.

I called Dottie at the service club and made arrangements to meet her that evening. We had coffee together, and after she closed the club we made love for over an hour. We had become very compatible and comfortable with each other. By now we both had learned the habits and desires of each other, and we grew closer together as time moved on.

Resting on my bunk one day in July I thought, what in the hell am I doing with my life. There's a war going on and I'm a soldier. I should be there in Korea. I joined the Army to see the world, and to experience everything that I possibly could including fighting, and now there's a war to fight. I'm getting a little tired of drinking too much, screwing everything that I can, hell I'm just wasting time and my life here in Germany. Rachel and the boy are gone totally out of my life. Why hang around and do nothing but drink too much and get into trouble. There's a war, and I want to experience real combat. I want to be able to hold my head high, and when I get home tell them that I fought for my country. As these thoughts raced through my mind I could feel a surging sense of patriotism, a burning desire to get in on the fighting, and the adrenalin was really flowing.

I figure I can put in an administrative request for transfer to Korea just like Skinner did to transfer to the Air Force. From the news reports they're really short of soldiers there, and to my way of thinking there's no reason that I can't go. The more I thought about it the better my idea seemed. I can't get out of the army until the war is over, so I'll go fight and speed up the process.

I saw the company clerk at noon time and said, "Ralph, you owe me a favor. I want you to type me up a Form 1049 requesting transfer to US Army Pacific, with duty station in Korea."

Ralph looked puzzled and replied, "I've never requested an inter-theater transfer, but I guess it is the same as any other type transfer.

All right, I'll have it ready for your signature before you go on shift this evening."

"Thanks Ralph, I owe you a beer or two for sure."

I slept for a couple of hours that afternoon then I cleaned up and went to the mess hall for dinner. The First Sergeant was on a three day pass to Berchtesgaden, so I knew that I'd have to wait until he returned for my request to be processed. I went by the orderly room and signed my request, Ralph then placed it in with some other papers for the First Sergeant.

Ralph said, "The First Sergeant will be back to work in the morning, so you should know something soon."

I went on to work. I had the early evening shift so I wasn't busy, and it turned out to be a very easy one. After work I went to the barracks and to bed.

Sleeping late the next morning I followed my usual routine and walked over to the snack bar and had coffee and donuts. I went by the Troop Information and Education office and caught up on the latest magazines and stateside information. I then returned to my room, shined my shoes and straightened out both my lockers. I could feel a growing sense of excitement as I thought about leaving Germany, and going to another part of the world. I thought if President Truman is going to extend my enlistment for the duration of the war, then I have to right to go to Korea and fight for an early duration.

I walked down to the mess hall and had lunch. I sat with Hodes and Pitts, and we discussed various items of mutual interest. Ralph walked by our table and said, "Ken, the First Sergeant wants to see you at one o'clock today in his office."

"All right, I'll be there, thanks Ralph."

Finished eating I casually strolled back up to the barracks. I thought the First Sergeant will tell me my transfer is approved and give me an expected date of departure, and I'll be on my way. I went upstairs and checked myself out in the latrine mirror to be sure I looked good and sharp when I saw Ironjaws. My boots were highly polished, my belt buckle glistened, and my haircut regulation style. I checked my watch and walked down the stairs to the clerk's office. Ralph informed Ironjaws that I was there to see him. He turned and told me to report to the First Sergeant.

I knocked on his door and heard that inimitable voice tell me to "Come in."

Walking quickly across his office I saluted and said, "Corporal Fisher reporting to the First Sergeant Sir."

Ironjaws returned my salute and grunted, "Stand at ease Corporal Fisher."

I relaxed a little and looked at him.

He leaned back in his chair, hooking his hands in back of his head and looking straight at me said, "So you want to go to fucking Korea do you? Do you really believe that the army is going to transfer you from Germany to Korea?"

Startled, I stammered and replied, "Why not First Sergeant? They have extended my enlistment for the duration. They need troops, so why shouldn't they let me go and fight?"

Bolting upright, his voice rising he replied, "You've never heard a shot fired in anger, or been shot at, or heard the whistle of death over your head, so don't be so damn anxious, your time will come." Glaring at me he continued, "Look you dumb ass, they're reactivating the Seventh Army here in Germany. They're rushing troops over here to Germany by the plane and boat loads, so there's no way in hell they'll transfer you to Korea."

Taking a deep breath he continued, "Our troops there have a job to do, and you have a job to do here, so the idea of transferring is out of the fucking question."

He stood up, then picking up my request for transfer he said, "Your request for transfer is denied!" Tearing my request in two he dropped it into his waste basket. Glaring at me he said, "Now get the hell out of my office, and go do your job, you're aren't going anywhere." Looking at me I knew he could tell I was pissed off.

I said, "It's not right!"

"Whether it's right or wrong doesn't matter one frigging bit, you still aren't going anywhere, so get your ass back to work," he replied.

I realized the futility of further arguing with him, so I saluted and said, "Yes sir First Sergeant." I did an about face and left his office. That ended my request for a transfer and I knew it. I couldn't win against Ironjaws, so I let it all go.

In August, Ray and I were at the club with several of the guys, dancing with the women and having a ball when Ray suggested we leave and go downtown and see what was happening. It was around nine-thirty so I agreed. Bell who was at our table also wanted a lift downtown.

"Let's at least finish our drinks here before we haul ass downtown,"

I said.

Ray picked up his glass of beer and said, "Okay, then let's chug-a-lug them."

We all three swallowed our drinks down. We then left the club and climbed into our Jeep. Ray was a little drunk, but he made it off the post with no problem. He was driving down the hill from the post with me in the front seat, and Bell sitting in the back seat. Since there was no chance of rain we had the top down. As we approached the intersection at the Rod and Gun club Ray swung the steering wheel too sharply to the right and hit the curb. He jerked the wheel back to the left and over compensated. The Jeep with its short wheel base flipped over, and then the lights went out for me.

I woke up on a gurney with someone pushing me down a hallway. I rose up on one elbow and looked around; the guy pushing me was a medic in white uniform. I was totally confused and bewildered. What in hell is wrong with me that I'm here in a hospital I wondered?

"What happened, and where am I?"

"You're in the 57th Field Hospital, you were in a Jeep accident," the medic replied.

I had a huge bandage over my right eye and could only see out of the left one. I had bandages on my hand, my chin, and my face. I asked the medic, "How badly hurt am I?"

He replied, "You're a little banged up, but you'll live. Your buddy is in worse shape than you are."

We turned a corner and he stopped at the elevator. I heard Ray calling me, "Ken, Ken, how are you buddy?"

I looked over, he was sitting on a bench outside the elevator, his left eye closed with a huge black and blue knot over it. His nose was broken and bleeding.

I said, "As far as I know I'm all right, how about you?"

"I'm screwed up, I think my collarbone or shoulder is broken, maybe both," he replied.

The elevator door opened and the medic began to roll me inside. Ray with two medics also entered the same car with us. Ray reached over and patted me on the shoulder. The car stopped and Ray and the two medics got off. The medic and I went on up to the fourth floor. He pushed me from the elevator to a room and I transferred from the gurney to a bed. I glanced at my watch it was eleven forty-five in the evening. Damn, we never even made it downtown for a beer. I wondered where Bell was, and if he had been hurt also? I fell asleep almost as quickly as my head hit the pillow.

Around six-thirty the next morning a medic woke me up. I got out of bed with pain shooting through my leg and shoulder. I walked out into the hallway and saw a sign indicating a latrine. I headed there and walked inside, after finishing I walked over to the mirror over the sink. I studied my face, it wasn't pretty. Bandages were all over my face and head. I wanted to throw up, but I just had dry heaves. I pulled the bathrobe over and looked at my shoulder, it was black and blue and swollen.

A medic came into the latrine and seeing me snarled, "Get the hell back in bed, and stay there."

I walked back to my room and sat on the edge of my bed. My uniform was on a hanger hung on a rack at the end of the bed. I wondered who had undressed me. I reached into my pockets and found a pack of cigarettes and my lighter. I pulled one out and lit it I looked again through my pants, my wallet was gone. I figured some sorry son-of-a-bitch in the hospital had stolen it. My ID card, ration card, and money were missing including the German Marks I had in my front pocket.

Shortly thereafter, a medic came into the room with a tray of food. He poured me a cup of coffee, and left a plate of scrambled eggs, two bacon strips and a piece of toast. I was starving so I ate it all very quickly.

I lay in bed for another hour or so before a doctor came through the ward. The doctor checked my blood pressure, pulse rate and my temperature. He said, "It's all normal, but we're keeping you here for three to five days for observation to make sure you're alright. Stay in bed for the remainder of today, you can walk around tomorrow."

I asked, "Where is my friend Corporal Washington?"

He answered, "He's alright, he's in a room two doors down the hallway. You can look for him tomorrow."

I lay around all day bored out of my mind. After supper, the medic on duty brought me a radio. Well, at least I could listen to the news, and some good country and western music.

A little after six that evening, Perry came to the hospital to visit me and Ray. He brought our shaving kits. I was happy about that I wanted and needed to brush my teeth, plus I needed a shave. I asked him, "What about Bell, is he alright, where is he?"

He said, "Bell jumped out of the jeep when it turned over, and he wasn't hurt at all."

We talked for a while longer then he left to go talk with Ray. Naturally, before he left he had to say, "Get your ass well and back to work." Pausing, he then said, "I have to leave now, I'll check in on you tomorrow."

Around eight o'clock that evening Dotty walked into my room. That was the best medicine I could have ordered. She pulled the curtain around my bed then moving closer she leaned over and kissed me gently on the lips.

She said, "I heard about your accident last night before I left the service club. I've been on pins and needles all day until I could get here."

Slowly lifting my arm, I hugged her neck. "Thank you sweetheart for coming to see me, I truly appreciate it."

She kissed me again and said, "Get well soon my love, I need you."

We talked for a little while longer. Then she said, "I have to go back to the club. I promise to come see you tomorrow night."

We kissed goodbye and then she left. I turned on the radio and listened to the news about Korea. The war was going badly for our forces. I believe that they need me there and here I am all screwed up and laid up in a hospital. I then listened to local Army news. Finally, some good country music began playing and I quickly drifted off to sleep.

The next morning when I returned to my room from the latrine, the medic had delivered my breakfast. On my tray were two pieces of French toast, syrup, and two links of sausage. They were all cold, but I was hungry, so I quickly ate it all.

I put on my hospital robe and left to find Ray. A couple of doors down I found him sitting up in bed. He looked terrible. A big cast on his arm, a large bandage over his eye, and his nose was bent out of shape. We greeted each other with genuine pleasure. I pulled up a chair and we talked for the remainder of the morning. We discussed the accident and how it happened, and agreed that drinking and driving just does not mix.

"Ray, did you hear that Bell jumped out of the jeep, and didn't get even a scratch?"

"Yeah, he was really lucky."

"We all were," I replied.

That evening around seven-thirty Dotty came by my room, I was sitting on the bed listening to the radio. She hugged my neck and kissed me. We talked for about an hour before she had to return to work.

"I should get released with the next day or two. So I'll see you back at the service club." She kissed me and left.

The next day Ray and I played several card games of hearts with two other guys in our ward. I enjoyed the game, and we won.

The following day they released me. I borrowed ten marks from Ray, and after walking to the front gate I caught a taxi back to the *Kaserne*.

After going through the main gate I went to the message center to see Perry. I told him, "I'm fine and I'm ready to go back to work. Ray is doing alright and should get released in about another week or ten days. They had to reset his nose, and he has a cast on his shoulder, but he's doing fine. The doctor told us we would have scars for the rest of our lives, but not too disfiguring."

Perry nodded and said, "Ken, you will take the day shift tomorrow."

I left and went to personnel. I obtained a replacement ration card and ID card. I had a few dollars buried in the bottom of my foot locker which enabled me to stay afloat until payday which wasn't too far off. Stopping by the service club I spend about an hour with Dotty. No one was in the club at that time of day, so I closed her office door and kissed her. I extracted her promise to see me that evening. I was as horny as a double dick dog in heat, if not more so.

When I arrived back at the company, I saw our Jeep still wrecked, but parked in the company parking lot. I inspected it from front to rear, it was in very sad shape. I entered our barracks and ran right into the First Sergeant as he was returning from the latrine. He saw me about the same time and said, "Just keep walking Fisher, straight into my damn office."

Damn, I knew I was in for another bad ass chewing. He led the way into his office.

I stepped in front of his desk, saluted and said, "Corporal Fisher returning to duty sir."

Ironjaws returned my salute and took his time studying my face. Finally, he said, "Fisher, in spite of my best efforts you are determined to fuck-up. You are a natural born fuck-up! I should kick your ass right now right here. I ought to bust you and Washington back to the dumb ass Privates that you both deserve to be. I made both of you Corporals, but neither of you have shown me that you'd make a pimple on a good Corporal's ass. You had better start walking a straight line, a plumb line. One more fuck-up out of you and your stripes are gone forever!" Glaring at me he growled. "Its best you believe me!"

Once again I found myself meekly saying, "Yes Sir, First Sergeant:"

He growled, "And get that god damn lipstick off your face!"

I saluted did an about face and hot footed it out of his office. Outside his office I used my handkerchief to wipe my lips. I went straight upstairs with my shaving kit. Ed was in the room, so I sat down on my bunk. We discussed all the details of the accident, our injuries, and my ass chewing by Ironjaws.

"Ed, how can I get the Jeep repaired and up and running?"

"I know a Kraut body man downtown. I'll check with him and let you know what he says," he replied.

That afternoon he went down town and got the guy to inspect the Jeep where it was parked, then took him back down town.

I saw Ed in the mess hall. He told me, "The guy will completely restore the Jeep in his shop for one hundred gallons of gasoline."

"That's great, and a deal. I have to work tomorrow, but if you'll pull it downtown to his shop we'll get it done." So the big restoration was in motion.

That night I went to the service club and waited until all the troops had left. Dotty went through her routine, turning off the lights and locking the door. I poured two cups of coffee and waited for her over on the couch. The seduction began and ended as it should. She was careful not to hurt my shoulder as it was still black and blue and ached. We lay on the couch with her holding me. We weren't talking just enjoying the physical closeness, in tune with each other's mood. Eventually, the passion fires began anew and we made love again. This time she was on top of me, slowly rising and sinking as I made up for lost time. Finally, with our passions sated we dressed and left the building. I walked her down the back stairs and kissed her good night.

Ray was released from the hospital seven days later. He didn't look too bad considering the beating he had absorbed. We took turns getting five gallon cans of gas filled. He would get ten gallons then take them to the body man in Ed's Jeep. Then I would get ten gallons and take them down. We had to be very sneaky. The Criminal Investigation Division would be all over our asses if they found out we were selling gas on the black market. We had to make several deliveries over several days before we delivered the one hundred gallons to him. Buying too much gas too frequently would be a dead give-away that we were up to no good. Our luck held out, we delivered the gas and our Jeep was ready. He had totally rebuilt and repainted it. It looked almost like a new one. I gave him forty marks extra for such a good job.

Ray and I picked up the Jeep and went to the Leopold and had a few beers—no serious drinking—and I did the driving. Returning to the barracks and in a covert show of defiance, I parked next to Ironjaw's parking spot in the company parking lot.

The next morning after breakfast, Ray and I walked together back to the company area and to the parking lot. He got in the Jeep and was ready to leave when I noticed two slender pieces of intertwined string tied to the bumper and to the steel runway planking that served as a parking barrier.

"Ray, look at this, my voice rising. Some asshole has tied string from our bumper to the planking."

He dismounted from the Jeep and came around to the front and saw the string. At that exact moment Ironjaws walked up.

He had a mean look on his face and growling he said, "I'm the asshole that tied that string to your bumper."

I swallowed hard.

He continued, "That thread will stay tied to your bumper until I decide to untie it. If some other *asshole* (he emphasized the word) wants to untie it or break it, he'll answer to me personally. When I tie a string to something, I mean for it to stay tied."

I looked at him, Ray was staring at him, and then we looked at each other. We both realized that Ironjaws had us by the short hairs. We had definitely lost this round.

Ray spoke first and said, "Ken, I've got to get to work, so I'll see you later." Turning he walked away and headed to the headquarters.

The First Sergeant looked at me and said, "I need a cup of coffee, let's go to the mess hall."

Together we walked down the hill to the mess hall. I added cream to my coffee, he just sugar to his. He selected a table and we sat down. He talked to me about the war in Korea, the new organizations coming to Europe, the new people we were getting into the outfit, but not once did he mention the Jeep. It was like it didn't even exist. Finally, our coffee finished we walked back up to the company. He went into his office, and I went upstairs to my room.

I thought, he's some man that First Sergeant. I admire him. He is direct when he wants to be, and subtle when he wants to be, but either way he makes his point and I always know what his point is.

In September, General MacArthur conducted the Inchon Landings in Korea. The 187th Airborne Infantry Regiment made a combat parachute jump, and the 1st Marine went ashore at Inchon. It was a total success. My military hero had once again proven his military genius. I thought if the First Sergeant had approved my transfer, I could have been there also. Instead of being in a Jeep wreck, I could be in combat. The way it looks the war will be won and over before I leave Germany.

General Dwight Eisenhower was in Europe, and things were changing. The US Seventh Army was reactivated in November and came back to Germany. They activated both the V and VII Corps. The Constabulary was assigned to one of the Corps, and the First Division to the other Corps. Several Armored Divisions were enroute from the states or preparing to come to Europe.

On the courier runs now I could always see large Army convoys on the Autobahns and secondary highways. Every day in the *Stars and Stripes* newspaper you would read about some units being out on maneuvers. Our small world in the 6087 SCU seemed to remain pretty much unchanged and unaffected.

While on duty in the radio room I received a call from Dotty. She wanted to see me that evening. I detected a sense of urgency in her voice, and queried her, but she denied that anything was wrong. Was it possible that she was pregnant? I worried about it the remainder of the day.

That evening I went to the service club and waited for the troops to clear out. She turned out the lights, locked the door and finished her nightly chores. I had gotten us coffee and sat down the couch waiting for her to finish.

Dotty soon joined me on the couch. As soon as she sat down she grabbed and hugged me, tears began forming in her eyes.

I was shocked by her actions. I kissed her face and stroked her hair. I held her close to me and asked, "Dotty, sweetheart what's wrong? Why are you crying, what's going on?"

She stopped crying for a moment and said, "They're transferring me to Heidleberg, I'm being reassigned to the service club there. It's a permanent move, and I don't want to go, I don't want to leave you."

My fears of her being pregnant evaporated immediately. Nevertheless, I was distressed by the news. I wasn't in love with Dotty, but I cared for her deeply. She had become one of my main emotional and physical supports after I lost Rachel. Was I now to lose her also?

I really didn't know what to say. Finally, I said, "Honey, Heidleberg isn't that far away. You can come here, and I can go there. We'll still be able to see and be with each other, not as frequently as we do here, but we will be able to do that. You can call me on the phone, and I can call you and that will help tremendously. When do you have to be there?"

"I have to be there Monday."

That left us three days. "Honey, I'm off tomorrow, maybe I can get someone to work a couple of shifts for me. Let's spend a couple of days together before you leave. You only have to pack your clothing and personal things, that shouldn't take too much time."

She sat silent for a full minute as I continued to stroke her hair and kiss her face and head. Finally, she replied, "All right, I'll meet you at the front gate tomorrow morning at nine o'clock. Can you be there?"

"I'll be there with bells on." I kissed her again, and then we left down the back stairs.

I went into action and contacted Roberts and Bell. They both agreed to cover my shifts. The next morning I went to the main front gate, she was there in a taxi waiting for me. I told the driver to take us to the castle across the Main River.

She waited in the taxi while I went to the Inn Keeper and rented us a room. I returned and paid the taxi driver. I took her small overnight bag, and my shaving kit and we went to our assigned room. It was surprisingly clean, nice and comfortable.

I returned to the front desk and bought two bottles of cold Rhine wine. He gave me two glasses and an ashtray. Back in the room I opened a bottle and poured us each a glass of wine. She sat on the bed and slowly began to relax as she sipped the wine. I drank my glass quickly and poured myself another. I sat down in the big chair in the corner, held out my arms and she came over and sat on my lap. I kissed her and hugged her to me. We were very comfortable together. I cared for her deeply, and truly hated for her to leave. We seemed to sense that we didn't have to talk, so we smoked, drank the wine refilling our glasses. Sitting on my lap and encouraged by the wine the passion fires ignited. Smoldering at first then exploding into a fiery, sizzling hot flame.

She unbuttoned her blouse then stood up and removed her brassiere, revealing her beautiful breast with their dark areolas, so firm and full. The nipples standing out erect, inviting me to kiss them. Then she removed her skirt and half slip. I removed all my clothing except my shorts. I turned the heavy bed covers back then picking her up and placing her gently on the bed. I lay down beside her.

We had never made love together in a bed before. We kissed and caressed each other fanning the fires of desire higher and hotter, the white hot flames of desire and passion enveloping us. I removed her panties and then my shorts. She murmured soft words of endearment and encouragement in Spanish, and tightened her legs behind my thighs. In spite of my slow movements we both climaxed as I could no longer restrain myself. I slowly moved from over her and lay on the bed. She turned and kissed me tenderly, softly saying something once again in Spanish which I did not understand—I didn't need to—her actions spoke louder than words.

I suggested to her we go for a sandwich at the Inn's restaurant. She agreed. We both took quick baths and dressed. We strolled into the bar and restaurant where I ordered us sandwiches and glasses of wine. The wine was chilled and the food surprisingly good.

After eating I bought two more bottles of wine, and we returned to our room. I moved two chairs onto the small balcony. Sitting there in the afternoon sun we enjoyed a magnificent view of Wurzburg across the Main River. I could see the top of the Ring Hotel, and a portion of the train station. On the surrounding hillsides grape vineyards covered all the tilled land. It was a peaceful pleasant, pastoral scene. I refilled our wine glasses. We spent the remainder of the afternoon talking, smoking and sipping the wine. It was an enjoyable, lazy afternoon, one that I will never forget.

Later that evening we returned to the restaurant for dinner. I ordered Chateaubriand with béarnaise sauce and baked potatoes for two. After dinner I stopped by the innkeeper's desk and managed to borrow a German radio. Back in the room I finally found the AFN station which had beautiful big band music playing. We made love again, and then fell asleep with her snuggled in my arms.

Saturday, we never left the castle. Eating all our meals in the restaurant and drank more wine. We both became a little more than inebriated.

A sensual haze enveloped us both; it was as if we had to make love in our desperate attempt to forestall the inevitability of Monday. We fell asleep once again with me holding her tightly in my arms.

Sunday morning we awoke and after baths I shaved and we went to breakfast. Returning to our room we cuddled on the bed exchanging soft kisses and caresses letting our passions rise. It was a surrealistic setting, consciously we knew we had to leave, subconsciously we attempted to delay it as long as possible.

That afternoon our passion spent, we reluctantly dressed and prepared to leave. I asked the Inn Keeper to call a taxi. After paying the bill we left. Our taxi stopped at the main *Kaserne* gate, and I gave Dotty a handful of Marks to pay the driver with. I held her in my arms and kissed her several times, she began to cry even as I begged her not to.

"Honey, call me when you get there and get settled in I'll be waiting to hear from you."

"I will, I will," she replied.

I turned away reluctantly and walked on through the gate and up the street to my barracks.

CHAPTER 18

Back to Soldering

Nearing the company I walked over to our Jeep, the string attached to the bumper was still there in place. It had been weeks since our encounter with the First Sergeant. He was a hard ass to be sure. I wondered if the man would ever let us drive the damn thing again.

Dotty left on Monday morning, and over the next several weeks she called me seven times, and I called her about ten times. Several days passed and she didn't call. I called several times, but she never seemed to be available. I realized that our affair as beautiful as it had been was now over. It had begun in 1948 for me, and had now ended near the close of 1950. My memory book expanded with page after page of us together, and I knew that I'd never forget her. They say that "Absence makes the hearts grow fonder," but at the time I thought it more realistic and appropriate to say, "Out of sight, out of mind." I reluctantly closed that Chapter in my book, it had been an exciting and beautiful one to me, and I hoped it had been for her also.

Our radio section went on several field exercises and I trained the new radio operators. Carlton received orders to rotate back to the states, and we had a good farewell party for him. The Company Commander received new rotation orders, and we had a company farewell party for him. A new Company Commander was assigned, and a new Executive Officer. We also had a new Signal Officer and an assistant Signal Officer. All the personnel leaving had orders for Korea. I wished it was me, but it didn't happen. Personnel changes in the outfit became the norm, rather than the exception.

In early December, Roberts was busted back to PFC for going AWOL. He was with some girl who was in a show troupe from England. He was absent seven days, but said it had been well worth it.

Ed received his paper work back with CID approval to marry Ericka. I was spending more and more of my time with Betty. She was during this time my one constant. I cared for her, and I knew she cared for me. We were comfortable with each other. In December, I got into a fight in the club, and they said it was my fault. I was busted back to PFC.

I went to see Ironjaws and told him it wasn't my fault. He listened patiently to my story then he said, "PFC Fisher, as I told you after you had the Jeep wreck, you are a natural born fuck-up. Corporal stripes don't even look good on your sleeves. They look too heavy and out of place. I'm a busy man, and I don't have time to listen to some dumb ass whine about losing his stripes. Would you please leave my office, and don't ever come back."

I said, "First Sergeant, why would I lie to you?"

Ironjaws stood up from behind his desk and said, "Fisher, I didn't say you lied, now get the fuck out of my office and go to work before I throw you out!"

Christmas 1950, came and went with nothing exciting going on. I pulled some extra shifts for the guys who wanted or needed it, no big deal. The war in Korea continued to rage and our casualties mounted. The battle lines continually shifted as they fought up and down the peninsula. Germany seemed to be flooded with new units and troops.

Sergeant Little and his girl friend Gisela were married, then he rotated back to the states. Gisela's daughter remained in Germany.

I looked forward to the New Year's Eve party as the next big event. Ray, Roberts, Hodes and I planned the evening. Sam Amato came in on the courier run, and was going to join us. We all got slicked up and left early for the club. The club manager had rotated, but the assistant manager had been promoted so things were much the same as always.

We drank beer and danced all evening with the ladies. Just before midnight the manager walked onto the stage and said he would count off the seconds to the New Year. He began at the thirty second mark at the stroke of midnight we raised our glasses and toasted the Army, and the New Year.

My thoughts turned to Rachel and the year we had toasted each other and our imaginary kiss right here in this very club. Time was slowly healing the wound, but I think it will remain like an incurable sore. I thought about our son, about her, their life in Chicago, and how they were. I had no answers, so I had a swallow of beer and refused to open that memory Chapter any further.

I poured myself another glass of beer and chug-a-lugged it. Damn, here I am drinking like an alcoholic, drinking like there's no tomorrow. I had better quit this crap or I'll be in big trouble. But how in the hell can I get away from drinking when everyone around me drinks all the time? I believe it is an almost impossible situation.

We all stayed until the club closed at one o:clockin the morning. Walking back across the street we looked forward to the New Year, 1951.

Right after New Year's, our company was told to move to the other end of the street. A new outfit was to move into our barracks. I think it was the 18th Engineer Company or Battalion. I really didn't care which, but it pissed me off that we had to move. Past the mess hall were two other barracks which had been vacated, so the plan called for our company to move there. Hodes and I went to the new barracks, selected our rooms, and posted our names on the room doors. Returning to our barracks we began to pack all our clothing and equipment, and moved it down the street. We also had to move our footlockers and wall lockers, but that required trucks. It was snowing and ice was all over the streets the day we moved. It took two full days for the entire company to relocate. The supply room, our weapons, racks and equipment, all the bunks, everything had to go. We loaded all the major items on trucks and drove to the new location.

It had been several weeks since Ironjaws first tied the string to our bumper. I went to see the First Sergeant the final day of our move. After receiving permission to go into his office I reported to him. Saluting smartly I asked Ironjaws, "First Sergeant, do we have your permission to untie our Jeep and drive it to the new company area?"

He returned my salute, and with a definite hint of a smile on his face asked, "Will the damn thing start?"

I assured him it would one way or another.

He asked, "Where's Ray Washington?"

"He's upstairs putting the final touches on his packing."

"Go get him."

I left his office and went upstairs to find Ray.

"Ray, we have to go see Ironjaws."

"What's it about?"

"It's about our Jeep. I think Ironjaws is gonna let us move it."

"It's about time he let us drive it again," he replied.

"I'm sure he won't make us leave it here in the old area."

We both went downstairs and reported to the First Sergeant.

He said, "Stand at ease." He stared at us with that menacing stare and said, "I'm not going to lecture you dumb asses on the hazards of drunk driving. You should've learned your lesson from your accident. Vehicle accidents kill more soldiers in Europe than all other reasons combined."

He reached into his desk and pulled out a pair of scissors. Handing them to me he said, "Go cut the string."

I took the scissors and went to the parking lot and cut the string. Actually, I could have just snapped the damn thing. I guessed he wanted me to cut the string for the symbolism of the act. Returning to his office, I gave him back his scissors.

He said, "You guys were lucky. Neither of you got seriously hurt. That may not always be the case. Take your Jeep and enjoy it. If you so much as get a speeding or parking ticket, I'll take the Jeep and drive it into the fucking river. It's best you believe me. Now get your asses out of here and get moved."

We saluted and left his office. Happily, we went to the parking lot and got into the Jeep. The starter was slow, and made a grinding sound as the motor turned over. It kept grinding and finally it started. Smoke streamed out of the exhaust pipe. We were once again in the transportation business. We loaded Ray's stuff into the Jeep, and a couple of other people's, and moved it all to our new barracks.

The following month I was promoted back to the rank of Corporal. I was one happy soldier. By this time I was the senior radio operator, and I knew my job. I made out the shift schedules and trained the operators. They had all been school trained in the states, yet at best they were neophytes in field operations. All of them could copy the code and send it around ten words a minute. I continued to work to make our section the best we could be. The new operators I gave additional training, and made them stay at it until they gained a great degree of operational knowledge and proficiency. With draftees it was not an easy task

A new Corporal, Ted Mathews, was assigned to our outfit. He had just been released from Walter Reed hospital after being wounded in Korea. Ted had been trained as a teletype operator, and was assigned to the message center. He quickly integrated into our group, and we all became friends with him.

Sitting around in the club Mathews who was my age would tell us about his experiences in Korea. He described one scene like this, "My unit was almost overrun. It was so bad that me and the radio operators, even the cooks were forced into the trenches." He had a swallow of beer and continued, "The North Koreans usually charged us in mass wave attacks. We fired our machine guns killing them by the dozens, and still they charged us. We wound up several times in hand to hand combat." He had another swallow of beer then continued, "The last charge was when I was bayoneted by a slope-headed chink." Shaking his head he said, "Almost all my company were killed or wounded in that battle."

I found it fascinating to sit and listen to him describe how he viewed the war, what it was costing in American lives, and his experience in the hospital. I was his age, and I envied him and his war experiences, but not his wound.

He said, "It was no picnic for sure. It was frightening; I can't explain how frightening a battle is. The silence at night, and the long dreadful wait for the next attack is horrible." He never could finish telling us how it felt to have your best friend next to you blown to pieces. I could only imagine such an event.

Mathews spoke about the mud, snow and ice, and the temperature hovering around zero or below. "Korea had frigid winds howling down through the valleys barreling south out of Manchuria, it freezes everything and everyone," he said.

I couldn't imagine it being any colder there than here in Germany in the winter time.

Ted said, "I was stationed on Okinawa in the Ryukyu Islands. I was a clerk in the Corps headquarters office. When the war first started I along with several others was thrown into the battle against the North Koreans. Eventually, our outfit was part of the forces that held the Pusan perimeter.

After the Pusan breakout, and the Inchon landing, I went north with what was left of my outfit. We were then absorbed into another infantry outfit. That's when I was in my last big battle. My company was trying to hold on to a hilltop when the Koreans charged across the ridge line in mass waves."

He paused for a moment and had a swallow of beer. "I remember that the radio operators, company clerks and cooks all grabbed rifles and was fighting from foxholes as we fought off attack after attack. The ground around my foxhole was covered with fresh snow, then it became red from the blood from wounded and dying men from both sides."

I interrupted him, "Let me order us another beer."

Ted continued, "I ran out of ammunition for my M-1 rifle, and the unit was being overrun. This North Korean soldier was right in front of my foxhole. I jumped up and grabbed my pistol just as he jammed his bayonet into my stomach. As I fell backwards into my foxhole, I shot the bastard in the head." He paused for a second, and had a larger swallow of his beer.

"I lay on the freezing ground all night. Sometime the next day the medics picked me up and moved me off the hill. I woke up in a big hospital in Japan, later on I was flown to Walter Reed hospital in DC."

Ted told us of weeks in the hospital at Walter Reed, and several operations to repair his stomach. "The wards were full of wounded soldiers. Many of them were in much, much worse shape that I was. Many of them had missing arms and legs, some of them paralyzed. They all seemed to deal with their problems in their own way. I'm from California and my family could only afford to make one trip east to visit me. But they were able to spend an entire weekend with me while I was there. After several operations I had recovered enough to be transferred to a hospital in San Francisco. My family was happy to have me so much closer to home. Their constant visits gave me the psychological lift that I needed, and I'm sure helped in my recovery. After I recovered, my family became really upset that I had decided to stay in the army, but they finally accepted my decision."

Meanwhile, we all continued to go to the club and do all the normal things which we had now been doing for a few years. Many of the faces changed, but for the most part our activities changed very little.

Ray and I got a Delinquent Report for being in an off-limits bar. Ironjaw's made us the company gardeners for thirty days. After our first weekend of pulling weeds he told us, "I'll make it easy for you men. You can paint my office and the Old Man's office, and I'll reduce your time by twenty days."

That was too good of an opportunity to pass up. We painted both offices the following weekend. After finishing the painting we reported back to the First Sergeant to tell him. I brazenly invited him to inspect our work.

Ironjaw's inspected both offices and in sarcasm as thick as molasses syrup said, "Gentlemen, I compliment your work ethics. When you two get out of the army, I highly recommend you both get jobs as professional house painters, specifically shit-house painters."

We both recognized his caustic wit, but we wanted to get off the detail, so we just nodded our heads, saluted and left his office as quickly as possible.

CHAPTER 19

I meet Elona

Ray and I drove downtown one evening to a new *Gasthaus* named the Golden Stallion, which had been declared on-limits to the troops. We ordered and had a great meal. They also had a band, and a small dance floor in the place. The customers were mostly German couples, some soldiers, and a few unattached women.

We sat drinking a beer and listening to the band when I noticed a young woman sitting with a couple at a table across the room. She was a young beautiful woman about twenty years old with dark black hair, and dark almost purple eyes.

I punched Ray in the ribs and said, "Look at that girl, isn't she beautiful?"

Glancing over at the table, he replied, "She's a doll, she's the best looking woman I've seen in Germany."

The couple at her table got up to dance, a German song. She gazed around the room, and I managed to catch her eye. Smiling at her I winked, she smiled at me and looked away.

"Ray, I'm going to dance with that gorgeous creature. Do you think she's German?"

He grunted and looked across the room again. "How in the hell do I know, she's in Germany, go find out."

The band began to play a waltz. Few people danced to it. Shortly thereafter they played a song I knew and liked, "*Old Buttermilk Skies*," I walked over to her table and asked her to dance.

She replied, "Sure, I'd like to."

I took her hand and led her onto the dance floor. She was about five foot six inches tall. I danced several tunes with her, she was an excellent dancer. She was so damn beautiful, I had to behave myself.

After dancing I returned to our table and said, “Ray, I think she’s that Hollywood actress Elizabeth Taylor. She looks exactly like her, and she speaks excellent English with hardly an accent. Look at those eyes, look at that body. She’s someone special.”

Ray smiled and said, “Go for it lover boy.”

Ray soon developed an interest in one of the unescorted women. A little later he told me they were leaving, and he’d see me back at the barracks. They left taking the Jeep. I danced again with the girl.

I learned her name was Elona Haufmann. While dancing I asked her, Will you meet me here Tuesday night?”

She looked at me as if I were a prime candidate for an insane asylum. “Why should I?” she asked.

“Well, we can have dinner, a drink or two and dance for a while,” I said.

She was slow in responding, but finally said, “All right, I’ll meet you here at seven o’clock Tuesday evening.”

We finished the dance, and I walked her back to her table. Shortly thereafter the couple paid their bill and the three of them left the nightclub.

I had another beer as I thought about how best to approach this lovely woman. She had definitely lit a fire in me.

The next two days were slow in passing. I could hardly wait for Tuesday evening to arrive. When it did, I put on my freshly pressed uniform, splashed on a dash of after shave lotion, and flew out the door. Arriving at the Golden Stallion about twenty minutes to seven, I located a table away from the band, sat down and ordered a beer.

She walked into the bar area at exactly seven in the evening. She saw me and headed for my table. I stood up, took her hand and kissed it, then I pulled out her chair and she sat down. I ordered her a glass of white wine, and another beer for myself.

She looked absolutely stunning, her hair falling in long large waves over her shoulders and down her back, a faint hint of light red lipstick on her lips. We exchanged small talk for several minutes. I learned that she had lived with her family in Kissengen, but they now lived here in Wurzburg. Her father was an optometrist, and her mother a school teacher now retired. She worked as a secretary in the US Military Government office located down town.

We danced several times, and then I asked her to order us dinner. She selected just a salad and bread. I ate, but I really wasn't interested in the food. I was absorbed in listening to and watching her as she selected and formed her words and sentences.

I asked, "How did you learn to speak English so fluently?"

She said, "My mother taught me, and I've learned even more since I began working in your Army's military government office."

We continued to dance and talk the evening away. Finally, it was time to leave. I attempted to get her to go to a hotel with me, but she refused. After conceding it was a losing effort, I was able to get her office phone number. I told her I would call her in a couple of days.

She said, "I have to go home now."

I walked outside with her and watched as she caught a taxi home. Once back inside I had another beer. The bar began to close, so I left and caught a taxi back to the post.

The next two days I worked the evening shift. I went to the club with Ray and the other guys, and just did normal routine things. The new barracks were not as well cared for as our old barracks had been. But, when someone screwed up which was almost daily, Ironjaws had them paint the hallways, the ceilings and even the latrine got a fresh coat of paint. In short order our barracks had a new face, and began to look really good.

I called Elona at her office and met her again at the Golden Stallion. We ate dinner, drank a few drinks, and danced several tunes, becoming better acquainted.

That evening I failed once again getting her to go to a hotel with me. It was becoming somewhat frustrating. My feelings for her were more than just casual, and the time I spent with her was becoming more enjoyable. Her resistance to going to a hotel with me had now become a personal challenge.

I called her on Friday and told her, "I'll be out of town for three or four days, I'll call you when I get back."

She accepted my statement without question.

Friday evening, Betty and I caught the train to Garmisch. We spent two and a half days there, we stayed at the White Horse Hotel where Ray and I had stayed. We went to the Casa Carioca night club, drank a few beers, danced, and really had a terrific time. We caught the cable car and went up the mountain to the Zugspitz lounge. I did not even consider drinking their Zombie drinks. We rented skis and made several amateurish runs down a beginners slope. I almost killed myself falling so often, but we had fun. I believed that I owed her this holiday trip having more or less promised her we would come to Garmisch together. Summing it up, it had been a most delightful holiday for both of us. With my pass almost up we caught the train back to Wurzburg. Ray picked us up in the Jeep, we then dropped Betty off at her apartment.

Back in the barracks I picked up and opened my three pieces of mail. I had a "Dear John" letter from my girlfriend back home. She had gotten married to some local guy. I threw it away, it was no big deal, and not really unexpected.

Christmas was rapidly approaching, so I sent the requisite cards home. The women decorated the Service Club, and the club manager the Enlisted Club for the holidays. These days the club was always busy with the men from the Engineer outfit plus the regular outfits. The engineers took up most of the table space. I received a call from Jack Taylor, he had made Sergeant. I congratulated him and knew he really deserved it. Roberts was promoted back to Corporal, he then took a short discharge and re-enlisted for six more years in the Army. The year 1951, was rapidly approaching.

I called Elona and made a date with her. I met her at the *Gasthaus* and took her to the club for Christmas Eve. I introduced her to all my friends. I saw Ironjaw's and his wife Inez at a table, so Elona and I walked over and I introduced her to him and his wife. He stood up as we approached his table. We shook hands all around and made a few appropriate remarks, then returned to our table. We danced several times as the band played mostly American music. I convinced her that evening to spend the night with me in a hotel downtown. Ray drove us down to the main gate where we caught a taxi to the Bavarian Inn, a fairly new hotel which had been declared on-limits to the troops.

While we were traveling, the driver spoke to Elona in German. With my limited knowledge of the language I couldn't decipher what he was saying. He seemed to be very harsh, and spoke in a belligerent tone of voice. I figured that he must be the type still wanting to fight WWII. There were still a few around, even this long after the war.

I asked Elona, "What's he saying?"

"I'll tell you later at the hotel."

The driver continued speaking to her, his tone becoming shrill and more belligerent. It pissed me off, so I tapped him on the shoulder and told him in a menacing tone, "Just shut up and drive!"

It must have ticked him off; he began to speed, and slid around a couple of corners. Finally, we arrived at the hotel, slamming on the brakes he slid to a stop in front of the driveway. I paid him and told him, "You're an asshole!" He glared at me then spoke to Elona. She spoke back to him in German, then we walked into the building.

I was fuming as I knew that he must have said something bad either about me, or about her. I stopped her in the lobby and asked, "What did he say?"

Hesitantly, she said, "He said, I should be ashamed of myself to be seen out with a filthy American soldier. He said all Americans are either Jews or Jew lovers. Then he called me a common whore."

That infuriated me, I asked, "Why didn't you tell me what he was saying? I would have kicked his ass."

She replied, "It's not important, he's just a bitter resentful old man."

Still upset, I went to the front desk and obtained a room for the night. It was located on the second floor. We went upstairs and I opened the room door and walked in. The room was spacious, a large bed, a big easy chair, table with a lamp and a radio, an ashtray, and the bathroom had a nice clean bathtub. I assisted her in removing her coat and sweater hanging them on a rack in the corner. I took off my overcoat and hung it up on the rack.

I said, "Make yourself comfortable, I'll go to the bar and get us something to drink."

I went to the hotel bar and bought three beers, a bottle of white wine, and picked up a wine glass then returned to the room. She had turned the radio on and tuned in AFN. I placed the drinks on the table then I took her hand drawing her up from her position on the bed. I pulled her close to me and for the first time, I kissed her. She responded to my kiss as our tongues touched lightly in their initial encounter. "Elona, its wonderful being here with you, so we have to make the very most of it."

She kissed my check and replied, "Ken, it wasn't because I didn't want to come here with you earlier, it was because I was afraid to."

I smiled, "Well, put all your fears to rest, I'm not a wild American soldier, I'm just a normal person who may be falling in love with you."

I bent down and kissed her again. I then released her, and removed my Ike jacket and necktie hanging them on the rack. I opened the bottle of wine pouring her a glass and flipped the top off one of the beer bottles. I sat in the easy chair and motioned for her to sit on my lap. She moved over in front of me and sat down. I pulled her closer to me and held her tightly. She draped her arm around my shoulder, then kissed me on the forehead.

She said in a low whisper, "Ken, I've never slept with an American soldier, or anyone else, so I'm nervous. Please understand, and be patient with me. I've never even been in a hotel room before, so this is all very new to me."

"I understand. There's no rush. We have all night and the evening is young," I replied. I looked into her eyes, they were so seductive, I felt myself sinking into their magic. I kissed her, and then I slowly began to unbutton her blouse. She offered no resistance. I bent her slightly forward and removed her blouse. I then unsnapped the clasp connecting her brassiere and removed it. Her armpits were cleanly shaven, her breast firm, full, flaunting in their beauty. I caressed them both, bending forward I tenderly kissed each in turn. I took each nipple and gently kissed it taking it in my mouth sucking lightly. She moaned, and pulled me closer. The passion fires once ignited now glowed red hot. A haze enveloped me, the need for release and gratification increasingly urgent. I undid the buttons on my shirt and removed it throwing it over the chair. I stood her up and she undid the buttons on her skirt and stepped out of it. I then removed her half-slip. I knelt and removed my shoes. She watched every move that I made as I removed my pants dropping them on the floor. She and I were left in just our underwear.

I picked her up and placed her gently on the bed. I lay down besides her pulling her closer to me. I then removed my shorts, and then her panties. I kissed and caressed her, the passion fires climbing, swirling, devouring us in its heat. I carefully and slowly moved over on top of her. The passion of the moment won out, and in short order I had an orgasm. She hugged me tighter and tighter reaching her own climax.

Slowly, my senses returned, and I kissed her lips then her face and said, "Elona, I love you."

She returned my kiss, and softly whispered, "I love you too."

Relaxing, I rolled to the side, my muscles unwound, my breathing slowed and my heartbeat returned to normal. Resting we talked for several minutes then we made love again. Afterwards we fell asleep with her head resting on my arm.

I woke early the next morning, my right arm numb. I slowly and carefully eased my arm from beneath her head. She moaned slightly as I pulled it away. I stared at her, she was the most beautiful woman I'd ever seen, and that included Rachel, and all my favorite movie stars.

I recalled the words of Chaplain Hodges who had told me that I would fall in love again, perhaps more than once. Perhaps, the heart really does have an infinite capacity to love, and to love again, and again. I eased out of the bed and sat in the easy chair. My mouth was dry and I had no coffee. Needing something to drink, I reached for my unopened beer and slowly eased the hinged top off. I took a small swallow and then lit a cigarette.

I watched her as she slept, and thought about so many things, the past, Rachel, the present and the future. Where was I headed? What did the future hold for me, for her and me? I had fallen in love with Elona, I didn't think that possible after Rachel. Should I think about putting in marriage papers? I knew that I couldn't treat her as just another overnight shack job. How long would it take the CID to process the papers, and complete the required background investigation I wondered?

Strange and unfamiliar thoughts forged forward. How would my family feel if I brought home a German war bride? Should I even care what they thought? Of course I had to care. I had to consider their feelings and thoughts. In the final analysis I had to be sure that I was doing the right thing, and that she was also making the right move if we decide to get married.

Finally, she began to stir, her eyes fluttering open. I watched as she felt around on my side of the bed, not finding me there she straightened out and sat up. Then seeing me she said, "Oh, I was frightened, I had a horrible thought that you had left me here alone."

I smiled and replied, "Sweet thing, after last night, you couldn't run me off with a big stick."

She laughed and got out of bed, totally nude without the slightest sense of embarrassment; she came over and sat on my lap. I kissed her face and lightly rubbed her back. I asked, "Did you enjoy last night?"

"Yes, of course. Last night was one wonderful night. I never knew that making love could be so much physical and emotional pleasure, and be so totally satisfying."

I suggested we go for breakfast. She agreed, so I waited as she took a bath in the bathtub. I then washed up, brushed my teeth and dressed. She was fully dressed when I finished. We walked down to the restaurant and ordered breakfast with coffee. We talked for about an hour as I drank several cups of coffee and smoked cigarettes.

Finished, we walked back to our room. She asked, "When are you going back to America?"

"I don't know. We have a war going on over in Korea, and my time in the army has been extended, so I have no sure way of knowing."

I walked over and gently eased her down on the bed. I sat beside her and kissed her. She returned my kisses with a passion that was both exciting and delightful. She slowly removed her clothing, and I ripped my uniform off in just seconds. I then consummated the wonderful act of love with her.

I then got up from the bed and had a drink of warm beer. I lit a cigarette, and poured the beer into the sink, it was flat. It was eleven-thirty in the morning.

She said, "Ken, we should get dressed and leave."

Reluctantly I agreed, and so we got dressed and walked out of the inn.

I hailed a taxi and asked her, "Where do you live? I'll have the driver take you home then drop me off at the *Kaserne* gate."

Surprising me she said, "No, have him drop you off first, and then he can take me home."

"Are you sure that's what you want me to do?"

She smiled and replied, "Yes, my mother and father might not want to see you bringing their daughter home at noontime on a Sunday after she's been out all night."

There was some logic in her statement, especially since this was Christmas Day. I gave her twenty marks to pay for the taxi.

When we arrived at the main gate, I kissed her and said, "I'll call you. Make plans to go to the club with me for the New Year's Eve dance and party." She nodded her head in agreement. I got out of the taxi and walked through the gate, the snow ankle deep, but it failed to dampen my happy feelings.

That night Ray, Roberts and I, plus several others went to the club for a few hours. The club was packed with the Engineers and people from our company. A couple of fights broke out, but the manager quickly broke them up and ejected the idiots. What a dumb ass way to spoil the evening.

The band was playing loudly, and with so many people laughing and talking it was extremely difficult to even hear people talking at our own table. When the band began playing their goodnight signature song we all struggled out the door and headed for the barracks. Celebrating holidays is tough!

Ed was in the room, and he had his usual bottle of cognac. Roberts also had bottle, so we gathered in Ray's room and opened the bottles with a couple of cola's for chasers. We had no ice, but that made no difference, it would have been nice, but it wasn't necessary. The holiday spirit filled the night air at least in the room. I went to my room about two-thirty in the morning. Ed was almost knee-walking drunk, so I half carried him down the hall and ensured he was safe in his bunk.

Most of us got up late the next morning. Breakfast had been extended for an hour, so we barely made the mess hall before they closed. The Mess Sergeant was pissed because we came in so late, but he agreed to feed us anyway. We were ravenous; we ate almost everything left on the serving line. Surprisingly, I didn't have a headache. I didn't know if that was good or bad. Pop Warner had tried to commit suicide after heavy drinking. I damn sure had no intention of being like him.

That day most of us just hung around the barracks. The guys who had to work made their shifts, so everything was normal. I spend part of the day shining my boots and shoes, and wrote a few letters. Later that evening Ray and I went to the service club and played several games of pool. I glanced over at the leather couch, pleasant memories filled my mind of Dottie and I. I wondered what has happened to her. I wished her nothing but the best and let it go. Eventually, we returned to the barracks.

The next morning Ray and I went to the mess hall early as we both had the day shift. After eating he opened his copy of the *Stars and Stripes* newspaper, and began to read as I finished my coffee and smoked a cigarette. The First Sergeant came through the serving lines and joined the two of us at our table. We exchanged the usual good morning pleasantries as he sat down and began to eat.

Ray spoke up and said, "There's an item in today's paper about the lynching of a black man down in Mississippi. Ken, you're from Alabama, do they really do things like that down in your part of the country?"

I looked at him, totally surprised he would ask me such a question. I reflected for a minute developing a response as I mulled over and formulated my answer. "The short answer to your question is yes, it does happen." I stopped for a moment.

"Ray, the Civil War has been over for eighty-six years, and colored people have been free for just that number of years. The South was almost destroyed during the war, and it has never fully recovered from that war. Where I come from, as a boy I heard stories of how white families were devastated, plantations, homes and farms burned to the ground, entire towns set afire and burned up, railroads, roads and industries totally destroyed. Our very old people who were little kids when all that happened, have long bitter, bitter memories. I guess they are all mostly dead by now, but they passed many of those hatreds and memories down to their kids, and their kids to their kids. The South had no Marshall Plan like they have here in Germany. Colored people had it equally hard after the war, probably more so, because they were all unemployed and homeless." I had a drink of coffee, a puff on my cigarette and considered my next statement then continued my response.

"Even today in 1951, down south the black and white races are totally separated. We don't go to the same schools, we don't eat in the same restaurants, don't go to the same churches, and don't sit on the same seats in public buses. There's a movie theater in the little Georgia town adjacent to my town that lets the colored people go to it, but only upstairs in the nose-bleed section, and the main floor downstairs is reserved for white people only. In my little town of Lynell, our movie theater does not allow them at all. The bus stations are like the train stations. They have separate waiting rooms, bathrooms and drinking fountains, everything's separated. White people don't mix with black people. It's almost like a sin to do so, other than perhaps overseeing a job, or explaining a work project." Pausing for a drink of coffee I continued.

"I lived in a rural area, out in the country. There my best and closest friends were two black boys. We used to hunt, fish, and go swimming together. We sat under shade trees and talked about things in our world, and dreamed of the future like all boys do. I have spent many evenings at their home, slept overnight in their house, and ate meals in their kitchen, but they never did in mine. It's not right, but that's the way it is. There are still many white people in the South who despise colored people. Some employers cheat them, and won't pay them a fair wage. Jobs for black men were, and are few and far between. The great depression made things much, much worse for my part of the country." I paused for another sip of coffee, and then continued.

"Look at the Army! Hell, it only recently integrated, so it and many other institutions in the United States aren't too far ahead of the South. Here in the army now and then you see a black soldier going with or married to a white European woman. You can see their kid's half-white half-black, half-breeds, the army accepts that. That couldn't happen down South. If it did crosses would burn on their front yard, and someone would probably get hung or shot. I can't picture even in my wildest imagination a black man with a white woman and a couple of half-white and black kids in my home town or a black woman with a white man and half-breed kids. Some day it may all change, maybe not in our lifetimes, but it has to change."

I had my last sip of coffee, crushed out my cigarette and said, "We'd better go to work, it's getting late."

The First Sergeant stopped me and said, "Fisher, that was a damn splendid explanation, and I'm glad that I heard it," he shook my hand.

His remark embarrassed me, so I left and went on to work.

I met Elona that evening and we went to a *Gasthaus* for a bite to eat and I had a couple of beers. We didn't go to a hotel. She said, "I have to go home early, my mother isn't feeling well."

I wished her mom well, and reminded her that we were planning to go to the New Year's party together. Before she left I gave her some marks for her taxi.

While I was still sitting at the bar I saw Betty and some Buck Sergeant from the Engineer Company enter the room. That sat at a small table and ordered drinks. I glanced at them occasionally, they were holding hands and appeared to be totally absorbed in each other. I felt a small twinge of jealousy, but it quickly passed. I cared too much for her to do anything other than to wish her the best. Eventually, she saw me. She said something to her boyfriend and they rose from their table and came up to me at the bar.

I said, "Hello Betty," and extended my hand.

She took my hand shaking it and said, "Hi Ken, I want you to meet my fiancé."

I shook his hand and introduced myself to him. Smiling, he shook my hand and told me his name was Earl something or other.

Betty turned to him and said, "Ken, is an old friend of mine, I've known him for over two years. He works in communications on the post."

We continued to make small talk, and I offered to buy them a drink. They declined stating they still had drinks on their table. I lied and told them I had to leave for work. But I was sincere in expressing my pleasure in seeing her, and meeting him.

I left them and caught a taxi back to the barracks. I dropped by the club which was still open for about another hour. I wanted another beer. Pitts was at a table with a couple of the guys, so I joined them. I mentioned to Bill that I had run into Betty at a bar with a guy from the Engineers.

He said, "Yeah, I know about the guy. He and Betty have been going out together for some time, and I think it is serious. He seems like a nice guy."

I digested that information and filed it away. We sat there for a while drank a couple of beers, and then drifted back down the street to our barracks.

The next morning I read the *Stars and Stripes*, and listened to the news about Korea on AFN, it certainly wasn't good. The Chinese communists were in up to their chink assholes in the war. General MacArthur was doing great, but we were being outmanned on the ground. I continually talked about the war with Corporal Mathews. As the battle lines shifted he would tell me if he had been in certain locations, and what it had been like. I felt I had been cheated out of participating in the war. But Ironjaws true to his word ran this frigging outfit, and what he says goes.

The big party day arrived. I checked the work schedule and made sure that everyone was aware of when they were scheduled to work. I was off New Year's Eve and day, so my personal schedule was in good shape. I called Elona and spoke with her for a couple of minutes.

"Honey, catch a taxi to the main gate, and I'll meet you there in the Jeep, then we'll go to the club," I said.

She agreed to meet me there at eight o'clock in the evening.

Later on I got all cleaned up and put on my best uniform, and my low quarter shoes. I jumped into the Jeep and drove down to the main gate. Hell, I was early so I stopped by the message center and checked in. Things were quite normal with no problems. I told Bell I'd be out at the gate for a few minutes, and then I'd be up at the club most of the night.

I walked out to the main gate and waited for her taxi to show up. I glanced at my watch, it was a few minutes after eight o'clock. I smoked a cigarette and stamped around to keep my feet warm. I heard one of the iron covers on the message center windows open. Bell looked out and saw me and yelled that I had a phone call. No cars were in sight coming up the hill, so I ran back to the building and he let me in. I picked up the phone, it was Elona.

"Hello sweetheart, where are you?"

"I'm at home, my mother is very sick, and I just can't come tonight."

Devastated I asked, "Can't your father take care of her?"

"No, he's too old and doesn't know what to do, so I have to stay home and take care of her."

It pissed me off, but I said, "All right, I hope she gets better. Call me tomorrow either here at the message center or at the company."

She promised to do so, and ended our conversation with, "I'm so sorry."

I immediately regretted what I had said to her. I bit my tongue. My remark about her father was probably crass, perhaps even arrogant. I thought maybe selfishness is one of my personality quirks. I got back in the Jeep and went to the club. The place was packed, and the band blaring out its best tunes. I finally located the table where Ray and the other guys were sitting. Many of them had their girlfriends, and the party was well under way.

Ray asked, "Where's Elona?"

"Her mom's sick and she had to stay home," I replied.

The activities were about normal, and several couples were dancing as the band put forth its best efforts. I really felt depressed, I had looked forward eagerly to tonight. I drank a couple of cognacs and cola, and my attitude improved greatly. As the evening wore on some of the troops were obviously getting tipsy, but the party didn't slow down at all. Ray was up dancing with his favorite local girl. She was a nice looking girl, about our age, and that was about all I knew about her. By the midnight hour I was getting a buzz on. I watched as the club manager headed for the microphone and made his spiel about counting down and saying farewell to the old year as we welcomed in the new one, 1951.

I was over twenty-years-old now and in spite of not wanting to my thoughts returned to this night two years ago. I thought about what might have been, what could have been, what I wish had happened. No use thinking about the past. I was torturing myself and I knew it. I drank a straight shot of cognac, and it burned my throat going down, but I didn't care. Now here I'm falling in love with another beautiful woman, but she's not with me tonight either.

I was originally due to get out of the army this July 1951. With Truman's extension I have no idea when I'll actually get released. If I'm truly serious about Elona, I best start thinking about our future. I really don't have any firm data on which to plan our future, I sipped another straight shot. It was now into New Year's Day, and I felt the effects of the cognac, so it was time for me to call it a night. I bid a few of the guys "Happy New Year," and headed for the exit. Back at the barracks I hung up my uniform, took a quick shower and went to bed. I heard guys all night stumbling into the barracks, laughing, loud talk and finally silence.

I woke up about eight in the morning, and noted that Ed wasn't in his bunk. After getting dressed I met Hodes and Roberts in the hallway, so we all went to breakfast. New Year's Day 1951, was a party recovery day for the troops just like each New Year's Day since I'd arrived here. Not much else was happening.

That afternoon I walked down to the message center and checked the radio room. I had no telephone calls and that didn't help my disposition. I told the clerk on duty that if I got a call to have them call the company as I would be there.

As I walked back to the company Ray pulled up behind me in our Jeep. I climbed aboard and we rode together the remainder of the way. Ray told me in his best Northwestern twang what a great night he'd had. He had spent the night at the Ring Hotel with his girlfriend.

A little later in the afternoon the Charge of Quarters came upstairs and told me I had a telephone call, and to take it in his office. It was Elona.

After exchanging greeting she asked, "Do you want to meet me this evening?"

"Yes, or course, meet me as six o'clock at the same hotel we stayed last time, the Bavarian Inn," I replied.

I cleaned up again, put on my OD's and left in the Jeep. I drove downtown and parked at the Bavarian Inn. I had arrived a little early, so I waited for her taxi to arrive. When it arrived she got out and I paid the driver. Elona and I walked inside and I went to the front desk and obtained a room for the evening. With my room key in my pocket we walked into the bar and restaurant area.

Several couples were seated around the room, and a small German band was playing a waltz. I escorted her to the bar and ordered a glass of white wine for her, and a beer for myself. I'd heard that Dinkerlacker was good beer, so I ordered one just to see if it was. I couldn't pronounce the name of the beer correctly, but the waiter corrected my pronunciation of the name.

"Ken, are you angry with me about last night?"

I looked at her and smiled, "No, I'm not angry. I was very disappointed that we couldn't enjoy the evening together, but certainly not angry." I leaned over and gave her a quick kiss on the cheek. "Now let's get a bite to eat."

I led her to a small table in the back of the room. We sat down with our drinks and she ordered us a German dish. It was some type beef and cabbage and was tasty and good. After eating we danced several slow dances.

"If you are ready, let's go to our room for a while," I said.

She nodded her head in agreement.

Once in our room she looked at me and said, "Ken, I'm so sorry that we couldn't be together last night. I wanted to make the party, and I wanted us to be together. I wanted to feel the beat of your heart as we slept together, but I couldn't come to you."

The look on her face was enough to melt my heart and make me forget all about any real anger that I might have had.

CHAPTER 20

I propose

Caressing her face I said, "Don't worry sweetheart. We'll do all that tonight and more. We have to catch up on what we missed last night, so I hope that you are well rested."

I kissed her again as she slowly unbuttoned her blouse and removed it from her shoulders. I removed her slip straps and undid her brassiere removing it as her full beautiful breast came into view. Tenderly, I caressed them both, kissing each of them in turn. She moaned and drew my face closer. I lifted her up and removed the remainder of her clothes. I quickly undressed placing all our clothes on the other chair.

Pulling her to me I hungrily kissed her again. I moved to the bed turning the covers back. With no hesitation she crossed to the side of the bed and lay down.

I lay down on the bed beside her.

She turned on her side facing me and I turned on mine. Our lips met again as we fed the flames of passion and desire. We made love as only young lovers can. Breathing deeply, we slowly recovered from the physical exertion. I moved back to my side of the bed.

I sat up and reaching over lit a cigarette. She had a satisfied smile of contentment on her face. I noticed tiny white marks on her upper thighs and abdomen.

"Darling, what are these tiny marks on your stomach and thighs?"

With a look of alarm she replied, "Those are called stretch marks. When I was younger I was really fat, by being so fat it stretched the skin and left those little marks."

I leaned over and kissed her stomach and both of her thighs and said, "I can't picture you as fat because you are so beautiful and slim now. Anyway, I love you dearly, stretch marks and all."

The evening wore on, and finally we went to sleep. The next morning after waking up I half cleaned up and partially dressed went to the restaurant for three cups of coffee. When I returned to the room she was awake. We drank our coffee and shared the third cup. We then took a bath together in the tub and played silly splash games.

Finally, we got dressed and I escorted her to the restaurant where we had breakfast and another cup of coffee. While I smoked we talked of various things of no consequence.

"Elona darling, we should consider getting married. I'm asking you to marry me. If you truly love me we should fill out the required paper work, and turn it in for the background checks and clearances we will need to get married."

She held my hand and said, "Darling, I do love you and I want to be married to you for all our lives, but let's just wait a little longer to be absolutely certain that's what we both really want to do."

I didn't argue the point, "Of course sweetheart, if that's what you want we can do that." Then I suggested we leave.

Walking out to the Jeep she stopped and said, "I'll just take a taxi home."

"Why would you do that?" I asked.

She responded, "I think it is the best thing to do. My mom is still sick, and I don't want to have to explain us and our relationship at this time."

I felt uncomfortable with her explanation, but I said, "Fine, if you think that is best." I gave her a hand full of German marks as she gave me a quick kiss.

"Ken darling, I love you so much, be a little patience we'll do what you want very soon, I do want to marry you."

The following week I took the radio team out on a five day communications exercise. We traveled up to the Fulda Gap and operated from there. Three operators were left at our base station, and I had four with me. The Signal Officer came to visit and inspect our site and operations. Completing his inspection and visit he complimented me, and jumped back into his helicopter and left for Wurzburg. We returned to Wurzburg at the end of the exercise. It had been a successful one, and

I felt that all the operators were now capable of operating a fixed base station and a mobile station.

January faded into February, snow covered everything. It was a cold brutal winter and I looked forward eagerly to springs arrival and some warm sunshine.

Elona and I continued to meet every chance we could, our love deepening and becoming more realistic. I still had not met her parents, but it no longer seemed too important. Some of the older guys were beginning to rotate back to the states, and most of them had orders assigning them to units in Korea.

President Truman's extension still prevailed. We received several new draftees in the unit all assigned to various sections. We picked up three in the message center with one being a radio operator. I gave him extra training, and got him up to acceptable speed fairly quickly.

In March I took a three day pass and Elona was able to arrange some days off from her government office job. I talked Ray into inviting his favorite local girl to go with us down to Garmisch. He agreed, so we four caught the train.

Elona and I spent many hours in bed as most young lovers do. It was a wonderful holiday. The Casa Carioca had great shows, more activities were available, and prices remained dirt cheap. But like all good things it had to end. We caught the train back to Wurzburg and Ray and I returned to the world of soldering once again. It had been a memorable three day pass.

In April 1951, we heard the news over AFN that President Truman had fired General MacArthur in Korea. I took that as a personal insult, as the General had been my military hero since his days on Bataan back in 1942. For weeks his firing remained the main topic in the news and on the air. Later, I read his farewell speech to Congress so many times I could almost recite it from memory.

Later than month I received a call from Betty. She said, "Ken, I want to talk to you about something very important. Will you come down to my house so we can talk in private?"

"Of course I will, but it's best if you let you boyfriend know that I'll be there. I don't want to have to fight with him."

"He's out on maneuvers, and will be gone for another two weeks, so you don't have to worry about that," she said.

"Okay sweet thing, I'll be there tomorrow evening around six."

I wondered what in the world Betty could have on her mind that she wanted to talk to me about. Whatever it is, I'll surely try and help

The following evening I took the Jeep and stopping along the way I bought six beers then arrived at her place a little after six. I knocked on the door and she let me in. I put the beer down and held out my arms. She stepped into my embrace, and I hugged and softly kissed her cheek. I then took off my jacket and sat down on the couch while she opened two of the beers and brought them over placing them on the small table. I took a swallow of my beer, and lit two cigarettes giving one to her. Looking again at her I thought, she is still a young and lovely woman.

"Now beautiful, tell me what's this huge problem, and what's the urgency?"

She had a swallow of her beer and said, "Ken, my boyfriend Earl and I are going to be married in three weeks. The CID has investigated all my background and I passed, so they approved our marriage. I'm scared. I don't know if I'm doing the right thing or not. All I know about America is from the movies and what I've been told. I only know American soldiers from here in Wurzburg. I don't know what to expect, or how I'll be received in America. What will the American people think of and expect from me?"

I waited for her to finish her remarks as she drew in a large breath.

She continued, "What if I get homesick? What if I want to come back home to Wurzburg? I have to talk to someone, you're my special friend, I trust and believe you and whatever you tell me."

"Come here Betty. Sit down beside me on the couch." She left the table and came over and sat down beside me. I tilted her head, and gave her a small tender kiss on the cheek.

"Betty honey, you have absolutely no problems worth worrying about. Since the end of the war there are a few thousand German girls who have married American soldiers, and gone with them to the states. If Earl stays in the Army, he'll be assigned to a military post where there may be dozens of German brides. You'll quickly know who they are, and make friends. You speak almost perfect English, you're educated, and you have excellent skills, you'll fit in anywhere." I stopped and had a swallow of my beer.

"America is made up of immigrants, so you'll be just one of millions who have traveled to America and became Americans. You're worrying needlessly. There's absolutely no need to bother yourself one minute longer worrying about marrying and leaving Germany. In fact, many small towns in the states are made up primarily with people of German ancestry."

She kissed me on the cheek. "Thanks Ken, I needed someone to tell me that. You're right I'm sure, perhaps I'm just being silly and thinking too much and too long about it all."

I replied, "You have a wedding coming up, that's what you should concern yourself with. Someday, you'll realize that going to America was your smartest possible move."

She rose from the couch went to the refrigerator and returned with two more beers which she opened and gave one to me. I pulled her over setting her on my lap. I put my arm around her and kissed her.

"Oh Ken, you, we shouldn't do this. It's wrong you know. I'm getting married, I love Earl, he's a good man, I can't cheat on him."

Releasing her I replied, "You're right, I'm wrong, and I apologize."

She moved back to her seat on the couch.

"Betty, I hope you now know that you really have no problem. You and Earl will have a good life, and have children together. You should go ahead and get married, and plan on a wonderful life and marriage. I'm very happy about it and happy for you. I wish you both the very best of everything. "

She smiled and said, "Ken, will you come to our wedding? It'll be at the post chapel. I'll call you later with the exact date and time."

"Of course I will, I wouldn't miss it for the world." I finished my beer and rose to leave.

She came up to me and kissed me, "Thank you Ken for everything, I'll never forget you."

I kissed her cheek, smiled and replied, "I'll never forget you either sweet thing. For sure you'll have a great life." I stepped out the door and closed it.

On my way back to the post I though again of the old adage, "A stiff dick has no conscience." I tried to tell myself that it didn't fit in this case because ours was a special relationship. I knew that Betty along with Dotty had been my emotional support crutches when I needed someone the most. Three weeks later on Saturday afternoon, Elona and

I went to the chapel to witness Betty and Earl's marriage ceremony. I even got to kiss the bride. I wished them all the luck in the world.

As a wedding present I gave her a bound photographer's book of Wurzburg before the war. The book also included several pages of pictures of Wurzburg after the war. I included a couple of personal pictures, one of her standing by the telephone center door, and one of she and I together by the phone center. I even included two pictures of her and me at the Zugspitz lounge in Garmisch.

Chaplain Hodges performed their wedding ceremony. I was surprised that he was still here. I introduced him to Elona. Betty and Earl left the following Monday, and I never saw or heard of either of them again. Several pages of delightful memories were cemented into my ever expanding memory book, and I closed another Chapter.

During the summer months Elona and I spent most of our time together. We visited museums, went to movies, had picnics and such. We did everything possible together. We were just two young people madly in love.

I continued to take the young operators out on field exercises as personnel within the company were being replaced. We received several new men who had already been in Korea and I talked with them constantly. I requested they describe their experiences during the war to me. My missing out on the war was like a festering sore. They told me about their experiences, the misery and muck of the war, and the frightening loss of life that occurs often within seconds. They spoke of men being wounded and freezing to death in the Chosin Reservoir area, and the loss of life during retreats. They spoke of the fear at night on the battlefield, and the cold of subzero weather. I listened and tried to absorb it all. I was too young for WWII, and now it seems I will miss Korea also. Well, so be it!

Meanwhile the war in Korea raged on. We had been fighting for over a year up and down the peninsula as the battle lines shifted back and forth. Our casualties continued to mount up. I followed the war in the newspaper and on the radio. Several more army divisions from the United States joined the 7th Army here in Germany.

The summer passed rapidly. The ominous gray clouds of fall and winter began to fill the skies. The snow and cold could not be far behind. I was twenty-one years old now, and mentally felt forty.

In September, Ed received his orders to return to the states. He and Ericka were married in the post chapel; half of the company attended, and we all wished them well. That evening we had a wedding party for them in the club. What a blowout that turned out to be. I think everyone got a little drunk including Ed. Ericka seemed to accept our antics and camaraderie. First Sergeant Ironjaws was also there, and had several drinks. Ericka was annoyed that Ed was getting loaded, but did her best to conceal it. I truly hated to see Ed leave; he was my roommate, one of my best friends and my mentor. I took his beloved picture of Bettie Page and had it framed and packed for him. I bought him two bottles of Five Star Cognac, and wrapped them in towels and packed them in a cushioned box, and gave them to Ericka for safekeeping. I made her promise not give them to him until they were back in the states

Ed's last words to me were: "Ken it's all copacetic. I'm pulling my last Hank Snow in Deustchland, Auf Wiedersehen." He hugged my neck and they left.

For me the company no longer seemed the same without him. But such is army life, you make friends and then they or you are reassigned. We had exchanged stateside addresses and promised to stay in touch. I never saw or heard from or of Ed again. I closed the pages on another great Chapter in my memory book.

November was the next big month. I took Elona to the mess hall for Thanksgiving dinner. We had a great time, many of the troops had brought their wives and children. There was a light snow, but nothing new in that. Elona and I continued to spend as much time together as our jobs permitted. The army closed her office in the army's military government building in downtown Wurzburg, but she quickly found another secretarial job with a German export company.

It was a time of continuous change. The city of Wurzburg was rapidly rebuilding. Many of the old bombed out buildings were torn down and hauled away. New houses and buildings were springing up in their place. The Marshall Plan was working exactly as planned.

December rolled around, and of course the holidays. I had passed my discharge date months earlier, and now I was well into President Truman's extension. The war continued to rage in Korea, so it didn't appear that I would be getting out of the army anytime soon. This became a matter of some concern as I realized that the army could issue me rotation orders at any time, and I would have to leave. I decided after the holidays I'd discuss marriage with Elona again, and we could file the necessary papers for her background investigation and clearance for us to get married.

Elona and I attended the normal Christmas party at the club. It was a lot of fun as they always were. I told her this year we would make the New Year's party, come hell or high water. Jack Taylor and Sam Amato both came to town for the party. I called and invited Grady, but he was too wrapped up with some *fraulein* to make it to Wurzburg. We all gathered in the club, most of the guys had girls some did not. Taylor and Amato had gone downtown and picked up a couple of nice looking women, and brought them to the party. It was shaping up to be one of the better ones.

We pulled three tables together with about twenty chairs, so we were set for the evening. Ironjaws and his lovely wife Inez showed up and joined our table. His wife Inez sat next to Elona and he sat on the other side of his wife, so I didn't have to pay too much attention to him as he was two chairs away. The hours sped by amidst the music, dancing and drinking. With the midnight hour almost upon us the club manager did his normal routine. As he counted the seconds down to midnight, we all stood and made a toast to the army, and to the New Year, 1952.

I drank a small sip of cognac and cola and continued to party. Ray and his girl friend were up dancing, so I asked Mrs. Baker the First Sergeants wife, to dance. She and I had a delightful slow dance. I also danced with Elona several times, but I was getting a little loaded and I knew it. Ironjaws appeared to be totally sober. I guessed he could hold his liquor better than me.

It was late when we left the club. Earlier that afternoon I had reserved a room downtown at the Bavarian Inn. Ray had also made room reservations. We all took a taxi to the Inn and went to the bar area.

Taylor and Amato had beaten us there with their girlfriends. I knew the party would liven up and continue. After a couple of drinks I made the decision that I had to go to bed. I'd had enough drinking and partying for one night. I told Sam that we were going to our room. I made sure my part of the booze bill was paid. Slowly, we got our coats and hats and left, finding our room with no problem. Elona and I were both tired, I gave her a kiss and asked, "Did you have a good time tonight?"

"Yes, but we all drank too much. Tomorrow, rather today, we're all going to be very sorry." I just nodded my head in agreement.

She said, "Let's go to bed I'm tired and sleepy." I gave her no argument. We undressed and went to bed. She snuggled in my arms, and in less than five minutes she was asleep. I closed my eyes and the party, the night, and the old year all became history.

Everyone lived through the holidays, and for once I was glad that they were over and behind us. I had to go on a three day field exercise the second week of the month. It went off without any problems. I continued to train our newer operators and keep them on their toes. I ensured that the mobile van was cleaned and serviced and ready for immediate deployment. All standard operating procedures were followed.

At the end of January Perry told me he had his rotation orders, and would be leaving on the 15th of February. That was a jolt, I considered him to be the absolute heart and soul of the message center, indeed of all post communications. Sergeant Perry knew more about communications than anyone I had ever met. I hated to see him go not only for the loss of his expertise, but he had become a personal friend of mine. He sold his 1946 Buick which he had for a few years to some Major in the unit. It was still a great looking automobile. He and his girlfriend of the past few years were married in the chapel and they left. We had a big blow out farewell party for the newlyweds in the club. I think he returned to someplace in Minnesota, or maybe he reenlisted.

Bill Pitts received his orders to rotate. He had reassignment orders to Fort Carson, Colorado. Bill told me that he was planning on reenlisting once he arrived back in the states. He had four years in now, and did not want to just throw them away. He said his wife was unhappy about his reenlisting as she did not like the army, and its long unplanned and unwanted separations. We had another great farewell party for him. That night he got into a fight with a guy from the Engineers. Pitts was a powerful man and he whipped the guy's ass in a flash. Two quick punches by Bill and the fight was over. It happened so quickly that very few people even know that there had been a fight. I wished him well, and expressed my appreciation for his friendship and assistance. He had been a good friend of mine for all the time I had been here.

A replacement sergeant came in and took Bill's job in the crypto room. A second sergeant came in and took over Sergeant Perry's job on a temporary basis. I continued to do my job, and made sure my section was ready for all contingencies.

One evening while Elona and I were at a local Gasthaus, I said to her, "Honey, we should put in our marriage papers now, so they can do whatever they have to do and we can get married." We discussed marriage and agreed we wanted it to happen this year and soon.

She seemed somewhat less than enthusiastic about the idea,

"Don't you want to marry me?" I asked.

"Of course I do. I love you completely, I guess I' m just nervous," she replied

The next day I went to see Ralph the company clerk, and requested the necessary papers to marry a German national. He gave me two forms to fill out, and several for Elona to complete. Her forms mostly requested information about her date of birth, place of birth, and lots of information on her family and addresses where they had lived and when.

I saw her the next night and gave them to her. I requested she fill them out and give them back to me as soon as she could. It was a week before I saw her again. She had the papers with her and they were completed. We spent the night at the Bavarian Inn and had a grand evening.

The following day I went to see the First Sergeant and after reporting to him, I told him I wanted to submit paperwork to marry Elona.

He accepted the papers glanced briefly at them then looking at me asked, "Is this what you really want to do?"

Somewhat surprised I said, "Of course, I love her, she loves me, we've been going together for over a year, why shouldn't we get married?"

"I didn't say you should or shouldn't get married, I asked is this what you really want to do. You have answered my question. I'll turn them in and let you know when they are approved or disapproved," he snapped.

I said, "Thank you First Sergeant." I saluted him did an about face, and quickly left his office.

I went upstairs to my room and lay down on my bunk. Thoughts were racing through my mind so fast they were almost making me dizzy. I knew that when I took Elona home my family would love her. So I have no problems there. It is still my intention to get out of the army when they release me. I had never contemplated making the army my life's career, or moving to any other place than back to my hometown. I'll have four years in the army soon, and I only signed up for three. The war is still raging in Korea, hell I might leave here and get sent there. That idea worried me, not for me, but for Elona. Where would she stay if I was deployed? I guess I had better begin to think more seriously about my future. Marriage is not a light step to take, especially one facing my uncertain future.

Ray came by the room and said, "Ken, I received my redeployment orders today. I'm leaving in May."

"Where are you being reassigned to?"

"I'm assigned to a replacement company at Fort Lewis, Washington, and I'm being discharged on May 31st."

"You mean you aren't going to another unit, but are getting out?"

"Yep, that's what the orders say."

"That's great news. It means that I'll get discharged also when they send me stateside. By the way, I put in papers to marry Elona."

"Congratulations Ken, you made a great choice."

We then exchanged home addresses and swore to stay in touch after our discharges.

"Ken, keep our Jeep and sell it before you leave. Just send me my half of whatever you get for it."

"Okay, you can bet on it."

May quickly arrived, and we had a terrific going away party for Ray. Taylor and Amato came in for the night, and most of the off-duty message center people were there. I guess we were all about half drunk by closing time, if they weren't then they damn sure weren't trying. Two of the troops carried Ray back to the barracks, and put him to bed, he was really stoned. I made it back under my own power.

The next morning Roberts, Hodes, and I loaded Ray and his duffle bag into the Jeep and drove him to the train station. Hell, he was still loaded. There were several other guys from the unit leaving today also, so I grabbed one I knew fairly well and asked him to watch out for Ray until he completely sobered up, He promised he would.

The sad moment arrived. Ray hugged everyone's neck and of course said he would see us all again. I helped him get aboard with his duffle bag and find a seat. The train whistle blew and the train began moving. I hugged his neck raced for the door and jumped off. I stood silently, watching his train fade out of sight, then I drove back to the Kaserne.

With the old gang being depleted the Kaserne and even the club lost much of its allure. I knew fewer people now than I did even one year ago. Roberts, Hodes and I hung out together and still did mostly the same old things. Taylor was brought back to Wurzburg to supervise the message center. I was glad of that, it eased my responsibilities, and I could spend more time off post with Elona.

The first of June I received a call to report to the First Sergeant. I went to his office and after receiving permission, I reported to him and stood at attention in front of his desk.

He said, "Stand at ease Fisher."

I relaxed and looked at him. He handed me some papers across his desk. Leaning forward I took them from him. Glancing quickly at them I knew they were my redeployment orders back to the states. My departure date was on or about the tenth of July. I was to report to Fort Benning, Georgia, for discharge on the last day of July 1952. I had a little over four weeks left in country.

"First Sergeant, what is the status of my papers to get married," I asked.

"I'll check on them and let you know as soon as possible." He relaxed back in his chair and asked, "Are you getting out of the army Fisher?"

I reflected for a moment then said, "Yes, First Sergeant. Four years almost to the day I guess is about enough time to serve my country, I'll get out."

"Well Fisher, I think you have the makings of a damn fine soldier. You've grown up quite a bit since you first arrived here, and the army needs men like you. I wish you would reconsider and change your mind. I'll let you know on the marriage papers."

"Yes Sir First Sergeant." I saluted him and left his office. I found out later that day that Hodes, Grady, Amato and Taylor plus all the guys who had came here with us were all leaving on the same day, and all with the same date of discharge.

I knew Taylor was reenlisting, and Roberts had already re-upped he was just rotating with us, all the others were getting out.

That night I met Elona and took her out for a bite to eat. We drank wine and I told her I had my orders to leave in July. I said, "Our paperwork is being checked on and it should be ready any day now. Are you happy?"

She smiled and taking my hand replied, "Yes of course, but I'm nervous and scared, the idea of leaving my country and going to a new one is scary,"

"Darling don't worry, things will be fine. You'll love the states and everything will work out fine for us. I plan to get out of the army, but I'm not sure what I'll do next. There are lots of opportunities in the civilian world, so we will be fine. My hometown may not have the best of opportunities, but we probably won't stay there anyway."

"Don't you like the army?" she asked.

"Sure, I like the army. It has afforded me lots of opportunities. I enjoy the army and the friends I've made. The army led me to you, for that alone I like it."

I suggested we return to our room, which we did. We partially undressed, and I sat in the big easy chair with her on my lap. I told her about the boat ride and what she could expect. I described how rough the North Sea is, and the Atlantic Ocean in the winter time, but that it should be nicer in the summer.

She smiled and said, "You're very excited about going home aren't you?"

"Of course, you and I will have a great trip on the boat, and on the train back in the states. You'll love it all I promise."

Smiling she replied, "If we're together, then it doesn't matter where we are."

I kissed her as we both finished undressing. I held her close to me and caressed her beautiful body as the blooming, burning flames of love and desire consumed us both.

Afterwards, I rolled over and relaxed a bit. Her arm was draped across my chest, so I picked up her hand and kissed it. I then got out of the bed and walked over and had a small drink of my beer. It was still cold. I lit a cigarette, and sat in the chair and thought about the challenges that were facing me and her.

She lay on the bed not saying anything, her eyes staring at the ceiling. Perhaps she's also thinking about her future with me and going to the states.

Damn it to hell, I never completed high school. Without at least a high school education my chances of succeeding in this world is drastically reduced. I have to get that diploma, but how will I be able to do that with a wife and working and maintaining a job?

I knew that I would have to get a job as soon as got home. I would have to find a place for us to live, buy some civilian clothes and a car. My relatives would be good for a week or so, but not for too long.

I guess it all means I will have to go to work in the cotton mill, at least until I can get my feet on the ground and get my goals set. I have the G. I. Bill and that will take care of the education cost. But just living takes money, and that creates one giant motivating force. Hell, I may never get out of the damn cotton mill.

Elona sat up and asked, "May I have a swallow of your beer?"

"Of course, it's not too cold but it's wet." I handed the bottle to her and she had a small swallow then handed it back to me. She lay back on the bed, and I lit another cigarette.

She closed her eyes again, and I wondered if she would drift off to sleep. I thought again about my immediate and long range future, and what it held for me. Back in my hometown most all the jobs were in the mills, and all businesses and people were dependent upon those employee's and their salaries. Where do I fit in?

My thoughts shifted and I wondered, do I really want to go home? Should I reenlist? Could I make the army my life's career? I had never even considered making the army a career. Joining the army was for me and most of my boyhood friends the proper thing to do. I suppose it was sort of expected of us. Hell, if we had not enlisted we would have been drafted. At least by volunteering we had our choice of services. But I had never had even the remotest idea of staying in.

Moving back to the bed I leaned over and shook her slightly. She immediately opened her eyes and smiled up at me. I grasped her arms, and then snuggled with her. She kissed me lightly and whispered, "I love you." We finished the night in the proper fashion. The next morning we were up early took a quick shower together then ate breakfast. She then caught a taxi home, and I returned to the Kaserne.

I was goofing off day-dreaming in the radio room when the phone rang bringing me back to reality. I answered it, and Ralph the company clerk said, "Ken, the First Sergeant wants to see you now!"

Normally, such an order would be terrifying to a young soldier like me, but the only thing I figured he wanted to see me about would be my marriage papers. I had already checked and received assurance from Chaplain Hodges that we could get married on one days notice.

CHAPTER 21

Blindsided

I drove my Jeep up to the company, and parked it in a spot next to the First Sergeant's. Checking in with Ralph, I was told to, "Report to the First Sergeant."

I knocked on Ironjaw's door and heard his gruff voice tell me to, "Come in." I walked over to the front of his desk, saluted and reported.

"Fisher, pull up that chair and let's talk."

That was surprising as we had never really engaged in light conversation. It isn't customary for a mere corporal to sit and talk with the First Sergeant.

"Go close the office doors also," he commanded.

That was equally strange, but I crossed the room and closed the door to the clerk's office then the door to the Commander's office. Returning to the chair I sat down. I wondered if I was in for an ass chewing for some reason or other.

"I received my reassignment orders today. I'll leave here the middle of next month. I'm going to Fort Riley, Kansas," he said

"Are you retiring?" I asked.

"No, I have over twenty years in this man's army. I am on indefinite enlistment so I'll stay for at least thirty years then I'll go back home to Arizona," he replied.

He said, "You've been away from Alabama for almost four years now, do you think race relations there have changed very frigging much?"

Stunned and puzzled by the question I asked, "What do you mean 'Change' First Sergeant, in what way?"

He growled, "I mean do you think god damn race relations and the frigging treatment of black people in the South has changed, or improved since you left?"

What a strange question I thought, as I tried to read his battle scarred face. "I don't know if they have or not. I doubt it. Change comes slowly in the Deep South. Race relations weren't a high priority item when I left, not even on a priority list, and I doubt if that's changed since I've been gone," I replied.

His black penetrating eyes just stared at me for a couple of seconds. He spoke again, "Fisher, do you remember the morning when you explained southern race relations and all its attendant problems to Ray Washington when I was sitting at your table in the mess hall?"

Not sure where this conversation was going I hesitated for a moment, and then answered. "Yes, I remember that conversation. I recall that you thought I had explained my understanding of that environment very well, and you told me so."

"Yes, that's true. You did, and I did say so." He replied.

He reached for a folder of papers on his desk. He opened it and removing several sheets began reading silently to himself. For a minute or two I sat and waited, and watched as his eyes raced across the sheets in front of him.

Looking at me again he said, "Fisher, I want to talk to you now as one man to another, not as First Sergeant to Corporal. I have watched you and Miss Haufmann for over a year. She's a lovely woman. You're both young and I believe truly in love with each other. These papers are your request to marry a German national. It's been approved. The only signature it needs to be final is the Company Commander's. Depending on the advice and recommendation I give to him, he will sign it either way, approved or disapproved." He stared at me for a few seconds.

In the gruffest of tones he said, "However, I'm not going to give him any fucking advice or recommendation. You're going to make the recommendation!"

Stunned, I just sat there and stared at the First Sergeant, my heart began pounding. I wasn't sure of what to say, or what question to ask, or why he spoke so harshly.

He spoke again, "Let me tell you the results of the CID background investigation of Miss Haufmann. After I finish you can read all the papers to be sure that what I tell you is accurate. Then I want you to take some time and think about what I tell you, and make a recommendation to me to give to the old man."

Puzzled and confused, I wondered what in the hell do I need to take time to do, and what should I think about, and what in hell is he going to tell me?

In a monotone he began by saying, "Miss Haufmann was born in Kissingen, Germany, in 1933. She lived there most of her life. Her father was an optometrist, he was also a Nazi Army officer, and was killed in the vicinity of Berlin in 1945. Her mother taught and retired from teaching high school."

He continued to recite facts he'd obviously gleaned from the papers.

He said, "She and her mother lived in a small house near what is now US Army Barracks in Kissingen. When she was sixteen-years-old, Miss Haufmann was raped by a black Army soldier from the transportation battalion there. The soldier was caught and court-martialed, and is now serving thirty-five years in Fort Leavenworth. Shortly thereafter her mother passed away. Miss Haufmann then moved here to Wurzburg to live with her older sister and her sister's husband. That's where she lives now"

He looked at me, I started to speak, but he waved his hand cutting me off.

"Let me finish then we can talk. As a result of being raped she gave birth to twins, a boy and a girl. They're about three or four years old now I'd guess. They are what you described to Washington as half-black and half-white half-breeds." He cleared his throat then continued. "There's no reason you can't marry her and take her and both children back with you to Alabama. That might create some racial problems for you down the road. You know that probably better than I do. She was just a young girl and there's nothing in her entire background that disqualifies her from going to the United States." He placed the papers back into the folder and closed it.

I sat in shocked disbelief and silence. I felt as if I'd been kicked in the stomach, and couldn't catch my breath. I could only stare at the First Sergeant.

Ironjaws opened the bottom drawer on his desk and pulled out two shot glasses and a fifth of whiskey. He poured both glasses full handing one to me. I accepted it and drank the entire shot without stopping. He did the same then capped the bottle, and returned it to the desk drawer. He lit a filter tip cigarette and handed it to me. I took it and inhaled deeply. I was unable to say a word.

Finally, I whispered, "May I read the report First Sergeant?"

He pushed the folder over to me, placing an ashtray onto his desk he pushed it over for my use.

There were only four pages to the report. I read them slowly, digesting every word and fact presented. A horrible feeling of helplessness spread over me, I'd had a similar feeling once before.

The First Sergeant didn't say a word as he reached down and refilled our shot glasses.

The report contained pictures of Elona and the two children. The twins were unmistakably bi-racial progeny. There were also pictures of Elona's father in his German army uniform, her mother, and of her sister and brother-in-law. I felt my eyes misting over with tears, a drop or two rolled down my cheek dripping onto my uniform. I closed the folder, reached over and downed the second shot of whiskey. I then lit one of my own cigarettes and looked at the First Sergeant.

"Fisher, I'm sorry, so frigging sorry," he said softly. He stood up walked around his desk and patted me on the shoulder.

"Why don't you take some time off, think about all of this, talk with Elona. Just don't make any hasty or stupid decisions. You have at least two weeks to make a decision, but you'll damn sure have to make this one!"

I reached up and patted his hand and said, "I understand, I know."

"May I have a ten day leave? I have lots of leave time accumulated, and this will take some time."

"Sure, whatever you decide I'll stand with you," he replied.

Handing him the folder, I stood up at attention, saluted him did an about face and left his office.

I went upstairs to my room and lay down on my bunk. Confused, I thought am I frigging jinxed? This is the second time I have loved and lost. What did I ever do to deserve this? Many of the other guys fall in love, get married and go home happy as a pig in shit, but not me. Since I arrived here almost four years ago, I've falling love with two beautiful women only to have both affairs blow up in my face. This tour has resulted in two broken hearts already, will there now be three?

I have to see Elona, but what can I say? What will I say, what should I say? What will she say? She hid all of this from me, and I have to know why. I realize I have some serious difficult decisions to make in the next several days. It was almost four in the afternoon when I got off my bunk. I walked down to the latrine and washed my face. I returned to my room, got my hat and headed for the club.

I was the only customer in the club as the manager had just opened it for business. I ordered a pitcher of beer from the waitress, found a table off in a quiet corner and sat down. As I sat there thoughts began racing through my mind in no particular order, just faster than I felt comfortable with. I would have to take into consideration the racial conditions that exist in my hometown, and in the entire South. As a son of the south, and understanding that part of the United States as I do, facing reality is one absolute requirement.

I knew that I wanted and needed to stay connected to my hometown of Lynell, even though I had left. That's where most of my family lives, and has always lived including me.

Today was the first time I'd seen Ironjaws exhibit any emotion other than anger or contempt. I also knew he had my best interest at heart. I knew he cared about me as a young soldier, and wanted only the best for me, and wanted me to make the right decisions.

I hoped that I would be able to make the best decision for myself, for Elona, and for the two children. I was glad that Ironjaws had demanded that I make this particular marriage decision. It's my choice, not some dumb-ass officer who knows nothing about me, about Elona, or about the South. I ordered another pitcher of beer.

My words to Ray about race relations in the south several months ago in the mess hall now returned to haunt me. I told him that the races didn't mix down South, I'd said that half-breed children wouldn't be accepted anywhere. That crosses would be burnt. I stated someone would likely get killed, and that would probably be me. That prospect didn't bother me, but the unfairness of it all was frustrating. I glanced around the room and noticed several soldiers had come into the club. I didn't know any of them, so I ignored them and they ignored me, that's what I wanted.

Then I saw Corporal Bell headed in my direction, the light reflecting off his half-bald head and ebony face. "Ken, is something wrong? What's going on?" he asked.

I smiled, "No nothing's wrong. I'll be on leave for the next ten days. Roberts will be in charge at the station, so you'll have to help out. He'll make out the schedule. You stay on the operators asses, and let me know if you have problems."

"Okay, I'll do it. Your girlfriend called twice. I told her I wasn't sure where you were. I have to go downtown, my girlfriend's waiting, and she gets pissed if I'm late," he replied.

I remarked, "You'd better hurry."

He got up from the table and said, "Have a ball on your leave."

"You can bet I will," I replied as he left.

I wondered if he too would have a little half-breed baby. What would happen to it? Would he take it back to the states? Bell's from South Carolina. When I took basic training there over three years ago I found they're like the rest of the South in their treatment and attitude about race. He would be stupid in my opinion to take a white wife, and a half black baby home. Catching the waitress's eye I ordered another pitcher of beer. The beer plus two shots of whiskey was having no effect on me, other than having to piss every twenty minutes.

I continued to sip my beer, smoke cigarettes and think about the immediate future. I didn't have much time to decide before I would be on a boat back to the states. I also knew that I had to be brutally honest with above all myself.

Although I could choose to settle elsewhere other than Alabama, I don't think that is realistic. I couldn't see me an undereducated southern boy in a strange northern city with limited funds, a wife and two kids, no trade and no job, as an acceptable option.

Realistically, and in my heart of hearts, I felt the decision was practically made. I couldn't and shouldn't move these little children to Alabama. Their lives would be miserable in my hometown. I visualized them in the small elementary school I'd attended. The teasing, taunts and insults from classmates would be deafening, degrading, and devastating for them. They would have no earthly idea what they were being harassed about. Even their inability to speak and understand English would contribute to and be a major handicap for them, and the community. Would the school board even permit them to attend any so called white public school?

I wouldn't permit them to be humiliated and subjected to that type denigration. The disrespect and contempt of the people in my community, and perhaps from my own family members would be devastating. Taking the two children to live in Lynell, Alabama would be a disaster just waiting to happen. I could marry Elona and we could go home, but we can't take the two children with us. On the other hand, what mother would abandon her children to follow a man to another country? How should I feel about that? To me, that would be contemptible and unacceptable behavior by any woman

No matter which way I look at this problem I'm screwed. I'm going to lose no matter what I decide to do. It seems an impossible situation.

I knew that Elona would be worried and wondering where am I. Why I wasn't returning her phone calls. But all that has to wait. I needed more time to wrestle with this nightmare before confronting her. It wasn't her fault, she didn't ask to be raped. Now I understand her reluctance to become involved with me, or to go to bed with me. Now it was clear why she never allowed me to take her home. All of a sudden it all began to make sense. Piece by bitter piece the puzzle came together. Even filling in the puzzle didn't furnish me an answer to my problem, what to do about the children?

I ordered one single beer. Finally, the alcohol began to take effect, and the drinking was catching up with me. I was getting loaded. I wanted the pain and uncertainty to be blotted out. It was time to go back to my barracks, so I finished my beer and left the club.

My Jeep was parked outside the company area, so I had left it there. Unsteadily, I stumbled down the street to my barracks, my mind and emotions numbed. I was overwhelmed with this last minute unbelievable news. I went straight to my room and lay down on my bunk. I dozed off but sleep did not come easily. Rolling over I kicked off my blanket, the room felt abnormally warm as sweat gathered on my forehead.

I loved Elona very much, but the children presented me with an impossible situation. Even through that are the results of a brutal rape, that doesn't change their color, and doesn't help in making a just decision. The booze seemed to tighten its grip on my mind. What would Elona say to me when she learns that I know about the children? Kids that were never mentioned, kids I was totally unaware of even though we are engaged. Our papers to get married are already approved. I only have to give the First Sergeant my decision to approve, and they would be finalized. I don't want to leave Elona, yet I dare not take two biracial children home with me. Not with the existing racial attitudes in my hometown, in my state, indeed, throughout the entire South.

Damn, damn, nothing, not anyone in my life, not my parents, my school teachers, not my military instructors, nor life experiences has taught or prepared me to make this type of decision, especially when it affects so many other lives.

Life with all it wondrous beauty can still be cruel and heartless. I realize life frequently presents us with difficult, disturbing, defining choices. Three years ago Rachel made her decision, and left me. Now life is presenting similar choices to me. When I make my decision about the twins, Elona will have to make her decision about us.

I can't begin to recall how many times as a boy I watched black people being ridiculed and humiliated. As a boy there was nothing I could do about it. Although I was embarrassed for them and hated it with a passion, as a boy I knew I couldn't stop or change it. So I had just kept my mouth shut, and my thoughts to myself. I was a good Son of the South.

Thinking about the twin's racial mix increased my fears. The thought of trying to rear and educate them in my hometown is frightening. Taking them home with me would be placing them at a tremendous disadvantage. They are just beginning their lives, and deserve the chance to succeed with no undue problems.

Eventually, my breathing slowed and I could feel myself falling asleep. Through a dream like haze I could see myself again as a small boy maybe nine or ten years old working in a cornfield with a black man I knew as Bob. Bob was middle aged, a sharecropper, and had three small children. Our neighbor, Mr. Belcher, had hired me to help Bob spread fertilizer around his corn. We arrived back at the loading wagon at the same time to refill our buckets with the commercial fertilizer. Mr. Belcher was standing there.

We both spoke to him, then Bob asked me, "How're you doing Ken? Do you need to take a rest?"

"No sir, I'm doing fine Mr. Bob. It's hot but we only have a little more to do today, so I'll make it," I replied.

Bob refilled his large bucket and returned to his area of the field. I finished filling my much smaller bucket.

Mr. Belcher said, “Boy, come over here, I want to talk to you.”

I sat my small bucket down and walked over to him. “Yes Sir?”

“Boy, I heard you saying Yes Sir and No Sir to Bob. I don’t like it. White people don’t say, Yes Sir and No Sir to black people. Do you understand that?”

Totally shocked, I looked at him and replied, “My grandpa told me to always say Yes Sir and No Sir to grown folks, so I ain’t done nothing wrong.”

A fierce scowl crossed his face, and he said, “That ain’t what your grandpa meant. He meant white people only.” His voice rising he continued, “If I hear you saying it again boy, I’ll send you home.”

That pissed me off, so I replied, “Mr. Belcher, I ain’t going against my grandpa’s teachings. People are people, and Bob’s color don’t make me no never mind, I quit!”

Grimacing, he reached into his pocket and gave me two half-dollars for two days work. I took them.

He said, “I’ll talk to your grandpa later.”

I left the corn field crossed the road and went home. I walked around to the back porch to find Papa.

Seeing me he said, “Ken, what are you doing home so early? Did you finish with the fertilizing?”

“No, Papa, I quit.”

A surprised but stern expression crossed his face, he asked, “Why did you do that?”

“Well, Mr. Belcher and I had a falling out about how I should talk to sharecropper Bob. He got mad and said I shouldn’t say ‘Yes Sir and No Sir’ to Bob”

Papa just looked at me without speaking, like he was thinking about what to say.

I spoke again and said, “Papa, you taught me to say Sir and Ma’m to grown folks, and that’s what I did today. If I was wrong, then you taught me wrong.”

Papa said, “Son, you did right, just keep doing and saying the right things and you won’t have any problems. Don’t worry about Mr. Belcher.”

I rolled over again. Elona, that's the south we would face if we go to Alabama. Mr. Belcher still lives where he did when that happened years ago,

Fully awake once more I rolled over and picked up my bottle of cognac and had a small sip. How in holy hell can this problem be resolved to everyone's satisfaction? My damn head hurts, and yet I'm no nearer to solving the problem of black and white kids than I was before.

A fitful sleep brought no peace of mind. The nightmares returned with a vengeance, with episodes of childhood incidents that I thought long forgotten. When I was a little boy maybe about six or seven years old, I saw a cross burning on a man's front yard in downtown Lynell. I was in the car with my grandpa and his brother, my uncle Charlie. My grandpa had stopped the car, and we watched the cross burn. I remember men with pointy hoods over their heads and faces walked around in the yard screaming bad things at the house. Their hoods and the burning cross scared me so I lay down in the backseat of the car and covered my face.

My uncle said to my grandpa, "It serves the man right, he shouldn't be whoring around with a black woman. I heer'ed he's got her pregnant."

I didn't know what he meant, so I just lay quietly and listened to their talk.

I heard my grandpa say, "If the man is very smart he'll get out of town in a hurry and keep looking back of him. The longer he hangs around the more the Klan is going to be after him. I heard yesterday that his old lady took the kids and moved back home with her ma and pa."

Uncle Charlie grunted and said, "There ain't nothing wrong with getting a wild piece of ass now and then. Chocolate nookie is pretty good, you jest can't flaunt it in front of people, especially in front of your old lady and expect to get away with it."

My grandpa spoke up and said, "Charlie, I never knew you slept with any black women! You were always a little wilder than the rest of us, but I never knew that."

Uncle Charlie laughed and said, "Well, back in the old days when I was a young buck, I did my share of hell raising and whoring around, and a little chocolate nookie now and then never hurt anyone."

My grandpa said, "Charlie, you oughta be ashamed of yourself to admit to such a thing, at least your wife Lilly Mae never knew about any of that."

Grandpa started the car moving again, and I got up on the backseat to look out the window. The cross was still burning. Black smoke curled upwards racing across the sky. We drove on until it was out of sight, but I never forgot the incident, or how scared those men with the hoods made me.

That's the Alabama that I remember and know. That was the attitude of most of the elderly town people. The very idea of taking Elona's two children home with me to Alabama is crazy and scary.

I rolled over in my bunk and realized that I could never get her to understand the present day racial attitudes that saturated the south, and specifically my hometown. The Civil War is long over, but the race problem is still there.

I love Elona and the idea of leaving her here is unacceptable, but the kids what about the kids? The people down south wouldn't accept them, or accept her as their mother or me as their step father. Nevertheless, Ironjaws will demand my decision soon, and time is closing in on me.

I woke up early in the morning with my head throbbing. In fact I hurt all over, as if I'd been beaten. My stomach churned. I must have recalled half of my childhood last night. What frigging nightmares! In the latrine I looked in the mirror, my eyes were red and sunken. I showered, shaved and finished dressing and went for a bite to eat. I met Roberts and Taylor at breakfast. They were all excited at the idea of us going home on the same boat. Just thinking about it did stir a sense of excitement. I went to the radio room and checked things out. Bell had things well in hand and there were no problems.

I called Elona at her office. She was frustrated and wanted to know where I'd been, and why I didn't call her last night. I explained that I had drunk too much beer and had gone to bed early.

I said, "I'll meet you later this evening at the Inn and get us a room." She reluctantly agreed.

I spent the day just sitting around thinking about my problems. I went up to the service club and played a solitary game of pool. I sat on the couch where Dotty and I had made love so many times. I ran my hand across the couch feeling the leather, memories crowding my mind about her, and I wondered if she were still in Germany. I 'm older now, but I don't feel a damn bit wiser. Rachel and I parted under different and unplanned circumstances, and it broke our hearts. Are Elona and I destined for the same fate? Am I frigging jinxed?

CHAPTER 22

The explanation

Back at the barracks I showered and dressed, splashed on a dash of after shave lotion and left. I arrived early at the Inn, obtained and paid for a room then I went to the bar to wait for Elona.

Shortly thereafter Elona came into the bar. She came to where I was sitting and kissed me on the cheek.

She said, "I've been so worried about you. You didn't call me back and I had bad thoughts."

I pulled her close and gave her a hug holding her tight and replied, "Don't worry sweetheart, I'm fine. I love you Miss Haufmann."

She sat down on the stool next to me, and I ordered her a glass of white wine and another beer for myself. We talked for a while then I suggested we go back to our room. I paid the bar bill, then we strolled to our room and went inside.

Once inside the room she turned around and threw her arms around my neck and said, "My darling, don't do this to me, not calling. I was worried sick."

I hugged her lightly and replied, "Please don't get so upset, it was just me and a few of the guys drinking, and I had too much to drink."

I knew that I couldn't talk about marriage and kids tonight. Tonight I determined would be ours for love. I wanted to enjoy the pleasure of our young bodies without the unwanted baggage of marriage, half-breed children, and decision deadlines.

She said, "Let's get in the tub and take a bath, I need one."

"Okay, let's get undressed."

I got up and removed all my clothing. I drew moderate hot water in the tub and she stepped into the tub first. I followed her and we sat down and splashed water on each other then soaped up and washed it all off. We got out of the tub and dried each other off and hung the towels up to dry. I sat down in the big chair and gently pulled her over on my lap. I kissed her and stroked her hair then held her close. My problem however continued to push to the front of my mind.

She leaned back, looked at me and said, "What's the matter Ken? You are so quiet, you seem different, what's the matter?"

"It's nothing really, I'm just a little hung over."

She pushed my hair back. I felt like a doomed man. She kissed my forehead, holding me close comforting me. I felt lousy.

I pulled her close and caressed her breasts and body, running my fingers through her hair kissing her face and lips. To me she was so beautiful. I thought again she looks just like that young lovely movie star Elizabeth Taylor. Elona's violet eyes, the full lips, her porcelain skin, the lush black hair even her figure, all were breath taking. Could I ever leave this woman I asked myself? Lord, you have certainly given me a problem that I might not be able to solve, a test that I might not be able to pass.

My ever ready dick seemingly sensing my problems, was not responding in its usual fashion. Dormant, asleep, ignoring the fact that such a beautiful woman was on my lap, it just lay immobile. What in the hell is happening to me I asked myself?

I asked Elona to turn around and sit on my lap facing me. She got up and straddled my legs. A few moves, and that did the trick. We wound up in bed and did what comes naturally to young lovers. Eventually, I got up and sat in the chair and sipped the rest of my first beer, then opened the second and had a swallow.

Setting up in the bed, Elona asked, "What's really the matter Ken?"

"There's nothing the matter sweet thing. I guess I still feel the effects of last night's beer drinking. Let's get dressed and go have a bite to eat."

"Fine, let's do that," she replied.

As we were eating in the bar area, Hodes and his girlfriend came in and joined us. The two girls began conversing in German, while Hodes and I had a casual conversation.

Hodes asked, "Ken, when's the big day? Am I invited to your wedding?"

I looked at him, and the girls immediately stopped talking. I frantically thought about an answer. Finally, I said, "We haven't set the exact day yet, and of course you're invited. You can be my best man."

"Well, best you set the date. We don't have that much time left before we go up the old gangplank."

I smiled and thought, hell, I feel like I'm walking off a damn gangplank.

We had another drink with them, and I suggested to Elona we go back to our room. We told them good night and left the bar area.

Back in our room Elona said, "Ken, there's something wrong. You're not yourself. You're very quiet, you seem preoccupied and worried. I don't know exactly why, but I can sense that something is bothering you. Did our papers come back yet?"

I looked at her and replied, "Yes, they came back yesterday. The First Sergeant has them. They only need the Company Commander's signature to be final."

She asked, "Are they approved?"

"No, they are not yet finalized."

Softly she asked, "Have you seen the papers yet?"

"Yes, I read them. They basically tell the story of your life."

Barely audible she asked, "Everything?"

I nodded my head yes, I did not want this conversation to go any further.

Her head sank and she began to cry, tears ran down her cheeks dripping onto her blouse. She said, "Then you know everything that happened."

I nodded my head, at a loss for words. I got up and pulled her close to me and hugged her. I pulled my handkerchief from my pocket to wipe away her tears.

"Don't cry darling," I said.

Words began pouring out of her mouth. "It was horrible. That big black soldier caught me and threw me to the ground. He held me down and ripped my clothes off then raped me. I couldn't get up, and he wouldn't stop. He left me lying there naked in the dirt. My vagina and legs, and my face and arms were bleeding. An old woman found me and took me home. They caught the man and sent him to jail, but that didn't change what had happened to me. I was so sick and afraid."

She was almost hysterical, tears now flooding down her face. I felt totally helpless. "Why didn't you get an abortion?" I asked.

She replied, "I didn't know I was pregnant until eight weeks later. I didn't even know what an abortion was. My mother was very sick then, and I had no one to care for her except me, and no one to ask for help. So I stayed with her until she died. By then it was too late for me, I was in my fifth month. I had no money, and there were no doctors in Kissingen as the war was just over."

"Elona, why didn't you tell me months ago? Why did you hide all of this from me?"

"I couldn't, I was too ashamed and too scared. I didn't want to lose you, so I didn't dare tell you. I was afraid you would reject me, or be ashamed of me and leave me. I thought I could find some way to let you know the whole story of what happened, but we never really talked, not like this."

"Elona, I've seen pictures of the children. They're beautiful little children."

"Now that you know, when we get married and go to America we will all go together as a family."

She, I realized had just exposed and laid bare the very core of our problem.

"Elona, we have to talk about this. I'm not sure that's possible."

She looked at me and asked, "What do you mean? I know a few women who married soldiers, they had children, and all of them left for America together."

I sat silent for a moment. I wasn't sure how to define, describe and detail explain the problems that I knew awaited us if we all went to Alabama together.

Finally, I said, "Darling, there is a difference. Your two children are a mixture of the white and black races. They wouldn't be accepted in my part of the country. They wouldn't be treated right. People there would hate them. They might not be able to go to a white school, or to a white church, or have white playmates of their own age. The schools for black children don't provide the best of education, so they can't go there. Most people would damn you because of their skin color, even though they would never know it was the result of your being raped."

She looked at me in horror. "How can people be so cruel to little innocent children?" she asked in an excited voice.

I quickly realized that I was incapable of explaining to someone totally ignorant of such things as black and white race relations, and how it exists in the South. I just raised and dropped my hands.

"Elona, I can't fully explain these things. All I can do is tell you that this racial intolerance exists in my hometown, in my state, indeed in all of the southern states of the United States."

I drank a large swallow of my beer. Our problem was now in the open in spite of my desire not to discuss it tonight. I realized that it was just as well, we had to discuss it sooner or later. We have to face the situation together, and we have to make a decision together based on realistic facts not desires.

For the next two weeks she and I discussed the racial problem. I tried to the best of my ability to explain to her the racial temperament and attitudes of southern people in the United States. I even attempted to explain to her the American Civil War, what led up to it, the fallout from it, and its long-lived aftermath.

I quickly realized that she couldn't comprehend the viciousness of some white people, or how blacks were viewed and treated in the South, and even in many of the northern cities and states. I also couldn't tell her that Hitler's Germany had viewed the Jewish people in much the same way, and the horrible outcome as their insane hatreds played out across Europe. She was just a child in those Holocaust years, and would neither comprehend, nor believe it happened here in her country.

During one of our discussions she said, "Ken, please meet the children. You must do this. You cannot and should not make a decision affecting all of our lives before you ever meet them!"

I knew that she was right, but I really didn't want to see the children. I had seen pictures of them. She finally convinced me to meet them. We agreed that she should bring them to the park in downtown Wurzburg at two o'clock the next day.

The following morning I went to the PX and bought a couple of appropriate children's toys and several candy bars. With a sense of foreboding and dread, I drove downtown to the park. I saw her sitting on the edge of the small fountain with the two children playing and splashing their hands in the water. I parked the Jeep, and with the toys and candy in hand I walked over to her.

She stood up as I walked up to her. I gave her a quick kiss on the cheek. The children stopped playing in the water and stared at me.

I said, "Hi kids, what are you two doing?"

They just stared at me. Oops! I forgot the kids didn't understand English.

I turned to Elona and said, "Honey, here are a couple of toys and some candy bars, will you give it to them for me?"

She took the candy and spoke in German to them. They quickly took the toys and candy. I picked up the little girl and kissed her cheek. She stared at me as she tore the paper from the chocolate candy bar. I studied her in some detail. She had dark eyes and a combination of straight and curly hair. Her skin was much darker than that of a totally white child. There was absolutely no mistaking that one parent had been black. I put her down. She was obviously enjoying the candy. I looked at the little boy, he had similar racial characteristics.

I turned to Elona, "Honey, they are darling little children. I would take them with me in a minute and love them dearly, but the people in my hometown would hate them, and hate you and me for bringing them there."

Tears immediately began to form in her eyes.

"Darling, please don't cry, I'm desperately trying to figure something out for us. Crying does not help, and furnishes us no answers."

I drove her and the children to her sister's house, and then returned to the *Kaserne*. I felt absolutely rotten, just as if I had cheated someone.

I begged her to consider leaving the children with her sister, to marry me and leave Germany. She remained adamant, she wouldn't abandon the children! Her sister had two small children of her own and couldn't manage two more, especially since they weren't hers.

She said, "I can't ask her to do that, and I cannot and will not leave my babies!"

I felt the pressure that we were running out of time. Although we loved each other, we both faced the brutal realization it was an impossible problem if I planned for us to move to and live in Alabama. My powers of persuasion were exhausted, I was exhausted.

Saturday morning I was off leave and had to stand a weekly stand-by barracks inspection, it was a snap for me as I had stood so many of them. As the First Sergeant left my room, he turned and said, "I want to see you in my office at one o'clock today Corporal Fisher."

"Yes Sir, First Sergeant."

After the inspection Hodes and I walked over to the snack bar and had a cup of coffee. Bell and one of the new radio operators who was also black joined us at the table.

After a sip of coffee, Bell asked me, "Ken, do you want to sell your Jeep:"

"Sure, do you want to buy it?"

"Yeah, how much do you want for it?"

"Make me an offer."

"I'll give you three hundred dollars cold cash for it."

I had a swallow of coffee, and appeared deep in thought as I weighed his offer. I said, "Make it three fifty and you have a deal, I'll even throw in forty-five gallons of gas coupons."

Smiling broadly he said, "Deal!"

We shook hands. He pulled out his wallet and counted out exactly three hundred and fifty dollars in script. I gave him my gas book, the key, and told him where it was parked.

Actually, I had completely forgotten about selling the Jeep. I was about to get caught like Corporal Sherron had been a couple of years ago. I was a little stunned that I had allowed myself to forget all about getting rid of our Jeep.

I guess with all my conscious thoughts on Elona and the twins, the Jeep had just slipped my mind. I'm really happy that Bell wanted and bought the Jeep. He eliminated what would have been a frantic effort on my part to sell it, and at the least advantageous moment.

CHAPTER 23

The Sword of Damocles

I glanced at my watch, it was a quarter till one.

"Hodes, I have to see Ironjaws, so I've got to leave."

"Good luck, I'll see you in the club this evening," he said.

I walked outside the snack bar, stopping, I looked around the quadrangle. It was all so familiar. I have been here since December 1948, and I know every foot of the area. I think in some weird way, I'm attached to the place, it has become home.

I looked across the area and could see our old barracks and the enlisted men's club where I had gotten really drunk for the first time in my life. I also realized that I was deliberately stalling. I dreaded having to see the First Sergeant this afternoon. I know he will expect my decision about marrying Elona today, and I will have to give him my answer.

Walking towards the barracks I agonized over what I would say to him, I truly wasn't sure in my own mind what decision I would make. I had wrestled so long and so hard over the issue of the kids. Kids are kids, they're the same all over the world, innocent and delightful. But they also have to fit into the society in which they live. Her children would never be able to do that if they lived in my hometown. Even as adults they would be shunned, unable to fit in with the while society, and neither with the black society. Being white myself they would have to be in my society.

I had talked so long with Elona trying to explain the racial atmosphere as it exists today, 1952, in the entire South. The US military has integrated, but Lynell, Alabama, has not. I have been unable to explain to her how dangerous I know it to be. In the South the racial culture extends even to ones state of mind. There is an unspoken, ineffable ethereal quality to it that's recognized and acknowledged by both whites and blacks—even if a word is never spoken—how in hell can anyone explain that?

Walking very slowly, I recalled how we met and later fell in love. I remembered all the good times and fun we had shared and enjoyed together. It has only been these past few weeks that our plans seemed to fall apart. Perhaps, I haven't been smart enough to adequately explain all the inherent difficulties existing in my hometown environment.

Her refusal to leave the two children with her sister here in Germany is the decision I truly expected her to make. In spite of my pleas and begging she was adamant. I admired her for her steadfastness, and that quality of motherhood that exceeds all others.

Had she done as I requested that decision would have haunted us for the rest of our lives. I know she would never truly be happy knowing that she left her two children behind in Germany, no matter the father. Even if we had other children they couldn't replace the twins. I understand it somewhat, because I wanted to see my son Kenny and I've never even had the chance to hold him. But I think about him often.

I suppose that I will always have to wonder what the boy looks like, what type man he will be, what his temperament is, and what directions his life will take. The only consolation I can muster is the situation is one that I didn't create. Rachel in her desperate search for safety and security made that decision. Now, she and I and the boy will have to live with it.

What a strange twist my life has taken. Worrying and wondering over a boy I've never seen, will never see, and headed for a meeting with the First Sergeant to make a lifelong decision about two baby half black kids that belong to the woman I now love. I can't lie to myself, and I haven't lied to Elona. I tried my best to explain what turned out to be for me unexplainable.

Slowly, I walked on towards Ironjaw's office, my mental state a nightmarish jumble of thoughts and emotions. I knocked on his door and heard him tell me to come in. I walked up to his desk, saluted and reported. He motioned me to sit in a chair next to his desk. I removed my hat and sat in the chair.

He looked at me and asked, "How was your leave?"

"It was fine, but the problems I have aren't resolved."

He nodded and said, "That's too bad, you and I are running out of frigging time for problem solving. We both will have our asses out of here and on a boat in less than two weeks."

I nodded my head in agreement, and looked at the folder on his desk holding my marriage application. He reached into his desk drawer and pulled out his bottle of bourbon whiskey.

Looking at me he asked, "Do you want a shot of some good stuff?"

"Yes First Sergeant, I would appreciate that."

He filled two shot glasses and pushed one over to me. I picked up the one and had a small sip of the whiskey, it burned my throat as it went down.

"Smoke'em if you've got'em," he said.

He lit a filter tip cigarette, and I lit one of my stronger ones and took a deep puff. I felt myself getting very nervous because I knew this was his way of telling me to relax, but I want an answer on the marriage issue. I downed the remainder of my shot.

He began extolling all the fine qualities of Tennessee bourbon whiskey. How it made a man smarter, and even added to his sexual capabilities. He explained the type of grains and the percentage of corn and mash from which it was made, and the type of wood they used to cook and age it with. I knew he was still trying to put me at ease, and I truly appreciated it. He then switched his conversation to the Army and military psychology.

"Fisher, there is a frigging system in the army that everyone has to go through if he stays in the military. You enlist and go through your early years, having fun and raising hell. You make a few stripes and lose a few, and have a lot of good times even if it's in wartime. But those wild oats are sown quickly, and you begin to grow up. One day you wake up and seemingly out of the wild-ass blue you understand the need for training and inspections. You even understand why short-arm inspections are conducted and are necessary. Then you'll want to get promoted, more pay, more stripes and responsibilities. You seek responsibility, and are responsible for your actions. You understand discipline, you give it, and you damn well demand it of your subordinates. You want to be all that you can be. You know almost everything about the army, you understand it all, and you finally join in making the system work. It becomes your life, and then you are part of the system. At that point, you are a professional soldier! Do you understand that?"

"Yes First Sergeant, I think I do."

He pushed the folder towards me and asked, "What's my recommendation to the Old Man?"

I picked up the folder and opened it. I reviewed the papers once again, looked at the pictures, and felt my eyes misting over.

"Take your time."

Then he said, "There is a fucking solution, you can immediately reenlist! The United States Army is the most democratic institution in the world. No one will ever question you, your wife, or the children. Skin color no longer matters, and the full authority of the United States government enforces that policy. Even if you reenlist today it's so late you wouldn't be able to get them on your travel orders for the states, but they could join you later somewhere."

The Sword of Damocles hung over my head. That long dreaded moment when I had to make a decision had arrived. With my heart breaking, and hands trembling, I took all the papers out of the folder and slowly tore them up, dropping them into the paper container beside his desk.

He poured us another shot of Tennessee's finest whiskey. He stood up and said, "Let's drink to the United States Army, and to its soldiers." Raising our shot glasses and lightly touching them together we drank the shots down without stopping,

He glanced at his watch and said, "The club's open, what say we go over and down a few for the road?"

"That's a great suggestion First Sergeant."

We left his office and walked down the street to the club. We found a table and he ordered us a drink. I requested cognac with cola, and he continued with bourbon and water. We didn't talk very much, just sat and watched the crowd. No one other than the waitress approached out table. Several of my friends were also there, but they stayed away from our table. I guess we had four or five drinks each over the next two hours, just sitting and watching the crowd and the few couples dancing to the jukebox.

Finally, Ironjaws spoke and asked, "Fisher, are you alright?"

"Yes, First Sergeant, I'm fine, getting a bit loaded, but I'll be fine."

He smiled at me and said, "All right, I'll be heading home now. I'll see you on Monday." He got up and pressed my shoulder in his huge hand and left the club.

After Ironjaws left, Hodes, Roberts, Taylor, Grady and Amato all joined me at the table. After exchanging greetings, I told them I wasn't getting married to Elona. I explained what had happened to her with the sordid rape episode. I explained it all and why I wasn't getting married. They seemed to understand why I couldn't take her two children to Alabama. I quickly pointed out that she was their mother, and would not leave without them.

Roberts spoke up and said, "I'm not sure the kids would be accepted back in my hometown in upstate New York either."

I ordered a pitcher of beer and glasses from the waitress. Everyone was quiet, seemingly absorbed in what I had related to them, as if they were analyzing what they might have done.

I was rather surprised at Robert's remark. He, Hodes and Amato were all three from up north. I knew they had their own conception, rather misconception of the South. To them it was a place of hillbillies, rednecks, and dumb asses.

Taylor patted me on the arm and said, "Ken, you're doing the right thing, they would never be accepted in Kentucky either."

Grady chimed in and said, "Ken, you and me are from the same hometown. There ain't no fucking way you could ever take those two little half-black kids home with you. The people would run all of you out of town so damn fast your frigging head would swim—if you got out alive—that is."

I looked at Grady and just nodded. Amato had nothing to say. I asked Roberts to call Elona and ask her to join us in the club. I gave him her home number, so he left and made the call. He returned to the table and told me he would meet her at the gate at six and bring her to the club.

I said, "It's almost six now you best leave."

He finished his beer then left, and within ten minutes he was back with Elona.

CHAPTER 24

Auf Weidersehen Germany

Elona walked in with a look of deep concern on her face, she appeared to have been crying. I stood up and gave her a brief kiss. She hugged me and kissed my cheek, tears welling up in her eyes.

I wiped them away and said, "Sweet thing, please don't do that. I'm hurting enough without seeing you cry also."

She replied, "I can't help it, life seems useless without you with me."

"Hush sweetheart, please sit down."

Grady said, "Ken, we've got to leave, we'll catch you later." I nodded in acknowledgement as Grady, Amato and Taylor left the table.

I ordered Elona a glass of white wine and a beer for me and the other guys. The band came into the club and began tuning up their instruments, and then left the stage.

"We haven't solved the problem of the children have we Elona?" She nodded her head in silent agreement.

"I'm leaving next week, I have no choice, I have to go!"

Again she nodded her head in silent agreement.

Robert and Hodes got up and told me they felt a wild evening coming on, and were headed down town for a last fling. Roberts stopped and turning around said, "I'll be back in time to take Elona to the gate."

"Thanks," I said acknowledging his statement. I pulled her closer to me. Sadly, we watched the people passing by laughing and having fun. I turned her face to mine and said, "Elona darling leaving you will be the hardest thing I've ever done. I'm not even sure if I can do it.

I love you more than I can tell. We're caught in a tragic, horrendous situation, not of my making or yours, but it is reality. If there is a way, I will come back, somehow, some way, I will come back to Germany."

She leaned over and kissed me. "I love you too Ken, you and the two children that I bore, no matter their father, are the most precious things in my life. Without you, I'm not sure of what I should do, but I must keep on for the children."

A little later I attempted to dance with her, but I was too tipsy to follow the music. So we returned to the table. I was drunk physically, but not mentally, there really is a difference. Time sped by and the band began to play, "Goodnight Sweetheart," the long time signal the club was closing.

Roberts came back for Elona, and we three walked outside the club. He had a Jeep, whose I didn't know. She climbed into the passenger seat. I leaned in and kissed her goodnight. "I'll call you tomorrow." She whispered, "All right."

Roberts started the Jeep and they drove away.

Sunday, Monday and Tuesday I didn't see her at all. She didn't answer my phone calls. On Tuesday I went to the finance office and exchanged all my marks and script for US Dollars. I bought a money order for one hundred seventy-five dollars and mailed it to Ray's address in Seattle, Washington, it was his half of the Jeep sale.

Finally, it was departure day. I got up at five o'clock, with my duffle bag all ready packed I went to the mess hall as soon as they opened, and ate a decent breakfast. Our train was due to leave at nine in the morning, so everyone had lots of time. Soon all the old guys came in, everyone who had arrived here with me four years ago was here. We all felt the exuberance and excitement of traveling and going home. I could even feel the excitement seeping through in spite of my sadness at leaving Elona.

They were all happy, talking and laughing. I wished that I could feel that happy, but I couldn't. I was the one unlucky son-of-a-bitch who had fallen in love not once, but twice, both times with incredibly beautiful women only to lose them both. I'm snake bitten! I shook my head as I thought about the past four years. I was just a kid when I arrived here, so young, happy and innocent. Now I feel older than dirt.

We all left the mess hall together, and moved back up the company street. A big bus was waiting to take about thirty of us down to the train station. We loaded our duffle bags into the baggage compartment down low on the side of the bus and slowly began boarding.

Seconds before I boarded, I heard someone call my name. I stopped and looked around and saw First Sergeant Ironjaws Baker walking towards me. He stopped in front of me, looked me in the eyes, took my hand and shook it. "Good luck Corporal Fisher,. You're a damn fine soldier!"

Damn, my eyes instantly misted over, I reached over and hugged the man. I said, "Take care old soldier, stay well my friend!" I turned and boarded the bus.

The big bus slowly pulled away. As we traveled through the post I looked at the antenna pole that I had been trapped on a couple of years earlier, and at the ugly steel covers protecting the windows of the message center and radio room. Out the gate and down the hill, the same streets we traveled in 1948. Most of the bombed out houses and buildings had been removed, and new construction well under way. The Marshall Plan is working here to be sure.

A million thoughts raced through my mind. Images of Rachel, Betty, and Dotty flooded my memory. They had all left, and now I was leaving, but Elona is staying, where in the hell is she?

Was Saturday night our last time together? Am I to leave without even seeing her again? Everyone was leaning out the windows, full of talk and laughter excited to be leaving, thrilled to be going home. Everyone it seemed had a bottle of cognac. They all began to drink, and I had a couple of small swallows when a bottle was passed my way. I really needed to numb this feeling of despair that hung over me.

At the station after off loading the bus we recovered our duffle bags, and waited to begin boarding the train. I looked around the station no one was there that I knew. Finally, someone shouted, "Load up," and the troops began to board the train. I waited until the very last, but finally I had to board.

I stood by a window close to the door and looked out. Taylor, Roberts and Hodes were in a seat close by. Grady, Amato and some other guys were in opposite facing seats. I had the most awful feeling that I can imagine, my emotions bankrupt, it was like the end of the world for me.

The train whistle blew. I looked out the window and saw a woman running towards the train, I knew it was Elona. She ran onto the platform frantically calling and looking for me. I leaned out the window and she saw me. She was crying, her arms reaching for me, our fingers barely touched. The train lurched forward and began its journey.

I hollowed out the window, "Elona wait, I'm coming!"

I think I went a little crazy. I turned and raced for the door thinking I'm going to get off. Screw the army, I can't do this, I can't leave her like this. Glancing quickly out the window I saw her sink to her knees her face buried in her hands.

Reaching the door I turned the handle, just as I was about to jump, I was jerked violently backwards. Taylor and Hodes had grabbed me and threw me to the floor. I struggled, kicking, and cursing them to hell and back, but to no avail. The train quickly picked up speed, finally they released me and I stood up. Looking back out the window in the distance I saw her small figure still on her knees. The train rounded a curve, Elona and the station were no longer visible. I felt sick to my stomach and thought I might puke right here in the door.

I looked up toward the sky and silently asked God why was I being punished this way? I didn't deserve this. I received no answer.

I found a space next to Roberts and sat down. H e handed me his bottle of cognac, I took a sip and returned it. Grady came by and said a few words to me, nothing important, just trying to cheer me up I guess. Taylor came by and said, "Let's go stand in the doorway."

I got up and we went to door and watched the countryside speed by. A guy came through passing out box lunches. We each took one. Naturally, it contained fried chicken, bread and an apple. I wasn't hungry but I had no idea when we would get our next meal, so I slid it beneath my seat. Taylor had a bottle of five star cognac and offered me a drink. I accepted his offer and had a large swallow.

"Thanks Jack, I needed that." He smiled, and had a swallow twice as big as mine.

The troops were talking incessantly it was like a game. What they were going to do first when they got back home. I began to think about that idea also.

What would I do first? What plan did I have, would I go to work in the mill? Would I be like everyone else that I knew who had been in the service and returned home. Get a job, get married, have kids, live a humdrum existence, live and die unknown and unsung in my hometown. Have I already had the great adventure and experiences of my life? Are my happy carefree traveling days over? Is this all in keeping within the great scheme of things? I think not! Dark, disturbing thoughts filled my mind as the wheels beneath me gobbled up the miles.

Many long hours later we finally arrived in Bremerhaven. We unloaded and after roll call we went up the gangplank and boarded the ship. A Sergeant on the deck told us which compartments we were assigned to. It all had a very familiar sound and feeling to it. My group selected our hammocks, and put up our duffle bags. Basically nothing had changed since our boat trip over almost four years ago. We followed the same routines back to the states as we had coming over. We had guard duty, clean up details, and of course trying to avoid the puddles of vomit in the stairwells and latrines. Card games were everywhere. I played a few games of hearts and some penny poker nothing serious.

Ten days later across the horizon the United States mainland came into view. We sailed pass the Statue of Liberty and docked in New York. Several dozens of people were on the docks waving and yelling up to the troops who were crowding the deck rails. Some of the soldiers apparently recognized their relatives who were waving and shouting. It was indeed, a most pleasant scene.

We finally made it off the boat and loaded onto buses to Fort Dix, New Jersey. There we were billeted and given instructions as to what we could and could not do.

The next day we were given passes, so Taylor, Hodes, Grady, Amato, and Roberts and I all went into Wrightstown to find a bar. We found one and harassed the waitress all in good humor. By midnight we were all three sheets in the wind. We caught a taxi and headed back to the fort. I was shocked at the high cost for beer, whiskey and cigarettes. Being away for almost four years from stateside bars had warped all my recollection of stateside prices.

The next morning we all went to breakfast together. After eating we sat around smoked, and talked about what to expect next. Taylor had orders for Fort Knox, Kentucky, so he knew where he was going. Roberts was waiting for his new assignment orders. Amato, Hodes, Grady and I were all getting out of the Army. Everyone exchanged home addresses, and swore to stay in touch with each other.

On Monday morning we had a formation in front of the barracks. There were five barracks filled with troops from our ship. They called out our names and told us to go see the personnel clerk in one of the buildings to get bus or train tickets and receive instructions on movement to our next post. Grady and I were issued bus tickets to Columbus, Georgia, and were departing that afternoon.

Back at the barracks we all met again to say our goodbyes. We pledged once again to stay in touch, just like Ray, Ed, and all the others had when they left.

Grady and I caught a military bus along with about thirty other soldiers that transported us to the local bus station. There we caught a south bound bus for Columbus and Fort Benning, Georgia. I had a window seat on the bus, and just sat quietly and viewed the countryside as we passed through state after state. We arrived in Columbus, Georgia, the following morning, and a military bus was waiting for us.

Dismounting from the bus, I stretched and looked around the station. It was apparent that nothing had changed in the South. There were still separate waiting rooms for whites and blacks. Separate drinking fountains and restrooms. The thought passed through my mind that even though the armed forces have become integrated, the South has not. The idea of racial integration hasn't even been considered. We boarded the military bus and were soon at the Fort. We checked into a replacement company and were assigned barracks, then told to draw bedding from a supply room. We did all that then found a mess hall and had a very decent meal.

The next morning we had a formation and were instructed to go to the personnel office where we would be briefed on our discharge dates, our GI Bill benefits, and review our personnel files. Grady and I were to be discharged that Thursday, which was the last day of the month.

We goofed off for about a day then we went back to personnel and received our final pay and allowances. We both received three hundred dollars mustering out pay. They gave us our Army form DD-214, and told us it was our most important document to protect it at all costs. We were then given our honorable discharges, and a bus ride back to the Columbus bus station.

I was out of the army at last. Almost four years has flown by since I first enlisted.

Korea was still a hot topic in the news, but peace talks had been initiated between the major parties involved. I apparently wouldn't be involved in that war. I guess I have missed my last big chance to fight for my country.

Grady and I bought bus tickets to Lynell, Alabama. We boarded the bus and sat quietly. We both were contemplating our futures, and perhaps reviewing our past. The roughly thirty-five miles between the two towns sped by rapidly. After numerous stops along the way we finally arrived in Lynell.

We along with most of the other passengers got off the bus. People rushed to grab their bags and suitcases. I just stood watching them and waited.

Grady and I finally recovered our duffle bags, and then shook hands first as welcome home, and then goodbye.

Grady said, "I'm happy to be back home, I'll come out and see you next week."

"Great, I'll be looking forward to seeing you. Take care."

Grady caught a taxi and left. I stood there for a few minutes longer getting reacquainted with the area. Nothing had really changed very much that I could tell. The bus station still had the same separate waiting rooms, separate bathrooms and drinking fountains, one for the white people, and one for colored people. The entire area looked run down, seedy and trashy. I knew for a fact that I had most definitely changed.

I thought what if I had brought Elona and the two kids back with me. What would be my next move? What would I do? Where would I go first?

The hot July sun was blazing down, and I was beginning to sweat. I shrugged my shoulders and admonished myself, as I knew it was wrong to think about what might have happened. I had to believe that I had made the right decision. Thinking otherwise would drive me nuts. I checked my wallet, I had a little over four hundred dollars. What would I have done with a wife and two kids, and so little money? Damn, I have to stop questioning myself like this!

CHAPTER 25

Home

I looked around for a taxi, and as I did one pulled into the bus driveway. The lettering on its side identified it as the 'Veteran's cab Co.' How appropriate I thought, after all I am now an army veteran.

I got into the cab and gave the driver instructions on how to get to my grandfather's house. I had found out it wasn't actually my grandfather's house. It was to my uncle's house I wanted to go. The old home place had been sold, and now he lived with his son and his family. My granddad had had a stroke which greatly reduced his ability to walk and talk.

The driver followed my instructions, and we quickly covered the four miles between town and the rural community where I had lived. We arrived at the large intersection where on the left was the little elementary school I had attended years ago, and on the right the local gas station and convenience store. I requested the driver to continue on straight and to drive a little slower. He seemed to sense that I had been gone for some time, so he slowed his speed considerably.

I saw that the one room barber shop on the corner had now become a relic, the roof caved in, windows missing and the door sagging lifelessly. Dying, decaying, dead, it sat alone in the field. Cotton and corn fields on both sides of the road were wilting in the hot summer sun. We drove past the old homestead and it appeared to be the same as when I left. Children were playing in the front yard, so some other family now lived there. The cotton fields that I had once plowed planted, and picked cotton now lay bare and fallow. I asked the driver to turn around and take me back to the large intersection. He did as I requested. I got out of the cab and paid the driver. He wished me luck and sped away. I took a moment to reacquaint myself with the area, I then picked up my duffle bag which contained all my earthly belongings, and walked down the road the short distance to where I knew my uncle lived.

I saw my grandfather sitting on the small front porch in a cane back rocking chair, a crutch on the floor beside him. He saw me as I got closer to the house and tried to stand up, he could not, but called out my name. I dropped my heavy duffle bag and ran onto the porch and grabbed my granddad in a bear hug and kissed his cheek and said, "Papa, I'm home, I'm really home!"

He held my hand and tried to speak, but he could hardly do so. He was home along. I went into the house got a chair and returned to the front porch and sat it alongside him. For about three hours we sat there with me doing most of the talking. Several cars passed the house, but I failed to recognize any of the occupants or drivers.

Papa said, "I'm going in and take a nap."

I assured him I would be there when he woke up. I opened the door for him and assisted him as he slowly made his way into the house. I walked over and turned on the television set and watched my first television program. It was absolutely amazing. I watched one show then turned it off.

I returned to sit on the porch. It was the first time in days, or perhaps years I was truly all by myself. No one to talk to or expected to respond to. I felt comfortable, but I could surely use an ice cold beer.

I had no civilian clothes, so I'll have to get some right away. That will be a strange feeling, as I haven't worn civilian clothes since I was at Fort Jackson four years ago. I'll also need shoes and socks, everything has to change.

Sitting there I recalled my motivation for going into the army. I wanted to travel and see as much as the world as I could, and to experience all the things this old world could offer me. I wanted to establish clearly defined personal goals for myself. Now sitting here, I don't have one damn clear goal, and no direction in my life. Where in the hell did I go wrong? I failed, and it's damn sure my own fault. Dejectedly, I thought three broken hearts isn't very much to show for four years of your life.

Shortly thereafter a school bus stopped in front of the house, and a small boy got off. He was my uncle's son. He had no idea who I was. I talked to him about an hour, then my aunt and uncle both arrived home from work. They were both employed in the cotton mill. We greeted each other in a display of love and affection. We hugged and kissed and all talked at the same time. Later that evening we sat in the small living room and talked until almost midnight. They both had to go to bed as they had to get up the next morning and go to work.

I slept on the couch that evening. I knew that I could stay with them as long as I wished, but there wasn't enough room, and it wouldn't be fair to them to do so.

But what to do was my major problem. I needed new clothes and a automobile as public buses did not run this far out. I sat every day on the porch with my granddad. We did not talk very much as it was exceedingly hard for him to do so for more than a few words. It gave me more than enough time to think about my past, and certainly about my future.

I also questioned what type of man am I? Was I really afraid of the racial climate here, or am I the one who is really prejudiced? Being from the south, reared in the south, do I have some deep seated subconscious prejudice that I neither recognize, nor dare admit? I should have married Elona and brought them all back here and told my relatives and the rest of the world to go screw themselves. But gutless me, I didn't!

I hung around the house all week talking with my grandfather and doing nothing. Saturday night my uncle and aunt took me to a restaurant down on the banks of the Chattahoochee River named the "Catfish House." I ate more fried catfish than the law should allow, and drank several Blue Ribbon beers. I think that restaurant serves the best food in the entire south. I brought a dozen beers back home with me

My uncle discussed my future, and wanted to know what I wanted and planned to do? I was truthful, and told him I truly did not know what I wanted.

He urged me to finish high school and to go on to college, and said that I could live with him until I completed school. I knew that I could do that using the GI Bill to pay for my tuition. It was a very kind offer, but I declined. I was twenty-two—years old now, but I didn't know what in hell I wanted to do with my life.

I went into town and bought some new clothes. I bought five pair of pants and cheap shirts, a pair of civilian shoes and some socks. I also had to buy a civilian belt and some underwear.

On Wednesday, Grady and a friend of his drove up to the house. We greeted each other, and he introduced his friend a guy named Jim.

Grady said, "Ken, let's go down to Bob Adam's beer joint and have a few."

I quickly agreed and said, "I could use one or better yet several cold ones."

In Jim's car we drove down some old country roads through the small town of Cusseta until we reached Lee country. My county was dry, and there was no alcohol to be had other than illegal bootleg moonshine. We reached Adam's beer joint and walked inside. I had been here years earlier long before I was old enough to drink. We sat on the stools, drank beer and talked all afternoon. Grady did most of the talking telling his friend all about his activities and experiences in Aschaffenburg and Wurzburg.

Grady had surprised the hell out of me. He had already gone to the employment office at the cotton mill and applied for a job, and had been hired as a loom doffer. He was to begin his new job the following Monday. While we were in the beer joint a white haired black man knocked on the back screen door.

The young bar clerk—a big fat slob—turned around and asked, "Whatta you want boy?"

The old man replied, "Bossman, I jest wants to buy a few beers."

The clerk snorted and arrogantly asked, "You got any money boy?"

The black man displayed his money and replied, "Yass sir bossman, I'se gots enough for six beers."

He wasn't allowed to come into the place, he could only stand out back and place his request through the screen door. I was pissed and embarrassed. I just bowed my head in disgust. Nothing has frigging changed, I wish I could tell Ironjaws that.

We all had a slight buzz on and decided we'd better leave while Jim could still drive safely. We drove back over those same old dirt country roads and arrived back at my uncle's house. I had bought a case of beer back with me. After having another beer each they had to leave. I shook hands with Jim and then with Grady.

"I'll check in with you in about two weeks," he said.

"That's great, be sure that you do. I'll need to see a friendly face by then." I never saw, or heard from Grady again.

I sat around well into my second week home doing nothing. I was in a funk and I knew it. The idea of going back to work in the cotton mill was absolutely revolting. It made me sick to my stomach. It wasn't the hard work, that didn't bother me. It was the monotonous total dead-end aspect of it that was repulsive. My choices however, seemed to narrow and shrink with each passing day.

I thought constantly about Elona, often about Rachel, and sometimes about Dotty and Betty. They had all played such a major role in my young life. Sitting here on this porch way down in Alabama it all seemed like a dream, something I had read about, not something that I had lived and experienced.

My uncle was compassionate and understanding and didn't push me to make an immediate decision. He had gone through a similar traumatic period back in 1945. My third week began much like the previous two with me still grappling with different ideas, trying to sort out my life and decide what I wanted to do, what direction to take.

I couldn't get the images of Elona on her knees at the train station, and of my two friends holding me down as I desperately tried to get off the train off my mind. It all appeared to be unreal, a nightmare in view of my present situation.

I heard a car pull into the driveway, so I got up and walked outside onto the porch. I almost fainted! It was John Hodes and another man. I jumped off the porch and grabbed him. We hugged each other both laughing with sheer joy. Words couldn't come fast enough as I wanted to know what in the hell he was doing way down here in Alabama, and why?

John looked so strange in his new civilian clothes. I'd never seen him other than in an army uniform. After we got over the shock and joy of seeing each other again he said, "Me and my buddy Steve are going to Miami Beach for a short vacation, and I decided to find you, and take you with us to Florida."

I couldn't believe it, John had driven all the way from Rochester, New York, and found me. I immediately said yes and agreed to go. I grabbed all my new clothes and stuffed them in with my uniforms in my duffle bag plus my shaving kit I was all set. This was an answer to part of my problem. John was to be my way out of my current situation.

I told Papa that I was going to Miami with my friends and would probably be back in a few weeks. I asked him to tell my aunt and uncle how very much I appreciated their letting me stay with them, and how much I thanked them for all their efforts. He assured me he would. I hugged his neck and kissed him. We jumped into Steve's car, and we were off for the beaches of South Florida.

After three flat tires, numerous wrong turns and detours, plus three cases of beer we finally arrived in Miami. We found a cheap hotel and rented a room for ten days and began to explore the city. Neither of us had ever been here, so it was all very new to us. We went to several nightclubs, numerous bars, and spent a small fortune on the taxi dancers.

John and Steve visited a couple of houses of ill repute that a taxi driver had recommended, but I passed it up. I just couldn't have sex in my present state of mind, Elona meant too much to me. One additional fact was I couldn't spend scarce money on a prostitute. We lay on the beach at Biscayne Bay and admired the ladies as they displayed their physical features. All in all we had a ball. One evening we drove over to Miami Beach to Martha Ray's Five O'clock club. It was fantastic but very expensive. John and Steve picked up a couple of college girls and took them to the beach. I went back to our hotel room.

Over on Miami Beach many of the hotels had signs out in front of their hotel stating, "No Military, no blacks or Jews permitted!" I found that to be utterly disgusting. I couldn't believe that here in America we had businesses that displayed that type of prejudice and bias.

Finally, our vacation came to an end. John and Steve had to return home, and I had to find a job. We said our goodbyes, and John and I swore once more to stay in touch.

They left and I checked my wallet to determine how much money I had left. I had fifty-nine dollars and some change. I had two paid up days left in the hotel. I had to find a job and fast.

I bought a newspaper and searched the help wanted ads. The Power Company was advertising for workers, so I caught a bus and went to their employment office. I was hired and told I would be working in their underground department. I had no idea what that was, but it was a job and that was what counted the most. I found out soon enough what the job was. The crew I was on had to dig ditches to lay cables through some of the hardest coral rock in the world. We started on top of the ground, and worked our way underground.

I became accustomed to swinging a fifty pound jack hammer around like a small tack hammer. It was the hardest work I had ever done in my life. It was harder than following behind a big ass mule plowing new ground. I lost weight and not wearing a shirt in the tropical sun I became as tan as any local Floridian.

On New Year's Eve 1952, I found myself sitting alone at a bar on Biscayne Boulevard in downtown Miami. I entertained myself by picking out the best looking of the taxi dancers and dancing with them. Ten cents a dance, but my heart just wasn't in it, and neither was theirs. The bar tender began counting down the seconds before midnight, finally he shouted, "Happy New Year," 1953, had arrived.

Seated at the bar and sipping a cold beer, I opened my indelible book of memories. I returned again to that year which seemed so impossibly long ago. Five years ago tonight, I had blown Rachel an imaginary kiss, she caught it and took it to her lips. We had loved each other so much. I thought did that really happen, or am I dreaming all this? In spite of our love we had allowed it to be taken away. I thought of Elona, Betty and Dotty, my mind filling and overflowing with images of past events and people.

I recalled First Sergeant Ironjaws Baker, how rough he was and of the aid and guidance he had given to me. I also remembered the harsh, bone-chilling ass chewing's he had also dealt out. I recalled him and me drinking straight shots of whiskey together as he tried to ease my pain and guide me through my decision making process about Elona and the twins. He was a very wise tough old combat soldier who tried to help a young immature soldier get through some rough times. I'll never forget him, and the lessons he taught me.

I thought of my young son Kenny, now living somewhere in Chicago. I hope he turns out well, and makes his mother proud that I am his father.

I had followed Rachel's instructions and had created this indelible book of memories, and dedicated a spot in my heart and memory to her and now to the boy. No one will ever be able to erase any pages from my memory book. I can open and close it at will and add pages to it, but even I cannot remove pages from it.

I ordered and drank a straight shot of cognac, the old familiar taste burned my throat, as even more memories surged forward.

I laughed as I recalled being stuck on the antenna pole wondering how I would ever get back to the ground safe and sound. I recalled my catching a dose of gonorrhea at the DP camp, and Betty taking me to the right doctor who cured me. Silently, I wished her and Earl her new husband well.

I recalled waking up in the hospital after our Jeep wreck, so hurt but yet so lucky. Never will I forget vivacious Dotty, and how we spend a weekend together enjoying our bodies, and the pleasure of each other's company. I wonder does she ever think about our affair, those carefree days and nights, and the fun we had together, or has she wiped me completely out of memory?

My beautiful Elona, how cruel life had treated her and us, perhaps also the twins. The image of her on her knees at the station, and my being thrown to the train floor are truly indelible. I can't erase them, and no longer want to. I ordered another straight shot of cognac.

Digging deeper into my memory book, I remembered my first visit to the Zugspitz, the magnificent views from atop the mountain, the cable car ride up and down the mountainside, the snow covered forest, and the joy I felt at being young and alive. I also remembered the Zugspitz Zombies, those treacherous drinks almost turned Ray and I both into zombies.

Seared into my memory book was Bertchesgaden with all its many ghosts. In memory's eye I could see once again the silent, shattered, shell-pocked emptiness of the Eagle's Nest. The once beautiful building that was Hitler's Alpine headquarters now totally destroyed. I recall the amount of graffiti on the walls and ceiling in the room where Hitler and Eva once danced. The magnificent panoramic view across the Alp mountain tops viewed through Hitler's huge glassless window. I remember seeing old black and white films of Hitler and Eva sitting on the rock wall, where my buddies and I had sat and drank beer all afternoon.

I felt rotten and I was beginning to feel my liquor, so I knew I'd better go back to my room. What a rotten ass New Year's Eve this one turned out to be, and I've only been out of the army about five months.

I wrote a couple of letters to Hodes, Ray and Sam Amato. After Hodes got back home he had gone to work for the telephone company. Ray was working in the aircraft factory out in Seattle, and Sam was working in an automobile factory once again making cars. Sam wrote back and asked me to come up to Buffalo and go to work with him. He told me he was making over a hundred dollars a week. That really sounded good as I was making less than fifty dollars a week in my underground job. It was an easy decision to make. Needing more money to move I wrote and told him I would save some money and then fly up.

I stayed and saved my money for six more weeks. I also went downtown and took the high school GED test as I had not graduated from high school before enlisting in the army. I passed with very high marks.

I had ten days vacation pay coming plus two weeks pay when I told them I was leaving the company. I collected all my pay and bought an airline ticket to Buffalo. That evening I called Sam and gave him my flight number and estimated time of arrival.

CHAPTER 26

A career decision

My first plane ride was to Buffalo, New York. I arrived at the airport and Sam was there to meet me. After much hand shaking and laughter we finally settled down. We went to the airport bar and had a couple of beers, and then caught a taxi to his house. He introduced me to his mom and dad and two brothers. His mom turned out to be a wonderful woman. She immediately liked me, after all I had spent some time with her mom and dad in Sicily. His father and both his brothers and I got along very well. His dad called me his second son.

In less than a week I found a job in the Aviation plant located in the suburb of Lackawanna. I also found a couple of fellow employees to ride back and forth to work with, things were definitely looking up. I made over a hundred dollars a week. I barely made more than that in a month in the Army.

Sam and I spent our spare time and weekends in and out of the bars chasing women and drinking booze. I enjoyed it all, but Elona was never but a thought away, she was always on my mind. It was a constant ache that I had no remedy for.

After about seven or eight months of screwing off it all began to wear thin. I continued to think about Elona and remembering my promise to her that I would return. It now seemed almost like another world—another place another time—and I guess it really was. I couldn't erase the images of us making love, or of her on her knees on the station platform.

One afternoon I was alone in a bar down on Main Street just drinking a beer, and contemplating my future. I found myself thinking more and more along certain lines of thought. I was twenty-three—years-old now, and needed to move on with my life. I could not continue to live with the Amato's and throw away all my money on booze and broads.

I ordered a fresh beer and remembered the things that Ironjaws had told me, especially the part about the military system, and what it demands from and of you before you become a part of it. The war in Korea is finished, truce talks had been going on for months and had resulted in a ceasefire agreement. I thought, maybe I should return to the Army, take a three year enlistment, and start all over again. It was the only avenue available to me that I knew of to return to Germany. Maybe just maybe, I can get back to Wurzburg and find Elona again.

I went to work on Monday and told my supervisor that I was quitting and leaving at the end of the week.

"What in the hell do you mean you're quitting? Where in the hell are you going? Why are you giving up a good paying job like this?"

"I'm reenlisting in the army."

"Fisher, you're frigging nuts! Korea is where they'll send you, and you'll get killed there, you're out of your dumb ass mind."

"I'm going back to Germany, maybe the long way around, but I'll get there,"

I didn't spend any more time justifying my actions. I didn't have to. I went home that night and met Sam. Then we went to one of our favorite bars, and had a couple of beers.

After several minutes of idle talk I said, "Sam, I'm pulling out of Buffalo. I'm going back into the army. Civilian life just isn't for me, not at this stage of my life."

A surprised look crossed his face, "Let me think about this overnight, hell I might go back in with you."

"Sam, you' re one of my best friends, you don't have to go, but do what you want to. Come Monday morning I'm reenlisting."

The next morning Sam and I got up and after we cleaned up his mom cooked us breakfast. I decided that I wouldn't go to work that day. I told Sam that I was going downtown and have a couple of beers that afternoon.

"I'll go with you, no 6087 man should ever have to drink alone," he said.

Sam told his mother that he and I were not going to work today. She got excited and started speaking to Sam in rapid Sicilian, which of course I couldn't understand a word she said. After about ten minutes of him listening to her and saying very little he said to me, "Let's go."

We walked out to Grant Street and caught the bus for downtown going to one of our favorite bars. I ordered us two beers.

"Sam, I have to go back to Germany. The memory of Elona is eating at me constantly. Nothing seems to matter; our affair isn't over for me. Civilian life holds no magic, the money is more than I've ever made, or had in my life, but I just throw it away. It doesn't mean that much, I spend it all on booze and women. What's the difference in our lifestyle here than when we were in Germany? You don't have to go, but I do!"

Sam gripped my shoulder and said, "Ken, I agree, let's do it, this civilian life is for the birds."

We shook hands on our decision.

CHAPTER 27

Reenlisting

On Monday morning Sam and I went to the recruiting station down town on Main Street. I pushed open the door and we walked in. I looked at the recruiting officer, well I'll be dipped in shit, it was Captain Tolliver from our old unit the 6087 SCU in Wurzburg. He recognized us both at the same time. He jumped up from his desk and came around the corner grabbed my hand shaking it, then Sam's.

"I hope you two guys are here to reenlist," he said.

"Yep, that's what we are here for," Sam replied.

I thought to myself, he must be a damn dud. He's still a Captain and in a recruiting station of all places. I assume the army doesn't think too highly of his combat and command potential.

"Captain Tolliver, I want to reenlist for Germany, and I want my Corporal's rank back."

"How long have you two been out of the army?' he asked.

"We were both discharged in July last year, it's now November, so that's roughly about sixteen months," I replied.

He frowned, "That's over a year, the best I can do is give you Private First Class Stripes."

Sam spoke up and said, "We'll take it. I don't want to go back to Germany, I want to go to Japan."

That stunned me. I thought Sam wanted to go back to Germany, but I had guessed wrong.

The Captain replied, "We can do that, you both can go wherever you want to go. I'll put it in your orders. After you reenlist you'll have to go to Fort Dix to take orientation training and get re-qualified on the infantry weapons, and then you'll be on your way."

I said, "Captain Tolliver, I don't want any screw-ups. I want to return to Germany. Fill out the paperwork and I'll sign them now."

He turned around and told his clerk to begin typing up our paperwork. The clerk a dumb ass Private looked at me and said, "So you want to go to Germany. Are you afraid of Korea?"

That really pissed me off. I reached over and grabbed him out of his swivel chair. I thought about slapping him, but instead I shoved him back into his chair.

"Private, you just do what the hell you are told to do. You are not required or expected to give your opinions or anything else. Your job is to take orders and just type, now do your frigging job. Do you understand?"

He just nodded his head, his face was pale with a scared look.

I added, "It's best you believe me!"

Captain Tolliver was speechless, he just stood there.

After two years of negotiations the Korean ceasefire had been signed on the twenty-seventh of July earlier this year. I had been in the army for most of that war, so I didn't need any smart ass lip from a dumb ass Private.

In about forty-five minutes all the paperwork was completed. Captain Tolliver read them over and gave a set for each of us to read. I read them carefully and made sure it stated I was reenlisting for Germany. I signed my papers, and so did Sam.

The Captain said, "Let's take the oath. Raise your right hands and repeat after me."

We both raised our right hands and repeated after him the oath that all soldiers take.

"I Kenneth Fisher do solemnly swear (or affirm) that I will support and defend the Constitution of the United States against all enemies, foreign and domestic; that I will bear true faith and allegiance to the same and that I will obey the orders of the President of the United States and the orders of the Officers appointed over me; according to regulations and the Uniform Code of Military Justice. So help me God!"

We had reenlisted for three years. I was back in the army, and on my way back to Germany. I'll find Elona again in Wurzburg her and the twins, and this time I won't let them go.

With the sure knowledge that I had done the right thing I felt a tremendous boost in my spirits and morale.

I turned to Sam and said, "Let's go to Fort Dix, I'm on my way back to Germany!"

Sam Amato and I shook hands. We had just reenlisted in the army for three years in the middle of November 1953. I was happy that we were able to regain the rank of Private First Class, after being out of the army for fifteen months. While a Private E-7 is at the bottom end of the chain of command, it's the base upon which you can build a military career. I'd been this rank before a couple of times, so I know what it takes to get promoted.

Standing there I thought, "Finally, I'll go back to Germany and find my sweetheart Elona. I don't give a damn what color her kids are. I promised her I'd return, and now I will.

After taking the oath of enlistment we both turned and shook hands with Captain Stanly Tolliver, as he congratulated us on reenlisting.

He said, "Why don't you guys go have a cup of coffee or a beer and come back in about forty-five minutes or so. We'll have your orders finished, and I'll have your bus tickets to Fort Dix, New Jersey, ready. Incidentally, what day do you want to leave Buffalo?"

Sam and I discussed the issue briefly.

"We'd like to leave one week from today, next Monday," I said.

"That's fine with me. Come back get your orders and tickets, and you're on your way," he replied.

We left the recruiting station and walked down Main Street to one of our favorite bars. It was too early for me to start on beer, or anything harder, so I ordered a soft drink.

Sam ordered a beer and exchanged small talk with the bar tender. I figured his stomach was tougher than mine. The bartender moved to wait on someone else, and we were silent for several minutes, sipping our drinks as the realization we were back in the Army began to fully sink in.

I thought about my family back in Alabama and Florida, wondering what they would think when I informed them that I was once again a member of Uncle Sam's military. I wondered also if my old friends John

Hodes or Ray Washington had reenlisted, or even considered doing so. I hadn't been in contact with either of them for several months, so I had no sure way of knowing. I thought about Pitts and Perry and my former roommate Ed Clarkston, and wondered if they were still in the military, or had they also gotten out of the Army, and faded back into the civilian world?

"Sam, how are you going to break the news to your mom and dad about being back in the Army?"

He appeared thoughtful for a moment then said, "I guess I'll have to come right out and tell them the truth. That'll give them a week to accept it, before we actually have to leave."

"That's probably the best way to deal with it. I just hope they don't blame me for you being back in the Army."

He laughed, "Well, we're both twenty-three-years-old now, and they know that I make my own decisions."

"I hope you're right."

Sam's mom took the news really hard. She cried and tried to get him to change his mind not knowing that it was too late. He was already on official military orders to report to Fort Dix. His dad was more realistic, and accepted the fact. He opened a gallon jug of his best homemade wine. The three of us managed to drink most of it that evening. I paid for that with an unbelievable headache the next day.

Sam and I called a few of the girls we knew to say farewell. We visited our favorite local bar on Saturday night to have a final drink with a couple of our friends, and called it a night.

Sunday we both packed our duffle bags. Then we got our uniforms ready to leave the next morning. I included a couple of pair of my nicer civilian pants and shirts, and a couple of pair of civilian socks in case the rules on civilian clothing had changed in Europe since I was there. I gave my civilian overcoat to his dad. Then I gave my three favorite phonograph albums to his brother. They were albums by Al Jolson, Mario Lanza, and Hank Snow.

Monday morning the family got up early. Sam's mom made us a big breakfast. While Sam expressed his goodbyes, I moved both his and my duffle bags out to the front porch. Sam's brother was there with his black Buick ready to take us to the bus station. I walked up the steps hugged his Mom and gave her a kiss on the cheek. She was crying as she hugged and kissed me.

I said, "Mrs. Amato, please don't worry, Sam and I will be fine. Besides, you won't have to make large breakfasts or dinners anymore."

Wiping her eyes with her small white apron, she smiled and said, "I love cooking for you two. Write us, and take care of yourself."

I shook hands with his dad and gave him a warm hug. "I'll write you and Mrs. Amato. I'll let you know where I am, and how I'm doing," then I left.

A few minutes later Sam joined me in the car, his brother slowly pulled away from the house. The trip took about fifteen minutes. We arrived at the bus station, unloaded our bags then shook hands and said good-bye to his brother.

We checked with the ticket clerk and confirmed we were to leave in twenty minutes. Boarding we found two seats in the back of the bus. We rapidly left the city of Buffalo, and headed toward Fort Dix, New Jersey.

"Sam, why did you choose to go to the Far East rather than return to Europe?" I asked.

"Well, I've been to Europe. I just want to go to another part of the world and see what it's like."

"I understand that. If I wasn't going back to find Elona, I'd go with you. I'm sure it's entirely different from occupation duty in Germany, it'll be a new world for you," I replied.

Sam and I still had Corporal stripes on our jackets. We finally arrived at the Fort Dix bus station. An army bus showed up and we boarded it. The driver drove us and four other new enlistees to a big administrative building where we were to be interviewed, and issued additional instructions on where to go and what to do.

We went through the in-processing procedures and were assigned to the same company. There we were issued some new and additional uniform items, and new boots and socks. We removed our corporal stripes from our jackets, and had new PFC stripes sewed on. I turned in my personal military records that I kept from my previous enlistment to the personnel clerk. Most of my old orders and field 201 file were intact, I wanted to have a continuous military record of my service for sure.

For the remainder of the month and into early December, we trained and re-qualified on all the small arm weapons the infantry used. Out on the rifle ranges the weather was horrible. Ice and snow covered the ground, and the temperature hovered around twenty-five degrees the day we qualified on the M-1 rifle. Lying on the frozen ground trying to aim a rifle at a small bull's eye target five hundred yards away was a nightmare. I squeezed the rounds off, and the guy at the target waved his red flag indicating that I had a Maggies Drawers. Simply put, I had missed the whole damn target. By the time I finished firing my second clip in the rifle I began hitting the target. By the end of the day—in spite of the cold—I had regained my expert rifle marksmanship status.

Eventually, we completed the orientation training and reported to personnel for new assignment orders. We were being released early to accommodate the pending holidays. I expected to have orders reassigning me to Germany, instead I received a devastating surprise.

`The personnel clerk said, "The Army won't honor your reenlistment request. We'll assign you based on Army needs."

I argued, "You're frigging wrong, my reenlistment orders say Germany."

He laughed and said, "See the Personnel Officer."

I told the personnel officer that I had specifically reenlisted for Germany. All my arguments were to no avail, they fell on deaf ears. I received new orders assigning me to a Signal company located at Fort Devens, Massachusetts. I was given seven days travel time, and received one month's pay plus travel expenses.

They honored Sam's request for Japan. Sam received his new orders to report to Fort Lewis, Washington, for further movement to Japan. He decided to forego any leave, and report in to Fort Lewis. The Army also gave him seven days travel time, so he decided to take the train west. We left Fort Dix together, and caught a taxi to the train station, where he bought a ticket to Tacoma, Washington. We then went to a local bar and had several farewell beers together.

Sam asked, "What are you going to do? Where're you going on leave?"

"Well, I don't want to travel to Alabama and then north again. I think I'll just return to Buffalo, spend a few days with your family, then catch a bus over to Fort Devens. What do you think of that?"

"I agree that's the smartest thing to do. Tell my Mom and Dad that I couldn't get a leave, and had to report in right away. "

I assured him I would and added, "I'll make it sound good."

"Sam, when our current enlistments are up, we'll both have almost seven years in the military. That's a lot of years to spend in the Army, and not make it a career."

Sam mulled that over for a minute, and said, "You're right, seven years is a damn long time for us to just throw away. I guess we'll have to take a fresh look when our enlistments are up."

"Well, you'll be in Japan and I'll be in Germany, if I can get there. But at least we can stay in touch through your family. I hope you have a good tour in the Far East."

Eventually, we had our fill of beer. We shook hands bear hugged each other then said our farewells. I expressed my appreciation to him for inviting me up to live with him, and how much I wished he was returning to Germany with me.

"Well, Sam old friend, I guess I'll see you again in about three years or so. Take care of yourself, and stay in touch. I'll let your mom know my address wherever I go and you do the same."

"You take care of yourself also. Have a few German beers for me, if you do get there, and if you see any of my old girlfriends, tell them I still love them"

Laughing I said," Sure buddy, I'll do that for you."

I really hated to see him go to Japan rather than Germany. I left him there, and caught a taxi over to the bus station, and bought a ticket for Buffalo. I arrived back in Buffalo the next morning. I caught a taxi to Spring Street, walked up to Sam's house and rang the doorbell.

His mother opened the door, seeing me she grabbed me, hugged and kissed me. She wanted to know where Sam was. I had to explain that he'd been sent to Fort Lewis, and was going to Japan. That deeply disappointed her, as she hoped that he would be able to return to Sicily, see her parents, and we two could stay together.

New Year's Eve I went to my favorite bar on Main Street. I found an empty stool at the bar and ordered a beer. It was about ten o'clock in the evening, and I appreciated being alone. I slowly sipped a couple of beers, and let my thoughts wander back over the past several years.

Opening my book of memories I thought about my first beautiful German sweetheart, Rachel, and our son Kenny. He would be about four years old. That special place in my memory book for her and the boy burned brightly.

I recalled First Sergeant Ironjaws Baker. He was a good man, and to me he represented the finest specimen of a professional soldier. Maybe someday now that I'm back in the Army, I might see him again. What a pleasure that would be.

My thoughts turned to the lovely and vivacious Dotty Gomez, the hostess from the Service Club. She with her beautiful body and engaging personality was so easy to love. I felt sure she'd be married by now. Some guy would be very lucky, without question.

Mentally, I turned more pages of my memory book. I thought about Betty, the switchboard operator. I recalled her escorting me to see the doctor when I had gonorrhea. I'd been so young and scared, and how much I truly appreciated her assistance. I hope she and her husband are happy wherever they are, and maybe have a house full of kids.

Lastly, I thought of Elona. Being honest with myself I know that she's the major reason that I'm once again in the Army. I had told her I'd return, and with a little luck, I will! I was right about not taking her and the twins to Alabama. Half-black children aren't welcome anyplace down South. That would have been a horrible mistake.

I also knew my second reason for being back in the army was because I was directionless. I had failed to develop personal goals. Now I was depending on the Army once again to restore direction and purpose to my life.

The time had slipped away from me, it was just a few minutes until midnight. Everyone stood up around the bar, and at the stroke of midnight they all shouted Happy New Year. The New Year 1954, had arrived. I drained my glass and left the bar, returning to Sam's house.

I spent two more days there. Finally, my time there came to an end, I had to leave. After tearful goodbyes and promises to write, I caught a bus for Ayer, Massachusetts.

I endured the long slow ride to Fort Devens, arriving there around mid-day. I caught an Army bus out to the Fort, and had the driver drop me off at the company that I'd been assigned to. I walked into the company orderly room, and found the company clerk alone in the office.

Introducing myself I asked, "May I speak with the First Sergeant?"

He said, "He, and the others are all out for coffee, they'll be back shortly."

I hung around, not having anything to do I read the bulletin boards, and everything else that was attached to the walls.

I asked the clerk, "What's the mission of the Signal Company?"

He replied, "I don't know, I'm not sure if we have a mission."

"Every unit in the Army has a mission, if it didn't, there wouldn't be a need for the unit," I said.

He looked at me like I was speaking a foreign language, and turned back to his typing.

Eventually, the First Sergeant returned from his coffee break. I met him as he entered the office and introduced myself. He invited me into his office and said, "Pull up a chair."

I pulled a straight back chair to the front of his desk and sat down.

He said, "Give me your personnel records."

I replied, "They were mailed from Fort Dix probably to the battalion personnel officer." He noticed that I had a three year service stripe on my left sleeve.

"You're probably right, so just tell me about yourself, and we'll go from there."

"I first enlisted in 1948, and took basic training at Fort Jackson, South Carolina. I went to Germany and was assigned to the 6087 SCU in Wurzburg, Germany. When I left I was the senior radio operator on the post and made the rank of Corporal. I was discharged last summer, and worked in Miami, Florida, and more recently in Buffalo, New York. I became dissatisfied with civilian life, so I re-enlisted with the expectation of returning to Germany."

I added, "The personnel officer at Fort Dix wouldn't honor my reenlistment orders returning me to Germany, so here I am at Ft Devens."

He snorted, and said, "Those idiots at Dix have no idea what in the hell they're doing. Well, we're a Signal Company here, and train on some different equipment than what you might have had in Germany. You'll learn it quickly, and I'll keep my eyes peeled for a slot for you to go overseas." He stopped and lit a cigarette.

He continued, "You're assigned to this company, 'A' Company. Get a room down in the first barracks and settle in. I'll see you tomorrow."

"Thanks, First Sergeant."

I got up and left the orderly room. As I walked away I thought, I guess the old army is disappearing. Formality, protocol and discipline seem to have all but disappeared. I guess First Sergeants like Ironjaws Baker are history. What a frigging shame!

After finding a place in the barracks I stored all my clothes in the wall locker, and set my things up in the footlocker. I then left, found the mess hall and had the evening meal. The next day I was introduced to their signal equipment.

They had the same type communications hut on the truck, and they operated mostly the same old equipment I had in Germany. Primarily, they operated radio teletype machines, plus a Morse code capability. It was no big deal for me to learn it quickly. I was thankful that I'd learned to type. Not much else had changed. I quickly found out that my transmitting and receiving skills had diminished considerably since I'd last used Morse code.

After duty, I often wandered down to the little town of Ayer, and patronized the local bars. To say they were not very exciting is no exaggeration. The booze was cheap, but the girls were older and mostly unattractive.

I stayed in the unit until the middle of April. In my short stay I had become friends with the First Sergeant. I was twenty-three-years—old, and after him I was the oldest enlisted man in the unit.

In late April, the First Sergeant using his influence with the battalion personnel officer was able to arrange for me to get orders going to Germany. I was one happy man! Finally, I'll get back to Elona, and this time I didn't plan to leave without her. I went to see the First Sergeant and said, "Thanks a million First Sergeant. You've been a good friend, I hope to see you again one day."

He laughed and replied, "Screw those personnel pricks in Dix, they all have their heads up their asses. Take care of yourself and have a good tour."

We shook hands and I left.

There were thirty-five men scheduled to go with me on a bus to Fort Dix for overseas processing. I was appointed senior man in charge of the troops for the bus trip. We had a two day stay at Fort Dix for out processing, then on to the Port of New York.

CHAPTER 28

Back in Germany

Our boarding the ship was uneventful. There was very little that had changed since my last trip on a troop ship some twenty months or so ago. Our ship for this journey was the U.S.A.T. Gen'l Ballou.

Tugboats slowly pulled us away from the dock. Relatives and friends covered the dock as they waved and shouted goodbye to the soldiers. Moving ever so slowly, we passed the Stature of Liberty and on out to the open sea.

Nothing had changed aboard troopships. After a few hours at sea dozens of troops became sick and were vomiting everywhere. Fortunately, I didn't get seasick. During the voyage we all had some guard duty and housecleaning jobs to perform.

Finally, our ten day crossing completed, we arrived in Bremmerhaven, Germany. The twin signs, one in English and the other in German welcomed us to Germany It was a much better crossing than my original trip, when it had been so cold and snowing. I was anxious to disembark, and get on my way.

I had orders assigning me to the 99th Signal Operations Battalion, stationed in Boblingen, which is a small town located not very far from the city of Stuttgart, Germany.

After a long train ride and another two day stopover in Marburg, I eventually arrived at my new unit. I'd been assigned to the Signal Operations Company within the Battalion. The unit was part of Seventh Army, and was located at Panzer *Kaserne.* The *Kaserne* had been a German army tank base during WW II. All the post streets were wide and cobble stoned. They were constructed to support heavy tanks and tank equipment. It could certainly support our radio truck equipment.

I reported in to First Sergeant, James Oliver, and received my barracks assignment, then my work assignment to the High Frequency platoon. He and I became almost instant friends. He wasn't that much older than me, maybe four years older. He was tall, slender, energetic, and young. He had earned his First Sergeant stripes in Korea during the war.

My platoon sergeant was Sergeant Jackson, who was black. He originally came from the Virgin Islands. He and I became good friends also. I was assigned as team chief on one of the eight radio teletype sets mounted on two and one-half ton trucks that we had in the platoon.

I was told more than once that the motto of the Seventh Army was: "Born at Sea, Baptized in Blood and Crowned in Glory." General George Patton was said to have coined the motto. I wasn't sure how true that was, but I never forgot it.

Our Company Commander was a former paratrooper from the 82nd Airborne Division. He was a Captain named Benny Cole. He was really a martinet, who reveled in pushing the troops to their limits, and imposing harsh methods of discipline, all for no apparent reason. He seemed to think that the harder he pushed the troops, the more of a leader he appeared or became. No one in the unit liked him. I don't think he even liked himself. He was in my opinion, an asshole from the word go. Unfortunately, you meet these types once in a while—perhaps too often—but they are around.

I quickly made many friends in the platoon. One of them was a tall lanky guy from Frostproof, Florida, named Bill Tindall. He was taller than me with sandy hair, a nice easy smile, and was a Private

Another new friend was a Corporal named Wayne Wilson. He hailed from someplace in the proud state of Indiana. Wayne was married, and he and his wife Roslyn lived off the post. I think he had two boys at that time. He and I both were in charge of radio teams. He loved country music, so if for no other reason, that made him my friend.

My unit as part of the Seventh Army, furnished field radio communications for it. I found out that the unit stayed on field exercises most of the time, either supporting one of the two Army Corps, or Army Headquarters There was always a sense of urgency to the training. We had three Lieutenants in the company, all recent graduates of West Point

Military Academy. I was glad of that, for they are usually the smartest, and best to work for and with.

. I quickly realized that the lazy, fun-filled days and nights back in Wurzburg and the 6087 SCU, had long since vanished, and would never return. Those days, and the events and people who were part of it, would remain as Chapters in my book of treasured memories.

I'm glad that I had the opportunity to be a part of those early days of the Army of Occupation, Germany

I intended as soon as I had built up enough leave time to take a furlough, return to Wurzburg and find Elona. That's why I reenlisted, and that's my goal on this tour back to Germany. I left here in July 1952, that's almost two years ago, a very long time to wait.

I wondered, am I kidding myself thinking she's still there, and still available. Is that a realistic expectation? I didn't know, but time will surely give me the answer. I hoped it would be the right answer.

I wrote a letter to my old army friend John Roberts's parents at the address he had given me back in 1952. I explained to them who I was, and that he and I were good friends from our earlier service together. About two weeks later I received a reply from his Mother. She informed me that he was now a Sergeant, and assigned to the Engineers located in Wurzburg. I could hardly believe it, the guy had actually come back to Germany, and was again in our old stomping grounds. What a pleasant surprise that was. I used the phone in the orderly room, and was able to place a call through to his unit. Luckily, I called early in the evening, he was in his barracks. The charge of quarters in his company located him, and in a few minutes he answered the telephone.

"Hi John, this is Ken Fisher. I'm back in Germany."

It was really a delight to talk to him again. We shared so many memories together. We exchanged happy greetings.

He said, "I'm now the company communications Sergeant and doing well, it's not a bad outfit."

I told him, "Sam Amato and I, reenlisted in November, and Sam has gone on to Japan, I'm now in Seventh Army in Boblingen."

"That's good, I don't know of anyone else from our old group reenlisting."

"John, have you seen Elona?" I waited with bated breath for his response.

"No, I haven't seen her since she showed up at the train station when we all left here in 1952."

"I'm planning to take a leave in November and come to Wurzburg. I'll spend a few days with you, and try to find Elona."

He was happy about that and made me promise to call and give him the date I'd arrive, and how long I'd stay. I assured him I would.

My unit went on a field exercise for two weeks in August. We would establish a base station, and then more often than not, be required to move to a new location in the middle of the night. It happened time after time as the units trained for wartime conditions, and battlefield expectations.

Bill Tindall and I went down to the little town of Boblinger, and met two nice looking women and stayed at a local hotel. The price of love-making had certainly gone up since I was last here. I made sure that I used condoms. I had paid the price several years earlier for not doing so.

The dollar mark exchange rate was somewhere around ten to twelve marks to the dollar, and was in a constant state of flux. That simply meant everything was more expensive. Bill made PFC, so he was happy with more money and increased responsibility. I was glad for him.

In September, I was promoted to Corporal, and that certainly made me happy. My pay increased by about one-forth, I needed the money. Wayne Wilson and I continued to spend lots of evenings in the club. He was fun to be with, and we enjoyed many lively stimulating conversations. He was a great guy, and never to my knowledge cheated on his wife. I admired him very much for his faithfulness and fortitude. Very few people I knew could do that.

CHAPTER 29

Searching for Elona

The first of November rolled around. I had accumulated thirty days of leave time, so I applied for ten days leave with my destination as Wurzburg. After it was approved I called Roberts and told him I'd be there on the tenth of the month for eight days. I packed an overnight bag and caught the train.

I was determined to find Elona. I had several pictures of her which I carefully packed in my bag. I knew that I might have a definite need for them. From Stuttgart to Wurzburg was a straight shot, and the ride took a couple hours. The trains hadn't changed at all, they still had the hard wooden seats, and small smut and soot-streaked windows.

I arrived in Wurzburg early in the afternoon. We pulled into the train station and I was absolutely astounded. This was a completely new train station. It was nice, much more modern than before. As I walked along the platform I noted that there were no longer any letters or pictures of missing people, and missing soldiers on the walls. I guessed that too many years has passed, people still missing will probably stay missing forever.

Roberts met me at the station. We saw each other about the same time. We grabbed and hugged each other like long lost brothers.

I held him by the arms and said, "John, you sorry ass, how the hell are you?"

He laughed and replied, "Ken, I'm fine, things are going great, how about you old friend?"

"I'm fine, and happy as hell to be back in Germany. It has taken a while to get here, but I made it."

John said, "I'm on a three day pass. We can spend some time together and go to the old *Gasthaus's.* Maybe find some of the old girls, and do it all over again!"

"That sounds like the best idea I've heard lately. Let's go find a hotel and rent a room for a few days."

He had a Jeep, which he said was his, so we climbed in and he drove over to the Bavarian Inn. I had over four hundred marks with me and some additional money in script. I figured that's sufficient money for my leave, unless I did something stupid.

"John, tell me how in the hell you managed to get back here to Wurzburg."

John, in his distinctive Northern accent replied, "I was assigned to Fort Hamilton, New York, from Fort Dix. I'd been there less than a year when I received reassignment orders back to Germany."

He paused, lit a cigarette then continued, "I came back through Marburg and received orders to go to the Engineers. I was surprised but happy to be back in our old stomping grounds."

Clearing his throat he then continued, "It's not a bad outfit. I got promoted here so things are going pretty good for me. Tell me about yourself and what all's happened since we last saw each other at Fort Dix."

"Well, Grady and I got out of the army at Fort Benning, Georgia, and went home to Alabama. Grady went to work in a local textile mill the week after we got home. I'd been home about three weeks doing nothing when John Hodes and his friend drove up. We three then went to Miami, Florida, for a vacation."

He interrupted me and said, "You mean Hodes drove from Rochester, New York, and found you, and you all went to Miami, Florida together?"

"Yep, that's exactly what happened."

He laughed, "Boy, would I have loved to have been with you guys in Miami."

"We did have a ball down there, John and his friend after a week of partying returned home. I found a job in Miami, and worked for six months. I then moved to Buffalo, and stayed with Sam Amato and his family for several months before we decided to reenlist."

I lit a cigarette and continued, "You won't believe who the reenlistment officer was at the recruiting station in Buffalo."

"Who?"

"It was our old Executive Officer, Captain Tolliver."

"Well, I'll be damned; he always was sort of weird."

We arrived at the Bavarian Inn. I noted that it hadn't changed in appearance whatsoever. John and I went to the desk clerk and obtained rooms. John paid for two nights lodging, and I paid for four. The price of a room per night had only gone up about five marks, so it was no big financial burden.

"John, let's put our bags in the room, and go to the bar and have a couple of cool ones."

"That's the best suggestion I've heard all day. Let's do it."

I had the weirdest feeling as I walked down the hall way. I thought about the many nights that Elona and I had been here together, the love that had been ours, the fun that we had, and how it all vanished in a twinkle of the eye.

We walked into the bar, it seemed to be exactly as I remembered it. I don't think even the furniture has been rearranged. The tables were the same.

"John, what do you want to drink?"

"What say we start with a cognac and cola?"

"That sounds good to me."

I asked the barkeeper for two cognac and colas. We then found a table and sat down.

I raised my glass, "This calls for a toast!"

John picked up his glass and said, "To old friends, may you live forever, and I may never die!" We drank to that

"Ken, let's get something to eat, we may have a long night. The booze may get to us too quickly if we don't eat."

"That's a great idea, plus I'm really hungry."

He ordered us something to eat, and we both ate quickly. John ordered us two more drinks. We began to discuss our current situations, and what the immediate future held for us both. We talked about everything and everybody under the sun for about two more hours as we continued to slowly sip cognac and cola.

Finally, I asked, "How's our old 6087 SCU doing these days, and how's the enlisted men's club?"

He replied, "I thought you knew that the 6087 has been deactivated, it's no longer on the post. It no longer exists as an active army unit as far as I know."

I was surprised; I couldn't picture the *Kaserne* without our old unit being there.

"Who's in our old barracks?"

"I'm not sure, but some unit from Seventh Army is in there."

"What about the enlisted club?"

He replied, "It's still there of course, and it's the same old Enlisted Men's club."

We had another drink; I noted it was getting along in the evening. The band was gathering on the bandstand and tuning up their instruments. I could almost swear they were the same musicians that were here on my last visit. I was probably wrong however.

John said, "Let's go over to the Leopold and check it out."

"Great, I'm looking forward to seeing my old honky-tonk hangout again."

We paid the bill and left the barroom, got into his Jeep and in just a few minutes we arrived at the Leopold *Gasthaus*. The only change I could readily observe was a couple of big flower pots out in front of the place. Strange emotions flooded up as I once again entered the place. I thought about the many times I'd been here. I recalled the time Ray and I had fought two other soldiers in the bathroom, and then had gotten away before the MP's arrived.

I brought Elona here once or twice, and each time we had an excellent, enjoyable evening. It really wasn't the best place to bring a beautiful woman, or any woman for that matter. The place inside was still the same, I went up to the bar and ordered two cognac and colas. I looked around the room not really expecting to see Elona, but I had to check. There was the usual crowd, just soldiers and girls. There were more girls than there were soldiers. That I considered rather unusual, it had never been that way before that I could recall.

John said, "Tomorrow we can have breakfast, then I'll take you out to the K*aserne* and show you around."

"Great, I really look forward to seeing my old stomping grounds again. John, I really want to find Elona, are you sure that you haven't seen her anywhere since you arrived back here?"

"Ken, I've been to all our old hangouts many times over, and I assure you I haven't seen her. I have no idea where she could have disappeared to!"

"Thanks again for the information."

"Let's dance with some of these girls, maybe we can find a couple to make out with tonight," he said.

I agreed, and looked them over with a jaundiced eye. They all appeared to be much better dressed than I remembered. I selected the one I considered to be the best looking, and asked her to dance. She readily agreed.

We walked out to the dance floor, and I gently pulled her to me. John had selected one, and he too was dancing. As the tune ended I saw that John was escorting her to a larger table. He then walked over to our table, picked up our drinks taking them to the new one. I escorted my dance partner to the new table, and invited her to sit down. She accepted my invitation. I thought some things never change, the mating game goes on!

John ordered us two more drinks, and a glass of beer and one of wine. My new friend introduced herself as Greta, and her friends name was Gisela. I thought of all the other Gisela's I had known in the past few years. Gisela obviously is a very popular name in Germany. John carried on a conversation with his girlfriend, and I turned to mine and engaged her in light conversation.

She asked, "Do you speak German?"

"No, I only know a few words in your language. You however, seem to speak excellent English."

She replied, "I studied it in school." We danced a couple more tunes and became fairly comfortable with each other.

I asked, "How old are you?"

She replied, "I'm twenty years old."

I took a closer look at her. She was about five foot four, long blonde hair and grey eyes. She had a nice body, and was very easy to look at. She had an engaging smile, nice white teeth, plus she was a damn good dancer.

"Do you work?"

"Yes, I have a part time job working in a clothing store in the afternoons. I make enough money to support myself."

"It's nice to be independent. Greta, would you like to spend the night with me? I have a room in the Bavarian Inn."

"I might. I don't usually spend the night with someone I just met."

"Well, think about it. If you agree, we can go there whenever you want to."

We danced again, and I ordered the four of us another drink. The two girls excused themselves and went to the bathroom.

John asked, "How are you making out,?"

"I think I might be doing alright, time will tell, I should know shortly."

He replied, "I'm right on target, and things are going smoothly with us."

I asked Greta to dance again. The tune was a nice old favorite of mine "Blue Skies." I pulled her close to me and kissed her lightly along her neck and her cheek. She responded by holding me tighter, and pressing her body a little closer to mine.

"Have you made a decision on staying with me tonight?"

She looked at me, smiled, and said, "Yes, I'll stay with you."

"Good."

The dance concluded we walked back to the table. I ordered us four more drinks.

I told John, "Things are fine, and it's a go for tonight."

"That's great, what do you say we finish these drinks and Hank Snow to the hotel."

"That sounds good to me."

I hadn't heard the old metaphor "Hank Snow" used to leave a place since I'd last seen Sam Amato. I was sort of surprised that John would remember the expression. I don't think the metaphor was ever in vogue outside our old outfit here in Wurzburg.

We finished our drinks, gathered up our coats and caps and left the bar. We managed to crowd into John's Jeep, and shortly thereafter we arrived back at the Bavarian Inn. John parked and locked up his Jeep, then we all went inside.

I suggested we have at least one more drink at the bar. They all agreed. I found us a table and ordered the round of drinks. I quickly looked around the room. Elona wasn't there.

We talked for about a half-hour then John said, "Gisela and I are going back to our room."

"We're leaving shortly also."

John said, "Ken, we can have breakfast here then we'll leave in the morning."

I nodded my head in agreement.

As Greta and I finished our drinks I asked, "Are you ready to call it a night?"

"Yes, I'm ready."

We picked up our coats and left the bar area, holding hands we walked down the hall. I stopped, unlocked the door and stepped into the room.

She walked in looked around, then said, "This is a nice room."

"I think so too."

I took her coat and hung it up on the coat rack back of the door and then hung my overcoat up with it. I took off my Ike jacket, and then my tie hanging them up also. The room décor hadn't changed much since I was last here. I had never stayed in this specific room, and I was glad of that. I gently pulled her over to me, and bending slightly gave her a gently kiss on the lips. She slowly responded as our bodies adjusted to each other.

I kissed her tenderly and said, "It's going to be a long night."

She replied, "It will be great night."

We undressed then moved onto the bed, and completed our act of intimacy.

Relaxing, she leaned over and kissed me softly on my lips. I remembered that I had bought and put two bottles of beer in my overcoat earlier, so I got up from the bed and retrieved my beer. I pulled the little hinged top off, and had a big swallow.

"Do you want a drink of beer?"

"No, I'm fine, I don't want any more to drink tonight."

Sitting down in the chair I motioned her to come over to me. She rose from the bed came around and I positioned her on my lap.

Lighting a cigarette I offered her one, but she refused saying, "I don't smoke, I've never smoked."

"That's good. Smoking does nothing for you except give you headaches, bad breath, and stains your teeth." I said.

I took another drink of beer and continued to smoke my cigarette. I looked at her and said Greta, "How much do I owe you for making love with me tonight?"

She looked sharply at me, and then slapped me lightly on my cheek. In an indignant tone of voice she said, “Ken, I’m not a prostitute, you owe me nothing other than respect. I chose to sleep with you tonight because I wanted to, not for money. I like you and I enjoy being with you. But my body isn’t for sale!”

I immediately apologized. “Greta, I’m very sorry that I asked you that question. I’m not accustomed to lovely women like you that doesn’t ask for money for a night of love. Let’s just forget that I ever asked the question, and go on from here.”

She nodded her head in agreement.

She asked, “How do you like Germany?”

“I like and enjoy it very much, I’ve been here before.”

She said, “You weren’t here during the war, you’re too young. When were you here?”

“I was here in Germany from December 1948, until July 1952.”

“Where were you?”

“I was stationed here in Wurzburg at the *Kaserne*.”

She appeared amazed that I had spent so much time in the city. She said, “You must know this city very well.”

“I used to. But I’ve been gone for a couple of years, so my memory is a little fuzzy.” I had another swallow from my beer.

“Did you have a girlfriend when you were here?”

“Yes I did, perhaps four of them.”

She giggled, “You’re not telling me the truth.”

“Sure I am, but they’re all gone now.”

“Where do you live now?”

“I live in Boblingen. Do you know where that is?”

She thought for a second then said, “No, I don’t know, it’s not close to Wurzburg?”

“It’s a small town on the outskirts of Stuttgart.”

She said, “That can’t be too far from here.”

“No, it’s about a two hour train ride.”

She asked, “Are you ready to go to bed?”

I was a little tired, “Yes, we can if you want to.”

She nodded her head yes.

She got up from my lap and went into the bathroom. I finished my beer and put out my cigarette. She returned, and I motioned for her to get into the bed first.

I rolled towards her, she moved and placed her head on my arm. I held her and gently rubbed her shoulder and arm. Not too much later she was asleep.

My last conscious thought was of Elona. Where is she, how can I find her?

Waking up I glanced at my watch, it was seven o'clock in the morning, I had really slept late this morning. Greta was still sleeping. I carefully got out of bed and went to the bathroom. I felt well rested and ready for today's activities. I quietly washed and dressed. Greta was still sleeping. I went to the restaurant and purchased three cups of coffee, and returned to the room. Greta was now awake.

I smiled and said, "Good morning, how are you today?"

She smiled, then stretched while still in the bed, and replied, "I feel great, I slept like a baby." I offered her a cup of coffee.

She accepted it and said, "Thanks."

"When you get ready we can go for breakfast together."

"I have to take a bath and dress, give me a few minutes, and I'll be ready to go."

I sat down in the chair as she went into the bathroom. I heard her fill the tub then the splashing of water. Several minutes later she came out and began to dress. She then brushed her hair and put on a faint hint of lipstick, and then she came over to me and kissed me tenderly on my cheek.

"You had best exercise caution, or else I'll have you back in the bed again, breakfast or no breakfast."

She laughed and pulled me to my feet. Together we left the room and went to the restaurant. John and his girlfriend were there, so we joined them. We exchanged the usual salutations and then ordered breakfast.

"John, are we still going out to the *Kaserne*?"

"Yeah, we'll go when we finish here."

We all ate slowly as the food was excellent.

"Greta, Are you going to be here at the bar tonight?"

"Do you want me to be here this evening?"

"Sure."

"I'll be here about seven o'clock. I'll meet you at the bar."

"Great, I'll be looking for you."

John then asked Gisela if she would be here.

"Yes, I'll be here with Greta."

We finished eating, and Greta said they had to leave, so we said goodbye until the evening. We ordered another cup of coffee.

"John, do you realize that you and I are now twenty-four-years-old. It was six years ago that we all first came to Germany?"

He was silent for a moment, then replied, "Ken, you're right. That seems like such a long time ago, and yet it all happened so quickly. I guess time flies when you're having fun, and we did have fun."

"Yeah, for the most part we really enjoyed ourselves. All the guys that we knew are now settled back into civilian life, and most likely married with kids. Here you and I are still boozing it up, and chasing F*rauleins* like we were still eighteen-year olds."

He laughed and replied, "I intend to make the army my career. When the time comes to get married, and the right girl comes along, I'll know it. Then I'll quit all the wild stuff and settle down."

"I also plan to make the Army my career. Maybe it's not the best of careers, certainly not the most lucrative. But it's all that I really know. Sometimes I feel like I'm trapped, other times I know it's what I truly want to do."

John said, "After you leave, I have only about a year or less left on this tour. Maybe if we both stay in the army, we'll meet again sometime, somewhere."

"I surely hope so."

"Me too," he replied.

"John, I came here to find Elona. But I would have come anyway once I found out that you were here. You're one of my best friends, and I treasure our friendship."

Grunting he replied, "I feel that exact same way." He lit a cigarette then said, "What do you say we go out to the *Kaserne.* I'll show you around, you can see what if any changes have been made."

"That's a great idea, let's go."

We split the costs of the breakfasts then walked outside to his Jeep.

I remarked, "Your Jeep seems to be a much better one than the one Ray and I had."

"This is a 1951 model, and it's much newer than the one you guys had. This one doesn't have the mileage and usage that yours did."

In defense of our old Jeep I pointed out that it had dodged its way through the war, and therefore it had a right to be ragged. John just laughed. We climbed into his Jeep. He turned around and then made several turns onto streets bringing us by the Ring Hotel.

He slowed down and asked, "You remember this old hotel don't you?"

"Yeah, I remember it well, very well. I've spent many happy hours in there."

He slowly drove past the hotel and around the big park. I had forgotten the street names, but as they came into view I recognized them. Finally, he turned onto the main street and went through the big intersection. I noted that the Rod and Gun Club was still open, and located in the same place.

He drove on up the hill, and I could see the *Kaserne* gates come into view. There were German police now as gate guards. They were known as Industrial Police, and were called IP's. John slowed down almost to a stop, and then slowly moved through the gate. I looked to the right at our old headquarters building. The tall antenna pole had been removed, the iron covers over the old message center and radio room had also been removed. There was a sign in front of the building identifying it as the headquarters of some unit, but he was moving too quickly for me to make it all out.

A feeling of deep nostalgia swept over me as I remembered the hundreds of days and nights I had spent in that building, and of the many events that had occurred there. It was hard for me to believe and accept the fact that I was once again on the *Kaserne*, at Leighton Barracks. I had truly figured that I would never see this place again.

We moved slowly past the old aircraft hangar, and I noticed three small army airplanes parked on the runway aprons. They appeared to be the small L-19's type planes that the army used for courier, reconnaissance, and other short distance missions.

John turned left past the fire station, and then right into the quadrangle. The gym was still there and the snack bar in its original location. The EM club a huge stone building was of course there. The barracks that housed the 6087 SCU and its personnel were there, but it had another unit as tenants. John drove past the old mess hall and up the street to our last barracks. They too had another unit, and other personnel were now billeted and assigned there.

I was somewhat overwhelmed as I viewed all the changes in organizations and personnel that had occurred in just two years. It seems everything in Germany now belongs to Seventh Army—that included me.

John said, "Let's go to the snack bar and have a cup of American coffee. We can check out the bowling alley, and then the old service club. The club will be open in about two hours, so we can go and have a few cold ones to start our day off the right way."

"That's a great idea," I said.

He parked by the snack bar, and we walked inside. The interior was exactly the same as it had been when I was last here. We went through the serving line obtaining two cups of coffee, then found a table.

We sat at the table slowly drinking the coffee, and smoked. I watched the crowd as they came through, almost as if I expected to see someone that I knew or recognized. I noticed two Service Club women come through the line. They wore the same type uniforms that Dotty had worn back in 1948. They both appeared to be older than either John or me.

"John, whatever happened to Corporal Bell who was with us in the old radio center?"

"I saw him about a week after I got back here. They were deactivating the unit, and he had reassignment orders for some other unit here in Germany. He had married his German girl friend from here in Wurzburg, but I don't know where he is now. He still had your old Jeep"

We left the snack bar and walked over to the bowling alley where a few people were bowling. I had the feeling that I should at least recognize one person, but that was again just wishful thinking. Things and people change and like it or not, you must accept the changes.

We then walked upstairs to the service club. It had changed very little since I was here over two years ago. Only the furniture had been rearranged

I walked around the room and checked it all out.

I said, "Let's play a game of pool that'll kill some time for us."

"Great, let's play a game of eight ball."

I racked the balls and invited him to break.

As he selected his stick and chalked up his cue, I walked by the black leather couch and touched it. It was the same couch that Dotty and I had made love on so many nights. I stood there for a few seconds recalling our many wonderful nights together. I heard the crack of the cue ball, and it startled me.

I watched as John ran about three balls off the table, then he missed and it was my shot. I ran two balls off then it was his turn again. He won the game, then I won two more games from him, before he conceded that I was the better pool player.

We hung up our cue sticks and left the service club. We walked across the quadrangle and into the EM club. I glanced at the spot that I had slipped on in the snow, and Corporal Sherron had sucker punched me that long ago night in December, 1948. We went up the stairs and into the club. It hadn't changed whatsoever since my last visit.

We found a table and John ordered two beers for us. I lay my pack of cigarettes and Zippo lighter on the table, he placed his beside mine. I looked around the room. Old memories swept over me like a high tide inundates Miami Beach.

"Ken, do you remember the night when you and I first came in here?"

"Sure, I remember that night. I still had black eyes from Sherron punching me, and you and I had more to drink than either of us could really handle, I think we were both half drunk when we finally went back to the barracks."

He laughed, "Remember John Hodes passing out at that table right there?" as he pointed to a table.

Laughing I replied, "Yeah, I remember that evening."

We both then began to recall events and incidents that occurred during the almost four years we had been here together. He would recall one incident, and I'd recall another. We laughed and continued to drink beer, as incident after incident was resurrected.

John left to go to the latrine, and I immediately began reminiscing about the many other nights I'd been here in the club. I looked at the table where I blew a kiss to Rachel, and at the dance floor where I had first kissed her, then at the table where Elona and I had spent our last few hours together two years ago. It was depressing!

Finally, John returned and said, "I think we should head back to the hotel, and perhaps have a bite to eat before the girls show up, if they really do show up."

"That's a good idea, I'll stop by the latrine, and then we'll be on our way."

I was glad to leave the club, a place that held so many memories for me, both good and bad.

We got back into his Jeep and left the *Kaserne,* returning to the Bavarian Inn. Once there we headed straight to the bar and restaurant area. We found a table and I ordered us both a cognac and cola.

John said, "Ken, I'll bet you a round of drinks that they won't show up tonight."

"John you're on. They'll be here not later than seven o'clock."

We both ordered a sandwich and ate as the local band began to tune up their instruments.

A little later the door to the bar area swung open, and both Greta and her friend Gisela walked into the room. They glanced around and spotting us, headed straight for our table. Both John and I stood up as they approached. I held out my arms and Greta walked into them and kissed me lightly on my cheek. We held their chairs as they seated themselves at the table. I immediately called the waiter and ordered a round of drinks for all of us. The waiter returned with our drinks, and extended the bill to me.

I said, "Give it to my friend, he's buying this round. Thanks John, ye of such little faith."

Greta began telling me about her day at work, and then asked,

"What have you been doing all day?"

"John and I went sightseeing and visiting old places where we used to go several years ago."

"Did you find them changed very much?"

"Some of them have, and some haven't changed whatsoever. Time changes everything even people. So I guess I have to expect some changes."

John and Gisela got up to dance, and I asked Greta if she would like to dance?

She said, "Sure."

We danced a couple of times and returned to the table. I ordered another round of drinks and paid for them.

Greta asked, "How much longer will you be in town?"

"I'm not really sure. Maybe three or four more days then I have to go back to Boblingen. Don't worry about me leaving, let's just enjoy the time that we have together."

She smiled and said, "I hope you find whatever or whoever you're looking for."

"What makes you think that I'm looking for something or someone?"

"I can see it in your eyes. I can't explain it, but it's there in your eyes," she said.

I replied, "You're a mystic, a mind reader, are you also a fortune teller?"

She giggled, leaned over and kissed me gently on the cheek.

We stayed at the table for about two more hours then John suggested we call it a night. I was a little tired, so I quickly agreed.

"Let's all have breakfast again tomorrow morning. Ken, if you'll take me back to the *Kaserne* you can keep my Jeep as long as you're in town, and save yourself some taxi money."

"Thanks John, that'll be a tremendous help to me. I'll bring it back to you, and I'll make sure that it's full of gas."

Greta and I left them, and went to the room. We entered and I removed my two bottles of beer, and sat them on the table. I removed my overcoat, and then helped Greta with her coat and sweater hanging them all on the door rack.

I pulled her to me and gave her a kiss holding her tightly to me. She returned my kiss. I released her and sat down in the chair, I then picked up one of the bottles of beer and popped the little top off and had a swallow. She sat down on my lap pushing my hair back, slowly leaning forward she again kissed me. I returned her kiss with passion and yearning. I still had that feeling of depression that began in the EM club, and couldn't seem to shake it

"Why don't you take your blouse and other clothes off, and make yourself more comfortable."

We both undressed then went to bed. We made love as only two young people can. I got out of the bed and moved to set in the chair. I took another big swallow of beer and lit a cigarette.

She came over sat on my lap and said, "I enjoyed that Ken, you're a good lover."

I smiled and said, "Thank you, you're not bad yourself." She lightly kissed me. We just sat there with her on my lap, I finished my one beer and opened the other. I drank a big swallow and lit another cigarette.

Greta looked at me and said, "Ken, you're somehow different tonight than you were last night, has something happened?"

I shook my head, "No, I had a long day, and I guess I'm a little tired tonight."

She said, "Do you want us to go to bed now?"

"When I finish my beer we can if you want to," I said.

I drank about half the beer then went to the bathroom. When I returned she was already in bed. I made sure the room door was locked then entered the bed with her. She leaned over and kissed me lightly on the lips and laid her head on my arm.

She said, "Goodnight Ken."

I whispered back, "Goodnight sweet thing."

I woke up around six-thirty the next morning, and quietly got out of bed. I watched her sleep as I lit a cigarette and sat in the chair.

I began to think of Elona, and wondered where in the hell can I find her. I really don't know where to begin looking. I know that she doesn't hang out in bars, or Roberts would have seen her. That leaves me very few locations to search. I guess the best thing is to take a few pictures of her, and inquire around some of the bars and restaurants and see if I have any luck.

Greta began to stir, eventually she opened her eyes, sitting up she saw me and said, "Good morning!"

"Good morning, and the top of the day to you."

"How long have you been up?" she asked.

"I guess about thirty minutes or so."

She rolled over got out of the bed, and went to the bathroom. I could hear her filling up the bathtub.

She called out, "Ken, come on in the tub with me."

I thought why not, I need a good bath.

"Okay, I'll be right there."

I removed my shorts and opened the door to the bathroom and tub. She was already in the tub splashing around. I stepped into the water, it was nice and warm. I slowly sat down as the water rose higher. She turned around and rising up slid over on to my legs and lap.

We soaped each other and played splash games, then made love in the warm water. We rinsed off and got out of the tub. We dried each other off, and I suggested we dress and go to breakfast.

As we were dressing she said, "Ken, you were mumbling in your sleep last night."

"Oh really, I never talk in my sleep."

"You were asking, where are you Elona?"

I looked at her rather dumbfounded.

She asked, "Is that the girl you're looking for?"

"Yes, she's the one."

"Is she your girlfriend?"

"Yes, at least she was. I want to find her again, but I'm not sure where to look."

We were both dressed, so I opened the door and we left the room.

We walked down the hall way and met John and Gisela as they were exiting their room. The four of us went to the restaurant, ordered and ate breakfast.

John said, "Ken, I need to go back to the company this morning, so if it's alright we'll go when we finish here."

"Of course, I'll take you back any time you want to go I replied."

John then told Gisela he wouldn't be able to see her this evening, maybe they could meet Saturday night.

"Greta, are you going be here this evening?"

"No, I have some things that I must do with my family. Maybe I can meet you again Saturday night."

"All right, I understand."

John and I paid the bill, and the four of us walked outside.

John kissed Gisela and told her, "I'll see you Saturday night."

As I kissed Greta, she whispered to me, "I hope you find your girlfriend Elona."

"I hope so too."

They walked away, and John and I got into his Jeep. John drove to the *Kaserne* and pulled up next to the curb by our old barracks. He put the gear in neutral and got out. I got out and walked around to the driver's side.

We shook hands and I said, "I have your phone number, so I'll call and let you know what day I'll bring your Jeep back."

"No sweat. I hope you find Elona. She has to be here in Wurzburg somewhere."

He walked into the barracks. I sat there for a moment or two and just looked around. John had walked into the barracks next to our old one. Where he had parked his Jeep was the exact spot that our First Sergeant had tied the string on my and Ray's Jeep to the planking. That scene still remained vivid in my mind.

I slowly pulled away from the curb and drove down to the gate. I stopped just prior to reaching the gate, and looked at the old headquarters building. A tall whip antenna was mounted on top of the building, and the spot where our antenna pole had been was now planted in flowers.

Driving on out the gate I headed downtown. I thought it best that I wait until later in the evening to visit some *Gasthaus's* and restaurants looking for Elona, I drove down to the big intersection glancing at the place that Ray and I had wrecked the Jeep. I drove on across the street and down into the city. Nine years since the end of the war, and Wurzburg it seems has been mostly rebuilt. The massive destruction I first viewed some six years ago has been removed. New office buildings and new homes has replaced most all of the bombed out ones.

I drove down by the park passing in front of the Ring Hotel. Memories of Rachel and I there, and the many beautiful evenings we had spent together flooded my mind as I slowly drove past. I drove across the bridge over the Main River and on up to the castle. I parked then got out. They now had a small beer garden on the terraced side of the castle overlooking the valley, and the river Main below. I walked in and sat at a table. Within seconds a waiter came to my table and I ordered a beer.

He returned placed the beer on my table and said, "I have today's copy of the "*Stars and Stripes*" would you like to read it?"

"Yes, *Danke Schon,*" then I paid him for the beer.

Placing my cigarettes and lighter on the table I read the front page of the newspaper. It was very familiar news; Seventh Army was in the midst of fall maneuvers, and both Corps were participating plus supporting units. I thought that's my outfit, a supporting unit.

The United Nations Command and the North Koreans were still arguing up on the DMZ. Several vehicle accidents had claimed the lives of four V Corps soldiers. A new American high school had opened somewhere around the town of Kaiserslautern. Kaiserslautern and

Grafenwohr had now become major training areas for units assigned to the Seventh Army.

Football was in full swing back in the states, and President Eisenhower had made a speech someplace. I lost interest in the news and laid the paper aside. I slowly began to sip my beer.

Looking across the valley I recalled that marvelous weekend Dotty and I had spent right here. I remembered how beautiful, vivacious and sexy she was, and how her fantastic body could stop a charging elephant in its tracks. I laughed as I recalled my pal Ed Clarkston, telling me that enlisted swine never made out with beautiful American women. I certainly proved him wrong on that point. I would dearly love to see and spend some time with her, but I knew that wasn't possible.

This trip back to Wurzburg has become a trip down memory lane in a sense. But, that's not the purpose of my trip, I have to find Elona.

For the next three days I stayed at the Bavarian Inn. I visited every possible place that I could remember Elona and I had been. I went to the Golden Stallion, the Leopold, even back to the EM club at the Kaserne. I showed the bar tenders, the waiters and waitresses and band members her picture and asked if they had seen her. My visit to the bars became nightmares, no one had seen her, or even recognized her picture. Each day became more frustrating as I continued reaching dead ends.

On Friday I drove downtown and went to the German company that I remembered she had worked for. I went into their company front office and spoke to a receptionist there.

I introduced myself, and showed her a picture of Elona. I asked if she knew her.

She smiled and said, "*Ja*, I know her, that's Elona, she used to work here."

My heart leaped into my throat. I asked, "Does she still work here?"

She shook her head and said, "*Nein,* she left the company many months ago. I don't know where she went."

Once again I had run into a dead end. I thanked the lady and left the building.

I decided to stop my search for now and return to Boblingen. I called John on the phone and was able to reach him. I told him I'd meet him in the EM club this evening and return his Jeep. He agreed to meet me there. I had lunch then found a gas station and filled up his gas tank.

I took a nap that afternoon, and about seven in the evening I drove to the *Kaserne* and parked outside the EM club.

I walked inside and into the ballroom. I selected and sat at a table well away from the bandstand. The club had quite a few people in it, but then it was Friday night. I recalled how we used to come to the club especially on Friday nights. I looked around the room, naturally there wasn't one person that I recognized. I hadn't really expected to. John came into the ballroom,and after spotting me came over to the table and had a seat.

I ordered a beer for myself, and a cognac and cola for him.

"John, I've been unsuccessful in my search for Elona." I told him the places I'd visited and the whole nine yards.

"Ken, I'm sorry that you weren't able to find her. I know what she meant to you. But I haven't seen her once since I returned here."

"Thanks John. I've decided to leave tomorrow morning and return to Boblingen. Are you really planning on returning to the Bavarian Inn tomorrow night and meet Gisela?"

"I might, she's a nice girl. But you know me, variety is the spice of life"

I laughed, "I guess you're right. However, if you do go and Greta is there, tell her I had to go back to Boblingen and left early."

"I will," he replied.

John and I sat there talking and sipping our drinks until about ten o'clock. I asked him to drive me to the gate. There I could catch a taxi back to the hotel. We put on our overcoats and left for the exit. I stopped and looked around the ballroom for a few seconds then left.

John drove slowly down to the gate and pulled outside next to the taxi stand. I got out of the Jeep and came around to his side. We shook hands, and I thanked him for the use of his Jeep. He bear hugged me, and I walked over and caught a taxi.

That evening I spent some time in the hotel bar. No one came in that I recognized, so I turned in early and went to bed. I was up around six in the morning and quickly took a shower, shaved and dressed. At seven in the morning I was in the restaurant and had a light breakfast.

I could catch an early train at eight-thirty, and that's what I intended to do. I paid my hotel bill, and caught a taxi to the *Bahn Hof,* I walked around the new station and compared it to the one that I had arrived at back in 1948. There was really no resemblance. I caught the train and in a couple of hours I was back in Boblingen.

My unit had just returned from a two week field exercise. All the equipment had to be cleaned, and the vehicle maintenance had to be accomplished. On New Year's Eve morning we had an inspection. The Company Commander, Captain Cole, at a company formation informed us that our camouflage nets were not up to his standards.

He said, "The Company will work today until all the nets are refurbished. If you don't complete it today, you'll work tomorrow on New Year's Day."

In my opinion the nets were in excellent shape, they needed no major overhaul or maintenance. I think he just wanted to show his authority, and what he considered his military leadership. He was an asshole, and had absolutely no recognizable qualities of leadership. I judged him against all the officers I had served under before, and he was a failure. I think everyone even the junior officers detested the man.

We worked all day on the nets, and half a day on New Year's Day before we were released. I had gotten about half drunk in our club the night before, went to bed and the New Year arrived, and I failed to even know it.

It was late in 1954, or early in 1955, the army changed its rank structure. I became a Corporal E-4. They also introduced Specialists ranks. The Specialists were primarily administrative personnel who were not involved with combat troops, or combat operations. An E-7 was now a Master Sergeant or First Sergeant. The pay for all ranks remained unchanged.

Early in 1955, I purchased a 1937 Mercedes convertible from one of the IP guards on the gate. I gave him two hundred and fifty dollars for it. It was in fairly decent shape. I bribed the motor pool mechanic, a friend of mine, into inspecting it and overhauling anything that needed repairing. After the mechanic finished, the motor purred. I put a twelve volt Jeep battery in it, and it never failed to start. Bill Tindall, and I drove all over the area in my new car. You had to manually raise and lower the top, but I usually kept it up. It wasn't much to look at but it ran, and that was all that I asked of it. We spent the weekends chasing the local beauties and seeing the sights.

In May, Peyton Stample, another friend of mine, and I decided to take a short leave and drive to Amsterdam, Holland. I took two five gallon cans of gas with me from the motor pool, and one five gallon can of water just in case. We loaded up the car and with our map in hand set off for Amsterdam. We wore our civilian clothes. It was now lawful for soldiers to wear them when they were off duty.

We left Stuttgart on the autobahn traveling through Koblenz, then Kohl, then on to Arnhein, finally reaching Amsterdam. We found a reasonably priced hotel on Rembrandt Square, and checked in for four days. To our pleasant surprise, there were bars and nightclubs all around the area. We had no problem finding things to do.

On our second day we decided to visit the famous Canal Street area. We had a taxi take us there. I was amazed, on both sides of the canal the houses had large windows like department stores back in the states. In each window there was a young woman in seductive wearing apparel. Many of them dressed in flimsy nightgowns which might reach to the top of their thighs, others in just panties and brassiere. The buildings were two and three stories high. On each side of their large windows they had attached little side view mirrors like those found on automobiles. This enabled them to see people approaching their window from either direction.

I turned to Peyton and asked, "Have you ever seen anything like this?" Naturally, he admitted he hadn't.

We walked a block down one side viewing the various ladies and trying to select one that we wanted to spend some money on. We crossed over the canal, and walked another block in the opposite direction.

Peyton finally said, "Let's select one and see what it costs."

Finally, I saw a beautiful red-haired girl in a window and said, "Peyton, this one's for me. I've never made love to a red-haired woman, I'm going in. If you find one you like and finish first wait for me out here on the street, and if I finish first I'll wait here for you."

He nodded his head in agreement, "Okay, go for it."

I looked again at the girl in the window noting that she wore only panties and a bra. She had beautiful legs, nice breasts, and a porcelain face, her red hair a mass of flaming beauty. She watched me from her position on the couch to see what I was going to do. I walked up the steps to her apartment and knocked on the door. She rose from the couch, quickly answered the door, and in perfect English invited me in.

I stepped inside, and she said, "Welcome to Amsterdam. You're an American are you not?"

Rather surprised, I said, "Yes, I'm an American. How did you know that?"

She replied, "I can tell by your hair, all American soldiers have very, very short hair. So you're easy to identify."

I laughed, recognizing the logic of her remark. My hair might be about a half inch long even on top of my head.

She said, "Would you like to make love to me?"

"Yes, how much will it cost me?"

She smiled, "It will cost you ten American dollars, and that's for one time only."

That was a little steep for a Corporal. But she was gorgeous enough, and I was horny enough to say, "Okay, let's do it!"

She led me into a small bedroom. She turned around and said, "Take off your clothes."

I began removing my clothes and shoes. She then led me to a small basin and turned on the faucet. She proceeded to wash my genitals with warm water and soap. My faithful friend immediately begin to stiffen. By the time she dried me, I was hard as a piece of granite rock. She then led me back into the bedroom.

"Do you have a condom?" she asked.

"No, I don't."

She reached into a drawer, and handed me a packet with one condom.

"Would you put that on for me please," I asked.

She smiled and said, "Sure, if you want me to. May I have the money first?"

"Of course, I should have thought of that."

I gave her a ten dollar bill in script. She turned and placed it in the drawer. She then removed her bra and panties.

She turned back to me and said, "Let's get on the bed."

I moved over on the bed to the far side and she followed. I lay on my side facing her. I leaned over and kissed her gently on the lips. She responded as our tongues played their own game of love. Her skin was flawless and smooth, as I traced out the contours of her body. I was determined to take my time, for I knew that once we began, I wouldn't last very long. She became excited and aroused, and began to return my caresses with delicate touches of her own. She kissed my eyes, bent and kissed my nipples and continued to stroke my body kissing me passionately. My resolve was weakening fast, I rolled on top of her and we began and consummated the act of love. I stopped moving and just lay on top of her.

Bending down I kissed her and said, "You're beautiful, and that was wonderful."

She said, "Do you want to do it again? This time it won't cost you any more money."

Not being stupid and still rigidly erect I said, "Yes, it'll take us longer, but it'll be better."

As I resumed my movements she responded, synchronizing her movements with mine. She kissed my face and said something in Dutch that I couldn't understand. I did understand her actions, and I followed suit with my best performance. I lay on her and said, "That was better than before, and I needed that second time around."

She smiled at me and said, "So did I."

She moved from under me and got off the bed, I followed her. She removed the condom, and led me back to the sink area and again washed and dried me off.

She then said, "You should get dressed now."

After I got dressed she led me to the door and kissed me gently on the cheek.

She said, "Have a good time in Amsterdam, and if you want to, come back and see me again before you leave."

I returned her kiss and said, "I'll do that."

I turned around and started down the steps. When I did two nuns and a priest approached her house. I had a mild panic attack!

They all three smiled at me, and in English said, "Good morning!"

With a very weak smile I returned their greetings, and kept walking. I spotted Peyton on the other side of the canal. I shouted to him and we met at the little bridge. We compared our experiences. However, I didn't tell him that she had allowed me to have intercourse twice, and only paying once. I knew he wouldn't believe me anyway. We caught a taxi back to our hotel stopping to have lunch in one of the many sidewalk café's that lined the streets. For the next couple of days we went to a different nightclub each night, drank and danced, and enjoyed the beauty and night life of Amsterdam.

Our furlough almost up, we had to return to Boblingen. As we traveled through Holland we could see the unbelievably beautiful tulip fields, acre after acre of multicolored tulips. There were red and white, purple, yellow and pink. It was a sight seared into my memory.

We arrived back in Boblingen, my car had made the roundtrip—with no problem whatsoever—not even a flat tire.

The latter part of the month we went on a three week field exercise in support of Seventh Corps. We primarily communicated via the radio teletype method, which only required the operators to have the ability to tune the transmitter to the correct frequency, and type.

At the end of the exercise I was called into the First Sergeants office. He said, "Corporal Fisher, you're going to the Seventh Army Non—Commissioned

Officers Academy in Munich. Pack your bags."

I left my convertible with Bill Tindall, and caught the train for Munich. I started the academy in 1955. For four weeks I devoted all my time and energies to the task at hand, which was simply to do well in the course, learn as much as I could, and graduate.

While there I toured and viewed the Dachau concentration camp just outside Munich. As I walked around the grounds I viewed the furnaces where it was said hundreds if not thousands of people had died. I was deeply and indelibly impressed with the horror of it all. The emotions and feelings I felt were ineffable. That people could be so sick, deranged, and perpetrate such inhuman torture on other human beings was almost beyond belief. But it did happen!

Finally my graduation day arrived. I was selected as the number three honor graduate. I missed being honor graduate by two and one-half percentage points. In August I walked out of the academy and caught the train back to Boblingen. The academy had given me a better understanding of what was expected of Non-Commissioned Officers. It was without a doubt, one of the best learning experiences I'd ever had.

Arriving back in Boblingen, I immediately went on a four week training exercise. The first of October I was promoted to Sergeant, and my pay increased significantly.

My friend, Sergeant Wayne Wilson, told me he was transferring to a Special Forces Group, located in Bad Tolz, Germany. He said "It's a new special type outfit, with a very different mission."

He had an older friend in the outfit who had talked him into joining the paratroopers. I kidded him and told him he was nuts, but he left anyway. He and I had a good evening together in the club the night before he left.

In late October I was sent to Koblenz, Germany, and tasked to establish radio communications there. I took my entire team, which consisted of me and three other men. We arrived and I reported to the acting First Sergeant. He was a Sergeant First Class, a rather lazy sort of a guy really. I had things up and running in no time.

I explored the little town of Koblenz and discovered that the French Army had been here earlier. They had lived upstairs in the same barracks I lived in. I was told stories of how they would empty their urinal pots out on the street besides the building. In short, they had acted disgraceful.

I was introduced to one of the city's finest nightclubs. It was there I met their singer, her name was Inga. She was tall, and had beautiful black hair, big brown eyes, and a figure that could stop a runaway tractor and trailer fully loaded. I managed to spend lots of time with her. We spent several nights at local inns, and other places that rented rooms. I became quite attached to her, and she to me. Ultimately her contract ran out with the nightclub, and she had to leave. We had an emotional parting, but we parted nevertheless.

A few weeks later I returned to Boblingen, and my friend Bill Tindall replaced me in Koblenz. In late November I was assigned duty as Platoon Sergeant of the high frequency platoon, Sergeant Jackson rotated back to the states.

I woke up early that first morning and recognized the responsibilities that I had inherited. I took a good look at myself, and thought about how I should respond as the new Platoon Sergeant. I considered how I should fulfill my responsibilities to the men assigned under me, and to the Commander who had placed me in this position. I recalled the wise words and lessons of First Sergeant Ironjaws Baker.

He had told me that there would come a day when a man would reach this point. He said, "You will become part of the system and at that point, you will be a professional soldier." He had said, "Seek responsibility and be responsible for your actions, be all that you can be." I recalled his words as if it were yesterday.

I took a good look at the men in my platoon. Most of them were draftees. They lacked discipline, training and guidance. I was determined to change that. I intended to change it immediately. I slightly distanced myself from the men under me. Not by being aloof, but by being more official, more military, and always more of the Sergeant. I treated them all as men. I played it straight with them, and demanded they be straight with me. It began to pay off, except for a few asshole draftees who insisted they remain problem children. I understood them, and I'd deal with them over time, one at a time.

CHAPTER 30

Second search for Elona

In late December I took ten days leave. I was determined to return to Wurzburg in one last attempt to find Elona. There wasn't a day go by that I didn't think of her. At night in dreams I would see her at the station crying as I tried desperately to get off the train. Next year my tour here will be up. I had to try again before it's too late. I packed a small bag with civilian clothes, shaving gear and stuff, and then caught the train for Wurzburg.

Once I arrived there I again marveled at the many changes that had taken place in the city. I thought it's a complete renovation since I first arrived here close to seven years ago. I was eighteen then, now I'm twenty-five-years old. Damn, so many miles, and so much has happened since that day so long ago. Only twenty-five, but I now had a few premature gray hairs along my temples. That fact alone made me shudder as I thought about the years passing so quickly, and knowing the years can steal and kill a young man's dreams.

I hadn't spoken with Roberts in several weeks, so I decided to call his outfit and talk with him. I called and the clerk that answered the phone said, "He's no longer here, he's been reassigned back to the states."

I wasn't totally surprised. He had been here longer than I had. I caught a taxi and instructed the driver to take me to the Bavarian Inn.

He said, "The Inn has closed for renovation, the Ram's Head Inn is another place where you can find a room."

I said, "All right, take me there."

He took me to the Rams Head Inn. It was a new place that I had never seen. I went to the Inn and rented a room for three days. I didn't want to commit myself for any longer than that.

It was still fairly early in the day. I caught a taxi and went to the Golden Stallion *Gasthaus.* I had my pictures of Elona with me. I showed them to the bartenders and to the waitresses, none of them professed to know her, or ever seeing her. I went to the castle across the Main River to their beer garden, no luck there. Then I checked with the inn keeper, he didn't know her.

I drank a bottle of beer out in the garden and reminisced about the weekend that Dotty and I had spent here, before she went to Heidleberg. It was getting late, so I went out front caught a taxi, and went to the Leopold bar. I checked there with the bartenders and waitresses all to no avail.

While at the Leopold I saw Greta and Gisela, both were sitting with young American soldiers. They appeared to be having a great time. I made no effort to speak to them, and Greta never saw me at all. That saved us both some embarrassment.

I spent the next two days going from *Gasthaus* to *Gasthaus*, I returned once more to the company where she had worked, that too resulted in failure.

It was New Year's Eve, and I was totally frustrated. I checked out of the inn where I was staying, and caught a taxi to the Ring Hotel, breaking my own vow.

I hadn't been here since the night that Rachel and I had said good-bye way back in 1949. That was six years ago. I was a little stunned to realize that the years had passed so quickly. I got out of the taxi and walked into the hotel. The lobby had been renovated, and looked modern and professional. A young girl was tending the front desk. I asked for a room for one night, specifically room number seven, and she obliged me.

I walked down the familiar hallway, and found the room. I unlocked the door and stepped inside. I looked around the room, noting that very little had changed since I was last here. There was a different table, but it too had several cigarette burns on its top. A new chair, the bed and sink looked the same, and new carpet. I sat my bag down, walked out the door and down the hall to the restaurant and bar.

I selected a table ordered a beer, and smoked a cigarette. I searched my memory to ensure that I had checked all possible places for Elona. I couldn't think of another place to go. Next July it'll be four years since I left here.

Perhaps I'm being totally unrealistic to think that a young beautiful girl like her would wait forever for a young soldier to return, especially from the States. She had two children to rear, and most likely by herself. To think she would hang around and wait for me, is asking too much. I had several beers sitting there by myself.

After paying my bar bill I returned to my room. I lay down on the bed and dozed off for about three hours. When I woke up I lay there and wondered, is this is the same bed that Rachel and I had spent so many nights on making love together. I doubted it, surely they would have gotten new mattresses since then. New Year's Eve was here, and I would obviously spend it alone. I wasn't depressed, just totally frustrated.

Returning to the bar I purchased four beers, and took them to my room. The room had a radio, so I turned it on and tuned in AFN. They were playing typical holiday music. I uncapped one of my beers and drank it slowly. I drank three more, then went back to the bar and bought three more. I drank two of them. I checked my watch it was minutes away from midnight, and the New Year.

I checked the minutes as they ticked away. The minute hand crossed into the New Year, 1956. I silently drank a toast to all the girls I'd loved and lost here in this ancient old city.

I had a swallow for Rachel, then another for Betty, another for Dotty, and a final toast to Elona. I then had a toast to myself, my future, and to the New Year. I lay down and went to sleep. The next morning I rose early, washed, shaved and dressed, then checked out of the hotel. I said goodbye to the Ring Hotel forever.

The train ride to Boblingen was uneventful. I made it back to my unit and signed in. I cancelled four days of my leave, and saved it for later use. In January we were again on field exercises. This one was extraordinarily long, six weeks we were out in the field. I pushed the young soldiers hard, and made them learn their jobs in spite of the fact some of them resisted all my efforts. Draftees are not the easiest people in the world to work with.

My convertible Mercedes continued to purr and take me everywhere I wanted to go. I even considered bringing it back to the states with me.

But I knew that I wouldn't be able to get the necessary maintenance parts for it, so I rejected the idea.

In early March I had gotten about half loaded one Saturday night and slept late the next morning. After getting up and dressing I walked outside to get my car and go out for breakfast. My convertible wasn't where I had parked it last night. I knew that I didn't loan it to anyone, so I was mystified as to where it could be. I checked with the charge of quarters, but he had no idea where my car was. I stayed around the barracks all day, but my car never showed up.

The next morning after work formation, and I had made all daily work assignments, I was called into the First Sergeant's office.

He asked, "Sergeant Fisher, do you know where your automobile is?"

"No, First Sergeant. I have no idea. It turned up missing yesterday. When I got up yesterday I couldn't find it, and it's still missing."

"I know where it is, come on with me," he said.

We walked out of the office to his Jeep. He climbed in the driver's seat, and I sat in the passenger's seat.

He turned to me and said, "Ken, I think you must have pissed someone off, or maybe you have pissed a bunch of people off."

Puzzled by his remark, I asked, "What do you mean?"

He replied, "You'll see when we get there."

He drove down the dirt road on the far side of the *Kaserne* heading to our rifle qualification range. The road widened about a hundred yards away from the range, and I saw what he meant.

There on the side of the road sat the smoldering remains of my Mercedes convertible. Some bastard, or bunch of bastards, had driven my car down here, and set the damn thing on fire. All the tires were burnt to a crisp. The top totally gone, the seats were but ashes. It was totally destroyed.

"First Sergeant, you're right I guess I really must have pissed someone off!"

I then uttered all my favorite curse words plus. I had no idea who could, or would have done this to me, neither did the First Sergeant.

"Well, we can use it here on the range for target practice, or get one of the krauts to haul it off and sell it for scrap metal."

The First Sergeant said, "I'll take care of it."

I was now reduced to walking, or catching a taxi. I never mentioned it to the platoon. But I never found out who had burnt up my convertible.

In late March we were scheduled to have a Company party. The platoon sergeant of the very high frequency platoon was in charge of making all the arrangements. He arranged a location off the post, and using company funds purchased all types of booze and beer, plus a little food. All of the company personnel attended the party which began about six o'clock in the evening. Around ten in the evening, a few of the guys had left for the barracks, and most of the married men back to their quarters.

It was about that time that the company commander stood up on a table and shouted, "I can whip any man's ass in this outfit!"

Everyone stopped talking, and just looked at the Captain. I saw immediately that he was about shit-faced. He had been drinking whiskey and some type mix all evening, and drinking quite a bit of it. The First Sergeant who was seated to my left sat quietly, and said nothing. The Captain walked down his table top and kicked everyone's drink off the table. Drinks were flying everywhere, glass shattered all around on the floor.

He said, "All you piss heads are scared shitless, and are afraid to fight a paratrooper."

None of the junior officers made a move, or said a word. He then jumped from his table over to our table, and stepped up in front of me.

He said, "How about you Sergeant Fisher. Have you got any balls, or are you just a scared little piss head also?"

Looking up at the Captain I said, "Captain, I think you've had too much to drink. Why don't you call it a night, and go home to your wife?"

He spit at me and missed, then drew his foot back to kick my drink off the table. When he did I reached over and grabbed his other leg and yanked. He fell crashing to the table, and the table tipped over. About four men jumped on him, and I saw several punches being thrown.

The First Sergeant went around the table, and someone hit him in the head, he went flying backwards, blood running down his face. I went around the table, and someone from the other platoon took a swing at me. I ducked and kicked him in the stomach. He folded like a used condom, and dropped to the floor.

I saw the Captain on the floor swinging and kicking away. Someone was swinging back at him. I saw him take a punch in the eye and blood spurted out of his brow. I thought, *why break up a damn good fight?*

I saw the platoon sergeant who had arranged the party with a broken bloody nose, he was standing to one side with a handkerchief to his face. Two men wrestling and swinging away plowed into me, I went head over heels and landed on the floor. I picked myself up, and continued to watch the fight. Shortly thereafter in rushed the MP's, whistles were blowing as they swung their nightsticks. I found the First Sergeant, grabbing his arm I led him out the back door. We both got away clean. It was a terrific party, and a great night.

The next day we had a new Company Commander. We were in a company formation, and the Battalion Commander chewed our asses for about fifteen minutes. We all accepted that with pleasure, at least we had gotten rid of the asshole, and things would return to normal, and had to get better around here.

We spent the better part of the next few months on exercises, and maintaining the equipment. I was approaching the end of my tour, and the end of my enlistment. I decided to take a leave, get away from the army for a few days and relax. I thought, I might return to Garmisch, and revisit the places Ray Washington and I had gone to so many years earlier. Then I thought, no, that's no good. I have too many beautiful memories of there. Then I thought, I might go to Berschesgaden, but I didn't want to go there alone, and I wanted to be alone.

I decided instead to go to Stuttgart, rent a room, relax and explore the city and its attractions. I'll just be a damn tourist for a week or so, and get away from all the military hum-drum.

Around the end of June I took a ten day leave listing Stuttgart as my destination. I caught the bus and after a short ride I was there. I called Special Services, and they recommended a hotel downtown called the Stuttgart Palace hotel. They assured me it had a bar and a restaurant. The amenities were very nice, the cost reasonable, and well worth it. I accepted their word for it.

CHAPTER 31

Destiny or dumb luck

I arrived at the hotel, registered in and was assigned a room on the second floor. I checked it out, and it was indeed very nice. A large bathtub and shower, double bed, a radio, telephone and writing table, plus two easy chairs. I had nothing but civilian clothes with me, so I could easily play the tourist. The first night I sat at the hotel bar and sipped beer until closing time, and listened to their band. I had an excellent night's sleep. The next morning I walked across the street and had breakfast, then returned to the hotel and had coffee in their little sidewalk café.

For the next two days I played tourist. I strolled around the city for several blocks around the hotel enjoying the sights, and observing the people. Eleven years after the end of the war, the German economy was definitely rebounding. The people were much better dressed, their cars newer, the streets cleaner, and the shops had more and better merchandise.

On the forth morning of my leave, I had gone across the street had breakfast then returned back to the sidewalk café. At a small table I ordered coffee and smoked a cigarette. I watched the people as they went about their daily activities. I observed this lady with three small children as they sat down at a table several feet away from me. I immediately noted that the larger boy and the girl were of mixed parents. They had either a black mother or a black father, but not both. They appeared to be about six or seven years of age. The smaller boy appeared to be about three or four years old, he was totally white.

I thought that's really odd. I studied the woman, and she appeared to be somewhat too old to have children so young. The longer I observed her the more I thought, I'd seen her someplace. She seemed strangely familiar. I searched my memory, but couldn't place her anywhere in my past. Puzzled, I ordered another cup of coffee and lit another cigarette. I watched as she glanced at her wrist watch, and then picking up the smaller child placed him on her lap.

I looked at the little boy, and the longer I studied him the more familiar he appeared. I shook my head, that's impossible. I've never seen these people before in my life, and that boy can't be anyone's child that I know. I continued to observe him, and then it dawned on me. It's incredible! He looks just like a small picture that my mother has of me when I was his age!

The hackles on my neck stood up, and I became slightly nervous. Mentally addressing myself, I said, "Sergeant Fisher, what are you thinking? Are you going frigging crazy? You don't know these people from Adam, and you're imagining things."

Lighting another cigarette I tried to relax, but I couldn't take my eyes off the little boy. He squirmed off the lady's lap, and walked over toward me.

I extended my hand and said, "Hello young fellow."

He grasped my hand and shook it, but he didn't speak. He then dropped my hand and walked over to the container holding flowers and smelled each of them. He had dark brown hair, and brown eyes, just like mine.

The two other children then began shouting, "*Mutter, Mutter*." A woman walked pass my table position, I couldn't see her face as the shrubbery hid it from my view. She walked over to the lady's table with her back to me. She reached down and picked up the little girl holding her and kissing the child. I became instantly alert. I sat up straight in my chair my nerves screaming. I recognized her even with her back to me, the woman had to be Elona!

I became so excited my arm jerked, and I knocked my coffee cup off the table. It shattered into smithereens. The woman turned around and looked at me. *It was Elona*!

She stared at me, and I stared at her. The small child slowly slid down her arms. She continued to stare at me with a shocked, disbelieving look on her face. Then in a barely audible voice, she said, "Ken?"

I stood up from the table and asked, "Elona, is it really you?"

The little boy came running to her and she picked him up. She continued to stare at me, as she slowly sat down on one of the wooden chairs.

"Hello Elona, it's me, I really am Ken Fisher!"

She looked faint as she just stared at me. The little boy was hugging her neck as she tried to hold him off.

She finally said, "Ken, is it really you? Tell me that I'm not imagining this!"

I moved away from my table, and walked over to her. I grasped her hand, "Elona, darling, I've finally found you. I'm indeed, Ken Fisher."

She just stared at my face, and slowly brought my hand to her lips kissing it. Tears filled her eyes as she continued looking at me.

She said, "This can't be, this can't be real, I must be dreaming!"

I thought, *she's more beautiful than I even remembered.* Her long hair was cut shorter, her face had a more mature look to it that enhanced her beauty as a full woman. One small barely noticeable crowfoot wrinkle ran outwards from her eyes. Her body still as slim and shapely as before. She turned and spoke rapidly to the other woman in German which I didn't understand. I did hear her say my name.

"May I sit down?"

She said, "Yes, yes of course, please do."

I pulled a chair over from another table and sat down. She reached over taking my hand again brought it to her lips kissing it. I took both her hands and kissed them. I immediately saw that she wore a wedding ring on her finger.

"Elona, darling, I've looked so long for you, and of all places I find you in Stuttgart. What fate has brought us together I don't know, but we're together now."

Tears filled her eyes, and rolled down her cheeks.

I reached over brushing them away, and said, "Darling, please don't cry, you and I have cried enough for a lifetime. We are by the grace of God, together once again."

She grasped my hand holding on to it tightly as words began pouring from her mouth.

She said, "Are you stationed in Stuttgart? How long have you been here, how long will you be here? Where have you been?"

I smiled and said, "Slow down darling. No, I'm stationed in Boblingen. I'm here on leave, I have six days left. I'm staying in this hotel, and I'm all by myself."

I was very nervous, my hands were shaking, so I lit a cigarette. I offered the other woman one, and she accepted it. I lit it for her. She was also staring at me. The small boy came to my knee, and I leaned over and picked him up. He sat quietly on my lap picking at the buttons on my shirt.

The other lady spoke to Elona and said something like: "*Remerkenswert ahnlichkeit*."

Elona replied, "*Bestimm*t."

I had no idea what they had said to each other.

Elona continued to hold tightly to my hand. She touched my temple and said, "My darling, you have gray in your hair." She then asked, "You have six more days here at this hotel?" I nodded my head yes, tears again filled her eyes, and I wiped them away.

"Elona, please don't cry, we've found each other again, now is the time to laugh, to be happy, now we can live again!"

The two other children were playing with the flowers, so the boy climbed down from my lap and joined them as they surveyed and smelled the flowers.

Elona stared at me and softly asked, "Do you want me to stay here with you at the hotel?"

"Yes, of course I do. I never want you out of my sight again!"

She continued to hold my hand, then turning she began speaking to the other woman. They talked for about five minutes as I sat quietly, not understanding anything they were discussing. She then turned and called all the children over to her and began talking to them, again in German. Each of them in turn hugged her neck and she kissed them. The smallest boy climbed on her lap hugging and kissing her. She said something to him and he squirmed down and walked over to me putting out his little hand. I accepted his hand and shook it.

Elona said, "Ken, kiss your son Kenny!"

I looked at her in shock. She nodded her head. I picked the little fellow up and stared at him for a full half minute, he began squirming, I then hugged and kissed him on the cheek,

I said to the boy, "You're a Fisher! Don't forget that," and put him back down.

The other lady took his hand, then saying something to the other two children they all four walked away.

I watched as they left. I looked at her and said, "Elona, I never knew that we had a child together. He's a beautiful boy. I'm thrilled to know that I'm his father, and you're his mother. How old is he now?"

She replied, "He's three years and four months old now."

I did some quick mental mathematics and calculated that he had been conceived around May or June of 1952.

She asked, "Can we go to your room now?"

"Of course, we have years to catch up on."

She rose and we entered the hotel together. I pointed out to her the bar, the restaurant, and some of the shops that were in the hotel. We caught the elevator to the second floor, and walked down the hallway to my room. I inserted the key unlocking the door. She then walked into the room. I followed her, then closed and locked the door.

I leaned against the door and watched as she walked around the room. She turned looked at me as I held out my arms to her. She ran across the room, and I grabbed her in my arms pulling her to me. She began crying again. I tilted her face and kissed her, tasting the salt from her tears. Her arms went around my neck as she kissed me passionately.

I whispered, "My dearest Elona, I've finally found you. I never thought I would. I'd almost given up all hope of ever seeing you again."

Tears came into my own eyes. I realized that it was a strange stroke of luck, or a playful destiny that had brought me here to Stuttgart at this exact moment in time.

I held her tightly and kissed her again. She kissed my tears away as she whispered, "My dearest darling Ken, I love you so much! I never expected to see you again. It's been so long, and so much has happened since Wurzburg."

I led her over to the table and sat her down in the small chair; I sat down opposite her and held her hands.

"Would you like a glass of wine?"

"Yes please."

"Wait here, and I'll go down to the bar and get us both a drink." She pulled my face to hers and kissed me again. I quickly left the room, and took the elevator down. I purchased a bottle of white wine and four cold beers, taking it all upstairs with me. She was sitting on the bed when I arrived back in the room.

I opened the wine and poured her a full glass. I opened one of the beers for myself.

Raising my beer in toast I said, "Here's to us once more!"

She raised her glass in return and had a sip of her wine. I came over and sat on the bed with her, and pulling her to me kissed her again. We slowly leaned over on the bed. I stroked her hair and kissed all her face and her lips. She held my head kissing my entire face.

She said, "Ken, I don't know where to start. All the things that have happened to us since we last saw each other in Wurzburg. Now you finally show up and walk back into my life, and that's what I prayed for! This is the happiest day of my life!"

I sat up and looked at her as she lay there on the bed watching me.

She said, "Tell me about yourself, tell me everything that's happened with you since you left."

"Elona, I called you for three days before I left, and you didn't take my calls. I had to leave. At the last moment, as the train began moving I saw you on the station platform, I leaned out the window my hand barely touched yours. I tried to get off the train, but my friends grabbed me and threw me on the floor holding me down until the train was moving too fast for me to jump."

Her hand stroked my face. She said, "I remember. I saw your friends John and Jack as they grabbed you and held you. I almost died that morning. If a broken heart could kill you, I'd now be dead."

I continued, "I went back to the states, and eventually I was discharged and got out of the army. I went home for a few weeks, and then I went to Florida, then to New York. I reenlisted in the army in Buffalo, New York. I arrived back here in Germany in 1954. I've been here since then. In 1954, I spent a week in Wurzburg looking for you. My friend John Roberts was also there, he told me he never saw you at all. I went back to Wurzburg again last year and spent several days looking for you. But you weren't to be found. I even went to the company that you worked for, and they told me that you had quit and left. They didn't know where you were. I went to every *Gasthaus* and restaurant we ever visited together, I showed them your picture, but no one could offer any help. I'd almost given up all hope. Now that I've found you, I'll never let you go again!"

She looked at me and listened, as I explained the last few years of my life. Tears again filled her eyes. I leaned over and kissed her again and stroked her hair.

"Tell me darling what the years have been like since then. Tell me where you've been, and why I couldn't find you. Tell me everything. Let's move over and sit in the big chair, I want to hold you close to me again."

We both got off the bed and moved to the big chair. I put my arm around her as she leaned over and kissed my forehead.

She said, "I didn't take your calls because I was too sick. I knew that you had to go, but that didn't help me. I had to see you again, so I went to the train station almost too late. I did see you, and we touched hands, then I saw them throw you to the floor as the train left. I just wanted to die!"

I stroked her face and kissed her cheek.

She continued, "My sister came to the station and got me, and took me back home. I stayed in bed for a week.

Then I found out I was pregnant. I was thrilled that you and I had created this life together. But without you, it all seemed so one-sided. I couldn't go to a *Gasthaus,* or a restaurant that you and I had gone together. If I did the memories of us haunted me, I saw you everywhere. So I never went to any of them. I just continued to work at the company, and took care of our new baby son."

I kissed her and said, "Thank you." Tears filled my eyes as she talked. She gently brushed them away.

She continued, "I waited for you and I prayed for you. You told me you would come back and I waited. Last year my brother-in-law who works for a big company was transferred to Stuttgart. All of us moved here together. I quit my job at the company, and came here with them. That was my sister you saw this morning, she took the kids home with her."

I recalled how I thought she appeared familiar to me. I had seen her years ago, and she and Elona have a definite resemblance.

She continued, "Next month it'll be four long years since I last saw you. Like you, my hopes of ever seeing you again had almost died. You were on one continent, and I on another. I went to work in a bank here in Stuttgart about a year ago. I rented my own apartment and Kenny I placed into a kindergarten every day. It was very hard as I didn't make a lot of money, but I was careful, and we were able to make it on my salary"

I pulled her face towards mine, and kissed her tenderly on her lips.

She said, "May I have another glass of wine?"

"Of course sweetheart"

She rose from my lap, as I got up and poured her another glass, and opened another beer for myself. I returned to the chair, and she sat back down on my lap, I hugged her and kissed her again. She returned my kisses with a passionate touch that I knew and recognized.

"Today, I almost fainted when I first saw you. I thought I must be sick and hallucinating. I couldn't believe that here you were sitting just feet away from your own son, and didn't know it. You were just feet away from me, and I didn't know it. I had prayed for years for you to return. God has answered my prayers!"

She leaned over and kissed me. With equal passion I returned her kiss, and the sexual fire and desires of old returned with a burning sense of urgency. I reached up and caressing her breasts as our tongues once again danced their own special dance of love. I slowly unbuttoned her blouse and she removed it, then I removed her brassiere and lay it aside. Her beautiful breasts rose and fell as her breath quickened. She rose from my lap and unbuttoned and removed my shirt. I stood up and removed my pants as she removed her skirt, half slip and panties. I removed the remainder of my clothes, and sat back down in the chair. She returned to my lap and kissed me. My erection was hungry and hard. I pressed it up against my stomach and pulled her closer to me.

"Elona, darling, I don't want to rush. You don't know how many times I've dreamed of holding you and making love to you, and with you. It's my dream come true, so I must make it last as long as possible."

She whispered, "I know. I've dreamed those very same dreams a thousand times over. I have dreamed of being in your arms, making love with you, holding you close to me, watching you sleep and knowing that we belong together."

I picked her up in my arms and moved over to the bed. I eased her down, and then lay down besides her. I kissed her and caressed her body. I kissed her beautiful breasts and teased them with my lips and tongue. The smoldering fires of desire climbing higher and hotter. I moved to the top of her as she opened her legs to me. She moaned and held my head as we began the wonderful journey together.

Within minutes I entered those fabulous short rows, and I told her I couldn't last. We completed our act of love. I reared up a little and kissed her again then said, "You're my dream come true."

I moved from on top of her, and just lay there my arm over her breasts. "Darling, I just can't believe that after such a long time we're once again together in a bed, making love like we used to. I can't believe that after looking so long, and in so many places, that I find you in Stuttgart. Now we're together again making love. It's almost unreal!" She rolled over on her side leaned over, and kissed my face.

She said, "Ken, I fell in love with you years ago, and I love you now, I'll love you forever. No matter whatever happens in our future, you and I are one person. Tears welled up and glistened in her dark beautiful eyes.

Looking deep into those mesmerizing violet pools of magic kissing them both, I said, "Yes, my darling, what you're saying is true. No one knows what the future holds for them, certainly not me. But we're the same, our hearts beat as one."

"Why don't we clean up a bit and go have a bite to eat."

"That's a good idea, I just realized that I'm hungry."

She went into the bathroom for several minutes then came out and dressed. I quickly cleaned up a bit then got dressed. Dressing into civilian clothes is so much easier and quicker than putting on an entire uniform.

We left the room and went down to the first floor on the elevator. I led the way into the restaurant. She ordered for us. She sipped a glass of white wine and I had another beer as we slowly ate our meal. I just wanted to stare at her, and hear her voice again. Four years of wishing, wondering, and wanting had ended in success. Finding her all my hopes and dreams had come true. My goal for reenlisting, and this tour of duty had been accomplished completely.

It was now early in the evening. I asked her, "Elona, are you going to be able to stay with me tonight, or do you have to go home to the children?"

"I'll stay here with you my love. My sister will take care of Kenny and the others until I return."

Leaning over kissing her cheek I said, "That's wonderful. So you have named our son Kenneth and you call him Kenny, that's a very nice name even if I do say so."

She laughed, punched me in the stomach and said, "I love the name and so does he."

"Are you ready to go back upstairs, I asked?"

"Yes."

Out in the hotel lobby she stopped and went into a small bookstore as I waited for her. She shortly returned and had a book inside a small bag. We went back upstairs via the elevator and entered our room.

I sat in the chair and she sat again on my lap.

"Ken, when you went back to your home did you find race problems there the same as when you were a boy?"

"Yes, my love, the situation there is exactly as it was when I was a boy. I was right, we could not have lived in my hometown with the two children. Believe me it would have been an impossible nightmare, a disaster waiting to happen. It would have been not only for us, but for the boy and the girl as well, and they're so innocent. I made the right decision, but it almost cost us everything."

Lighting a cigarette I continued, "Nothing has changed down South. The prejudices there will be there it seems forever. Someday it may change perhaps, but not in my lifetime."

She asked, "Even now we couldn't go there and make it our home?"

"My love we would never go there. I intend to remain in the army, and the army doesn't care who or what you are as long as you can soldier and do your job. I'm a professional soldier now, and the army is my life. It's not an easy life, but it's my life! I love the army. All that I am, and all that I'll ever be, I owe to the army. I love you like no other, and I always will, but the army is my home."

She hugged my neck kissing me and said, "You're my world!"

She truly surprised me saying, "Darling, let's take our clothes off."

She stood up and began removing all her clothing. I immediately undressed completely. She then pushed me back into the chair, and reaching over she removed the small book which she had just purchased downstairs. It appeared to be a small bible, but it was in German, and I couldn't make out the title.

She took my hand and placed it on the cover of the book.

She then placed her hand on top of mine and said, "I Elona Haufmann, followed by several words in German."

She then leaned over kissing me and said, "My love, we're now one person. Nothing can change or destroy that."

Deeply moved, I pulled her to me and said, "Yes, sweetheart you're right."

A question that I knew had to be asked kept pushing itself to the front of my mind. I also knew that it had to be answered before she and I could go any further.

I tilted her head up and asked, "Elona, why are you wearing a wedding ring? I didn't give it to you, you didn't wear it before. Please be completely honest with me, and tell me why you're wearing it now."

She looked at me with a sudden look of despair and anguish. She said, "Ken, please hear me out, and let me explain it all."

I just nodded my head and said, "Please do."

She began, "Next month it'll be four years since we last saw each other. I waited for you, and I prayed for you and your return, but you never came back. For over two long years I stayed in Wurzburg working, waiting, worrying and hoping. Meanwhile, I had three children to care for. We finally moved to Stuttgart. I had lost all hope of you ever returning. America is a long ways away from Germany."

I caressed her cheek and stroked her bobbed hair as she continued.

"When we arrived here I found a job in a big bank. I work in their English translation department. I met this young man who is a junior vice-president in the bank. After I had been there several months he continually asked me to go out with him. I wasn't getting any younger, so finally I relented, and I did go out with him. One thing led to another and we dated only each other. He met my three children, and I explained them all to him. He understood perfectly, and accepted them without question. He loves the three children, and they all adore him. He asked me to marry him, and only after I had exhausted all hope of ever seeing you again, I consented. We've been married six months this month. Now he's attending a banking seminar in Zurich, Switzerland, for two weeks. He left here yesterday morning."

She now had tears running down her cheeks, and I slowly wiped them away as I listened to her explanation. I realized that once again, I was facing another losing situation.

She continued, "When I saw you this morning my whole world turned upside down. I'm caught once again in a situation I have no control over."

I pulled her to me and kissed her gently on the cheek. I could feel her heart racing as she sobbed quietly against my chest. I took a big drink from my beer, and lit a cigarette.

"Sweetheart, I have to think this situation out. I must think it through and find some answers to it. Do you love your husband?"

I realized that once again I was involved in a covert love affair. The first time with Rachel who had promised to marry another man, and now my lover Elona, who is married to another man.

Softly she replied, "Yes, I do love him, but not like I love you. I have told you so many times in so many ways how much I love you, and you know it. What you and I have, and always had, is more than my feeble English can describe or explain. The words I said and swore just moments ago are as truthful and pure as I know how to say them."

She pulled my head over kissing me on the cheek.

I held her close to me and said, "Darling, why must our love be so very hard and difficult. Why must everything go wrong for us?" I slowly shook my head in dismay.

I had another big swallow of beer and lit another cigarette. I pulled her against me and just held her close. Neither of us spoke for several minutes.

"Do you want to stay here with me for the remainder of my leave? I want you to."

She raised her head and replied, "Yes, I want to. I have to stay with you! In my mind we're one person. I can't let you leave me again, not like this."

"I have six days left here. If you stay with me then its best we simply stay in the hotel. There's the possibility that one of your friends, or one of your husband's friends, could see us together if we go out, and that would cause you unnecessary problems You would have to explain to them, and to your husband who I am, and why you're with me. We can avoid that problem by staying here. They have a bar, a restaurant, and a women's clothes shop downstairs, you can get whatever you need here." I had a swallow of beer and said, "Staying here will also give us more time together, and more time to solve our problem."

She said, "Yes, we can do that, I will do that."

I hugged her to me and asked, “Would you like another glass of wine?”

She nodded her head, and I refilled her glass. I suggested she and I take a bath together. She readily agreed. We both went to the bath room and I filled the tub with very warm water. She entered it first and I followed. I soaped and bathed her, and she in turn soaped and bathed me. It was such a delight, she was still one of the most beautiful women I’d ever seen.

We got out of the tub and toweled off. Then I lay on the bed and pulled her close to me.

“Elona, do you remember the three days we spent together in Garmisch?”

“Yes, my love I think of it many times. The fun we had with your friend Ray and his girlfriend. The happiness we shared. At that point in our lives we had no problems that were so terrible, or so big we couldn’t handle.”

“Sweet thing those were the days indeed.” I rolled over and kissed her on the eyes. We made love again, and then we both fell asleep.

For the next four days we stayed in the hotel. We ate all our meals in the restaurant, and spent a few hours each night in the bar. It was a time of idyllic charm and beauty. Three of the nights they had a band, and we danced like we had several years earlier. We talked about our problem of her marriage, but we never developed or advanced an answer to the problem. Neither of us spoke of the future beyond my leave. Each day she would call her sister and check on the kids, and I suppose tell her sister about us.

On the ninth morning of my leave, I woke up early got out of bed and sat in the chair. I watched her sleep as I smoked a cigarette.

In her eyes we were truly joined as one. Quietly, I sat there and thought about our situation.

I posed question after question to myself, and produced no acceptable answers. I could develop no quick immediate legitimate solution to our problem of her marriage.

Eventually, I arrived at a decision. One I didn’t like, but a decision I had to make, and one that would permit us to go on with our lives. I went into the bathroom took a shower and shaved. When I returned she was awake. I suggested to her that we go have breakfast. She promptly agreed.

She took a bath and then got dressed. She wore the new outfit that I had purchased downstairs in the dress shop the day before. She was absolutely stunning in it. She was quieter than normal, and I knew that the weight of our problem was on her mind, as it was on mine. After eating, I drank a couple of cups of coffee and smoked a cigarette.

She said, "Let's go back to our room." I agreed, we rose and left the restaurant.

Arriving back at our room I turned on AFN listened to the news then turned it off. I sat down in the big chair, and she came over to me, I gently pulled her down onto my lap.

I kissed her on the cheek and said, "Elona, sweetheart, with all my heart I love you, but I must leave tomorrow, and we have to make our decisions today."

She hugged me and said, "My dearest love I know. We have talked enough. You make the decision for us, and I'll do whatever you say we should do!"

"I'll be twenty-six-years-old in just a few more days, and you'll be twenty-four. Hopefully, we both still have a long life ahead of us. The decisions we make now might hurt, but they will allow us hopefully to have good lives. You must agree with my decision, or it's worthless and means nothing."

She hugged my neck and laid her head on my chest. She was slightly trembling, I held her closely as I continued, "You are now legally and morally married, and you do love your new husband. He loves you and the three children, and you said they adore him. I cannot in good conscience disrupt, or destroy your lawful legal marriage."

Taking a deep breath I continued, "I'm a professional soldier, and the life of military wives is hard, often difficult, and even lonely at times as the army sends me to strange places. Such times would be difficult for you and the children, and hard for me to accept. I'll leave tomorrow, and you must go home and live with your new husband. You and he must build your lives together, and assist the children as they mature and grow into adulthood." She sobbed, clutching me as I continued.

"Life has dealt us a cruel hand. Nevertheless, we must accept and play the hand we've been dealt. Tomorrow, we'll part again forever. But this time we truly know that we share together a love that will endure. Continents and oceans may and will separate us, but we know we're just a heartbeat away from each other. If we're ever to achieve peace of mind and soul, we must do this. We must kiss each other goodbye tomorrow, and go our separate ways. I probably will never return to Germany, and I'll make no effort to ever do so again. Germany gave me great happiness, and then snatched it all back. This country hasn't been good to me! You're mine and I'm yours, to deny that would be to deny our love for each other."

I took another deep breath and felt her sobbing. I felt like crying myself. But I knew that this was the only honorable, decent and logical decision that I could make. I couldn't upset and destroy her marriage. I couldn't disrupt the children's lives, and my own.

My heart was breaking. Silently, I cursed the Goddess Aphrodite. Three times now I have experienced this horrific pain. I guess I must be a sucker for pain.

I said, "Will you do this one last thing for me Elona? My darling will you help me tomorrow, as we part will you walk away from me, and don't look back? Just kiss me goodbye, and I'll leave."

She began crying even more as she buried her head on my chest, I held her close to me and tried to calm her down.

She said, "It's not fair, it's not right, it's not fair!"

I brushed the tears from her cheeks.

"Ken, I'll do whatever you say, with all my heart I'll try and do this. I know that you're right, but that doesn't help. Nothing can help me!"

I replied, "We have made the hard decision. We must put this behind us now, and spend the remainder of our time together like the young lovers we once were, and are once again. We won't discuss or even think of tomorrow. We must enjoy today the pleasure of being together. We must support each other in this, or we'll surely fail."

She nodded her head in agreement.

We ate our meals together, and I bought one bottle of wine and several bottles of beer taking them to the room. We drank and made love, and drank some more. I was completely sober, and so was she. She laid nearly on top of me on the bed caressing me, and listening to my heartbeat. I caressed her and whispered sweet things into her ear. We both knew that this was our last night together.

Midnight came and went. Neither of us was sleepy, neither did we attempt to sleep. I held her as we talked mostly about our past times together. We laughed, reminiscing and recalling things that we had done and experienced together.

The hours sped by, and daylight stealing along on its delicate feet danced swiftly through the window curtains. Finally, I got up from the bed and had another drink of beer. I had two bottles left. There was less than a half of a bottle of wine left. I drank another swallow of beer, as I steeled and fortified myself for today's departure.

I went into the bathroom took a hot shower and shaved. I dried off and walked back into the room. She lay there wide awake watching me. I made no effort whatsoever to dress. My bus left at six in the evening, so I had nothing but time. She got up and went into the bathroom, took a bath and returned.

I suggested we go have a bite to eat, she nodded in agreement. We both dressed and went down the elevator to the restaurant and had breakfast. Returning to our room I followed my routine and sat down in the chair, she almost automatically sat down on my lap.

I held her close to me. There was so little left that we could say, our emotions exhausted, both hearts broken. I think we were both lost in the fog of sadness and despair that had settled over our room. I had to somehow break this suffocating morbid feeling of impending disaster.

I tilted her face up kissing her, then I smiled and said, "Smile at me, tell me you have enjoyed our holiday together, tell me you loved having sex with me again, or I'll kiss you until you faint."

She giggled and said, "Yes, my wonderful lover to all those things. These six days will have to last me a lifetime, but they have been the happiest days of my life. God has answered my prayers."

I had no beer left, so I poured a glass of wine and took a sip. She took the glass from me and turned it to where my lips had been also taken a sip. I lit a cigarette and smoked it as we enjoyed small sips from the glass of wine. It was early afternoon now. I became nervous and restless, as I knew our time left together was evaporating rapidly.

She looked at me and said, "Kenny, will you make love to me once more?"

I kissed her and replied, "Darling, you just try and stop me from doing so."

I caressed her breasts and kissed her neck and ear. I slowly unbuttoned and removed her clothing. I removed my shoes and took my clothing off. Together we moved over to the bed. We lay across the bed and caressed each other. She said, "My dearest darling, make me pregnant, give me another baby, give me a baby girl!"

I remained silent and continued out act of love. The act consummated I kissed her and she said, "Thank you my darling."

Rolling to one side I relaxed a bit. I glanced at my watch and said, "Sweetheart, we must get dressed now."

Rising from the bed I went to the bathroom then returned and put my clothes on. She continued to lie on the bed.

She finally got off the bed and said, "I will not bathe until tomorrow. Your seed my darling must stay where you planted them."

There was no reply that I could possibly make. What could I have said? I would never know if she became pregnant or not.

I put my socks and shoes on then I put my excess clothing and my shaving kit back in the bag that I had brought with me. She again wore the new outfit that I had bought her a couple of days earlier. She was absolutely gorgeous in it. She brushed her hair and applied a little lipstick to her lips. I walked up behind her, and took her in my arms. I lifted her hair and kissed her softly on the back of her neck, then gently kissed her along her ear and neck. She clasped both my hands raising them to her lips and kissed them.

With tears in my eyes I said, "We must go now my darling."

Silently, she nodded her head in agreement. She picked up her small shopping bag, and I picked up my bag and walked to the door. I stopped and turned, she had not moved. I looked at her she had tears in her eyes. Tears immediately filled my own eyes again.

"Come darling, we must not torture ourselves, we have agreed that we must do this if we're ever to have a life."

Slowly, she moved toward the door and we left the room. We rode silently down the elevator. She waited as I turned in the room key and paid for my lodging. We then walked together out to the sidewalk café.

She said, "Ken, can we please just sit here for a few minutes?"

I nodded yes, and sat down in a chair. She sat down beside me and held my hand. I lit a cigarette as my hands were rather shaky. I still had tears in my eyes as did she.

I smoked the cigarette, extinguishing it in the ashtray and said, "We must go now my love."

I stood up and she stood up with me arm in arm we moved to the sidewalk. I turned and took her in my arms kissing her with all the love and passion that I had within me. She returned my kiss, holding my head and began crying again.

Gently pulling her arms from around my neck I said, "Please go now dear heart, while I'm strong enough to leave."

She turned and slowly walked down the street.

I watched as she walked away. Once again I was absolutely devastated. I watched her as she crossed an intersection, then she stopped and turned around taking several steps back in my direction.

I waved her to go on. She stopped, turned again, and walked on out of sight.

My long beautiful love affair with Elona had reached its conclusion! My memory book grew ever larger with more pages of wondrous beauty than I ever thought possible. I slowly and irrevocably closed that tear stained Chapter.

I caught a taxi to the bus station, and then the bus back to Boblingen, arriving back at my barracks a few minutes before ten o'clock. I was dead tired, and had not slept in hours. I went to my room, throwing my clothes off, I laid down on my bunk and immediately fell asleep.

The sound of reveille woke me up. I was no longer a tourist. I was back in the army again. I lit a cigarette and just lay there remembering all the events that had just taken place. It's weird I thought, *the strange destiny that guided me to Stuttgart fulfilling my reason for being here in Germany, and then mockingly snatched it all away.*

I knew that my decision was the right one. In spite of a broken heart it was right. I consoled myself with the thought that I'd at least found her, and my new son. She will do well, and in time she'll have a great life. Now I have to determine new directions for my own life, seek new horizons, establish and crystallize fresh goals, and move forward.

CHAPTER 32

Leaving Germany again

I was coming to the end of my tour, and my enlistment would be up in November. I had to review my options and determine what I wanted to do. For sure I was ready to leave Germany. It no longer held any fantasies, fascination, or future for me.

During August and September my unit spent most of its time in the field on exercises. The troops were rotating back to the states, and new draftees were filled the vacancies. Bill Tindall and I spent lots of time together, chasing a few of the skirts down town and drank a little booze together. He was a good friend of mine.

Eventually, November arrived, and I began gathering my belongings together to leave. The platoon planned a farewell party for me over in the EM club. The big night arrived, and about twenty men showed up for the party, plus several men from the other platoon. Someone called for a speech, I declined, but they continued to insist I make a speech. So I consented.

Naturally, I told them how much I enjoyed working with them, and how important their work and efforts contributed to the platoons success. Reaching the end of my remarks, and in sort of an afterthought, I said this, "I would also like to express my appreciation to the sorry son-of-a-bitch that burned my frigging Mercedes convertible. I was going to get rid of it, and you simply saved me the trouble. Nevertheless, whoever you are you're a gutless, cowardly bastard, and you do know who you are. Other than that, we've all had a great time." I lifted my beer and said, "*Prosit und auf wiedersehen!*"

I left the next afternoon for Bremmerhaven. The train ride was as boring as could be expected. The seats were still hard, cold and uncomfortable. Arriving at last to Bremmerhaven we walked up the gangplank, went to our compartment, selected a hammock and left our duffle bags. I dreaded the ten day voyage back to New York, as this was my forth time to make the boat trip. We had about three hundred men aboard the ship, and were told we were going to Liverpool, England, and pick up another eight hundred men who were stationed there.

I felt the ship move away from the dock, and then slowly move out toward the open sea. I walked up top side and back to the rear of the ship. I watched with a deepening sense of sadness as the view of the port slowly receded in the distance. I lit a cigarette then leaning against the rail, I slowly smoked it. I thought, I've spent the better part of six years in Germany. It had given me four beautiful women, two of them I loved with every fiber of my being. I conceived two sons in this country, one I've seen, the other I'll never see. It then broke my heart twice, and broke it unmercifully. I won't let that happen to me again ever!

Standing back from the rail I looked across the endless whitecaps, the rising, falling, disappearing waves, and at my last sight of Germany as it slowly sank beneath the horizon. I knew that several complete Chapters in my life had ended, but they were safely stored in my memory book, and my military journey still has a long way to go.

I flipped my lifeless cigarette into the ocean, turned and went below. I never returned to Germany, and I never wanted to! My enlistment was almost up. I knew I would reenlist for sure. I also had to develop and set new goals for my career, and in my life. I knew with an absolute sense of finality that Germany and the life I knew there, and the women I had met and loved, was irreversibly and irrevocably finished.

I won't look back. Instead my new goal is to make Master Sergeant by the time I get twenty years in the army. That's realistic and doable, now all I have to do is make it happen!

I wondered where Sam Amato was these days. As far as I know he's still in Japan. I wonder if he'll also reenlist or get out. I'll have to write Mrs. Amato and find out.

The ship moved along and in no time we were well out into the North Sea. Eventually, we arrived at Liverpool, England, and our ship docked there for two days.

The first day we were there one of the ship's crew told me and another Sergeant that he was going ashore and have a few drinks, and asked if we wanted to join him.

I immediately told him yes, the other guy also agreed to go ashore and visit an English pub.

We both went downstairs; I found some civilian clothes in my bag and put them on. The other Sergeant did likewise. We both met the crewman back on the top deck, he led as we walked down the gangplank and out of the dock area. The crewman caught a small taxi and gave him instructions to the Fox and Hounds pub. We walked inside, and the crewman ordered three pints of ale.

"What does this stuff taste like?" I asked.

He replied, "Its good, some of it stronger than beer, and some weaker, but all in all, I think you'll like it."

I took a big swallow it was rather bitter. I took a second swallow, and it was a little better than the first. The three of us quickly consumed our drinks, so I ordered another round. Then I realized that I didn't have any English money. I explained to the Innkeeper that I had only American money. He assured me he'd accept it, so we had another round of ale. Around midnight we were all about half loaded, so we caught a taxi and returned to the ship.

I woke up the next morning with a splitting headache. I searched my shaving kit and found some aspirins. I headed for the latrine and swallowed three of them down immediately. I then shaved and cleaned up. I wandered through the compartments until I found the galley. I had a decent breakfast and several cups of black coffee. My headache eased off and I felt much better. I went up topside smoked a cigarette, and saw that busses were arriving with the troops who were to come aboard our ship.

Eventually, all the troops were aboard and the lines were cast off. The tug boats began to move the ship away from the dock, and out once again to the open sea. The next ten days were the longest and most miserable of my life. I had no friends to talk with, plus I was made a compartment Sergeant, which I didn't want to be.

I opened and reopened the pages of my memory book. I knew without a doubt that my sweetheart Rachel, my friends Betty, and Dotty, and even my beloved Elona were all gone forever out of my life.

I didn't regret that it had all happened, only that it ended so badly for three of us. Marriage now had no appeal for me whatsoever.

I was standing alongside the rail deep in thought when a SFC walked over and we began talking. He introduced himself as SFC Larry Watkins.

"I'm SGT Ken Fisher, and it's a pleasure to meet you."

He said, "I'm returning to the 82nd Airborne Division, stationed at Fort Bragg, North Carolina. Where are you headed?"

"Well, I have to reenlist at Fort Jackson, South Carolina, and I have no idea where I'll go after that."

"If I may make a suggestion, why don't you enlist for the Airborne, then you'll take jump training at either Fort Benning or Fort Bragg." He lit a cigarette and continued, "It's a three week course, you're young, so you'll have no problems with the physical training."

"I'll have to think about that, I really haven't even thought about or considered going into the paratroopers."

"You know you make an extra fifty-five dollars a month in hazardous duty jump pay when you're airborne."

"I didn't know that, but I could use the extra money for sure. I need a car, and I need one quickly," I replied.

"I've been in the paratroopers for eight years, and I bought and paid for my first new car with my jump pay."

"Let me think about that, it sounds good for sure." We then went downstairs and had lunch together.

SFC Watkins and I continued to spend some time together as the ship slowly crossed the Atlantic Ocean. He continued to encourage me to commit to the Airborne.

Finally, we arrived at New York Harbor. Once again there were lots of people along the dock all hollering up to the troops, and the troops shouting back at their relatives. That's always a nice scene to witness. We unloaded from the ship, and I processed through Fort Dix, and then caught a bus for Fort Jackson, South Carolina.

Eventually, I arrived in Columbia, South Carolina. I hadn't been here since I completed basic training some eight years earlier. Nothing seemed familiar. I along with several other soldiers caught a military bus out to the fort. I got off the bus at the replacement company and reported into the orderly room. There I met the company First Sergeant.

He welcomed me to the company and said, “Sergeant Fisher, you’ll be in charge of your barracks, and of the first platoon which is in there. It’ll be only for a few days. Are you getting out, or are you reenlisting?”

I replied, “I’m reenlisting.”

He asked, “Are you going for the Signal Corps, Infantry or what?”

I noted that he had master jump wings on his uniform, so without really thinking about it, I said, “I’m going Airborne.”

He extended his hand, and I shook it.

Three days later I reported to the personnel officer who was going to swear me in for my third enlistment. I had requested a six year enlistment. My reasoning I guess went something like this, I had seven years in the Army already; a six year enlistment would give me thirteen. My career would then be set in concrete with no more second guessing myself. I wasn’t sure that I was making the best decision, but it was a decision and one that I would have to live with like it or not. The idea of buying a new car and having the extra money with which to pay for it without going broke every month was very, very appealing.

CHAPTER 33

Jumping out of airplanes

The young Captain said, "Raise your right hand and repeat after me."

"I Kenneth Fisher do solemnly swear (or affirm) that I will support and defend the Constitution of the United States against all enemies, foreign and domestic; that I will bear true faith and allegiance to the same; and that I will obey the orders of the President of the United States and the orders of the officers appointed over me; according to regulations and the Uniform Code of Military Justice. So help me God!"

He read the oath as about a dozen of us repeated it. He then shook each of our hands and congratulated us. I had forty-five days leave coming, so I decided to take thirty of them. I received a months pay and a small reenlistment bonus of a few hundred dollars. I also received new orders to report to the 82nd Airborne Division Signal Battalion in Fort Bragg, North Carolina. There I was to receive paratrooper training, and then be assigned somewhere in the battalion.

I caught a bus downtown to Columbia and got off on what I would call, "Automobile Avenue" There was several new and used car dealerships on the street, and I needed a car. My family had always preferred Fords, so I headed for the Ford dealership.

There I was met by a salesman who greeted me and said, "How are you Sergeant, are you looking for a new car?"

"Yes I am, but I'm not sure what I want."

"Well, let me show you the finest cars made today."

I followed him around the lot as he showed me the latest models and explained all their features. Finally, I selected a 1957 Ford Fairlane. It was blue and white with leather seats. He and I began haggling about the down payment I'd have to make to buy the car. Finally we agreed that I'd make two hundred dollars down payment, and monthly payments of forty-five dollars a month for thirty-six months. I signed the papers and counted out two hundred dollars in fifty dollar bills, and gave them to the salesman. There went my reenlistment bonus. Two days later, I slung my duffle bag into the trunk, left Fort Jackson and headed for Alabama.

I spent about ten days in Alabama visiting with my uncle and his family. My grand dad had passed away some time earlier, and that was a bitter disappointment to me. I enjoyed driving around my hometown, and going to the local beer joints and honkytonks down in Lee County.

Once in a while I would meet someone that I had attended school with, or some other boyhood friend. A few minutes of conversation with them, and I quickly realized that we had almost nothing left in common. A few school memories, and that was it. We really lived in two different worlds. Their concerns and problems weren't mine, and I never discussed any concerns of mine, of which I had very few. They were all married or divorced, had children and worked in the local cotton mills.

I made no effort to locate my friend Kelly Grady, who had been with me on my first tour in Germany. I don't know why, but I just didn't want to see him as just another civilian who had left then returned, and now was just another thread in the fabric of society. Someone did mention to me that he knew him. He was married, and had three kids, and worked on the midnight shift at the Lynell Textile Mill. Other than a few shared memories from Germany, I knew we too had very little left in common.

I left and drove down to Miami, Florida for a few days to visit with an Aunt and Uncle who lived there. I stayed with them, and I went to my first horse race, greyhound dog race, and enjoyed betting on my first game of Jai Alai. I also got Florida driver's license

Tiring of the leave I drove up to Fort Bragg and reported in early. I reported into the company I was assigned to and met the First Sergeant.

His name was Sam Harper. He was a large man, a WWII, and Korean War veteran, and a master parachutist.

He welcomed me into the company, shook my hand, and said, "We're glad that you're here. You'll be going to jump school in two weeks, and then you'll take over the Signal platoon."

I replied, "Glad to be here, and I'm looking forward to the school, my assignment, and to the company."

Our barracks was the old WWII wooden, two stories, coal heated and no air conditioning type. I was assigned a small room called a Cadre room as I was a Sergeant. Two rows of bunks lined either side of the main floors both up and down stairs. Most of the men in the platoon were draftees, and they for the most part, apparently did not want to be in the army. I had met many of their type before, and really didn't look forward to serving and working with them.

I met the Battalion Commander who welcomed me into the outfit. He was a Lieutenant Colonel named Weber. He had a sly, wolfish look about him that I didn't really like. But I had no real reason to dislike or distrust the man.

I began to hear all sorts of things about the division, about how it was nothing but a cardboard and starch display unit for the big brass. I hoped that wasn't true. I thought, if it's true, how could Captain Bernie Cole back in Germany think it was such a hot, bad ass outfit? Surely, just jumping out of airplanes doesn't make you a tough bad ass.

I met the men in the platoon, and the present platoon sergeant.

He said, "Glad you're here, I'm leaving. I have a new assignment, and I wish you lots of luck in the company."

"Wherever you're going I wish you good luck also. I'm glad that you'll be here until I at least finish jump school."

He showed me around the area then we went to the motor pool where all the platoon radio vehicles were located. They had the old radio huts much to my delight, as I knew them inside and out. I considered myself sort of an expert on their deployment and operation. Monday rolled around and dressed in my PT shorts and boots, I reported into the jump school. I was told that we had physical training, and then we'd begin classes on parachuting.

The PT wasn't a problem until they began the morning run. We left the school area and turned right, ran down the street all in a massive formation. I think there were about six hundred guys in the class I was in. We ran past the little buildings that my platoon used for operations, and then we were to run around the division area, some several miles.

A tall Lieutenant about six foot four, skinny as a rail led the group. He would stand out in front of the formation before we began the run and shout out, "We're going to run like gazelles today! What are we going to run like today?"

All the men shouted back, "Like gazelles, Sir!"

I thought what a silly crock of shit this is. I'll run as far and as fast as I have to, and not one frigging step further. They then had all the tall men in front of the formation, and all the shorter men to the rear. That simply meant the men in the rear of the formation had to run almost twice as fast as the front people just to keep up. The formation was about eight to ten men across.

We began the morning run, and for about the first five hundred yards I felt great. Then my problems began, I was giving out of breath. I quickly realized that I was in sad physical condition and in trouble on this run. Not participating in physical training in years, I was in no condition to run four or five miles. Coming off a long leave did absolutely nothing to help my physical condition.

I was located in the middle of our long formation, and I could see guys falling out alongside the street gasping for breath. Many of them would begin throwing up and some were even crying. The medical ambulance that always followed the formation would stop and check them out. About a thousand yards into the run I realized I could run no further. I like the others stumbled over to the side of the road gasping for breath. The pickup truck came along and the men falling out of the run climbed aboard, and were trucked back to the training assembly area.

When we returned to the training area I was singled out and told to report to the school office. I went to the office opened the door, and stepped inside. A couple of the jump instructors were there, and one short fat Captain who was sitting back of a small field desk.

I walked over to the desk and asked, "Did you want to see me Captain?" He stood up from his desk, he was much shorter than me.

He said, "I understand Sergeant that you fell out of the run this morning, is that right?"

"Yes sir, I was unable to complete the run."

His face grimacing, he snarled at me, "What makes you think you'll ever complete the run? What makes you think you can be a paratrooper?"

I was surprised at his attitude and nasty tone of voice. I replied, "I'll complete the run because I want to complete the run. Being a paratrooper doesn't mean you will fight longer, harder, or make you more motivated than any other soldier. To me Sir, the parachute is nothing but another transportation system. It's like a train, a plane or a truck, just another means of transportation to get you to a desired location."

He glared at me not really appreciating my remarks.

Then he said, "I have a special fondness for Leg Sergeants. So I'll be on your ass until you quit, or until you graduate. I prefer you quit, and save me the trouble. I don't think you'll ever graduate."

We were in his small office alone now as the two instructors had left. His attitude and remarks had really pissed me off.

I said, "Captain, I don't give a rat's ass about your preferences. And I don't give a rat's ass if you like me or not. If riding my ass is your job, then do your job, and I'll do mine."

His face distorted, he snarled, "Get the hell out of here, and find your formation."

I left the office and found the section I was assigned to. We began our daily parachute training. We did physical training, and trained on the towers and practiced parachute landing falls. The next morning we had PT then we began the run again.

As we passed my platoon building all my platoon was standing alongside the street and they were singing, "Old Leg Fisher ain't gonna make it, ain't gonna make it. Old Leg Fisher he can't run no more." They kept singing until the formation passed on around the corner.

I accepted and appreciated the humor of it all and ran on. That day I made a few hundred more yards than the day before, but I gave out again. I didn't see the Captain that day. Our training continued.

The end of the second week I was called into the office again to see the Captain.

He smiled at me and said, "Well, Sergeant, you have made three out of ten runs, so you must be ready to quit."

I stared at him for a few seconds then said, "Captain, I have no intention of quitting. Next week is jump week, why should I quit?"

His face contorting he snapped, "You ain't gonna be here next week. I'm flunking you out. You can recycle with the next class if you have the guts to!"

"That's not fair Captain. I made the last three runs. The fact I missed the first seven just means I was in poor physical condition, and I'm now getting into shape"

With sarcasm dripping from his voice like cold syrup, he growled, "What do you want me to do, give you jump wings?" With that he threw a pair of novice jump wings at me.

Instinctively I raised my hands, and the wings hit me in the face. The sharp little tack points on the back of the insignia stuck in my cheek. I pulled it away, and a drop of blood was on my finger. I touched my face again, and another drop of blood was on my finger.

I stared at the Captain and said, "You're lucky you're an Officer, you are very fucking lucky!" Wiping another drop of blood off my cheek I said, "I'll be back for the next class, and I'll be looking for you. Its best you believe me!"

I left the office and the school, I walked across the railroad tracks and up the street and went to see the First Sergeant. I told Harper that the Captain in charge of the jump school had recycled me for the next class.

He was disappointed but said, "No big fucking deal. We're leaving shortly for three weeks maneuvers down in Louisiana, so you can go when we get back."

"Great," I replied.

The original platoon sergeant left, and reported to his new assignment at Fort Campbell, Kentucky. I was made platoon sergeant even though I hadn't graduated jump school yet.

For the next couple of weeks I trained the platoon and made sure that each rig had all the supplies it was supposed to have. I ensured the operators knew what they were supposed to do. Finally, we left for Southern Louisiana. I had been on dozens of these type exercises with the Seventh Army, so it was no big deal for me.

Down in Louisiana, each evening after we had selected our overnight bivouac site, I would leave our area and run. I would find old trails and roads, and run for about three or four miles then turn around and run back. I could feel my lungs expanding with more air filling them. My leg muscles strengthened, and I lost a few pounds of weight. I felt good and I was ready, even eager for jump school.

The exercise over the Division returned to Fort Bragg. I quickly had all our equipment back in shape and ready for the next operational deployment. I reported back to jump school. Unlike my first attempt the runs now were a breeze, I made them with ease. Our third week was the jump week. We were scheduled for four day jumps, then one night jump. We loaded aboard an old C-124 Globemaster cargo plane. Troops loaded both upstairs and downstairs in the plane.

First Sergeant Harper came down to the assembly area at the parachute issuing point, and volunteered to be the jump master on our plane. We all drew parachutes at the parachute shed and put them on. Harper and the jump instructors checked us and our equipment out. We boarded the plane and finally took off. The plane flew for about thirty minutes, and then began its approach to the drop zone.

We were jumping on Normandy drop zone that day. Harper had placed me in front of the jump stick, so I was to be the first one out. The door light was red when he turned and faced us. He raised his hand palm out which we had been taught meant 'get ready,' he then gave us the hand signal to stand up, then hook up, then the signal to sound off for equipment check. Each man checked the man in front of him, and confirmed he was hooked up correctly and ready to go.

Harper issued the command to: "Stand in the Door."

I shuffled forward just a couple of feet, turned and placed my hands on both sides of the door. We were at twelve hundred and fifty feet altitude. I looked down as the ground features sped quickly by. I thought what in the hell am I doing here? To deny I was scared would be a lie, I was flat ass scared. Then the little light on the door frame turned green, and I jumped!

I tumbled around as the propeller wash tossed me about. I counted one thousand, then two, three, and four thousand. I looked up as my parachute blossomed open, I jerked to a stop. Then slowly I began my descent to the ground. I watched the other chutes opening as they all began their descent. To say I was one happy soldier when I knew my parachute had opened, and I was safe would be a gross understatement. We continued to make our jumps over the next three days culminating with the night jump on Friday night.

Saturday morning we assembled at the jump school and received our jump certificate, and our set of novice jump wings. First Sergeant Harper came over for the ceremony, and personally pinned my wings on. As we stood there talking the school Captain came by.

He stopped in front of me and said, "Congratulations Sergeant, I knew you'd make it."

I responded, "Captain, don't ever sell a Sergeant short whether he is a Leg or not." He stuck out his hand for me to shake. Ignoring his gesture, I turned and walked away.

For the next several months we had small exercises on the post. We received some new smaller radio equipment and trained on it. The barracks was another matter. We were required to have little wooden blocks made for our footlockers, and then we had to have our underwear and towels draped over them in a specific manner. The blocks were sitting on a wooden platform that fit in the bottom front of the footlocker. It was all neat, pretty, and uniform. It was also phony as hell, but without the blocks and platform you were in trouble. I thought the local carpenter must make a small fortune in selling wooden blocks and footlocker platforms. Our field caps had plastic rims in them to make them stand up, and the rims would hurt your forehead. We had to blouse our boots so that our fatigue trousers were fashioned in an acceptable way. Our fatigue field uniforms had to be heavily starched and pressed. It was a dog and pony show that absolutely defied logic for such a famous fighting division.

I had a Private First Class named Jack Gaskin in my platoon, he was really a nice young guy. I think he was from someplace in Georgia. He was full of piss and vinegar and enjoyed raising hell all the time. He reminded me of myself, and some other young soldiers I had served with several years earlier. He got drunk on guard duty and was caught, the company commander busted him back to Private. In about a month I got him promoted back to PFC. We went out on a post exercise and he got drunk, stole a vehicle from the aggressor detail, and got caught, and was busted back to Private again. I really liked his southern accent and humor. But he was a natural born fuck-up.

Two months later I went to see First Sergeant Harper and told him, "I want to get Gaskin promoted back to PFC."

Harper laughed, "Ken, that Gaskin shithead is a total screw up. I can't justify promoting him."

I decided to let it go for awhile. I recalled the wise words of First Sergeant Ironjaws Baker as he explained the army, and its system to me many years earlier.

I was told that we had a big inspection coming up. It's called the Inspector General inspection. (IG) It's an annual inspection to determine the operational status of the troops and equipment.

I pushed the men doubly hard, and they responded magnificently. We had our vehicles in tip top shape, and our communications equipment was the best it had ever been. Finally, the battalion formed on the parade field and displayed all of our equipment. I reported to the inspector, and followed him and the battalion commander as they inspected the troops and equipment. I responded to several technical and tactical questions the IG asked of me. With the inspection over he congratulated me on the platoon appearance, and the equipment's readiness condition.

Two weeks later I was promoted on the "Outstanding List" to Sergeant First Class E-6. I was proud, justifiably proud of myself. In just over three years I had earned promotions from Corporal to SFC. However, I quickly found out that my jump pay of fifty-five dollars a month wouldn't cover my cost for the car, the insurance, and its maintenance. Since I was now making more money, I didn't let it bother me at all.

We received a new replacement in the company and it turned out to be my old friend Wayne Wilson, from the 99th Signal Operations Battalion, back in Boblingen, Germany. He had just returned from an extended tour of duty with the Special Forces Group in Bad Tolz, Germany, and was now assigned to the Division.

We had a great reunion. We went out and drank several cold beers as we brought each other up to date on our activities for the past couple of years. I told him about Captain Cole trying to whip the company, and had instead gotten his ass whipped, and was relieved the next day. We laughed about that for sure.

Wayne was unhappy about being in the Division, and planned to transfer to the Special Forces Group located over on Smoke Bomb Hill. He and I talked about the situation here in the company. We also discussed the phony blocks in the footlockers, the starched fatigues, and the plastic rim caps. It was enough to make any man want to leave.

Wayne said, "Ken, why don't you put in the paperwork and we can both go over to SF." Lighting a cigarette he continued, "There they treat you like men, train you professionally, and demand your best possible efforts."

"Wayne, that sounds like a great idea. I'm sick of this every weekend in the motor pool, and the phony crap in the barracks. How do I or you know if I request a transfer that SF will accept me?"

"They're expanding, and they'll accept only Sergeants and higher. They have no Second Lieutenants at all in the outfit. So it's a very professional group."

"What's the mission of the outfit?"

"I'll try and sum it up. Their mission is: to infiltrate by land, sea, or air into enemy territory, and to organize, train and develop indigenous forces, and deploy them in accordance with the Commanders orders."

I replied, "That's one hell of a mission."

Wayne put in his transfer papers the next day and left the following week. I then placed my transfer papers in. The next day I was told to report to the Battalion Commander.

I reported to the Commander and he said, "Stand at "Parade Rest." He then asked me, "Sergeant Fisher, why do you want to transfer out of the Division?"

"Truthfully Sir, I'm tired of spending every weekend in the motor pool supervising a bunch of draftees, who don't care at all about the equipment, or for being in the army. I'm also tired of the phony wooden blocks I have to maintain in my footlocker, and the Mickey Mouse blousing of my boots. I'm tired of the starching and pressing of my fatigues. I want to go to an outfit that trains for their mission, and not worry about the next inspection, or the next parachute display for some visiting dignitary."

He glared at me. With venom dripping from each word he snarled, "Sergeant Fisher, I made you a SFC, and I regret that. You have no loyalty at all."

His face grew red, and the veins on his forehead were now prominent. Continuing he said, "I don't know if I can stop your transfer or not. But I'll disapprove it, then it'll go up to Division and then to Corp if need be."

"Sir, I'm sorry that you feel this way, after all I'll still be airborne and in the army. What difference does it make where I serve?"

He didn't answer me. Instead he said, "If Division disapproves your transfer, I'll get that stripe back, I'll get you busted one fucking way or the other!"

I was stunned by his truculent remarks. It seems my original evaluation and impression of him had been correct.

Staring at me, his face grimacing he snarled, "Dismissed!"

I saluted him and left his office. I went up to the NCO club and drank some beer for a few hours. Wayne met me there, and I told him all about the reaction of the Battalion Commander to my request for transfer.

He thought it was funny as hell and told me jokingly, "I'll pray for you."

CHAPTER 34

Joining Special Forces

The following week my transfer came through approved. I piled all my uniforms and personal clothing into my car, and drove over to the Smoke Bomb Hill area, and signed in at the Special Forces Group.

I was now in another new outfit, and would have to make new friends. Perhaps learn new equipment, plus whatever else the unit had to teach me. I was twenty-seven-years old, and there was still a lot of the world I hadn't seen, and many things that I still wanted to experience. I was enthusiastic and receptive to my new assignment.

I reported in to my new outfit and was assigned to Charlie Company. I met my new First Sergeant, Bill Barkley, and the new Commander, LTC Wayne Bearor. I moved into the barracks, and had a bunk in the open bay area.

There I first met SFC Arthur Taylor. Everyone called him Art. In my opinion he wasn't a piece of art. He was about six foot-two and weighed about two hundred twenty-five pounds, and was one rugged looking individual. He hailed from London, Kentucky. We became friends as we both were from the south, and spoke much the same language.

I met dozens of new men, they were all with few exceptions Sergeants and higher. That put just about everyone around the same pay grade. We were all on "A" teams which consisted of twelve men. I attended classes almost every day as I learned the mission and capabilities of the teams and the unit. I also taught radio communication classes. We all cross trained in other MOS specialties, and became quite proficient in more than one skill. We jumped primarily at night out on the several drop zones located at Fort Bragg and Camp McCall.

Gone were the phony plastics and wooden blocks so prevalent in the Division. Here we trained to fight, and to win. Not many demonstrations were put on. No one in the Army cared a damn about us, except us. Other units called us: "Snake eaters," Sneaky Pete's, and several other profane and less than appreciative names. The names rolled off us like water, for we knew that we were among the best the nation had in its military arsenal.

I had a Top Secret security clearance, so I was assigned as a security guard for a top level planning conference that was held in the Group gymnasium. I was the inside guard at the entrance door as a Lieutenant General was addressing the group of officers.

He said, "I've been a Division commander, and a Corps commander, and I know how to deploy and fight a tank division, and I know how to deploy and fight a Corps. But I'll be dammed if I know how to deploy and fight a bunch of men playing guerrillas."

I never forgot his remarks as the years ahead would prove him out of step with military warfare as it was being conducted.

I made many friends, especially a guy named Jason Raymond. He was from Pennsylvania. He was tall about six one, and around 185 pounds. He was married, but having problems staying married. He, Art and I hung out quite a bit together.

We three were at the Main post NCO club one evening downing a few cold beers, and the subject of wives came up. I had no experience with them, so I wasn't participating in their conversation. Art and Jason were talking about wife problems. Art was divorced, so he had some basis for his comments.

Jason spoke up and said, "Damn women, you can't live with them, and you can't live without them, plus they possess that one indispensable commodity which we all have to have."

"I agree, why don't you do like me and Ken, just use the "Four 'F" system," Art replied.

That drew my immediate attention. I had never heard of such a system, and certainly didn't think I employed it, whatever it was.

Jason asked, "What in the hell is the Four F system?"

Art laughed and said, "Find'em, Feed'em, Fuck'em and Forget'em!"

I cracked up with laughter. We all had a good laugh at the four F theory. It was happy hour at the club, so we set there until closing time, and by then we were all about three sheets in the wind. We made it back to the barracks just fine. As I lay on my bunk a little later I recalled the theory, and thought that might just very well be the best one around. I'd had my share of heartaches and neither planned nor wanted to go through such emotional disasters again.

I quickly learned that discipline in Special Forces was a little more lax than in a regular army unit, and certainly different from the Division's pony show. Here you were treated as a man, as a soldier, and were expected to act like a man and a soldier. Most of us were about the same age, and all of us were senior Non Commissioned Officers, so everyone did what was expected of them.

On the A and B teams you quickly found out who knew or didn't know their jobs. If they failed to learn their jobs quickly and proficiently, they would soon be shipped out to other units. The officers were professional and knowledgeable. They realized that one day their own life might depend on the skills and abilities of their team NCO's. The younger NCO's were taught and guided by the senior NCO's. We all continued to cross-train in other skills becoming proficient in more than just our primary jobs.

About six months after I had joined SF, I went downtown Fayetteville alone, and stopped in at a favorite SF bar on Hay street. It was called "Sammy's Bar." The owner was a small rather fat guy named Sam. He was an admirer of all airborne troopers, especially those from WW II. On his wall he had a big picture of Major General (Slim) Jim Gavin, who had been a major player in the birth and development of the United States Airborne. He also had a big picture of a legendary soldier of the 101st Screaming Eagle Division of Bastogne fame, Master Sergeant Joe Marino. Joe and a movie star were together in the picture, and to my thinking he was the more handsome of the two. Marino, had been a technical adviser when they made a movie about Bastogne, or whichever battle it was. Marino was also in our outfit, and became a personal friend of mine.

I had several beers. It was about nine in the evening when I decided to drive out to the small town of Spring Lake, and visit with my friend Wayne Wilson. He and his family lived in a small trailer park. I drove out of town on Bragg Boulevard and was cruising along about fifty miles an hour when a police car pulled up behind me flashing his red lights. I pulled over to the shoulder of the road and stopped. He got out of his car came up to my window and requested my license and insurance. I showed him both.

He said, "Sergeant, you were driving rather erratically, and I smell alcohol on your breath."

He then spotted a half full bottle of Scotch whiskey I had in the front seat. He asked, "Have you been drinking that?"

"No I haven't. It's been in my car for a few days, but I haven't been drinking it today."

He said, "Get out of your car!"

I got out of my car; he handcuffed me and said, "Get in the back of my car."

I thought, oh shit! Now I have big problems. He took my keys and locked my car up after removing the half-filled fifth of Scotch liquor. He then turned his car around took me back down town, and booked me into the Cumberland County jail.

The next morning a man from my company came down and signed me out of jail. I was issued a court summons and a date to appear. I then was given the keys to my car, and told where it was located. I could visualize my hard won stripes disappearing. It was Sunday morning, so I stopped at a drive in and had a bite to eat. Then I went back to the barracks. Jason came by my bunk and naturally tried to cheer me up, Art came by and added his two cents.

The following morning I was told to report to the Group Executive officer. I walked up to the headquarters and reported to the Executive Officer.

He chewed my ass out, up one side then down the other for getting locked up. He finally slowed down long enough to ask me, "What happened?"

I said, "The police officer stopped me, and I had an open bottle of liquor on the front seat. Then he arrested me for speeding, drunk driving and having an open container of liquor in my car. But I wasn't drunk at all, and I wasn't speeding."

He glared at me and said in a very nasty, sarcastic voice, "Well, let's just wait and see what they say and do when you go to court. If you're found guilty, I'll take at least one of your stripes, and maybe two." Then very snottily he said, "Dismissed."

I saluted the XO did an about face and left his office. For the next few weeks I trained with my team and did the normal everyday activities. I worried about the trial and losing stripes. They were so damn hard to make, and even harder to keep it seemed. I was informed one morning after the work formation that the XO wanted to see me. I walked up to headquarters, and reported again to the Executive Officer.

He told me, "Stand at ease." Then he pushed a two page document over and said, "Sergeant Fisher, read this and give me your evaluation."

I picked up the document and saw that it was from the Signal Battalion in the Division. It was from LTC Weber, the Battalion Commander. I read it and it was embarrassing. He accused me of being disloyal, unprofessional, and an unfit drunken bum.

Placing the paper back on the desk I said, "Colonel, I don't think the man likes me very much." I cleared my throat then said, "Colonel, when I got to the division last year I was made platoon sergeant before I even graduated from jump school. I turned the platoon around, they hadn't passed an IG inspection in years, and I made them pass with the highest grade they had ever received. I was promoted to SFC, and there was only one E-6 stripe allocated to the entire division, and I made it" He stared at me, and I continued, "The Commander got pissed off when I requested transfer to Special Forces. That's the reason, and the only reason, he's written this nasty ass letter."

The XO stared at me and said, "We'll wait and see what the court says, as I told you earlier, if you're found guilty I'll take at least one stripe, dismissed!"

I walked out of the building and thought, *what a dirty, rotten son-of-a-bitch that Weber turned out to be. He's really trying to get back at me for leaving the division. I hope on his next parachute jump the bastard streamers in!*

Ten days later I reported down to the court house and checked in with the clerk of the court. I was scheduled for an eleven o'clock hearing but they were running late.

I strolled around the hallway. The police officer who had arrested me came up to me and said, "Sergeant Fisher, do you have an attorney to represent you in court this morning?"

"No, do I need one?"

He laughed and said, "Yes, you do. Let me tell you what. Give me one hundred and fifty dollars, and I'll get an attorney to represent you. Maybe he can work something out to reduce the charges."

"Are you bullshitting me or what?"

"No, give me the money and wait here for me."

I thought well, maybe he can help me, so I gave the officer one hundred and fifty dollars and he walked away.

I walked into the courtroom sat down, and listened to a couple of cases that were being tried. Each of the cases involved soldiers charged mostly with petty driving offenses. All were found guilty and fined. Then the court clerk called my name out. I wondered where in the hell is that attorney? Have I been taking as a sucker or what? I walked up to the front of the court, and some civilian walked up beside me, we both stopped. I glanced at him and had no idea who in the hell he was, or what he represented.

The clerk read out the charges to the court. I listened very carefully. I was charged with driving with an expired out-of-state drivers license.

The man beside me spoke up and said, "Your Honor, this Sergeant has an expired Florida State Drivers license, and because he is active military, the license is valid. He doesn't have to renew it until he returns to the state of Florida."

The judge asked the police officer who had stopped and arrested me, "Is that right officer, is that the only charge against him?"

The police officer replied, "Yes, your honor."

The judge looked at me and said, "Sergeant, I fine you court costs of thirty-nine dollars and fifty cents."

I walked over and paid the clerk, picked up the paperwork and left the courthouse. I didn't speak to, or know the name of the attorney. I was happy that I had gotten Florida driving license when I was in Miami even thro they had expired already. It had cost me one hundred eighty-nine dollars and fifty cents for a phony charge.

I thought so much for justice for soldiers in Fayetteville, and Cumberland County, North Carolina.

I was pissed as much about the cost to me, as I was about the very idea that you could actually buy your way out of charges. I then calmed down and realized it was to my benefit. The total cost is a hell of a lot less than what it would have cost me in stripes, time and money. I got in my car and drove back out to the Fort. I parked outside the headquarters building walked inside, and requested to see the Executive Officer.

After receiving permission, I reported to him saluted and said, "Sir, I've just left the court house, and here are the results of my trial." I passed the court papers over to him.

He read the papers, then glaring at me said in a very angry voice, "Sergeant, you paid someone off!"

I replied, "Sir, are you saying the judges, police officers and attorneys in Cumberland County can all be bought and paid off?"

Glaring at me he realized he had backed himself into a bad verbal corner. He said, "No, that's not what I'm saying, but the charges on your original arrest report were different than what this paper says."

Looking him in the eyes I replied, "Sir, that's true. But the arresting officer realized that he had made a huge mistake and corrected it. The judge being a judicious and fair man realized that my driving license from Florida though expired is a valid one as long as I'm on active duty."

He continued to glare at me, finally he laughed and growled, "You lucky bastard, get the hell out of here!"

I couldn't help but smile as I saluted him did an about face and left. As I walked out of the building I knew I was indeed one lucky bastard to get away this easily and that cheaply.

Jason and I went downtown that night drank a few beers and found two local girls and spent the night in a motel down on Bragg Boulevard. The four "F's "were a splendid operational system for both of us.

Meanwhile, Art got married for a few months, and then got divorced. He had moved off the post to an apartment, and now he was back in the barracks. I rode his ass mercilessly and continuously.

One evening Art and I went to the main post NCO club for happy hour. We were sitting in the stag bar area, I was drinking scotch and water, and he was drinking bourbon and water.

I said, "Art, you're from Kentucky. Did you ever know a man named Jack Taylor from some little town called Neon, Kentucky?"

He looked at me sort of funny and replied, "I had a first cousin named Jack Taylor, why do you want to know?"

"I used to know and serve with a Jack Taylor over in Germany. What does your cousin look like?"

"He was about six foot four, skinny as a rail, and meaner than a pissed off rattlesnake."

"Art, you used the terms had and was, what did you mean by that?"

"Jack was killed in Korea in December1952. He was in the same division I was, the 3rd Infantry Division when he bought the farm." He stopped had a drink then continued, "I have some pictures back in the barracks of him, I'll show them to you later tonight."

I had that sinking feeling that his cousin was my old friend from my days back in Wurzburg. I hoped like hell I was wrong, but more often than not my gut feelings are correct. Eventually we returned to the barracks. We walked to his little cadre room. He reached into his wall locker and pulled out a small photo album. He flipped through a couple of plastic covered pages, and then handed the book to me.

I looked at the yellow faded picture he showed me, and sure enough it was my old friend Jack Taylor from Wurzburg. I studied the picture, Jack was in uniform, a Corporal, and wearing the old EUCOM patch. He was standing outside the EM club at the foot of the stairs in Leighton Barracks, Wurzburg, Germany.

I closed the book and handed it back to Art and said, "Art, Jack was one of my best friends when this picture was taken. We spent almost four years together. I'm so sorry to learn that he was killed in Korea."

Art replied, "Me too."

"I'll see you in the morning," I said.

Leaving Art's room I went to the latrine then returned to my bunk area. I undressed, hung up my uniform, and slid beneath my sheets and blanket. My mind was filled with pages from my memory book of Jack Taylor and I, so many years ago. I recalled him slapping the MP on the train as we traveled to Marburg. I remembered him offering to beat up the Corporal that beat me up. I had indelible memories of him and John Hodes jerking me to the floor as I tried to jump off the train in Wurzburg. Swallowing hard, I finally fell asleep.

The next day I sat down and wrote to Ray Washington and John Hodes and made them aware that Jack Taylor had been killed in Korea back in 1952. I explained that I was in the same outfit with Jack's cousin, and that's how I had found out he had bought the farm. It was a tough letter to write.

Jason and I went over to the 82nd Division NCO Club on a Saturday night in June to check it out and see what was happening. There were the usual scenes. Some younger Sergeants were there with their wives, and some with their girlfriends. We sat at the bar which was in the front of the building, the small ballroom and dance floor was in the back part of the building. I ordered us both a scotch and water as that had become our favorite drink.

"Jason there isn't too much happening around here. I guess we should go back to the main post club."

"I agree, hell there's nothing here for us at all."

"Let's finish our drinks and then we'll go."

About that time I saw this man come out of the ballroom area dressed in a civilian suit. I thought, I know him. He passed by without looking at me and proceeded to the latrine.

I said, "Wait here for a couple of minutes, I think I know the guy that just went to the latrine, I want to check him out."

I left my drink at the bar and walked into the latrine. The man I sought was washing his hands at the bathroom sink. He didn't glance up as I entered the room, so I stared at him. I had been right in my initial recognition, it was indeed, LTC Weber.

I tapped him on the shoulder and said, "Hello Colonel Weber, what are you doing here in the NCO club?"

He turned from the sink, a big smile lit up his face and said, "Sergeant Fisher, how are you? Boy, it's good to see you again."

He stuck out his hand in handshake fashion; I ignored his proffered hand and again asked him, "What are you doing here in the NCO club?"

He smiled again and said, "I'm retired now, and I'm selling life insurance."

I asked, "Are you making many sales here in the club?"

He replied, "A few, hopefully it will pick up later."

"Weber, why did you write such an asshole nasty letter to my new commander in Special Forces about me, and about my personal character?" I asked.

He appeared to pale a little and stammered, "That was a mistake. I really didn't give it too much thought before I wrote it."

"You're right, it was a mistake. You described me as a sorry low-life character, everything short of calling me a drunken asshole. I didn't appreciate it then, and I don't appreciate it now."

He stammered, "I apologize for that."

"It's too late!" I hit him in the stomach with all my might. He doubled over and fell on the floor; the poor bastard was out like a light. There was just the two of us in the latrine, so I reached down and picked him up by the back of his shirt collar and drug him about four feet away sitting him on the commode. I turned around and walked out of the latrine.

I rejoined Jason at the bar and said, "Let's get the hell out of here." We both finished our drinks and left the club.

The following week our A team spent five days out at Camp McCall training area. We conducted some demolitions cross training, and night parachute operations. We set up drop zones and had small aircraft fly over, locate the drop zone and parachute out cases of C rations.

The following Saturday afternoon Jason and I decided to go to Raleigh, North Carolina, and attend the local dance at the American Legion Club. We got there about seven in the evening, the dance had already begun. We both picked out a couple of women that were together and invited them to dance. We danced several times with them. They were from Selma, North Carolina, and apparently came here to see what they could pick up also. I suggested to the one I was dancing with that we go to Fort Bragg to the club. She checked with her girlfriend and she agreed. My friend was named Laura.The other girl named Edna suggested we go in both their car and mine.

I told Jason, "You ride with Edna, and I'll take Laura in mine, and we'll meet at the main post club." He agreed.

Laura and I got into my little Ford. I then took a drink of beer from a bottle I had opened earlier. It was still cool. I offered her a drink and she accepted it.

"Laura, why don't you come over closer to me, let's not be strangers."

"All right," She slid across the seat moving closer to me.

I drove out of town, picked up state highway 410 and drove south to Fayetteville. I maintained my speed between seventy and seventy-five miles an hour reaching Fort Bragg and the club in fairly short order. I escorted her into the club and to the main ballroom. I saw Jason and

Edna, so we joined them at their table. I ordered a scotch and water for myself and Jason, and two margaritas for the girls. We stayed, drank and danced until the club closed.

Jason said, “Let’s all go down to the Tropical restaurant and have something to eat.”

I replied, “That’s a good idea, I’m starved.”

The girls both agreed. We left Edna’s car in the club parking lot, and the four of us went to the Tropical restaurant down on Bragg Boulevard.

We arrived at the restaurant, and the place was packed. There were very few restaurants in the Fayetteville area, and the Tropical restaurant was the best of the few located on the boulevard. I think almost everyone I knew in Special Forces was in the restaurant that evening. Taylor was with some woman over in the corner booth, opposite him was Bert with a very nice looking woman.

I waved to Doug and Vick, then to Doc and Jaw, then to Johnson and Hap. Mo and Rocky were also there. I shouted to my friend Billy Bowles setting in a booth with some good looking blonde. I walked over and talked with him a couple of minutes as we waited for a table. He and I got along well. He told me he and his girlfriend were getting ready to leave, I could have his booth.

My friend Billy Walton was also seated in a booth alongside the wall. He was deep in conversation with someone I didn’t know. Everyone was talking, and the jukebox blaring. The noise for such a small place was deafening. Over in another corner I spotted PFC Jack Gaskin from the division signal battalion. I excused myself with Laura, and walked over to say hello to him. I could tell he was about two sheets in the wind. He had some young girl with him, and she was cute as a doll.

I said, “Hello Gaskin, how the hell are you?”

He jumped up grabbed my hand shook it and replied, “Hi Sergeant Fisher, I’m doing great.” Turning his shoulder he said, “Look, I’m a PFC again!”

I laughed and replied, “Keep up the good work, and you’ll make Master Sergeant before I do.”

He said, “I’m on orders to go to Okinawa, I’ll see you when I get back.”

“Good luck, keep your ass out of trouble for a change.”

I then walked back to Jason and the girls. I waved to Mel and Johnny in one of the booths.

Laura pointed out Billy's empty booth, we managed to quickly claim it. We waited for the busboy to clean the table, and then we ordered breakfast. After eating breakfast I suggested we find a motel room. Motels were as scarce as hen's teeth in town, so we had a problem.

Jason said, "Let's go to the Prince Wilheim hotel downtown, we might be able to get rooms there."

I drove downtown parked the car, and we walked into the hotel on Hay Street. I walked up to the desk clerk, I was shocked it was one of the Sergeant's from our company.

"Sergeant Brooklyn, what in the hell are you doing here?"

"Hi Ken, I work the night shift on the weekends, man I need the money."

I knew Lou was married with two or three kids, and I guessed he really did need the money.

"Lou, we really truly need two rooms for tonight, do you have a vacancy?"

A pained look crossed his face and he replied, "Ken, I'm not supposed to rent rooms for one night stands to the troops."

"Lou, it's after midnight, no one will find out, hell we'll register as Mr. and Mrs."

Lou reluctantly agreed as Jason and I both signed in the register as Mister and wives.

We had rooms up on the fourth floor. I escorted Laura up to the room, then returned to my car and got a bottle of scotch out of the trunk. I kept it in a small overnight bag for safety. I returned to our room. When I entered the room she was already undressed down to her slip. I mixed two drinks of scotch and water, and she and I slowly drank them. We turned on the TV and watched it for a couple of minutes, then I turned it off.

I sat down in the big chair in front of the small writing table and asked her to come over. She did and sat down on my lap. I kissed her and caressed both her breasts. Laura kissed my forehead and pushed her chest forward as she encouraged my manipulations.

She surprised me by saying, "Ken, I like you. You're quite, gentle and considerate."

I looked into her light green eyes and replied, "I like you too Laura. You're a very lovely woman. You have a beautiful body, a quick mind, and you like sex, that makes you very special."

She laughed and replied, "That's all you men think about is sex, sex, sex."

I laughed, "No, I also think about other things. Offhand, I can't remember what, but I do think about other things."

With that I picked her up and moved over to the double bed. I lay her down. With all preliminaries out of the way we consummated the reason we came here to begin with. A little tired, I held her in my arms as we fell asleep.

I woke up with the telephone jingling off the hook. I got out of bed walked over to the table and picked up the receiver. "Hello!"

Jason was on the line, "Ken, let's get cleaned up and dressed and then take the girls for breakfast."

"Okay, give us about thirty minutes or so, and we'll be ready. I turned back to the bed and Laura was awake watching me.

"Good morning sweet thing. Do you want to get dressed, and we'll all go for breakfast?"

She yawned and replied, "It's too early to get up on Sunday morning, but yes, I'll go."

"Give me about ten minutes in the bathroom, and then you can have it."

I walked into the bathroom, and took a quick shower, brushed my teeth with my fingers and dried off. I walked back into the room.

"All finished," I remarked.

She moved from the bed, and into the bathroom. I could hear the tub being filled. I picked up my bottle of Scotch and had a small swallow. More to kill any oral germs I might have, and to freshen up my breath rather than any desire to drink so early.

In about fifteen minutes she walked back into the room. She looked as fresh as a dew covered morning lily. With us both dressed, I called Jason on the phone, he and Edna were ready to go.

"I'll meet you down at the car in five minutes."

Laura really looked great as we went down the elevator and out the door. Jason and Edna were waiting. We got into the car, and I drove out to a restaurant on the boulevard where we had breakfast.

Edna peering through her cloud of cigarette smoke said, "Laura, we need to head back to Selma this morning. I have some things I need to do today."

Laura replied, "All right, we can leave whenever you want to."

Jason said, "I hope you girls enjoyed yourselves last night. Personally, I had a great time."

I leaned over and kissed Laura on the cheek and remarked, "So did I."

We finished our coffee and cigarettes, loaded back in the car and rode out to the Fort and the main club. Edna's car was right where she had parked it. I parked besides her car, and the four of us got out.

I turned and saw that Jason had Edna in an embrace. They were kissing each other like young lovers—I guess they were. Laura then gave me her phone number, I told her I'd call. They got in their car and slowly drove away leaving us standing in the parking lot. It was around noontime, so we walked over and entered the club.

There were a lot of troops in the bar and at tables in the main ball room. We chose the bar area. I ordered two scotch and waters for Jason and I. We sat down on the barstools and discussed our evening with Laura and Edna. We agreed that it had been a most pleasant evening and morning. We had one more drink before we went back to the barracks.

Wednesday of that week our team was to parachute in at Camp McCall and conduct escape and evasion operations, map and compass problems, plus radio communications. We jumped in about eleven o'clock in the evening. After getting all the team together we set up our operating base. I hung my poncho between two tree limbs, shaping it to protect me from any rain. Next, I blew up my air mattress, unrolled my sleeping bag and lay down and went to sleep. I woke up about four in the morning, rain was coming down in torrential sheets. My air mattress had partially deflated during the night, and my sleeping bag was getting soaking wet. I sat up pulled my boots back on then got up and tightened the parachute cord lines holding my poncho in place. Jagged lightning flashes ripped across the sky tearing the clouds apart, followed immediately by rolling rumbling, claps of thunder. It was a bad storm.

I blew my air mattress up again, and doubling it I sat down intending to wait out the rain. Sleep was now impossible. I lit a cigarette and just stared out into the dark, miserable, wet Carolina night. I was twenty-eight-years-old now, still in the prime of life and doing what I had grown to love—soldering!

It was a wonderful time to reopen my book of memories, and review some of the pages I had stored away across the years. I sat there in the darkness smoking, listening to the rain pound onto then bounce off my poncho. I thought again of my beautiful Elona. I felt sure that she was well, and her life with her husband was hopefully a very good one. I thought of our son Kenny, and could only wish him well. Leaving her and making the decision to not interfere in her new marriage was a tough one. But I know it was the right one.

I then thought of my first sweetheart, my breathtaking Rachel. She, so young, so lovely and we were so much in love. She too has my son, and he's also named Kenny. I realized that it had been almost ten years ago since she and I first met and fell in love. A dark cloak of sadness, coupled with a sense of failure invaded my consciousness. The night grew darker, the rain fiercer, and more depressing. My son would now be either eight or nine years old. The wounds of our parting were long since healed, but the memory of she and I remained.

My thoughts then turned to lovely Dotty, she with the gorgeous body and sparkling personality, what a beautiful sexual love affair we enjoyed. I still think the man who married her was very lucky.

I recalled Betty and her journey through the war, and ultimately her finding happiness with an American soldier named Earl. She was my personal friend, and would all ways be. I cared for her very much.

I thought about all the men back in the old 6087. I hoped they were all well and living productive and fruitful lives. They were all good men. Back then they were young and irresponsible like me, but still good men. The storm slowly began to pass.

Morning arrived, and we found enough partially dry pine limbs to build a small fire and dry our clothes and boots. The sun came up shining brightly and helped tremendously. We completed the exercises and were trucked back into the garrison area. The weather was hot as hell. July in North Carolina, is almost as bad as the heat in Alabama, and South Georgia, although not as humid as the climate in Florida.

After completing the exercise and returning back to Bragg we took a day off to get our equipment back in top shape, and to get our laundry taken care of. Jason, Art and I went to the Main club and had a few drinks. Hap Arnold came in the bar room with a young woman he introduced to us as his fiancée. I stood up shook her hand, and congratulated both he and her.

She was a nice looking woman, and was wearing one of the shorter skirts that seemed to be in vogue these days. Her legs weren't too bad either. We all sat for a couple more hours drinking, talking and laughing. Hap got up and went to the latrine. I watched as Jason leaned over and whispered something to the girl.

She laughed, and I heard her say, "I dare you!"

I glanced up and saw Hap coming back into the bar area, at about the same time Jason leaned over and lifted up the short skirt the girl was wearing. Bending down he kissed her in or around her pubic area. She began laughing and giggling, and more or less held his head there.

Hap walked up and saw the whole thing. He sat back down and didn't say a word. They finished their drink then they left. The following day he broke up with her, and he never spoke to Jason again. True love, when less than true, does present its problems.

The months passed and Christmas rolled around. The new main post NCO club had opened and it was an instant success. Jason, Art and I spent many hours in the new stag bar area. Happy hour was the best time of the day, and drinks were also the cheapest.

Every morning several of us would drive down to the club restaurant and have breakfast. The club made the best shit-on-the-shingle (SOS) ever produced. We ordered it almost every morning.

I knew one of the bar waitresses, her name was Debby. I first met her back in Boblingen, Germany, in 1954. At that time she was married to a Sergeant in Wire Company of the battalion. She was a beautiful young girl, with long black hair, dark eyes and slender as a reed. I think she had at that time two or three children. I learned earlier that she was now divorced. She was the best waitress the club ever had. She and I talked often, with her always asking and wanting to know, "When are you going to get married Ken?"

I always replied, "When I find a beautiful woman who owns a liquor store, is rich, and is a nymphomaniac."

We laughed together, and were good friends.

New Year's rolled around and most of the troops spent their time at home, or on leave.

Jason asked me, "What do you want to do for New Year's Ken?"

I thought for a few moments and replied, "Hell, there isn't too much to do. I guess we can go to the club and have a few."

"I guess you're right, let's get dressed and we'll go."

We both took showers, and put on our best sport clothes wearing a tie and jacket went to the club.

By midnight we were both about half shit faced drinking scotches and water. Happy hour I thought ended early that evening, or perhaps that was just my imagination. At midnight we all stood up, in the main ballroom, the band leader was counted off the seconds to the New Year. I stood up with the rest of the people and thought about the past ten New Years, and tried to remember where I had spent each of them. I couldn't in those few seconds recall where I'd spent them all. I think my worst one ever was spent alone in Miami back in 1952.

About one in the morning Jason said, "Ken, I'm getting loaded, let's go back to the barracks."

"My friend you aren't alone, let's go."

He drove us back to the barracks, and we called it a night. 1959 had arrived.

In January the unit began to reorganize, and our company received several new officers. We began to receive classified briefings, and told we were going on a classified mission of some great importance. Jason and I were reassigned to the company headquarters section. He was the weapons man, and I was the communications sergeant. A surgeon was assigned to our unit, and our training intensified. At this point in time none of us had any idea where or what we would be doing or going.

The new army ranks of Master Sergeant E-8 and Sergeant Major E-9 had recently been introduced into the army rank structure. We had a new E-8 named Hart take over as First Sergeant in the company. We all sat around and discussed where the hell we were going, and what we were going to do. No one had any answers!

January merged into February and our training intensified even more. We began taking classes learning to speak and understand French and Laotian languages. To be honest, I don't think I had ever heard of a country named Laos. We were told that our operation was code named, "Operation Ambidextrous." We all had either secret or top secret clearances, and became heavily involved studying the country of Laos.

Laos is a small country in Southeast Asia, formerly a part of French Indochina. We had a brilliant young West Point Lieutenant who spoke about five languages teach us both French and Laotian. We were all excited about our upcoming mission. Finally, we would get out of Bragg for a while and perform the tasks we all had trained so hard to master. We read such books as the "Ugly American," also the "Praetorian", and the "Centurion." All the men in the unit were under strict orders not to mention, or even to breathe our mission or mission destination.

Late in February Taylor said to me, "Let's take a three day pass and go up to DC check out the women, visit some monuments, and see the sights."

I thought that's a good place to visit and spend some time, so I replied, "That's a great idea, let's go next weekend."

We made plans all week to take off Friday night, and have off for the next three days. Taylor was off that Friday, but I had to work until around five in the evening. I arrived back at the barracks took a quick shower and jumped into my civilian clothes. Taylor was not in his room, so I drove down to the club looking for him. He wasn't there, but the bartender told me he had been there and was getting loaded. I checked a couple of the club annexes, and then the Division NCO club, he was simply not to be found. I went back to the barracks, but he wasn't there. I left a note on his room door that I would be in the club waiting for him. I had no frigging idea where he was.

I stayed at the club until it closed then I returned to the barracks. My note to Taylor was still attached to his door. Pissed off, and disgusted I went to bed. About five o'clock the next morning the Charge of Quarters came to my room and woke me up.

Rearing up in my bunk I asked, "What's up?"

He said, "Sergeant Taylor's in jail out in Lillington, and he wants you to come get him out."

"In jail! What the fuck is he in jail for?"

The CQ said, "I'm not sure, but he has his little dog, Killer with him. He sounds drunk as hell on the phone."

"Fuck'im, I'm not going to Lillington this time of the morning and bail his ass out. I'll go get him when it's daylight. If the asshole calls again tell him I'll be there later this morning."

I rolled over, and tried but failed to go back to sleep. Here we are supposed to be on three day pass in DC, and he's in frigging jail in Lillington, I was disgusted.

I got up about six-thirty, and after showering and cleaning up I went to the club and had a quick breakfast. Jumping in my car I left the post. I picked up state route 210 and shortly thereafter I arrived in the small town of Lillington. I drove around several streets before I found the city jail. It was eight-thirty Saturday morning when I parked my car, walked over and entered the building.

I walked into the front office and there sat a deputy Sheriff. He had his feet up on the desk leafing through a nude girlie magazine.

I said, "Good morning Sir, do you have a Mister Taylor here in jail?"

Slowly raising his head he casually looked me up and down, then leaned over and spit a mouthful of either snuff or tobacco spit into his trash can and asked, "Who wants to know?"

"I'm Sergeant Fisher from Fort Bragg, and I'm here hopefully to get Mr. Taylor out of jail. What's he charged with?"

He yawned, revealing yellow, jagged, tobacco stained teeth then replied, "He's charged with driving under the influence, speeding, and resisting arrest."

I thought, oh shit, Arts in big trouble! "May I see him?"

"Sho, come on back here with me."

I followed him to the back part of the building, and saw my friend Taylor stretched out on a bunk. He was asleep. The deputy banged on the cell bars with his nightstick and finally Taylor woke up. I heard a dog barking a couple of doors away, and figured it was Art's dog, Killer.

The deputy said, "Yo friend is here to see you Mr. Taylor, so git yo ass up!"

He then turned and walked back up to the front of the building. Art saw me and came over to the cell door. I stared at him and saw that he had a big knot on the side of his head.

"Taylor, what in the hell happened? How in hell did you get over here in Lillington drunk and in jail?"

Art stared at me through glazed bloodshot eyes and said, "Where's Killer?"

"I think the deputy has him in another cell, or someplace here in the jail."

He said, "I got drunk at the club and picked up this woman, and brought her home here to Lillington and ran into her husband. He and I had an argument, and he called the law. They stopped me before I could get out of town, so here I am."

"Well, let me go back up front and talk to the deputy, and see if I can get your sorry ass out of here."

I walked back up to the front and saw the deputy.

"Sir, what will it take to get my friend out of jail?"

He looked at me and said, "Son, he has two choices. One: he can pay me the fine, or two: stay in jail and go to court."

"How much is his fine?"

"It's fifty dollars on each charge, and twenty-five dollars for his damn mutt."

"What did his dog do to get such a big fine?"

"That's for the dog's room and board and upkeep."

"Let me check with my friend, I'll be right back."

"Take your time, he ain't going anywhere."

I walked back to Taylor's cell and said, "Art, it's going to cost you one hundred-fifty dollars, and another twenty-five dollars for Killer." He began cursing and kicking at the cell doors.

"Art, shut the fuck up, and let's get the hell out of here!"

He finally quieted down, and I went back to see the deputy.

I said, "My friend will pay the fine, and we want to leave."

He rose from his desk walked over and picked up a ring of keys, then walked down to Taylor's cell. I walked right behind him.

He unlocked the cell door and said, "Sergeant Taylor, come on up to the front. Pay yo fine, and you can go with yo friend. But yo car will have to stay until you or someone else can drive it. You're still drunk, and you damn sho ain't gonna drive it today!"

The three of us walked back up to the deputy's desk.

He turned and said, "That'll be one hundred seventy-five dollars."

Taylor said, "Where the hell is my dog? I won't pay a frigging penny until I get my dog."

The deputy replied, "Mr. Taylor, you had better just pay yo frigging fine, and watch your goddamn mouth, or you'll be back in that cell for a long time."

I said, "Art, just pay the fine and shut up."

The deputy handed Art a manila envelope which had his bill folder, car keys, ring and watch inside it. Art pulled out his billfold then his watch, ring and change.

The deputy reached over and said, "Just give those car keys to me boy."

Art handed the manila envelope back to the deputy. He placed it back into a desk drawer. Taylor counted out the correct amount of money and handed it to the deputy.

The deputy said, "Y'all wait here."

He left and shortly returned with Killer. The little cockle spaniel looked to be all right. He spotted Taylor and ran over and jumped up on his legs. Art picked up his dog, and I held his arm as we turned to leave.

Taylor stopped, turned around and said to the deputy, "I want a receipt for my money."

The deputy glared at him, then spit into his trash container. With sarcasm dripping from every word he said, "Boy, yo sho nuff better fuckin' leave while I'm still in a good mood!"

I pushed Art on out the door.

I finally got his big ass in my car, put Killer in the back seat and left Lillington. All the way back Taylor kept telling me what had happened to him last night.

I said, "Well, thanks a lot asshole, our three day pass is shot. There's no way we can go to DC this weekend. I'll find someone and come back and get your car for you."

We finally arrived back to the barracks. Art and Killer went into his room, and straight to bed.

I found Jason and asked, "Will you go with me out to Lillington and drive Art's car back?"

"What the hell is his car doing in Lillington?"

"Art got drunk last night and picked up some woman. He took her home to Lillington. Then he met her husband and they got into a fight. The local cops got involved and he wound up in jail."

He laughed and said, "Sure, let's go now."

We drove back to Lillington, and without any trouble I was able to get the car keys from the deputy.

As I turned to leave his office the deputy said, "Tell yo friend Sergeant Taylor, to keep his ass out of Lillington, or else I'll lock him up and throw away the frigging key!"

I replied, "I'll be sure and advise him of your kind and thoughtful remarks."

He glared daggers at me as we left.

After we got back and parked Taylor's car, Jason said, "Let's go down to Sam's bar and have a few."

I replied, "That sounds good to me, after that dumb ass deputy, I need a couple."

We drove downtown and I parked my car in a space on Hay Street. Doc, Bert and Bob were inside, so we joined them for a few cold beers.

I told them about Taylor's misadventure last night. We all enjoyed a laugh at his troubles. The legendary Marino came in the bar, and the conversation increased in volume as jokes and laughter echoed and bounced around the barroom.

After a few hours of sipping beer I said to Jason, "We'd better head back to the base before we both get shit faced."

He agreed, so we left and returned to the barracks.

That evening I suggested to Jason we go to the club and see what we could pick up. We both showered put on fresh clothes and went to the club. My friend Debby was the hostess in the bar area. I kidded around with her for a while, and then Jason and I moved out to the ballroom. The place was filled with people, some out of town band was playing and they were pretty good. We surveyed the area and noted there were several women that were there unattended. I knew we had a chance to make out.

I chose several women and danced with them. Jason also danced with several different women. The evening wore on and neither of us had scored whatsoever. Closing time was rapidly approaching, so in disgust we gave up and called it a night.

Jason said, "Sometimes chicken, and sometimes feathers, tonight we got the feathers."

During March and April our training continued to intensify. Our cross-training increased as we continued to master the intricacies of each other's MOS. We flew down to Eglin Air Force base in Florida and conducted a night jump, and trained on guerrilla tactics in the swamp and pinelands on the base. We also did some small boat training. I was happy as hell to leave there as the heat and humidity made life miserable for us all.

In May we all gathered out on Normandy drop zone. We were going to execute several parachute jumps in advance in order to maintain our jump status and jump pay while we were gone. We were jumping from helicopters. Jason and I jumped seven times that one day, it was a great day for parachuting.

CHAPTER 35

Introduction to the Orient

Operation Ambidextrous had been renamed to "Operation Hotfoot," and was about to be implemented. In May we began to tidy up our affairs and made sure we had sufficient civilian clothes to hold us for at least six months. We inventoried all our supplies and ensured that we had all the items we anticipating needing to perform our mission. Final briefings were given, and in June we were given orders to execute the mission.

"Our mission was: to organize, train and develop the Laotian military forces into units capable of defending their country."

We all gathered at the Green ramp over on Pope Air force Base, all ninety-six or so of us dressed out in civilian clothes. All our baggage was stored aboard the plane. Our supplies had been loaded earlier. We were to fly out in two C-124 Globe Masters. It's an old double deck aircraft, with four engines, and flies very slowly.

Around midnight we were all standing around talking and waiting for the order to board the aircraft when a sedan pulled up. I immediately saw the front license plate which had three stars on it indicating that a Lieutenant General was in the car. Out stepped legendary World War Two Commander, Robert Sink. Everyone in the Airborne knew about General Sink. He had been the commander of the 506th Parachute Infantry Regiment, an element of the Hundred and First Airborne Division. They were one of the units that defeated the Germans at the battle of the bulge in Bastogne, Belgium, in December 1944. Back then he was a full Colonel, now he was the Eighteenth Airborne Corps Commander, and our boss.

The group gathered around his car, as he addressed us for about ten minutes. As he spoke, I recalled my trip to Hitler's Eagles Nest in Berchestgaden, Germany, in 1949. I remembered someone in his unit had carved their unit identification in the window jam there in May of 1945. Finally, he wished us all success and Godspeed as we began our mission.

We loaded the planes and strapping ourselves in the canvas seats, the planes slowly taxied out to the runway, and one after the other took off. Jason and I and several others sat around and talked about the mission, and just about everything else we could think of. As the night wore on I found a spot and went to sleep. Trying to sleep on the plane was tough to do, the drone of the engines was deafening with people stepping over and around you all night long it's nigh impossible.

Eventually, we landed at Travis Air Force Base just outside Fairfield, California. We unloaded and gathered in a group then received a short talk from our boss The Boss was a Lieutenant Colonel, and one of the Army's best officers. We loaded up on three Air Force busses and were transported to our temporary quarters.

I remarked to Jason, "This place is damn hot and humid, I hope it cools off at night."

He replied, "Well, this is my first trip west, so I have no idea what the hell the weather is like around here."

Bert Kettle laughed and said, "If you palefaces can't take the heat, stay the hell out of the kitchen!"

"Bert, you're sweating just as damn much as I am."

We found our barracks and dropped off our hand bags and then headed for the Officers Club. The club was very nice and the drinks there were just a bit higher than the prices back at the NCO club on Fort Bragg. Since we were incognito civilians we were allowed into the Officers club. We all ordered our drinks and sat around talking about what we should do next. The Boss had told us we would be here for two-three days and we could go into town if we wanted to. The next day Jason, Bert, me and Bob Evening our intelligence man headed to San Francisco and Fisherman's Wharf. There I had my first taste of raw oysters, I loved them.

Bert said, "Ken, I'll bet you a beer that I can eat a dozen oysters faster than you can."

"That's a bet." I called the waiter and ordered two dozen raw oysters. In just a moment he returned and had two dozen raw oysters on the half-shell. Bob was elected to judge our contest.

Bert said "Wait a minute," then he placed one drop of hot sauce on each of his oysters.

Bob said, "Go!"

I immediately chewed and swallowed down the first oyster then another and another, all the while I'm watching Bert as he was chewing and swallowing as fast as he could. I beat him by one full oyster. He bought the beer and issued a second challenge for another dozen. I reluctantly accepted.

He ordered two dozen more raw oysters, put on his hot sauce then we began. He beat me by four oysters. I bought the beer and refused to eat any more. We strolled around the area, then Bob suggested we return to the Air Base. We arrived back at the base and checked in the barracks. I showered, made up my bunk and lay down. It was evening now and the heat was stifling. I lay there and felt the sweat rolling from my armpits and from my forehead. I took a towel out of my hand bag and wiped the sweat off. As soon as I did, I'd sweat more. It was a long miserable night to be sure

We all got up rather early as the time zone change had not kicked in our biological clocks yet. Everyone cleaned up shaved and were dressed. It was still dark outside. We caught a military bus over to the mess hall.

Jason said, "I hope to hell they have some hot coffee this time of the morning."

"I'm sure they will, hell even the Air Force drinks coffee."

We arrived at the mess hall, they were open but not serving. We convinced the mess officer that we were legitimately authorized to eat in his mess hall, so he let us have some coffee.

Bob spoke up and said, "I'm hungry, so I'm staying here until I get fed."

Bert said, "I'm not too hungry, so coffee is fine with me."

I said, "Bert, you ate enough damn oysters to last you for a couple of days, but me, I'm hungry."

Finally, the mess officer had the serving line set up and he allowed us to pass through. We all ate and returned back to our barracks. It was early in the morning and my shirt was soaked in sweat and sticking to me. I wasn't alone everyone else had the same problem.

Jason spoke up, "I wonder how in the hell the people who live out here all the time make it in this heat and humidity?"

I replied, "Jason, I lived and worked in Miami for about six months, you get acclimated and accustomed to the heat and humidity, then it doesn't bother you too much. It's when you're not accustomed to it that it hurts you the most."

We screwed around all day and tried to stay cool, which proved to be an impossible task. The Boss told us we would be leaving the next morning. That was good news to all of us.

The following morning we were all up early had breakfast and bused out to the airplanes. Our flight schedule was to fly to Honolulu and refuel, then on to Wake Island refuel, then Okinawa refuel there, and then our final leg on to Bangkok, Thailand. We boarded the planes and our plane taxied for takeoff. The pilot in our plane saw that the other plane had one outboard engine on fire. He called the other pilot and made him aware of it. The decision was made for us to go ahead, and the other plane with most of the supplies and a few personnel would get repaired and follow us later.

On our flight from Pope Air Base I had become friendly with the loadmaster of the aircraft. He was responsible for the correct loading, tonnage and placement of all cargo on the aircraft.

After we gained our cruising altitude of ten thousand feet over the Pacific Ocean, he came up to me and said, "Ken, I have to do a tunnel check, would you like to go with me?"

I said, "Mr. Loadmaster, I don't see any damn tunnels on this aircraft, what in the hell are you talking about?"

He laughed and replied, "I mean I have to check the engines out on each wing, do you want to go with me. You're airborne, so being out in the wing shouldn't bother you at all."

That remark appealed to my personal pride, so I in a cavalier manner replied, "Sure, I'll go with you lead the way."

He walked over to the left wing of the plane, and removed two or three of the panels from the wall laying them aside. He turned and said to me, "Come on."

He crawled up into the wing. I entered the opening and there was a walkway that let out to the engines. He walked along and I followed him. He stopped back of the first engine and checked it out with his flashlight. As I stood there looking around the side of the engine I could see the Pacific Ocean ten thousand feet below us. He then moved on out to the second engine. I very reluctantly walked behind him. He got down behind the second engine and inspected it with his light. I was able to stand up right behind the engine. I was glad that we both had ear protectors on as those huge engines were deafening.

As I stood there looking down at the ocean, I thought this has to be the dumbest damn thing I've ever done. Walking around inside the wing of an airplane flying at ten thousand feet over the Pacific Ocean, I should have my frigging head examined.

We walked back to the wall and I crawled out of the wing.

The loadmaster replaced the panels and said, "How did you like that?"

"Truthfully, I don't care for tunnel checking worth a damn. That's not the type work I would enjoy doing, but I guess someone has to do it."

He laughed and said, "I'll check the other wing later."

I was glad of that, my days of walking around in the wing of a flying airplane over an ocean, or over land for that matter is finished.

Several hours later, we could see the islands of Hawaii slowly come into view. I spotted the world famous Diamond Head. As our plane slowly decreased altitude the beaches came into view, and Pearl Harbor was spotted. Inside we would race from one side of the plane to the other as the guys would hollow out what they were seeing. The little windows were invaluable for us. We landed at Hickam Air Force Base in Hawaii. We were permitted to leave the airplane and go to the terminal area, where we bought soft drinks and snacks. Several of us walked around the area and tried to absorb as much of the scenery as we could from our location.

The plane was refueled and we loaded back on. We took off for our next leg of the trip to Wake Island. After several hours of flying we finally arrived at Wake Island. We all got off the plane and discovered much to our delight a bar. It was called "Drifter's Reef." Everyone poured into the bar, and the two bartenders were literally overwhelmed. I ordered six beers from the bartender and finally got them. The beer was San Miguel and cold. I gave two to Jason and two to Bob. We all chug-a-lugged the first one down, Bert came by with six beers, so he shared his with us. I think I wound up drinking three beers in a very short time. Someone finally shouted okay men let's go. We disposed of all the remaining beer and walked back over to the plane. Drinking so many beers so fast had given me a buzz for sure.

Our next leg was to Okinawa. After several more hours of flying we landed at Kadena Air Force Base, Okinawa. We got off with our little hand bags and were bused to barracks in Sukiran. I think we were to stay here for maybe one day.

I said to Bob, "Let's take a shower. I think we'll feel a hell of a lot better." He agreed so we pushed and shoved our way to the showers. I think all the men had the same idea.

That evening we were allowed to go to the NCO club or officer's club, both was not too far away. US money was the medium of exchange on Okinawa so Jason, Bob and I caught a small taxi and went to the "Top Three" NCO club. It turned out to be very nice.

Jason said, "Let's eat something, I'm frigging starved."

"I agree, box lunches just don't satisfy my stomach."

Jason and I ordered lobster and baked potato. I had one large lobster and two smaller ones, a large baked potato, rolls and a salad. The total cost was less than four dollars. I thought now this is my kind of place. Bob had been to the Orient during the Korean War, so he ordered fried rice and sushi. This was my and Jason's first exposure to the Orient, and to native oriental people.

Around eleven o'clock that evening we decided we had observed enough and drank enough, so we caught a small taxi and returned to the barracks. The next morning the entire group was informed that due to some international inquiry we were being held up from proceeding on our journey. Our stay was now for an indefinite period. We were allowed to leave the base and check out the island. Severe restrictions were placed on us as to whom we could talk, and what we could say.

Several of the men in our group had good friends that were stationed here on Okinawa in the Special Forces Group. They exchanged visits and we received the lowdown on where to go and where not to go, and what to do. Our stay on Okinawa extended into two weeks. We went to the clubs and especially the American Legion Post. We also went downtown, and the three of us spent a few dollars on girls in the little village of New Koza.

I confirmed that whether you have sex in Germany, Holland or New Koza, Okinawa, a piece of ass is still a piece of ass, and if you're an American soldier, it surely won't ever be for free!

Eventually our group was given clearances to proceed on our journey. While we had been stalled here on Oki our second plane had arrived with all our equipment and the few troops that were on it. All the team leaders reported to the Boss that the troops were present and accounted for. We loaded up again, and finally took off for the next leg of our journey to Bangkok.

We landed at Don Muang airport Bangkok, and checked into a hotel for the night. We were not allowed to leave. The next morning several World War Two cargo aircraft arrived at the airport. They were the famed C46's and C-47's belonging to Air America.

Bob Evening said to me, "Well, Ken let's get our ass to work and get this crap reloaded on the other planes." Our entire group worked in unloading and transferring our bags and equipment from one plane to another. Finally, we accomplished it all and the planes took off with the group.

We flew at a low altitude over some very rugged jungle country and eventually landed at our destination, Vientiane, Laos. The short runway, the area, and the capitol city looked like the backwaters of the orient. The heat was unbelievable, the temperature well over one hundred degrees. You could stand in the shade and your clothing would be soaked in minutes.

We were trucked out to an area containing several small huts, there we unloaded our bags and moved into the huts.

Jason said, "Ken, I hope like hell this isn't where we're going to live for the next six months."

"I hope not also. This place is for the frigging birds." I looked up at the ceiling, several Gecko lizards raced across. I had heard of them, but never seen the creatures before. I was told they have little adhesive pads on the bottom of their feet which enabled them to walk and run upside down on the ceilings. I figured they are good for mosquitoes, flies and other insect control.

The Boss said, "Fisher, set up a radio station and get ready to open up a net."

We had several "A" teams that had been dispatched to several towns across the country. The teams had gone to Pakse, Savannakhet, Luang Prabang, and a couple other towns. One or two teams were to stay in the Vientiane area. We stayed in the huts several days. All the teams with their equipment were now in their operational areas.

The Boss said, "We're moving into a house in town, and we'll all be living in the same house."

I said to Jason, "I hope like hell you don't snore."

"Guess you will damn sure find out soon enough."

The next day we did move into town and into a house. It had two stories and about six bedrooms. Jason, Bob and I were in one room, and my fellow radio operator Dave McMillen, and the senior enlisted man Hart had another smaller room.

Dave and I set up an antenna. I built small wooden racks to hold our radios, and then established communications with all the teams in the field. The Boss stayed on everyone's ass to do right, and make sure we didn't give away our true status.

The Boss said, "Fisher, I don't give a damn if you and McMillen drink or don't drink, but I want the communications done accurately, and I want it done when it's supposed to be done."

"Sir, I promise you the communications will be done on time, we'll do whatever it requires to make sure of it".

Jason returned that evening from a supply run and said, "Ken, I'm as horny as a double dick Billy goat lets go to town and see what's available."

Experiencing the same primal urge I replied, "That sounds good to me let's go."

We left the house and walked down toward town. The streets were dirt, and mud puddles were everywhere from the rains. We had to walk everywhere. The boss had a vehicle, a Land Rover, but we walked. We found a little café that had a sign in French advertising beer, so we stopped there and ordered a beer.

Jason did the ordering, I laughed as he tried to combine English, French and Laotian at the same time.

Jason, "You'll never make it as a linguist, hell even I didn't understand what you're saying."

He grunted, "Screw you, you do the ordering next time."

I paid the woman in Kip which was their official currency. The beer was bottled and warm. Not even a hint of ice, or any cooling device anywhere in sight.

I said, "Jason, drinking hot beer on a day with hundred degree temperatures is not my idea of a fiesta."

"You'd better get used to it as we're here for the next six months."

While we were sitting there Bob joined us and said, "Let's go to the "White Rose" they have beer, and there are some women there worth checking out. It's also a massage parlor."

"Bob, you lead the way as I have no damn idea where the place is."

"It's on Main Street on the way out to the airport, it's not very far."

We finished our beers and left. We walked down the main road, past huge pot holes in the crumbling asphalt all filled with mud and water. We arrived at the White Rose and walked inside. It was just a little tin roofed hut with a couple of seats, and a small bar top. Bob, who had a better command of the language than we did, ordered us three beers. Two girls came out of the back room, and just hung around the bar area. An old lady also came out,

Bob said, "She's the Mama San, the boss, she runs the place and the girls."

I took a close look at the mama san. She was a little woman about four foot three or four inches high. She had a black sarong type wrap that was draped around her, and came up to just above her breasts and extended down almost to the floor. Her eyes were black, and her hair also dark black. She said something to one of the girls and then laughed. She had no teeth, and her gums were bright red. A thin trickle of what appeared to be red spittle oozed down her chin.

"Bob, what the hell is that stuff she's chewing?"

Bob glanced at the woman and replied, "She's chewing betel nut, it's a little like chewing tobacco. I think it may have some narcotic effect to it as most of the natives chew it."

I replied, "Well, it sure looks like hell, her entire mouth is red."

I shifted my attention to the young girls that were still in the bar area. Beauty contest winners they weren't. There was however a certain amount of native beauty to them, but I think you would have to be really desperate to consider sleeping all night with one of them.

Jason said, "Bob, why don't you check it out and see what they are willing to do, or not do whatever the case may be."

I chipped in and said, "You might want to inquire about prices also."

Bob mixed in English, Laotian and French as he spoke to the little woman. She appeared to listen intently to what Bob had to say. I thought his language attempt hilarious, but I couldn't do any better.

Poking Jason in the ribs, I asked, "What the hell did he say?"

Jason laughed, "Beats me. I just hope we get some decent action out of the deal."

I replied, "Well, for sure I'm not getting laid, it's a hand job or nothing at all."

Bob turned around and said, "We can get a head job for one hundred Kip each."

Jason spoke up and said, "I'll take it!"

"Bob, how much money is that?"

Bob replied, "I'm not really sure, a couple of dollars I guess."

I had about five hundred and fifty kip in my wallet, so I said, "I'll go for that also."

Jason gave mama san his one hundred kip. She said something to one of the girls who came over taking Jason by the arm, and led him into one of the back rooms. I gave mama san my one hundred kip. She spoke to the other girl who came and led me back through the hut. The room she led me to was very small and had one very small bed in it. She had me lie down on the mattress as she leaned over and unbuttoned my pants. She in quick order completed her task. I buttoned my pants and went back to the bar area. In about two minutes Jason rejoined us in the bar. I ordered three more beers. Jason and I drank ours as we waited for Bob to return. He wasn't gone long. Bob returned and resumed his seat at the little plank bar.

I said, "Well, gents that did afford some relief, but it can't replace an American woman, but it's our only way to go until we get back to the land of the big PX."

Jason spoke up, "We just got here. I'll wait and see what you say about three months from now."

Bob replied, "Remember that old saying, 'All the girls are more beautiful at closing time,' or something like that. Well, when we're here long enough they'll all begin to look like movie stars."

I replied, "I hope the hell we get out of here before any of that shit happens."

We had a couple more beers, then walked up the street and through the little town. Not much was going on, so we returned to our house. The boss was sitting in the main room in his little short pants reading a magazine while drinking a Gin and Tonic. Dave was over on the radio set, and had the earphones on. I could see he was copying something down. I walked over and observed he was copying groups of numbers. Eventually, he finished and then translated the numbers into words then gave the boss the message. It turned out to be unimportant, so the message was disposed of.

Jason said, "Ken, let's have a Gin and Lime juice."

"I've never drank that type of mixed drink, but I'm game."

We both found a clean glass, and got ice from the small refrigerator we had. Jason poured a really stiff shot into his glass and then a similar amount into mine. He then opened a large bottle of Lime Juice, and filled both glasses to the brim with it. We stirred up the mix and I took my first tentative taste of the drink. To my pleasant surprise it was really good. Bob mixed himself a drink.

The three of us sat down, and in no time at all we had consumed a complete fifth of Gin and two bottles of the lime juice. I felt a little tipsy, so I said good night and went upstairs to bed. I woke up the next morning and didn't have a hangover, so that became my favorite drink as long as we were in country.

Jason and Bob made the supply run to the teams out in the field. Bob purchased team supplies from the small commissary located over in the American Embassy compound. The American civilians, and there were many attached to the Embassy, and the Program Evaluation Office and its other programs, complained that we were buying all of their food supplies, and other items from their local exchange. The problem was solved by increasing the amount of supplies coming from Bangkok to the Laotian exchange.

The boss said Fisher, "I want you to make a trip to each of the field teams, and check out their communications setup."

For the next several days I flew from one team location to another. I checked out their operations assuring myself that they had protection for their small crypto capabilities. I spend the night at each location, then moved to the next. It was a fun trip to be sure.

I reported back to the boss, "All the teams are in good shape, and are performing their mission in an outstanding professional manner." I then said, "I flew over the Plaine de Jarres, and you really have to see that. The pilot was flying really low over the plains and you could look down and see these huge earthen jars. Some of them are really huge and whoever made them must have had some plan in mind for their use, but damn if I can figure it out."

The boss responded, "I've seen them they're impressive, I don't think anyone really knows who made them, or for what purpose."

The monsoon rains began. I had never seen such rain. Virtual solid sheets of water came down. We had a small well out in the front of the house, and before the rains began, the water level in the well was about ten to twelve feet below the surface of the earth. In about one hour the well was filled and overflowing. Until you see and experience Southeast Asian monsoons, you just can't imagine that much water coming from the sky. The Mekong River was flooding. That's a damn big, wide river to be sure. The Chatahoochee River in my hometown would look like a tiny creek compared to the Mekong River.

We had a house boy who cleaned up the place, washed dishes and clothes. We had appropriately named him "Charlie." Charlie thought almost everything we did was extremely funny. He was always laughing at us. One example was when our surgeon gave one of the guys a shot of penicillin in the ass for something he had caught. The guy dropped his pants and shorts, and the Doc prepped the cheek of his ass with alcohol. He then plunged the hypodermic needle into his cheek. He jumped and hollered, and Charlie collapsed in laughter. I guessed he had never seen someone get a shot in the ass before.

Charlie came in one morning with a little monkey. He had tied a rope collar around its neck and was leading it around. Well, we sort of adopted the monkey, he lived in our house and everyone fed him. One day he got loose from his rope collar and ran out of the house and climbed up the porch column and the low roof.

The boss shouted, "Fisher, catch our damn monkey!"

I was over by the radios, so I ran out the back door and was dashing around the side of the house when I saw the boss on the front porch trying to talk the monkey into coming down. I stopped and watched both he and the monkey. The monkey just sat on the roof edge, and stared at the boss. The boss reached up to get him, when he did the monkey began pissing. He pissed all over the face and head of the boss. In spite of piss all over his face and head he caught our monkey, I ran back inside the house and got the collar. To say the boss was pissed off or pissed on, is to put it very, very mildly.

The boss glared at each of us and said, "Not one god damn word of this, or I'll bust your asses back to privates."

He washed up, changed shirts and left. As soon as he left he rest of us were laughing our asses off. To think our boss, the best LTC I ever knew had just gotten pissed on by a monkey.

I told Jason, "That monkey's cute and a lot of fun, but don't ever let the little bastard get above your head."

He replied, "We really should let him go."

"Well, he's not really ours, he belongs to Charlie."

Bob came by and said, "Ken, I'm going to buy a motor bike why don't you buy one. I'm tired of walking everywhere I go."

"How much does a motorbike cost?"

"About a hundred dollars or so more or less."

"Where can we buy a motorbike?"

"There's a store here in Vientiane that has them they're from Japan I guess."

"Well, let's go take a look and see what they're like," I said.

Bob and I walked downtown and found the little store. Sure enough, they had small one seat motorbikes for sale for about one hundred dollars. We each bought one. The speedometer indicated it would go eighty kilometers per hour, but I was never able to get mine to go faster than seventy kilometers per hour.

About a week later I came rolling up to the house, and noticed the boss and several others standing around the well. I parked my motorbike walked over and asked, "What's up?"

The boss said, "Look down in the well."

I leaned over the rim and looked down. There floating face down in the water was our little monkey.

Puzzled, I asked, "How the hell did he get down in the well?"

Jason replied, "He either fell in there by himself, or else someone threw him in the well."

I said, "No one here would throw our monkey in our own damn well. So it had to be someone outside of this group. Our monkey would never fall in the well, he was too smart."

Charlie, fished him out of the well and disposed of his body. We never solved the mystery of how he got into and drowned in the well. We surmised that someone did not like Americans.

My buddy Ed MacNerry came into town from Pakse for a few days rest and relaxation. I took him around town and showed him all the sights. His tour took about ten minutes. He stayed in an extra bunk in our house and ate what and when we ate.

On his second day I said, “Ed, let’s go down to the White Rose get a massage and get your pipe cleaned out.”

Ed replied, “That sounds like a winner to me.”

We both climbed on my bike and headed down the road to the airport. Ed was sitting on a pillow on the book rack over the rear wheel. I pulled into the yard of the White Rose and parked.

Ed ordered us two beers. The mama san brought them and they were cool, not cold, but cool.

“Where are the girls?” Ed asked.

“They’re here. Sometimes they may be sleeping or whatever.”

He smiled, “It’s that whatever I should be worried about.”

“Ed, the most beautiful girls in Laos are working here in this place, be careful that you don’t fall in love.”

He said, “I’ll bet they probably all chew betel nut, and have no frigging teeth.”

“That may be right, but with no teeth think about the great gum job you can get.”

Yeah, “But how would I explain a betel nut red dick?”

“Who do you have to explain it to?”

“To my shack job in Pakse.”

“You have a shack job there?”

He smiled, “No, not really. There’s one girl that I pour the pork to every now and then.”

“You damn sure hid her when I was there.”

Before he could reply, two of the young lovelies came out and walked behind the bar. I spoke to both of them as I had seen them before.

“Ed, take your pick. They’re the best this town has to offer.” I could see a look of disappointment cross his face.

“Well, we don’t have to rush do we?”

"No, there's no hurry as a matter of fact, I have four more months to do around here, so take your time."

Ed ordered us two more beers. I realized that he didn't want anything to do with the two girls.

I said, "Let's go to another place and drink a little gin." He agreed, so we both climbed back aboard my motorbike and headed into town. I stopped at the Chinese restaurant. We had a plate of fried rice, and a bowl of birds nest soup. The Chinaman cooked the best food in town bar none.

After eating we finished our drinks of gin and tonic. The price was reasonable and he had ice.

About an hour later I felt the booze, so I said, "Ed, we'd better head back to the house while I can still drive my motorbike."

"Let's have one more for the road and then we can go," he replied.

I being a most gracious host agreed to his idea.

We had one more drink then Ed bought a double drink and put it in a tall glass. Ed took it with him when we left the place.

We climbed back aboard my motorbike and I said, "Ed, hold on we're both a little shit faced, so I'll be careful."

Ed laughed, "Ken, I've got faith in you and your driving, just don't make me spill our drink."

As we roared away from the Chinaman's, I began thinking about the long wooden bridge that I had to cross from the main street to get over to our street. I knew that the bridge, an old bridge with wooden runners on it wasn't safe. It spanned a filthy canal that was filled with feces, garbage, and almost anything else you could think of. The wooden runners had holes in them, some of them at least eighteen inches long and one to three inches wide. It required careful maneuvering to get around them with the small motorbike tires.

We drove on down the street, and I slowed down as I approached the bridge. I was going about ten kilometers per hour as I entered the bridge. That was my normal speed in crossing this particular bridge. I apparently over estimated my ability, or under estimated the amount of alcohol I'd consumed. I was on the right runner and where I normally veered to miss the hole I drove right into it. The front wheel sunk into the plank and the bike flipped over. I went flying through the air landing on the opposite side of the bridge. Dazed, I tried to get up. Then I became aware of this little old woman standing right above me. She was laughing as if our accident was the funniest thing she'd ever seen. Her mouth and gums a dark shade of red, dried red spittle lined her lips, and a thin trace trailed down both sides of her chin. I looked around for Ed. He was sitting in the middle of the bridge laughing, saying, "I didn't spill a drop, I didn't spill a drop!"

Ed was holding the glass with our double shot of gin in it. I could see he wasn't hurt, and that was a big relief. The little old woman walked away still laughing wildly to herself. I slowly got up then picked my bike up. It had no major damage.

"Ed, we only have a few hundred yards to go, are you still willing to ride with me?"

Ed laughed, "Hell yes! What the hell does a rough landing mean to fucking paratroopers like us? Let's have a drink before we start again, just in case. I might not be so lucky next time."

I sat down on the side of the bridge, Ed sat down beside me. We drank the entire drink, smoked a cigarette and I asked, "Ed, are you ready to try again?"

Ed was from New Hampshire, and in his best imitative Southern drawl said, "Sho nuff podner!"

We climbed back on my bike and it started immediately. I slowly maneuvered my way across the remainder of the bridge. We arrived safely back at our house with no further mishap.

Jason and the Boss were sitting in the big room, and both had a drink. I found my bottle of gin, and made Ed and I both a drink of gin and lime juice.

The Boss said, "Fisher, what's wrong with your elbow it's bleeding?" I looked at my elbow, and sure enough it was bleeding. I pulled out my handkerchief and wrapped it around my arm and said, "Ed and I turned the bike over, I guess that's how I hurt my arm."

He growled, "You're damn lucky you didn't kill yourselves, you're both half drunk!"

I wisely chose not to answer, because I knew it was true. Ed stayed another day then returned to his team. Bob and Jason continued to deliver supplies to all the teams in country. The communications network was working fine, and the problems were few. Our mission of organizing, training and developing the Laotian troops into a reasonable fighting defense force was proceeding right on schedule.

Several of us were sitting around in the big room at our house discussing our new President, JFK. We wondered what new changes if any, he would make in the military, and specifically with the Army's Special Forces.

Bob said, "You guys know that we're only allowed 180 days of temporary duty before you are permanently assigned don't you?"

I replied, well, we'll be here about that amount of time in just a few weeks. I don't think they're going to assign us here on a permanent basis, and I damn sure hope they don't."

The Boss walked in about that time, and Jason asked him, "Sir, what's the story on our TDY, are we going to stay over our 180 days?"

The Boss said, "We're working on that with the Pentagon. I think we'll be extended for a short period of time." He followed that up with, "Are you in a hurry to go someplace Raymond?"

Jason laughed and replied, "No Sir, we were just sitting around and talking about when we would be returning to Bragg."

The Boss said, "Don't worry, you'll get back when you are supposed to get back." He then walked over and drank a glass of canned orange juice.

The Boss turned and asked me, "Do you want to go down to the Chinaman's and have a bite to eat?"

"Yes sir, he's got the best food in town, let's do it."

Three other guys all volunteered to go. We finished our drinks and loaded up the Rover. I drove down to the restaurant where we had a fine shrimp and fried rice dinner then returned to the house.

The next afternoon Bob came back from a supply flight, and had a baby black bear with him. The bear was about ten inches tall, weighed maybe twenty pounds and had a huge head. He brought him to the team house and led him upstairs to where he, Jason and I slept. I was on my bunk reading a magazine, and Jason was taking a nap on his bunk. Bob led the bear into our room. The little bear walked over to Jason's bunk, reared up on his short legs, and licked Jason on the face.

Jason woke up and saw this big bear head looking at him. He hollered. Rearing up he swung his fist at the little bear hitting it on the head. The baby bear fell over on the floor almost unconscious. Jason jumped off his bunk, and Bob began shouting, "Don't hurt the bear, don't hurt the bear!"

I had watched all this happen. I thought, that's one of the funniest things I'd ever seen. We both got Jason calmed down. Finally, he saw the humor of the situation and laughed. That evening the Boss came home, and the next morning the bear was gone back to the wilds of up-country Laos.

Christmas came and went. New Year's Day was just another day for us. The troops were training and operations proceeding on schedule. I lay on my bunk on New Year's Eve after I'd had two drinks of gin and lime juice. I allowed my memory to drift back across the last several years. Here it is 1960, and I've been in the army almost eleven years. So many wonderful and tragic things I've experienced since I first enlisted way back in 1948.

In memory's eye I visualized my beautiful Rachel, the vivacious Dotty, the lovely Betty, and my beloved Elona. All four beautiful women, all four whose lives and mine had crossed, and then separated along the path that destiny had chosen for each of us. I recalled the face of my son when he was just three years old back in Stuttgart. He would be seven now. I thought of the son that I had never seen, nor would I ever see in Chicago. He would now be about eleven years old. There are so many memories, so many years, so much water has flowed beneath the proverbial bridge. I finally fell asleep.

Our TDY had been extended, we now were scheduled to return to Bragg at the end of January. Toward the end of the month the replacement teams began arriving, and as soon as they were positioned with our teams we all gathered in Vientiane. I sold my motorbike to one of the new guys, taking only a slight loss in price. Some of the officers from our team including the Boss were remaining with the new teams for command continuity. We all briefed our replacements and made sure they were on top of the situation then we headed for the airport. Operation "White Star" the new operational code name for the mission was in full operation.

Once again we caught Air America C-46 and 47's for our flight to Bangkok. There we stayed in a hotel overnight and waited to board the one C-124 Globe Master cargo plane that was to take us back home.

The next morning we loaded onto busses and motored out to Bangkok Airport. We loaded aboard the aircraft found seats and stored our baggage. The load master told us we were being delayed for a while. We left the aircraft and stayed on the tarmac. The sizzling tropical sun bore down on us like an open door of a blast furnace. Most of the men tried to sit underneath the wings of the airplane in the shade, which was the only shade available. We sat there for about three hours while we waited further instructions. I looked at Jason and he was haggard looking, Bob looked the same way, and I'm sure that I also looked equally haggard. Finally, a Jeep rolled up and we saw that it was the pilot and copilot. A loud cheer went up from the group, we knew that finally we would be on our way back to the land of the big PX.

Jason growled, "It's about frigging time for them to show up, I'll bet they were sleeping off a drunk in the hotel, while we're sweating our asses off here on the tarmac."

"You're probably right my friend, but they're the pilots, so we have to depend on them."

The loadmaster shouted, "Load up."

We once again loaded onto the aircraft. I slumped down in the little canvas seat, I wiped sweat from my face with my handkerchief, then rung it out, a little puddle grew at my feet.

"Look at that Bob, not only my clothes but even my handkerchief is saturated with water." He just laughed.

The engines began to turn over and after several starts all four engines were running smoothly. We strapped ourselves into the little bucket seats. The big plane began to move forward slowly then turned around after reaching the end of the runway.

"Jason, where're we going first?"

He shouted back, "We're flying into Hong Kong. Spend one night there, then Tachikawa Air force base in Japan. We'll spend the night there then fly on to Wake Island."

I replied, "That'll take us about a week on this plane."

He smiled and reached into his small bag and pulled out a fifth of scotch. He opened it and took a large drink. He offered it to me but I declined. Bob had a drink then Jason put the bottle back in his bag.

The plane began to move forward, the big engines revved up as it gained takeoff speed. I glanced out the window and watched as the ground sped beneath us. With a surge the plane lifted off the ground, finally we were headed back home. Bangkok, Thailand, slowly disappeared from our view.

Card games began immediately, little groups of men spread out over the floor of the plane playing hearts, and pinochle even a penny poker game had started.

After flying for several hours the plane cut back on the engines and we began descending.

As we made a huge turn to line up with the runway Bob said, "Ken, look out the window, the runway extends out into the frigging ocean."

I glanced out the window and sure enough it appeared that the runway jutted out into the ocean. The plane continued to turn and descend. I looked out and you could see row after row of apartments on the hillsides. Believe it or not, you could actually see the people in their rooms and windows. They were waving at us as we slowly passed around them. That's how close they were. On our final approach it appeared we were just above the waves. Finally, to everyone's relief we touched down on the runway and rolled to a complete stop. Our Executive Officer, Major Rigsby, briefed us.

He said, "We'll be here overnight. Hotel arrangements have been made for us. You're free to roam around and buy whatever you want, but woe to the son-of-a-bitch who fails to make our take off. The bus will leave our hotel tomorrow morning at exactly eight o'clock."

After reaching the hotel, Bob, Jason and I decided to have some suits and shirts made, if we could get them back before eight in the morning.

While checking in I asked the clerk, "Do you know a tailor that makes suits, and could make us a couple and deliver them before eight in the morning?"

He assured me that he did. "There is a tailor shop just five doors away from the hotel, tell the owner you are staying in this hotel."

The three of us walked up to the shop, and I said to the tailor, "I want two suits made, two shirts and matching ties, and I need them by seven o'clock tomorrow morning."

The tailor in excellent British English replied, "I promise you'll have them by then."

He measured me. Then I picked out the colors and the material I wanted. He then proceeded to measure both Jason and Bob. My suits were going to cost me twenty dollars each, and the shirts five dollars each.

He said "I'll give you the ties and a belt free."

After we left I remarked to Jason, "I don't think he'll get six suits and shirts done by tomorrow morning, I only saw two other people working in his shop."

Jason replied, "Well, if he doesn't, we're out nothing. We don't have to pay him until he shows up with the suits."

"That's true, but we'll also be out the suits."

Jason grunted, and said nothing.

Across from the hotel we spotted a jewelry store advertising Rolex watches. We stopped in and checked out the merchandise. We all three wound up buying a Rolex watch. My watch cost me exactly seventy-nine dollars.

Bob said, "Let's go have a beer in the hotel bar."

We both agreed to the suggestion, and walked back to the hotel entering the bar. We slowly drank beer for a couple of hours then left to find a good restaurant. We found one named the Crown Restaurant and Pub. We enjoyed a very good Chinese meal, and drank hot Chinese tea with it. We caught a taxi back to the hotel and went back into the bar. Jason selected us a table and ordered three beers.

The waiter brought over the beer, and in a soft conspiratorial tone asked, "Would you gentlemen like some young women for the evening?"

I looked at both of them and asked, "What do you guys think?" They looked at each other, and then back at me.

I said, "I think I'll pass on this one. Hell, we're only going to be here overnight, I don't want to get screwed up by some local prostitute."

Jason replied, "You're right, I'll pass on this one also."

Bob replied, "Ass is ass, so I think I'll get a shot of Chinese ass while we have the chance." He then told the waiter to have the girl meet him in our room upstairs.

Bob got up and left the table.

I said, "Well, if he gets laid I hope like hell he uses a condom, and if not then maybe he'll just get a hand massage."

Jason replied, "I don't have any condoms do you?"

"No, I don't have any either. That automatically cancels us out of having sex in Hong Kong."

We sat there and sipped beer for at least another hour. It was getting late. I said to Jason, "Let's go upstairs and check out the room. Hopefully, Bob will have the woman out of there."

"Okay, we have to get up early in the morning if we are going to get our suits and get something to eat before we take off."

We caught the elevator and rode up to the fifth floor. We walked down the hallway to our room. I opened the room door as it was unlocked, I stepped into the room and up on the sink was a small Chinese girl. I stared in disbelief, she was perched on the rim of the small sink bathing herself. I walked on into the room and Jason followed me. Bob was lying on the bed naked as the day he was born.

He said in a very irritated voice, "What the hell, don't you guys ever knock before you come into a room?"

I replied, "No, not when it's our room too."

The little Chinese girl began chattering something in Chinese. She jumped off the sink and put her pajama pants on. She completed her dress and darted out of the room.

I laughed and said, "What the hell was that all about?"

Bob replied, "I don't know, I guess you guys scared her. "Jason said, "Scared her my ass, her looks alone scared the hell out of me!"

I remarked, "Bob, you sure know how to pick'em."

He snapped, "I got what I wanted."

Jason replied, "Hell you've been up here with her for over an hour, that's time enough."

I said, "The hell with it, I'm going to bed." I took the bunk and they had the beds.

I woke up to a knock on our room door. I glanced at my new Rolex watch it was six-thirty in the morning. I walked over to the door and opened it. It was the tailor with a rolling rack full of clothes with him.

He said, "I have all your suits ready for you to try on."

I swung the door open and replied, "Come in."

He rolled the small rack into our room, and handed me two shirts and two suits and said "Try them on."

I slipped on the shirt and it fit perfectly, then I put on the first suit it also fit perfectly. I tried on the second shirt and suit, and they were truly tailor made for me. I paid him the money in US dollars.

Jason got up and tried on his suits, then Bob. I could hardly believe it, they all fit perfectly. He had overnight made all six suits, shirts, ties and belts. I thought, these Hong Kong tailors must be the most talented and fastest tailors in the world.

The tailor left and we washed up and dressed. The tailor had given us wooden coat hangers to carry our suits and shirts on and that was a very big help. We packed our small bags and went down stairs to grab a quick bite to eat before the bus arrived. We arrived back at the airport and loaded the plane. A roll call was conducted and happily everyone was present. We were then delayed for several hours for some aircraft maintenance problem. Finally, our plane slowly took off, and I swear it skimmed the waves as we lifted off the runway. We were headed for Japan.

About three hours into our flight, a fire started in the right outboard engine. The load master instructed us to put on our life preservers. He then performed a tunnel check and the fire was extinguished. The pilot feathered the prop. Now we were flying with just three engines.

I said to Jason, "I'll take a shot of that whiskey now if you don't mind."

He replied, "Okay, me too."

We both had a stiff shot of whiskey, and he returned the bottle to his bag.

I walked over to the door and looked out the window; the dead prop looked so odd.

The load master walked by and said, "No sweat, we can make it on three engines, we just won't get there on schedule."

"I don't care how many engines it takes, or how many hours, just as long as we get there," I replied.

He said, "Tachikawa is sending out two SA-10 seaplanes to escort us on into the base."

"Can those two planes hold all of the troops?"

"I don't think so. If we go down out here some of the troops will have to spend the night on rafts."

I just looked at him as he walked away.

I glanced over at my friend SFC Johnson, a big black man. He was wiping his brow and praying.

I walked over and said, "Big John, it's too late for you to pray. You should have been doing that in Pakse, and left those little Laotian women alone."

He growled, "Get the hell away from me. You and the others are the big sinners, it's all you guys fault, now we gonna answer to the man upstairs."

I laughed and walked away. I laughed more to help him relax than any other reason. I glanced out the window, the sun had almost disappeared. Darkness slowly extinguished the horizon, and enclosed the plane. I watched the engines, you could see sparks flying from the exhaust pipes. I was concerned, but not frightened. I figured that if this big plane goes down in the ocean at night some of us aren't going to make it. Many of the men were sleeping, so I sat in my seat and dozed off.

Jason punched me on the shoulder waking me up and said, "The little seaplanes are here, they're both flying just behind and below our plane."

Looking out the window I could see their wing lights a thousand feet below us.

I said to Jason, "Let's have another drink of that rotgut shit you call scotch."

He replied, "You don't have to drink it me boy."

I smiled and reached for his bottle, I had a stiff drink, and then he had one.

Suddenly, we felt the plane pitch forward and the engines slacked off. Jason and I looked at each other. I thought, *oh shit, we're going down in the ocean!*

Someone shouted, "I see the lights in Tokyo."

We all crowded around the windows and sure enough the lights in Tokyo loomed bright. You could almost feel a sense of relief racing through the plane. The pilot made a couple of banking turns, and then we could see the runway rushing up to meet us. The plane landed and after a couple of rough bounces slowed down and continued to roll smoothly down the runway. I think a collective sigh could be heard from the group. We rolled to a stop, and the engines were turned off.

An Air Force major came aboard and said, "Gentlemen, you will be bused from the plane to the mess hall, and then we'll take you to the barracks you'll be quartered in for your stay here at Tachikawa Air Force Base. Take only the items you need with you."

Bob said, "I for one am damn glad to be down on solid ground once again."

Jason responded, "That goes for both of us."

I said, "I think everyone on the plane is happy to be back on the ground again. I wonder how long we'll be here before they get the airplane ready to fly again."

Neither of us had an answer. After eating we went to the barracks we were to stay. I was tired so I took a hot shower and went to bed. Several of the guys cleaned up and went to the officers club on the base. The next morning we were informed we'd be here for at least two days.

That evening Jason, Bob and I went over to the officers club to have a few cold beers. While sitting at our table I saw a young Captain that I recognized from my days in the 99th Signal Operations Battalion in Boblingen, Germany. He had been my platoon leader, and was then a first Lieutenant He saw me at the same time and rising from his chair came over to my table.

He extended his hand and said, "Sergeant Fisher, what in the world are you doing here?"

I stood up shook his hand and replied, "Hello Captain, the last time I saw you, you were a first Lieutenant."

He said, "How in hell are you, what the heck are you doing here in the officers club, and in civilian clothes?"

He wasn't belligerent, just truly curious.

I frantically thought for an answer then replied, "I'm out of the Army. I'm on a Geodetic Survey Team, and we just stopped by here for a couple of hours." It was the only damn thing I could think of to say.

He looked at me, laughed and said, "I really don't believe that."

I saw Major Rigsby sitting at a nearby table, he glanced at me, and I motioned for him to join me.

He immediately came to my table and I said, "Mr. Rigsby, this young Captain whom I know from my army days doesn't believe we're on a geodetic survey team, could you perhaps convince him that we are."

The Major said to the young Captain, "Please step over here with me for a minute."

He led the Captain away from our table to an empty spot in the room and talked to him for a few minutes. He then went back to his table and the Captain returned to his. I had no further problems with the Captain. He did however glance at me frequently with a very puzzled look on his face. I really liked the guy and felt badly about the ruse I was conducting, but the security of the mission was paramount.

Eventually, we left the club and went back to our barracks. The next day was uneventful. We heard that the parts needed for the plane engine had arrived from Kadena Air Force Base on Okinawa, and we were slated to fly out the following morning. Before boarding our plane we had a roll call. One of the senior sergeants missed our flight out of Tachikawa, but he did catch a commercial jet to Honolulu and caught up with us there. It cost him one stripe.

We took off on schedule and flew to Wake Island, there we refueled, bought all their beer and then flew on to Hawaii. We refueled there and spend one night for the pilots to rest. We left the following morning and flew to Travis Air Force Base, California. The next day we flew back to Pope Air Force Base on Fort Bragg, North Carolina.

It had been a long round trip journey, and my first exposure to the Orient had been a good one. For me it was a far different world from the old European world I had experienced in Germany. I was glad to get back to Bragg, get my car and take a leave.

I took a ten day leave drove down to Alabama and spent a couple of days with my relatives. I then drove down to Florida and visited my relatives there. I returned to Bragg with one day left on my leave. I went to the NCO club with Art Taylor and made out that evening with a lovely young lady. I took her to the Tropical restaurant for a late night breakfast, then to a motel. I returned her to the parking lot at the club early the next morning. American women are still the best looking, and the most challenging in the world.

CHAPTER 36

Moonshine, Ironjaws and Orders

In April, several of us were selected to go to Dahlonega, Georgia, to the Army's Ranger camp to conduct training. It was nice to get away. We did a little rope climbing, river crossings, map and compass training and goofing off.

One evening Master Sergeant Hoskins who was in charge had everyone kick in a couple of dollars to buy a gallon of white lightning moonshine liquor and twelve soft drinks for chasers.

He returned in less than an hour. "Ken, I have a gallon of what the guy said was the best moonshine in the county. Let's have a few snorts and see how it tastes."

"I don't care very much for moonshine, but I'll have a couple shots of it."

It was very chilly, so the guys had built a large bonfire from old dead tree branches. The fire really felt great as the cold winds whistled down through the mountain valleys of North Georgia. We sat around the fire, and everyone poured themselves a drink of the whiskey in their canteen cups then mixed it with some cola. It didn't taste too bad, so everyone just kept tapping the gallon jug. I guess there were about nine of us sitting around the fire drinking. I began to feel a little dizzy, and I stopped drinking. The master sergeant who had been drinking heavily began to talk louder and louder, then suddenly seemed to go berserk.

He hollered out, "I'm going to bust all your heads in." He grabbed a large pine limb from our firewood, and backing up defied anyone to come near him.

I said, "Sergeant Hoskins, take it easy. We don't need to get into a damn fight over nothing. Put the log down and let's talk things over."

He cursed and swung the big limb at me. I jumped back out of his way. As I carefully watched him, he suddenly keeled over, passing right out.

I said to Sgt Smith who was with us, "Smith, help me get him over onto his air mattress."

We picked him up and placed him on his air mattress. I covered him up with his poncho. I figured if it rains at least he'll have some protection, and maybe sober up. I returned by the fire and felt my stomach churning. My head began hurting, and I immediately realized that we had some bad, rotgut moonshine. I walked away from the fire and the group, and began throwing up. I became weak and slowly sank down to my knees and continued retching. I stayed on my hands and knees for about ten minutes. Finally, I had what is known as the dry heaves. I was trying to throw up, but nothing came out. I was one sick soldier. Eventually, I was able to get back on my feet and walked back to the fire.

I said, "You guys leave that rotgut shit alone. Sarge went a little goofy, and I'm sicker than four hundred hells."

Sgt Smith picked up the jug, walked away a few steps and poured it out on the ground. We must have drunk at least half of the gallon.

We all went to bed. I had my poncho tied between some small trees, and my air mattress and sleeping bag were underneath it. I lay down and cursed the day I drank that damn rotgut moonshine. My bed began spinning. I rolled over and attempted to throw up again, but it was just dry heaves. Finally, I fell asleep.

I woke up the next morning just as the sun peaked over the hilltops. Several song birds were singing their good morning to the world song. I got up and put some more wood on our fire which was almost out. I picked up the liquor jug, and it had maybe two ounces of whiskey still in it. I poured that over the fresh logs on the fire. The fire exploded in a burst of flames, embers and smoke. I thought that crap is almost as powerful as gasoline. No frigging wonder we all got sick.

Then I put some water for coffee on the edge of the fire. We had instant coffee and some sugar, so we were in good shape. I saw Hoskins stirring, I watched as he slowly got out from under his poncho.

He looked over at me and said, "Ken, what the hell happened last night? I don't remember a damn thing."

"Sarge, we were drinking that damn rotgut and you went nuts. You then passed out and we put you to bed. I got sicker than a dog and threw up. Several of the other guys were throwing up, so we poured that damn moonshine out."

His eyes were red, and he was pale as a ghost.

"Do you want a cup of instant?"

He just shook his head in the affirmative. I got his canteen cup mixed a cup of instant coffee for him, gave it to him and he slowly sipped it. Two minutes later he bolted from the fire and began throwing up. For the next five minutes he bent over retching black looking crap as his body continued to reject the booze.

He finally returned. I said, "Hoskins, you should know better than to buy moonshine that only cost eight dollars a gallon. That has to be made out of battery acid, or lye, or something else that'll kill you."

He just looked at me, he was too damn sick to even respond.

Two days later we returned to Fort Bragg. Reassignment orders for about twenty men came out. They were all being reassigned to the Special Forces Group on Okinawa. I wasn't on the orders. Art Taylor and several of my friends were. We had a small farewell get together at the NCO club, and they left on leave. It was early1960, when Art left. I requested and received a three day pass. I had nowhere to go in particular, but I figured I would goof off for a couple of days. The first morning I was on pass in the barracks, and I picked up a copy of the Eighteenth Airborne Corps newspaper, "*The Paraglide.*"

I began to read through it. I noticed they were having a retirement parade the next day. I read through the list of people who were retiring, and a name suddenly jumped out at me. The article stated that one of the retirees was a Command Sergeant Major Howard Baker. He was retiring after thirty-two years of military service. I knew that had to be Ironjaws Baker, my old First Sergeant from the 6087 SCU back in Wurzburg, Germany. The ceremony was scheduled for eleven o'clock the following morning. I had to be there for this one for sure. This would be my last chance to ever see him. I damned sure didn't want to miss his retirement!

The next morning I got up early and ate breakfast in the mess hall then returned to my barracks. I spit shined my jump boots until they looked like glass. I polished my belt buckle and selected my best starched and pressed fatigue uniform then I got dressed. I drove up to the Corps parade field, parked my car and walked across to a position alongside the reviewing stand. The Division band was playing several John Phillip Sousa tunes which all soldiers know the beat by heart.

There were six soldiers that were retiring and being honored at the ceremony. I looked for the tallest man. To my great delight it was indeed Ironjaws Baker. He didn't see me. To the left of the reviewing stand were several rows of chairs which had been sat up for the ladies and other guests. I walked over to the chairs and looked for Mrs. Baker, but she wasn't there in the group. I was a little surprised and hoped that she was still alive and well.

Finally, the ceremony began and I waited for them to read out the individual awards and retirement orders. They began with some Colonel who was retiring after twenty-eight years service.

Then they began to read out Command Sergeant Major Baker's service and awards. He had joined the Army in 1928. He had jumped into Normandy with the 82nd Division on D-Day, and then had jumped into Holland with the 101st Airborne Division. He had served in Korea been wounded there, and had won his second Silver Star there. He had two Silver Stars, three Bronze Stars with the "V" for Valor device, four Purple Hearts, and numerous commendation and service medals. He was completing thirty-two years of continuous military service. He was then awarded the Legion of Merit. He was still the most impressive looking soldier I had ever seen.

I watched him as he stood ramrod straight, I was so glad that I had served under him. He was in my opinion, the epitome of what a soldier should be, and can be.

When all the retirees were saluted, the troops began to pass in review. When the battalion passed the reviewing stand in company formations the parade and the ceremony was complete.

I walked over by the steps leading up to the reviewing stand and just waited. The men on the stand began to come down the steps. I stood to the side then I saw Ironjaws come down the steps. He didn't notice me as he was responding to some remark from the Colonel. He finished speaking with the Colonel, they shook hands and he began to walk away.

I called out, "Sergeant Major Baker," he stopped and turned around facing me.

He stared for a moment, and then a look of recognition, and a huge smile spread across his face as I stepped towards him.

In that deep inimitable voice that I remembered so well, he said, "Well I'll be dammed, Ken Fisher!"

He grabbed me and gave me a huge bear hug. I hugged him back, and knew that I had a country mile wide smile on my face.

I said, "Sergeant Major, how in the hell are you?"

He held me out from him with his two huge hands and said, "Fisher, let me look at you. I can't really believe that you're here at Bragg. I thought you got out of the Army." He removed my cap and said, "Damn, you have more gray hair than I do."

I laughed and replied, "Sergeant Major, it's been a long time since our days together in Wurzburg. A lot of water has gone over the dam since then. Where's Mrs. Baker I don't see her here at your retirement?"

"Inez is at home in Arizona. She told me she'd seen enough of parades, and I could make this one alone."

I laughed and replied, "I'm sure she has seen enough parades of all types. Where are you going now?"

"I'm catching a plane this evening around six for Tucson."

"Do you have your own transportation to the airport?"

"No, I don't."

"I'd be happy to take you. Would you like to go have a drink with me to celebrate your retirement?"

"Sure, I'd love to have a few frigging drinks with you and catch up on your career."

"Great, let's go to my car." He had only a small briefcase with him, so I asked, "Do you have any other bags or luggage you need to pick up?"

"No, I took my one bag out to the airport yesterday and checked it through. I'll pick it up when I get to Tucson."

We both got into my car, and I drove over to the NCO club. We went into the stag bar area, and I located a table over in a quiet corner.

"What would you like to drink Sergeant Major?"

"I'll take Jack Daniel's and water."

I ordered his drink, and ordered Scotch and water for myself.

He stared at me, smiling a huge smile said, "I just can't believe you're back in the army stationed here at Fort Bragg, and a Sergeant First Class no less."

I laughed, "It's a long story, but I'm stationed here with the Special Forces Group." Our drinks arrived and we raised them in toast.

I said, "Sergeant Major, I offer a toast to the best First Sergeant this Army ever produced, and the finest Sergeant Major I've ever known!"

He laughed, tapped my glass with his and sipped at his drink.

He said, "I toast the United States Army, to all its soldiers, and to you being back in the Army!"

"I'll drink to that for sure."

We settled down in our seats and Ironjaws said, "Tell me Ken about yourself, how you came back in the army."

"Well, Sergeant Major let me begin about eight years ago. I got discharged down at Fort Benning, and went home to Alabama. But I had no goals, and no direction in my life. I was screwed up about leaving Elona. I sat around the house about three weeks trying to figure out what the hell I should do. John Hodes from our old company showed up one day, and we went to Miami for a vacation."

I took a drink then continued, "John went home, and I went to work. I couldn't get my girlfriend Elona out of my mind, and I tried to figure out a way to get back to her. The Army was my only possible avenue to get back to Germany. I left Miami, moved to Buffalo and worked there for a few months, then I reenlisted in the Army. The reenlistment officer was our old XO Captain Tolliver."

He laughed and said, "That shithead Tolliver."

I continued, "Korea was finished, and by a sheer stroke of luck I was sent back to Germany. I was assigned to a Signal Operations Battalion in Boblingen, and I stayed there almost three years. While there I returned to Wurzburg twice looking for Elona, but I couldn't find her. One day near the end of my tour I decided to go to Stuttgart for about ten days leave just to get away, play tourist and relax from continuous field exercises."

He said, "Wait a minute," and he ordered us two more drinks.

I continued, "I was sitting at a little sidewalk café in front of the hotel I was staying and this woman shows up with three kids. Two of them were of mixed race, and the youngest of the three was totally white. I saw this young woman walk up to the older woman and I recognized her, it was Elona.

"To make it short, she had married a young executive in a German bank six months earlier. It had been four years since I'd last seen her. She and I did talk, and we discussed the future. We also spent some time together. However, we mutually agreed that we should go our separate ways. I returned to the states and reenlisted for the airborne, took jump training here at Bragg, then went to the 82nd then to Special Forces, and that brings you up to date on me. By the way, our old outfit the 6087 had been deactivated by the time I returned there in 1954."

"Ken, that's a great story, and I'm damn glad that you decided to come back in the army. The Army needs men like you!"

"Thanks Sergeant Major. What are you going to do now that you're retired?"

"I intend to catch up on my fishing. I intend to set beneath a shade tree on the Salt River, and just let the rest of the fucking world drift by."

"That sounds like an ideal way to spend your retirement," I said.

"I have my own house in Arizona, and all our kids and grandkids are there. The wife and I want to spend a lot more time with them, and watch them all grow up. We're both tired of traveling around the frigging world, and tired of moving every two or three years. After thirty-two years in the army, I'm stacking arms forever!"

"Sergeant Major, you have certainly earned your retirement. I wish you and Mrs. Baker long happy lives, and the very best of everything."

We sat there in the club for about three more hours and discussed everything we possibly could. I learned he had gone to Korea in December 1952, and had picked up one of his four purple hearts there.

I said, "Sergeant Major, I'll run back up to the barracks and change into civilian clothes, so we can go to the airport when we need to. Getting caught off-post in fatigue uniforms around here is an automatic court-martial offense."

"Let's have another drink before you go," he said.

I called the waiter and ordered us both another drink. We slowly drank the drinks. Then I returned to the barracks and slipped into some comfortable civilian clothes. I drove back down to the club and rejoined the Sergeant Major.

I said, "Would you like to get something to eat before we go? You know the airlines will serve you only snacks and peanuts."

He replied, "Let's you and I have another drink together, probably our last one then we can eat."

I agreed with that, and he ordered us two more drinks. We finished our drinks and went into the restaurant. We continued to talk as we ate.

"Ken, there is one final thing I'd like to ask you, and I know you have the answer to my question."

"Fire away Sergeant Major."

"Do you remember that Corporal that whipped your ass your first night in the outfit?"

I laughed, "Yeah, of course, you're talking about that asshole Corporal Sherron."

"Yeah, that was his name. My question is, how did he get so beaten up that night after he had whipped your ass?"

"Sergeant Major, I've never told anyone else this, but I knew he was drunk that night, and after everyone went to sleep, I snuck down to his room and beat the shit out of him with my old combat boot."

Laughing, he pounded the table with his fist, "I frigging knew it, by god, I just knew that you had to do it. By damn, you've just confirmed it! I wanted very much for that to be you. I wanted it that morning I chewed your ass out about it."

I just laughed. That was a good memory in my book. We talked about him tying our Jeep to the planking. Then we talked about me being trapped on the antenna pole. It was a wonderful, beautiful stroll down memory lane for both of us. I'm still a young soldier, and he's completing a career that began before I was even born.

He glanced at his watch and said, "Ken, I guess we'd better head for the airport. I'll check in a little early and make sure my flights on time."

I picked up both checks and said, "It would be my honor to buy you dinner." I paid the bill and we drove out to the Fayetteville Regional Airport. He checked with the ticket clerk and was told his flight would be leaving right on schedule.

We stood around talking for almost thirty minutes, then they announced his flight was boarding. We waited until all the other passengers had boarded then he had to go. We shook hands and bear hugged each other. I said, *"Sergeant Major Baker, I thank you with all my heart for everything that you taught me, but most of all, I thank you for being my friend."*

He bear hugged me again and replied, "Ken, take care of yourself. This old world is a dangerous place, stay safe and be well. Who knows, we may meet again someday. I surely hope so!"

He turned walked out the gate and boarded the plane. Seeing him again after so many years was one of the most memorable and pleasant events of my life. I added more pages to my ever expanding memory book. The Chapter on Sergeant Major Howard Ironjaws Baker, like so many other Chapters, was irrevocably closed.

I slowly drove back out to the fort, old memories crowding and filling my mind. I parked my car and went into the barracks. It was still early evening, but the booze had made me tired. I lay down on my bunk closed my eyes and dozed off.

Bert came by and kicked my bunk and said, "Get up you lazy ass, let's go to the club and get a beer." I slowly rolled over and then sat up on the side of my bunk.

I said, "Chief of all Redskins, I've been drinking all afternoon, but I could handle a cold beer."

He replied, "I'll drive."

We got into his car and he drove us down to the club. We went into the bar area, and he ordered us two beers. The club was crowded and noisy, but we finally found a table.

After we sat down Bert said, "I heard today that there's a bunch more people coming out on orders for the First Group on Okinawa, I hope to hell I'm on'em."

"Me too, I'm a little tired of Bragg for a while."

"Ken, when are you going to get married?" I looked at him in amazement.

"Married! Bert, the thought has never crossed my mind. I operate on the 'Four F' system. Besides, if the army wanted me to have a wife they'd issue me one," I replied.

He laughed and ordered us another beer. Bob and Jason came into the bar and joined us at the table. Bob mentioned that he'd heard the same rumor that Bert had.

I asked, "When are we going to find out about the orders, have you heard a reporting date?"

He replied, “I heard they’ll be out next Monday, and the reporting date is sometimes in June.”

Jason said, “I hope I’m on’em. I’d like to get the hell away from Bragg.”

I said, “I hope Okinawa is bigger than what we saw last year and bigger than Wake Island. One plane load of troops and we almost drank the island dry.”

My friend Billy Bowles and some good looking lady came into the bar and sat at another table, we all exchanged greetings. We slowly sipped our beer and talked for another couple of hours, then we headed back to the barracks.

CHAPTER 37

Okinawa, Isle of fun

The next day orders did come out, about forty of us were selected to go to the First Group on Okinawa. Most everyone was very happy to get out of Fort Bragg for a while. Everyone who was leaving requested several days furlough to go home, or to go wherever they wanted before reporting in on the west coast for onward movement to Okinawa.

One of my friends who had been in Laos with us on one of the "A" teams Sergeant First Class Ralph Slaughter from Nitro, West Virginia, said to me, "Ken, why don't you come up to my house and spend a couple of days with me, and we can fly out to the west coast together."

"Thanks Ralph that would be a nice thing to do. I have to take my car home to Alabama, then I'll catch a bus to Atlanta and fly up to Charleston. Can you pick me up there?"

"Sure, just call me and let me know what flight you'll be on, and the arrival time." He then gave me his home address and telephone number in Nitro.

Everyone on the orders left Fort Bragg around the same time going their separate ways. I headed south out of Fayetteville on US highway 301, through South Carolina eventually Georgia then Alabama. It was about a seven hour drive until I reached Lynell, Alabama. I stayed with my Uncle and Aunt for a few days. While there I visited with a few cousins and a couple of friends.

Once again I failed to see Grady, an old ex-army friend of mine. I did learn he was still working in the cotton mill, and now had four children. I left my car with my Uncle for his use and care then caught a bus north to Atlanta.

I went to the airport and purchased a ticket for Charleston, West Virginia. The flight took off on time and landed in Charleston right on schedule. Ralph was waiting for me. We picked up my duffle bag and he drove us to his home in Nitro. He introduced me to his mom and dad. They were very nice people, and treated me like I was part of the family.

Ralph and I had a few cold beers that evening, and as we talked he shocked the hell out of me when he said, "Ken, I'm getting married day after tomorrow."

I stared hard at him and replied, "Ralph, who're you marrying? I never knew that you had a girl friend here in Nitro?"

"It's a girl I've known for quite some time. She was married once before, and has a young daughter."

"Well, the little girl doesn't matter. Congratulations my friend, am I invited to the wedding?"

"Yes, of course you are, you can be my best man."

I said in a joking manner, "Well, you know you still have time to change your mind, we can catch the plane early tomorrow and be on the west coast before sundown."

He laughed, "No, I'd never do that, she means too much to me for me to do something like that."

I replied, "I'm teasing of course, but you had your chance."

We drank another beer, and then turned in for the night. The next morning his mom made us a wonderful breakfast. Ralph left to go see his girlfriend, and I spent some time with his father. His dad told me all about West Virginia, relating tales that went back to his own childhood. I found him to be highly educated, and most informative. It was indeed a very pleasant discussion.

Ralph came home and had lunch with me and his dad. While we were seated at the table Ralph said, "Ken, I mentioned to my girlfriend Shirley what you said about us leaving early today for the west coast, she got pissed!"

Stunned, I replied, "Ralph, I'm sorry to hear that. Of course you told her I was just kidding didn't you?"

He shook his head and said, "I guess I did. Anyway she's pissed at you, and said that you can't attend our wedding!"

Staring hard at him I replied, "Ralph, I'm really sorry about this. I hope you know that I was just kidding you, don't you?"

He shook his head in the affirmative and said, "I know you were, and I should have told her, but it's too late now."

"I'm embarrassed, I'm truly sorry this happened, and I know it's all just a misunderstanding. But, if she feels that way I damn sure won't be at your wedding."

Ralph's dad spoke up and said, "Ken, you and I can stay at home and drink some good homemade West Virginia whiskey. I have a couple of things that I'd like to show you."

"Thank you Mr. Slaughter, I'd love to sip some of the states famous whiskey with such excellent company as you."

Ralph spoke up and said, "That's settled! Ken, let's you and I go to the local carnival its downtown tonight."

"That sounds good to me. I haven't been to a carnival since I was a little boy."

That evening Ralph and I drove downtown Nitro to a small park. There the carnival was all set up, and people were walking around playing the various games and riding the large Ferris wheel. We parked and walked into the area. Kids were chasing each other, and the older ones all seemed to have a huge stick of cotton candy. I noticed one smaller boy who had pink cotton candy plastered across his mouth and most of his face, but he was truly enjoying it.

He smiled at me and said, "This is really good."

We played a couple of the games, winning nothing. I finally knocked over a moving duck and won a small doll. I turned and gave it to a young girl that was watching us. Her face lit up with a huge smile, and off she dashed to show her mother.

Tiring of the carnival we left, and Ralph picked up a dozen cold beers on the way back to his house. His dad joined us for a couple of beers then went to bed. Ralph and I drank another beer, then we called it an evening also.

The next morning we had a wonderful breakfast, and I enjoyed some of the finest West Virginia ham that I'd ever tasted. After breakfast Ralph and I left to go pick up his suit and boutonniere, plus a bouquet of flowers for the bride.

As he was driving I said, "Ralph, what would you like for me to give you and your bride as a wedding present?"

He was silent for a moment then replied, "Nothing really, Shirley, my fiancée, said she didn't want anything from you."

"Ralph, I'm really sorry that your girlfriend thinks so harshly of me. What I said to you was of course just a frigging joke, and it has turned out all wrong."

"I know, and I feel bad about it also, but you know women once they make up their minds it's all over."

"Yeah, I guess so."

Once back home we had dinner, then he and his Mother dressed for the wedding. I congratulated Ralph on his appearance, and wished them both all the best of luck. His dad and I opened a fifth of his whiskey, and we toasted his son and the new bride.

He said, "Ken, let me show you my collections."

"What type do you have sir?"

"I have a coin collection, and a phonograph collection."

First he showed me his coin collection. It was a fantastic collection. He had coins dated back to the mid eighteen hundreds. He had dozens of albums holding various denominations of coins. He would explain them to me and estimate their current value. I was amazed at their age and value, and fascinated by his knowledge of the various coins.

Then he showed me his record collection. I think he must have had two huge trunks loaded with records. They extended back to the earliest days of recorded music. He had an old hand wound record player, and he'd occasionally play one of records. I listened to singers and bands that I'd never heard of. But it was fascinating to hear those long ago singers and musicians, and their songs and music. Finally, we both began to feel the effects of the whiskey, so he suggested we call it an evening. I quickly agreed.

The next day he and I rode around the country side as he showed me that part of his state. It was a very pleasant day. That evening Ralph came home, and he and I talked for a while. We had to leave the next morning, so we went to bed early.

We told his parents goodbye, and I expressed my appreciation for their kind hospitality. We arrived at the airport, and caught our plane to San Francisco. Six hours later we landed in San Francisco and stayed in transient quarters at the Presidio. Several of the guys were already there, and they all were planning their evening activities. My friend

Jason was there, so he and I decided to go to a nightclub and see what it had to offer.

We caught a taxi then found a nightclub, and watched a couple of strippers wrap themselves around a pole simulating various sexual acts. I said to Jason, "This is about exciting as watching paint dry. Let's go some other place, this is boring as hell."

"I agree let's go."

We visited a couple more night clubs, and they basically all presented the same type show, so we called it a night and returned to the base.

The next day Bert, Jason and I went down to Fishermen's Wharf and ate raw oysters until they oozed out our ears. Some of the other guys who were traveling with us were on the Wharf, and they were all eating various dishes of fish. We pulled a couple of tables together, drank a barrel of beer, and ate more raw clams and oysters. That night we hit the clubs again, and knowing we had to leave early the next day we curtailed the evening activities early.

The following morning everyone loaded their bags and was bussed to the airport. After checking in we climbed aboard the big jet and took off for Okinawa. We landed initially in Honolulu for refueling staying there for about four hours. We didn't have enough time to explore the place as we really would have liked to.

We took off again, and after several more hours of flying we landed at Kadena Air Force Base, Okinawa. A bus met us and we were taken to Sukiran and billeted in quarters there. Jason and I were assigned to the same room.

As we unpacked I said to Jason, "Well, I guess we're home for three years, I hope they turn out to be good ones for us."

He replied, "It'll be a good tour. I heard that prices here remain pretty cheap about the same as last year plus there's loads of women, so we'll have a good tour."

Bob came by the room and said, "I dropped by personnel, and I'm going on to Taiwan. I'm going to be on the resident team there."

I remarked, "I didn't know we have a resident team there."

He replied, "Sure we do, and there's a resident team in Korea also."

Jason said, "I guess we'll all find out what we'll be doing by tomorrow."

I heard someone calling my name, and I said to Jason, "I bet you that's Art Taylor."

I stepped out into the hallway, and sure enough it was Art. We shook hands as he welcomed me to Okie. Soon the hallway filled up with the people assigned here already, looking for their friends who had arrived with us. I ran into several of my friends who had been with us in Laos and back at Bragg, and had been assigned here on the island earlier.

Art said, "I have a job as the bouncer at the Top Three NCO Club, and it's the best club on the island."

I replied, "Art, I can't picture you as a bouncer, did that deputy sheriff in Lillington recommend you for the job?"

Scowling he replied, "Screw you!"

We finished hanging up our clothes and put all the proper items in our footlockers. Then I hauled out my boots, shoes, shoe polish and brushes and positioned them the army way.

Finally, we were finished, and I remarked "I'm hungry as hell, where's the mess hall?"

Art replied, "It's just across the street, let's go."

So the entire group of us strolled over to the mess hall and had a fine meal by any standard. After eating and returning to the barracks, Art changed clothes for his night job as club bouncer.

Jason said, "I'm going to take a shower and go to the club, do you want to go?"

"Of course! Hell, you'd be lost without me helping you find your way back home."

We both took showers, and dressed in our civilian clothes caught a small taxi to the Top Three Club.

We arrived at the club which was located up on a hill. Inside it was really nice. It was just as it was when we came through here last year. They had a large bandstand, good sized dance floor, and lots of tables. Along several of the walls were lines of slot machines. I noticed that there were several American dependent wives who were playing the machines. A few soldiers were also playing the machines. I had never played the slots, so I looked forward to the experience.

After finding a table, Jason and I ordered a beer. The waitress brought us a San Miguel beer bottled in the Philippine Islands, I had drunk the beer before, and it is damn good. For the next few hours we just sat there and talked with the various soldiers we knew that came into the club. We saw several of our friends that had been here for several months already. Art walked by, and he really looked good. He had on a deep red jacket, a black tie and sharply pressed black trousers. I told him he was very impressive looking.

Art sat down at our table. “Ken, I’m going with the head hostess.” He then pointed her out. She was indeed an outstanding looking woman. Rather tall for an oriental, smooth skin, slender and very well built.

“Art, my compliments on your choice of women, if I get a chance I’ll have to back door you,” I said.

He scowled and replied, “Better not, I’ll whip your ass.”

I said, “Well, if you feel that way about it forget it, it’s her loss”

We stayed until the club closed. A little loaded we walked to the foot of the hill and caught one of the hundreds of tiny Japanese taxis that cruise the island looking for GI’s to transport. We reached our barracks with no difficulty.

Monday we were assigned to the various companies. Jason and I went to C Company. Ralph and several others went to the other companies. We all drew our rucksacks and field equipment. We spent our first day getting everything in good shape and completing our personnel in-processing procedures.

Jason had mail waiting for him in the company mail room. He picked it up and came upstairs.

“Ken, I have this letter from my lawyer, open it and let me know what he says about my frigging divorce.” He handed the letter to me and lay down on his bunk. I accepted the letter, and sitting down on my bunk I slowly ripped it open.

I read the letter through and said, “Jason, there’s no good news here. The lawyer says his letters to your wife have all been returned as undeliverable, and he has no other address. He wants to know if you have an updated address for your wife.” I handed the letter to him.

He let out a deep sigh and said, “Well shit, how in the hell am I supposed to know where she is, she was in South Carolina, and I’m in Okinawa.”

“Jason, you’re from Pennsylvania why don’t you file for divorce there, and claim she deserted you, or skipped town or something.”

“You have a point. I’ll check with the Judge Advocate and see what he says.”

"Well, keep the letter it might be useful as evidence, or as a supporting document down the line. By the way we have to make a parachute jump tomorrow morning down on some golf course in the middle of town. Fortunately, we'll be jumping choppers so it won't be too bad."

Later that evening we cleaned up and headed for the little village of New Koza. We had been there last year when we came through on our way to Laos. We caught a cab and shortly arrived in the little village. We walked down the dirt streets. Bars were everywhere, all you had to do was select one. Jason selected one and we entered it. There were a couple of small tables. The boss mama san came out, so we asked for two beers. She brought us two San Miguel beers. They weren't cold but they were cool.

We drank the two beers and ordered two more, then two young girls showed up. We spent the early evening in their company, where we both performed our required military duty then returned to the barracks.

The next morning we boarded a truck and rode to the marshalling area which was on a corner of the drop zone. There we drew our chutes and put them on, and as our stick was called six of us loaded on to the H-34 helicopters. It took several minutes for the straining engines to gain the right jump altitude.

The drop zone was named Awase Meadows, it was the local golf course. I think we were up somewhere about one thousand feet when the light turned green and one after another we jumped. Happily all of us landed on the course, and missed the little streets and its myriad of electric lines that crisscrossed the area.

I landed next to Mike Jacobson, an old friend of mine since 1957. He was one of the first persons I'd met after leaving the division. I really liked him. He was a veteran of the Korean War having jumped with the Parachute Regiment during the Inchon landing. We rolled up our chutes placing them in the kit bag then walked together back to the marshalling area. Mike was in A company as was Ralph Slaughter. I saw Ralph in the marshalling area and we had an opportunity to talk for a few minutes. Finally, with the jump completed we loaded the trucks and returned to the company.

Jason and I were assigned to the same "A" team, and I was very happy about that. I met dozens of new guys in the outfit and quickly realized that most of them were true professionals. They knew their jobs, and they knew several other jobs as well. We spend lots of time in team training. We conducted area studies, and our 'B' team area of operations was the country of Korea. We studied the country until we knew almost every village and town in it. We knew where the rivers were and their names, the dams, bridges and the electric grids, almost everything except the language. We half-heartedly tried to learn the language, but it's so guttural and harsh it was nigh impossible for us to master. Certain phrases we knew, but over all we never did learn to speak Korean. During the summer and fall months we made several training trips to Korea, Thailand, Taiwan and the Philippines. We jumped in and conducted small exercises. It was a terrific learning experience, and gave us exceptional exposure to the countries of Southeast Asia.

The summer passed and Thanksgiving was a big event. Lot of the guys was invited to their friend's house that was lucky enough to have their wives and families with them on the island. Jason, Art and I, and most of the bachelors ate in the mess hall.

Looking over his big cigar Art said to me, "After we finish why don't we go downtown and get a steam bath and massage."

I asked, "How much does it cost?"

"About two dollars, it all depends on what all you have done."

"It sounds good to me, how about you Jason?"

He grunted, as he finished up a turkey leg, "Fine with me."

We finished our meal then walked out to the street and caught one of the omni-present taxis. The driver drove around the Airbase then to highway one. Art told him where and when to stop.

We stopped at a little house alongside the highway, and Art paid the driver. The three of us walked into the place.

The Mama San behind the little counter smiled and asked, "You want steam bath?"

I said, "Yes, we also want a massage."

She smiled and said, "Okay, you pay two dollars please."

I handed her two one dollar bills. She called out something in Japanese, and a young nice looking girl came from behind a curtain. She took me by the hand and led me to the back of the building.

She turned around and said, "Take off clothes please."

So I undressed. I hung my pants shirt and shorts up on a hangar. Then I sat on a small bench and removed my shoes and socks.

She opened up this big wooden box on the side of the room indicating I should step inside. I stepped inside the box and sat on the small stool that was there. She closed the lid on one side of my head and then the other. She then wrapped a small white towel around my throat, then walked over to a small switch device mounted on the wall turned it on. I immediately felt the steam streaming into the box. The steam wasn't so hot that it burned, but it was hot enough to produce instant perspiration. I could feel the sweat running down my arms and legs. She was using a small towel to wipe my face and forehead as sweat began to pour down my face. I remained in the steam cabinet for about ten minutes,

I said to the girl, "That's about enough."

She walked over and turned the switch off came back and removed the towel from around my neck. I stood up and I swore I felt ten pounds lighter than when I had first stepped into the box.

She led me over about four feet away from the box and had me sit down in a large tub filled with water. She then began washing me. She washed off my face first then the upper part of my body. She had me stand up and then she washed the lower part of my torso. As she began washing me I had an erection. It had immediately sprung to the position of attention in magnificent fashion.

She giggled and said, "Your thing like boy san, number one."

I replied, "Maybe it likes you too much, because you're number one."

She just smiled and continued to administer the bath. She had me step out of the tub, and she began drying my body off. When she finished drying me she led me to a small table with clean fresh towels on it, and indicated that I should lie down on it, which I did. She then began to massage my body beginning at my toes, worked up my legs and then my back, shoulders and neck. It really felt good. She then stepped up on a small stool and stepped up onto my back. She then began to walk up and down my back, and I swore her toes were as nimble and educated as her fingers had been. Eventually, she climbed down and told me to turn over. I did and she covered my mid section with another towel. My erection had lost none of its rigidity, so naturally the towel looked as if it had a tent peg under it. She began again to massage my legs beginning at the toes and worked up my legs. She bypassed my groin area working on my chest muscles then my neck and finally my face.

She appeared to be nearing the end so I asked her, "Why you no massage my friend?"

She giggled again and said, "I give him good massage for two more dollars."

Trapped, I said, "All right, let's do it."

She expertly performed her massage. Then she said, "Finee!"

I sat up and began to put my clothes back on. I handed her two additional dollars.

She said, "I number one, yes?"

I kissed her on top of her head and replied, "Yes, you're number one."

I walked back up to the front of the building bought a beer and found a chair. I was there about two minutes when Jason walked out and joined me.

"Jason how'd you like the bath and massage?"

"I loved it. It beats the hell out of the 'White Rose' in Vientiane by a mile."

"I agree with that, I think I must have sweated all the booze out that I've drank since we got on the island," I replied.

He grinned, "So did I."

"Yeah, I also got a hand massage for two bucks, how about you?"

"Yeah, I got the same thing."

Art came out and said, "Well boy's, how did you like that?"

I replied, "That's the best four dollars I've spent in a long time."

We caught a taxi to the American Legion where Jason and I put ten dollars worth of quarters apiece into one slot machine, and lost it all. Art left to go to the Top Three club where he was on duty in the evening. I told him we'd see him later at the club.

The Legion was filled with people. Lots of GI's and a couple of Marines were sitting at the tables drinking and talking. Marv, Fred and Dan were at one table and Mike, Bert and Jake were at another. Smoke filled the room in spite of the labors of the air conditioners. We sat there about two more hours sipping San Miguel and just bullshitting. Personnel in the room constantly changed as people left and others came in. Most of the time all the slot machines were played constantly, now and then a jackpot would be yelled out.

Jason and I left and went up to the Top Three.

I said to Jason, "What say we get a bite to eat, it's been a long time since dinner, and I'm hungry as a Florida alligator."

"Me too, that sounds good to me."

I ordered a lobster dinner and he had a T-bone steak. The cost was just three dollars and fifty cents.

I remarked to Jason, "You just can't beat the meal and the price."

"Yeah, and you can't beat the calories that we just put down also."

We stayed there for about one more hour then went back to the barracks. November passed, and December rolled around. We were scheduled for a two week exercise in Korea. Our Group Commander believed that we should train and live in Korea the way we would if we were actually deployed on a combat operation. That simply meant we'd have to live in their huts, or out in the open woods and eat whatever they ate.

Our team Sergeant was a young Master Sergeant E-7 from California of Spanish extraction. His name was Tony Domingo. He was the best team sergeant, and one of the best soldiers I was ever to meet. He was married to a lovely girl from California named Juliet and had three children. They lived off post in one of the Wherry housing developments. Tony was a Silver Star winner from the Korean War, and seemed to be an expert on almost every job on the team. We trucked over late in the evening to Kadena, and a C-130 cargo aircraft was waiting. We loaded our rucksacks and parachutes aboard. That was all the equipment we were taking with us. We climbed aboard and the big bird took off.

A couple hours later the plane load master came back and told us to begin getting ready. We had about thirty minutes before reaching our drop zone. A couple of men from the Korean resident team were to set up the drop zone lights for the pilot. We began to put our parachutes on, and then our rucksacks which we attached below our reserve chutes. In my rucksack in additional to clothes, shaving kit and cigarettes I had packed the team radio and the generator. My rucksack weighted it seemed about one hundred-fifty pounds.

We were flying at twelve hundred and fifty feet, the proper drop altitude. The cargo side doors opened and the red light was on. We went through the preparatory commands, and I stood in the door.

Looking out the night was as black as pitch, and not one light anywhere in sight. The air at that altitude was unbelievably cold. My hands although in gloves seemed to freeze immediately. I became so cold in just two minutes that my entire body began shaking. I leaned out and I could see that we were well off the proper flight path as the DZ lights were off to my right.

The load master came back and said, "We have to make another pass."

I stepped back away from the door. I couldn't believe that the pilot had missed the entire drop zone. Tony came up and shouted into my ear, "We have a reserve pilot from the states, he's getting in his flight time requirements."

I hollered back to Tony, "If the son-of-a-bitch misses the DZ again, you'll have to throw me out, as my ass will be frozen solid."

Tony just laughed.

The pilot made a wide turn, and then straightened out for the next pass over the DZ. I stood in the door and again looked out. My eyes were watering as the prop blast hit my face in a fury. I could barely see. Finally I made out the lights well out in front of the plane. I looked at Tony as he held up one finger, which indicated I had one minute before jumping. We were hooked up to the static line, and everyone was crowding the door behind me. Everyone was freezing as the frigid air ripped through the plane. The temperature had to be down around zero, or below at this altitude. I couldn't feel my fingers as I gripped the sides of the plane door. The light turned green and I jumped.

The prop blast grabbed me and threw me head over heels. Then my chute popped open, I stopped the wild falling then began a slow descent. I looked around and could barely make out the rest of the team as they also were floating down slowly. With no moon at all the darkness was complete.

Looking down towards the ground I could barely see that it was white, so I knew that we'll land in snow. I released the drop cord holding my rucksack so that it would land before me, and I wouldn't land on it and get hurt, it fell about fifteen feet below me. As I drew closer to the ground I prepared to make a parachute landing fall. I heard rather than saw my rucksack hit the ground then I landed. I hit like a sack of shit. I fell one way then another; finally, I was flat on the ground. Damn, that was a rough landing I muttered to myself. I got up unbuckled my chute rolled it up stuffing it into the parachute kitbag. I found my rucksack picked it up and began walking towards a set of headlights that suddenly came on. The resident team would take the parachutes and send them back to Oki.

I met Tony and Jason as they were heading towards the truck that would pick us up.

Tony asked, "Ken, have you warmed up yet?"

"Hell no, I'm freezing my balls off. That frigging reserve pilot has no idea how damn cold it gets standing in the door at night in December over Korea, and probably doesn't care."

Jason who had been standing in the door opposite me spoke up "Kenny, I'm with you. Making a double pass at night is a crock of shit. Especially, when the only frigging lights for miles around are the little DZ lights"

We linked up with the Korean army forces that were to participate with us in the exercise, and for the next two weeks we roughed it. We slept in huts, in the woods, and in some Korean homes, and even in cellars as we evaded the opposing forces out to capture us. We had to buy and eat the local food.

I hate Kimchi, which is a Korean dish of pickled cabbage. It stinks, stinks, and stinks! However, I would eat it if it was the only thing we had. We hiked up more damn hills than the law should allow. Korea is hills and more hills. Very few trees remained as the forest had not yet fully recovered from the war. Finally, the exercise was over. We reported in to K-36 which was the airfield we were to fly out. The airfield itself was a few old buildings all filled with shell and bullet holes from the war. We caught our C-130 and headed back to Oki.

Christmas and New Year's rolled around. On New Year's Eve Art and I were together at the Top Three club. He was the bouncer that night, and I was having a few Scotch and water drinks. A Japanese band was playing, so I listened to them as they played popular American songs. At midnight they began their countdown to the New Year. Art had left the table to check on something or other, so I was by myself. I caught the waitress's eye and ordered another drink. All the horns, whistles and shouting began as 1961, was born. I thought, here I am thirty-years-old going on thirty-one. Time does fly by, and the passing years can wreck all a young man's dreams.

I allowed myself the luxury of opening my wonderful memory book and turned the pages back to 1948. I closed my eyes, and in memory's eye I saw again my beautiful Rachel as I danced with her, and threw her a kiss so many years ago. I thought of her and I in the Ring Hotel, so young, so much in love, and it all had been snatched away from us so abruptly.

I recalled sparkling Dotty, so sexy, and so loving. I remembered Betty who had helped me through my medical crisis, and hopefully found happiness in the states.

My thoughts turned to Elona. We too loved each other, but nothing had ever worked out for us, it just wasn't meant to be.

Lastly, I thought of the two sons that I knew were mine. Rachel would be thirty-two now, and Kenny would be eleven or twelve years old. I wondered what he looked like. I thought of my other son also named Kenny, he would be about eight years old now. Neither of them would ever know me, and I'd never know them. How strange I thought, the destiny that controls and shapes our lives. I swallowed my drink and ordered two more from the waitress. I thought no use torturing myself, I closed my memory book, and watched the festivities.

The months sped by and we continued to conduct off-island exercises. In September Tony and our Company Commander plus a couple of other guys were sent to South Vietnam as a survey team to make an estimate of the situation, and then report on present conditions. They returned, and their report was bleak. The communist Viet Cong called the VC were over-running the villages, and terrorizing the native Montagnards in the central highlands of the country. They also were creating havoc in the delta region. They were a definite threat to the survival of the South Vietnamese government.

Jason and I were placed on a new team with a Master Sergeant Medic as the Team Sergeant. I knew him as one of the better medics, but I didn't think he was team sergeant material. I knew all the other team members as they were all from C Company. We really didn't have to train very much together as we were all highly qualified professionals in our own jobs. The lowest ranking member of the team was a buck sergeant.

The Team Leader was a Captain named Sidney Brunkhalter, a seasoned professional who knew his job.

November rolled around and our team was alerted along with an "A" team from B Company to go to South Vietnam. Our team began a limited area study as we tried to learn as much as we could about the country. Everyone knew that the French had lost the Indo-China war, and had been run out of the country. But the intelligence information we had was old, and not too damn useful.

CHAPTER 38

Vietnam at the beginning

In the latter part of November 1961, we left Okinawa and flew by C-130 aircraft to Tan Son Nhut airport in Saigon, South Vietnam. We were all dressed in civilian clothes, mostly slacks, boots and shirts. We landed and as the aircraft taxied to the terminal the tailgate of the airplane opened and the heat wave that rushed through the airplane was unbelievable. The temperature was over one hundred degrees Fahrenheit.

The first two full Special Forces "A" teams ever assigned to South Vietnam for duty stepped out onto the tarmac, and gathered our equipment together. A couple of old trucks pulled up and we were transported to the Military Advisory and Assistance Group headquarters. We were shepherded into a large room and given a briefing on the country, the situation in the country, and basically our mission while in country.

Our mission as it turned out was a simple one: "We were to recruit, organize train and develop village defense forces, so that they would be able to defend themselves against the Communist Viet Cong."

The briefing officer made a statement that here in Nam, we could continue to learn and perfect our unconventional warfare skills. Your job he said, "Is not to fight a war, but to train others to fight their own war."

We were told we would be working for Combined Studies which was a section within the MAAG headquarters. Instructions were given us to go to the paymaster in the finance section draw two hundred dollars then buy some civilian clothes. We were to be considered civilian employees, not US military. Jason and I went to the pay section which was run by the US Navy. I thought that rather odd, but then I didn't know very much about MAAG's. We checked in with the pay section, and there I met US Navy LTJG Henry Hamby.

Hamby was about six foot two, dark hair and slender. I detected an obvious southern drawl and accent in his voice. I suspected he was from either Georgia or Tennessee, maybe even Alabama. He was in charge of the finance section for the MAAG.

He asked, "Let me see your paperwork."

I said, "You're supposed to have a payroll already made up with about two dozen names on it for pay purposes, and we're all Army personnel."

"Well, I damn sure don't have it, and without it you won't get any money from this office."

Jason said, "Screw it, we'll check back with the section chief and let him handle it."

I replied, "Fine, we can get the money and buy clothes tomorrow." We walked away from the pay office, and went back to the briefing room.

We were assigned to stay in a local house identified to us as House Number Ten. We were free for the remainder of the day. Several of us caught a couple of taxis and went downtown Saigon to the main street. It was Tu Do Street. We found seats at a small sidewalk café and ordered beer. They served us a beer named Bier 33. It wasn't very cold, and was a very poor excuse for beer.

The girls of Saigon were surprisingly nice looking. They wore long pajamas covered with a thin silk like material. I learned it was called Ao Dai, the traditional Vietnamese dress for women. We indulged in what was later entitled "bird watching," which was nothing more than watching the girls stroll by.

The streets of Saigon were filled with rickshaws, small taxi cars, motorbikes, scooters and bicycles by the hundreds were everywhere. French architecture was prevalent, and most of the natives seemed to speak French. I should have paid closer attention when I was studying French. We sat there for a couple of hours then caught a taxi back to house ten.

The next morning we were told to go to the pay section and get our clothing allowance, go into Saigon and get some clothes. Jason and I went together. I saw the Navy Lieutenant Hamby again.

I spoke to him and asked, "Do you have our name on a pay request yet?"

He laughed and replied, "Yep, it came in this morning. I have no problem with paying you guys. But I have to have the paperwork to cover my ass, it was nothing personal." He then said, "Let me buy you two a beer."

So we followed him over to a small canteen where he bought three bottles of San Miguel. It was cold and taste great. The three of us sat at a table and drank two beers each. He told me he was from Smyrna, Georgia, a suburb of Atlanta, so I had been correct in my estimate of his orgin. He turned out to be a really nice guy. He mentioned that he was shacking up with a beautiful Chinese Eurasian girl.

I said to him, "Henry, it might not be best for you to shack up someplace outside of a major hotel."

He remarked, "So far it's been safe."

"Well, you've been in Saigon longer than I have, so I guess you know best. If your girlfriend is as beautiful as you say, I hope I get a chance to back door you before I leave here."

He laughed and replied, "She's a blue water woman. For you ground pounders, that means she only makes it with sailors."

"She'll never know what she's missing," I replied

We finished our beer thanked him for the drink and left.

Jason and I walked downtown and on Tu Do Street found several stores that sold clothing. We both bought bush hats, denim type trousers, a couple of long sleeve shirts and a jacket. We both looked ready to go big game hunting in the Serengeti in East Africa, rather than chasing the bad guys out here in the jungles of Southeast Asia.

The other team began to organize their operations, and was being stationed here in Saigon. Our team was briefed and told we were to split into two six man teams. One half of the team would go to Hua Cam in Danang, which was up north, and the second half would go to Bam Me Thout which was more in the central part of the country. Operating in the country was Air America, which was the same airline that operated in Laos when we were there. We boxed up some old weapons that were given to us for training and arming the natives, and everything else we had with us then caught an old reliable Air America C-47 cargo plane and took off for our destination.

We arrived at the small airport in Bam Me Thout and a young agency guy named Dave Smith met us. We loaded up all our equipment and trucked into the city to a small hotel that he had rented for us. We hauled all the boxes of weapons and equipment up the stairs to the different rooms that we had. By the time we completed that I was soaking wet with sweat, everyone was. The heat and humidity was so high that you could sit down in the shade, and not even blink your eyes and actually sweat through your clothes.

Dave had a three-quarter ton vehicle, so we all loaded on to it and drove out to the small village of Buon Enao. The village was about eight kilometers outside the little town. The village was populated with members of the Rhade tribe. They are Montagnards. I think their name roughly translated would be 'Mountain People'. There are several different tribes of them who inhabit the central highlands of Vietnam. We called them "Yards" for short.

We were to train the villagers in a new program called the Civilian Irregular Defense Group and teach them how to defend and protect their village and crops. My friend, SFC Paul Reynolds, a highly trained Special Forces medic, and Dave under the direction of a Colonel in Saigon had initiated the CIDG Program They both had established great rapport with the Rhade tribe that we were to work with. We drove through the gate into the village, and I noticed that the village was surrounded by a ten foot high fence made out of sharpened bamboo poles. There were several large houses in the village and several smaller type buildings.

Dave said, "The bigger buildings are called long houses, and several families live in each one of them."

The long houses were totally built out of bamboo. At several locations in front of the huge huts there were logs that had been fashioned into stairs. Carved out steps were in the logs leading up to narrow doorways.

Dave spoke to the village chief and then turned and said to us, "We're going to have an alert so you can see the villagers respond." He then picked up a wooden mallet and struck a gong that was hanging from a nearby tree limb. When he did that the native Yards began pouring out of their huts and forming up into platoon like formations. I watched in disbelief as they formed up, some were carrying old French rifles, some had spears and bow and arrows, and a few were armed with long swords. They were all dressed in loin cloths, and all of them were barefooted. It resembled something from an old Hollywood jungle movie. I knew however, that this scene involved life and death issues not just for the natives, but for we Americans also.

Jason said, “Ken, we’re in a world of shit if we’re supposed to fight a war with these guys and their weapons.”

I smiled at him and replied, “Jason, we’d better do a super fast job of training, and getting these guys armed, or we’re all going to be worm food.”

They concluded their alert and the natives drifted back into their long houses. We loaded back into the truck and went back to the little town.

That evening Jason and I walked across the street from the hotel to a local bar. Underneath my shirt I had a loaded forty-five caliber pistol and so did Jason. We sat down at a small table and I ordered two beers. Naturally, they brought out bier 33’s. They were warm, but that’s all that we had to drink, so it had to do. We were the only two customers in the small place. We both sat with our backs to the back of the building so we could watch the street in front of us. Jason sat on the back side of one side of the table and I sat on the other. I watched the gecko’s racing across the ceiling and walls. The way those little lizards could run across the ceiling upside down was amazing. As I watched them their little tongues would dart out, and in a flash a fly or some other type insect would disappear. It had now become dark.

A little woman switched on the ceiling light, which had to be about a twenty-five watt bulb. The dim light shone maybe three feet outside the table. In just a few minutes the bulb was swarmed with insects flitting around. The geckos were having a feast.

Jason asked, “Are you ready for another beer?”

“Sure, we have nothing else to drink, and nothing else to do, so let’s have another one.”

The woman brought us another beer. I lit a cigarette and blew smoke up towards the closest gecko, but he wasn’t bothered or distracted whatsoever. All of a sudden the light went out!

Jason said, “Ken, get down!”

He then turned the table over, our two beers crashed to the floor breaking both bottles. I immediately hit the floor and grabbed for my pistol cocking the trigger, I stared into the dark street but saw no movement whatsoever, there were no incoming rounds. The light as suddenly as it went off came right back on. I looked over at Jason he was on the floor and had his pistol out. I heard laughter behind me it was the old woman pointing at us and laughing, as red betel nut juice trickled down her chin. I felt rather sheepish as I slowly released the hammer on my pistol, and got up from the floor. I placed it back in my waistband and picked up the table. Jason got up and told the woman to give us two more beers.

I looked at him, laughed and said, "We may look stupid, but you can't be too damn careful. I would rather look stupid than look dead, because I acted stupid."

We finished the two beers and walked back across the street to the hotel. All seven of us discussed what the training plans were for the next day. The agent wanted to give out the weapons that we had brought with us to the natives, and begin small unit tactics training, and build a small firing range. He was the boss, so that's what we'd do. I finally went to bed and just lay there as the sweat rolled down from my forehead and my armpits. In spite of the heat, I eventually fell asleep.

The next morning we all managed to grab a bite to eat, and I had a cup of what they said was coffee. We went out to the village. The village chief had all his warriors present waiting our arrival. We began to give out the old rifles that we had, and issued them a limited amount of ammunition. Using Vietnamese interpreters we began explaining basic squad tactics, and how we wanted them to operate in squad and platoon sized formations. We also used a blackboard and chalk to draw the positions. We demonstrated and explained the various weapons. We took them out to a cleared part of the jungle and set up small targets for them to practice firing.

Going through one or two interpreters you never knew what the final instructions really were. Teaching small unit tactics continued for two more days then we began taking them out on patrols. They were great in the jungle, but they had absolutely no sense of noise discipline. I would stop and have the interpreter tell them not to be laughing, or coughing or talking. It really was wasted effort on my part.

We conducted several day and night patrols always going further out than previously.

The fifth day of our training in the village we were explaining ambushes, when all of a sudden they all got up and disappeared into the long houses. We finally discovered the reason for their disappearance. A small monkey had entered the village and was watching us from a tree. The natives thought the monkey was laughing at them. We ran it off by throwing sticks until it left the village. I watched as it disappeared into the tall trees. All the natives then returned to the training site.

Jason and I took a larger patrol out for a daytime exercise. I was up front with the selected patrol leader, and Jason was near the rear of the patrol. The patrol leader stopped and kneeling down motioned for quiet. I turned and hand signaled Jason to come forward.

He quickly reached my position and asked, "What's up?"

"I don't know."

I heard a loud noise off to my left, the little Yard looked in that direction then pointed out to me a huge elephant standing in a growth of bamboo. In the tall, thick canes it was almost invisible. The elephant swung his trunk and just stood there looking at us.

"Holy shit Jason, look at the size of that damn elephant!"

The Yard leader touched me on the army, and indicated that we should very slowly move back away from where the elephant was feeding.

Jason said as we were walking away from the area, "We're armed with .30 caliber carbines; if that elephant gets pissed at us, we don't stand a damn chance."

"Friend, you're absolutely right. Let's just keep walking a little faster, and hope like hell he ignores us."

The elephant resumed doing whatever elephants do, and ignored us completely. We never knew if the elephant was tame or not, but he was alone in the jungle, so he got the benefit of the doubt. We worked our way back to the village, and called it a day.

Dave came up to Jason and me as we were checking in all the weapons and ammunition and said, "Hey guys, I'd want to go tiger hunting tonight, and I'd like for you two to go with me."

I looked at him to try and determine if he was joking or serious, and apparently he was really serious.

Jason asked, "How do you plan to go tiger hunting at night?"

Dave replied, "We can take the truck and a spotlight, and just drive down some jungle trails, shine the light around, and you can pick up all kinds of animals by their eyes."

I asked, "What type weapon will you be using?"

"I have a high-powered rifle I'll take, and it'll stop an elephant, so there's no problem."

"Ok, I'll go after we get something to eat."

Jason said, "All right count me in."

We all drove back into town and grabbed a quick bite to eat at the local greasy spoon, or maybe it would be better to say the local slippery chop sticks joint.

Darkness swept in swiftly, silently settling over the landscape as the sun disappeared beneath the horizon. The three of us got all our gear together, and loaded up the little truck.

Dave told Jason, "You drive, I'll carry the rifle, and Ken can take care of the spotlight.

He gave Jason directions, and we immediately headed out into the jungle on small little animal trails and foot trails the natives used. We drove for about forty-five minutes or more. We stopped and shut the motor off. I stood up in the bed of the truck, and holding a twelve volt battery in one hand, and with the other I shone the spotlight on first one side of the trail and then the other. I was stunned at the amount of wildlife you could see by the numbers of eyes that suddenly appeared out in the brush. Dave didn't identify any of them as a tiger or anything else. Personally, I had no frigging idea what a tiger's eyes would look like in the dark.

"Dave, what in the hell does a tiger's eye look like at night?" I asked.

"They are big, very bright, sort of orange and red," he replied.

I thought this is really dumb, out here in Viet Cong country at night hunting tigers. I should have my ass kicked for agreeing to this. Any good VC will know it's those crazy Americans out here at night in a damn truck. We slowly moved along the trail as I kept the spotlight shifting along the trail on both sides.

We stopped and suddenly Dave said, "Listen, do you hear that yelping?"

"Yeah, I hear it."

He said, "That's a tiger."

"I thought tigers roared?"

"They do, but at night they yelp."

"Well, I have to take your word for it, I damn sure don't know."

Suddenly, two large eyes reflected by the spotlight shone like twin rubies in the darkness. Dave swung his rifle around and fired. The twin eyes disappeared. I thought, man I hope he hit whatever it was. If it's a tiger and he missed or injured him that tiger will be pissed off, and might charge and tear our asses up. My little carbine might stop a big rabbit, but that's about all.

Dave said, "Ken, come on down with the spotlight and let's walk over there."

I handed him the battery and the spotlight then climbed down from the truck I retook the spotlight and battery as we slowly and cautiously approached the area he had fired into. I saw a huge animal lying on the ground; I didn't see any tiger stripes.

Dave spoke up and said, "Damn, it's a mule deer." I walked up closer, and it was indeed a huge mule deer.

Jason walked over took a look, and then backed the truck up. The three of us struggled to load the huge deer aboard the truck, finally we succeeded.

Dave said, "Let's get the hell out of here everything else will have left the area by now."

"I hope that means the VC also," I replied.

Leaving was good news to my ears. We turned around and slowly drove back our original route into town, and then out to the village. We gave the deer to the village chief.

The chief and several other yards lit a bonfire and immediately skinned the deer. I estimated that it weighed between two and three hundred pounds dressed out. The next day they had a big feast. The big mule deer weighted well over two-hundred plus pounds, and the entire village was fed. That was my first and last tiger hunt!

We stayed in the little town for over three weeks organizing, training and equipping the natives. Then we were instructed to pack up and catch an Air America plane to Danang and rejoin our team. Another "A" team from the Special Forces Group on Okinawa replaced us.

We flew into Danang airport. There were some American helicopters there, several South Vietnam airplanes, and three American C-123 cargo aircraft. We taxied to the terminal stopped and unloaded the aircraft. A truck with our team medic driving showed up. We loaded all our gear aboard and headed into Danang

I shouted, "Hello Bacsi, long time no see, how the hell are you?"

He laughed and said, "Hello Ken, I'm well how are all you guys?"

"We're fine, just glad to be back with the rest of the team."

He drove us to a house in downtown Danang where our half of the team was to be briefed. Then we were to go out to the training compound outside town called Hua Cam. After the briefing we loaded back up on the truck and drove about three miles outside the city to the training site. There were several buildings in the training area. The buildings all were built from rough lumber, and had tin roofs, open windows, all on concrete slabs. Air conditioning was something to dream about. We unloaded our baggage, and selected a cot in the building designated as our team house.

I selected a bunk noting it had a mosquito net already on it. We were no longer in civilian clothes; we were now in our fatigues and wearing our army rank insignia. I think there were too many SF teams now in country to continue the charade of being civilians. Since we were in the field and with no other head gear to wear, we wore the Green Beret. After years of wearing them covertly, they were now our official head gear in Vietnam, and all around the world, compliments of President JF. Kennedy.

We had a few dozen men and women Montagnards we were to train in village defense, and civil actions procedures. There was also a company of South Vietnamese army Aspirants to train in military procedures. They were equivalent to our army second lieutenants. As additional security we had a Chinese Nung company of ex-army personnel who escaped out of China many years earlier. It was without question, a multicultural diverse group.

The next day we began training in earnest. There were three and four classes being conducted all at the same time. Weapons training, medical training, squad tactics, company tactics, even well digging. We taught it all as we worked at least twelve hour days. At night we had the Yards guard around the perimeter of the camp. Occasionally a few incoming rifle rounds would come in, and the camp would come alive.

Christmas was rapidly approaching, but here in the middle of nowhere, there was no evidence of it. The training continued as we sent out patrols and sometimes night ambushes. Large violent military actions at this time were rare in Vietnam. Occasionally we would hear of a South Vietnamese army unit and the Viet Cong having a major battle. Christmas Day passed really without notice. For New Year's some of the guys were going into the team house in Danang, take a break, drink a little booze, and perhaps find a local beauty to spend some fun time with. I was designated to stay in the camp for the evening, and to sleep with the trainees in their building that night.

I said to Jason, "Have a few cold ones for me."

He laughed and replied, "I'll have more than a few for you, but only after I drink all I want for myself."

I replied, "I hope you have a damn rotten ass hangover tomorrow."

They all left for town. Here in camp was just Bud our weapons man, and me. The sun slid silently behind the hilltops. The night rushed in with its cacophony of sounds, its heavy stillness, and uneasy quiet. I checked all the guard posts several times to ensure they were manned, and the guards awake. I then went to the barracks I was to sleep in with the Yards. I selected a spot next to the door and against the wall. That gave me a little extra room to sleep and space to keep my weapon and combat harness gear close.

Around eleven o'clock that evening I finally lay down in the barracks on my small gray blanket. I lit a cigarette and smoked as rivulets of sweat trickling down from my forehead and face. I contemplated my present situation, and began reviewing my life up to this point.

I'm a long time, and a long way from the cotton and corn fields of Alabama. When I left there in 1948, I never really expected to find myself in the jungles of South Vietnam, a country that I had never even heard of. Even so, this is what I have trained to do, and I love it.

I glanced at my Rolex watch it was midnight. The year 1962, tiptoeing silently across the dark, ominous landscape arrived right on time.

As sleep slowly began to overtake me, I opened my memory book and reviewed several pages. I recalled those six wonderful days I had spent with Elona in that faraway city of Stuttgart, Germany. I thought of meeting Sergeant Major Ironjaws Baker again after so many years, and what a pleasant reunion that had been. I slowly closed the pages, and embraced the beckoning, welcoming arms of Morpheus.

About two-thirty in the morning, I was awakened with someone shaking me saying, "Ken, wake up, wake up, the team Sergeant has been killed!"

I woke with a start and recognized one of our demolition men. I said, "What the hell are you talking about?"

Sergeant Eversharp has been killed!"

I asked, "How did it happen, are there any other of our guys dead or wounded?"

"No, he was done in by a grenade someone threw in the room he was in with some other people. All of them are hurt, but I think he's the only one dead."

I just stared in the dim light at him, "What do you want me to do?" I asked.

"Nothing I guess. I was told to let you and Bud know it happened."

I said, "Let's go up to our place and make some coffee."

I picked up my blanket, weapon and harness, and leaving the yard barracks we walked up to the team house.

"Light the Coleman stove put on some water, and we'll make some coffee." In a few minutes we had hot water, so I put a spoon full of instant coffee in my canteen cup and filled it. I added a shot of scotch whiskey to the mix and stirred it all. I sat down on my cot and said, "Tell me what happened at the house."

He began to tell what happened, and it turned out to be not a very pleasant scene.

He said, "Someone opened the door to the room where the Sergeant was with several other people and tossed in a live grenade. The room is a shambles with blood everywhere, parts of people lying around, and everyone confused as to who did it."

I remarked, "Well, we still have Britain, our Intel Sgt, he can take over the team if necessary."

We three sat there drinking coffee and scotch, and talked until daylight. I checked with the Yard leader of the group, and told him we're leaving for a couple of hours. We got into the Jeep and drove back into town. We drove into the little compound, and the place was flooded with people.

I saw Jason and asked him, "What's going on?"

He said, "The Air Force police are here, the CID people are here, and people are flying in from Saigon to investigate what happened."

Several Vietnamese army officers and police were also present. I walked over and looked at the room where the accident had occurred. It was a bloody mess, and the walls were full of grenade shrapnel holes.

I walked back over to Jason and asked, "What did happen here last night?"

Jason lifted his hands, and just shrugged his shoulders. Finally, most of our team left. We went back to the training area. A Major from the First Group took over all operations. We also had our intelligence sergeant John Britain, continue as the team sergeant.

We continued to train and run patrols. I was on one patrol and we were walking around a huge rice paddy when we received incoming fire. I heard the sound of the bullets as they cracked and whined over my head. I thought to myself, some son-of-a—bitch is trying to kill me. It was the first time I had ever been shot at in my life. It's not a pleasant feeling. I crouched down on the edge of the rice paddy as my boots sunk deeper into the mud, water poured into them until they were overflowing. A few of our men fired back and the firing ceased. We continued on with the patrol.

About two months later after several weeks of continuous training and teaching, Jason and I caught an Air America plane and flew to Saigon for a couple of days of Rest and Relaxation. We dropped loads of money in Tu Do street bars. We ran into Henry Hamby, the Navy money man; he was with his lovely Vietnamese-Eurasian girl.

He shouted over to us and said, "Hey Ken, I won't be wanking my log tonight."

I hollered back, "You'll be sorry, you'll be in the damn dispensary in a couple of days."

We both walked over, and had a quick drink with him. His girlfriend was indeed a very lovely woman. She displayed the best physical and facial features of the Caucasian and Oriental races.

"I'll be heading out to sea again in a few weeks. We're going to Japan, then to the Philippines, then back to Charleston."

I said, "Henry, when you get back to the states, and get your first piece of wonderful American nookie think of me, way the hell out here in the middle of fucking nowhere fighting for your freedom, and your right to get some good American nookie."

He laughed, "Ken, at that moment you'll be the last person on earth I'll be thinking of."

Jason spoke up, "Henry, I'm with you. I wouldn't be thinking of that dipshit either."

I raised my beer in salute. I said, "So long sailor boy," and then we left.

We caught a taxi to a restaurant over to Cholon, the Chinese section of Saigon. We had a great meal, several drinks, and made out with a couple of lovely young Chinese women. They charged more than the Vietnamese women. Finally, with our passes up we returned to Hua Cam, and the war.

In late February a civil action training group was assembled and sent out in the field. We had another team now assigned with us, and two of their men were to accompany two men from our team. There were about fifty Yard men and women plus the four Americans in the group.

They left on Saturday and were due to return on Tuesday. Most of our guys had gone into Danang on Saturday and would spend the night. I remained out at the camp and alternated on the radio as we maintained twenty-four hour contact with the team out in the field.

Early Sunday morning as I sat by the radio sipping a canteen cup of coffee and smoking a cigarette, the radio came alive, and I answered it.

I heard Jim on the other end, he was screaming, "We're under attack, we're being overrun, send help!" I could hear weapons firing in the background.

Then the radio went silent. I called and called for about ten minutes but received no response. I called the Air Force for helicopters over at the airport, but they refused to get involved. I thought, if I can get the helicopters maybe I could get the Chinese Nung company, and head for Jim's location. I sent the assistant radio operator to notify someone at the team house in town, and make them aware that our field team is in trouble.

In short order the Major showed up and organized a combat search and rescue team. He also was able to get the choppers from the Air Force. Jason was the senior enlisted man, so he was going out with the team. I told them what had happened, and we had the map coordinates where they were supposed to be. The team left and searched for several hours before they finally located the remnants of the group. It appeared that the group had indeed been ambushed and overrun. Jim and Willie were both found dead. The two men from the other team were missing. Both bodies were recovered, and the remainder of the civil action group brought back to Hua Cam.

As we sat around the team area Jason spoke up and said, "Well, Ken, that makes three members of our team that's bought the farm. This is turning out to be a very costly operational mission for us."

"Yep, plus we still have two men missing, Fred and Greg we don't know where they are, or what condition they're in."

Richard Wallace, an attached member from the Saigon team said, "Maybe we'll find them, but we can't count on it."

I poured myself another scotch and water and said, "I feel so damn tired, and I really haven't done that much today. Guess I'm either getting old, or not getting enough of the right food."

We had Vietnamese cooks and ate with the trainees most of our meals. A few days earlier I had been down by the outside kitchen and watched them as they prepared the food. A truck had brought in several bags of rice and some fish. They were large fish and appeared to me to be tuna. I watched as they cleaned the fish. I noted that for several inches up from the tails the fish were infested with maggots. The fish cleaner chopped off the section that contained the maggots, and continued to prepare the fish. We all had fish and rice for dinner.

Several days later I went to see our medic. "Bacsi, I feel like shit. All I want to do is sleep and rest. I'm not eating anything at all, and I'm losing weight like crazy. Something has to be wrong with me."

Bacsi said, "Lay down on your bunk."

He then pressed my abdomen which hurt like hell, and stared into my eyes. Finally, he said, "You have hepatitis, or yellow jaundice. Your liver is enlarged, and your eyes are yellow. What color is your urine when you piss?"

I replied, "It's pure gold."

He said, "I'm sending you to the hospital in Saigon."

He told the Major that I had hepatitis and had to leave. I packed all my stuff together and left it with Jason. I took a small bag that contained my shaving kit some cigarettes, and a couple of changes of underwear.

I caught an Air American cargo plane and landed at Than San Nhut airport. There I was picked up and taken to a hospital in Saigon. They quarantined and isolated me in a room. All I wanted to do was sleep. They weighed me and I topped out at one hundred-thirty pounds. Damn, I had come into country weighing one hundred forty-five pounds. I stayed there two days then I was picked up in an army ambulance and driven to the airport. I was told I was being medically evacuated to the Philippines by C-130 aircraft.

An Air force medic strapped me down on a stretcher. There were several other military personnel on stretchers. The stretchers were attached to racks in the cargo area of a C-130 Hercules cargo plane.

The load master came by and said, “We’re having trouble starting a couple of the engines, we’re going to start them by racing up and down the runway.”

I was too sick and weak to care. So I said, “Fine with me, do what you have to do.”

I heard the engines revving up, and then the plane began moving. It seemed to be at takeoff speed when the engines reversed and the plane slowly stopped. It turned around and began gaining speed in the opposite direction.

Again it slowed and turned around, the loadmaster stopped by me and said, “We’re okay, we have all four engines running now.” I gave him a thumbs-up sign then fell asleep.

I woke up with some guy shaking me saying, “Wake up we’re here.”

Groggily, I looked at him and recognized him as a medic. I replied, “We’re where?”

He said, “We’re at Clark Air Force Base in the Philippines.”

I immediately went back to sleep. When next I woke up I was in a hospital bed in the hospital at the Air Force base. I looked around and the entire ward was filled with Americans, all suffering from miscellaneous illness or injuries.

Early the next morning some guy came through the ward, he woke me up and said, “Get up you have to go for a test.”

I got up and put on a bathrobe then followed him down a couple of corridors.

I went into a little room and a nurse was there who said, “We’re going to inject a dye into your arm, and then in about thirty minutes we’ll take a blood test. This is to determine how well your liver is functioning, or not functioning.”

I replied, "That's fine with me; let's do whatever it takes to get me well again!"

She rolled up my sleeve and injected some type dye into my right arm and said, "That's it just have a seat for a little while."

I sat down in a chair and fished for a cigarette in my bathrobe. I finally found my pack and lit one up. I began to fall asleep again, and the nurse came over and removed the cigarette from between my fingers.

She said, "You don't want to burn yourself do you?"

I groggily shook my head. I was so damn tired and weak. I managed somehow to stay awake, and finally the nurse called me over and took some blood from my left arm. I was then told to return to my ward.

Later in the morning a medic came by woke me up and said, "Drink this," as he shoved a glass at me.

I asked, "What is it?"

"It's a double malted milkshake."

"Is it chocolate or vanilla?"

He got nasty and replied, "What the hell's the difference, just drink the damn thing."

I glared at the nasty ass and drank it down slowly, but completely. I handed the mug back to him and said, "Thanks a fucking lot, you need to get a sense of humor."

I lay down and went back to sleep. An hour or so later they brought lunch into the ward, I was awake and figured I had better eat something. I didn't remember the last time I had eaten solid food. I uncovered my tray and had a huge helping of mashed potatoes and brown gravy with a small piece of roast beef. I had one bite of the roast beef, but I managed to eat about half of my potatoes and gravy. My appetite had just completely vanished, so I slept the afternoon away. I was awake when they brought the evening meal around. I had another milkshake and more mashed potatoes and gravy, plus a slice of roast pork. I couldn't eat the pork, but I managed to eat most of the potatoes and I drank all the milkshake.

This went on for two weeks before I slowly began to recover. I no longer slept so much and I was hungry. I ate everything they brought to me whether I liked it or not. One of the doctors had told me earlier that I had to eat in order to get my liver functioning correctly. I wanted to get well, get the hell out of the hospital, and back to Nam with my team. Each week I took the dye test. In the fourth week the doctor told me that my liver was again functioning correctly, and that I could go back to Okinawa.

I told him, "Sir, my unit's in South Vietnam, that's where I came from, and that's where I want to go back to."

"All right, orders will be cut and you can leave this weekend."

"Thank you Sir."

I heard later that day on the radio that two American soldiers who had been captured earlier had been released, and both were back in American hands.

I walked down to the weight room and stepped on the scales, I weighed one hundred thirty-six pounds, so I was regaining my weight. I again felt good and my appetite had returned to normal. I caught the plane, and a few hours later I landed in Danang, then caught a ride to the team house downtown.

There I ran into Bacsi. He had come in to pick up some supplies, so I rode out to the camp with him.

He greeted me and asked, "How do you feel Ken?"

"A hell of a lot better than I did when I left here," I replied.

"What type treatment did you receive in Clark?"

"I took dye tests, and ate tons of food, drank malted milkshakes, and gained a little weight back," I replied.

He said, "That's the normal treatment. You know that you can't drink any booze for a year, don't you?"

I looked at him in disbelief. "Horseshit, the doctor didn't tell me that!"

He laughed and replied, "The doctor should have told you that. But it's a fact that you have to give your liver time to recover, and that means no drinking."

I had too much respect for Bacsi and his medical knowledge and experience to dispute or argue with his advice. We arrived back at the base camp and I reported to the Major in charge.

He welcomed me back and asked, "How do you feel?"

I replied, "I feel good."

"Great, you'll be going on recon patrol tomorrow."

I ran into Richard and Jason, they had just come off patrol. They had gotten into a firefight with several VC, and had lost two men. We sat around and talked for several hours, they were both drinking scotch and water. Jason confirmed that the two team members captured earlier Fred and Greg was indeed our guys, and they were safe.

I turned in for the evening as I was still weak. The next morning I ate two cans of C-rations and drank a cup of instant coffee. We had a small briefing and received our mission assignment. I got the small radios and checked them out, they all worked. Richard was in charge of the mission, so he and I selected the Yards to go with us. We loaded up on three H-34 helicopters and took off for points west.

The American pilots landed at the designated landing zone, and we all jumped off the chopper and moved out smartly into the jungle. Richard was up front of the patrol, and I was bringing up the rear. Richard and I were in sight of each other so the patrol was going smoothly. We crossed a small stream and I experienced my first encounter with blood sucking leeches.

We stopped after crossing and I said to Richard, "I think I have some damn leeches on my legs."

He said, "Hell, I know that I do."

We stopped the patrol and established a perimeter defense. I unlaced one boot and took it off. I removed my sock and sure enough I had four leeches on my left leg. Blood was running from each one of the bites they had made, they were still attached to my leg.

Richard said, "Light a cigarette and stick the hot end to them, they'll let go."

I did that and one by one I was able to get the leeches off my leg. The blood continued to run from their bites. I checked my other leg and had three leeches, using the same procedures I removed them. Dick removed six leeches from his feet and legs. That evening we set up an overnight camp. Richard said, "Ken, I'll take the late shift, you stand guard until one in the morning, and I'll take over."

"That's fine with me."

We settled in for the night, and then everyone ate cold rations and drank water. The Yards ate their little packs of rice and fish, and I had a can of pork and beans.

At one in the morning I woke Richard up and said, "Things are fine, everything is quiet, no problems so far."

I stretched out on the jungle floor and immediately fell asleep. I knew that I didn't have the energy that I did before contracting hepatitis.

I felt someone shaking me. I woke up and heard Richard whisper, "Ken, wake up we've got visitors!"

I rolled over and had my weapon ready. I pulled on my web gear with my grenades and magazines.

Richard whispered, "We have some people over on the left of us. I don't know how many there are. Help me wake the Yards up and let's get ready."

Silently, I crawled from one position to the next and woke our Yards up. They were good troops and remained silent. I checked my own equipment; I had four grenades, and ten magazines of .30 caliber carbine ammunition. I had three sets of magazines taped back to back for quicker changing. There were twenty-two of us, so I felt we were in decent shape for a firefight. I lifted up the green tape over my watch and checked my Rolex. It was four in the morning.

Richard crawled over and said, "I'm going to take six guys and circle to the left and set up. You take six men and circle to the right and set up. The Yard team leader will stay here with eight men."

I nodded in agreement, crawled over and selected my six men. We crawled our way around our perimeter, and set up positions about fifty yards away on the right flank. What we had set up was an ambush within an ambush. The VC had one remaining escape route, and that was to their rear.

Just before daylight firing started over on the left side, then it switched to the front of the main position, we had no targets so we all held our fire. I heard people hollering and then people appeared to our front running in our direction. I opened fire with my carbine. I saw bright flashes as the VC returned our fire. One man jumped up in front of me firing in our direction I cut him down with two rounds. Four more people appeared running in our direction their rifles firing on full automatic. I could hear the bullets as they cut through the grass and small trees, snapping over my head. I shot two of them and the Yard next to me cut down the other two.

Suddenly, all the firing stopped. We all remained in our positions. No one was moving, and only a low moan could be heard from the area in front of us. I turned on my PRC-10 radio set and called the base.

Johnny was on the base radio. I very quietly said, "Base, this is PT Two, we're in a firefight at our overnight location. No other info available. Stay alert, out!" Johnny confirmed receipt then went silent.

Daylight arrives agonizingly slow in the jungle, and today was no exception. I crawled around, we had two Yards with flesh wounds. I managed to stop their bleeding, put bandages on their wounds, and they were fine. I called on the radio to Richard. He had a little Yard with him who had his radio.

He came on. I said, "Dick, we have two yards wounded, and at least four dead VC and one wounded in front of our position. I radioed base and have informed them about the action."

Dick replied, "We have no friendly wounded. We have seven VC dead, we caught them cold. We're coming back in to the center position."

I checked my leg which was burning, and saw that I had a bullet hole through my pants leg. I lowered my pants and saw that I had a red streak across my thigh where a bullet had passed. I was very lucky as it didn't hit me at all, just left a blister in its path. Cautiously both groups converged back to our original positions. The fight seemed to be over. We counted thirteen VC dead at the cost of two Yards wounded.

As the radio operator I reported the information back to the base station. The Major who was waiting by the radio made the decision that our position was compromised, and we should get extracted. He gave us a map coordinate to rendezvous with the choppers. We picked up five AK-47's, and some ammunition from the dead VC plus several other odd type weapons. Dick cautiously led the group to our pick up point, and the choppers showed right up. We loaded on the choppers and returned to the base without further incident. I had just engaged in my first firefight, my first live ambush, and I had killed my first man. There would be more, a lot more!

Richard and I briefed our team then we went to see Bacsi for whatever he could give us to stop the bleeding from the frigging leeches. He gave us some antibiotic salve and band aids. Those bites bled for three more days.

I took a whores bath, and made a cup of instant coffee.

Jason came by and said, "Would you like a cold San Miguel?"

I growled, "You know damn well I'm not supposed to drink anything for a year, why are you frigging torturing me?"

He replied, "Screw those doctors, they don't know everything."

In spite of knowing better I replied, "Yeah, you're right, let's have a cold beer."

He opened the little kerosene refrigerator, and pulled out two cold beers. We sat there for two hours drinking cold beer. It had never taste so good.

We had another team from the First Special Forces Group join us in Hua Cam. We now had almost three full teams here and operations continued. Our tour of duty was drawing to a close, so we slowly turned over most of our functions to the other teams. About this time President Diem of South Vietnam was assassinated. We all were restricted to the camp and couldn't leave. This continued for a few days then the restriction was lifted.

In May, we loaded aboard a C-130 and took off from Danang for Okinawa. A few hours later we landed at Kadena Air Force Base, and was met by a small bus that took us back to what we found out was our new barracks in Chibana. We eventually located all our personal belongings left behind six months earlier. We were assigned rooms and reverted back to normal army garrison duty.

That first night back as I lay on my bunk before going to sleep I thought about what I considered an abnormal situation. One day you're fighting for your life and killing other men, then in less than twenty-four hours you're back in the normal world. No one trying to kill you, women and booze plentiful, life's good, and how are you supposed to act. Can the average person kill or try to kill people and watch his friends die, then less than twenty-four hours later act like a normal person? I didn't have an answer, but I knew that was what me, and Jason, Dick, Bud, Bacsi, and all the rest of us were supposed to do, and was expected to do. I wasn't sure about it, but I knew that's asking an awful lot of the troops.

Jason and I went to the Top Three club and drank beer, ate lobster and shrimp until I thought we'd burst. We then went down to New Koza, found our favorite girls, and spent the night.

The next day to my surprise my old friend Wayne Wilson showed up assigned to the group. He was fortunate, he had his family with him and had quarters over in the dependent housing area. I was glad to see him. He was a damn good friend, and I had known him longer than anyone else I knew still on active duty.

Ralph Slaughter finally got his wife Shirley and their little girl over, and moved into quarters. I finally got to meet her. She was a very lovely young woman with a beautiful little girl. She and I became very good friends and remain so.

More troops had been received into the Group, and we were expanding in size. I heard that there were new Groups being formed back at Fort Bragg, and the Fifth Special Forces Group would be going to Vietnam. By this time the First Group had suffered maybe a half-dozen soldiers killed in action in Vietnam. There were some soldiers from the Seventh Group also killed. I thought Special Forces is taking a beating. We seem to be the only combat unit in the country fighting the Viet Cong. Military history reports later showed that during that time period we really were the only American ground combat forces in Vietnam.

CHAPTER 39

Vietnam explodes

The troops were being shifted around and reassigned to different "A" and "B" teams. I was assigned to a newly formed "A" team. Happily, I had the best team sergeant in the army as my team sergeant once again, Master Sergeant E-7 Tony Domingo.

Sergeant Major Ironjaws Baker was the epitome of First Sergeants and Sergeant Majors, but Tony Domingo was a work of military art when it came to team sergeants.

We also had a new Team Leader, and a new team Executive Officer. The team leader was a young Captain, a West Point graduate, and as I later learned a brilliant tactician and leader. I was happy about that as West Point officers had always been lucky for me. He had recently completed language school, and was fluent in Korean. I thought that's great except we aren't going to Korea any more. We're now fighting in South Vietnam. He was three years younger than me and a natural leader. The more I learned about him only increased my respect for his abilities. In time, I would have followed him to hell and back. His name was William P.Leadenham III.

Our new Executive Officer was a young first Lieutenant. He was a good man, and adaptable to all the various situations that occur, or seem to occur in Special Forces. He was knowledgeable and eager to learn from the old soldiers on the team. We still didn't have second Lieutenants as they simply didn't have the required experiencc. IIis name was Jamesl Larson. He and I became good friends.

Our team slowly came together as we added the personnel required to fill out the twelve man team. We trained together, jumped together, and participated in training exercises together as we learned the individual strengths and weakness of each other.

We received orders to move the company back to Sukiran, so we packed up all our belongings and moved back to Sukiran. The summer passed quickly. Vietnam was ablaze now with more and more Special Forces teams going into country, and deploying to places with names you've never heard of, and could hardly pronounce. Every few days we'd get the word that some friend of ours, or someone we knew had bought the farm, or had been wounded.

Bob Evening flew over from Taiwan. He was sick with something or other. Jason and I visited with him in the local military hospital. He had lost considerable weight, but his feisty spirit was still there and on exhibition.

Jason finally hit a small jackpot on the slots at the Top Three club, and about six of us drank the whole amount up in one evening. He and I and another friend of ours nicknamed Moe spent many evenings in New Koza chasing the girls. Life was fun and good!

Art decided he was going home on leave. I said, "Art, if you go to Alabama and pick up my car, you can have it if you make the remaining payments."

He agreed to do so. I wrote my uncle and told him Art would be there to get the car, and to release it to him. I then gave Art a letter of introduction to my uncle.

In early September our team was selected to go to Nam. Jason was on another team this time out, and I hated that. The Old Man, Captain Leadenham, gave us all a team briefing then we loaded our gear and headed for Kadena Air Base. Once again we boarded the best of cargo planes, the C-130 Hercules, and took off for Tan San Nhut airport in Saigon.

A few hours flight and we landed. We taxied to the terminal area and the pilot raised the tailgate of the plane. That sudden rush of heat and humidity is really unbelievable. It's like opening the door of a hot stove oven, and feeling the rush of heat in your face. In the few months that I'd been gone I'd forgotten how ghastly hot and humid it was in this part of the world. In just a few minutes of lifting bags and equipment I was soaked with sweat. Tony and the Old Man went into Saigon for a meeting with the Combined Studies people.

We had a young medic on the team named Gene Kelly, and a senior medic named Homer Wolfe, they were talking, so I joined their conversation.

"Gene, How do you like this heat?"

He laughed; I'll never make it in this heat for sure."

I replied, "You'll get acclimated to it in a couple of weeks, and it won't bother you at all."

He replied in his slow Alabama drawl, "In a pig's ass. I'll never get used to this heat, look at me, I'm soaked through already."

"We all are, look at Melvin, he's sitting in the shade on his ass doing nothing, and still he's soaking wet." Melvin Capone was our intelligence sergeant.

Homer spoke up, "I can handle the heat, I just want to get off the tarmac, and go someplace and have a cold beer."

Just as he finished speaking Tony rolled up in a civilian truck and shouted, "Load it up and let's move out."

We quickly loaded our rucksacks, handbags and equipment on the truck and piled on. The team and our equipment weighed the truck down for sure.

As Tony drove into Saigon he said, "We're going to a new house the agency has rented for us."

Lt Lawson was sitting in the right passenger seat up front. He spit out a big wad of tobacco juice. It streamed back and landed right in Frenchy's face. I saw that and began laughing. Frenchy began cursing, and wiping.

Frenchy Lapew was our second radio operator. When the truck stopped for a stop sign I leaned over and said to the Lt, "Don't spit any more its flying back into the truck"

"Okay, I didn't even think of that."

We finally arrived at the location of the new house, and Frenchy immediately began talking to Lt Lawson complaining about the tobacco spit hitting him in the face.

Lawson listened and said, "I'm sorry, I didn't realize that the spit would fly back." That seemed to end the matter.

Jack Bagette, the light weapons man said, "I guess we need to unload the truck and move our stuff into the house."

Tony said, "Take your stuff upstairs and pick out a bed, put your stuff on it, but don't unpack anything, we won't be here long. Ken, take Lou and go find us some cold beer."

"Great, everyone kick in three dollars, and I'll get the beer,"

Lou Brooklyn, the other weapons man and I caught a small taxi and went to the MAAG compound. I bought two cases of San Miguel and picked up four bags of ice. I ran into Henry Hamby. He was still in charge of the Navy finance office.

"Hello Henry, what in the hell are you still doing here? I thought you Navy guys wanted to stay safe out at sea. You're supposed to be in Charleston getting some great American ass."

He laughed, "Ken, you dumb ass how are you? They cancelled my orders, so I'm here for a few more months. What in the hell are you doing back here again?"

I replied, "We're running this frigging war, and they needed some real fighting men. So I came back once more.

Henry turned serious and said, "This is sort of getting out of hand, your outfit is losing men almost every day, and there's no one else here helping you guys out in the boonies."

"There are a few Air Force people here, and they should be in support of the camps we have, and some Army helicopter people here also," I replied.

He said, "I think they should send in the Marines and get the job done right."

"Screw the Marines. But we could surely use more fire power. Maybe they'll send over the Parachute Combat team from Okinawa. Anyway, I've got to go, I'll see you come payday."

"Are you guys still on Per Diem?"

"Yeah, you don't think I'd do this shit for free do you? I'll be here to get mine soon." Laughing, I turned and walked away.

Henry hollered, "Take care of your shaky ass."

Lou and I caught another taxi and returned to the house. I walked in and shouted, "Men get a bucket or something and put this beer on ice. In less than five minutes we had one whole case iced down, we waited less than five minutes for it to get cold.

I sat down next to Lt Lawson. He asked, "Ken, where do you think we'll go?"

"I have no idea, the agency could send us anywhere in the country. I hope we go to the central highlands. I like working with the Yards, they're good people."

"What are they like?"

"They are small people usually dressed in loin cloths. Most of them live in what we call long houses. The women wear some type sarong and they're nice also. They farm using water buffaloes. They fish, hunt, farm and just want to live in peace and be left alone."

I took a swallow from my beer and continued. "The VC take their rice crops, and make them live in fear all the time. They also try and recruit them into their communist organization. You'll like them when you meet them."

Later in the afternoon the Old Man, Captain Leadenham, returned and said, "Men, you can go to town tonight and get something to eat. But get your asses back here this evening. Drink if you want to, but stay straight, and don't get into any trouble. We'll be here for a couple of days, so just unpack what you need and nothing more. Go by the finance office and change some money, don't spend it all, we have six months to go, so be smart!"

Tony, Lou, Frenchy and I caught a taxi and went downtown Saigon. We sat in one of the little sidewalk café's bird-watching for about two hours on Tu Do street. The beer they served was still Bier 33, and it still taste like juiced up water. We were setting at the little sidewalk café table, and to my surprise who comes walking by but our friend, SFC Billy Walton.

I called to him, "Hey Billy, come on over and have a cold one with us."

Billy had a large grin on his face, as he walked over and pulled up a chair. We shook hands all around, and I ordered him a cold beer.

"Billy, old friend where are you at in-country?"

"Our team just left the Tin Khan-DakTo area and moved down to Song Mao, we're operating out of there now."

I said, "Our team just got back in country, and we don't have a destination yet. But I'm sure that it'll be somewhere in the rice paddies."

Tony asked Billy, "Who's your Team Leader this trip?"

"We have Major Barton, and he's a good one."

We all knew the major, and agreed that he's a damn good man.

I asked him, "How are Jim and Mike and Red getting along, are they all right?"

Billy laughed, "Yeah, they're all doing fine. Jim is having a lot of trouble getting along with Herman the German."

I immediately searched my memory, but couldn't place anyone by that name or nickname.

"Billy, who in the hell is Herman the German, do I know him?"

Billy laughed and said, "Herman the German is our pet monkey. Where we're staying in Song Mao, we're in an old French house and have ceiling fans in our rooms. Anyway, Jim hates our monkey and Herman hates Jim, in short they just don't get along. When Jim walks through the room Herman hides and jumps on his head, and pulls his damn hair then runs like hell. Jim, when he can, catches Herman throws him up on the fan. Herman sets up there screaming. Jim turns on the fan, and Herman hangs on for dear life until it finally throws his little ass off, and he lands up against one of the walls. When he does recover he sets there and screams at Jim for a couple of hours."

"Another thing that Jim hates about Herman is Herman likes to play with his little dick. He in effect gives himself a hand-job a few times every day. Everyone thinks it's funny except Jim. Well one day Jim had Herman on the fan, it was spinning and threw him off. He landed on Mike's head, and bit and scratched the hell out of him. When that happened Jim grabbed his pistol and began shooting at Herman. Mike already bleeding thought sure as hell Jim was going to shoot him. Jim missed Herman and Mike altogether. Me and the rest of the team laughed about the fight between Jim and Herman."

I could just picture my old friend Jim throwing that monkey up on a fan and turning the motor on.

Billy still laughing said, "The war is still going on, I'll let you know the final winner."

Tony said, "Let's go get something to eat, I know a fine French style restaurant that serves good food, and they have a small band. I went there when I was first here."

"Great idea, let's go, my stomach thinks my throat's been cut it's been so long since I've eaten."

Lou said, "I'm game let's do it."

Billy replied, "I've eaten already. You guys have a great evening, and a good tour. I'll probably see you back on Okinawa, or at Bragg."

We shook hands all around, and then caught a small taxi. Tony gave the driver instructions as we zipped through the streets of Saigon. He finally stopped at a restaurant named 'Le Cegull'.

We walked inside and it was indeed very nice. They had a Vietnamese band playing, and a beautiful Eurasian girl was singing a song in French. She had a very good voice and her French to my uneducated ear appeared to be perfect, but what the hell did I know. We ordered a chef salad and a shrimp dinner. Surprisingly, it was very good. I had two beers as they were serving San Miguel. The price was about double what it should've been, but it was cold, the meal good, so we couldn't complain.

We remained at the nightclub for about two hours. Tony suggested we leave. We split the bill then walked outside and caught a taxi to the house. Most of the troops were there, Melvin Capone and Homer hadn't returned yet.

We opened a beer then Captain Leadenham who was reading a book looked up and asked, "Where did you guys go this evening?"

I replied, "We went to a nice night club called Le Cegull, we had a good meal and listened to their band for a couple of hours then came home."

Lou spoke up and said, "I'm in love with the singer, so if you go there lay off her, she belongs to me."

Tony laughed, "Lou, she didn't look at you once all evening, she doesn't know you exists."

Lou laughed and replied, "She will me boys, she will."

The captain said, "Best you all get some sleep, I think we may be leaving here tomorrow."

We all turned in about midnight. About two in the morning I heard Melvin and Homer come in, they stumbled up the stairs talking loudly and finally went to bed. The next morning we all got up early and one by one cleaned up and got dressed. We caught three taxis and went down town to get something to eat. We found a restaurant that served eggs and buffalo steak, so most of us ordered that. The eggs were good, but the steak was tough as boot leather. Since we were unsure when we would eat again everyone ate their entire meal.

We didn't leave that day. Early in the evening I suggested to Tony that we go to Cholon and see what the Chinese were up to. We washed up, put on clean uniforms and caught a taxi to a nightclub that we'd seen advertised. It turned out to be a very pleasant evening.

Tony said, "I think the Chinese women are the best looking women in the Orient."

"Well, they're certainly good looking in this place."

We both tried to make out with a couple of them all to no avail. Disgusted I said, "Let's get the hell out of here, they just want us to spend money with no chance of getting anything in return." Tony agreed, so we paid our bill and left.

The next morning the Old Man and the XO caught a taxi and went to MAAG headquarters. Shortly after noon they returned and said we're leaving in about an hour. We packed all our stuff and after loading the vehicle headed for the airport. We caught a C-46 Air America plane and flew into Pleiku.

There we loaded onto H-34's and began a long journey up to DakTo. My old friend from the legendary 101st Division, Master Sergeant Joe Marino, was the team sergeant at the camp. We were to be satellited on their team until final disposition of our own team was determined.

We unloaded from the choppers and I heard Joe hollering, "Welcome aboard we can use some help."

They had several buildings made of planks and bamboo. We were quickly assigned places to sleep. Thankfully we had air mattresses which came in very handy. My old friend Ralph Slaughter was the senior medic in the camp. I spent lots of time with him. They were training a company of Yards, so we immediately pitched in to help. They were teaching small unit tactics, ambushes and counter-ambushes, weapons training and marksmanship. At night ambush patrols were sent out and stayed all night at various locations.

We stayed with them for several days before the agency told us we were to go further south and then west and built a camp. We would be going west of Pleiku next to the Laotian border. We selected a company of Jarai Yards to go with us when we left DakTo. We loaded up on two and a half ton trucks and slowly pulled away from the camp. We traveled down highway fourteen for a couple of hours until we finally reached a sign placed by Cpt Leadenham that indicated a small road that led straight out to a village named Plei Mrong. We turned onto the dirt road and traveled west until we reached the village. We pulled into the area then drove past the village out to the edge of the jungle, finally coming to a stop when it was virtually impossible to go further.

Captain Leadenham got out of the cab of the truck he was riding and said, "Men, this is where we'll build our camp. The first thing you need to do is set up personal defensive positions. Then find yourselves a place to sleep for tonight."

There was an old crumbling wooden building that had been built by the French many years earlier. It had a few tin sheets still on the roof so we moved into it. As we moved in several large snakes, some rats and millions of spiders moved out. We exhausted the few cans of insect spray we had. We had folding canvas cots so we set those up then hung mosquito nets over them to protect ourselves from what I believe are the biggest, meanest mosquitoes in the world.

I looked around and said to Tony, "If we have to build here look at all the trees we're going to have to cut down or blow down. We'll play hell and have a lot of hard work to do before this place becomes a livable, defensible camp. We should name our camp, Camp Plei Hell."

"I agree, but what the hell that's our job, we'll get it done. I like the name also, I hope the Old Man does."

The Old Man began to assign various tasks to each of us. We began work cutting down small trees and hauling them away, and the team demo people began to blow the larger ones down with C-4 explosives. The Captain talked with the Province chief and we began recruiting natives to join the CIDG program. We hired the natives to build huts for us. It was amazing how quickly they could find bamboo and build a house. The roofs were covered with overlapping layers of bamboo leaves, and they never leaked even in the hardest rains. We sent a truck out with guards to find and bring back more bamboo. The one wooden house we build with a concrete floor was the dispensary. Both of our medics, Gene and Homer set up shop and began right away treating the local natives, introducing them to the miracles of modern military medicine.

Homer also began building a team shower for us. Prior to that, we washed off in a small stream, while in it you had to be careful not to get leeches. Those little blood sucking bastards were everywhere. Our little group of trainees grew. The only bad thing about them was we didn't know if they were really VC, or just natives wanting to defend their own villages. We gave them marksmanship training, teaching them how to aim and hit what they were aiming at. It was a task to be sure. At night we would take up their weapons and ammunition as we were unsure who was who. Better to be safe than sorry in our situation.

My turn for patrol arrived. I was scheduled to take out an ambush patrol. Lou was to take another out in the opposite direction. Tony and I sat down in the kitchen hut and planned out the evening.

He said, "Ken, Take about fifteen men and one radio, check in when you get to your position. If you run into trouble fire a flare and we'll get to you."

"Tony, if I get into trouble I won't be firing flares, I'll be firing live ass rounds."

I got all my Yards together and told them we're spending the night out in the woods, so take only what you need for the evening. As I waited for nightfall I thought this is really weird, I'm taking men out maybe to fight for their lives, and I can't speak one word of their language, and they can't speak a word of mine. I hope things go all right for all of us.

Night always comes early in the jungle. I spoke briefly with the Captain, and then I led the men out the main gate. We headed east then circled around then headed west. We moved steadily but quietly through the jungle undergrowth, thorns grabbed at me every step I took, gradually tearing my trousers to shreds. The lead man in front of me stopped, the designated Yard leader came back to me and indicated we should change directions. Not speaking his language, I read his hand gestures. I couldn't understand why we needed to change our route, but I shook my head affirmatively. He led off and I followed him. We finally reached the spot I wanted to stay and set up in a defensive perimeter. We were overlooking a trail that led past our camp, and on to the village. I placed men on both sides of the trail, and hoped like hell they would stay quiet.

The jungle at night is a weird place, filled with creepy, crawly creatures, and unnerving sounds like none you've ever heard before echoed and reechoed through the trees and tall elephant grass. About two in the morning I heard someone or something coming through the brush. I shook the Yard leader, he sat up and after turning his head back and forth, made a motion to indicate it was a large animal. I just nodded at him. Whatever it was, it was big, and I knew that tigers existed around here, so I remained apprehensive.

The noise faded away into the night, and I lay back down. I couldn't sleep as the mosquitoes practiced their dive-bombing, techniques, and were trying to eat me alive. I lay there with all my senses alert, and just thought about things going on in my life.

Here I am thirty-two-years-old and headed on the downside of twenty years in the military. My hair was now about one-third gray and two–thirds brown. Not married, and no desire to get married, still doing what I loved to do most of all—soldier. I dozed off and then I felt the Yard shake me, he pointed off to the faint light that indicated the sun was about to come up. I nodded to him, and he began to wake the troops up. We moved back towards the camp, another night was completed with no action.

On the way back the chief Yard stopped me and pointed to the location we had changed directions last night. The area was covered with punjii stakes. I was amazed at the number of stakes in the ground and how effectively they could have blocked troops from moving through the area. Punji stakes are sharpened bamboo stakes usually with fire hardened tips, and often covered in human feces. If they stick you it'll result in you being out of action for an indefinite amount of time. They were placed in all directions, so you couldn't move if you were in the stake field. They are an infantryman's nightmare!

We arrived back at the base with no incident. I released the troops, and they went to their tent and did whatever they wanted to do.

I saw Tony and said, "We had a good patrol nothing happened. We failed to contact any VC, but we did run into a huge punjii stake field."

"Good, get some sleep and then help Frenchy with the radio setup."

I washed up a bit then lay down on my bunk, in no time I was sound asleep. I woke up with Homer singing. As I listened to him I knew he had been drinking. I spoke up and said, "Homer, what did you do with the money your mama gave you for singing lessons?"

He replied, "Wise ass, I used it to buy some nookie."

"I hope you got some good stuff, because you damn sure can't sing," I said.

Homer asked, "Do you want a drink of scotch?"

Now fully awake I replied, "Sure, I never turn down a free drink of scotch." He brought over his bottle and handed it to me. I sat up and took a small drink. It hit the spot and dispelled any lingering desire to sleep.

I checked my watch, it was two o'clock in the afternoon.

"Homer, when are you going to have the shower completed? I could surely use a shower right about now."

Homer replied, "I have the framework up for the bathroom and the shower, so I should be finished in a couple of more days, or a couple more weeks."

"Well, if you need some help let me know, I can drive a straight nail," I replied.

Lou came into the building and said, "Guess what we're having for dinner tonight?"

Homer started to reply. I interrupted him and said, "Let me guess. I predict we'll have boiled rice and either turtle or chicken necks."

"Bingo," replied Lou. He picked up the bottle of scotch and had a big drink of it. Setting the bottle back down said, "Thanks Homer."

I got out of my bunk and pulled the mosquito net back, finding a towel I slipped on my shower shoes, and with my shaving kit I left for the mud hole down at the little stream. Sitting down in the slow moving water, I splashed water on my upper body and began to apply soap to my face, chest and arms. I rinsed the soap off my face and opened my eyes. There stood two little native boys watching me bath. I spoke to both of them and they just laughed and giggled as I stood up to complete my bath. I was naked, but none of the women were in sight, so I didn't mind the boys staring at me. Before I completed my bath Lt. Lawson joined me and took his turn sitting in the stream and being stared at by the boys. I was never really sure what they found so amusing in us bathing. They all bathed in the same water hole as we did.

The next day we had two journalists show up at the camp. One was named Cecil, and the other David or something like that. They spent the night and just talked to all of us. I felt it more of a fishing for an article tour than anything else. They didn't volunteer to go on any patrols with us. I really didn't expect them to, neither did I want them to!

I spoke to Captain Leadenham and suggested to him, "We build a radio room and put it underground. That way the equipment will be safe, and the operator will be able to operate even if we come under attack."

He thought for a moment and asked, "Where do you propose to put it?"

"I think about five feet from the building next to that big tree which may give it additional protection." I then pointed out the exact location I proposed.

"Okay go ahead and put it in."

I got three Yards from the group and a couple of shovels and picks. I drew an outline on the ground and told them this is what I want. They understood and began digging. It continued to amaze me how much information you could exchange even without speaking one word of each other's language.

Tony came by and said, "I want you to give the trainees a class on small unit ambushes today.

I knew the subject well, so I didn't need a lesson plan. I told Frenchy that I'd need him for two hours on my classes. I thought what a strange way to teach. I had a blackboard and some chalk to outline positions and movements. I spoke in English, and then Frenchy my fellow radio operator would convert my remarks into French to a Vietnamese who then would translate it into Montagnard. I never knew for sure what information was reaching the Yards, but we all hoped for the best.

The following week a well known author dropped by our camp. He stayed with us three or four days and went out on a patrol with Baggette. I never learned his name. I think he enjoyed it all, I learned later that he was the author of a famous book entitled something or other 'Diary.' He then wrote another Diary book. I later read the book and noted that he covered his participation in the patrol extensively. He had written several Diary types books going back to WWII. I think a couple of them had been made into movies starring John Wayne, but I wasn't sure.

Tony came through the barracks and said, "We're going to complete the fence around the camp today, and keep working until it's finished."

I moaned as he said that, I didn't like handling barbed wire, but I knew we had to complete the fence. We all joined in and over the next several days we installed a thirty-two wire double apron fence around our entire compound. The troops were then engaged in building a berm, and a fighting trench around the camp inside the fence.

Tony got promoted to Master Sergeant E-8, and I was promoted to Sergeant First Class E-7. We split half a bottle of scotch together in celebration.

I said to Tony, "I'm not sure that I'm getting anywhere fast. I reenlisted in November 1953 as a Private E-7, and now ten years later I'm again an E-7, is that progress or what?"

Tony laughed and replied, "I would say that's about three hundred dollars worth of progress."

Melvin and Lou were heavily engaged in installing our eighty-one millimeter mortar. Lou built a long wooden arrow and lined it with small flashlight bulbs and hooked up batteries so if we were attacked at night we could aim the arrow in the direction of the attack, and coordinate our defenses with any supporting aircraft.

Gradually Plei Hell was rounding into shape. Homer reported the dispensary operational, and he and Gene worked daily on the natives as they came in with all their various ailments. They pulled teeth, lanced boils, treated cuts and other medical conditions. There was a daily line of people from several villages to be treated. He also completed our toilet and the shower. We had two fifty gallon drums of water mounted on 2x4's, heated by the sun. It worked and we could finally wash up without worrying about leeches.

We were sitting around in our kitchen at the makeshift table when Kelly said, "I'm taking a bunch of Yards to town and get some supplies, does anyone need anything?"

"Buy a couple cases of beer and bring them back, if you go by the "B" team in Pleiku," I said.

He rounded up several Yards and left for Pleiku.

Tony said, "Ken, get a squad together and make a recon around the area, go out about a mile and see what's going on if anything."

Lou spoke up, "I'll go with you Ken, let me get my gear."

"Okay, I'll be gone for a couple of hours or more, we leave in fifteen minutes."

I got a squad of Yards together and issued them carbines, and got them armed and ready to go. Lou was there ready to join us. We left out through the back gate and went down the trail. About five hundred yards out of the camp I led the way out into the dense jungle area and headed west for about half of a mile then turned south for about a mile. We ran into another trail that looked well used. I crossed it and motioned for the squad to follow me. We walked alongside the trail for about a thousand yards, I could see nothing unusual, so I deviated away from the trail and headed back toward the camp. We began to cross a large half open field when I saw we were walking into a large punji stake area. I stopped the patrol and motioned them to go back the way we came.

Lou was walking several feet away from me.

I glanced over towards him and said, “Be careful Lou, this looks like ambush country.”

He looked toward me, and as he took another step the earth disappeared from beneath him. I knew immediately that he had fallen into a punjii pit. I halted the patrol, and on my hands and knees I slowly crawled over to where the pit was.

Fearfully, I peered over the side. I was afraid I’d see Lou impaled on the huge sharpened bamboo spears they placed in the bottom of the pits. As I reached the pit’s edge I could hear Lou moaning. Leaning over I looked down, Lou was lying at the bottom of the pit. He had indeed hit the stakes, but they had been here for a long time, maybe years. They were all old and rotten, so when he fell on them they just crumbled and broke.

I softly called down, “Lou, Lou, are you all right Lou?”

He finally answered, “Yeah, I think so. I just had the wind knocked out of me.”

“Can you get up?”

“Yeah, I’m okay now.”

He stood up, shook himself and looked up, he was about twelve feet down from the top of the hole. I told him to hold tight for a few minutes. I had the Yard leader put out a perimeter defense and told him to wait for us. I look my pistol belt and the pistol belt from the Yard. I had Lou throw me his up from the hole. I buckled them all together and lowered it down to Lou.

I said, “Lou, grab the belt and walk yourself up the side of the hole until I can grab you.”

Lou pulled on the belts, me and a Yard together hung on while he slowly walked up the side of the hole. Finally, he got near the top and I grabbed him pulling him over the rim. We sat there for a few minutes as he relaxed and settled his nerves.

"Lou, you're one lucky bastard, it's good that those stakes are so damn old and rotten that they broke," I said.

He weakly smiled and replied, "Lady Luck smiled on me today for sure. One week to go before Thanksgiving, and I don't want to miss that."

I gathered the squad together, and we slowly made our way back to the camp.

I released the men and Lou and I went to the kitchen. Tony and the Captain were there, so I related what had happened. While we were sitting there talking the sound of a loud explosion some distance away was heard.

We jumped to our feet and the Captain said, "That sounds like the road to our place." Grabbing our weapons and gear we raced over to the old Jeep that we had been given, we pushed it off to start, and then jumping on it, raced out of camp.

In the distance we saw our old two and a half ton truck, several men were grouped around it. We slowly drove up to it, and I saw Gene Kelly lying over on the ground.

The Captain raced over to Kelly checked him out and turning to Tony said, "He's all right."

We all knew immediately what had happened. The truck had run over a Chinese land mine and had a double wheel blown off. I immediately set the men up in a semi defensive position, then I inspected the truck. The front set of double wheels of the truck had hit the mine. When it exploded it blew both sets of tires and wheels off the truck. The truck was tilted dangerously to one side above the hole that the mine had gouged into the ground.

Fortunately the truck was loaded down with hundred pound bags of rice and construction material. If it hadn't been loaded it would have blown the truck up and over. I walked over to Gene and spoke to him. He was obviously very shaken and nervous; I lit a cigarette and gave it to him. Gene had been driving, and his position was the second closest to the explosion. He had been blown out of the truck, and had several cuts and bruises.

Tony spoke up and said, "Well, we know the mine wasn't here when he left out this morning, so that means someone, or some group placed the mine later".

I said, "That also means we have someone who's watching us all, and knows just about everything that we're doing."

Captain Leadenham said, "That we expected, out here in the middle of nowhere, it means we just don't know who in the hell we can trust."

Homer treated Gene for his cuts and bruises, and we sent him back to camp in the Jeep. All of the Yards had been sitting on top of the bags of rice, and none of them had suffered any injuries.

We formed two columns one on either side of the road as we slowly walked everyone back to the compound. We all knew that we had a new major problem. Each time now when we sent out a vehicle on the road we would have to check the road first for any additional mines or booby traps. That created ideal ambush conditions.

We arrived back at camp. Gene and the Captain were in the dining room going over every aspect of the explosion. I got a beer out of the kerosene refrigerator, it wasn't freezing but it was cold and that's all I wanted. I got a second one and handed it to Tony. We sat quietly and listened to Gene excitedly relate his ideas about the mining. I quickly finished my first beer a San Miguel and got another one. I was tired and thirsty from the patrol, and now this land mine explosion.

Gene said, "Two more SF men were killed in action a couple of days ago some place down south of Saigon."

I asked, "Do you know who they were?"

"No, the medic over in Pleiku told me about it, but he didn't remember their names."

I replied, "That's really, really nice, you get your ass KIA and no one remembers your damn name."

I walked out of the hut and went to the bunkhouse. I took off my combat gear and went to the radio room. I walked down the three steps to the radio and turned it on. I checked in with Pleiku and informed them of the landmine explosion; they had no traffic for us, so. I turned off the set and went back to the house. I lay down on my bunk and dozed off for a few minutes.

Lt Lawson came by, woke me up and said, "Do you want to eat?"

I looked up and replied, "What's on the menu?"

"Tonight the chef is offering rice pilaf, rice and buffalo balls, fried rice and fish heads, boiled rice and chicken feet, plus hot San Miguel."

"That's a terrific menu. May I invite some of my friends?"

"Sorry, tonight is just for members only," he replied.

"What happened to the cold beer?"

He said, "That's all been consumed. Homer just drank the last cold one."

I replied, "That pill-pushing prick, he's so damn inconsiderate."

Tony walked over to me and said, "Ken, I have converted this old M-1 rifle and some cartridges so we can fire 60 millimeter mortar rounds from it. You're going out on patrol tomorrow, so I want you to take it."

I picked up the old familiar rifle and looked at the cartridges. The lead round had been removed and they were converted to basically blank cartridges. The old rifle grenade launcher had been fitted to the rifle and the mortar round would fit on the launcher. I could see no reason why it wouldn't work "Tony, I see no reason why it won't work. You tested it, so I'll be happy to take it, hell I might have a need for it."

He said, "I had one of the local women make little vests that will fit the Yards. They'll wear the vest and carry two rounds each, one in front and one in back."

"Okay, it'll go with me tomorrow. George Higgins will go with me." George was the team heavy weapons man, and a good one.

The next morning I got together my previously selected twenty man recon patrol and left just after daylight. I planned on making a wide sweep to the west of the camp. I ensured that the rifle and the mortar rounds were loaded and assigned to two Yards. I had one man carry the radio I was wearing my combat gear, and didn't want to be weighted down with excess equipment. We left as the sun casts its first light across the jungle tops. By the time daylight filtered down to the jungle floor we were nearly a mile away from the compound. We reached an old deserted Yard village. All the long houses were deserted, the natives had all simply disappeared. I saw a scruffy hound dog skulking around the edge of the clearing staring at us. There was also a cairn that seemed to represent a marker of some type.

On the hard ground besides several huts were crude drawings. They depicted American helicopters and fixed wing aircraft. I figured that this must be a training area for the Viet Cong. They must teach classes just like we do.

We passed around the village, and I turned northeast and proceeded for about one more mile. I halted the patrol and told the lead Yard to set out a perimeter guard, and then have the men eat. I had a can of C-rations with me. I had selected Ham and Lima Beans which was my favorite, they are very salty but tasty. I searched my pockets for my P-38 can opener, but couldn't find it. I pulled out my TL-29 knife and quickly had the can open. I ate the beans in nothing flat, then buried the can and the small spoon. The Yards began chattering, and I spoke to the leader and cautioned him to quiet them down. He did and only the native sounds of the jungle could be heard. The little native Jarai Yards were very good trainees. We stayed in that one position for a few hours.

I spoke to George and said, "When we stop for the night I'll stay up until one in the morning, and you can take over for the remainder of the night."

He replied, "That's fine with me, whatever you want to do is good."

We remained at that location for most of the afternoon, then just before dark I moved them out again. I turned back southeast and went for about a mile before I found a hilltop that I wanted to stop and setup for the night. I positioned the men and pointed out their fields of fire, they all seemed to grasp what I in gestures and English tried to tell them. I radioed back to camp and told them where I thought I was.

Later in the evening I could hear off in the distance drums beating. I thought, this shit is totally unreal. Beating drums in the middle of the night in the jungle, if it wasn't so real it would make a great scene for a movie.

I crawled over to George and said, "Have you ever heard any such shit as these damn drums beating way the hell out here in the jungle?"

He replied, "This crap is scary."

The hot humid air hovered close to the ground, and the never ending mysterious sounds of the jungle continued unceasingly. I slept fitfully, never really asleep and not really awake. I rolled over facing the ground pulled my jacket over my head and lit a cigarette carefully guarding the end of the cigarette so that the red tip wouldn't glow.

About an hour before daylight I watched as the Yard leader woke the men up one by one. He came back and told me in sign language that we had two men missing along with their weapons and ammunition.

I counted the men and sure enough two men were gone. I motioned to him that we would move immediately. It wasn't yet daylight, but I knew we needed to move. I led the way as I wanted to be sure we went in the right direction. It was extremely slow moving.

Off in the distance I heard a bunch of monkeys or birds screaming and carrying on. I stopped the patrol and called the leader.

He joined me and said, "VC, VC" and pointed out that they were heading in our direction.

I motioned for George, and he quickly joined me. I said, "George, we have some VC headed in our direction, I don't know how many, but we have the high ground and the trail runs just below us. Let's let them walk right up to us and then we'll open fire. Take ten men and setup a position just past where I'll be. We'll fire first then leapfrog back past you and reload, you blast them, and then leapfrog back past me."

He grunted, "Okay," and left.

We waited quietly in the dim light as I watched the trail. In about thirty minutes I saw figures headed in our direction. The leader saw them at the same time and tapped me on the arm.

He murmured, "VC." I nodded my head in agreement.

I counted about twelve of them. I found some comfort in the fact that we outnumbered them, if they were the entire group.

They came closer. I observed they weren't too alert, the two men in front was the two trainees who had left sometimes last night. I waited until they were ten feet away from my position, I reared up and began firing, the entire platoon minus George and his group began firing. Both of the trainees dropped. I immediately threw a grenade over towards the end of their group. It exploded, and I heard men screaming and yelling. I had shot up my entire magazine.

I immediately switched magazines and motioned to the yard leader to follow me. One by one the men got up and followed the two of us. I moved past George and his men. We all found new positions, and began reloading our weapons. In less than a minute seven men began running down the trail firing their weapons up the hill in our direction. I threw a grenade toward them and it exploded in a blinding flash. George and his group opened fire, and for a few minutes the sound was deafening.

As suddenly as it had begun, it stopped. Several more minutes passed. The Yard tapped me on the arm. He indicated he was going down on the trail and check out the situation. I nodded my head affirmatively.

He slowly worked his way down the hill. Then I heard two shots ring out. I waited, I saw the Yard, he motioned for us to join him.

I sent one squad down, they appeared safe then I and the others joined them on the trail. I counted fourteen VC all dead. I looked at the two trainees, they both had a bullet hole right between their eyes. I knew the chief yard had just placed those there. We gathered up all their weapons and ammunition.

As I stood there looking down at the muddy, mangled, motionless bodies, an almost forgotten quatrain from "The Rubaiyat" came to mind:

"Ah make the most of what we yet may spend,
Before we too into the Dust descend,
Dust into Dust, and under Dust to lie,
Sans Wine, sans Song, san Singers, and sans End."

What a weird thing to think about and remember at this time and place. These little guys have however, spent all that they had.

I led the patrol back along a small ridge line. After we reached the top I said, "George, radio the camp and tell'em we're coming back in and report on the ambush. Make the conversation quick and short, and let's get the hell out of here."

George made the radio contact, then I very quietly led them back to our camp. We arrived early in the afternoon and I reported to Tony and the Captain. I gave them a full briefing on everything that happened. We had recovered several weapons and four Chinese stick grenades.

I said, "The two trainees were the lead men in their group. They obviously knew where we had sat up last night. I guess they figured we wouldn't move out of there before daylight. It proves once more that we have VC in among the trainees."

That evening we all sat around in the little hut and drank a few beers. Homer was telling jokes, and he was a natural at telling jokes. Tony and I were talking about an upcoming operation.

He said, "There are a few old American T-28's over on the airfield in Pleiku. The Vietnamese fly them. I hope we can count on them for air support in the future."

"What the hell are they there for, if not to support us?"

The Old Man spoke up, "We plan to take about half of the trainees and cross over the Ronhing River and run some patrols. We need to find out what the hell is over there."

I asked, "When do you plan on going?"

"Right after New Year's. I have laid on some American helicopters from the 281st Company to take us over there, and the Vietnamese are going to bring a battery of 105mm Howitzers here to our camp to lend support in the case we need it."

I remarked, "Seems like you have it all planned out."

He smiled and said, "I do."

I opened another San Miguel and drank it with pleasure. I was tired, so I walked over to our hut took my clothes and boots off and lay down on my bunk. Christmas Day was just a couple of days away. I closed my eyes and sleep came quickly.

The team leader had planned a big Christmas party for the Jarai natives in the next door village, and the other small villages in the local vicinity. He bought two large water buffaloes which the natives were going to cook for the party.

The night before Lt. Lawson was drinking a big orange drink. He left to go to the latrine. I watched as Homer poured some grain alcohol into his drink and shook it up. The Lt. returned picked up his drink and had a big swallow.

He looked at the drink and said, "Damn this taste good, I really must be thirsty for it to taste this good."

I replied, "Well, it came all the way from Saigon, so you should enjoy it."

I watched as he took another big swallow. He finished the entire drink and by then he was knee-walking drunk. Lawson began laughing and talking and hanging on to people. He didn't realize how drunk he was. Tony and I helped him back to the sleeping area placing him on his bunk. He was out like the proverbial light.

Tony said, "That's a rotten ass trick to spike his drink with grain alcohol."

"Yep, it is a dirty trick, but he needed to relax anyway, and tonight he'll get a good night's sleep for sure."

The next morning the two buffaloes were tied to four bamboo poles erected in a small clearing. The four poles represented the four compass directions, and the natives began beating their drums and gongs as they danced around the buffaloes.

I thought this is unreal. *It's a throwback to some ancient civilization, I can't believe in this modern day and age that men still dance around poles, beat drums, and sacrifice animals. But they do!*

I watched in awe as the dancing and chanting continued. Large earthen jugs of rice wine were brought out, and long straws made from thin reeds inserted down their necks were used to suck the wine from the jugs.

"Tony, I dare you to try it."

Tony stepped up picking up a straw and inserted it into the neck of the jug. He began to suck on it, and I could see the liquid traveling up the straw.

He had several swallows and remarked, "It's not that bad, it won't replace San Miguel, but it isn't bad."

I picked up a straw and tried several swallows of the wine. It really wasn't too bad, better than Biere 33 for sure.

There were over two hundred adults and twice again as many children all playing games laughing and dancing.

Our team leader had a couple thousand small packets of salt, and he began handing them out to the natives. Once they realized what was in the small paper packets they mobbed him. I thought damn, he's going to get crushed to death unless we get him out of that crowd. George and I waded into the crowd and led the way for him to get away.

The local village chief was now dancing around the buffaloes. He had a four foot long curved sword which he manipulated with a dexterity I'd never seen. The drummers and the gong beaters increased their intensity, and their sounds bounced around and echoed throughout the area. The chief danced faster around the buffaloes, approaching them closer and closer. Tension increased as the drums grew louder, the gongs beat faster, and the crowd moved closer. I watched intently, mesmerized by the pageantry.

He was behind one of the buffaloes, suddenly he swung his long sword cutting the tendons behind one of the buffalo's legs then he cut the other. The drummers went wild. The chief swirling and shouting, he then did the same to the second buffalo. With their tendons cut neither of the buffaloes could stand they slumped to the ground. Other young men moved in quickly, and cut the throats of both buffaloes.

As we Americans watched in awe and amazement, they immediately began to skin the buffaloes. Huge palm leaves were laid out on the ground, and as they carved the buffaloes they placed the meat on the hopefully clean palm leaves.

A huge bonfire was build, and the natives began cooking sections of the buffalo. I continued to take swallows out of the rice wine jugs. Capone had made a Santa Claus suit out of the orange panels of re-supply parachutes; he was wearing the suit, and handing out cans of cola to the natives. He showed them how to open the bright red cans, and they really had a ball. Much later in the evening the feast began. I cut a large section of the cooked meat sprinkled salt on it and began eating. It was tasty but tough, or else I'd had too much rice wine. All the natives ate, and our team filled up on roasted buffalo.

I was beginning to feel a little tipsy from the wine, so I left the feast and went back to our hut. I went to bed with a full stomach, and an aching head. I had a headache and diarrhea for the next four days.

Christmas came and went, and all our efforts were now directed toward getting the troops and equipment ready for deployment across the river.

We were sitting in our little eating hut when I asked Captain Leadenham, "Who're you taking with you on the operation?"

"I'm taking Homer, Tony, Lou, and George. We'll be gone for four days. So you guys have to hold the fort here."

Lt Lawson spoke up and said, "Captain, you're leaving me with a bunch of misfits, maybe I should go with you."

The captain smiling replied, "Lieutenant, you had better keep these guys in line and straight while I'm gone."

Lawson laughed and said, "There's going to be some changes made! I have a harder job than you do, these guys are impossible."

I spoke up and said, "Lieutenant, we'll make it easy for you, why don't you go to Saigon on pass, and we'll run the damn outfit. That way you get away clean, have fun, and nothing can go wrong."

He looked at me and replied, "I wish."

It was all in good humor, so we continued to plan the operation.

New Year's Eve night I went to bed early. I thought I'll probably be asleep when 1963 arrives. I had drank a forth of a fifth of Scotch, and my head was swimming. As I lay there I thought, here I am seeing and experiencing things that I never thought possible. Animal sacrifices, people killing people, booby traps and land mines, languages that no one understands, jungle people in loin cloths, punjii stakes, rice wine and animism. I never expected this.

Most of the world is at peace, but here in the jungles of Southeast Asia there's a lot of killing going on, and much more killing still to come. I hoped that the recon patrol would go off well with no one injured. I had absolute faith in the Team Leader and the Team Sergeant, so I knew they would do well. I easily fell into a deep sleep.

The next morning the choppers from the Helicopter Company came roaring in and landed in the little landing strip we had carved out. Captain Leadenham and Tony got all the little Yards loaded onto the craft and one by one they took off. The entire first company departed. That left us with just one company to defend the camp plus the few artillery people. As we stood there watching them load you could see the eyes of the Yards get bigger and bigger. This was the closest they had ever been to an actual flying machine.

Melvin said to me, "Ken, those guys have a lot of guts to get on a machine they know absolutely nothing about."

"You're right, I imagine they're scared shitless, but they got on anyway. I just hope they all come back alive."

We walked back over to the camp and I watched as the Vietnamese artillery unit set up its howitzers and stacked their shells around the guns. I called on the radio to Pleiku and reported that the patrol had left on schedule. My old friend Wayne Wilson from Germany, and the 82nd Division was on the radio, so I exchanged some small banter with him for a few minutes. He was the "B" team communications chief located in Pleiku. Radio security was no big deal in those early days of the war.

Lt. Lawson came up to me and said, "Ken, Lt Till, the Yard commander wants to arm about eleven of his men with weapons and ammunition while the other company is gone, what do you think about that?"

I thought for a moment and replied, "I guess it'll be all right, we don't have many people to defend the camp since the other company and half of the team is gone."

He left and I mentioned to Melvin that some of the Yards would be armed that night, so keep a sharp eye out.

I went to bed about eleven that evening as the moon completed its long slide below the horizon. Melvin was on duty as the walk around alert guard within the compound. I listened to the myriad sounds of the jungle as they echoed and reechoed through the damp, dark, still night air. I fell asleep easily as it had been a long exhausting day.

Suddenly, there was a tremendous explosion at the end of our building, that and a blinding flash of light jolted me awake immediately. I jumped off of my cot and heard a tremendous amount of machine guns, recoilless rifle fire, automatic rifle fire and grenades exploding. Bullets were smashing through our hut, the rounds cracking as they flew over and around my head. Our camp was under a major attack! I grabbed my pants and slid them on, then my boots, and finally I swung my combat gear on and grabbed my carbine. In the flash of exploding rounds I saw that everyone in the building was up and moving. I dashed out of the building and a burst of automatic rifle fire cracked over my head, I doubled over and ran to the mortar pit.

The mortar had a four foot wall of sand bags surrounding it for the mortar and gunner's protection. I jumped into the pit knelt down behind the bags and made a quick estimate of the situation. With the moon long gone it was dark, so frigging dark. I could see from the gun flashes that all incoming fire was coming from mainly one direction. I could also see several shadowy figures advancing towards the pit and our billets. I fired a full magazine at them seeing several drop. I reloaded a new magazine and continued firing.

Machine gun rounds with green tracer bullets began chewing into a sandbag next to me, and sand flew up into my face. A hand grenade blew up several feet away from my position, and I felt the shrapnel tearing into the sandbags. I wiped more sand from my face and spit it out of my mouth.

I was joined by Melvin and Jack. Lt Lawson joined us as we threw grenades at the approaching figures. Flash after flash tore through the night sky as grenades and recoilless rifle shells exploded in and around the camp and its perimeter. The sound of rifle bullets screaming as they passed over our heads. Round after round slammed into the sand bags. Several of the bags on the end disappeared as they were chewed apart by the machine gun fire.

I shouted to Lt Larson, "Our Yards aren't armed, so anyone with a weapon has to be VC, kill anyone you see armed!"

Melvin hollered over to me, "The mortar sights have been screwed with, it's no good!"

I shouted back, "I'll get the sixty millimeter mortar." I left the pit and raced to the building and picked up the little hand held 60mm mortar. I also grabbed a box of mortar shells and drug it along the ground behind me.

As I went around the corner I met Frenchy. I screamed to him, "Get in the radio hut, call Pleiku and tell'em we're under attack, request air support and tell'em we need it now!"

I moved the little mortar into an open firing position, and without any charges on it I dropped a round down the tube. I had the tube aimed almost straight up and the round fired, I watched and shortly thereafter I saw it explode down back of the wire fence. I fired the entire box of rounds moving the tube slightly after each round to cover more territory.

The sound of the mortar firing had deafened me I could hardly hear anything. I quickly ran out of shells. I ran back to the mortar pit. Grenades were exploded much closer to our position than before. Lt Lawson hollered fall back to the generator, we moved out quickly leapfrog style as we covered our move.

Once we were all there I told Jack, "I'm going to check on Frenchy, let's hope he got Pleiku and help is on the way."

As I left the generator area I heard three men talking and laughing over to my left front close to the small ammunition dump we had built and stocked. I took a grenade off my harness, pulled the pin and threw it in their direction. I lay close to the ground and watched it explode, there was no more laughing.

I got up and ran towards the radio hut entrance, before I reached the steps an explosion went off on my left and I was violently knocked to the ground. I lay there a few moments trying to regain my breath and senses. I couldn't feel my left arm. I reached across my body with my right arm. I wanted to know if I still had an arm. I felt the whole arm then my hand. My hand was numb and wet with blood. I could feel a long gash across the palm and heel of my hand. I opened my first aid kit and took the dressing out wrapping it around my hand. I couldn't tie it, so I stuffed the ends of the dressing underneath. I located and picked up my rifle then went to the radio pit.

I entered the small bunker in the ground, Frenchy was working both radios. He was sending Morse code out on the RS-1, and calling on the voice radio.

He stopped for a minute and said, “Ken, I can’t raise anyone, no one is answering me at Pleiku!”

I replied, “Frenchy keep trying, we’ll take care of things on top, you just keep trying to get some air support. Tell them to send that damn Vietnamese Ranger Company also.”

I then had Frenchy tie the ends of my dressing. I ran back to the generator, and the group was still there. I went to the bunker and picked up what I thought was a box of 60mm high explosive mortar shells, it turned out to be smoke shells.

I said to Jack, “Hell, let’s fire these, maybe we can smoke those bastards to death, or blind them for a while.”

We began firing the box of smoke shells. Bright flashes continued to tear through the night sky as explosion after explosion ripped shook and reverberated around the compound.I glanced at my Rolex, it was three o’clock in the morning. I thought daylight can’t come too fast for me, we’ve been fighting now over two hours. Suddenly the firing slacked off.

I said to Lt Lawson, “They’re probably regrouping and getting ready for another assault.”

We all checked our web belts for magazines, and our harness for grenades. I was in fairly good shape. We could hear water gurgling and splashing, I realized it was the water barrels for our shower.

Jack said, “Son of a bitch, they’ve ruined our shower.”

I replied, “Jack, those barrels are the least of our worries right now. We still have to worry about saving our nasty asses!”

Melvin spoke up and said, “I think I hear an airplane!”

He and Gene ran to the mortar pit switched on the arrow lights and swung it pointing west. They realized that there was no plane, so they turned off the little flashlight bulbs and returned to the generator.

More grenades exploded, their flash ripping through the darkness, and automatic rifle fire filled the night once more as the VC began their second assault on the camp. I glanced toward the front gate and saw three dark figures sneaking along. I pointed them out to Gene and Jack, they moved forward and shot all three of the bastards.

We had been fighting now for several hours when we all heard a plane fly over.

I raced to the radio hut and Frenchy said, "It's a plane that flew up from Saigon, it's not a fighter or bomber it's a flare ship. I'm in contact with the pilot."

I replied, "Frenchy, flares aren't going to help us too fucking much, stay in contact with the pilot and see what else is happening."

The pilot dropped a couple of flares. The artificial light revealed that half of the camp had been blown to pieces as the flares gracefully floated to earth. Shadowy figures could be seen at different locations inside and outside the fence. I saw several figures moving down on the outside of the fence line. I took a deep breath and squeezed off several rounds at them. I saw one of them drop.

We moved away from the generator. Lt Lawson said to me, "You go around to the right and I'll go around to the left, I'll meet you on the other side of the house."

"Roger."

Cautiously we left the area, I moved carefully around the front of the team house and saw that the Yards tents were still standing half erect.

Even in the dim light I could see bodies lying all over the place. The trench line looked totally caved in. I stepped gingerly over several bodies and quickly realized I couldn't tell who was who. The VC was dressed like our Yards mostly in black pajamas. Chinese stick grenades were lying all over the ground. I looked down towards the artillery unit and they seemed to be all right. I couldn't tell if they had casualties or not. I didn't see any outgoing fire from their position.

I met Lt Larson, he said, "Holy shit, what a mess this is!"

I replied, "Hell, we can't see half of it, wait until daylight then we'll really know. As far as we know they're still inside the camp, be careful, shoot first, and we'll ask questions later!"

I glanced at my watch it was about four in the morning. I wished like hell the sun would come up, but we still had a while to go yet. All of a sudden a tremendous explosion sounded on the north side of the camp. Automatic rifle fire screamed over my head, and I heard bullet rounds slamming and ripping through our building. I crawled around to that side but couldn't see anyone.

Another burst of machine gun fire cracked over my head, and I saw for the first time multiple green tracers coming from the north fence line. The machine gunner was sweeping his fire across the camp.

I crawled on my belly and hands and knees toward the fence, as he fired another burst. I squeezed off an entire magazine in the direction of the firer then another. The tracer rounds stopped coming in. Firing gradually slacked then stopped. The third assault was over, and the VC began fading back into the jungle.

About six-thirty the first faint rays of daylight made it's prayed for appearance. I heard in the distance a siren and saw headlights coming through the village of Plei Mrong. I found out they were reinforcements from Kontum, they were very welcome indeed. The operator on another Special Forces "A" team north of us in Kontum had heard Frenchy's radio calls, and had sent out reinforcements to us.

A few minutes after seven it was full daylight and the flare airplane left for Saigon. Shortly thereafter helicopters began arriving at our little strip. Vietnamese officers and some American officers arrived from Pleiku. Lt Lawson was handling all the visiting officers.

The assault on Camp Plei Hell was finally over. Six Americans and less than two hundred trainee Yards had fought off an estimated 400 man battalion of VC. Lt Till and his eleven Yards were missing. I suspect they were the inside VC force that led the assault.

To my knowledge Plei Hell was the first Special Forces camp that came under direct assault in Vietnam.

My hand was throbbing as I walked around the camp observing that over half of the camp had been destroyed. Bodies were everywhere. Arms and legs were lying around divorced of the bodies they once belonged to. I found the body of one of my favorite Yards a squad leader. His hands were bound with wire behind him and he had been shot between the eyes. I walked down to the wire on the north side where the last assault had began, and saw that the VC had placed a bangalore torpedo explosive underneath the barbed wire in an effort to blow out the fence. It had failed, the wire was badly burnt but had only a few strands broken. Next to the wire was a man with half his head blown off, I had no idea if he was VC or one of our trainees. I picked up a AK-47 automatic rifle next to him which meant he was VC for sure. Several other VC lay dead around the area.

Almost all the team had suffered some type of injury. No one was seriously wounded and I said a small prayer of thanks for that.

The helicopters from Pleiku after leaving our camp flew over the river and picked up Captain Leadenham and the other members of our team, and the Yards and flew them back to the camp. That took about thirty minutes to accomplish. I briefed the team leader and Tony for over an hour. Captain Leadenham was then tied up in examining the camp and talking to the B team officers. My hand hurt like hell, so I told Lt Lawson, "I'm going in to Pleiku and have the Doctor there take care of my hand. Gene and Homer are treating the wounded Yards."

He agreed with me, so I caught one of the helicopters returning to Pleiku airfield. I went to the "B" team and saw the doctor there who cleaned out my wound, sewed up my hand then put on a clean dressing and bandage.

I ran into Wayne Wilson, "Wayne, you sorry ass! Where in the hell were you people when we were calling you all frigging night?"

He replied, "We couldn't hear you. We heard the firing and the explosions, but we couldn't pick-up any radio signals."

"Well, something is definitely wrong, Kontum heard us. Frenchy and I both tried to get you on both radios, and we never got an answer. I think you guys were scared shitless, and wouldn't even turn on your radios. Why the hell didn't you guys send reinforcements out to us, if you heard all the firing?"

He shrugged his shoulders and said, "Ken, I'm not in charge. To make up for it I have a bottle of Chivas Regal scotch, we can drink that together."

"Well, that will certainly go a long, long ways towards making up for your scary ass non-support."

Wayne and I sat there for a few hours as I recounted the fight for our camp, and we drank half of the bottle. I found a bunk and went to sleep; I was a little drunk and totally exhausted. The next morning after having breakfast I managed to catch a helicopter headed out to our camp and returned to Plei Hell.

I think our final figures for the camp were twenty-four trainees missing, roughly thirty-five to forty men killed and about forty wounded. All the dead were laid out inside the camp wrapped in the standard issue for them, cheap gray blankets. Old men and women would come to the camp to identify their sons or brothers and slowly carry them away. The VC and trainees all were removed. It was a sad, sad sight to witness. I had no idea that this scene would be duplicated many times over in the years ahead.

As we quickly began to rebuild the camp, a good friend of mine from the B team came out to replace one of our weapons men who had gotten ill and returned to Okinawa. The replacement's name was Benny Polina. He was a nice young Italian from Fort Lauderdale, Florida. He blended in well with our team and everyone liked him.

An author and newsman named Johnny Roswell came out and spent several days with us. He interviewed each member of the team, and even went on a short patrol to get the feel of the tasks involved. He had spent some time earlier with another Special Forces Team from Okinawa, and had photographed and interviewed each of them. As I understood it he was a contract author, and sold articles to several major magazines and newspapers. He was personable and everyone on our team liked him and enjoyed his company.

Later on we learned that he had written a major article on Vietnam, and on our camp defense for a major monthly magazine. It was published in the March 1963, edition. We later obtained copies of the magazine. On the cover is a picture of our Team Leader and two Yards, they were out on an operation. We all read the article and found it to be essentially correct, and fairly accurate in its portrayal of the assault on Plei Hell.

Meanwhile, we had received several cases of anti-personnel mines which we were going to place between our original barbed wire fence and a second one we were installing around the camp. In addition we were going to place punjii stakes in between the two fences. Those additional defensive measures would surely help in the next assault on the camp—and there would be another one.

One morning, Tony, the Old Man, and I were sitting in our bamboo kitchen having a late cup of instant coffee when we heard an explosion down toward the west fence.

Captain Leadenham looked at me and asked, "Is someone training with explosives today?"

Tony said, "No, but Benny is laying anti-personnel mines."

It hit us all at once, that's the cause of the explosion. We raced out of the kitchen and ran towards the fence and saw Benny lying on the ground. He had obviously stepped on one of the mines he was installing. We all stopped about twenty yards away. We didn't know for sure where he had laid the mines.

Tony said, "Wait here!"

Without hesitation, and with no regard for his own safety, he began to walk slowly out into the mine field towards Benny. He studied the ground in front of him, then stepped forward one step at a time. I crossed my fingers saying a silent prayer that he wouldn't step on another mine. Benny lay writhing in agony on the ground. Tony finally reached him. Bending over he picked him up and slung him across his shoulders. He turned around and stepping back in his original tracks brought him back to us. Benny's foot was severely injured with blood everywhere, the bottom half of his combat boot blown off. Captain Leadenham and I grabbed him, and the three of us rushed him to our dispensary.

Homer, the medic was there, he knew what had happened and he immediately went into action. He removed the remnants of the boot and washed Benny's foot off in alcohol, then gave him a shot of morphine to lessen the pain.

Homer said, "His foot's numb!" He began cutting away at the shredded flesh. Meanwhile Frenchy radioed Pleiku for an evacuation helicopter. Benny was in intense pain obviously fearing that he had lost a foot. Homer was magnificent as he attended to the injury. He was as cool as any skilled doctor could be as he operated on Benny's shattered foot. He completed the debridement, and put on a dressing and bandage. We got Benny up to the landing strip, the chopper was there waiting. Benny left for Pleiku, and ultimately on to Walter Reed Army Hospital.

About two weeks later the Old Man called the team together and said, "Gentlemen, the Chief of Staff of the Army is coming here to inspect our camp, which means we have to put this camp back together and look sharp. I'm having a couple of loads of gravel brought in from Pleiku, and we're going to spread it out on the roadway from the team house to the front gate to help hold down some of the frigging dust. Everyone is going to have to help, and we are still running patrols and ambushes, so stay sharp."

I remarked to Tony, "If the Chief of Staff wants to see us, and the camp like it really is, why in the hell should we try and make it something it isn't. Let him eat dust like we do."

Tony laughed, "Ken, you know the army, it'll only be for a couple of hours. A dog and pony show, then we'll go back to our normal activities."

Sure enough a week later the Chief of Staff of the United States Army, and a dozen other high ranking officers and civilian officials from Saigon showed up. They flew in by helicopter. We had a small area so we were all lined up outside the team house as he inspected us, and told us what a fine job we had done in beating back a battalion attack.

Finally, he and the entire entourage with him left for Saigon and on to Washington. We who remained knew the fight wasn't over. The endless patrols, ambushes, firefights, casualties, mines, death, and punjii stakes dominated our days and nights. We lost several more of our Yards, and killed a larger number of the VC.

We had about a month left in country, and I was tired. This had been a long tough tour, and so much has happened since our arrival. I thought about our accomplishments. We had built our camp, carving it out of the jungle, a dispensary, a schoolhouse, living quarters, camp defenses, and defended it all. We had paid for it in sweat, blood and lives.

I knew that other Special Forces teams were doing the same things throughout the country, and they too were having their share of problems. We were still operating under Combined Studies in Saigon, but were told that the 5th Special Forces Group would be taking over operations in the country. I think half of the SF teams on Okinawa were already in country, or getting ready to come back in country. The First Group had suffered numerous battle deaths since we first arrived here back in sixty-one, and there seemed to be no end in sight. We and the other Special Forces teams were however, wiping out the VC across the country.

Two weeks before we were due to leave, we planned a ceremony to dedicate the new schoolhouse and the dispensary. The village chief wanted to have a huge sacrifice for the occasion. Captain Leadenham bought two more huge water buffalo. They erected their four decorated compass poles. The villagers were all invited, and their kids showed up by the dozens. The buffalo were tied up to the poles, and the dancing and gong playing began. Several Vietnamese officials showed up for the ceremony plus various officers and the ceremony began.

Once again amidst all the pagan pageantry, the chief hamstrung the two buffalo, and then their throats were cut. Young men skilled at their task quickly skinned them both, and cut them into sections. The big buffalo roast began. Jugs of rice wine were offered, and we all had a few drinks of it

Our replacement team arrived from Okinawa and we packed up our personal belongings, and equipment that we had brought from Okinawa. We loaded aboard a truck and went to Pleiku. We left Camp Plei Hell behind us—way behind us—but with deep lasting pride in our efforts and accomplishments.

Our experiences as a team gave birth to an unbelievable bond between the team members. That bond was born under the glare of exploding shells and grenades, forged in the heat of machine gun fire that fed on buildings, chewing its path through sand bags, elephant grass and bodies, shaped by the sounds of dying men along many a long and lonely trail, nurtured to full bloom by the blood and lives shed at nameless jungle coordinates. That bond would endure for the remainder of our lives.

We cleared out in Saigon. We went to the finance section to get paid. I asked for Hamby, but he had shipped out. We were paid, and then the agency gave each of us a brand new nine millimeter pistol as appreciation for our services.

One day later we boarded a C-130 cargo plane and a few hours later touched down in Kadena Air Force Base, Okinawa. We were met by a bus and found out that our company had moved to Machinato, Okinawa

I told Tony, "The first thing I want to do is get a hot steam bath and a massage, and then have a big lobster dinner, some ice cold San Miguel beer, and then think about getting laid someplace."

He replied, "That sounds like a great plan of attack, I might just do that myself."

George asked, "Are you going to the club tonight?"

"I am indeed. First, we have to find out where we live get a bunk, and then some clothes, then we can go." Tony, Lou, Melvin and Frenchy all had their wives on the island, so I knew they would be going home to their quarters and families.

We were told which rooms were ours, and what container had our bags and clothing in it. We finally located it all and lugged it upstairs. I hung up everything in the wall locker and went to the latrine and shower. I stood for about thirty minutes beneath the hot water as it cascaded over me. I could feel the dust, mud, sweat and leech bites washing away. I shampooed my hair twice, and finally felt totally clean. I went back to the room and put on a pair of civilian pants and shirt, I even wore my civilian loafers.

I sat on my bunk and thought how strange it all seems. For months you are constantly alert, aware of everything around you. You're always listening, looking and searching for clues or indicators that you're about to be attacked; *the next day you're back in the civilized world, where the slot machines are the only place where you hope to make a killing.* Life goes on I guess, and life is for the living!

George and I finally got ready and went up to the club. The place was jumping, the band playing, couples dancing, and the slots jingling. I spotted Jason and Art sitting at a table, so I walked over to them.

Jason saw me first, jumped up and hollered my name, "Ken, you sweet mother—huncher how the hell are you?"

We laughed as we shook hands with each other, and I replied, "Hello old friend, I'm fine, just glad to be back on the island, how are you?"

"I'm doing great, we're all fine, when did you get back?"

"We got back about two hours ago. We had to locate all our clothes, our room and all that stuff."

Art gave me a big bear hug and said, "Welcome back Ken! We heard you got hit are you all right?"

"Sure, I'm fine, I received a nasty cut, but otherwise I'm well."

George joined us, and they shook hands all around.

"Gentlemen, I'm really hungry. I haven't eaten all day just waiting until I could get here, and have a good meal for a change."

Jason said, "Let me buy you dinner as a welcome home present."

"Jason, that's very nice, and I appreciate it, if you want to, be my guest."

The waitress came by and I ordered a lobster dinner. I had a cold, and I mean cold San Miguel beer. I had another beer before my dinner arrived. The lobsters were the best I had ever had, or else I was just so hungry and glad to be back it super enhanced their taste.

After dinner I became very sleepy, I had about four more beers then decided that I'd best call it a night. They all were headed to New Koza, but I was just too tired.

Jason said, "Ken, why don't you go back and get some rest. I'll tell the girls you're back on the island and will see them later."

"Thanks Jason, you are one good man. Tell my girl not to butterfly until I can get there."

They caught a taxi and left. I caught a second taxi and went to our new barracks. I had a slight buzz on from the beer, so I wearily went to bed. Sleep came easily and quickly. The next day I asked Art about my car.

He said, "I have it, and its running great. I made five payments on it. If you want it back, I'll give it to you for the five payments."

"Great, I'll take it."

He replied, instead of giving me the money there's a watch that I want downtown, you can buy that for me instead."

"What kind of watch is it?"

"It's a gold Rolex."

"It must be nice, how much is it?"

"A little over five-hundred dollars."

I looked at him and asked, "Do you really want to pay that much for a watch?"

He laughed and replied, "Sure, you should see the watch it's a beauty."

We got into my car and I drove downtown Futima. We went to a store named Sax Fifth Avenue. I looked at the watch he wanted and it really was a beauty. It was real gold and weighed a couple of ounces. I gave the clerk five hundred dollars and Art kicked in the remainder, and walked out of the store acting like a damn proud father.

Later that month I had an auto accident. I hit a drunken Okinawan who had staggered out in the street, and into the path of my car.

A few days later the Group Sergeant Major approached me and asked for my driving license, then said, "Sergeant Fisher, your driving days on Okie are over. It might not have been your fault, but the old man thinks it was. So it's better you not drive any more on island."

I replied, "No big deal Sergeant Major. I have only a few more months to go here, and I'll be rotating back to Bragg. I'll let Lou Brooklyn keep it until I leave."

I handed him my Okinawan driving license. He tore it up and let the paper shreds fall into the street. Taxi cabs were plentiful and cheap, transportation wasn't that important or hard to obtain.

I ran into Lou and asked him if he would keep my car until I rotated. He agreed to do so. That solved my automobile problem.

The following Monday Captain Leadenham called our team together in the team room and said, "We're all going to take SCUBA training beginning next week. The training will last for three weeks, and will be given by a Navy Seal team. Once we complete their training, we'll give them parachute training. They'll make SCUBA divers out of us, and we'll get them jump qualified."

Mike spoke up, "What's SCUBA?"

Tony answered, "That stands for Self Contained Underwater Breathing Apparatus."

We began SCUBA training the following Monday morning with some other members. The navy team began our training with a two mile run along the beach and sand dunes. I thought I'd pass out, I was so badly out of shape.

I said to Captain Leadenham, "Six months in the jungle existing on rice, fish and buffalo meat doesn't prepare you for running two miles on a beach."

He laughed and replied, "Don't worry, you'll be in shape in a week."

I grunted, "I hope."

Then we began working out in the swimming pool. We swam and we swam. We practiced with the air tanks and practiced exchanging air hoses underwater. We had to swim without tanks for twenty-five yards underwater without surfacing. Holding your breath for that time and distance was a tough grind to be sure. We were placed into two man teams. Jason and I were one team. The second week we loaded onto RB-12 rubber boats and taken out in the ocean, there we began practicing diving for real. As our training progressed it became easier and easier. I could now make the runs without experiencing breathing problems, and handling the equipment was a snap. Each day we would have what they termed a recreational dive. They would let the teams go down to whatever depth we desired within reason, and just explore the ocean floor, or observe the myriad of sea life that exists off the Okinawan Island.

On our second recreational dive Jason and I went down about eighty feet. There we observed a deep ditch that was gouged into the ocean floor. I motioned to him let's go check it out. He gave me a thumbs-up sign, so we went deeper. I was gliding along above the coral rocks and ocean floor about ninety feet down when out of the side of a coral rock a huge Moray eel came out and glided up towards me. It scared the fatal hell out of me, and I headed upwards. Jason saw the eel and followed me up. That eel was one scary looking creature, and I wanted nothing to do with it. Sea snakes were plentiful. We had been told that they wouldn't harm you. Just leave them alone and they'll leave you alone.

On our next recreational dive, down about sixty feet we ran into a huge grouper, at least I think he was a grouper. The big fish was about four feet long and looked to weigh maybe two or three hundred pounds. He outweighed either one of us, but he was friendly. He stared at us for a moment, then slowly swam away.

In our final week we were to complete the course by swimming in from a mile off shore from rubber boats. We were to simulate attacking ships docked in Naha harbor. This was to all take place at night.

"Jason, this shouldn't be too hard, hell we can swim a mile for sure."

"Yeah, but at night, and you have to be down fifty feet for that mile, and you only have a compass to go by."

That Friday evening we put on our air tanks got aboard the rubber boats and went out a mile from the harbor. There the navy team tied balloons with a small flashlight attached to it on a sixty foot rope to the back of our tanks. We were set to go. We both checked our compasses and determined the azimuth to the harbor. The lights from Naha harbor could barely be seen from where we were to begin our dive and swim. Jason and I sat upon the edge of the boat, then falling over backwards we entered the water. It was a dim moonlit night, and despite the darkness at the surface we both were pleasantly surprised at how well we could see beneath the surface.

We slowly swam down until we reached the required fifty feet. I looked up towards the surface and could barely see our little light floating on top of the surface. We then checked our compasses and agreed that we had the correct azimuth to get to the harbor. We began the swim; we were side by side and continued a slow swim toward the harbor. After several minutes into the swim, I felt a tug on the line attached to my tank. I stopped and motioned to Jason that we needed to go up. We both began our ascent and reached the top in short order. The rubber boat was there with the Seal crew in it.

He hollered out to us, "You guys are headed in the wrong direction!"

We had swam about three hundred yards straight out to sea. Jason looked at me, and I looked at him.

I said, "Well, I'll be dipped in shit, how in the hell did we misread the compass so badly?"

Jason replied, "Dammed if I know."

We both shot another azimuth, and with a wave to the crew we sank again beneath the waves. We reached our desired fifty feet and again checked our compass. We began our swim much more vigorously to make up for the time we had lost going in the wrong direction.

Finally, we reached the objective and slowly surfaced. We were only a hundred yards or so off target. Both of our air tanks were getting low on air, I was happy just to make it. We swam on in to shore, loaded up on trucks then returned to the base. The following Saturday we received our certificates of completion of SCUBA diving.

The following Monday airborne training for the Seal team began. I was to assist in the physical training part of the program, and take jump master training at the same time. We were to jump them out of helicopters, and from C-123 cargo planes. Tony was a Master parachutist and a qualified skydiver, so he was to conduct the jump master training for several of us who needed it.

We all jumped with a Griswold container. The bag had a heavy piece of equipment in it. We jumped six times and acted as jump masters on the jumps for the Seals. We all graduated, receiving our master jump wings, and the Seal team received novice jump wings. At that time I already had over forty-four jumps catalogued in my jump log.

Meanwhile, the entire Special Forces Group was involved in either training for deployment to South Vietnam, or supporting teams that were deployed. Casualties continued to mount in our outfit, and the list of KIA's continued to lengthen. I had already lost several very close friends to action in that country.

The group had now increased to almost twice its size since I had first arrived back in 1960. We now had more "A" teams than ever before. We learned that back at Fort Bragg they had four Special Forces Groups, plus a training group. I thought back to the late fifties when I knew almost everyone in the old original Group. Now I would be lucky to know two in ten persons. Almost daily we would hear of a friend of ours getting wounded, or killed in Nam. It seemed it was the old hard core Special Forces troopers leading the way that were getting killed or wounded. They were from our group, or the fifth group which was now in Nam.

Jason, Art and I were sitting in the Top Three club soaking up some suds when Tony and Sam Trout came in and joined us at the table. We talked about everything imaginable.

"Tony, you know it seems odd that Special Forces is the only major ground fighting force in Nam, and there are no other major combat units involved. Are they trying to get us all wiped out?" I asked.

"I don't fucking know. But I do know this, unless the teams get more and better support, we can't win this by ourselves," he replied.

Sam, who had also recently returned from Nam spoke up "Our team ran into some North Vietnamese regulars plus VC, so they're stepping up their combat forces and fighting strength, we have to also."

"We need close air support, and we need back up forces when we get into deep shit, I remarked. I guess that the people in Washington know what they're doing, but that doesn't seem to help when you're in a fight for your life, look at what happened to us at Plei Hell, we received absolutely no help."

Jason said, "Remember Ken when we first went to Nam back in 61, and that Major said 'this is the only war we have, let's keep it going?' "

"Yeah, that was Harry something or other. I think he's getting his wish."

Looking around the table I realized that we were all considered combat veterans. Tony had been in the Korean War, and now involved in Vietnam. Sam had been in WW II, and now in Nam. Art had been in the 3rd Infantry Division in Korea, and now in Nam. Only Jason and I were recent combat veterans. Opinions and solutions were passing around the table. Of course it didn't amount to a hill of beans, as we were just the people who followed orders, and carried them out.

The PA system came on and said, "We're in Condition Two, all personnel are requested to leave the club."

We all knew that typhoon warnings had been issued earlier in the day. A typhoon was on the way, perhaps heading for the island.

Jason said to me, "Let's get a typhoon fifth of scotch, and head for town."

"That's the best idea I've heard lately," I replied.

We all left the club. Jason and I bought a huge typhoon fifth of Scotch, caught a small taxi and went to New Koza.

"Jason, let's get a steam bath and massage, then find us some beautiful women, and we'll ride out the typhoon in style."

"Ken, that's a marvelous idea. I wished I'd thought of that."

I laughed, "You smooth talking devil, I think you planned all this shit including the typhoon."

The narrow streets of New Koza were as familiar to us as the streets in our own compound. We exited the taxi in front of the steam house. We walked in and the Mama San greeted us like long lost friends, I guess we really were. I told her what we wanted, and she happily furnished us two girls for the bath and massage.

I went into the little steam room and began to remove my clothing. A very pretty girl whom I had not seen before came into the room. She seemed embarrassed to see me nude. I walked over and sat down in the steam box as she wrapped towels around my neck. Then she turned up the steam. I swear, I lost all the recent beer that I had drank. Sweat was pouring out of me. She continually wiped my face and forehead. Finally, the steam bath was over; I got out of the box and stretched out on the table. She hurriedly placed a large towel over my midsection. She began to massage my toes then my leg muscles and back. She slowly worked her way up my neck, and it felt wonderful. I felt as limber as a rag. I turned over and she began to massage my legs working her hands up my body.

My dick was in its normal state, but like a good soldier reared up to full attention in appreciation of her efforts. She worked her manipulations around it, and didn't touch it at all. I felt cheated!

I took her hand and placed it on my erection, and said, "My friend needs a massage also," She reached for her bottle of oil and poured a small amount in her hand. She rubbed her palms together then she removed the towel altogether.

She said, "You pay two dollars more."

I nodded in full agreement to her request.

She slowly began to massage me then giggling she said, "You Papa San up here, pointed to my head of partly gray hair, but you boy san here as she pointed to my erection."

She continued to massage me. I thought gray hair or not, I'm only thirty-two, that's not old in anyone's book that I know of. I could feel the tension building as I was getting to those fabulous short rows. Her efforts were quick and complete. She began giggling as she grabbed a wet towel and cleaned the oil off my stomach and chest.

I paid her the amount due. I dressed walked out and waited for Jason. He came out shortly. We sat down at the table and ordered a cola and ice and had a couple of drinks together from our bottle.

We left the steam house and walked down to our favorite bar. My favorite girl Taeko was there, and Jason's girl Michiko was there. We all went back to the room that they had for the girls. Jason and I changed into the kimono type robes they furnished. They brought out water and ice and he and I began to enjoy the best drink in the world.

As we sat there drinking and fooling around with the girls, the rain picked up in intensity. The winds increased in speed, and the little houses with their tin roofs began to shake. You could hear miscellaneous objects flying around in the street outside.

"Jason, it doesn't get any better than this. Two lovely women, a typhoon fifth of scotch, some ice and water, and two good friends, what else could a man possibly want?"

He laughed and replied, "Nothing that I can think of. Let's enjoy it while it's available."

We both had a drink to the occasion, and Jason leaned over and kissed his girl friend. I wrapped an arm around my girlfriend and suggested to her we retire to her room.

She agreed. I said to Jason, "We'll be back in a little while."

Taeko and I went to her room, and I performed my military duty. Finished, I said, "Let's go back to the other room, I need another drink."

She called out something in Japanese to Michiko, and listened to the answer. Jason and his girl were sitting on little cushions on the floor with the table in front of them. We joined them pulling up cushions to sit on. I reached over for my glass, put some ice in it then poured a stiff shot of scotch topping it off with water, and stirred it with a bamboo straw.

I raised my glass in toast to Jason and said, "Here's to a long typhoon, and may the scotch hold out to the end."

"I'll certainly drink to that," he said.

"Do you want to play some records," Michiko asked.

"Sure, what records do you have?"

She got up and left the room, then returned with a small record player and several records. Jason took the records, and I took the player plugging it into the wall socket. Jason placed a record by Bing Crosby on the player. I turned the volume down to a decent level. We then played a record by Elvis Pressley, followed by one by Hank Williams. Jason finally turned the player off, and just in time, the electricity went out. We refilled our glasses.

The wind was howling and whistling through the small streets buffeting the building, I surely hope this house stays up and stays together. I could hear sheets of tin covering the roofs making slapping, flailing noises off in the distance. The rain was coming down in torrential sheets, yet the building had no leaks whatsoever. By an oil lamp we sat there for another couple of hours drinking, talking and playing cards with the two girls.

I realized I was getting a little loaded, so I said, "Goodnight, I'm going to bed." We left and went to bed. I went to sleep immediately.

The next morning I woke up early. The tin roofs still flapping, the wind and rain howling. Taeko heated some water and made us both a cup of instant coffee. She had a can of condensed milk, so I poured some in my cup. She placed four teaspoons of sugar into hers, and stirred it vigorously. I turned on her battery radio and tuned in AFN. The radio announcer stated, "We're in condition two, and will be so for several more hours." I turned off the radio and had another cup of coffee. I heard Jason and his girl over in the other room.

I shouted, "Jason, I'll meet you in the other room for coffee."

"Be right there."

I made another cup of coffee, and put on my small kimono robe and went to the other room. Jason joined me as we both smoked and drank our coffee.

Looking over my cigarette I said, "We're still in typhoon status, so it looks like we'll be here another day."

He replied, "Good, let's see if we can get something to eat."

I asked, "Where're we going to get some food?"

He called Michiko and she came quickly into the room. She looked as fresh this morning as she did the previous day.

Taeko came in and said, "We can have some soup and rice."

I replied, "That's good." The four of us had some type of soup and rice for breakfast and lunch. I turned the radio on again, and heard the announcer say that the typhoon alert had been downgraded.

I said to Jason, "Well, old friend, it looks like we better get our asses back to Machinato."

We both got dressed walked outside, and sure enough the taxis were running again. We caught a cab and returned to the barracks.

Jason remarked, "We'd better get cleaned up and get back into uniform."

I replied, "Well, we still have well over three-fourths of a typhoon fifth we can drink later on."

We both taking our shaving kits and towels, hit the shower room. I finished showering then shaved and went back to our room and dressed. Nothing was going on in the company.

"Jason, let's go to the club and get something to eat."

We caught a taxi and went to the club. The damn place was packed with troops, their wives and girlfriends. We found a table and finally had some solid American food to eat.

A couple of days later in the team room, Tony who had a black belt in Karate said to me, "Ken, why don't you take up karate. I have a good time, and it helps keep you in shape."

I replied, "Where do you train, and what do you do?"

"I go to the dojo right outside the gate, it's not expensive and we have a great time. We do exercises, perform the karate dances, and compete against each other and against other dojo's," he replied.

I thought for a moment and said, "All right, I'll take it up. When do you go again?"

He replied, "I go tonight. So you need to buy yourself a uniform and we'll go together."

That night I went by Tony's house, and together we caught a taxi and went to his dojo. I bought a training uniform from the owner, and changed into it. For the first twenty minutes we simply did stretching and breathing exercises. I stood to one side and watched the others as they began to compete in the bouts.

As the evening wore on I observed that some of the Okinawan students were playing almost for keeps. They were kicking each other, and hitting each other with almost maximum force. I chose not to participate that evening in the bouts. A couple of night later I did participate in the bouts with other lesser trained opponents. Each time I went to the dojo I would spend about a half-hour punching a plank that stood outside that had been wound in rope. This I was told was to toughen up your knuckles. Ultimately, it did.

Tony said, "Ken, I'll work with you until you begin to understand what you're doing, and develop some ability to defend yourself. You also need to learn how to attack your opponent."

"Thanks Tony, I damn sure need someone to help teach me this program before I get kicked to death."

For the next several weeks I worked out with Tony and felt like I was beginning to learn the basic ideas of karate. My hands and knuckles toughened up, and my arms became almost immune to pain from hand blows. One evening I was competing with another young guy, and when I kicked him, I felt my right big toe snap. I knew I had broken it. It began swelling and turning blue. For the next several weeks I just did the exercises.

One day in late June Jason said, "Some of the guys want to go fishing tomorrow with DuPont spinners, do you want to go?"

"What the hell are DuPont spinners? They must be a new lure, I've never heard of them."

"You just wait and see."

The next day several of us checked out a RB-12 rubber boat, and Jason secured some quarter pound blocks of C-4 plastic explosive. We went fishing. I had never seen this before, but it worked. We put the fuses in and dropped them overboard. The block would sink down to around twenty-five feet before it exploded. We would wait a few minutes and fish came floating up to the top. What happened was the concussion from the blast killed the fish, and they floated topside.

We fished for about an hour and filled the bottom of the boat with large and small fish. We drove the boat over to a small village and gave them all the fish except five of the largest ones. That evening we built a fire on the beach and cooked all five. Jason and I took the truck and bought some beer to wash the fish down with.

I remarked to Jason, "I like the efficiency of the DuPont spinners, but it really isn't sporting to just blow them up."

He replied, "This isn't for sport, this is to make sure you get some fish, and don't go home with a wet ass, empty handed and hungry."

After eating all the fish and naturally drinking all the beer, we took the boat back to the boat shed, cleaned it up and signed it back in.

The next evening after training was over, I talked Lou into going down on highway one and getting a hot steam bath and massage.

"Lou, you owe it to yourself to participate in the finer things in life, and a hot bath and massage is surely one of the finer things."

"I agree with you, it's one of the finer things, but if my wife finds out I'm a dead man," he said.

"Lou, she'll never know, hell we won't be there that long."

Reluctantly, Lou agreed. He had my car, so we climbed in and he drove down highway one to my favorite steam houses. Mama San was happy to see us, and offered us her two best girls. I followed my normal routine, and after dressing I had a beer as I waited for Lou to come out. Finally, Lou strolled out and sat down with me.

"What took you so damn long?"

He laughed, "Ken, that doll fell in love with me, and wouldn't let me leave."

"Horseshit, she fell in love with your money."

"It doesn't matter, she's a number one girl." He dropped me off at the barracks and went on to his quarters.

The next day two more teams from the unit left for Vietnam. We were there as they loaded the trucks to go to Kadena. We shook hands all around, and I wished my old friend Shultz good luck and God speed. Two days later two teams returned to the Group from Nam. They had six wounded on the two teams.

We began a program of Counter-Insurgency training. I said to Lt. Lawson, "Hell, we don't need this training. I've had two tours fighting these frigging insurgencies. This is guerrilla warfare, and the thing you do is simply kill the bastards, and leave them to rot in the jungle where they originated."

He replied, "I agree, but we have to take the training, maybe we'll learn something new."

"I'm sure we'll learn something new, I always do. I just hope it's something useful and practical. Anything that can help save team lives I want to learn, especially if it will help save my own life,"

The training turned out to be interesting and even helpful. The instructor knew his stuff and his explanation of why certain things happened was very interesting. I even enjoyed the course.

CHAPTER 40

Back to the Land of the big PX

My tour and time on the island was rapidly running out. Several of the guys had already received rotation orders. All of them were returning to Fort Bragg to one of the Special Forces groups. I looked forward to returning to the land of the big PX.

Art and I received redeployment orders the same day, and were returning to Bragg. I had orders to return to the 7th SF group, and he had orders to return to the 3rd SF group. We had a big going away party. Wayne Wilson was there, Ralph Slaughter was there, Captain Leadenham and Lt Larson were there. Bert and many of our original group that had come over together in 1960, was also on orders back to the states and made the party.

I asked Jason, "When are your orders coming up?"

"I don't know. I guess any day I'll get mine. I hate to leave, I like it over here. Since my divorce, I've had more fun than I've had in years. When I get back to the states, I'll make every damn effort to get back over here."

"Well, old friend, it doesn't matter where you are, we'll all go back to Vietnam. The 5th Special Forces group is now running the show in Nam, and our Group seems to be more in general support these days."

The day after the party I went to see Lou and picked up my car.

"Thanks Lou for taking care of my car. It's old now, and has heavy salt damage from being on the island, so I'll probably swap it when I get to the states."

"No sweat Ken, your car saved me a small fortune in taxi money."

Laughing, I replied, “Glad that I could help.”

I drove the car down to Naha port, and turned it in for shipment to Oakland Army Terminal in Oakland, California. I then packed all my personal things into a box for further shipment to the 7th Special Forces Group at Fort Bragg, North Carolina, and turned it in.

We began to clear post the following week. That required we get clearance from all debts, or any other type obligation before we could leave the island.

Art and I went to the Top Three club, then to the American Legion to get cleared. SFC Melvin Capone from my old team was the manager of the Legion so he joined us. We began drinking beer and before we left the Legion we were both half shit-faced. We ran into SGM McCain, our company Sergeant Major. He chewed our asses up and down. We accepted the ass chewing as due us, and went ahead and continued our clearing.

We cleared the library, the PX, the Red Cross and every damn office it seemed on the island. I was surprised that I didn’t have to clear the steam bath, massage parlor and my favorite mama san, but they weren’t on the list.

Art and I went to the transportation office and picked up our airline tickets for the flight back to San Francisco. He was on a different flight than me, he was flying out a day later than I was.

“Art, I’ll wait for you in San Francisco, before you get there I’ll pick up my car, and I’ll meet you at the airport.”

“Okay, you better wait for me, we’ll drive across the states together, so make sure you wait.”

“No sweat, I’ll be at the airport. I don’t want to drive across the states alone.”

I spent most of the next day visiting with friends, and saying so long. We refused to ever say goodbye in SF. Goodbye has a tinge of finality to it that we neither needed, nor desired.

The next morning those of us leaving caught a bus over to Kadena and loaded onto a Boeing 707 jet plane. The plane was loaded with troops, mostly Marines and Air Force personnel. The hostesses stayed busy meeting all the demands of the troops, and the requirements of the aircraft crew. We flew for several hours and landed in Anchorage, Alaska. There we unloaded and moved into the terminal. The plane refueled, all the troops reloaded, and we took off for San Francisco.

After arriving in San Francisco the troops began to go their separate ways. They rushed to the airline ticket counters buying tickets for every imaginable stateside destination. I caught an army bus over to Oakland Army base. I checked in with the civilian who was in charge of the holding lot where the automobiles were parked after arrival from overseas. I spotted my little blue and white ford, and produced the necessary proof that it was mine. The man released it to me.

Before I left the lot I checked the oil, it was low and dirty. I checked the tires, and they were mostly bald and needed air. I checked the body, and it was rusting in several spots. The upholstery was stained and worn. I thought, I really don't want to drive this old wreck across the states, it wouldn't make it. I made an instant decision to trade it in on another model.

The civilian told me where several car lots were located. I started the car and drove down several streets, and saw a large used car lot. I drove into the lot, and a salesman came out to greet me. I was in uniform, so he knew that I wanted to trade in my car.

He stuck out his hand and said, "Hi Sergeant, how are you? Are you looking for another car, what would you like to do?"

I shook his hand and said, "Hello, I want to trade mine in on another car, I'd like to get a 1957 Thunderbird."

"Let's take a look at your car"

"Go right ahead."

He walked around the car and said, "I see that you've just come in from Okinawa, you have some salt damage by the rust, and it's an older car."

I knew that he had observed the Okinawa license plate on the rear, and of course I couldn't argue with his remarks.

"I know all that. I want to trade it on a Thunderbird. Do you have a 1957 Thunderbird?"

"Let's go in the office and check the records."

I followed him into his trailer office, and he thumbed through his records. He turned to me and said, "Sergeant, I don't have one on the lot, maybe I can find one for you."

"How long will that take you? I don't have a lot of time to look for cars."

It was afternoon now. He replied, "Just a little while. Have a seat and let me call around."

I sat down in a chair and lit a cigarette. He made several calls then turned to me and said, "Sergeant, I've been unable to locate a 1957 Thunderbird. I've found a 1959 model that has low mileage, and is I'm told in great shape. Would you like to take a look at it?"

"Sure, bring it around and let me see it."

About a half-hour later a young man drove into the lot with a black 1959 Thunderbird. I knew they had just washed it as water still beaded up on the rear window and trunk. I walked around the car and noted it needed at least two tires. I checked the trunk and the spare tire was flat. I then opened the hood and checked the oil it was dirty. The odometer reflected thirty-seven thousand miles. I started the motor, and it purred like a baby cat.

The dealer said, "I'll take three thousand for it."

"How much will you give me for my car?"

"I'll allow you eleven hundred for it."

I'll take it if you replace three of the tires, change the oil and filter, and give it a lube job." He agreed to do so.

We went to his office and he drew up the purchase contract while his mechanics serviced the Thunderbird. I signed it, and gave him the title and keys to my old car, and drove off the lot.

I returned to the San Francisco airport area, and found a hotel room for the evening. Art was due in the next day around noontime. I had lots of time to kill. I didn't want to just blunder around San Francisco as I didn't know the city. I followed the informational street signs and was able to find my way to Fisherman's wharf. I had a dozen and a half raw oysters, and a nice fresh garden salad. It was great just sitting there watching the tourists as they wandered from shop to shop, and to watch the kid hustlers as they worked the crowd. I divided my attention between the Sea Lions and the crowd. Watching the crowd I thought how strange, here are all these people having fun, sightseeing and safe, while a war is raging on the other side of the world. These people seem oblivious to the fact that American men and boys are being wounded and killed daily, in a far off country that perhaps they've never even heard of. I guess JFK will wake them up sooner or later, and let them know what's really going on.

I drove back to the hotel, parked and locked the car up for the night. No longer hungry, I walked into the small hotel bar. I ordered scotch and water, and found a seat at a three person table against the wall. I had my khaki uniform on. My Green Beret, cigarette pack and lighter I placed on the table.

There were two women and a man seated at the bar, and another two couples sitting at other tables. One couple got up and left, as I ordered another drink and lit a cigarette. The man and one of the women at the bar began talking loudly to each other. I surmised they were getting into an argument. I hoped they didn't, as I surely didn't want to hear a family argument on my first night back in the states.

The second woman at the bar got off her barstool and came over to my table and asked, "May I sit with you? I don't want to get into an argument with that man."

Being a natural born southern gentleman, I said, "Of course you may." I stood up and pulled out a chair for her. She sat down, and I moved my Beret and cigarettes out of her way.

"May I buy you a drink?"

Looking at me through heavy mascara laden eyes she replied, "Sure, I'll have a glass of wine." I walked up to the bar and ordered her a glass of wine, returning I placed it in front of her.

"Thank you. The woman at the bar is my girl friend, and that's her boy friend, but they're having an argument, and I don't want to get involved."

I replied, "It's obvious they're arguing."

The man at the bar shouted at the woman, "You phony bitch!"

The lady at the bar got off her stool came over to my table, and said to me, "Did you hear what he just called me?"

Looking at her I said, "Yes, I heard what he called you."

"Well! Are you going to just sit there and let him call a lady names?"

I looked at her like she was frigging nuts—she might have been.

"Lady, I don't know you and I don't know him and your argument or fight with your husband or boyfriend is yours and yours alone, not mine."

Glaring at me she said, "You're one sorry ass soldier. You won't even fight for a lady."

I stared at her in absolute stunned amazement.

I said, "Lady, the Army didn't train me, and doesn't pay me to participate in bar fights, family feuds, or gang bangs. Tell the bartender and let him handle it."

Her face grimacing, she snarled, "Fuck you!"

I smiled at her and said, "The idea does have a certain physical appeal to it, but not here, and not now."

She whirled around, and went back to her seat at the bar.

I asked the woman sitting with me, "Are all your friends like that?"

She laughed and replied, "No, I think she might have had one too many drinks today."

The lady at the bar and the man resumed their conversation. Within ten minutes he had his arm around her, and she was kissing him.

I pointed out their activities to the lady at my table and said, "Seems like your friends have made up, and all's right with the world."

She smiled and replied, "That's normal for those two."

The woman at the bar returned to my table, and said to the lady with me, "Are you leaving with us?"

"Yes," she replied.

She stood up and stuck out her hand. I stood up accepted it, and shook hands with her.

I said, "It's been a pleasure meeting you, and your friend."

She smiled and replied, I'll stay with you, if you want me to."

"That's up to you, it's your decision."

"If I stay, it'll cost you."

"Oh!, How much?"

"One hundred dollars!"

Smiling I said, "No thanks. Have a great evening."

She smiled in return and said, "Thanks for the drink, good luck Sergeant."

She and the other woman with the man left the bar.

The bartender came over to my table bringing me a new drink and said, "This one's on me, that woman's a dingbat."

I laughed, "Thanks for the drink, and I most definitely agree with you."

Finishing my drink, I said good evening to the bartender, and went up to my room. I took a hot shower, dried off, then turned on the television set. I watched a couple of shows, and the news then turned both the set and the lights off and went to sleep.

The next morning I woke up early. I cleaned up and put on a clean pair of khaki pants and shirt. I polished my jump boots again until they glistened. I went downstairs and had breakfast in the hotel restaurant, it was very good.

I left the restaurant and walked over to the elevator to go back up to my room. The door opened and the two ladies from the bar last night with two men were getting off the elevator. Neither man was the one from the previous evening. They both looked at me, and appeared to not recognize me. Small world I thought, I didn't speak to them.

I checked out of the hotel and drove over to the airport. I found a reasonably close in parking space, and went into the terminal. I found the gate where I expected Art to come in. I checked the flight information board, and his flight was on schedule. I found a seat and sat down. I began to read the paper I had picked up at the hotel. There were but two small articles on the combat actions in South Vietnam. They were on the back pages of the paper. Finished with the paper I lay it aside.

I studied the people as they rushed about the terminal. I thought, an airline terminal is the one sure place you can see some weird sights. People in all manner of dress, all types of baggage, barefoot kids, monks, jerks, you name it, and you'll see it in an airline terminal.

I walked over to a food stand and bought a cup of coffee. I sat on a stool and let it cool. Over a cigarette I continued to study the crowd. Finally, it was time for Art's plane to arrive. I walked over to the window and watched. Sure enough his plane taxied up to the gate on time. I stepped back and watched the passengers as they came through the gate, finally I saw Art. I walked over and greeted him. We shook hands as he stepped away from the crowd. We then went to the baggage section and recovered his B-four bag.

I led the way as we left the airport to the automobile parking lot. We walked out into the lot and I said, "Art, I don't remember exactly in which line I parked my car." He began to look for the blue and white Ford.

"How can you be so damn dumb as to forget where in the hell you parked your car?" he asked.

"It's not too hard to do. We're back in the states and everything's all new. Leave your bag here and go down that line, and I'll go down this one, holler if you find it," I said.

I was standing by the black T-bird, but he had no idea that it was my car. He went down the line, and I picked up his bag and placed it in the trunk of the T-bird. When he was down at the end of the long line of cars, I got into the T-bird started the engine and drove down to where he was standing. As I pulled up next to him I said, "Get in Art, if they stole my damn car, I'll just take one of theirs." Art looked at me like I was absolutely insane.

"Ken, you're off your frigging rocker! I'm not stealing a car. We wouldn't get five miles before they had us in jail."

"Art, I'll drive like a bat out of hell, and we can be out of Frisco in thirty minutes, and on our way to North Carolina."

He placed both his hands on his hips and said, "There's no way in hell that I'm leaving here in a stolen car. Where in the hell is my bag?"

"I put it in the trunk of the car."

"How did you do that? Let me get the damn thing."

Turning the motor off, I got out of the car and went to the rear and opened the trunk. He looked inside and saw that my bags were also in the trunk.

Art looked at me with a quizzical expression on his face and said, "Ken, you son-of-a-bitch, you traded cars!"

I laughed at him and said, "Yeah, I did. How do you like it?"

He slowly walked around the car, inspecting it with what I considered to be an expert eye.

He finally remarked, "It looks like a nice one, how many miles on it?"

"Around thirty-seven thousand."

"Great. Let's get on the road to Bragg." He got back in the car and began to inspect the interior.

"Art, we have electric windows, leather seats, air conditioner, radio, all the nice things. I bought it for three thousand, and he gave me eleven hundred for the Ford, so it's not a bad deal."

"Well, the trip home will let you know if you have a good deal or not."

I headed out of the city picked up Highway One, and drove south.

"Ken, let's stop someplace and buy some whiskey. We can have a few, and we'll have it tonight when we stop."

"That sounds like a good plan to me. The next little town I see I'll pull over."

As we continued to drive south I stopped in a town called Half Moon Bay and found a liquor store. We both went inside. Art bought a fifth of Jack Daniel's Bourbon, and I bought a fifth of scotch. We bought several bottles of cola to go with the booze then headed south again. He immediately opened his bottle and had a drink. I took a small swallow as he opened a cola and passed it to me.

I switched places with Art, and he drove for a while. We finally reached the small town of Carmel and found a motel. We checked in for the night. It was a beautiful little town. We were next to a marina, and the boats were beautiful at night with all their lights on. We sat outside the motel at a small table and chairs. We drank almost half his fifth of bourbon before we called it a day, and went to bed.

We woke up late the next morning, and I had a splitting headache. I opened my shaving kit found my aspirins and took three of them. I walked over to the other bed and shook Art awake. He could barely wake up. Jet lag, that devil of intercontinental travel had its grip on both of us. Finally, Art got up and waited until I got out of the shower. He took a shower as I shaved. He recovered his bag from the car and changed into a fresh uniform.

"Art, let's get something in our stomachs before we get on the road again."

He growled, "Hell yes, I haven't eaten since I left Okie. I had a small snack on the plane, I'm starving."

We went to the first restaurant we spotted and both ordered breakfast. To my great surprise and delight they had on their menu creamed beef on toast (SOS) I ordered that with two eggs over light on top of the SOS. I added a dash of Tabasco sauce, and the meal was terrific. Art ordered a T-bone steak and two eggs with potatoes. By the time we finished breakfast I felt alive and ready to roll again.

Art drove first and we went to San Luis Obispo, somewhere around there we picked up highway fifty-eight and headed east. We stopped for the day in a place called Indio. We checked into a small motel, then found something to eat, and went back to the motel. We watched the television for awhile and drank the remainder of Art's fifth of bourbon.

"Art, now you can have a man's drink. Try this scotch." I twisted the cap off the bottle and took a drink."

He reached for the bottle, took a swallow, made a face and said, "This taste like horse piss!"

"Art, old friend I accept your analysis. I personally have never drunk horse piss, so I don't know what it tastes like."

"Screw you, he growled!"

We drank less than a third of the fifth. He chased it with colas, and I used only ice and water. We called it a night and went to bed.

He woke up first the next morning, then woke me up and said, "Get up lazy ass and let's get on the road."

Pulling myself up I took a quick shower, shaved, brushed my teeth and dressed. We checked out of the motel, and resumed our journey east on highway ten. We bypassed Phoenix and then on to Tucson. We stopped along the way, bought another fifth of whiskey and continued driving.

Driving out of Tucson I was on a long desolate stretch of highway, speeding along about eighty-five miles per hour when out of nowhere an Arizona highway patrolman caught up with me and pulled me over. The patrolman got out of his car and walked up to mine.

"What's the hurry fellows?"

I replied, "Officer, we just returned from South Vietnam, and we're in a hurry to get back home. I know I was speeding a little, but it's been a long time since I was home."

"You might not make it going as fast as you were driving."

He took out a small booklet from his rear pocket placing it on top of my car. I assumed he was writing me a ticket. He then checked my driver's license. All I had was expired Florida state license.

He said, "I don't think this license is worth a damn, but I'll give you guys a break. I'll let you go without writing you up. But you had best slow down before you kill yourselves, or someone else."

"Thank you officer, I'll slow down. I really don't need a speeding ticket."

He got back in his car and drove away.

I turned to Art and said, "Well, we got away with that. Guess we better slow down for the rest of Arizona."

"Hell, we'll be in Texas pretty soon. Screw these Arizona hicks."

I slowly pulled away from the side of the road and maintained the legal speed limit for the next several miles. Inevitably, I found that once again I was exceeding the speed limit, but I kept a close watch on the rear view mirror for anything behind me.

We entered Texas at El Paso, and continued east on Highway Ten. We stopped and had lunch then continued east. Art was driving and the highway was really deserted. Just before we reached a small town called Ft. Stockton, I glanced at the speedometer and the needle hovered around eighty-five miles per hour. I heard a siren back behind us.

Art cursed and said, "Dammit Ken, I think we're gonna get stopped again!"

Disgusted I said, "Oh crap!"

Sure enough the Texas Highway Patrol car pulled up behind us as we pulled over to the side of the highway. The officer got out of his car and came up to ours.

He said, "Fellows, you're driving pretty fast aren't you?"

Art spoke up, "I don't think we were that much over the speed limit officer."

The officer then asked, "Which one of you owns the car?"

I spoke up and replied, "It's my car officer. I just bought it two days ago in California. We're both just returning from Okinawa, and we're anxious to get home. My grandmother is dying, and I want to get home before she does."

He looked at me, smiled and said, "That's a wonderful explanation. I used that one myself several years ago. It didn't work for me then, and I don't think it'll work for you now." He then asked, "Have you been stopped by a patrol since you left California?"

Art spoke up, "No sir officer. We've tried to maintain the correct speed all the way. I guess I just got careless, and was speeding a little on this long lonesome stretch."

The officer smiled at Art, and said to me, "Get out of the car and come around over here."

I opened the door and came around the car stopping in front of the officer.

He said, "I want you to do something for me."

"What do you want me to do Sir?"

"I want you to look on the top of your car right here." He pointed a finger to the roof of the car. "I want you to read out loud what's written there."

The hot Texas sun was beaming down, and sweat began rolling down my face as I peered at the roof of the car. I looked closer, and sure enough there was pencil writing on the roof of the car.

I began to read the inscription: "Stopped outside Tucson on 10/02/63, @ 90 MPH." I read it out loud, and then looked at the officer.

He smiled, then said, "Now you soldier boys wouldn't bullshit an officer of the law in the sovereign state of Texas would you?"

I knew we were trapped. I looked at the officer and said, "Officer, what the hell can I say, you caught us fair and square!"

He laughed and replied, "Well, one thing you could say is Mr. Officer, have a drink of my fine scotch whiskey, that I have open on the front seat of my car for a start."

I said, "Art, hand me that bottle of scotch."

Art opened the door and stepped out with the bottle in his hand. He twisted off the cap and said, "Mr. Officer, would you like a drink of the world's finest scotch?" He handed the bottle to the officer.

The patrolman said, "Here's to us kicking some ass in Vietnam."

He took a big swallow of the scotch, then took another smaller swallow, and handed the bottle to me. I took a big drink.

He said, "You guys better be careful. There are some real assholes in the patrol out here. So just watch your speed."

He walked away then drove off in his patrol car. When he left I spit on the writing on the roof, took out my handkerchief and rubbed all the writing off the roof.

"Art, that sneaky bastard in Arizona really did us a big favor. He set us up for he knew we're going to speed somewhere between Arizona and North Carolina."

"Either way Ken, that's twice we've gotten off. So maybe we best slow down a bit."

"Art, look at the road there's nothing for miles and miles but desert and hills and dirt. But you're right. Let's slow down and make it in one piece."

We slowly drove away from the road stop, and gradually increased the speed. I got in the back seat and told Art that I was going to catch a few Z's. I lay down and slowly dozed off. I woke up about an hour later. I reared up in the back and looked around we were still out in the prairie country, no other cars were in sight.

Art was driving and staring straight ahead at the road. His left arm was on the door sill with his hand inside at the top of the window. The window controls were in the middle of the console between the two seats. I slowly and deliberately reached over and lightly pressed the button that raised the window on his side.

His window rose slightly, his arm got caught and he hollered, "What the hell!" He jerked the wheel, and the car swerved sideways, he then straightened it out, as it seesawed back and forth across the road. He slammed on the brakes, and the car began to slow down.

I spoke up and said, "Art, I just wanted to see if you're really awake."

Needless to say, Art cursed me using every obscene word you can say in the English language. I thought it funny as hell, but it was really a very stupid thing to do.

We finally decided to call it a day just outside San Antonio. We found a motel, checked in, and then found a liquor store. I bought a fifth of whiskey and a bunch of bottle colas. We found a restaurant so we both ordered bar-b-cue and a baked potato. The bar-b-cue was good, and the sauce was excellent. The motel had a lounge, so we went there after returning to the motel.

We sat in the lounge for a couple of hours sipping beer, and I played the jukebox listening to the latest songs and artists. I heard some new guy named Johnny Cash, he was great. Of course I played my favorite, Elvis. Nothing was really happening. We left the lounge went to our room, and called it a night.

We were up early the next morning and checked out of the motel. We found a nice little family type restaurant and had a decent breakfast. We drove all the way to Mobile before we stopped for the day.

I remarked to Art, "My ass is worn out from sitting in this car seat."

"So is mine, but we don't have too much farther to go."

We found a nice seafood restaurant and had a great meal. I ate Cajun food for the first time, and found it to be delicious. We then had coffee.

Peering through Art's nasty cigar smoke, I said Art, "Tomorrow we'll get to Montgomery. I'll take you to the airport, and then I'll go see my family down in Lynell for a few days. I'll probably drive down to Miami for a few days, then I'll head back to Bragg."

Art replied, "Say hello to your Aunt and Uncle in Lynell for me, and tell'em I made it all the way with your Ford."

We turned in a little early that night, and were both up early the next morning. In just a few hours we were in Montgomery. I found the airport and dropped Art off. I waited until he had purchased his ticket to Lexington before I left.

I then drove on over to my home town of Lynell, Alabama. I spent several very enjoyable days with my aunt and uncle. It was a great time, and I really enjoyed being home again. I drove by the old cotton fields that I had plowed, planted and picked as a boy, but they were now bereft of all crops.

I then drove down to the creek that I went fishing in as a boy. The creek seemed much smaller than I remembered. Parking the car I got out and walked deep into the woods. I found an old log and sat on the creek bank, and leaned back against a tree. Closing my eyes I opened my wonderful memory book and leafed through the pages. I recalled me and sharecropper Bob fishing here, and up and down the creek. I looked around the woods, and remembered the nights of possum hunting, and days of squirrel hunting that I did here in these very same woods. The remembered smell of wild honeysuckle vines filled my hungry nostrils with a heady, exotic fragrance I had long missed, but never forgot. I lay back on the tree trunk and lit a cigarette. As the smoke slowly drifted aimlessly skyward, I thought all these wonderful memories, and my life could have ended in a split second back in that god forsaken jungle spot called Plei Hell. But it didn't. I stood up, looked once more around this old familiar forested spot, then returned to my car.

I placed flowers on family graves in the local cemetery. I also ran into a few friends that I had known from my school days. Once again, we had very little, if anything left in common. They were fat, happy, safe and secure in their world. But it seemed to me that I lived and operated entirely in another.

To me my world and that of all my Green Beret friends and fellow soldiers consisted of parachutes and planes, weapons, training, and continuous studying of the tactics of unconventional warfare.

Leaving Alabama, I then drove to Fort Lauderdale and visited with my aunts and uncles who lived there. It was nice to be back in Florida. The little house that I had purchased last year for my mother was a typical stucco home so prevalent in that part of the state. I had bought it sight unseen based on the recommendations of my relatives. It was supposed to be a good deal. My mom had moved here from Alabama, but she indicated to me that she most likely would return to Alabama to be with her friends. That was cause for some concern, as I had a small mortgage on the property, and didn't want it to sit unoccupied.

The skin show on Fort Lauderdale beach was better than ever. At thirty-three years of age, I certainly appreciated it, perhaps more than ever. I renewed my driving license, and I even won a few bucks on the greyhounds and Jai Alai.

One evening I was sitting in a bar over on Highway A1A just sipping a few cold beers. I thought, I accomplished my original reason for reenlisting a long time ago. I found Elona and the circumstances were such that it was really impossible for us to get together again. I'm sure she's happy, and the kids are well and growing up to be good citizens. Now I'm heading back to Fort Bragg, and who knows what destiny and the future holds for me. I've been lucky so far. I've completed two tours in Vietnam, and have only a few physical scars to show for that. I've got a few years in grade now, hopefully I'll achieve my goal of making Master Sergeant by the time I get twenty years in.

I hate the idea of staying a damned old bachelor all my life, but after experiencing two failed love affairs marriage might be too much. Maybe, just maybe, one of these day's I'll meet the right woman, get married and settle down to a normal life. Have kids and teach them everything I know. I'll give them all the things that I never had as a child. Oh well!

I finished my beer and went home. Tomorrow is another day, and I still have years to go, and miles to travel before this journey ends.

My uniforms were clean and ready to go. I packed my bag and said all my goodbyes. I aimed the little black T-bird north to Fort Bragg, North Carolina, and to my next military assignment, and next challenge in my life.

Stopping at a service station before I left town I had the oil and filter changed, the tires rotated, and the car lubricated. After paying the station attendant, I once again headed North on US Highway A1A.

I was anxious to get on the road and get back to Bragg, and see what my old outfit had in store for me. I had heard that the Fifth Group had moved its entire headquarters to Nhatrang, South Vietnam, and were now directing all SF operations in the country. That had to be an improvement. Surely I thought, they'll have enough supporting units and resources to get the job done. I knew for sure however, that Special Forces alone could neither pacify the entire country, nor win the war by itself.

I was deep in thought as I drove. I thought the war in Vietnam might soon be over if we keep killing the VC as we have in the past. I may never go back there. I have a couple years left on this enlistment, and then one more six year tour and I'll go over twenty years and be eligible for retirement. I guess I'll wind up as a bitter old bachelor, not married, and no children. That's an unpleasant thought, but I never want to experience a broken heart again.,

I wasn't paying close enough attention to my driving as I should have. I was going through the little town of Pompano Beach when this idiot ran a red light, and I swerved to miss him. He clipped the front of my bumper. I stopped and pulled over to the side of the street.

The other driver got out, walked over toward my car, and began berating me.

Getting out of my car I said, "Sir, I didn't run the red light you did!"

He was a fat man, not too tall, partially bald, and red faced. He replied, "I had the damn right of way, and it's not my fault."

"Mister, you're at fault, I didn't hit you, you ran into me."

At that moment a city policeman walked up and said to the fat man, "I saw the entire accident, mister it was your fault."

The man turned even redder and began sputtering then said, "This god damn snowbird ran the light, and caused the accident."

"Mister, don't call me names, and the officer saw you run the red light." He then without warning took a swing at me. I ducked his arm and grabbing it I twisted it behind his back and slammed him down on the hood of his car.

I then released him and said to the officer, "Do something, this guy is nuts."

The officer grabbed the man's arm and said, "Cool down mister before you get locked up." He then turned to me and asked, "What do you want to do?"

I checked out my bumper and replied, "Nothing, I'm on my way to North Carolina, and I don't have time to worry about this jerk. Charge him if you want to, or let him go, but I have to leave."

He said, "Go ahead and go. Don't worry about this. I'll take care of it."

I got back in my car and drove away. As I drove I thought damn, Art and I drove completely across the United States, and never had the slightest bit of problem, and in less than ten miles I have an accident. Oh well, crap happens!

On through West Palm Beach then up to Fort Pierce, then barreled on towards Jacksonville. I stopped at a convenience store and bought a bag of ice and a twelve pack of beer in anticipation of stopping for the night. This had been a long haul, and I was a little tired. I made the decision to stop and spend the night south of Jacksonville. I found a reasonably clean looking motel, and pulled in for the night.

As I was checking in with the motel clerk, two young girls came into the office and began to fill out a registration form for the clerk. I glanced at them. They were identical twins, blonde and young, perhaps in their late teens or early twenties, and definitely attractive.

They were dressed identically, both were in yellow shorts and a white halter top. They were built like brick shithouses, in short, they were gorgeous.

I paid the clerk, and he gave me the room key. Leaving the office I found my room, unlocked the door and took in only my shaving kit and a change of underwear and a shirt. Then I went back to the car for my beer and bag of ice.

The two girls came out of their room two doors from mine, just as I was about to reenter mine with the beer. They both smiled and said hello to me. I returned their greetings, and went on into my room. I filled the small sink with beer then covered the cans with ice. I knew that it wouldn't take too long to get the beer really cold. I walked outside to my car figuring I'd find a restaurant, and get a quick bite to eat. I watched the two girls as they got into a Oldsmobile convertible and drove away. They were very good looking women, I wasn't sure that I had ever seen identical twins before. Guess there's a first time for everything.

I spotted a small restaurant that advertised fresh catfish, and I knew that's what I wanted. I pulled into the restaurant parking lot and walked inside. I found a table and sat down. I ordered a cold beer and a fried catfish dinner. It was delicious, and I truly enjoyed it; catfish are my favorite fresh water fish. The waitress came by my table and removed the empty plate. I ordered another cold beer as the front door swung open, and the blonde twins walked in.

I watched as they selected a table they then ordered a beer each. I walked across the room to the jukebox, and deposited a quarter into the slot. I studied the selection menu and selected Johnny Cash's "*Ring of Fire*," then three songs by Elvis, and finally a wonderful old sentimental favorite by Hank Snow entitled, "*I'm Moving On*." I returned to my table and finished my beer. I ordered another from the waitress, and listened to the last of my selections.

One of the twins got up from their table and walked over to the jukebox. I wondered with some interest what type selections she would make. I also wondered does your choice of music reveal any personal psychological, or character traits. That's something to ponder over. She made her selections and glancing over at me smiled. I smiled back, and raised my beer bottle in a semi toast to her. Her first selection was Elvis singing: "*You ain't nothing but a Hound Dog*." I thought that's me, I'm horny as a double dick hound dog in heat. The next record came up and it was Cash's "*Ring of Fire*." Then a couple of artists I had never heard before sang their songs.

Finishing my beer I decided that I'd return to the motel, watch a little TV, then call it a night. The long haul from Fort Lauderdale to here had really made me a little tired. I left a tip for the waitress, and walked by the twins on my way to the door. They both looked up and smiled. I smiled back at them and left the restaurant.

Arriving back at the motel I parked and locked the car and went into my room. I checked the beer in the sink, it was really cold. I picked up one and popped the top on it. It really tastes good. I took off all my clothing except my jockey shorts, and then I flipped on the television and watched a show. The set had little rabbit ear antennas, and the picture was very poor quality. It was sort of boring. I turned it off and turned on the radio located on the small night table by the bed. I tuned in to a local country music station and just listened to it for a while.

I closed my eyes and let my thoughts drift across the pages of my memory. I had so many beautiful memories, and so many bad ones, to separate the two would be impossible. The images of people who had walked into and out of my life crowded forward as if in a giant parade.

The remembered faces of those I knew in Wurzburg, and those from Boblingen, Germany. I could see Charlie our houseboy in Laos. Then the beautiful red-haired prostitute in Amsterdam, my friend the Yard who was shot between the eyes, Jim and Willie, and the Mama San in the steam house on Okinawa.

What a weird assortment of people parading across the pages in my mind. There was no rhyme or reason for the diversity of people, and faces that came into my mental viewfinder.

Even as I pictured those people, there was also a parallel page of memories. I saw again my lovely Rachel, and Dotty, Betty and Elona. As quickly as they appeared they faded, and more violent images took their place.

I saw again Benny's shattered bloody foot, the destroyed trenches, the bloody deep gash in my hand, and the death dealing violence of exploding grenades. Lou falling into the punjii pit, our camp with dead mangled bodies, and body parts everywhere, the worry etched face of Captain Leadenham.

Looming large was the frightening ugly face of a moray eel at ninety feet beneath the ocean surface. Involuntarily I moaned. I shook my head opened my eyes, and made them all disappear.

Suddenly a knock on my door roused me further from my reveries. I wondered who in the hell is knocking on my door, and what could they possibly want? I was in my jockey shorts and not prepared to open the door. I thought whoever it is they're invading my privacy, and they deserve no frigging respect from me. Actually it pissed me off that someone was knocking on my door. I was rather tired and feeling the effects of several beers, and didn't need visitors for whatever reason.

Getting up from the bed I walked over to the door and opened it. The twins were standing there. They were a wonderful reason to open the door! I was hidden by the door as I had only stuck my head out to see who was there.

They both smiled, and one of them said, "Hello, can we borrow a couple of beers from you?"

Smiling back I said, "Sure! But you have to drink them here in my room. Florida motel law expressly forbids guests to pass beer from one room to another."

The second girl giggling spoke up and said, "That's fine with us we'll do that."

"Well, at the moment I only have my shorts on. Give me a minute and I'll slip on my pants."

The one twin who had spoken first replied, "Oh please, don't get dressed for us, we'll just pretend that you have your swimming suit on." With that she walked into my room and her sister followed. All thoughts of me being tired from driving disappeared as if they had waved a magic energizing wand.

Motioning to my sink I said, "The beer's cold, and it's in the sink."

The one girl walked over and removed three beers from the sink, drying them off with one of the small face towels hanging on the towel rack. She handed one to each of us, then she put three hot beers back into the sink. I popped the top on my beer, and the twins both followed suit.

"What do I owe the pleasure of your visit?"

One of the twins spoke up and said, "We knew you had beer as we saw you bring it in before we went to eat. So we thought it would be nice to have a cold beer with you, so the evening wouldn't be so boring."

"That's very nice of you two to think of livening up my evening. My name's Ken. What are your names?"

The one twin spoke up and said, "My name's Nicki, she spelled it out, and my sisters name is Micki, and she spelled out the name."

"Please, won't you two have a seat?"

The girl named Nicki sat down on one side of my bed, and Micki sat down in the small chair at the table. I sat down on the opposite side of my bed.

"Where're you girls from, and where're you going?"

"We're from Cleveland, Tennessee, and we're going to Miami Beach," Micki said.

"Have you been to Miami before?"

Nicki replied, "No, this will be our first trip there."

"You'll love it, the beach is beautiful, the night life is great, and there are a million things to see and do." I got up from the bed walked over to the little table picked up a cigarette and lit it.

Micki who was seated in the little chair asked, "Are all the men on Miami Beach built like you?"

I smiled at her and said, "I don't know if you're poking fun at me, or complimenting me, but the answer is no, you'll find all shapes, sizes and types. As beautiful as you both are, you'll have no problem in selecting whomever you desire." I walked over replacing my half empty beer with a full cold one, returned and sat down on my side of the bed.

Nicki bounced my own question back to me asked, "Where're you from, and where're you going?"

"I'm from Fort Lauderdale, and I'm headed to Fayetteville, North Carolina."

"Are you in the army?"

"Yes, I'm in a unit called Special Forces."

She laughed and said, "I saw some of those guys on television the other day, with their funny little green hats."

I replied "Those funny little green hats are called Berets."

"What rank are you in the army?"

"I'm a Sergeant First Class."

She laughed and said, "I love Sergeants!"

I replied, "I love blondes, especially identical twins."

Nicki reached over and ran her hand across my face, then asked, "Would you like to kiss me?"

I reached up taking her hand, held it in mine and replied, "Of course, every man in the world would like to kiss someone as beautiful as you."

She moved across the bed on her knees, rearing up a little placed her arms around me, and gently kissed me on the lips. Her tongue slipping easily into my mouth engaging my own in a delightful dance of love or lust, or both.

I pulled her tightly against me feeling her breast press against my naked chest. The kiss ended, but she didn't pull away.

She whispered, "I liked that" and kissed me again. Through mere reflex my hand drifted up to her breast, and I gently massaged it. My best friend immediately roared to life, in seconds my erection was as hard as a piece of coral rock.

Micki, who was still in the chair at the table spoke up saying, "Nicki, I have to go back to the room to check on something, I'll be back shortly."

Nicki, mumbled something as she continued to eat me alive with kisses.

I heard the room door close. I pulled back and checked. I turned back to Nicki, pulling her over closer to me, and gently pressed her against the bed.

"Why don't you take your top off?"

She without replying sat up and removed her halter top, she wore no brassiere. Her beautiful breasts tumbled out full and inviting. I kissed each of them teasing the nipples. I unbuttoned the side button on her shorts, slid the zipper down and slowly removed them, and then I removed her panties. She was a true blonde, her pubic hair a matching color to that on her head. I gently kissed and caressed her body as the sexual fires exploded, burning brighter and hotter. If she had any imperfection it was a very tiny mole on the left side of her left breast. My best friend was now as hard as railroad steel. I removed my briefs and moved over on top of her.

We then engaged in the wonderful act of physical love for several minutes, both reaching a mutual climax. I kissed her, and told her how wonderful and beautiful she was.

She giggled and said, "I hope all the men in Miami are like you." I rolled over to one side.

She sat up and said, "I'd better go check and make sure Micki is all right. You stay right here, and I won't be gone but a minute."

"All right, I think you and I should make love at least once or twice more tonight."

She laughed, and after dressing kissed me on the cheek and said, "Bless your lil' heart, we will sugar. I'll be right back."

She left the room, and I finished my beer and got another one from the sink. I refilled the ice in the sink from the bag, and added two more beers to the mix. I wasn't sure if she would come back or not, so I sat in the chair and lit a cigarette.

I heard a tap on the door and it opened. Nicki came into the room and said, "See, I told you I'd be right back."

I smiled and pulled her to me as she sat down on my lap. I pulled my erection up and out of the way. She kissed me, and I returned her kisses with equal passion. I slowly removed her top. Her breasts were truly a work of art. I thought, all women should have breasts these beautiful. I kissed each of them nibbling gently on the nipples. Then I noticed that she didn't have the small mole! I knew immediately that this was the twin Micki. I wondered what game are they playing? Maybe they're just out for kicks, and maybe this is their way of having fun.

Either way, I'm one lucky bastard to make love to such beautiful women. I picked her up and walked over placing her on the bed, and slowly removed her shorts and panties. Except for the tiny missing mole on her breast, she was absolutely identical to Nicki. I kissed and caressed her body as the sexual fires of desire swept higher and higher enveloping us both in its lustful flames. We made love, and I was able to prolong the action longer than earlier. My erection was magnificent in its rigidity. We finished in a mutual climax. I held her to me kissing her face and forehead, she passionately returned my kisses.

Finally, she spoke and said, "I guess I'd better go check on Micki, she doesn't like to be alone too long."

"I guess so. It's not good for a beautiful young woman to be alone in a motel it's too dangerous," I replied.

She got up and quickly dressed. She leaned over and kissed me gently on the cheek and said, "That was great sugar, I'll see you in the morning."

Returning her kiss I said, "Sleep well."

I didn't wake up until seven in the morning. I took a quick shower, shaved and then dressed. I walked outside and saw immediately that the twins had already left the motel. I turned in my room key, got in my car and drove away. I stopped at a local restaurant and had breakfast. As I sat drinking my coffee watching my cigarette smoke curl towards the ceiling I thought about the twins. They were beautiful, and I truly appreciated whatever game they were playing.

I drove on up to Fort Bragg, North Carolina, arriving there later in the afternoon. I was on Bragg Boulevard, and confirmed that the Tropical restaurant was still there. There were many new businesses built on the boulevard since I'd last been here. I drove on out to the Fort, and then to my assigned Special Forces Group area and headquarters building. I turned in my records and was then assigned to a company. I checked in with the First Sergeant, who told me I would stay in the barracks but just for tonight. He further explained that I would be moving to one of the Bachelor Enlisted Quarters tomorrow.

After finishing all the necessary processing, I went to the NCO club to get a bite to eat, and see who all I would run into. The first person

I ran into was the waitress Debby, my friend from Germany. She ran over gave me a kiss, and welcomed me back to Fort Bragg. We talked for a few minutes before she had to return to the bar.

I followed her into the bar, and there sat my buddy, Art Taylor.

He appeared to be a little tipsy. He stood up, calling out my name, "Ken, you sweet mother, let me buy you a drink."

We shook hands, looking around I saw that everyone in the bar was someone I knew. I spent the next ten minutes walking around the barroom and shaking hands with old friends. I shook hands with Billy Walton then with Billy Bowles, then Bert and Jaw, on around the room. Some of them had returned recently from Okinawa, but most had just returned from South Vietnam. Finally, I sat down at the table with Art, Doug and Vince. They were all drinking beer, so I ordered a round of beer from Debby.

Art told me he was living in the BEQ over by the golf course, and had an individual room there. He said, "Most of the senior bachelor NCO's live in the BEQ, and the Sergeants and below live in the barracks."

"I've never heard of senior sergeants having their own rooms and quarters, but it has to beat the hell out of living in the barracks."

We stayed there for about two more hours catching up on things around the Fort, Fayetteville, and more specifically on things going on in Special Forces. I learned that there was three groups now at Bragg, and one group the 8th SFG was now located in the Panama Canal Zone. There was also a SF training group for all the new people who were coming into Special Forces.

Art surprised the hell out of me when he said, "Ken, you're talking to the First Sergeant of Headquarters Company of the 3rd Group. Diamonds are trumps, and I expect a little more respect out of you."

"Well, I'll be dipped in shit, miracles never stop happening around here." I congratulated him on his latest promotion and new job. Then I added, "Son, you'll have to earn my respect. I bailed your shaky ass out of jail."

He grunted, "Screw you!"

I drank a couple more beers, and then pleaded being tired and left the club. I drove back up to the barracks found my bunk for the night and went to bed.

The next morning I checked in with the First Sergeant who assigned me as the company senior communications sergeant.

He said, "Go get yourself set up in the BEQ, get all your stuff put away, and check in with me tomorrow."

Leaving the unit I drove down to the club and ordered breakfast. I ran into Command Sergeant Major Hoskins who was also eating breakfast. I hadn't seen him since we returned from Dahlonega, Georgia, in 1960. I joined him and we had breakfast together. We shared a good laugh as we recalled the rotten moonshine whiskey he had bought, and how we both had gotten so damn sick from drinking it.

He said, "Ken, I'm Sergeant Major of one of the new Groups now, and I'm looking for Team Sergeants. We need some solid team sergeants with combat experience. Are you interested in coming over and taking a team?"

"Sure. I'm interested in having my own "A" team, but I don't think the group will release me as I just reported in."

"Well, keep it in mind. Things change around here so rapidly you never know what'll happen next."

I found the right people and was assigned a room over in the BEQ where Art and several of my other friends were also staying. I moved all my clothes into the building made up my bed put everything in place then stood back and inspected it all. It passed my inspection with flying colors.

I heard car tires screaming around a corner down on the street, and wondered who in the hell is that nut. I glanced out the window, and saw that it was my buddy Art. He was driving a 1957 pink and white Thunderbird.

Raising my window I hollered down to him, "Hey Art, the way you're speeding you must have stolen that car."

He laughed and replied, "No, this is my car. How do you like it?"

"It's beautiful. I'll swap you mine for yours."

"No way, my car is a better car then yours, mine's a classic."

"If you keep spinning around corners, it'll be a classic pile of junk"

I walked downstairs met Art, and looked his car over. It was really a beauty. He had the hard top on. It was just the model I wanted to buy when I arrived back in California.

Art said, "Here's the keys take it for a spin, and let me know what you think."

Accepting the keys I sat behind the wheel, adjusted the seat and started the engine. I pulled away and slowly drove around several blocks, it was really a great car, and I wished like hell it was mine. I returned to the barracks, and Art was standing on the sidewalk waiting for me.

"Art, you have a great car I really like it. How much did it cost?"

"Fourteen hundred bucks, and it's worth every bit of it."

"I agree, it really is a nice car."

Three days later my friend Jason showed up from Okinawa. He had taken a thirty day leave and gone home to Pennsylvania spending some time with his family. I was delighted to see him again. He was also assigned to a room in the BEQ that Art and I were in.

He had purchased a 1963 Thunderbird, and was as happy as a new father with it. Now the three of us had Ford Thunderbirds, Art had a 57, I had a 59, and Jason had the 63.

Art suggested we find out which was the faster automobile. The race was to be around two blocks and back to the starting point. We raced and he won.

He laughed and said, "Ken, I told you my car was faster."

"You were just lucky this time."

Jason said, "Okay Art, see what that piece of junk can do against a real car." They raced, and Art won again.

We loaded into my car and went over to club annex thirteen, and sipped beer for a couple of hours. Naturally, we had to listen to Art telling us over, and over what a terrific car he had, and how we were too inexperienced to drive against him.

We all returned to the BEQ, cleaned up, and went to the club for the evening. I was slightly dismayed at the number of unescorted women who were there. With so many of the troops deployed to Vietnam, some of the wives and girlfriends were being less than faithful. We all made out that night with women we had never seen before.

In November, President Kennedy was assassinated in Dallas. I was off that day and stayed glued to the television. The next day we had a mandatory formation for all the troops, and were informed that our Commander-in-Chief had died. It was a sad day for all America, indeed for the world. Then Oswald was killed. Art and Jason because of their height and military bearing, was selected as honor guards that walked alongside the President's caisson as it moved through the streets of

Washington. A Special Forces Sergeant Major placed his Green Beret on the grave of the fallen president in Arlington.

We all made it through the holidays. In late January Jason called Ms. Landers at the Pentagon. She arranged for him to get reassignment orders back to the First Group on Okinawa.

Ms. Landers was the Pentagon official in charge of all Special Forces assignments. If you ever needed, or wanted to go to a different location, or Special Forces assignment, she was the one person that could truly make it happen. She was instrumental in so many senior sergeant assignments it would be difficult to list them. She helped so many people so many times, that we all loved her. She was always compassionate, caring, concerned, and official.

I think my friend Master Sergeant Billy Walton was her favorite. He always got the assignments he asked for, and it was always back to Nam for him. He thrived on the challenge of combat. I admit it can become addictive. You study and train for years, then train and study some more. When you have the opportunity to put it all to the ultimate test, you go for it.

Tactics and techniques change, and you had better adapt and change with them. Weapons and the instruments of war evolve and change, some don't. You adapt and you win. I thought about the punjii stakes, they're as effective today as they were when a caveman first placed them outside his cave thousands of years ago.

A bunch of us old timers planned a party for Jason. We all met at the NCO club the following Saturday. Naturally, it was happy hour, and the drinks were half-priced. Actually, it was just an excuse to have a party. Any flimsy excuse will do when you really want to party.

As we sat there Jason leaned over and asked, "Ken, what are you going to do? Are you staying here at Bragg, or coming back to Okinawa?"

I thought for a moment and replied, "Jason, I don't really know. I might stay here a few more months and see what happens. I would like to make E-8 before I move on again. Hoskins wants me to come to his Group and take a team, I might try that." Jason left two days later.

I remained where I was for a couple of months. The First Sergeant informed me that I had been reassigned to a new "A" team, that would be going to Vietnam within two months. I didn't mind that. I just hoped that I would get on a good team with some experienced officers and team members.

We were getting a lot of new people into Special Forces these days. Most of them were neither highly trained, nor knowledgeable about Special Forces and its missions. I could only hope for the best.

I joined the new" A" team. Most of the team personnel I didn't know. All of them were much younger than me. The Team Sergeant, who outranked me, had recently joined the organization from the 82nd Division. I didn't question his dedication, just his experience and combat knowledge.

One evening a few days later, I was sitting with my friend SFC Billy Bowles in the club stag bar having a couple of cold beers, when this Sergeant First Class whom I didn't know came up to me and asked, "Are you Ken Fisher?"

Looking closely at him I said, "Yes, I'm Ken Fisher."

He stuck out his hand and said, "I'm Joe Tolomeo. I'm in the 6th Group as a radio operator."

I shook his hand and asked, "What can I do for you Sergeant?"

He replied, "I want to go to Vietnam on an 'A' team as a radio operator. I was told that you're on a team that's heading over."

"Yeah, that's true. I'm on a team that's going over in about three or four weeks. But what has that got to do with you wanting to go to Nam?"

Joe said, "Sergeant Major Hoskins told me about you. He sent me over here to see you, and to talk about me swapping jobs with you. He wants you to come over and be an "A" team Sergeant in the group."

I looked at Joe with renewed interest. I asked him, "Joe, do you really want to go to Nam as a radio operator?"

He smiled and said, "Yes!"

"Have you been to Nam before?"

He shook his head no.

"Have you been in combat before?"

"No, I haven't. But I want to, and this is my chance."

"Sergeant, it just might be your chance to get frigging killed. You know they're not playing over there, it's not a game." I had a sip of beer, then said, "Operating a radio might be the least of your team responsibilities."

"I know."

"Are you sure that's what you want to do?"

He nodded his head yes.

"I'll talk with the Sergeant Major tomorrow, and he'll let you know what's going on."

He bought me and Billy a beer, shook our hands and left.

Billy who had already completed two tours in Vietnam, and had himself been wounded said, "Ken, he's a new guy, and wants to prove himself. This is the only way he knows how."

I just nodded, I knew Billy was right.

Billy then said, "Ken, take Hoskins up on this. You should be a team sergeant, and he needs them. Hell, anyone can be a radio operator."

Again I just nodded, as I mulled it over in my mind.

The next morning I called Hoskins on the phone and asked him, "What's the situation with Tolomeo."

"Ken, the man has never been in combat and he wants to go now. He's afraid that if he doesn't the war will be over, and he'll miss out. Ken, I want you over here as a team sergeant. I have it all set up with TJ in your group. All you have to do is go see him. Let him know you want to come over, and it'll happen."

"All right, I'll check with TJ today, and if it's a go I'll be there tomorrow. If I come over tomorrow have Tolomeo over here tomorrow, so he can meet and integrate into the team as my replacement."

"No problem, he'll be there."

I walked up to group headquarters and went in to see TJ Black, the group sergeant major. TJ and I had been friends for several years, and were on a first name basis. He had been one of the team sergeants when we were on the classified mission in Laos.

He rose from his desk and gave me a bear hug, shook my hand and said, "Ken, how in the hell are you? It's been a while since we've seen each other."

I shook his hand and replied, "TJ, I'm doing good, been back here now for a couple of months, and watching all the changes taking place in SF."

We had a cup of coffee together, and I asked, "TJ, what's the story on the personnel swap with Tolomeo in Hoskin's Group?"

"Ken, Hoskins has the new group, and few experienced personnel for the teams. He needs help. Hell, you've been to Laos, and now to

Nam twice already, he needs your experience and steady hand, plus you'll make E-8 in no time."

"All right I'll go. If I can do some good and help teach the younger troops how to stay alive, and how to win, then we all win." I stood up and said, "I'll go get my gear and tell the team leader. I'll report to Hoskins today." We shook hands and I left the headquarters.

I went down to the company and told the First Sergeant, then my team leader, that I'd been transferred to the new group, and my replacement would be in today.

The team leader replied, "I don't like it, but I guess things will work out for the best."

I said, "I don't know my replacement. I just met the guy once, but I hope he'll be a good man for you." We shook hands and I left.

Going back up to group personnel I picked up my personal records, and new orders reassigning me to the sixth group. I then reported into the sixth and saw Hoskins.

He assigned me to a company and then to an "A" team as the team sergeant. During January through March my team was involved in extensive field exercises as we trained. I had a First Lieutenant Sully as the executive officer. He was an eager gung-ho guy. He was very intelligent and eager to learn. The team leader was a black Captain who had limited experience in special operations, but was willing to learn his job. We spent several days on exercises in Uwharrie National Forest, and the team slowly began to gel and segue into a cohesive unit.

In early March, I had a call to go see the Sergeant Major. Hoskins pinned a set of Master Sergeant Stripes on me, and gave me my promotion orders to E-8. I was one happy paratrooper. I had advanced from Private First Class to Master Sergeant in just over ten years, from 1954 to 1964. I was proud of myself, and ahead of my personal goal. The orders also changed my MOS to Operations Sergeant.

Hoskins said, "Ken, you're going to Intelligence Analysts School in Fort Holabird, Maryland. You'll be in the next class, so get your stuff together.

"What part of Maryland is the Fort located?" I asked.

"Downtown Baltimore" he said.

CHAPTER 41

Ft Holabird and Erin

In late March I loaded up my little Thunderbird with civilian clothes and uniforms. I left Fayetteville on Interstate Ninety-five. I drove through Richmond, around Washington, and then to Baltimore through the Harbor Tunnel. To my pleasant surprise I quickly found Holabird Avenue, and located the Fort with minimum effort.

I checked into the school office, and was delighted to learn that approximately twenty-four Special Forces personnel were also in my class. Roy Lane was there, Mike West and Bucky Comer were there. I thought this is quite a collection of men for one class.

After locating a room and a bed I recovered my clothes from the car, and made sure I hung them up, and was all squared away.

Then I drove across Holabird Avenue to the Hooligan Inn. I walked inside and most of my friends were already there. I joined them at the bar. Mike and Roy had been with me on Okinawa, and had also spent a tour or two in Nam. So we had a lot in common.

Roy, "How long have you been here?"

"I got here yesterday, I checked in early."

West spoke up and said, "I got here this morning."

Bucky and Jerry Willis were talking to two women at a table. One look at the women and I wasn't impressed.

I met the tavern owner, a lady named Betty Butler. She was around forty-years-old I guessed, and very pleasant. She seemed to enjoy the soldiers very much. They also spent a lot of dollars there, so that had to improve her attitude. There was a back room to the tavern, and Betty told me they occasionally had a small band. Couples danced primarily on Friday and Saturday nights. Several of us had a bite to eat and sipped beer for a couple more hours. I left, and returned to the billets at the fort.

Classes began on Monday morning. The instructors were all Majors and Lieutenant Colonels. I think they recognized that we were all combat veterans, and not young kids, so none of us had any problems. The courses of study weren't extremely difficult, but they did require some study as many of their intelligence techniques and terminology were unique, indeed rather exotic.

Friday, many of the guys especially those who were married all made plans to return to Fort Bragg for the weekend. I had no reason to drive the six hour one-way trip. So I decided to stay in Baltimore and look around the city. I'd never been here before, so it was all new to me.

Saturday morning I had breakfast in the small mess hall, and then drove downtown. Eastern Avenue was an interesting place. I found a small tavern named 'Busby's Downbeat' and had a cold beer. I listened to the bartender as he talked with another patron that he apparently knew. They were talking about a famous stripper. Apparently the patron had seen her show, and was raving about how beautiful she was, and what a fantastic body she had. I personally had never seen her, but I was aware of who she was.

I also learned that an area called the "Block" was the place for nightlife over on Baltimore Street. I left the bar and got back in my car. I checked my city street map and located Baltimore Street then drove over there. I parked and found a bar and walked inside. I knew I was in the right place as there were several guys hanging around, and either four or five women were in the place. I had a beer then left and drove back to the fort.

That afternoon I took a nap then took a hot shower and cleaned up. I decided to wear one of my two Hong Kong suits. I chose the blue one with matching tie and monogrammed shirt. I spit shined my loafers, and finally I was ready to hit the town big time.

I drove over to the Hooligan Inn and walked inside around seven in the evening. I sat at the bar had a cold beer and a Polish sausage sandwich. Roy and Mike walked into the bar, and the three of us sat at a table watching the crowd.

Roy said, "Let's go down to Baltimore Street, and see what's going on there."

Mike replied, "I'm game let's go."

So we got into Roy's car, and he drove down to Baltimore Street. He parked alongside the curb, and we walked into one of the taverns.

We found the bar, a large circular one in the center of the room, and I ordered us a drink. I looked around the darken room and noted that there was nothing but women in the bar, and by their appearance and activities I immediately assumed that we had walked into a lesbian bar.

About ten minutes into our stay, Roy began talking with one of the girls, and in no time he had his arm around her waist, and they were laughing and talking together. Roy was two stools away from me sitting on the other side of Mike.

I said, "Mike, I think this is a lesbian joint otherwise there would be some men in here with all these women."

He replied, "You're right, look at those two dancing together."

I turned and looked at the two women dancing together. The one mannish looking woman was leading the much younger girl. They were doing everything short of intercourse on the dance floor. It was a rather disturbing sight.

Roy was having a ball with the young woman he was entertaining.

I mentioned to Mike, "Roy is having fun, and possibly making out with this one."

Mike replied, "Roy better watch his ass, or one of these dykes will do him in."

Just as he finished his remark, a mannish looking woman walked up to Roy and tapped him on the shoulder. I looked at the woman. She was wearing blue jean pants, a lumberjack style shirt, and had a large metal belt buckle depicting a cowboy on a bucking horse. Her hair was short, almost a GI haircut.

Roy turned around. The woman grabbed him by his shirt front, and said rather loudly, "If you don't want your balls cut out, leave my woman alone!"

She then raised her right hand. She was holding a four inch knife. She moved it even with Roy's groin and growled, "I mean it asshole!" Without hesitation, Mike grabbed the woman by the wrist twisting her up and around into the bar. The knife fell to the floor.

He said, "You two get the hell out of here!"

I said, "Let's go Roy."

We walked up to the door, I turned and waited for Mike. He called the woman a nasty name, and shoved her out towards the dance floor. Several of the women began moving up towards the front of the bar. Mike walked through the door as I held it open. We both then walked outside. We got into Roy's car, and the woman who had threatened him came out of the door screaming and cursing at us. She again had the knife in her hand. We drove away, and left her still screaming.

Speaking to no one I said, "That's my first time in a lesbian joint and my last. Besides, all the women were ugly as hell."

We drove on for a couple of minutes and found a bar that was normal and had a couple of beers. Naturally our conversation was about the dyke who had the knife.

"Roy, how in the hell would you ever explain to the Group Commander how you lost your balls, if that bitch had used the knife?"

He laughed and replied, "I guess I would have to tell him I was defending my honor, or some shit like that."

Mike grunted and said, "Or some shit like that wouldn't get it. But it didn't happen, so no sweat."

I asked Roy to drop me by the Hooligan Inn as my car was still parked there. They planned to go to some bar out on Pulaski highway that Roy had heard about.

As I got out of the car I told Mike, "Keep Roy the hell out of those lesbian bars, he'll get you into too much trouble."

I walked back in to the bar. I glanced at my watch, it was only ten-thirty in the evening. I selected a seat at the bar. Betty was there, so I ordered a beer. I heard a band playing in the back room, so I assumed some people must be dancing. I paid for my beer, then I walked back to the dance hall. There were several couples dancing, and several people seated at tables around the dance floor. I selected a small table, and had a seat. As my eyes became accustomed to the dim lights, I glanced around the room. I didn't see any of my friends from school, so I assumed all the dancers and people were local civilians.

There were three women sitting together about three tables away from me. I naturally had to observe them much closer. One was red haired, one a brunette and the third a blonde. I couldn't see the blondes face, but the other two were nice looking. They appeared to be in their late twenties or very early thirties. As they moved their hands around I could see that none of the three were wearing wedding rings, which I found encouraging. I didn't particularly care for the first two, but the blonde I thought might be more interesting, if I could just see her face.

I decided to walk up to the band and request a particular tune. That would allow me to see her as I returned to my table. I walked up to the bandstand and requested the band leader play, "*Sentimental Journey*" and dropped a dollar in his small kettle. I turned and walked back towards my table. I saw the blonde's face. I almost stopped in mid-stride she was so beautiful!

I could feel my pulse speed up as I looked at her. Damn, she took my breath away. The band played a couple more songs then took a break. I figured hell if I'm going to meet her, I'd better figure out how.

Getting up from my table I walked over to theirs, "May I buy you ladies a drink?"

The redhead immediately said, "Yes," the brunette said "yes," but the blonde said, "No thank you."

I turned and asked the waitress to bring the ladies whatever they were drinking. She brought three Gin and Tonics.

I then asked them as a group, "May I join your table since I'm alone?"

The redhead said, "Yes," the brunette said "If you want to," and the blonde didn't reply.

I walked over to my table recovered my beer, then joined them at their table. After setting down I introduced myself to them,

"My name is Ken Fisher," and shook hands with each of them.

The red head said, "Hi, I'm Ethel," the brunette said, "I'm Doris," and the blonde said, "Hello, I'm Erin."

"What are three beautiful women like you three doing sitting here by yourselves?"

Doris responded, "We just stopped by to have a drink, we heard the band so we came back here."

"Well, I'm glad that you stopped by for a drink. I thank you for permitting me to join you. It has been a rather boring evening."

Ethel spoke up and asked, "Where's your wife?"

I replied, "I'm not married."

"Do you live in Baltimore?"

"No. I'm in the Army, and I'm here at Fort Holabird for a few weeks of school." That seemed to generate some interest on their part.

The band returned to the dancehall and began playing again. The band played one tune, and then began to play my request. I asked Erin to dance. She very reluctantly agreed to do so. I led her out to the dance floor, and we began to slowly dance to the music.

I asked, "Erin, are you married?"

She looked at me with a slightly puzzled expression and said, "No, I'm divorced."

I responded with a smile and said, "That's good. I don't especially like to dance with married women." I looked at her, and her grey-green eyes were mesmerizing pools of beauty. I found it extremely difficult to take my eyes off her face. I hadn't been this fascinated with a woman in years.

I asked, "Do you come here often?"

"No, I think I might have been here once before a long time ago."

The music finished and we walked back to the table. I managed to hold her hand as we returned to the table. We sat down, and at that moment I saw Bucky standing in the door. I called him over and asked him to join us.

He said, "Sure, Jerry is with me."

I replied, "Bring him in too."

Doris and Ethel seemed delighted, but Erin seemed annoyed. But I knew that I couldn't entertain and keep the interest of three women by myself.

I devoted all my time to Erin and finally, reluctantly, she seemed to show some interest in me. We danced several more times, and she seemed to loosen up just a bit. I was fascinated by her beautiful smile, and the whitest teeth I think I'd ever seen. Her blonde hair appeared to have been professionally done, and her outfit was the latest fashion, not that I know a damn thing about ladies fashions. I had also noted that Erin had a fantastic body on her. I couldn't remember any woman that I knew having a sexier body than she did. She was about five foot six, a couple of inches shorter than me, and she was very well developed.

Bucky and Ethel seemed to really hit it off. I found out Ethel was a widow as her husband had died in an auto accident. Doris was married, so she and Jerry had a more restrained conversation. As the evening wore on I asked Erin if I might drive her home. She politely declined. I thought it best not to push the issue.

The band finished their gig for the evening and put away their instruments. We all drifted back out into the bar area pulling two tables together.

"Erin, will you come here again?" I asked.

"Why should I? This isn't my type of place," she said.

I looked into her eyes, they had a mischievous glint to them as she smiled at me.

"I want you to come back because I'll be here, and I'd like to see you again."

"How do I know that you're not lying to us about not being married?" she asked.

I smiled and replied, "Erin, I have no need or reason to lie to you. What would I gain by lying? If I were married, I seriously doubt that I'd be here at all. I would have gone back to Fort Bragg to be with my wife for the weekend." She just smiled that mysterious smile, and let the remark pass.

Bucky and Ethel really seemed to be a twosome. Betty came over and announced last call for alcohol. We all ordered one last drink.

I said to Erin, "I hope you'll come back. I would really love to see you again."

Bucky spoke up and said, "Next Saturday they're having a charity event at the Fort Holabird NCO club, we should all plan to go there."

I jumped at the idea, and suggested to Erin that she and her friends should come. We could go together and participate. She wouldn't commit herself.

Bucky said, "I'm taking Ethel home, so I'll see you guys later."

We all walked outside. Erin and Doris after telling us how much they enjoyed the evening thanked us, got into a late model car and drove away. Jerry and I got in my car, and I drove back to the billets.

Jerry said, "I have a bottle of whiskey in my room, and there's a soft drink machine in the hallway, also an ice machine. Would you like to have a couple for a nightcap?"

"Sure, hell it's Saturday night, and there's nothing to do tomorrow, so let's have a couple." We went to his room then walked down the hall and bought three colas from the machine. He scooped up a bucket of ice and we went back to his room.

Jerry made us both a drink. I lit a cigarette and sat down in the small chair in his room. He sat on the side of his bed.

"Ken, I met this young woman tonight before we came back to the Hooligan Inn. She's something special. I made a date to meet her tomorrow."

"Congratulations Jerry. I hope things work out for you. To get your full attention so quickly she really must be special. Bucky seemed to really like the girl Ethel, I guess he made out tonight. He took her home about two hours ago, so I guess he stayed overnight with her."

"It damn sure looks that way, good for him."

We sat there and talked for a couple more hours drinking about half of his whiskey then finally called it a night. I was getting a little tipsy and knew I should go to bed.

I walked down to my room, took off and hung up my suit. I went to the latrine, and cleaned up a bit. I thought about my friend Jerry.

He had enlisted in the Canadian army in 1939, and had gone to England. There he trained with the Canadian army. He served with them for a couple of years. Later, he had been wounded in Italy. They found out his real age in the hospital and were going to discharge him. He transferred over to the American army, and remained there for the rest of the war. Jerry had enough years in now to retire, and he was talking about doing just that.

I thought about Bucky, he was younger than us, and a little wild. He drank too much, but was proficient in his job, and wasn't afraid of anything or anyone. He was a good man.

Finally, I thought about the beautiful woman, Erin. I hadn't been this attracted to a woman for years. To me, she was really something special. I recalled her dancing eyes, delightful laugh and dazzling smile. I sincerely hoped that she and her friends will come back to the Inn, and we can get together again. With pictures of her floating through my mind I went to sleep.

Sunday morning came around, and I woke up with a slight hangover. I took a shower, shaved and got dressed. I was too late for breakfast in the mess hall, so I drove off base and found a restaurant and had breakfast. I went back to the base and read the Sunday paper, "*The Baltimore Sun*". Then I read all my lessons of the past week. I reviewed a few manuals and text books in preparation for the coming week. The instructors had used many new terms in describing activities that were fairly common. But we had to use their terminology in the exams they gave every day.

The second week began, and the lessons became more demanding. We learned the intelligence cycle inside and out. We studied interrogation techniques, information analysis, and other elements of intelligence.

I had no idea if Erin and the other women would be at the Hooligan Inn or not, but I kept a positive attitude and hoped for the best.

Saturday morning I found a service station and had my little Thunderbird washed and waxed. I screwed off all day and finally that evening I showered and shaved for the second time that day. I wore my grey Hong Kong suit with monogrammed shirt and tie. My black loafers looked like glass. I threw on a dash of after shave lotion, and felt I looked as sharp as I possibly could. At eight o'clock that evening I drove over to the Inn.

I walked in and the band in the back room was playing. I glanced around the bar, and only a few people were there. Rather dejected, I walked back to the dance hall and looked through the doors. I immediately saw Erin and Ethel with Bucky. I immediately headed for their table. Erin saw me and flashed that brilliant smile. I knew she recognized the pleasure that must have registered on my face. I joined them at their table, and Bucky immediately ordered me a drink. He and his girlfriend Ethel were drinking tequila, and chasing it by sucking on lemon slices. Erin was sipping on a gin and tonic.

I sat down at the table looked at Erin and said, "I'm so happy that you decided to come tonight, I've been worried all week that you wouldn't show up."

She smiled and replied, "Ethel asked me to come so she could meet Bucky, and she's my friend."

"Well, if she got you here, then she's also a friend of mine." I drank my drink rather rapidly and ordered another; I lit a cigarette and offered one to Erin.

She refused saying, "I very seldom smoke if ever. I don't really like cigarettes."

"Well, it's a very bad habit, however I've had the habit for several years. But I do enjoy it."

She replied, "To each his own poison."

We danced a couple of tunes, then Bucky suggested we all go to the Holabird NCO club, and find out what the charity event was all about. I agreed as that meant I would have more time with Erin. We all entered my car, and I drove over to the club. We walked into the lounge. I didn't know what to expect, as I'd never been here before. It was a nice club, not overly large, but comfortable and intimate. Bucky found us a table, and the four of us sat down. I ordered a round of drinks.

About five minutes later a man in a red jacket came up to me, and told me I was under arrest.

He said, "You're sitting at a table that only permits tobacco chewing, and you are smoking." He held up the edge of the table cloth, and sure enough there was a small sign attached that said tobacco chewing only.

I played their game, and he led me off to jail. It was a small area with plastic bars and ribbons around it. I stood inside the enclosure and looked around for Erin. She was talking to the main jailer, and he was obviously telling her the bail rules. I saw that she gave the man a five dollar bill. He announced to the crowd that the prisoner from table twenty was being bailed out. The crowd applauded. I felt sort of silly, but it was all for charity, so I played the game.

I was released, and went back to the table. I thanked Erin for bailing me out and gave her back the five dollars. We stayed for another hour, then I suggested, "Let's return to the Hooligan Inn and listen to their band for awhile." Happily, they all agreed. So we left the NCO club. I never knew what the charity was for, but it didn't matter.

Arriving back at the Hooligan Inn we walked into the dance hall. I saw Jerry at about the same time he saw me. The four of us joined him and his girlfriend, whom he introduced as Lillian. Jerry ordered us a round of drinks, and I asked Erin to dance. She accepted my invitation, and we danced two complete tunes. As we danced I pulled her a little closer to me, and kissed her alongside her neck.

She pulled away and said, "Please, don't do that. We're out in public."

I replied, "Would you like to go somewhere more private?"

She smiled, "No, that's not a very good idea."

It was still early, so I knew we would have a long evening. I ordered the table another round of drinks, but Erin insisted that she didn't want another.

Around midnight, Bucky said he was taking Ethel home.

I looked at Erin and asked, "May I take you home?"

She shook her head and replied, "No, that's not a good idea. I'll have Bucky and Ethel drop me off at my place."

I walked her out to Bucky's car, which was parked back of the club. I waited until Bucky and Ethel had gotten into his car. I pulled Erin closer to me and asked, "When may I see you again?"

She replied, "I'll try and get here Wednesday night, is that a good night?"

I said, "Any night that you can get here is a good night for me."

She leaned forward and kissed me on the cheek, and said, "Thanks for a nice evening out. I hope to see you Wednesday evening."

They drove away, and I returned to the bar in the club. I ordered a Scotch and water, and struck up a conversation with Betty the owner.

Betty poured herself a drink and said, "Ken, that beautiful blonde might be too high class for you. She might go for a Colonel or General, but I don't think Sergeants are her style."

"Betty, you might be right. But for now there are no Colonels or Generals around here—she's stuck with a poor ass Sergeant—me!"

"Well, Sergeant Fisher, I wish you good luck."

Lifting my drink in salute I replied, "Thanks a lot, I need all the luck I can get."

School started up again on Monday, and once again we were deeply engaged in mastering the mechanics of combat information and combat intelligence. Differentiating between information and intelligence seemed to be a problem for several members of the class.

I heard on the local news that my military hero, General of the Army Douglas MacArthur had died. I really felt bad. I had admired him since I was a little boy and had first heard of him in 1941. I had a copy of the speech he had given at West Point accepting the Thayer Award a couple of years earlier. He had given the speech without any written notes, and to me it was equal to "*Lincoln's Gettysburg Address*" as a beautiful and enduring American oration. Captain Leadenham, my former team leader in Vietnam knowing my admiration for the General, had given me a recording of the speech.

Wednesday finally arrived. After classes and after dinner, I cleaned up and dressed in a casual outfit. Around seven-thirty that evening I drove over to the Inn, parked the car and went inside.

Betty was there and said, "Hi Ken, you're in luck, your girlfriend is back in the back with Bucky and his love."

I smiled and replied, "Thanks Betty, I'm glad that you're looking out for this old low ass Sergeant's welfare."

She laughed, "I just hate to see a grown man cry."

I walked back into the dance hall area and saw Erin with Bucky and Ethel. They were laughing, and seemed to be enjoying themselves very much. I walked over behind Erin placing my hands over her eyes and said, "Guess who?"

She responded, "I don't have to guess, I recognize your voice, it's Ken."

I laughed, "Bingo, you win the prize for the evening."

Bucky spoke up and said, "What a hell of a prize you are."

"For that, I won't give you any more test answers next week, so you'll fail," I replied.

I sat down and ordered a drink for the table and asked Erin, "How've you been since Saturday?"

"I've been okay, working and doing all sorts of normal things, nothing really out of the ordinary."

"That's great, where do you work?"

"I work in the Federal Reserve Bank here in Baltimore."

"That sounds like a very important job."

Bucky walked over to the jukebox, inserted some coins, studied the menu then made several selections. His first selection was a love song by Jerry Vale, and then one by Tony Bennett, both beautiful songs and by great artists.

I asked Erin to dance and she accepted. There were about four other couples in the back, they all got up and began dancing. I pulled her closer to me, but made no further advances. She was a good dancer, better than I was and I told her so. We sat back down at the table while Bucky and Ethel danced a couple of tunes.

"Erin, do you have any children from your marriage?" I asked.

"No, I don't have any children, would it bother you if I did?"

"No, It wouldn't make any difference to me, I think you're a beautiful woman, and if you had children, I'd certainly accept them."

She asked, "How much longer are you going to be here in Baltimore?"

"I think we have about three more weeks, and then we'll return to North Carolina."

"Did you know that Bucky has asked Ethel to marry him?"

A little shocked I replied, "No, I didn't know that, he hasn't mentioned that to me. Not that he has to, but that's a surprise." Pausing, I continued, "They really haven't been going together very long, but I guess when the love bug bites you time is of no major importance."

She said, "Maybe it was love at first sight, do you believe in love at first sight?"

I gave her a long steady look and replied, "Yes, I do believe in love at first sight. As a matter of fact, I believe in love."

She smiled and said, "You're a romantic."

"I don't know what a romantic is, but I do believe in love, it's one of our strongest emotions. Wars have been fought for love, sacrifices have been made in the name of love, indeed to love and be loved is one of our deepest desires. I once had an Army Chaplain tell me that every person has an infinite capacity for love, and I believed him. Do you believe that a person can love more than once, or love more than one person?"

She softly replied, "Yes, I believe that."

The evening passed too quickly, and the bar began to close. I asked, "May I drive you home?"

She declined, and said, "I'm spending the night with Ethel, so I'll ride home with her and Bucky."

"May I see you Saturday night?"

"No, this weekend I'm taking my mom and dad out to my brother's house, and we're going to just spend some time together. So I can't make it this coming weekend."

"Well, let Ethel know when you're coming back here, she can tell Bucky and I'll know."

"All right, I'll let Ethel know."

We all left the Inn and walked out back to Bucky's car, they got in first. I stopped and pulled Erin to me, and tilting her face upward kissed her. She was a little resistant, but gradually relaxed and kissed me.

I said, "Good night beautiful, I hope to see you soon."

I didn't see Erin all week. The following weekend Roy Lane and I drove over to Washington, D.C. and visited several of the national monuments. My first trip to Arlington National Cemetery left me deeply impressed with its quiet beauty and simplicity. I thought someday I'd like to be buried here, if the army will permit me. The Lincoln, Washington, and Jefferson memorials all were truly impressive. After viewing the memorials we returned to Baltimore, and stopped in at the Hooligan Inn.

There were a few of our classmates at the bar and the small band in the back was knocking themselves out. Most of the SF personnel had returned to Fort Bragg to be with their families over the weekend. I knew Jerry and Bucky both were spending time with their girlfriends here in Baltimore.

I suggested to Roy that we go over to a famous restaurant that I'd heard about, and get a really good seafood meal. He agreed, so we got into my car and using my city map I located the approximate address of Hausner's Restaurant on Eastern Avenue. I drove downtown and found it. We located a place to park on the street, and joined the line of customers that were waiting to be seated inside.

Once inside we entered the little bar located on the right entrance of the door, it seemed to be more of a stag bar than a family bar. They had this beautiful painting of a nude woman back of the bar, and she was truly lovely. We had a quick drink, then we were escorted to our table.

I was amazed at the amount of beautiful statuary that was in the room. There were several gorgeous paintings, and many other works of art. It was truly a top of the line restaurant, and probably the finest in all of Baltimore. The meal was equally as impressive, and their deserts were unparalleled as to their size and beauty. I didn't however purchase desert after a huge meal of baked salmon and crab cakes.

Monday rolled around, and we had two weeks left before graduation. The examinations became more frequent, and the intensity of the instructions increased as we approached the climax of the course.

On Wednesday we were presented with a new class entitled: "Lessons from Vietnam." The instructor was a Major, and he began by telling us several things that our forces were doing wrong in Vietnam.

He said, "Let's take the assault against Camp Plei Hell out by the village of Plei Mrong for example. This was the first Special Forces camp attacked since our forces were introduced into the country. Their mistake was not to have a second wire fence inside their first one. If they had they could have channeled the attackers rather than allowing them free rein once they breached the main fence."

I raised my hand.

The major said, "Yes, Sergeant Fisher?"

Standing up behind my desk I said, "Sir, I detect a fallacy in your reasoning."

The Major replied, "Why do you say that Sergeant?"

"Sir, had an internal fence been constructed so as to channel the attackers, it stands to reason that it would also by its very construction, channel the responses, and the location of the camp defenders themselves!"

He replied, "Sergeant, your answer suggests that you have limited experience, and know very little about fixed camp defenses."

An audible moan could be heard from the class, as most all of my Special Forces classmates knew that I had been at Plei Hell.

I asked, "Sir, have you ever constructed a camp in the jungle, fortified and defended it, while training natives who can't understand one word of English, and who know nothing about weapons, defenses, or combat operations?"

He stared hard at me, then gruffly replied, "No, I haven't. Have you?"

I stared at him a few seconds, smiled and replied, "Yes I have!" Then I sat down.

Wednesday evening I was in my room when the building CQ came to my room and said, "You have a phone call downstairs."

I went down to the office answered the phone and it was Bucky.

He said, "Ken, Erin is over here at the Inn, why don't you come over for a while."

I'll be right there, I said. I dashed upstairs, cleaned up a bit, brushed my teeth and dashed a splash of after shave lotion on my face and left for the Inn.

They were sitting near the rear of the bar area at a small table, so I joined them there. We all exchanged greetings, and I ordered a fresh round of drinks for the table.

I asked Erin, "How've you been this past week?"

She smiled and said, "I've been well, how about you?"

"It's been a very long week. I missed seeing you I missed being with you, so therefore it's been a lousy week."

She laughed and replied, "Well, I missed seeing you too. Does that make you feel better?"

"Only if you promise not to ever make me suffer like that again." She smiled and just patted my hand.

Bucky spoke up and said, "Ken, Ethel and I are getting married this June, and we want you to be best man."

I feigned surprise and replied, "This is rather sudden. Are you two kids sure you want me at your wedding?"

Ethel said, "Ken, Erin is going to be the bridesmaid, and with you as best man it'll make the wedding much more memorable."

"Well, if the army doesn't have other plans for me, I'd be delighted to be at your wedding. What date have you selected for the big event?"

She replied, "It's on the second Saturday of the month, we'll be married around noon time."

I walked back into the dance hall part of the Inn and deposited several coins in the jukebox, then selected several songs that I thought appropriate for the evening. I played a couple of Dean Martin's songs then a couple of instrumentals, and finally one by Elvis Pressley. I invited Erin to dance and she accepted.

All of the tunes I selected were for slow easy dancing, so I pulled Erin closer into me as we began dancing. As we began the second dance I kissed her alongside her neck and said, "There's no one here but us, so don't plea the public is watching."

She just smiled at me.

I then said, "Erin, I think that I'm falling in love with you, I'm not sure if that's good or bad, but it's true. I truly missed seeing you last week, in fact I was miserable."

She looked at me and gently pulled my head down and kissed me. I returned her kiss with a passion. We danced another tune then returned to the table.

"Erin, may I take you home this evening, or do you have to baby sit the sweethearts here?"

She laughed and replied, "Sure, you can take me home."

We stayed a little while longer, and then we called it a night.

She got into my car and gave me directions as I drove to her address. I parked and walked her up to her apartment on the second floor of a small apartment building.

We stopped at her door and I asked, "May I come in for a nightcap?"

"No, I don't think that's a good idea. We don't know each other that well, and we have lots of time."

I said, "That would give us more time to get to know each other, don't you think?"

She smiled and said, "No, I'll see you Friday night." With that she kissed me goodnight, unlocked her door and stepped inside.

I returned to the Inn, Bucky and Ethel were still there. I had a quick word with them and left for the barracks. It was midnight. I went to the latrine then went to bed. Thursday and Friday we had psychology classes. Late that afternoon we had an examination on the two days presentation. It wasn't too difficult, not even tricky.

Friday night I went to the Inn and met Erin there along with Bucky and Ethel. Doris was also there. This was the first time I had seen her since we first met. I exchanged greetings with all of them. We then moved back into the dance hall and found a large table. Shortly thereafter Jerry and Lillian came into the room and we pulled another table together, a small impromptu party began. The band was playing and couples were dancing. It would be a fun evening.

My friend Danny Rhodes joined us, and he and Doris seemed to get together rather quickly. About an hour later Danny and Doris left together.

I remarked to Erin, "All your friends seem to be making out just fine. Bucky and Ethel are getting married, and now I hear that Jerry and Lillian are also getting married. Do you think that's some type of a trend, an infection, or maybe an indicator that you and I should also get married?"

She laughed and replied, "No, I don't think so. Maybe they have more in common than we do."

I replied, "I think we have a lot in common, we're both young, unmarried and attracted to each other. I think that's commonality enough."

She looked at me with a very serious look and asked, "Ken, are you proposing?"

"I don't know if I am or not."

She leaned over and gently kissed me and replied, "Ken, let's take our time, you've never been married and I have. We don't want to make a mistake. Mistakes are easy to make, and often very difficult and costly to correct. I made one the first time, so I want to be very sure before I ever get married again."

I looked into her beautiful grey-green eyes and replied, "I understand what you're saying, and I agree with you. I certainly don't want to make a mistake, and I don't want you to make a mistake. Let's just both wait and see where our relationship leads, and find out what's in the future for us."

She nodded her head in agreement.

She said, "I told my dad that I'm dating an army guy who jumps out of airplanes. He said, "He has to be crazy, and you must be crazy for dating him."

"Well, I surely hope he really doesn't feel that way."

She smiled and replied, I don't think he really does. However to a degree, I agree with him. Jumping out of perfectly good airplanes wouldn't be my cup of tea."

"I'd like to meet your father. I probably would get along very well with him, and with your mother. All my family loves me, so I can't be a monster."

I leaned over and gave her a tender kiss on the lips. Public or not, she accepted it as our tongues touched briefly, enhancing the beauty of the moment.

Around midnight I suggested that we leave. We bade the rest of the group good night and left the dance hall. Betty was back of the main bar, and as we left I winked at her and gave her a thumbs-up sign.

She smiled and mouthed the words, "Good Luck."

I drove Erin home to her apartment. She asked if I wanted a cup of coffee.

"Certainly, I could use a hot cup of coffee this time of the night."

She unlocked the door, and we stepped into her apartment. It was a one bedroom one bath type apartment, and was in my view very tastefully decorated. There was a small loveseat in the living room and a small table. I took a seat on the small couch and lit a cigarette. Erin found and brought me an ashtray. She then put on a small pot of coffee on the small electric stove in the kitchen area. Shortly thereafter she joined me on the small couch, and set the two cups of coffee on the small cocktail table.

I pulled her close to me and said, "Erin, I really am in love with you, but I'm a little confused as to how you feel about me. Maybe I'm just kidding myself, and hoping that you care for me."

She kissed me tenderly on the lips and replied, "Ken, I do care for you. I may be falling in love with you also, but I'm so afraid of making another mistake. I couldn't stand facing my family and friends, and telling them I made another mistake. I couldn't face myself and know I had made another stupid mistake. So I hope that you understand my reluctance and resistance to romance."

I caressed her face and kissed her on the forehead and replied, "I do understand, I'd also hate to make a mistake. I promise you we'll take our time, and find out if marriage is really for the two of us. We have no reason to rush into anything. We'll be out of school next Friday, and then we'll return to Fort Bragg. We'll have the graduation ceremony next Friday morning then get released. Would you like to come to the graduation ceremony?"

She replied, "Sure, I'll be there. I know that Ethel and Lillian will be, so you guys will have lot of admirers."

I kissed her passionately on the lips and she returned my kiss with equal passion. My hand reflexively moved to caress her breasts. She had large breast they were full and round. I caressed the one tenderly and she moaned slightly. The flames of passion now stoked burned red hot, and as the flames swept higher I felt that primal urge for release.

Erin pulled back from me and said, "Ken, we mustn't do this, I can't do this. It's not right, we have time for this in the future!"

Stunned I replied, "Erin darling, if you say stop, we stop. I don't want to, but I love you too much to rush you into having sex if you're not ready."

I reached over and picked up my cup of coffee and took a small sip. I then lit a cigarette and leaned back on the small sofa.

She put her hand on my face and said, "Ken, I'm so sorry, I shouldn't have let you go this far."

I smiled at her and said, "Erin, its okay, perhaps it's me that has gone too far, and pushing too hard. As you said we have lots of time to make love. It's late, so I'd better leave for tonight. How about me picking you up tomorrow night around six, and we'll go out for dinner?"

She replied, "That's a good idea. I'll be ready, and I know a good German restaurant we can go to."

She rose from the small couch, and I gently pulled her to me giving her a quick kiss, she returned it with an equal fervor. She then again apologized to me for allowing us go so far.

"Don't worry about it darling, I'll make up for it one of these days a dozen times over."

She walked me to the door; I kissed her good night and left. I drove back to the Fort parked my car and went upstairs to my room. I took off my clothes and hung them back into my locker. As I lay on the bed I thought about Erin and tried to truly understand her reticence about making love. Finally, I conceded that perhaps she's right. Why should she have sex with a man that she really doesn't know? Oh well, time will tell us both if we are right for each other or not. I finally fell asleep.

I began dreaming that Erin and I were in some unknown beautiful place, soft music playing, and somehow we were both naked. The bed we were on was soft and enticing. I kissed her and she returned my kisses with a hungry intensity. In my dream she pulled me on top of her. We began that beautiful physical journey to sexual fulfillment. We made love for several minutes and then it all ended.

I woke up from my dream, and realized that I'd just had in medical terms, a nocturnal emission. I recognized it in more earthy, manly terms as a beautiful wet dream. I got out of bed removed my shorts, cleaned up a bit and went back to bed minus my underwear. No big deal!

The next night I picked up Erin at six in the evening, and after giving her a hello kiss she instructed me on directions to take. We went instead of the German restaurant to a seafood restaurant out on Bel Air road. The name of the restaurant was the "Blue Harbor." I was introduced to my first crabs there, and they were absolutely delicious.

We then went to a lounge out on Pulaski Highway, had a few drinks then danced for a couple of hours. I suggested we drop by the Hooligan Inn and see what's going on there. She gave me street directions, and I finally arrived back at the Inn. Bucky and Ethel were there, so we joined them for about two hours. I then drove her back to her apartment. I didn't go in as I didn't want a repeat of the previous evening. I kissed her good night, and we made a date for the following Tuesday evening.

Tuesday morning at our "lessons learned" class the Major I had suggested was wrong in his approach to camp defenses was again our instructor. He began his class by asking me to stand. Puzzled, I stood up.

He said, "Sergeant Fisher, I was totally unaware that you were one of the defenders at Camp Plei Hell. I talked with our tactical department and they all agree with your reasoning. I stand corrected, and I applaud you for correcting me, and indeed, for the great defense of your camp."

I replied, "Major, This school is for teaching, and we all learn something every day from each other."

Tuesday evening I picked Erin up, and she suggested we go have a bite to eat at a German restaurant. She directed me across town to a family type restaurant named Spitzenkrantz's. I had a couple of German beers with my meal, and she had a small glass of wine. As we ate I comparing the food here with the dozens of meals that I'd consumed during my years in Germany. Truthfully I could tell no difference—or else I had long forgotten. After leaving the restaurant we drove down to the Inn and had a few beers with Jerry and Lillian. I then drove Erin home, she promised to be at the graduation ceremony on Friday morning. I kissed her good night and returned to the barracks.

Wednesday and Thursday nights I stayed in the barracks and reviewed all my notes and notebooks. I spend a lot of time on photo interpretation. Friday morning we had a final course examination lasting about two hours. I knew I passed, so I had no worry there. At eleven in the morning we fell outside on the small parade field dressed in our Khaki uniforms. The men with the Green Berets were so obvious in the formation other than just their berets. They were older; most of their chests were filled with ribbons and decorations, some covering three wars. The other troops were younger, and had few if any ribbons or badges, but I knew they too would get their chance at combat one of these days.

I looked over at the spectators stand and saw Erin, Ethel, Lillian and Doris. I noted also that several of the wives from Fort Bragg had made the trip for the ceremony.

A Master Sergeant from San Juan Valley, California, who was in a reserve Special Forces Group, was the honor graduate. We marched by in a small review parade, and then we were released from the school.

Many of the SF men gathered over at the Hooligan Inn some with their wives, and several of us with girlfriends. Everyone was having their favorite drinks, and making remarks on the course of instruction we had just completed. One by one the crowd began to thin out. We bid those leaving so long, see you later.

Finally, there were just eight of us left, me, Jerry, Bucky, Danny and the four women. I suggested to Erin that we leave, and I'd take her home. She agreed, so I said so long to the group. As we left I was stopped by Betty.

She hugged my neck and said, “Ken, I’m happy to have known you, I hope you’ll come back to Baltimore again, be sure and stop by and say hello to me.”

I hugged her back, “Betty, I promise you I’ll be back, and for sure I’ll stop and have a drink with you.”

We then left, and drove over to a small restaurant and had a sandwich.

“Erin, I have your address and phone number, so I’ll call you often, and when I can I’ll be back up here to see you. I don’t know what the future holds for me or for us. I hope it will be kind to us both. I love you and I want to marry you, and I hope you feel the same way. If you really don’t you should tell me now, and I’ll just leave.”

She grasped my hand and replied, “Ken, I do love you, you are the most exciting person I’ve ever met. You’re kind, compassionate, understanding and a little wild and crazy, and I do want to marry you. I only ask for a little more time. I want you to meet my family first, and for them to meet you. I desperately want this marriage to work for us both, do you understand that?”

I smiled kissed her cheek and replied, “Of course I understand. Fort Bragg is not a world away. Between me calling and coming up here we’ll make it all work for us. I’ll be back for Bucky and Ethel’s wedding, and between now and then I’ll call you on the phone. You have a number where you can reach me, so we should be able to overcome any problems that may develop.”

She placed her hand on my face caressing it she said, “I do love you.”

We left the place and I drove her home and walked her to the door then we kissed, an emotional kiss as we both realized I was leaving at least for a while. Then I left.

I arrived back at Fort Bragg and my BEQ later than evening. I unloaded all my clothes placing them back into my room. Since it was still early I drove over to the main NCO club. There I met Art, and told him all about the school. Then I told him I had met the woman I wanted to marry.

Art said, "Ken, don't screw up like I did, make sure this is the woman you really want, otherwise you'll find yourself in divorce court with lots of problems."

"Well, I hope I don't make a mistake. Erin has been married before, and she doesn't want to make another mistake, so hopefully we can make this all work."

Art asked, "Is she good sexually, is she good in bed because that's also very important?"

I looked at him, and for a moment I didn't know how to answer. Finally, I said, "Art, to be truthful I really don't know, we've never slept together!"

He stared at me in amazement and said, "You've got to be shitting me! You mean you were up there that long, and never slept with her?"

I laughed at his look of incredulity and replied, "Yeah, that's what I mean, I've never slept with her!"

Art shook his head, "You dumb ass, I haven't taught you a frigging thing."

I laughed, "Art, you damn Kentucky redneck, after two screwed up marriages you can't teach me shit."

"Well, you've got me there. But I do think you should sleep with her before you get married."

"I will, I will, but it has to be the right time for us."

I had another drink with him, then I'd had enough. I said my goodnights and left returning to the BEQ.

I took a quick shower in my little bathroom and finally went to bed. I lay there thinking about all the things that were occurring in my life. I thought I'm thirty-four-years-old, thinking about getting married for the first time, and really don't have a pot to piss in. I don't make a lot of money, I have several years left yet in the army before I can retire, I owe for a car, and a house in Florida. I'm not sure that I make enough for us to live on. I began to feel miserable as I contemplated the future with Erin. I wanted to have children, and I wanted to be able to give them all the things that I never had, and bring them up to be educated, responsible citizens. Finally, I fell asleep.

Saturday morning I slept a little late and missed breakfast in the mess hall. I drove over to the club and had my favorite breakfast, SOS topped with two eggs over easy.

While in the club my old friend Billy Walton came by the table and had a cup of coffee with me, we talked for a while. He was on his way back to Nam. Ms. Landers in the Pentagon had assured him he'd be out on orders shortly

Another old friend Billy Bowles stopped by the table, and we talked for several minutes. He told me he was getting married in the near future. I didn't mention to him that I was also thinking about getting married. Billy I knew had been married once before, but it hadn't worked out for him. We shook hands, and I wished him luck as he left.

Another friend of mine Jim Parnell, stopped by the table and drank a cup of coffee with me. Looking at me over his steaming coffee cup, and thick cigarette smoke he said, "Ken, I need a favor, hopefully you'll be able to help me."

"Just name it my friend, I'll do whatever I can to help."

"This afternoon I have to take my girlfriend out for a visit to see some people, and as you might know she has two small kids. I need you to baby sit them for a couple of hours."

I stared at him in total disbelief. "Jim, I've never baby sit kids in my life. What in the hell would I do with two small kids in the BEQ?"

"Just let them watch television, and they'll be no problem."

"How old are they?"

"They're four and five."

I thought for a moment and asked, "What time do you want me to do this?"

"I'll bring them over about three and pick them up around six this evening."

I thought, *other than going tiger hunting at night in Vietnam, or walking around inside an airplane wing at ten thousand feet over the Pacific Ocean, this has to be one of the dumbest things I've ever consented to.*

"All right, bring them over around three, and I'll be there."

I left the club and drove back to the BEQ. I went upstairs and changed my clothes and went back downstairs. I pulled out the water hose and washed my car, the little black T-bird really looked good. I drove off-post, found a car wash and using their vacuum cleaner cleaned out the inside. I was proud of my little car. I drove back to the BEQ went upstairs and decided to take a nap.

I woke up with someone pounding on my door. I got off my bed and opened the door, there stood Jim with two little kids. I looked at my watch it was two-thirty in the afternoon. I looked at him and then at the two kids, they both had bright red hair, freckled faces, and beautiful little smiles.

"Jim, you're early."

"I came early because I wanted to make sure you'd be here."

I looked at him and said, "I told you I'd be here, why do you have so little faith?"

He laughed and replied, "I knew you would be, but I need a few extra minutes."

"You asshole, you just wanted to get rid of the kids early that's all."

He laughed and said, "Don't use that language in front of the kids, they repeat everything they hear."

I replied, "They'll have to take their chances, after all this isn't a kindergarten."

He smiled, and held his nose, "You can say that again. See you later."

I took the kids into my room and said, "Sit here on the bed and watch television."

They both climbed up on my bed as I turned on the television set. The small 17 inch black and white screen lit up as I turned to a comedy show, and they began to watch it. Jim and I shook hands, then he left.

I sat down at my small table and pulled out a book I had begun to read. It was Edward Gibbon's, "The Decline and fall of the Roman Empire." The two children began arguing. I put my book aside and tried to calm them down. The little girl began crying and complaining about something her brother had done. I didn't see him do anything, so I really didn't know what to say to him.

I picked her up and held her in my arms and tried to comfort her, finally she stopped crying. I set her back over on my bed then I changed the channel on the small television. I found another kiddy show, and that seemed to mollify them at least for now. I knew that I couldn't read my book, so I just lay it aside.

A few minutes later the little boy said, "I have to tinkle!"

I interpreted that to mean he had to go to the bathroom.

The little girl said, "I have to tee tee too."

The little boy jumped off the bed and raced for the bathroom, the little girl right behind him. They both entered the small bathroom and shower and closed the door. I jumped from my chair and dashed to the bathroom. The little rats locked the door. They were laughing, giggling and shouting.

I said, "Will you two please come out of the bathroom?"

They were laughing and the girl said something I couldn't understand. For the next five minutes I begged them to come out of the bathroom, all my pleas were unsuccessful. I then remembered that the bathroom window was raised, and only the thin screen was between them and the outside of the building, I wasn't sure if it was latched.

I immediately developed nightmares of them undoing the one small latch and crawling out on the ledge that separated the second floor from the bottom floor. The ledge was about fifteen feet above the ground. I knew if they went out on it they would fall and get seriously hurt, or worse.

I begged them again to unlock the door.

But they just laughed, giggled and shouted, "No, no, no!"

I knew I had to do something, but what?

Finally, I hit upon a quick solution. I walked over and put the top latch on my room door, then went into my small living room and raised the window in the room. Unlatching the screen I lay it aside, I stepped out onto the small ledge then turned around and lowered the window. I walked along the ledge towards the bathroom, finally I got there.

The two kids saw me outside the window and began laughing and screaming. They then unlocked the door and ran back into my room. I was satisfied with that, as I knew they couldn't get out of the room, my plan had worked.

I pushed the little screen in as the latch was on the inside. I then pulled it away from the window, raising the window higher I stepped into the bathroom. Then I closed the window and latched it. Both kids were setting on the bed laughing.

In a mock reprimanding voice I said, "You two are bad locking the door, you know better than that."

The little girl spoke up and said, "I have to tee tee."

I lifted her off the bed and took her into the bathroom pulled her little pants down and sat her on the commode. She completed her action, and I pulled her little pants back up.

We walked back into the room, and the small red haired boy said, "I have to tinkle."

I walked him into the bathroom lifted him up and unzipped his pants. I waited as he urinated, then I zipped his pants up and we returned to my room. I went back into the bathroom and made sure that I had closed and locked the window.

I looked at them, they both looked like little red haired angels. I asked them, "Are you hungry?"

They both jumped off the bed, and began jumping up and down shouting, "Yeah, Yeah!"

I put my shirt on and holding their hands we all went downstairs to my car. We got in the car and I drove down Bragg Boulevard to MacDonald's. I got them both a hamburger and a milkshake. I had a milkshake myself. I hadn't had a milkshake since my stay in the hospital in the Philippines over two years earlier. I lit a cigarette and smoked it while they finished their meal.

Finally, they finished, so I emptied the containers, cups and wrappers into the nearest disposal bin, and we returned to my room in the BEQ. I looked at my Rolex it was five o'clock in the evening, I had one more hour to go if Jim arrived back here on time.

The little girl lay back on the bed, and in a few minutes she was sound asleep. A few minutes later the little boy was also asleep. I was one happy relieved person to see them both sleeping. I turned off the television.

I picked up my copy of the magazine and read again the article about our big battle at Camp Plei Hell in early 1963. That team was now all scattered. Some were back in Nam; some were here at Bragg, while others were back on Okinawa. I didn't know where Bennie Polina was. I last heard that he had been discharged out of the army on disability, and gone to work for some federal agency in Washington, D. C.

I checked my watch again it was six o'clock. I hoped like hell that Jim and his date would show up on time, and take the kids home. I walked over to the small refrigerator I had in the room, and rescued a cold beer and popped the top. I sat back down in my chair and slowly drank the beer and smoked a cigarette. I heard someone coming down the hallway then Jim appeared with his girlfriend.

She was a lovely red haired woman. He introduced her to me as Emanuell. At least that's what the name sounded like. They woke the two children up, and made them ready to leave.

Jim shook my hand and said, "Thanks Ken for babysitting, I owe you a favor."

"Jim old friend, I won't do this again, you owe me big time."

He laughed and replied, "Ken, you're an expert baby sitter. You might consider making this a part-time job for yourself."

Laughing I said, "Yeah, get the hell out of here."

Jim, his girlfriend and the kids all walked away

I rescued another beer and sat down relaxing for a few minutes. Jim didn't know it, but I actually enjoyed the kids.

I heard Art coming in he was hollering out my name coming down the hallway. I just sat there, and finally he walked into my room.

"Hello First Sergeant would you like a cold beer?"

He walked over to the refrigerator pulled one out, and popped the top. He then sat down on my bed and asked, "What in the hell have you been doing all day?"

"Art, you won't believe this, but I've been babysitting Parnell's girlfriends two kids all afternoon."

He looked at me suspiciously and said, "Are you bullshitting me?"

"No, I really did baby sit her two little kids, and they were a bit of a problem."

I then told him how they locked themselves in the bathroom, and I had to go out on the ledge, rip out the screen and get them out.

He laughed and asked, "Did you whip their little butts?"

"No, I took them to MacDonald's, filled up their little guts with hamburgers and milkshakes and they fell asleep."

He just grunted and replied, "Let's go up to the club and see what's happening."

"That sounds like a good idea to me. Let me take a quick shower and get dressed, and we'll be on our way."

"I have to shower and change clothes also, so take your time."

"Art, when I get dressed I want to use your telephone to call my girl in Baltimore."

"No problem, you can use it anytime. I get the bill monthly, so I'll be able to identify your calls from mine."

He left and I jumped in the shower and took a quick hot bath.

After showering and a light shave I got dressed and walked over to Art's room. He was in the shower, so I picked up his phone and dialed Erin. A couple of rings and she answered the phone. We talked for about twenty minutes and I told her I'd be up there the following weekend. I'd arrive around midnight as I'll leave Fayetteville around five in the evening.

Jerry had told me of a motel that was new and easily accessible in a location I was familiar with, so I told her I'd call her from there. With all arrangements made I kissed her goodbye over the phone and hung up.

Art was ready to go so we got into his little T Bird and drove over to the club. The place was almost packed. I think almost everyone I knew was there with their wives, or girlfriends. The stag bar was filled with people. Happy hour was about over, and it seemed everyone was trying to get an order in before it ended. I was able to get a couple of beers for Art and I.

We moved out to the main ballroom, and found an empty table and had a seat. The band began playing and couples were dancing. I saw Jerry and some woman cutting a rug out on the floor. Art spotted a woman he knew, so he left to go dance with her. I was content to just sit and watch the crowd. They were a fascinating group to be sure. I made no effort to make out with any of the women.

We sat there for about two more hours slowly sipping our beer, as Art blew cigar smoke rings toward the ceiling.

Looking over his cigar he said, "Ken, let's go down to the Tropical and get a bite to eat."

"That sounds good to me let's go."

We left the club and drove down the Boulevard. The restaurant was also packed with people. I checked my watch, it was just after midnight. Art and I finally found a table and ordered breakfast. After eating we drove back to the BEQ and called it a night.

Monday morning around six o'clock, Art and I went to the club for breakfast. We were sitting at a table waiting on our order when Sergeant Major Hoskins joined us.

He and Art were old friends as they had been in the 101st Airborne Division and the 11th Airborne Division together on earlier assignments.

They were talking when Hoskins turned to me and said, "By the way Ken, I wanted to tell you that SFC Tolomeo, and his team leader was both ambushed and killed last week in Nam".

I stared at him in disbelief. I said, "Damn, I told him that was a dangerous place and he could get his ass killed. I'm damn sorry to hear this. I feel terrible about it; maybe I shouldn't have traded positions with him."

Art spoke up and said, "Ken, it's not your fault, he wanted to go, and he knew what he was getting into, so don't blame yourself."

Hoskins added, "Ken, it was just his time to go, there's nothing you or I can do now, so forget it, there'll be lots more."

I still felt bad about Tolomeo, but they were both right. I said a silent prayer for him and dismissed it from my mind.

I spent the week in classrooms with my team, and on Thursday night we all participated in a parachute jump out on Salerno drop zone. I screwed around on Friday, and took off a couple hours early heading north on I-95 to Baltimore.

I got to Baltimore around nine-thirty that night. I found the motel which was aptly named the North Motel. It was new, fresh and centrally located around the streets that I knew. After registering into the motel I called Erin, she was thrilled to hear that I was already in town. I asked her to meet me at the Hooligan Inn. I washed up a bit then threw on a dash of after shave lotion and headed for the Inn.

I walked in and the bar was crowded with soldiers. I knew several of them from Bragg, so we all greeted each other, then I bought a scotch and water for myself. Betty came by hugged my neck, and welcomed me back to the Inn, and to Baltimore.

"I'm meeting that high class blonde in just a few minutes."

She laughed and asked, "Ken, are you serious about her?"

"Of course, I love the woman, and I plan to marry her."

She smiled and said, "Ken you're too military for her. She's a nice girl, but she knows nothing about the army or army life. Your marriage won't last six months, if she does marry you."

"Damn, Betty, you don't seem to have a very high opinion of me."

She laughed and said, "Oh no, I think you're a great guy, if I were younger I'd marry you myself, but she's a big city girl, intelligent and beautiful. Army life just isn't for her."

Smiling I replied, "I hope you're wrong, because I'm going to marry her."

"I wish you and her all the luck in the world."

"Thanks!"

About that time Erin walked into the bar, and after spotting me headed in my direction. Two of the younger soldiers began hooting and making asses out of themselves as she walked by them. She ignored them, and walked on up to the bar where I was sitting.

Standing up from the barstool pulling her to me I gave her a quick light kiss and said, "Hello darling, it's wonderful to see you again." She sat down on my barstool as I stood. Turning around I ordered her a gin and tonic.

She asked, "How have you been?"

"Just fine, not too much going on at Bragg, training, going to classes and making sure my team is up to date on everything. I've been very anxious to get back to Baltimore to see you again."

She smiled and replied, "It's been a long wait for me also. I wish you were still in school here."

"Well, honey that school's over for me. The thing we need to do now is determine if we want to get married or not. You know, and I know that I love you, and want to marry you, the sooner the better."

She said, "Let's wait a little longer and make sure that you and I want to get married, and I know for certain that I'm not making another horrible mistake."

"I agree that we should be certain, but I'm certain now. We're wasting time by being too careful and waiting too long. Let's go get a bite to eat, and then we can let the evening take care of itself."

She smiled and replied, "That sounds good to me, let's go."

She directed me to a place called the "Woodshop." It was a bar and grill. We both had a sandwich and I had a beer, she had a glass of orange juice.

I asked, "Where would you like to go from here?"

She replied, "What do you feel like doing this evening?"

Smiling at her I replied, "I feel like making mad passionate love to you all night."

"She smiled, patted my face and said, "Sweetheart, we have a lifetime to do all that."

I replied, "Each day we wait is lost, one that we can't make up." She didn't reply so I said, "Let's go dancing someplace for a couple of hours."

We then drove out to a nightclub on Pulaski Highway. They had a small band, so we danced until about eleven o'clock in the evening. She had taken a taxi to the Inn, so I drove her to her apartment.

She asked, "Would you like a beer or a cup of coffee?"

"Neither. I've had enough to drink for today. I'll just drop you off and come get you tomorrow morning. We can go for breakfast together if you'd like to"

She leaned over and kissed my cheek and said, "That would be wonderful!"

I parked outside her apartment, then walked her up to her door and kissed her goodnight. After she entered her apartment and locked her door, I left returning to the North Motel.

I walked into my room and checked the beer that I had placed into the sink, and covered with ice when I first arrived. Most of the ice had melted, but the beer was ice cold. I rescued and popped the top on one of the cans, and sat down in the big easy chair in the corner flipping on the television. I watched a little news and then some rerun of a show. I lit a cigarette and drank another beer.

I knew that I loved Erin, and wanted to marry her. I also knew that I was over all of the heartaches of the past, and they no longer affected me. I heard someone pounding on my door. I walked over and peeked through the little hole and saw Jerry and Bucky.

I opened the door and they walked in. Jerry said, "Bucky and I just got into town. We left late, so it took some time to get here."

"I've been here since about ten tonight, I left before you two, I didn't know that you guys were coming up this weekend."

Bucky said, "I wasn't coming up, but Jerry wanted me to, so I rode up with him. We saw your car so we knew where you were."

I gave them both a cold beer. We sat and talked about an hour then they left for their room. I slowly undressed and went to bed.

The next morning I woke about seven-thirty jumped into the shower, shaved and got dressed. I drove over to Erin's apartment, and she was ready and waiting. We found a nice restaurant and enjoyed a great breakfast. We then spent the day sightseeing. We went to Fort McHenry, the grave of Edgar Allen Poe, and several other historical sites around the city. I dropped her off at her apartment so she could get ready for the evening. I returned to the motel showered and got dressed. I had my blue Hong Kong suit on so I felt good. I picked her up and told her we were to meet Bucky and Ethel and probably Jerry and Lillian at the Inn.

She kissed me on the cheek and remarked, "That's nice, and it'll be like old times with all of us there."

"Erin honey, the old times was just a few weeks ago, so that makes it not old times, instead it's continuing the good times."

She laughed and said, "I suppose you're right."

We all met at the Inn. Ethel reminded me that she and Bucky were getting married in two weeks, and I'd better be there.

"I'll definitely be there, unless the Army has other ideas."

We found a table in the back room as the little band began playing. We danced most of the evening away. Finally, when Betty said last call for alcohol, we had our last drink then drove over to an all night restaurant, and had a bite to eat.

Again tonight I walked Erin up to her apartment door and kissed her good night, then returned to the motel. I had a cold beer and thought about the two of us. I knew that I wasn't being too pushy or demanding. I also knew that I was exercising restraint in the sex department. I wanted Erin to be receptive to the idea of sex and to enjoy it uninhibited. She was a beautiful woman, and in the full bloom of life, but I also knew that she had to accept me, and our relationship in all its facets, for it to be a happy one for the two of us.

Sunday we spent the day together, and around three that afternoon I took her back to her apartment. We sat around and talked for a little while. I kissed her goodbye, and told her I'd see her in two weeks, as I would be back for Bucky and Ethel's wedding. I promised to call her during the week.

I left Baltimore and traveled through the Baltimore Tunnel and then around Washington and into Virginia. I stayed just above the speed limit, and had no trouble with the patrolmen.

The following week Art came by my room and said, "Ken, I got my phone bill today. You must love to talk to your girl in Baltimore, you have a three figure bill for the month."

"Art that could be any figure, from one hundred dollars to nine hundred and ninety-nine dollars. Do I need to sit down when you tell me the amount?"

Art laughed and replied, "Nah, it's not all that bad, just one hundred and eighteen dollars."

"Well, that's a little more than I figured, but not as bad as it could've been. Let me write you a check for that amount." I sat down and wrote him a check.

I spoke to Erin a couple of times during the week and once over the weekend. The following week I called her on Wednesday and told her I'd be in Baltimore that Friday night, and would stay at the North Motel.

I saw Bucky on Thursday and he said, "Ken, I just received orders sending me to Okinawa to the First Group."

"Well, that's a tough break with you getting married this weekend. When do you have to be there?"

"I have to be there on the twentieth of the month, I'll have just enough time for a short honeymoon, then I have to leave."

"Well, you'll enjoy your tour over there, the cost of living is relatively cheap, and lots of things to do if you get to stay on the island. When I left there last year most of the teams were either going or coming to or from Nam."

He said, "I can get Ethel over there in about six months they tell me, so that'll help keep me straight."

"Ethel's a good woman, too damn good for you, but she made her choice. I hope she likes it when she does get there."

He laughed and said, "I'm sure she'll like it. It's her first trip out of the states, and going to a warm tropical climate. That beats the hell out of these cold northern winters."

"You have an excellent selling point," I replied.

Bucky and I drove up to Baltimore on Friday night and checked into the North Motel. He had his dress blues for the wedding, and I knew he looked great in them. I planned to wear a civilian suit and tie. I called Erin from the motel, she was at the apartment waiting for my call. I told her to catch a taxi to the Hooligan Inn, and I'd meet her there. Bucky called Ethel, and they also planned to meet at the Inn. Bucky and I went over to the Inn, and in about fifteen minutes both the girls arrived. I found us a table back in the dance hall, and ordered us all a drink. We danced for a couple of hours then Betty began to close the place down. I drove Bucky and Ethel back to her apartment leaving them both there. I then drove Erin to her apartment and we both walked inside.

We got inside the apartment, and gently pulling her to me I gave her a long passionate kiss.

I said, "Darling, these separations seem to be getting longer and harder to take. I think we should set a date for our marriage, tell your family, and I'll tell mine, and we'll just do it."

She kissed me again and said, "Ken darling, just give me a little more time, then we'll get married."

"All right, whatever you say." I had a cup of coffee with her, and then I kissed her good night and left.

Returning to the North Motel I rescued a cold beer from the sink that I had placed earlier. It was very cold. I sat down in the chair turned on the television and watched it for a few minutes. Frustrated, I finished my beer and went to bed.

The next morning I went to a local restaurant and had breakfast. I went back to the motel and Bucky was there. His wedding was scheduled for three o'clock in the afternoon at a church over on Bel Air Road. I then called Erin who told me she would meet me at the church as she was coming with Ethel. I agreed with that.

"Bucky, have you told Ethel that you're on orders for Okinawa yet?"

"Yeah, I told her last night. She took it hard, but she understands that I have no choice. I also told her I'd get quarters there in a couple of months, and she'll come over and join me. We're going to Niagara Falls for a five day honeymoon, and then I'll leave from there. She'll return here to Baltimore."

"You should have a great honeymoon, after all, it's the place for honeymooners," I said.

Early that afternoon we both began to get dressed for the wedding. We had a couple of beers, and finally I drove us over to the church. It was a beautiful old church. Once inside the church I saw both Ethel and Erin. Erin was dazzling in a pink dress, and Ethel looked great in a light blue outfit. Finally, the wedding began and within thirty minutes it was all over. Many of their mutual friends were there, and they were lined up throwing rice on the couple as they exited the church. They left, the crowd left, and only Erin and I remained.

I said, "Let's go to the Woodshop and have a cold drink and perhaps a bite to eat." She nodded in agreement, so we left in my little black T-bird. She gave me directions on how to get there.

While sitting at a small table, I said, "Darling, you're thirty-one now, and I'll be thirty-four in a couple of months. I truly think we should get married and began to have a family, if we're to ever have one."

She smiled leaned over kissed my cheek and said, "Sweetheart we'll do that, and soon."

We danced a couple of tunes then left and went back to her apartment. I parked and locked the car out on the street, and we walked into her apartment.

She went to the small refrigerator and brought out two beers. I opened them both and sat down on her small couch. She placed an ashtray in front of me and I lit a cigarette.

She sat down next to me and I said, "It was a lovely wedding, I wish them a long and happy life."

She replied, "I wish them all that also."

"Jerry and Lillian are getting married next week, but I don't know where." Pausing for a second, I said, "I think they'll keep it small and personal, perhaps not even in a church."

She said, "I didn't know that"

"I think Jerry is getting ready to retire, and maybe move to Canada to live. He has friends up there from WWII, and no family here in the states, so I think that's where he'll go."

She replied, "I didn't know that, but it does makes sense."

Finishing my beer I rose from the little couch and said, "Guess I'll go back to the motel and get a good night's sleep."

She appeared surprised as she stood up and asked, "Why so early?"

I replied, "I'm trying to comply with your wishes, and wait for both sex and marriage, and so leaving makes it easier for both of us."

She had a hurt look on her face, but I was also hurting. I kissed her and turned for the door.

Stopping, I turned around and said, "I'll call you tomorrow morning, and we can go for a bite to eat."

"I'll be waiting for your call."

I closed the door walked out to my car and left. I arrived back at the motel and went to my room. It was only ten-thirty in the evening, but I was sort of frustrated and didn't want to go anywhere else. Opening a cold beer I sat in the chair. I turned on the television and watched a dumb ass show for a few minutes then turned it off, and turned on the motel radio.

I was just sitting there listening to some good country music sipping my beer, when I heard a light tap on my door. I got up wondering who in the hell is knocking on my door? I walked over and looked out the little peep hole, it was Erin.

I opened the door and she stepped into the room. I wrapped my arms around her kissing her.

She held me close and whispered, "Darling, you shouldn't sleep alone tonight!"

"Thank you sweetheart, you shouldn't sleep alone either. It's time we satisfied the hunger that we both have. It's time we stop teasing and torturing ourselves. It's time for love and more love."

I went to the sink and recovered two beers, opening them I gave one to her. Then I sat down in the chair. She walked over, and I pulled her lightly down on my lap.

She smoothed my hair back, kissed my forehead and said, "I do love you Ken, but I'm so afraid of making another mistake."

Kissing her lightly on the lips I replied, "Darling, we all make mistakes, some serious and some not so serious, but we do make them. Marriage is a very serious step, and too often taken too lightly by too many couples. Like you, I don't want to make a serious mistake in marriage. But there comes a time when you must make a firm decision, and stand by it. If you make the wrong decision you suffer and pay for it, if you make the right one you prosper from and are happy with it. But you have to make one!"

She nodded her head silently in agreement with me. She pulled my head down slightly and kissed me, our tongues lightly touching, performed their own dance of love. My hand inevitably slid up to her breasts. I massaged one of them, and she moaned as I continued my gentle massage. Our breathing deepened, and the passion fires now lit began flaring hotter and higher.

I reached up and began to unbutton her blouse, she aided in removing it. I then removed her brassiere and her beautiful breast fell free, her dark areolas and taunt nipples stood out in splendid relief. I kissed each of them in turn. She kissed me again, moaning as I returned her kiss. I picked her up and walked over to the bed and placed her gently on one side. I then unzipped her skirt and removed it, then her slip and her panties.

She gazed at me as I slowly removed my shirt and tie, then my pants and shorts, her green eyes reflecting desire and love. I moved to one side of the bed and she turned towards me. I kissed her and caressed her body. I nibbled on each breast and with each nibble and kiss the flames of passion soared higher and brighter as the need for consummation overtook us both. We engaged in that most physically satisfying of all human activities. I moved to one side and allowed my heart to slow down, and my breathing to return to normal. She turned and kissed me.

We talked for a while then made love again, finally we fell asleep holding each other. It had been a wonderful day and night.

I woke up fairly early the next morning, Erin was still asleep. I got up and went to the bathroom. When I returned she was awake.

She smiled at me and said, "Good morning darling."

"Good morning sweetheart, I hope you slept well."

She replied, I haven't slept so well in a very long time."

I said, "Would you like to take a bath?"

"No. I don't like motel bathtubs, but I'll freshen up a bit."

With that she got out of bed. I was thrilled by the beautiful body she had. Her hair appeared not to have a strand out of place, and with not an ounce of fat on her she was stunning. She reappeared from the bathroom and came over to me. I immediately wrapped my arms around her and gave her a kiss.

She returned my kiss with equal fervor, as I picked her up and returned to the bed. We made love again, and I was able to make up for some lost time. We then went for breakfast, and then returned to the motel for a couple of hours.

Finally, I had to leave to make that long boring trip back to Fort Bragg. I checked out of the motel, and promised to call after I got back to North Carolina.

I kissed her and said, "I love you Erin, you're mine, and I'll never let you go."

She kissed me and said, "Yes darling, things will work out for us I promise you."

She got into a taxi and slowly drove away. I climbed in the little T-bird and aimed it south to North Carolina.

I called her later that evening after I reached the BEQ. I told her how happy I was that we had finally consummated our relationship, and how much I loved her. She appeared happy and expressed her love for me. I promised to call later in the week.

The next morning I learned that our company was going on a field training exercise to Pisgah National Forest to practice our skills in mountain climbing. We would be gone for two weeks. I immediately called Erin and told her about the exercise and that I'd call her as soon as possible. She seemed to understand and accept my position.

The summer rolled on and fall arrived with all its brilliant colors and cooler weather. It's a most beautiful time of the year. I went to Baltimore every two weeks and spend the weekend with Erin. My little T-bird was racking up the miles. I was now approaching one hundred and ten thousand miles on it. I had replaced all the tires once since I bought it. I kept the oil changed, and conducted all other preventive maintenance, and it continued to perform beautifully.

I went to Baltimore the first weekend in December and met with Erin. We decided we would be married on the fifteenth of the month.

She said, "Ken, you have to meet my parents before we get married. Let's go to their house and meet them."

"Darling, that's fine with me, I'm sure that we'll all get along wonderfully," I replied.

We left my motel, and she gave me directions to her parents' house. We walked in and she introduced us. Her father was about six foot one or two, and her mother was much shorter and a little on the heavy side. Her mom made us a cup of coffee, as we all sat at the morning breakfast table.

I explained to them that I was a professional soldier, and had been in the army for almost fourteen years. I discussed that part of my life, with them both doing more listening than talking.

Finally, looking at her father I said, "Sir, I would like your permission to marry your daughter Erin!"

Staring at me with a look indicating I was lower than whale shit, and not worthy of his daughter, he replied, "She's old enough to make up her own mind, whatever she decides I'll accept. I trust her judgment. If she accepts you, then I'll accept you."

I replied, "Then the decision is hers. If we get married, I hope to measure up to all your expectations of a son-in-law."

We talked for a little while longer, then Erin and I left returning to my motel.

That evening we went out for dinner, and then to the Hooligan Inn. The band was playing and the place was packed with soldiers and civilians. We managed to find a small two person table over by the dance floor. I ordered us two drinks. Betty the owner came by our table pulled up a chair and sat down. I told her that Erin and I were getting married later this month. She congratulated us and wished us the best. Erin and I danced several times, and then decided to return to her apartment. She changed clothes as I sat on the little couch and had a beer and smoked a cigarette. She returned and sat on my lap.

Kissing her gently I said, "Honey, I think we'll be very happy as a married couple. We both are old enough and mature enough to know what we want, and to appreciate what we have. Let's have a small wedding, maybe two other people with us, and that's it."

She smiled that beautiful smile and said, "Darling, I agree completely with you. My first wedding was a church wedding, this time I want a small one."

"Then that's settled."

We watched a television show together and I had another beer. Finally in mutual consent we went to bed. We made gentle passionate love, and finally fell asleep.

I left on Sunday returning to Fort Bragg. On Monday, I found out that out entire company was scheduled for cold weather training for two months at Fort Greely, Alaska, beginning on the second day of January. I quickly did some mental calculations. I had requested leave for fifteen days beginning on the fifteenth of the month. My uncle in Fort Lauderdale had reserved us a hotel room over on the beach, so I had some obstacles to overcome to make all this work.

That evening I went to bed a little earlier than usual, I was tired from all the day's activities. Sometime during the night I began to dream. Night time dreaming wasn't a normal occurrence for me. In my dream I saw again beautiful Rachel, she with her familiar mysterious smile.

She said, "Kenny, this is the right thing to do, keep me and our son in your memory book always, and be happy." She faded from view.

Then I saw Elona. She leaned over kissed me on the brow and said, "Ken, this will make you happy, and that's all I ever wanted. It's now your time. Don't ever forget us, enjoy your life."

I woke up startled, my heart pounding, my forehead wet with sweat, wildly I looked around. I realized I was in my bed in the BEQ, and no one else was here. Was it my subconscious, a crazy dream, or what? Strangely enough I felt truly at peace with myself, and with my pending marriage. Did I really dream what I think I did or not? I really wasn't sure. But I knew it was the right time for me, and with the right person.

All my heartaches and disappointments from the past would remain forever buried in the past. I was still a young man, and still had a career to complete, a marriage to make, so all my thoughts and efforts were now focused and directed towards my future.

CHAPTER 42

Marriage and Panama

Arriving back in Baltimore on the fourteenth, I met my friend Danny who was to be my best man. He had driven up, and I was to return to Bragg with him. The T-bird I would leave with Erin since she didn't have a car. We both went to the Hooligan Inn and had a couple of drinks.

I said to Betty, "Tomorrow is the big day; Erin and I are getting married in some little town outside Baltimore."

She congratulated me and said, "Ken, I'll bet you fifty dollars that your marriage won't last six months."

Smiling I said, "Betty you have a bet."

She replied, "Put up your money!"

She then got out an envelope and placed fifty dollars inside it, I gave her two twenties and a ten. She placed them into the envelope and sealed it. She then wrote on it payable to Ken or Betty June $20^{th,}$ 1965.She placed it into a small safe, turning to me she said, "That's the easiest fifty bucks I've ever made."

I laughed, "Betty, I don't mind losing fifty dollars. But I would hate like hell for my marriage to fail within six months. My best advice is not to count your chickens before they hatch."

Danny and I went to a restaurant and had a bite to eat. I called Erin and let her know that I would pick her and Doris her bridesmaid up tomorrow at five in the evening.

She agreed and said, "Darling, don't drink too much this evening, tomorrow is a big day for us." I assured her that I wouldn't. I was too excited to drink very much.

Danny and I returned to the Inn, had a few more beers then returned to the North Motel, and watched a couple of television shows. We went to bed fairly early that evening.

Waking early the next morning I rolled over and lit a cigarette. I lay in bed and thought about my marriage day. I loved Erin very much, and knew that things would work out for us. I also knew that the army makes strange and unusual demands on its soldiers, and on its military wives. I felt that Erin was strong enough, and intelligent enough, to overcome all the difficulties that the future might present to us.

Getting up I went to the bathroom took a hot shower then shaved and slipped on a comfortable pair of pants and shirt. I heard a knock on the door and opened it to Danny's smiling face.

He said, "Good morning sucker, are you ready for the big day?"

"Certainly, they should make my wedding day a National holiday, but I don't think they will."

We then went out for breakfast. The day passed slowly and finally Danny and I drove over to Erin's apartment. She and Doris were both there, and both were dressed for the wedding. Erin wore a bright pink dress, and Doris was dressed in green. When I saw Erin I fell in love with her all over again. She was dazzling!

We took my car and drove to a small town somewhere outside of Baltimore. Danny was driving, so I had no idea where we went. We entered a small chapel and met the Reverend who performed the ceremony for us. I had only attended a couple of weddings before, so this was all new to me.

I said, "I do!" Then slipping a ring on her finger, I kissed my lovely bride.

We left and Danny drove us all to the Hooligan Inn. Betty had told me she was having a small reception for us and a small buffet.

We arrived there, and to my total surprise two young Buck Sergeants from my 'A' team back at Fort Bragg were there. They had hitchhiked from Fort Bragg carrying a case of C-rations as a wedding present. They then presented Erin and I with two mess kits complete with eating utensils. The kits were marked His and Hers.

I truly appreciated the gifts, especially since they had physically carried them so far. I sincerely thanked them both. Danny and Doris were getting along very well, and shortly afterwards Danny said they were going to leave us newlyweds to ourselves. We thanked them both and they left. We stayed for perhaps another hour, and then after thanking Betty for the reception we left for the North Motel.

I parked the car and we walked up to the door. I unlocked it then bent and lifted Erin up in my arms; I pushed the door open with my foot, and carried her into the room. I put her down as she wrapped her arms around my neck kissing me.

I returned her kiss with equal fervor and whispered, "I love you Mrs. Fisher."

She softly replied, "I love you too Master Sergeant Fisher."

She sat down on the bed, and I sat in the chair.

I said, "Let's go over our flight plans again. I'll leave here tomorrow with Danny and return to Fort Bragg. Monday, I'll fly into Atlanta and wait for you to join me there. Then we'll fly together to Fort Lauderdale. Monday, you take my car and drive out to Baltimore airport park it in a secured lot, then fly to Atlanta."

She nodded her head in agreement. I continued, "We'll stay in Fort Lauderdale until I leave on New Year's Eve. I'll return to Fort Bragg, and then go to Alaska on the second day of January. You'll stay with my family in Fort Lauderdale and leave there on the second and fly back to Baltimore." She again nodded in agreement.

I opened a bottle of champagne and filled the two glasses that Doris had given us. We drank a toast to our long and happy marriage. We finished the bottle, and then I slowly undressed her and then myself. We made beautiful love twice then fell asleep as I held her snuggled close to me.

The next morning we got up then bathed and dressed. I drove us to a small restaurant for a bite to eat then back to the motel. Danny was there waiting for me. I got my bags and locked the door. I then gave Erin my car registration and keys. We kissed each other goodbye, and I watched as she drove away.

I got into the car with Danny, then he headed south to Fort Bragg.

"What kind of evening did you have with Doris?"

"Ken, I had a fantastic evening. We left and went dancing then I took her to my motel room, and we made love all night."

"Danny, you realize that she's married, don't you?"

"Not to me," he said.

"You're a back door artist."

He laughed and replied, "Ken, me boy you take it where you find it."

"That's irrefutable logic, I can't argue with that."

Monday, Art drove me out to the airport in Fayetteville, and I caught a plane for Atlanta. I arrived about two hours before Erin's plane was due to arrive. We both had to change planes in Atlanta. Her plane arrived on time, and I met her at the gate. I hugged and kissed her, and she blushed as people around us either stared or giggled.

"Ignore those people darling, we're on our honeymoon!"

She replied, "I agree," and kissed me with abandon. We walked over to the National Airline gate, and shortly thereafter boarded our plane, and headed south for Fort Lauderdale.

We arrived at the Fort Lauderdale airport and my Uncle and Aunt were there to meet us. I introduced Erin to them both, and then I hugged them both giving my aunt a kiss on the cheek. My uncle then drove us over to the Misty Moon hotel on Fort Lauderdale beach.

He pointed out a car parked in the lot and said, "That's my other car, you can use it while you're here," handing me a set of keys. He then gave Erin the key to our room, and invited us for dinner that evening.

"Where should we meet you?" I asked.

He replied, "We'll meet you at the Hotel Yankee Pride which is just a few blocks down the street at seven o'clock."

"Great, we'll be there." I shook his hand and he and my aunt drove away.

We went into the hotel and checked in. We were on the ground floor facing the ocean which I was very happy about. "Honey, this is a very nice hotel room. We have a huge double bed, television, telephone, radio, refrigerator, bathtub and shower. I think we are really going to enjoy this honeymoon."

Erin walked over and said, "I promise you we will."

As her kiss became a little more passionate my friend immediately responded with a rock hard erection. I lifted her up and deposited her on the bed. I then slowly removed all her clothes. She watched me with those beautiful gray green eyes as I rapidly removed all my own clothes, throwing them all on the floor.

I then dove over onto the bed, she bounced upwards a little from the shock of my sudden weight on the bed.

She hugged me and said, "You're crazy."

I replied, "Perhaps, but I'm your crazy husband."

I kissed her and caressed her breasts and then her body, the lustful, roaring fires of passion overtook us both. If I thought I was going to make this a long session I was kidding myself. In less than five minutes I was in the short rows, and nothing could wait. We completed what we both wanted so badly. Then we just held each other as a sense of normalcy returned.

I rolled away and said, "Erin my darling, you're trying to kill me, I'm as weak as a kitten."

She giggled and replied, "You're a wild tiger, just wait until tonight."

"Let's go for a swim in the ocean," I said.

"That's a great idea."

She went into the bathroom then came out and opened her suitcase extracting a bathing suit. I waited as she put it on. Then found my own swimming trunks and put it on. We picked up a couple of large towels and walked about twenty yards out onto the beach. I spread the towels out on the sand, and then we waded out into the water. We swam for a little while then returned and relaxed on the towels. I smoked a cigarette as we soaked up a little sun.

Finally, returning to our room Erin drew a tub of water and invited me to join her for a bath. I thought that's a marvelous idea.

It was getting late, so I suggested we dress and go to the other hotel early and have a couple of drinks before my uncle and aunt arrived. She agreed, we dressed in very casual outfits and left our hotel.

We met them and had a terrific evening. They loved Erin, telling me so individually. The next several days were an absolute delight. Christmas Eve and Day were a holiday on the beach, but like all holidays and vacations, it drew to a close too quickly.

On New Year's Eve, I got up early in the morning and woke Erin up. We went to the restaurant and had a great breakfast. We then returned to the room, and with a little coaxing I convinced her we should make love again. We did, and then I slowly began to pack my bag. She also packed hers.

A little later my uncle and aunt showed up and I gave the car keys to my aunt and she left in the car. My uncle then drove us over to the airport. He and Erin walked me to my gate. I thanked him for all his help and hospitality. Then I kissed Erin and told her "I'll see you around the first of March."

She had tears in her eyes as I held her close to me, she murmured in my ear, "I love you, I love you."

I boarded my plane for Atlanta and after changing planes there, I flew on to Fayetteville. There I caught a taxi and went back to the fort. My beautiful honeymoon was over.

Two days later my company loaded up on a plane at the Green Ramp on Pope Air force Base, and took off for Alaska. We landed in Seattle and went to Fort Lewis. There we went to a warehouse and drew all our winter clothing and gear. I was familiar with some of it as I had spent considerable time in that icebox of the world, Korea.

We then flew on to Eielson Air Force base in Alaska. We were billeted in quarters there and given briefings on our mission, and how we were to accomplish it.

My team minus the team leader was to jump in at night, go across country and reach a designated spot within a certain timeframe, and then be picked up. We were to take minimum C-rations with us. We would receive re-supplies as we reached and supplied the map coordinates for an airdrop, and established a drop zone. If we failed to makes the locations and set up a drop zone, we wouldn't eat. That was a powerful incentive. We were to jump just after dark.

There would be eleven team members, and an attached member from another Company who would be jumping in with us. I checked and rechecked the team for the proper gear, and finally we were ready to go. We were trucked out to the airfield and loaded aboard a C-130 aircraft. It took off and flew around about forty-five minutes. The loadmaster gave me the four minute sign. We all hooked up and checked our equipment. We had rucksacks and Griswold containers hooked on to us with all our equipment. I was the jumpmaster, so I told the first man out to head for the end of the drop zone and wait while I rolled up the stick.

They shuffled to the door, and the light turned green. I yelled go, and the men jumped out the door. The crew chief had told me the temperature at jump altitude was sixty below zero. I jumped last and even with all my arctic clothes on, I was freezing cold. The air was heavy, so we all floated down slowly and gently. I could see the men below me as they were rolling up their chutes and heading for the rendezvous point.

I landed gently in the snow, and my chute slowly dropped to one side of me. I rolled it up and put it into my kit bag. Slinging it over my shoulder and my rucksack I headed for our rendezvous point. I arrived there and began to count the jumpers. We had twelve jumpers, and I could only count eleven. I lined them up, and everyone was there except the attached soldier. Everyone began calling his name, but we heard no reply. We spread out in two's and walked the drop zone, but couldn't find him. I conferred with the Lt and we agreed to build a large bonfire, and continue the search until we found him.

The remainder of the night was spent in called for and looking for the Specialist from the other company, all to no avail. Full daylight finally arrived, and we broadened our search. I heard a call from the far side of the drop zone, so I headed in that direction. I was wading through about two feet of snow; the going was slow and very tiring. Finally, I crossed the crest of a small rise, and then I knew what had happened to the young soldier.

From my position I could see the young soldier hanging from a tree about twenty feet above the ground, and about fifty yards off the drop zone. I waded on over and joined the two guys who were standing there. Looking up I saw that the paratrooper had landed in the tree and somehow several of his shroud lines had wrapped around his neck. In his efforts to free himself he must have slipped from the branch and hung himself.

He had now been there for several hours, and with the temperature hovering around fifty-five degrees below zero he had frozen.

I cursed as this exercise was starting off on a very bad note. I sent one Sergeant over to the LT with the news. I also directed the team set up the radio and call the base station at Fort Greely, and make them aware of what had happened. An hour later a helicopter arrived and took the body of the young paratrooper away. The LT filled out an official report on what had occurred, and all the circumstances surrounding it. Finally, we were set once again to begin the exercise.

For the next four weeks I think our team skied, and walked over a third of Alaska. Conditions were at best miserable. We would build small fires and melt the snow for drinking water, and for heating water to make a cup of C-ration coffee. We received a couple of aerial re-supplies and made our designated points on schedule. A helicopter stopped by and delivered the mail to the team, and we gave him the few letters we had written.

I wrote to Erin and described Alaska and our activities to her. Then I suggested she and I consider having children when I returned. I wanted to have them before we got too old, and while we were still young enough to really enjoy them. I hoped she would agree.

We returned to Fort Greely, and took an additional two weeks of cold weather training at the Northern Warfare Training Center. Then our exercise was over.

We boarded a plane and made our way back to Fort Bragg. I returned to the BEQ and went to Art's room and called Erin. Art was on a thirty day leave, I guessed he had gone home.

We exchanged greetings and expressions of how much we had missed each other. Then she said, "I got your letters, and I think you are going to get your wish earlier than you might have thought."

Puzzled I replied," Darling, I have no idea what you're talking about, what do you mean?"

She giggled, "Darling, I'm pregnant, we're going to have a baby!"

I was shocked into silence.

She said, "Say something!"

"Darling, that's wonderful news, I'm thrilled at the idea that we're going to have a baby. I hope that it's a boy."

She said, "Well, I hope that it's a girl."

"Either way honey, I'm very happy that you're pregnant. That Florida honeymoon was really magical. I wish that we were there right now." I asked, "Have you told your mom and dad yet that you're pregnant?"

"No, I wanted to make absolutely sure that I am before I tell them, and I wanted to tell you first."

"That's a good idea, no point in shaking them up if it turns out to be not true," I replied.

She laughed and said, "Oh, it's true alright."

"Honey, to change the subject, I'll find us a place here in the Fayetteville area, and when I do you can come down. The army will arrange for a packer for your things and move it here, all you'll have to do is drive down."

She replied, "That's an easy thing to do. Just hurry and find us a place, I need you and I want to see you."

I promised her I would, and after several more minutes of conversation I hung up the phone.

The next morning I saw Jerry, and he and I went to the club for breakfast. I told him I had to find a place to live. He volunteered to drive me around the various subdivision areas and help me out. We checked out several apartment complexes, and I found nothing that I really wanted. He then drove by a subdivision called Montclair, it was all new houses.

Jerry said, "Ken, let's take a look at the new houses. Hell, it's just as cheap to buy as it is to rent, and you'll build up equity in your house."

There were several streets in the subdivision, and he drove down the main street. I saw that my old friend Sam Trout lived in a very nice corner house, and I saw a couple of other senior sergeant's names that I knew on mailboxes.

I noticed one nice model house that had a carport, columns on the front porch and a decent yard. We pulled into the drive way after seeing the house was open for inspection. We walked through and I thought it was very nice. While we were there the salesman came in, and immediately began his sales pitch.

I asked, "How much of a down payment will I have to put down to buy the house?"

He replied, "Nothing! You have the GI bill, and that'll take care of it."

Jerry spoke up and said, "Hell Ken, go for it, Erin will love the house."

I turned to the salesman and said, "Draw up the contract and I'll take it."

We drove over to his small house trailer office, and he filled out the papers. I signed them right then. He in turn gave me the house keys and we shook hands. Jerry and I left. I looked over the papers more closely, and they all appeared to be correct. I had a thirty year mortgage at forty-four dollars a month.

I mentioned the amount to Jerry.

He said, "That's no problem, just cut out a few cases of beer, tighten the belt a little, and you'll have it."

I immediately began to worry, here I have a new mortgage and still had a small mortgage on the little house in Florida, and my T-bird wasn't paid off. I thought holy shit, how am I going to make it on my salary? Then I realized I would get a housing allowance, and separate ration money, so just maybe I'll be able to do alright.

I couldn't wait to call Erin and tell her that I had bought a house. Then I began to sweat a little. What if she doesn't like it? What if it's the wrong color, or too small or too large? The what if's were ruining my day. We got back to the BEQ, and I thanked Jerry for all his help. He dropped me off and left.

I went to Art's room and using my duplicate key I opened his door and picked up the phone. I called Erin, happily she was in.

We exchanged greetings and then I said, "Darling, I have a big surprise for you."

She hesitated and finally asked, "What is it?"

"Honey, I bought a new house here in Fayetteville."

She exclaimed rather excitedly, "What?"

I repeated what I had said, "Honey, I bought a new house."

I then began to describe what the house looked like and how it was situated, I tried to make it as appealing as I knew how. I finally ended the conversation by telling her I would send her a detailed map how to get to the house from Baltimore. I completed all the necessary paperwork at Group personnel, and the people at Fort Holabird arranged for a furniture mover to pick up all her furniture and stuff from her apartment in Baltimore, and transport it here to Fayetteville.

Erin left early Saturday morning on her drive to Fayetteville. My little hand drawn map was perfect in detail, and as I was sitting on the front porch of our new house, I saw my beautiful black T-bird driving up the street. I stood up and watched as she drove into the driveway. I dashed out and helped her from the car, and gave her a big kiss. I hadn't seen her since New Year's Eve, and I was overjoyed to see and hold her again. We must have kissed three or four times, I was so much in love with her.

I patted her stomach and asked, "Darling, is my son there?"

She laughed and said, "No, your daughter is there."

She really was a little heavier around the middle. Probably not noticeable to anyone that didn't know her, but I could tell the difference. We walked up to the steps and onto the porch. I picked her up and carried her into our first house. We entered the small living room, and she reached over pulling my head to her kissing me.

"Darling, I hope you like our new home," I said.

She replied, "Honey, if you like it, I like it."

"When will your furniture arrive?"

"It should be here today. The moving guy yesterday told me they would be here by six or seven this evening."

I glanced at my watch it was three-thirty in the afternoon. I asked, "Would you like a nice cold beer?"

She replied, "Sure, that would be refreshing after such a long drive."

I got two cold beers from the new refrigerator which came with the house, and then I walked her through the house. We had three bedrooms, a small den, and a kitchen dining room combination. I continually asked her how she liked the house?

She would reply, "If you like it, then it's perfect."

At five that afternoon I drove up to a pizza place and bought a large pizza. I returned to the house and Erin and I sat in the dining area on the floor and had pizza and beer. About six-thirty that evening a large truck pulled up in front of the house and after confirming he had the right address the two men began to unload the furniture and moving it into the house. Erin and I both directed them to the various rooms. Finally they finished and left. We inspected the house again together, and it seemed pitifully short of furniture.

"Darling, we have to buy some more furniture, we have only one bed and a table and chairs and a few other things."

She smiled at me and replied, "We have to buy a baby bed and things for the new baby, let's not worry too much about all the other stuff."

I nodded in agreement.

"We don't even have a mail box. I'll have to go get one tomorrow and put it out by the end of the driveway." I added, "We don't have a washer and dryer we need to get those also."

She said, "Let's go make up the bed, and get things ready for the evening."

"That's a wonderful idea, we definitely have to have a place to sleep."

Together we approached the bed. I began to place the sheets in military fashion on the bed tucking and folding them in like it was an army bunk.

Erin looked at me in amazement and said, "Where did you ever learn to make up a bed, look at the way you're doing the sheets!"

I stopped and probably with a look of disbelief on my face replied, "Honey, what do you mean? Look at how neat and folded they are."

She laughed and said, "Ken, you're impossible, I think I'll have a job teaching you how to be a good housekeeper."

I shook my head in amazement as she undid the fold and tucks I had made with the sheets and bedspread then made it up her way.

We then put away all the dinner ware, the silverware and kitchen utensils. We unpacked a few more boxes, and then gave up for the night. I had another beer as we sat on her small couch. I pulled her to me and whispered in her ear sweet nothings, and nibbled on her ear lobe. I hadn't had sex for two months, so I was no longer concerned with the house. I wanted to satisfy this hunger for her, and I wanted to do it soon. I think she got the message.

I pulled her to me and kissed her a very loving kiss, my erection was almost out of control. It was still early, so I suggested we go into the bedroom. She agreed with me. I sat my beer down and after putting out my cigarette we walked back into our bedroom.

I hung small blankets across both windows, then I pulled her to me and kissed her again, our tongues played games as the sexual passions built, and the flames swept higher and hotter. I caressed her breasts and pulled her into me. She responded with equal passion, holding me around the neck she returned my kisses. I unbuttoned her blouse and removed her brassiere, then I unzipped her skirt and it dropped to the floor. I removed my shirt and then my pants. I slipped off my loafers and then my shorts. I knelt in front of her and pulled her panties down. I kissed her stomach which I knew held my child, and then slowly kissed my way back up to her face.

She held me close to her and said, "Ken, I love you so much."

I picked her up and lay her gently on the bed, and then I moved to the other side. I slowly caressed her entire body, the smooth contours of her breast and stomach, the firmness of her legs, I slowly moved as we began that wonderful journey. I was very slow and deliberate, as I knew nothing about making love to pregnant women.

Spent, I rolled from on top of her and said, "Darling, I've waited for over two months for this, and now you exhaust me in just a few minutes, it doesn't seem fair."

She giggled and replied, "Honey, you can do it again, the night's young, and we have all night."

Bravely I responded, "I intend to do just that."

We went back into the small living room and had another piece of pizza and I opened another beer. I turned on the radio and picked up a country music station. They were playing a beautiful Jim Reeves tune. He had been killed recently in a plane crash, and the world had lost one of its best singersr. They followed that with a Patsy Cline melody, "*I fall to Pieces.*" She had to be the best woman country singer ever in my opinion. What a shame that she too had passed on in a plane crash. What a beautiful unforgettable voice she had!

We talked for about an hour, making plans and deciding what we needed in the house and what we didn't. We talked about the coming baby, and what we should name it. No decisions were reached on either names for a boy or a girl. I reached over and picked up Erin's beer which she hadn't touched. I then proceeded to drink hers. She suggested we go to bed, and I immediately agreed. We went back to our bedroom and removed the few clothes we had on and lay down on the bed. I immediately kissed her and caressed her and my ever dependable buddy became his normal self as he became excited in anticipation of a more intimate environment. We made love as I tenderly and gingerly lay on top of her. I didn't want to do anything that would hurt her.

The next few weeks were hectic, we bought some of the things that we needed for the house, and I bought a mailbox and put it out by the driveway. I was very proud of the mailbox. I had my name on it. For the first time in my life, I really felt something represented me—and of course Erin.

My buddy Alton called me and told me he was getting married and wanted to borrow a suit, Alton was much heavier than I was. I told him he could borrow one of my suits, but it wouldn't fit. He insisted it would. He drove out to the house and I loaned him a suit and tie. Alton was drunk as hell when he arrived at the house. He loved moonshine, and through his local connections bought the finest moonshine that North

Carolina had to offer. I had a couple of drinks with him. He left and as he was backing out of my driveway he ran over the mailbox totally destroying it. He stopped got out of the car then began to apologize. I waved it off, and told him just to replace it when he returned from his wedding. I watched as he drove down the street weaving back and forth. I hoped like hell he didn't have an accident.

The next day Art drove out to my house and shocked the hell out of me, he had gotten married again when he was on leave. He had married a school teacher who had a Masters degree from The University of Kentucky.

Congratulating him I said, "Art, you bastard, you only have a high school education, that woman is so damn much smarter than you, how in the hell are you going to make her happy?"

He laughed and replied, "Ken, you don't have to be a genius to make a woman happy. A college education cannot replace experience. My experience and mastery of bedroom techniques will ensure that I make her happy, this is the last time for me."

I shook his hand again and said, "The very best of luck old friend."

He and Erin became very good friends. I was very glad that she liked and appreciated most of my close friends, even though they, like me, were a little rough around the edges.

The first of May I received orders reassigning me to the Special Forces Group in Panama. I was shocked, so I went to see Hoskins. He explained that he had absolutely no control over the orders and I had to go. I was further directed to attend the East Coast Defense Language Institute in Washington, DC, for two months to learn Spanish. I broke the news to Erin and she was somewhat upset. She was five months pregnant now and it was obvious. The baby was due in September, so I knew that I would be able to attend the school, and be home for the birth of the baby.

My mother had returned to Alabama, so my little house in Fort Lauderdale was vacant. That solved my immediate problem of where Erin would stay during her pregnancy while I attended school. I immediately took all necessary procedural steps to get our household goods moved, and then I had the problem of selling the house.

I contacted the agent who had sold me the house and he purchased it from me for the exact price I had paid for it. He picked up a fewdollars equity, but I didn't mind that. I had a trailer hitch put on my T-bird, then I rented a small U-Haul trailer, and loaded up most of the clothes and our personal things. Reluctantly, we left Fayetteville.

I drove down to Lynell and introduced my beautiful bride to my family there. I even took her to the "Catfish Restaurant" and introduced her to fresh water catfish. She didn't like the catfish. I accused her of being spoiled by the crabs of Baltimore. We left Alabama, and drove on down to Fort Lauderdale.

My little house was next door to my aunt's. She had supervised the arrival of our furniture two days earlier. I immediately unloaded the little trailer, and then I began to clean the house from top to bottom. I used sprays and disinfectants, mops and soaps and made it hospital clean for the arrival of the baby.

I had two aunts and uncles close by, so I was comfortable with Erin staying in the little house alone. I left her the T-bird, and caught a plane to National Airport in Washington. Once there I caught a taxi to the hotel where I would be staying with three other guys from the group, who were also on orders to Panama.

We began school and our instructors were all Cuban refugees who were all college educated. They all had other occupations prior to their arrival in the United States. My favorite teacher was a Cuban lawyer. He was patient and deliberate in his language skills. I telephoned Erin twice a week. She told me she was getting bigger and heavier, otherwise she was doing fine.

In July I received word that my old friend Master Sergeant Billy Walton, had been all shot up in Vietnam. The way I heard it, he was on a deep penetration operation attacking a company of Vietcong and North Vietnamese when they got into some deep shit. He was in the Binh Dinh province which I knew was along the South China Sea. He had gotten into some type of a hellacious firefight with some NVA regulars, and had been shot to hell somewhere around Bong Son. I also heard he had been rescued and was in a hospital somewhere. I said a silent prayer for my old friend, and hoped like hell he'd make it all in one piece.

In August my roommate Don Caraway, who had a car and I drove over to Baltimore for the weekend. Don had also attended the Intelligence course at Fort Holabird in a class after me. We drove up to the Inn and both walked inside. Betty was back of the bar. She immediately hugged my neck, then Don's.

She said, "Welcome back you guys, Ken how are you, and how's your wife?"

Laughing I returned her hug and said, "I'm fine and she's fine. She's down in Fort Lauderdale waiting arrival of our baby."

I immediately ordered Don and I a beer, as we found a seat at the bar. She stood there and talked with us for about fifteen minutes.

Betty said, "Ken, I have an envelope for you."

She left and came back with the envelope containing the fifty dollar bet we had made months earlier. I opened it and the one-hundred dollars were there. I had forgotten about our bet.

I laughed and said, "Betty, I tried to tell you that Sergeants do marry beautiful high-class women."

She replied, "You certainly did. You got lucky and I congratulate you once more."

We rented a room that evening over at the North Motel, and I took Don out to the Blue Harbor restaurant on Bel Air Road. We had a great crab cake dinner. Sunday we drove back to Washington and back to school.

We all graduated at the end of August. I felt reasonably comfortable in basic Spanish. I was certainly no expert in the language. I flew home on National Airlines and landed in Miami. I walked out of the gate and there Erin was waiting for me.

I grabbed her and kissed her with pent-up passion and happiness. The baby was due almost any day now, and I knew that I had just made it home in time.

She asked me, "How was school, and how did you like Washington?"

I replied, "School was fine, Washington streets and most of the housing is a national disgrace, otherwise it was alright."

I drove us back to Fort Lauderdale. The little house really looked good. The next door neighbor had mowed the grass for Erin, and the house itself sparkled inside. She had a baby bed in one bedroom and little plastic butterflies on a wand above the bed. I was thrilled with the idea of it all.

I was home a few days when Erin and I went to the bank. Once inside she turned and said to me, "Ken, my water just broke. We need to go home *now*!"

I must have been stupid as I had no idea what she was talking about. We immediately left the bank, and I drove her home.

She said, "Honey, I'm fine. Why don't you go back to the bank and complete your transactions, I'll be fine."

"Are you sure darling?"

She nodded her head in agreement.

I left and drove back up to the bank. In twenty minutes time I had completed all my business and left. I arrived back home and Erin wasn't there. I immediately checked for her small suitcase with its night gowns and stuff, it was gone. I rushed over to my aunts house and she wasn't there, neither was her car. I called the hospital and found out that Erin had just been admitted to the hospital pending childbirth.

Later that afternoon I went to the hospital and waited until almost eleven o'clock in the evening before the doctor came out, and presented me with a beautiful little brown haired baby girl. I wanted a boy, but who could resist such a beautiful baby girl. I was allowed to visit with Erin. She appeared to be in better shape than I was. She was calm and held the little baby in her arms. I didn't hold the baby as I was afraid I would drop or hurt it. I called her mother that night, and told her she was a grandmother again, and had a granddaughter. She and my Father-in-law were thrilled. Three days later Erin was released from the hospital. I was the most careful driver in the world as I slowly drove her and the baby to our home.

I had another ten days of leave left. I spent it all with Erin and the baby. I hand washed diapers, and changed them, fed her baby formula, and talked to her. I played her great country music on my little stereo. I wanted to make sure she grew up to appreciate good music.

I complained to Erin that the baby had blue eyes.

She said, "All little babies have blue eyes when they're first born, they will eventually become whatever color they will be."

I wasn't totally convinced, but I had to accept what she said, hell I didn't know. The army had told us that Erin and the baby couldn't travel to Panama until the baby was six weeks old.

My leave was up, so I took the little T-bird and drove to Charleston, South Carolina. I checked in at the Air Force base and turned in my car for shipment to Panama, and then caught a four engine propeller plane for Panama. The flight was long and boring, about seven hours with young soldiers, wives, and squalling kids. I surely hoped that our baby didn't do like all these were doing.

I arrived in Panama in October, and was assigned as team sergeant on an "A" team in B Company. I had lots of old friends there also. Ralph Slaughter and Bert were there. The personnel Sergeant Major Del Soto and I were long time friends was also there. That was another great thing about Special Forces, wherever you went in the world, you would have old friends there. I had to wait until mid—December before Erin and the baby she had named Erin Katherine would arrive on the Isthmus.

I met them at Howard Air Force Base, on the Pacific side of the Canal Zone. I was never as happy as when I first spotted them coming down the steps from the plane. Erin looked terrific. She had regained her figure and was as shapely as ever. I swear my dick stirred a little at the sight of her coming down the steps. I had not had sex since May, and to say I was horny would be the world's biggest understatement. I rushed over and pulled her to me and kissed her, she had the baby in a little cradle. I was afraid I might hurt her, so I backed off.

"Darling, you and the baby finally got here, this has been the longest eight weeks in my life waiting for you two."

She laughed and replied, "Ken, it's been a long tough wait for us also, your daughter needs her father to be sure."

We got into the little T-bird, and I drove across the Isthmus to our new quarters at Fort Gulick. All our furniture had been delivered two days earlier. I had sat it all up in our quarters, and everything was ready for her to arrive. I had even gone to the commissary and bought groceries. I had bought two air conditioners from a guy who had left and installed them in our house. I had one upstairs and one downstairs. The temperature and humidity in Panama is very similar to that I experienced in Laos and South Vietnam.

That first night was a night for love-making. We went to bed and I pulled her to me as we exchanged kisses. I kissed and caressed her breasts and her stomach. I allowed the passion fires to build as they became more demanding. Finally, we made love slow and deliberate. We rested a little while and talked then I made love to her again. She in the bloom of womanhood was equally as passionate and hungry. It was a wonderful reunion of bodies, passions, and emotions.

The one thing I couldn't get was a clothes dryer. We had to wash diapers and such and hang them on a line to dry. Eventually, I was able to get one from a downtown Colon Sears store by mail order. It finally arrived and made life much easier.

In January on a Sunday afternoon in preparation for a jungle warfare class I had to attend, we had a large formation and a class on guerrilla warfare given by some Major. Prior to going out to the class me and my next door neighbor named Herman Simpson drank about a half-fifty of whiskey. I guess we were both about half shit faced when we arrived at the class. I was sitting on the top back row of the bleachers listening to the Major. The hot tropical sun bore down upon our heads, and I was getting dizzy. He made a statement to the affect that when you are in a firefight, if your buddies are wounded you just leave them. I knew that was wrong. I stood up in the row, raised my hand and asked for recognition.

The Major said, "Do you have a question Sergeant?"

I responded, "Not a question sir, but if I may be so bold, your statement that you leave your team mates behind, is totally wrong. By doctrine we don't do that, and there're several reasons why you don't." As I was speaking I swayed a little.

The Major noticed it and asked, "Have you been drinking Sergeant?"

"I had a couple of small drinks earlier this morning."

Almost snarling he said, "You're dismissed from the class, report back to your unit!"

I left the bleachers, found the company driver and returned to Fort Gulick. The next morning I had to report to the Company Commander, a Lieutenant Colonel.

Glaring at me he asked, "What happened Sergeant Fisher?"

I said, "The Major was teaching incorrect doctrine. His instructions violate all that I have been taught for many years in Special Forces, and two combat tours in Nam, so I corrected him."

He then asked, "Were you drunk at the class?"

I replied, "No sir. I had a couple of drinks yesterday morning, but sitting in the hot sun made me a little dizzy."

He dismissed me, and I joined my team in the daily activities.

The next day I had to report to the company commander again.

He said, "Sergeant Fisher, reports indicate you were drunk. So I'm giving you Article fifteen and fining you fifty dollars pay for drinking on duty." Clearing his throat he continued, "You're now assigned to help write the Course of Instruction for the Jungle Warfare School that's being initiated at Fort Sherman."

Two Captains and I wrote the course of instruction for the school. I made sure that correct Special Forces Doctrine, and personal jungle warfare experience from Nam was included in the manual.

Soon after we finished writing the course I was selected to go on a Mobile Training Team to the Dominican Republic. Four Majors, plus a Sergeant First Class and I were to assist in training their General Staff. It was a six week mission. I knew that the other wives would help Erin, so I wasn't worried.

The firefight conducted earlier on the island had been quickly extinguished by the 82nd Airborne Division. We flew to the island, and for six weeks gave them classes on organizational structure, the chain of command, plus various other military subjects. The training completed, we returned to Panama.

I was then given a new assignment. I was assigned as the First Sergeant of Headquarters Company of the Group. Never having been a First Sergeant I studied every manual I could find on Company administration. I recalled and thought about all the things that I'd learned from First Sergeant Ironjaws Baker so many years earlier, and then all the things that I'd learned from observing other First Sergeants. I mastered it all in short order. I segued from Team Sergeant to First Sergeant with relative ease.

We had an army command inspection coming up, so with my company clerk we took all the company records apart, and put them back together correctly. With numerous manuals as guides, the mess sergeant, supply sergeant and I corrected every deficiency in the company administration we could find. They held the inspection, and my company received the highest marks in the entire Southern Command. I received a letter of commendation, and was placed on the outstanding promotion list to Sergeant Major.

The Group executive officer assigned a new Master Sergeant as the company First Sergeant, and reassigned me to the liaison office at United States Army South.

I then had to move the family and all our belongings, from the Atlantic side to Fort Clayton on the Pacific side of the Isthmus.

Meanwhile, I had sent Erin and the baby home to Baltimore to see her family, and to introduce them to their new granddaughter. While she was gone I supervised the movement of all our belongings to the opposite side of the Isthmus, the Pacific side, and into a new set of quarters. I got it all accomplished with very few mishaps.

I sold my beloved little black T-bird to a native Panamanian. It was truly worn out. The body was rusting away in several places, and most of the electric windows no longer worked. I met this sergeant who had just arrived in Panama, who had a fairly new 1967 Ford. He said I could have it if I took over the payments. I jumped at the chance. Erin and the baby returned to Panama and our new quarters, there we lived a normal life.

Later on I intuitively felt that Erin was no longer happy in Panama. I approached her on the subject. She admitted that she wanted to be back in the states. I had the orders prepared, and she and I and the baby flew back into Charleston. Little Kathy was very happy as we took off. As she sat on my lap she looked out the window, and suddenly somehow realized that she was in the air. She scrambled over to Erin sat on her lap and hid her face. She stayed that way for most of the flight back to Charleston. I had shipped the Ford earlier, and it was there waiting for us when we arrived.

I drove us down to Fort Lauderdale, but had enormous difficulty in finding them a permanent place to stay. I had sold my little house to a family friend earlier, and he now lived there. I found them a temporary apartment before I had to return to Panama.

A couple of weeks later Erin called and told me that she had purchased us a house in Plantation, Florida. I recalled that as a local town on the western outskirts of Fort Lauderdale, sparsely populated, and rural in nature, it sounded great to me. She and the baby moved into the new house, and had our furniture delivered.

Erin was becoming a master in handling all the details of home making in the military. I really felt bad that I wasn't there to assist in the multitude of things that I knew had to be accomplished.

CHAPTER 43

Vietnam again then Korea

A couple of months later, I received reassignment orders to the Special Forces Group in South Vietnam. I knew that sooner or later I would return to the war. My friends Bert, Ralph, and Herman all got orders to return to Vietnam at the same time.

That evening as I lay on my bunk in the barracks, I thought well, I'm now thirty-eight-years-old. I've been out of Nam since 1963. It's a little over five years since I last ran a combat reconnaissance mission, or setup and executed an ambush, or fought my way out of one. I hope that I still have a lucky touch.

I worried about Erin and Kathy the baby, but I also knew that I had to redirect my thinking as I headed back to Nam. Mission success, taking care of the troops, plus staying alive would have to be my major concerns, and in that order.

I was fully aware of the recent Tet Offensive, and its cost to us, and to the North Vietnamese. We had wiped out over forty thousand of them in the first ten days during that battle. We also lost several hundred of our own. I thought about the fact that we had now been fighting there since November 1961, when our first two "A" teams were introduced into the country. That was almost eight years ago. We should have won this war long before now. The frigging Washington politicians were not trying to win. But they didn't seem to fully and truly realize the cost to our military, and to the country.

Most of the men who had arrived here in Panama at the same time as I did were also getting reassignment orders, and most of them to Nam, a few back to the states.

I left Panama, flew into Charleston, and then caught a flight to Fort Lauderdale. Erin and Kathy were at the airport waiting for me. The love of my life Erin looked so beautiful standing in the airport lobby.

Little Kathy recognized me immediately and ran to me. I picked her up and said, "Kathy, you still remember your dad, that's wonderful, as I gave her a big kiss."

Erin walked up hugged and kissed me, she had tears in her eyes as she hugged me tightly.

"Hello darling, you are more beautiful than ever, and I've missed you so very much," I said.

She laughed, and replied, "We have missed you also my love." Kathy leaned over and began to lick my face and laughing, as I wiped at my cheeks. I put her down and she held onto my hand.

I pulled Erin to me and kissed her again and said, "I love you Mrs. Fisher!"

She kissed me back and replied, "I love you too Sergeant Fisher."

Kathy began jumping up and down shouting "Carry me daddy, carry me." I picked her up, and we slowly walked out to the parking lot.

Erin drove us home, and I was delighted with the house that she had purchased for us. It was in an elegant neighborhood, and near all the needed services and facilities. It was located within a few miles of my relatives, so I felt comfortable about that. I had thirty days leave, then I had to report to San Francisco for further flight to South Vietnam.

During times like these the days pass unbelievably swift. Before we could fully become reintegrated again as a family my time to leave arrived. I made a new will and power of attorney for Erin, and ensured that she had all the necessary information that she needed to cover any event.

My aunt baby sat for us my final night at home. Erin and I went to a beautiful dinner club on Hollywood Beach had dinner and watched the show. Finally, we returned home and went to bed. We held each other as we fell asleep. The next morning my aunt returned Kathy to us, and the three of us drove to the airport. I kissed little Kathy goodbye even though she didn't understand any of what was happening.

Holding Erin close to me I said, "Darling, don't worry I'd be fine, and I'd be back in thirteen months. Just take care of yourself and the baby." Nothing I could say could stop her tears.

She hugged me and kissed me and said, "Ken, darling, be careful, Kathy and I need you, and we both love you."

Finally, my plane began boarding, I kissed her goodbye and went up the stairs, I turned and waved goodbye to her and Kathy. My flight flew nonstop to San Francisco.

I had a couple of days before my flight left for Saigon, so I called up my old team sergeant Tony Domingo. Tony had retired after twenty plus years in the army, and two wars. He now had a small business in the city. He met me at the airport. We grabbed each other in bear hugs coupled with smiles and laughter. I was happy to see him again. We sat in the airport bar and had a few drinks together.

Tony said, "I was Sergeant Major of a project when I rotated back to the states. After four tours in Nam, I decided to retire and try my luck in the civilian world before I got too old."

"How's your business doing?"

"Hell, I'm making money, I make home deliveries of whiskey and beer, and it's growing." He then said, "You would be shocked at how much damn booze these civilians drink."

"Tony, I congratulate you on your success here in Frisco. After your military career you deserve to make it good."

"How about spending the night with me and the family?" he asked.

"Sure, I'd be happy to. We have a million things we can talk about since we last ran jungle trails together, and fought off those damn leeches."

He drove us out to his house. I took my bag inside and met his wife again. I hadn't seen her since Bragg several years earlier. She and Tony had either four or five children together, and they were all over the place. After eating a light dinner we sat around and talked until about midnight. That's three o'clock in the morning for me East Coast time. We drank a little and finally called it a night. Tony brought me up to date on current operations in Nam, and the things to be careful of. He briefed me on some new weapons, tactics and equipment they were now employing in country. The war continued to evolve.

The next morning after a light breakfast Tony drove me out to the airport. We had coffee together and continued to discuss the war, and our role in its progression. Finally, he had to go to work.

We shook hands and bear hugged each other. His final words to me were, "Ken, old friend take care of yourself over there, we've lost too many of the good ones already. Be careful!"

"Tony, I'll do my best, we need to either win, or get the fuck out of that place. I'll call you when I get back to the states."

He left and I checked in with the airline, I had about two more hours to kill.

Eventually, I boarded my plane for Saigon. The entire plane was loaded with soldiers, and I didn't know one damn one of them. I had a window seat, so I read a couple of magazines and smoked. I looked out the window at the endless Pacific Ocean below. It had a familiar, friendly look to it. To me, it was very different from the cold Atlantic Ocean, or the blue Caribbean, even the green Mediterranean Sea. Once in a while I dozed off for a few minutes, and then woke up.

I thought about the war. *Our casualties now numbered in the tens of thousands. We bombed for a while then stopped for a while, and the NVA would rush supplies and more troops southward along the Ho Chi Minh trail. It was a stupid policy; it was a policy that wouldn't let us win. Our combat commanders had their hands tied, yet our troops continued to be killed and maimed.*

My train of thoughts continued. I knew I was thirty-eight-years—old now, and wasn't the hard charging young sergeant first class that first came into the country seven years ago. My responsibilities and recent duty assignments now reflected an army propensity for Senior Sergeants towards command supervision and unit management, rather than the tactics, techniques, actions and energy needed and utilized at the "A" and Recon team levels. What ultimate assignment I'd get, I'd just have to wait and see.

The plane landed in Saigon. I had a couple of days before going on to Nhatrang, and Special Forces headquarters. I ran into a couple of SF guys I knew. We all went downtown Saigon together, and found a small table at a sidewalk café on Tu Do street. The street looked the same as ever, except it was more crowded than ever before. There was more of everything including American soldiers.

An old friend Rocky Newhart came by and we bear hugged and shook hands and talked for a while. He was out of the army and flying cargo planes in country. That really surprised me. He was a good man, and had been with us in Laos on the first Operation White Star teams nine years earlier.

He left, and I sat back down and ordered a Biere 33. The frigging taste hadn't changed in all the years that I'd been gone. As I sat there I looked around Tu Do Street, the main street in Saigon. It was filled with young men eighteen to thirty years old hawking any and everything you wanted. I thought these damn people don't want to fight, don't want to win, and won't win. I thought these thousands of young men should be in the South Vietnamese army fighting, instead of hustling on the streets of Saigon.

I thought our American troops are their age, and are fighting and dying for them, and they aren't worth it. You could go down any street off Tu Do Street, and the sidewalks were filled with refrigerators, television sets, Hi Fidelity radios, new tires, air conditioners and batteries.

You name it, and it was all there for sale, and all stolen from the US military. It was at that moment that I experienced my first real doubts that we would win this war.

I shook those dark thoughts from my mind, and returned to watching the street activities and bird watching. The women still wore their Ao Dai's, and still appeared shapely, appealing and oriental.

Rocky came back down the street and asked me if I wanted to fly into Nhatrang with him. He was leaving shortly, so I said yes. I got my B-four bag and joined him as he had a plane load of cargo to deliver. We went to the airport and took off. A couple of hours later he landed in Nhatrang. I had been through here many years earlier, but I didn't remember anything about the city. I caught a Jeep ride over to the Special Forces Group and reported into personnel.

My old friend Del Soto was the group personnel Sergeant Major. He had left Panama about four months before I did. After handshakes he told me to report to the group Sergeant Major. I knew that Command Sergeant Major Modo was the main man. I also knew him from Okinawa several years earlier. I didn't have much use for him, but I considered him harmless.

He told me that he didn't have a Sergeant Major position open right then, and I was on the promotion list, and would be promoted shortly. I left the problem up to him. I had no idea what he needed or where. I found a bunk in the transient quarters put my B-four bag there, and walked around the headquarters complex.

I ran into my old friend Melvin Capone who had been with our team at Plei Hell. We greeted each other with laughs and handshakes. He was now a master sergeant, and was in charge of the enlisted men clubs. To myself I said, "Melvin, that's not the job you need," but then it wasn't up to me to make that decision.

The next morning I checked in with Del Soto who said, "You probably will be going to the Combat Orientation Course." I asked him, "What in the hell is that course?"

He replied, "It's for all the SF men coming into, or back into the country. It's a refresher course, and a PT course to insure that the troops are trained and up to speed prior to assignment."

"Who's running it now?"

"There's a SFC that takes care of things there at the compound, but the training is out on Hon Tre Island just off the coast here in Nhatrang."

I asked, "What's with the Sergeant, is he rotating?"

Del replied, "No, he's complaining that too many of the men outrank him, and he wants to go to an A or B team in-country."

"Well, Del, it is up to you and Modo where I'm assigned."

I wound up being assigned to the COC course.

The course was actually moderately demanding, and did help some in getting the younger troops oriented towards the difficulties they would face as they went to their assignments in country. I knew some of the Sergeants involved in the Recon School. They were tasked with teaching the in-country free world military forces reconnaissance tactics and techniques.

My old friend Mike West, who had gone to school with me at Fort Holabird in 1964, was there as an instructor. Most of the instructors had one or more tours in-country, and were considered experts in reconnaissance. Most of them had served on "A" teams in country, and many of them had tours with other lettered projects within the Command.

I went to my first in-country briefing up at headquarters and learned more about the SF setup in country. If I heard the briefer correctly, he said we have one-hundred and eight "A" teams in-country at ninety-six locations, plus others in the Mike Forces, and still others in the lettered projects.

I thought damn, how it's all changed from the first two teams in 1961, to this many now. I knew also that the Special Forces list of KIA's and WIA's had also grown tremendously since those earlier years. After the briefing I returned to the COC course and the Recon school compound. Troops continually rotated into and through the COC course, and I hoped that it helped them as they assimilated across the country into all the different war fighting projects that was going on.

One afternoon, I was in the little club on the compound having a cold San Miguel beer, and in walked my old friend Sergeant Major Billy Walton. We shook hands had a bear hug and after exchanging greetings, we had a cold San Miguel beer together.

Billy said, "Ken, I'm in the Command and Control project, We're running recon operations across the border plus other things, it's great, but we're also losing a lot of good men."

I replied, "Billy, I'm know about your operations, and I know many of the people in the project. But like all actions you win some and lose some. That can't be avoided."

He then told me about several mutual friends that had been killed that I didn't know about. I was shocked to learn that so many had been killed in one attack on their compound, it happened at one of the compounds north of us. We had another couple beers, and talked about several other people that we both knew.

I said, "Billy, it's been a long war for Special Forces. I don't see an end in sight, but we'll keep fighting as long as they tell us to, or until we kill all the bastards and win."

He replied, "Ken, we'll win for sure. We can't afford to lose. The NVA has never seen the day they can win against us."

He had to leave, so we shook hands again and Billy left.

I found out that my old friend Jerry who had gone to Intelligence school with me in Baltimore was now at the headquarters compound, and was in charge of the boats and scuba gear there. I went up to see him. We had a great reunion.

"Jerry, what in the hell are you doing back over here, you're supposed to be retired and living in Canada?"

He laughed and replied, "Ken, I was bored stiff in Canada. The army sent me a letter asking me to come back on active duty for a few years, so I said why the hell not, so here I am."

"Well, I'm damn glad you're here in Nhatrang, you're too damn old for running around in the boonies."

He laughed and replied, "Kid, this old man still has his shit together, and can run with the best of them."

"Jerry how's Lillian these days, and where is she while you're over here?"

"She's fine; she's back in Baltimore while I'm over here." He then asked, "How's Erin?"

"She's well, I guess you know we had a little girl together, she's three years old this year. We bought a home down in Plantation, Florida, which is a suburb of Fort Lauderdale, and she and the girl are there."

"No shit, I didn't know you two had a baby. I thought you might be shooting blanks."

"No way, she got pregnant when we were on our honeymoon, I do good work."

He laughed, "Congratulations Ken. Damn a lot has happened since we went to Fort Holabird together, and that was only a little over four years ago."

I replied, "Times flies when you're having fun."

We walked over to the club and had a couple of beers together. I felt good about him being assigned to the compound. He should be safe, he has already had his share of wars and wounds. We discussed ideas of him and Lillian visiting us in Florida in the winter time, and Erin and I visiting him and Lillian in the summer time in Canada. It really sounded like a great idea.

I heard that one of my old friends had been overrun at his camp in Lang Vei. He had the most distant camp from Saigon. Reports were that for the first time Russian tanks had been used in the assault against his defenses. He made it out alive along with many of his team. This had happened earlier this year. Those tanks added another huge dimension to the war being waged by the NVA.

About this time I also heard that my moonshine drinking buddy Alton, had been killed during a firefight. I really hated that. I recalled that he had replaced my mailbox after he ran over it while drunk, and on his way to getting married. It was depressing, so many of my old friends were getting killed. Many of them were on their third, fourth or more tours of duty here. Eight years of constant, continuous, combat takes its toll on any unit and its men. We have been fighting here more than twice as long as we did in World War Two.

Christmas came and went, and the war raged on from one end of the country to the other. We had an almost nightly mortar attack on the compound, but no one was ever seriously injured in the attacks. The war was being waged by the different projects, the Mike forces, and most of all by the individual "A" teams that were strategically placed across the length and breadth of the country. We continued to add to our KIA roll. The conventional units in country was also fighting, and winning all of their major battles.

In February I was promoted to Sergeant Major. I knew it was coming nevertheless I was proud as hell to make it. I thought to myself, I didn't do too badly. I went from Private in 1954, to Sergeant Major in 1969. It had taken me less than sixteen years to make it. My personal military goals had now all been achieved and exceeded.

I went up to headquarters to see Jerry and have a cold beer with him. While we were just sipping our beer he said, "Ken, I'm going on an operation. They need a flame thrower man, and I used to work one of those back in Italy in the big one. When they give the word, I'll be gone for about four or five days."

"Jerry, you shouldn't go on the operation. Hell it's been years since you operated a flame thrower. Besides, you're too damn old to run through rice paddies, or up mountain sides."

He laughed and replied, "It'll be over in no time. I'll see you this weekend, and we'll drink a few together."

I smiled, "Okay old friend. Be careful, and take care of your ass, I'll keep the beer on ice."

We shook hands, and I left returning to the school compound.

Sergeant Major Modo rotated, and the new group Sergeant Major was my friend Ron Baxter who had been one of the team sergeants when we first came here. I hadn't seen him since I left Okinawa. I was glad he had the position.

A few weeks later the Sergeant Major of the School had some type illness, and was shipped out to a hospital someplace. I had a call from Ron to come see him. I went to his office and after exchanging greetings, we caught up on each other's activities since we had last seen each other.

Ron asked, "How old are you now Ken?"

"I'm almost thirty-nine now."

He said, "I want to you to take over as Sergeant Major at Recon, I checked with the school Commandant and he agrees."

"I suppose that's as good a job as any other, if that's what you want, then its fine with me."

He then said, "Ken, I want you to honcho the school and the instructors, you do the administration and supervise the unit. The instructors are much younger than you are, and it's their job to instruct, and to run the recons, let them do their jobs." He paused and lit a cigarette. "You and I haven't run a combat recon since 1963, and you and I aren't the young studs we were back then, so don't do anything foolish."

I smiled and replied, "I know my limitations Sergeant Major!"

Leaving his office I ran into my friend Richard. I hadn't seen him in a few years either. We both went to the club and talked for over an hour. He was now the Sergeant Major of one of the Mike Forces. I thought he was one of the better team sergeants I ever knew, I had tremendous respect and admiration for him.

In March, I escorted one of COC groups up to their orientation briefings at the Group headquarters. Settling down in the back I listened to the Colonel who was giving the briefing. He mentioned an operation that had taken place down in the seven mountains area.

He said, "One of the men, a Master Sergeant, had been killed by a sniper as he was carrying a flame thrower up the mountain." He coughed, and then said, "The man was a WWII man, and had served in the Canadian army before transferring to the US Army during the war."

I immediately knew who he was talking about, he meant Jerry, my old friend. I raised my hand and stood up.

The Colonel said, "Yes Sergeant Major?"

I said, "Sir, was that the scuba man?"

He looked at me and nodded, "Yes!"

I walked out of the building and found a seat outside the door. I lit a cigarette and felt an overwhelming sense of disbelief. I just couldn't believe that Jerry had gotten killed on a mission he shouldn't have gone on, one that I told him not to go on. I thought about his wife Lillian back in Baltimore waiting for his return, does she know yet?

I was pissed! This damn war has killed enough of my friends and wounded dozens more. The politicians should either let us win it, or pull us the fuck out!

I went back to our compound and started drinking. By late that afternoon I was drunk as a skunk, and a couple of the sergeants took me to my room and put me to bed. I woke up the next morning with a devastating headache, I was sick for the next two days.

A few days later my old friend Art Taylor came into the compound, he had just arrived back in-country. He also was now a Sergeant Major, and was taking over one of the Mike Force units. He stayed with me for about three days. He had mail in the headquarters, so he got it and returned to my room. It turned out that it was a cassette. His wife had recorded her mail on a small cassette and sent it to him. He had a small tape recorder player with him. So I left him in my room as he listened to her electronic mail. I thought, boy that's really neat.

Art and I talked for hours about everything. He now had a small baby boy with his school teacher wife. I told him about my baby girl, Kathy.

He said, "Ken, things have really changed for you and I since the old days."

"They damn sure have. One thing we're both getting a hell of a lot older." Pausing I lit a cigarette, then continued, "It looks like you and I no longer use the Four F theory anymore."

He laughed, "Some days I think maybe we should have stuck to that system."

Chuckling, I replied, "No, those days are all over for us. I found the love of my life, and I'm happy."

Laughing he said, "So am I, but you crazy bastard, you'll fuck up one of these days, and she'll run your ass off."

I replied, "No way, no way!"

He moved on up to his unit, and I continued at the school.

The following week I received a letter from Lillian. She wrote and asked me what had happened to Jerry? I thought long and hard about the type of reply that I should write to her. Finally, I sat down and wrote her a two page response. I explained what had happened, and expressed my deepest sympathy for the loss of her husband, and the loss of my friend. I never heard from her, or of her again.

I was sitting at my desk one day in the compound, and who should walk in but Major James Larson. I jumped up from my desk, as we grabbed each other in a bear hug then a big handshake. I hadn't seen him since I left Okinawa back in 1963.

"Major, let's go over to our little club and have a beer together."

"Let's go, I'm damn hot and thirsty."

We walked across the compound together, and asking a million questions about events since we had been in Plei Hell together so many years earlier.

I quickly brought him up to date on myself and current events. He told me he had a couple more kids now for a total of four kids. He had pulled a tour in Alaska, and was happy as hell to be back in decent even hot weather again. We spent the remainder of the afternoon in the little club sipping beer and talking. We had supper together in our mess hall then he left for the evening.

He came back to see me over the next two days, and we spent many pleasurable hours remembering our earlier tour, and our days together on Okinawa, and enjoyed the pleasure of each other's company.

Finally, he had to leave, so we said all the proper things and he returned to his Special Forces unit somewhere down south.

I was sitting at my desk about a month later, late one afternoon writing out a citation for a combat award for one of the instructors when the phone rang. I picked it up and it was my friend Art Taylor.

"Hi Art, what's up?"

"Ken, I'm up here at Group. The transient barracks next to our Mike Force is full. We just returned from an operation this morning, and I had this young medic Corporal on my team for the operation. He's rotating back to the states for discharge tomorrow, do you have an extra room where he can stay tonight?"

"Sure, I have an extra bunk, if necessary he can stay with me in my room for one or two nights."

Art said, "You know, he looks a lot like you did about twelve or fifteen years ago."

Somewhat confused by that remark I replied, "What in the hell do you mean he looks a lot like me? Are you frigging drunk or something?"

Art laughed and said, "No, I'm not drunk. I'm just telling you this kid, looks a lot like you. Of course he doesn't have your gray hair, or your fucked up face, other than that he does."

I said, "Well, I'm glad that the kid doesn't have gray hair, and a fucked up face.

Why don't you bring him down here to the compound. I'm finished for the day, and I'll buy you and him a beer in the bar."

"Okay, I'll go get him, and we'll be there shortly."

I hung up the phone and leaned back in my chair, and wondered what in the hell has Art got on his mind. That is rather stupid telling me some corporal looks a lot like me. What in the hell is he trying to prove, or what's he thinking? I think the bastard just wants me to spring for some beer. Oh well, I couldn't find a better drinking partner, or friend to drink with than him. I told the clerk I was leaving and would be over at the bar.

I walked across the compound and entered our bar. It was a small building, but we had a jukebox, two slot machines, a small bar, and about six small tables and chairs. I bought a San Miguel, and found a table over in the corner of the room. Most of the cadre was out on recon patrols with the trainees, so the bar wasn't crowded.

I had drunk about half my beer when I heard a Jeep pull into the compound and park outside the bar. I figured that it was Art. I was right, in a minute or so, he came into the bar followed by a young corporal. I got up and shook hands with Art. He then introduced me to Corporal Sanders.

I shook his hand and asked, "How are you Corporal?"

"Hi Sergeant Major Fisher, I'm fine. I'm on my way home, been here for a year, and I'm outta here tomorrow morning."

"That's great, I'm glad you made it, where's home?"

"I'm going back to the Windy City, Chicago."

"That's a great city I hear, but I've never been there," I replied.

"Let me buy you guys a beer." I walked over to Master Sergeant Holloway who was running the bar for today, and bought three San Miguel beers bringing them back to the table.

At that moment the clerk came into the bar and said, "Sergeant Major Taylor, they want you back in your unit right away."

Art stood up and chug-a-lugged his entire beer in one continuous drink, then said, "Ken, take care of the Corporal, he did a great job on the operation, he patched up a lot of men, I've gotta run."

"No sweat, take care of yourself," I replied.

Art immediately left the bar jumped in his Jeep and left.

Through my cigarette smoke I looked at the young man, and I could see just as Art had a surprising resemblance to me as I looked many years ago. His height, weight, eyes, hair, all appeared the same as mine maybe fifteen or twenty so years ago I thought.

"What's your primary job Sanders?"

"I'm a medic."

"School trained I suppose?"

"Yeah, I went through Special Forces medical training," he replied.

"What made you choose to go into the medical field?"

"My dad's a physician's assistant in a hospital in Chicago, so I sort of drifted into the medical field. But I want to be a doctor. I plan to go to medical school on the GI bill, and become a doctor when I get out next month."

He had a swallow of his beer then continued, "Rather than waiting for the draft I enlisted, so I could get my military obligation out of the way. I'm twenty-years-old, and now I can go to college and not worry about being drafted."

"Well, that was very smart thinking," I said.

"My dad was a medic in the army during WWII, and after he got out he went to work in the hospital," he said.

"That war was several wars and a long time ago, your dad must be pretty old by now."

He had another swallow of his beer and said, "Yeah, he's up in the years now, but he keeps working, he loves his job."

I said, "If you love your job then it really isn't work, it's a labor of love."

"Is your mother still alive?"

He laughed and replied, "Oh yeah, my mom's still alive. She's much younger than my dad, and she's the one who keeps my ass straight."

I smiled, "Moms are usually that way, and they normally rule the roost."

"I know a couple of guys named Sanders, what was your father's first name?"

He replied, "Harold."

"Don't know him," I said.

He said, "My Mom's name is Rachel, she's German. She and my dad met a couple of years after the war, and got married in some little German town called Wurzburg. I guess it was one of those wartime romances."

My bottle of San Miguel slipped out of my hand to the floor and shattered. He had floored me with the name of his mother, and where she got married. I was absolutely stunned by the information.

"Sanders, what's your first name?" I asked.

"It's Kenneth, but my Mom calls me Kenny. Let me get you another beer." He walked up to the bar and bought two beers.

In shocked disbelief I sat there. I know who he is, this young Corporal. He's my own son by my German sweetheart Rachel, over twenty years ago. He's twenty-years-old, born in 1949, its 1969. The numbers fit, all the names and events fit.

My God, I thought is this possible? Have I returned to this fucked up country only to meet my own son whom I never knew, never saw before, and he has absolutely no idea who the hell I am?

He returned to our table with the two beers.

"Thanks, I don't usually drop my beer."

He laughed, "Well, accidents do happen."

"Would you like to see a picture of my family he asked?"

"Sure, do you have recent one?"

"Yeah, this was made last year just before I came over here."

He reached into his pocket pulling out his wallet, and flipped a couple of plastic holders then said, "Here it is, it's dad, me and mom," handing it to me.

I accepted his wallet and looked at the small family picture. I looked first at the father whom I recognized in spite of the twenty years. Kenny was in the middle, and his beautiful mother Rachel was on the left. I stared at her. The years had been kind, and she was still an extraordinarily beautiful woman, only forty, and still in the prime of life. A hundred memories of she and I flooded through my mind. I closed his wallet and handed it back.

"You have a lovely family I said."

About that time a mortar shell exploded in the compound. It was a normal Viet Cong harassment tactic, walk a few shells across our compound and the headquarters compound. I knew that there would be a second one, and maybe a third.

I shouted, "Kenny, get on the floor!"

He sat frozen in his chair with a stunned look on his face. A second shell exploded some dozens of yards away. I grabbed Kenny and threw him to the floor covering him with my own body. The third round went off outside the building. I felt the shock wave and heard the roof and back of the building being peppered by shrapnel. Then silence!

I slowly rose up from the floor with Kenny still beneath me. His chair lay on its side with a huge hole through the chair back.

Sergeant Holloway got up from the floor, walked over to us and asked, "Sergeant Major are you guys all right?"

I pulled Kenny to his feet and replied, "Yeah Bob, no sweat. It looks like we now have an open bar the entire back of the building is ruined."

Sergeant Holloway laughed and replied, "Screw the Cong, they're lousy gunners anyway."

Kenny just stood there with a pale look on his face.

"Are you all right Corporal?" I asked.

He stared at me, and finally replied, "Sergeant Major Fisher, you saved my life, look at that frigging chair, had I stayed there three seconds longer I'd have that hole in me!"

I hugged the boy to me and said, "Don't sweat it Corporal, you're alright, and that's all that matters. I don't think they will shell us anymore tonight."

I walked up to the bar and bought two more beers for us. Kenny sat down in another chair and at another table. I walked over and played the jukebox. I wanted to make him feel things were back to normal. I selected the tune "*Purple Heart*" a Sergeant friend of mine in one of the 'A' teams had wrote the song and made the recording back in Nashville. I heard the counter battery fire from up at the headquarters firing off a few rounds.

Kenny and I sat there and talked for about two hours. With so many conflicting emotions I was getting a little loaded. He drank a lot less than I did, which I was thankful for. During our conversation I found out all about his mother. I knew she was well, and her marriage had evolved into a sound one.

He told me about his mother during WWII, and her escape from Berlin. But I knew the story better than he did. He told me how his parents had gotten married in a hospital chapel in Wurzburg, Germany. I knew that part much better than he ever could.

I recalled the day she got married, and I got drunk for two or three days. I knew she was pregnant then, but she had to leave anyway.

He had no earthly idea I was his father. I was determined to leave it just that way. He informed me that he had no brothers or sisters that he was an only child. I felt some personal perhaps selfish pleasure in that information.

SFC Urich walked into the bar, he was one of our instructors and was off for two days after completing a long patrol. He was about half shit faced. He bought a beer, and then sat down at one of the other tables.

A couple of minutes later he spoke up and said, "Sergeant Major is he your son?"

I glanced at Urich and replied, "No, I don't have a son, and I've never seen him before. He's just passing through, and needs a bunk for tonight. He's spending the night here, and he's going home tomorrow."

SFC Urich just grunted.

A few minutes later he got up to leave and said, "Well, he damn sure looks like you."

I laughed and replied, "Urich, you need a couple more beers to improve your frigging eyesight. Then you'll think I look like Clark Gable."

SFC Urich grunted again, and left the bar.

I suggested to Kenny that he spend the night with me. I said, "I have an extra bunk in my room which I use for people passing through, so the bed is yours for tonight."

He quickly accepted my offer.

"Wait here I have to go across the compound and check in, I'll be back in a couple of minutes.

He nodded in agreement.

I walked over to the medic's office. Smith was the medic on duty. I said, "Smitty, I think I got nicked by a piece of shrapnel check out my shoulder."

Smitty looked at my shoulder and said, "You sure did."

I had a slight cut across my right shoulder where a thin sliver of shrapnel had passed. The cut had stopped bleeding, and I wasn't worried about it. He swiped it with alcohol then placed a small dressing then a band aid on it, and I went back to the bar.

It was almost midnight, so I suggested to Kenny that we go to bed. He quickly agreed. We left the club and went to my room, I pointed out which bunk was his. I turned on the small window air conditioner, and the room quickly cooled off. He took off his uniform and boots and went to bed.

I had brought a bottle of beer with me so I sat on my bunk. The dim night light flickering as the generator produced electricity fluctuated. My cigarette smoke slowly drifted to the ceiling, as I thought about this whole crazy frigging situation. Truth is truly stranger than fiction, and destiny continues to surprise.

He was lying on his back sound asleep. I studied his face, and I could see the soft lines and facial contours of his mother. He had a beautiful smile just like Rachel had. I could see the hair just like mine, and his attitude and comments I might have made years ago. I knew from his comments, and by the photograph that without a doubt my decades ago German sweetheart Rachel, was his mother, and I'm his father.

I also knew without a doubt he had absolutely no idea I was his father. I thought at least he's safe, soon he'll be back with her. He's leaving here tomorrow, and will be back in the states in less than forty-eight hours. With so many crazy mixed up emotions, I finally went to bed.

Early the next morning I woke up and then Kenny got up. I took him to breakfast in our mess hall, and in our Jeep returned him to group headquarters.

He got out of the Jeep, turning he thanked me for a place to sleep last night and said, "Thanks for taking care of me Sergeant Major Fisher, what's your first name?"

I smiled, and a little hesitantly replied, "Well Corporal, oddly enough I have the same first name as you do, it's Kenneth, and my friends call me Kenny."

"Wait a minute, let me get a picture of you."

He opened his bag and pulled out a small camera. I stood in front of the jeep as he snapped a picture of me. He stopped a young soldier passing by, and had him take a picture of the two of us in front of the jeep.

"I'll never forget you, or my tour in Vietnam," he said.

I shook his hand and replied, "I hope you never forget. It's been my pleasure son. I won't forget you either. Tell your Mom she raised a good boy. Promise me that'll you'll tell her I said that!"

"I promise, I will."

"Take good care of yourself, go home and get that doctor's degree, or I'll come to Chicago and kick your ass."

"I promise I will. Good luck Sergeant Major," and then laughing saluted me, and walked away.

I drove over to the Mike Force, and found out that Art and his company had left earlier this morning on another combat operation somewhere down south. I drove back to our compound.

I walked into the bar and several people whom I didn't know were there drinking, the jukebox blaring, and the slot machine jingling. I found a small table over in the corner sat down and lit a cigarette.

I thought what a crazy mixed up fucking world this is. I fathered a son in Germany over twenty years ago, he was born in the states, and I finally meet him here in this God forsaken country. He had no frigging idea who I am. Yet, I feel I know him as if I'd always known him.

How strange, I have now met both my sons. One was a small boy back in Stuttgart, and the other here in this damn country. How sad that neither one of them knew I was his father, nor will they ever know me. Destiny does play strange tricks on us earthlings.

At least I know that his mother will know that I'm alive and well, and she'll know that I know who he is. In spite of the passage of years, we'll share that together.

The months passed swiftly and my tour was coming to a close. I received orders reassigning me to the ROTC unit at Miami, Florida. I thought what a crock of shit this is. I would be off jump status, and assigned to a leg outfit. I was disgusted. I knew that Erin would be thrilled, but my military career still had a ways to go. The only thing I can do from here is wait until I get back to the states then call the Pentagon and see if I could get the orders changed. I didn't know what my chances would be, but I wanted to go back to Fort Bragg, and stay in Special Forces on jump status. Besides, I know nothing about universities, or teaching college student's military science.

As the end of my thirteenth month in country approached I made the local rounds in Nhatrang, and said so long to the many people that I knew. With several of them we downed a few beers together. I cleared group headquarters, and then caught a helicopter ride down to Cam Ran Bay Air Base. I had to spend two days there waiting for my particular flight back to the states. The base was a beehive of activity as troops were entering and leaving the country. I met several SF personnel returning in country, and a couple that were also leaving. We exchanged salutations, and any other pertinent information that we could with each other.

Finally, my plane arrived, and I along with over two hundred others slowly boarded the big World Airlines jet and settled in to depart Vietnam. I had a window seat up front, so I just watched out the small window as the plane revved up the engines and slowly moved out to the taxi strip. It turned around and with a gradual increase in speed lifted into the hot tropical air, we were airborne. The plane passengers broke out with a loud cheer as the plane left the ground.

Instead of cheering I looked down at the rapidly receding shore line around the base, and then at the ocean as we continued to gain altitude. I thought it's the last day of November. I first came to this country eight years ago this month, and how many thousands of our men have we lost since then. It was sobering, and depressing to say the least. In my heart and mind I knew we could have won this war long ago, but the arm chair politicians wouldn't let us.

My military hero General Douglas MacArthur, had said it best when he told Congress that: "*In War there is no substitute for Victory*." I knew that unless we changed our war fighting policy, we would never achieve victory here.

We landed at Kadena Air Base on Okinawa, and had six hours stopover for refueling and some minor maintenance. I called my old company, "C" Company of the first SF Group to contact my buddy Jason Raymond, but he wasn't available. I left word if he returned to let him know I was at the terminal. I then caught a small taxi to New Koza, and walked into a bar that I remembered from six years earlier. I drank a cold San Miguel beer, and looked around. Everything was familiar, but none of the girls were the same as when I was last here. With a sigh I left, this was no longer my area of operations. I caught a small taxi and returned to the air base.

The troops slowly began reloading onto the aircraft. I waited until almost the last when I heard a shout, "Ken, Ken!" I turned around it was my buddy Jason. He grabbed me in a bear hug as we shook hands.

"Jason, I didn't think I would get to see you, were you shacked up?"

He laughed and replied, "No, I was just goofing off, how the hell are you?"

I laughed and replied, "I'm fine just left Nhatrang, and now I'm headed back to the land of the big PX."

We continued to talk for another fifteen minutes, then I had to board the plane. I shook hands again with my old friend then I boarded, and the plane left for San Francisco.

Several hours later we landed at San Francisco, the troops unloaded and headed in every direction looking for the different airlines, and their flights home. I headed for the baggage section to pick up my B 4 bag. I had a small bag with me with nothing but my shaving kit, military records, and some cigarettes in it. I was a little tired as it had been a long almost sleepless flight for me.

As we moved through the terminal there were several groups of what I guess they called hippies, some of them were shouting at the troops, and making nasty degrading remarks, and calling us names. I ignored them as the fools that they were.

I entered a small corridor along with an elderly gentleman and his wife. As we walked along a big hippy came through from the other end. He had a ragged ass beard, long filthy hair, big rings hung from both ears, dressed in ridiculous clothes, he even looked stupid.

As he walked towards me he began to make remarks, then as he approached within a few feet of me he spit at me. I ducked his spittle, and swung my bag at his head. It knocked him up against the wall, as he rebounded I hit him with the best karate punch I had, and he hit the floor with a sodden dull thud. He was out like a light, blood spurting from his mouth and face, three of his teeth lay on the floor in front of him.

I stood over him as the gentleman and his wife approached, the old gentleman stopped and patted me on the shoulder.

He saluted me and said, "Semper Fi Sergeant Major, that was good work, screw these cowardly, scummy bastards!"

Smiling at him, I replied, "Semper Fi Sir, it was my pleasure. Please step around the garbage." I turned and continued my trip to the baggage room.

Recovering my B-4 bag, I then called Erin. I caught an Eastern Airlines plane for Atlanta, there I changed planes and flew into Fort Lauderdale, Florida. Finally I was home.

Erin and Kathy met me at the airport, and what a happy reunion we had. The house was beautiful, Erin had maintained it superbly.

After a week at home I called the Pentagon and spoke to a Master Sergeant who worked in the Special Forces assignment branch.

I said, "I have orders assigning me to the University of Miami ROTC unit, and I don't want to go there. Can you change the orders and send me back to Fort Bragg?"

He laughed and replied, "Sergeant Major, I have more E-9's and E-8s looking for jobs at Bragg than there are positions. There's no way that you can get there."

Dismayed I replied, "Well, where else can you send me other than to the university?"

He said, "You'll have to take the job there at least until something else comes open. But don't hold your breath, the war in Nam is winding down, and we have a surplus of personnel to deal with."

That really pissed me off, so I replied, "Dammit, don't tell me the fucking war is winding down I just left there. I want out of this damn assignment, so help me!"

He replied, "I can't."

"Let me speak with Ms. Landers!"

"She's not available, she's out of town. Call me again in about two months, and I'll see what I can do for you."

The bastard then hung up.

I was on a thirty day leave, so for the remainder of the month as we approached the holidays were a wonderful happy time for the three of us. I bought a Christmas tree and decorated it Christmas Eve, so when

Kathy got up the next morning her first sight would be of it, and the toys underneath. New Year's Eve I obtained a baby-sitter and Erin and I went to a dinner club over on Fort Lauderdale Beach called Marina Bayside. They had a show, and we enjoyed a delicious seafood dinner. Outside the yachts and smaller boats with all their lights ablaze lent a magical element to the scene. At midnight we all stood and had a drink. The pages of my memory book tugged at me, begging to be opened. I absolutely refused to do so. Instead I had a drink, and kissed Erin as the year 1970, arrived right on time. The holidays came and went.

After New Year's I reported into the University, to the Military Science department and met the senior officer there. The Professor of Military Science was an elderly Colonel. He was of the Infantry branch, so I felt good about that. He had been in the latter stages of World War Two, then Korea, and had been wounded in Vietnam, so we had an awful lot in common. There were three other enlisted men assigned, and a LTC, a Major, and four Captains. It was a large staff to be sure.

My jobs as it turned out was a simple one, ensure efficient administration of the unit, and occasionally teach a class on various military subjects. We had a large number of people, over a thousand in the course. I figured that most of them were trying to avoid the draft.

One day some Hollywood personality showed up on campus and gave a speech. She had quite a turnout, mostly the hippies and other dumb, cowardly types who really had no idea of the world, and what was truly going on. I ignored her and the idiots who attended her talk. They were not worth a minute of my time.

I called Fort Bragg and spoke to TJ, then to Britain, and then I called Hoskins who now was with the 18th Corps. None of them could help as senior NCO's were everywhere looking for an SF assignment.

By early 1972, I'd had my fill of ROTC. President Nixon had ended the draft, and within two weeks our number of students dropped by half. I was right many of them only joined to escape the draft.

I called the Pentagon, and now being out of Special Forces, I had to talk to the Combat Arms Branch. I spoke with some sergeant who told me I could go to Korea. I immediately accepted the assignment.

I went home that evening and told Erin that I was getting orders to go to Korea for a thirteen month assignment. She was upset and distraught at the idea of having to leave our home, and waiting for me once again to return. I understood her situation and her concerns, but I had to get out of that academic environment. I was smothering there, and felt like a scuba diver operating on empty air tanks.

We put our home up for sale, and fortunately the market was receptive. We were able to sell it quickly, and at a nice profit. In a few days my orders came through, so we had all our furniture shipped to Baltimore.

We left and drove up to Fort McPherson in Atlanta, Georgia; there I reenlisted for six more years. I received a small reenlistment bonus which I gave to Erin. We arrived in Baltimore, and spent a few days with her family. Then she rented a small townhouse, and we moved the family in there. I drove down to the Hooligan Inn to see Betty again, and maybe have a few beers together. But it was no more, it had closed, and someone else had another business in its place.

I spent another week with Erin in Baltimore, then I had to catch a plane for Seattle, Washington. She and Kathy took me to the Washington Baltimore Airport where I kissed them both goodbye and quickly boarded the plane. I was never in favor of long drawn out goodbyes, they're too emotional.

I flew nonstop to Seattle and reported into Fort Lewis for further shipment to Korea. The company First Sergeant informed me that I had a four day delay before further movement. I went to the NCO club and drank a few beers. While there I had the brilliant idea to find a phone book and see if I could locate my old friend Ray Washington. I hadn't seen him since he left Wurzburg over twenty years ago. I walked over to the phone booth found the phone book, and thumbed through the W's. Much to my delight I located a Ray Washington listed in one of the suburbs. I called the listed number, and a woman answered the phone identifying herself as his wife. I explained who I was, my name, and my relationship to her husband.

She expressed genuine surprise, and said, "I know you. Ray has spoken so many times about you. Where are you now?"

"I'm in Fort Lewis, and I'm on my way to Korea. I've got three more days here then the plane should be ready to go."

"Oh my! Ray is deer hunting down south in the Woodland area."

"Well, that's too bad. I guess we'll miss each other. I really hate that, it's been so long since we last seen each other."

"Ken, call me early tomorrow morning, he's supposed to call me tonight, and I'll let him know you're here."

"Well, I don't want him to stop his deer hunt. But I'll call you tomorrow morning. If he calls and can't get back, just tell him hello for me, and that I had to Hank Snow to Korea."

She laughed and replied, "I know that expression he told me about it. I'll certainly tell him."

I said my goodbye, and hung up the phone.

I sat back down at the bar and ordered another beer. I thought back across the years to the late forties and early fifties when Ray and I were together in the 6087 Station Complement Unit in Wurzburg, Germany. We had been best friends, and had so much fun together. We were just eighteen years-old, and the world was truly ours. I recalled him wrecking our Jeep, and both of us in the hospital. We had gone to the DP camp together, and I caught gonorrhea. I thought about the two of us getting into fights at the Leopold Bar, and other places. I recalled me telling him about racial conditions in the south that I grew up in. I recalled our First Sergeant Ironjaws tying our Jeep to the metal planking, and daring us to break the string. I remembered our trips to Garmish together, drinking Zugspitz zombies getting drunk, and exchanging bed partners.

We had a lot of great memories together. I hoped he would forget deer hunting and come home. Screw the deer, he could hunt them anytime. I had one more beer then walked over to the barracks where I was assigned for my stay here and went to bed.

I woke up the next morning to the sounds of the bugle playing reveille. My biological clock hadn't made the adjustment to the West coast time, but it really didn't matter. Soon, I would be even more separated from East Coast time. I got out of my bunk and headed for the shower then shaved and dressed. I found the local mess hall, and had a decent breakfast then a couple of cups of coffee.

I now had over twenty years in the army, and could actually retire at any time. But I'm only forty-two-years-old, and still certainly in my opinion, a young man. I finished the coffee, and slowly walked back to my barracks. I was sort of depressed and could think of no reason to be. Of course I hated to leave Erin, and my daughter once again for a year out of our lives, but I had no choice in the matter. I shrugged off the feeling and forced myself to cheer up.

Around nine o'clock in the morning I called Ray's house. He answered the phone, and I recognized his voice immediately.

"Ray, this is Ken, how in the hell are you?"

He laughed and replied, "Ken, you old warhorse, I'm fine, how are you old friend?"

"Ray, I'm well and on my way to Korea. I found your name in the local phone book, and thought I'd call. This is my first chance in years to talk with you."

Ray replied, "I'm so happy that you came through Seattle and Fort Lewis. How long will you be here?"

"I'll be here three more days then I fly out. I hope you didn't stop your deer hunt because of me."

"No, the hunt wasn't that important, I can go anytime, but it's not every day that I get to see an old friend. Where are you I'll come and pick you up?"

"I'm at the replacement company here at Fort Lewis, and that's about all I know. When you get here just stop at the gate and ask the MP, and he'll tell you how to get to the replacement company."

"I'll be there in about an hour, have your stuff ready, and I'll pick you up, you can stay with me for a couple of days."

"Okay, I'll be ready. See you when you get here!"

I walked across the street and saw the First Sergeant.

I told him, "I'm going into Seattle and spend a couple of days with an old army buddy. I'll be back in two days in case you need me for any reason, here's my friend's phone number." I gave him Ray's telephone number.

"Have fun Sergeant Major, and check in with me when you get back," he said.

I went back to the barracks, picked up my shaving kit and a clean set of underwear placing them into my small bag. I then walked over to the mess hall had a cup of coffee and smoked a cigarette.

The head cook came out and sat at the table with me, and wanted to talk about Vietnam. He hadn't been there, so I didn't want to talk to him. I answered a few of his questions then finished my coffee and left.

I walked outside and just looked around the street. The old WW II barracks were still in use, and apparently holding up well. The mess hall was of that vintage, and it appeared good for many more years. I saw this pickup truck drive around the corner and stop at the orderly room. I waited, and sure enough Ray got out of the truck and walked into the orderly room. Shortly thereafter he walked back outside, and by then I was almost at his truck.

He turned in my direction and I said, "Ray, you old bastard here I am!"

He laughed and shouted, "Ken, damn you look good!"

We walked towards each other, and meeting we embraced in a big bear hug then a handshake, and smiles a country mile wide.

"Ray, you look great, it's wonderful to see you again after so many years."

He laughed and replied, "The same for me old friend. I haven't heard from you in a couple of years or so. I was worried since I knew that you were in Vietnam the last time you wrote."

"I apologize for that. The army has kept me on the move and busy, so I let my letter writing slip I guess. The main thing is we finally get together again after about twenty years or so."

We jumped into his small pickup, and he slowly drove off the post. He drove onto either an interstate or parkway, and headed in the direction of Seattle. While driving to his house he asked a million questions. Most of them required too detailed of an answer to fully respond, so I gave partial answers as I knew he would ask them again later. We finally arrived at his house. He had a nice brick home, and a manicured grass front yard. He led the way as we walked into his house.

His wife met us. She said, "Hello Ken, it's really a pleasure to finally meet you." She hugged me then a quick kiss on the cheek.

I smiled and said, "Hello, it's my pleasure meeting you."

Ray led the way into the den area and said, "Ken have a seat, let me have your bag." I handed him my small bag then removed my cap. I took a seat at the small table.

His wife asked, "Would you like a cup of fresh coffee?"

"I surely would."

She sat out three cups and saucers, and then poured out three cups of coffee. The coffee had a tantalizing fresh aroma to it. I poured a small amount of cream from the little pitcher into my cup and stirred it.

Ray took a seat, and then he introduced his wife as Imogene to me.

"Ray, I know her name from your letters years ago. I just wasn't sure if we would ever meet."

We sat and talked for maybe an hour before Imogene said, "Well, I'll leave you two alone to catch up on things; I'll be back in a couple of hours." With that she left and went out the side door.

Ray looked at me and said, "Ken, I don't where to start. Why don't you tell me about yourself, and what all the hell you've been doing since we left Wurzburg."

I replied, "Ray, that's a tall order, and would take my entire two days to do. Let me just hit the highlights for you."

I then told him of my leaving Wurzburg, going home then back to Germany and finding Elona then leaving again. I touched on Vietnam, and then my marriage to Erin. I ended my story by simply saying, "Now I'm going to South Korea for a thirteen month tour, and after that I don't know what'll happen, or where I'll be."

"Oh, I almost forgot, I met First Sergeant Ironjaws Baker again back in 1960, and we spent several hours together. He was retiring after thirty-two years in the army. After he left Wurzburg he went to Korea in 1952, and had gotten wounded for the third time. We had several drinks together, and I was there for his retirement parade."

Ray laughed and said. "Old Ironjaws, I'll never forget him. He was one of a kind."

Smiling I replied, "Yeah, he was surely that."

Ray said, "That money you sent me for my half of the Jeep sure came in handy. I was about broke with no job, and then that money order arrived. That kept me going until I went to work at the aircraft factory."

"Corporal Bell, remember him. He bought our Jeep. I almost got caught like we caught that asshole Sherron," I then explained what had happened.

We sat there and talked the rest of the day. Imogene came back with three young boys. Ray introduced them to me. They were fascinated by the ribbons and badges on my uniform, and the stripes on my sleeve. They were like all young boys, military uniforms, and such things are exciting and mysterious to them.

Imogene made dinner and we all had a regular family dinner. It was a pure delight spending time with Ray and his family. I hoped that someday my family and his could have such a get together, but only my uncertain future would reveal if that were possible.

Around eight o'clock that evening the boys had completed their homework, so they took their baths and went on to bed. Imogene came into the den where Ray and I were still talking, and said she was going out and get us some more beer.

We had polished off the better part of a twelve pack already. She left and shortly returned with a case of beer, placing it in the refrigerator. She joined us for another hour of conversation, and then bid us goodnight.

Ray and I sat there in his den until one o'clock in the morning discussing everything under the sun and drinking beer. We relived all the things that we did so many years earlier. By midnight I think we were both more than a little loaded. I really began to feel the effects of the change in time from the East coast. Finally, we gave it up and both went to bed.

The next day Ray and Imogene gave me a guided tour of Seattle. It was an enjoyable and educational tour. That evening followed the pattern of the previous evening. Ray and I sat there for hours discussing our years together in Germany, our trips to Garmish, friends, and events. Finally, we called it a day and went to bed.

The next morning after showering and shaving, I got dressed and joined the family for breakfast. I shook hands with all the boys, and told them to do well in school, and expressed other proper motivational ideas. Finally, I hugged Imogene, and expressed my pleasure at finally meeting her, and how lucky Ray was to have married such a lovely lady.

She hugged my neck and said, "Be careful, and write to us, and let us know where and how you are."

I assured her I would. Ray and I got into his truck and he drove me back to Fort Lewis and the replacement company. He stopped in front of the company, and we sat and talked a little while.

"Well Ray, I guess I'd better go. I thank you very much for the time I had with you and your family. You have a beautiful family. I'll stay in touch with you, and maybe one of these days we'll all get together again, both of our families."

Ray looked at me, and then sort of choked up a bit said, "Ken, you're still my best friend ever. Take care of yourself and stay in touch, give my regards to Erin and the little girl."

We shook hands, and I got out of the truck. He restarted his motor and slowly drove away. I watched as his truck drove out of sight. I thought my old friend of my youth, very much the same, and yet so different now from then. I knew that I too had matured, and aged in both years and thought since those long ago carefree days in occupied Germany. I also thought how lucky I am to once again meet an old friend of mine from so long ago.

My plane took off that evening, and some ten hours later I landed in Seoul, Korea. We were then trucked to the 2nd Infantry Division replacement company. I stayed there two days and was interviewed by the Division G-3 Operations Officer.

I explained to him that I'd been in Special Forces for fourteen years. I really had no idea of the composition of an infantry division, and I didn't want to be the Operations Sergeant of the division. He was a former Special Forces officer, and agreed with me. He suggested that I take the position of Operations Sergeant of the 3rd Brigade in the division. I quickly accepted that.

The next day I was driven out to Camp Howze, and to the headquarters of the brigade. There I reported in and met the brigade commander, and then the brigade sergeant major. I was introduced to the brigade operations officer and his small staff. I felt fairly comfortable in Korea, as I remembered some of the area studies I had completed years earlier while in the Special Forces Group on Okinawa.

The following week I read the mission of the unit then determined what the operations section was required to do. I checked out all out communications equipment, and interviewed all the assigned personnel. Most of the men in the brigade were draftees, and true to form many of them didn't want to be in Korea, neither did they want to be in the army. That wasn't unusual. I would just have to work with them, and do the best that I could. We went on several exercises, and I was able to better ascertain the quality of the personnel I had.

About three months after I arrived in country the brigade commander, and the brigade sergeant major both rotated back to the states. We got another full Colonel as the commander, a West Point officer named William Green, and he was a damn good one. He proved to be one of the best Colonel's I'd ever met.

I was assigned temporary duty as the brigadc sergeant major until the new command sergeant major arrived. The job certainly had its drawbacks. I spent the first hour, and sometimes two hours each morning escorting soldiers into see the commander for disciplinary problems. Six days a week I did that, everything from fighting in the village, to drunk on duty, to possession and use of drugs. It was an absolute nightmare.

I often wondered how in the hell would First Sergeant Ironjaws Baker have handled these troops.

Colonel Green was a splendid commander, fair, totally military. But we both were fighting a losing battle with the troops we had assigned. I was on the promotion list to become Command Sergeant Major, and I hoped that the new sergeant major would show up before I was promoted.

The last of our army combat troops had been withdrawn from Vietnam earlier this year. The last combat unit was the Special Forces Command and Control North, and I knew in my mind that the South Vietnamese army couldn't hold out. That left a bitter taste. I knew too many good men had died, and even more had suffered injuries to let it all go down the damn drain as the politicians were doing.

I received a letter from a friend of mine back at Fort Bragg telling me that my old friend Sergeant Major Billy Walton had retired at Fort Bragg in February, and had conducted a freefall jump on his retirement day. I was very glad that he had made it all the way through, but I hated like hell to see him leave the active duty ranks.

Part of my job was teaching a class on equal opportunity and race relations every Saturday. It was an easy class to teach, but the young soldiers were bored stiff. Race relations in the division, and in the brigade were certainly not the best; in fact they were the worst I had ever seen or experienced. But we did with what we had. I remained in the command job for four months, and finally the new guy showed up.

We got a Command Sergeant Major Charles Jacobs who had extensive combat experience going back to the Korean War plus Nam. He had been in Special Forces for several years, but I had never met him. Special Forces during the war had grown from a few hundred to several thousand, so the days of knowing almost everyone in Special Forces had long since vanished. We quickly became friends on a first name basis. I returned to my operations job, and I also managed to spend considerable time up on the demilitarized zone with the brigades Infantry Battalion.

Meanwhile, I wrote daily to Erin, and encouraged her to be patient, that I'd be home in a few months and we'd be together again. I truly missed her and Kathy. That was the worst part, missing out on so much of their lives. I mailed Christmas cards and presents home to them both, but that was at best a poor substitute for not being there.

In June, I was sitting at my desk in the operations section when my phone rang. I picked it up and Erin was on the line. I was shocked that she had called me, and that she had been able to reach me in my office. After greeting her I could tell by the tone in her voice that something was amiss.

"Erin, something's wrong what's going on, is Kathy alright?"

She said, "Yes, Kathy is fine and growing bigger. I need to talk to you. I had a phone call yesterday from some ROTC sergeant in Wisconsin, who said he wanted to welcome us to the university there. I had no idea what he was talking about. Do you know anything about us going to Wisconsin?"

I was stunned and replied, "No darling. I have no idea what they're talking about. I have four more months left here, and I haven't received orders for anywhere." Pausing for a moment I said, "I'll call the Pentagon Monday, and find out about this. For sure I know nothing about it."

She said, "Ken, I don't want to go to Wisconsin. I won't go there! I want no part of Wisconsin. When you call the Army, tell them we don't want to go there."

I assured her that I'd definitely do that, and promised her we wouldn't go to Wisconsin.

She gave me a kiss over the phone then hung up.

I was totally amazed that someone would call my wife, and tell her I had orders for a university in Wisconsin. Especially since no one had advised me, and I had no orders for such an assignment. I had absolutely no intention of going back into ROTC, and certainly not to Wisconsin. ROTC is a wonderful program, but not for me.

That night there was a big fight in the enlisted men's club. It degenerated into a bad racial problem. The MP's came and locked up about a dozen men from the unit. The commander, Colonel Green, the brigade sergeant major, and I were there trying to quell the problem. Finally, it ended, and the Colonel closed the club for the evening. I thought this isn't the army that I know. I was disgusted with the quality of most of the men we had in the outfit. The draft was over, but it would be a while before the volunteer army concept would be fully in place. Until then the dregs of the draft would have to serve out their enlistments, and the army would continue to suffer.

Monday morning I called the Pentagon and spoke to some master sergeant in the combat arms section.

I said, "This is Sergeant Major Fisher in the 2nd Infantry Division in Korea. I've been told that I may be coming out on orders for some ROTC unit, at a university in Wisconsin, and I want to check it out."

He replied, "Let me check, hold on for a moment."

I waited and waited and finally he came back on line and asked

"Are you Kenneth Fisher?"

"Yes."

"Yeah, you're on orders for ROTC duty in Wisconsin."

"I don't want that assignment; I want to go to Fort Bragg."

He laughed and said, "Sorry, there are no vacant non airborne E-9 slots at Fort Bragg, they are all filled."

I replied, "I'm on the promotion list for Command Sergeant Major, I don't need to go to an ROTC unit, that doesn't fit my rank."

He then got snotty and said, "Sergeant Major, you have to take that job until you get promoted, or else retire!"

I took a deep breath and replied, "Listen you leg son-of-a-bitch, I won't take that frigging job. If I have to, I'll fucking retire! With assholes like you in the puzzle palace personnel section, I don't need this bullshit anymore. I'll see you in the Pentagon. When I leave here I'm coming there, I'll get those fucking orders changed!"

I slammed the phone down. I walked across the street and spoke to the brigade office clerk, and instructed him to type up my request for retirement, just leave the retirement date blank.

That afternoon I was told to report to the brigade commander. I checked in with Jacobs then reported to the commander.

Colonel Green said, "Have a seat Sergeant Major."

I sat down in the small chair in front of his desk. I noticed that he had my request in front of him.

He asked "Why are you requesting retirement now? I thought you would at least stay in for twenty-six years."

I replied, "Sir, I want to stay in for thirty, but they're sending me to an ROTC unit in Wisconsin until I get promoted to Command Sergeant Major. I really don't want any part of ROTC, and the university scene, and no damn part of Wisconsin."

He replied, "That would probably be for only a few months, and then you would be reassigned as soon as you are promoted."

"That's true, but I missed one year out of my wife and little daughter's life in Nam, another one here in Korea, they're now in Baltimore. I would have to move them to Wisconsin, and then a little later move them again to wherever the Army sends me. My daughter's schooling would be all fucked up, and it would be just one move after another. The army has multiple problems coming out of Nam, and it's changing with the volunteer army coming in. I'm not sure that I fit any longer; maybe it's time that I retired."

Taking a deep breath I continued, "I'm from the old army school of discipline, and today that doesn't seem to fit any more. So maybe it's time for me to go."

He replied, "It's true, the army is changing, and discipline isn't what it was, or what it should be, and what it will be again. But the army needs the institutional knowledge that you have, and can carry forward into the volunteer army concept."

"Sir, I understand that and agree with you. But there are other younger men than I that will pick up the load and make it all work. We always have, and hopefully we always will."

Colonel Green gave me a long look and said, "All right Sergeant Major, I'll sign your papers if you're sure that's what you want."

"If I can get my orders changed I'll stay in, otherwise I'll go." I stood up and said, "Colonel, that's what I want."

I then saluted him, he returned my salute. I did an about face and left his office.

That night I went to the little club, and the brigade sergeant major and I, with a couple of master sergeants tried to drink the club dry. We were unable to do so, and the next morning I had one horrible headache and hangover. I knew that I would live however; too many headaches and hangovers in the past gave me that knowledge.

CHAPTER 44

Leaving the land of the morning calm

My day to leave finally arrived, and Jacob using the Old Man's sedan drove me down to Seoul to catch my flight.

As we rode along he said, "Ken, I don't blame you for retiring, this will be my last tour also. I have twenty-seven years in now, and I've about had enough. The army is really changing, and it has problems now that we never had before. It'll take a long time to recover from Nam"

I replied, "Well, the army is definitely changing, and the all volunteer army is on the way, and I really don't think that I truly fit in anymore. I've had a ball and enjoyed every bit of it. I have seen quite a bit of the world, and made hundreds of friends. I wouldn't change a thing in my career, even if I could. All that I am, and all that I'll ever be, I owe to the Army. I left the cotton fields of Alabama a dumb ass kid, and now it's time to leave the Army."

Arriving at the airport, he stopped and let me out. We shook hands and I thanked him for driving me down.

He said, "I'll see you back in Fayetteville one of these days."

I nodded in agreement and said, "You bet."

We then wished each other the best of luck, and he slowly drove away. I walked into the terminal, checked my baggage and still had a one hour wait before boarding the plane. I walked over to one of the concession stands, bought a Korean beer had a seat and lit a cigarette. I slowly drank the beer and smoked maybe two cigarettes as I watched the troops passing through the terminal. It was all so familiar, so many different airports in so many different countries, over so many years. Finally, we boarded the plane, and the big jet roared down the runway, we were airborne.

I had pushed the seat back and fallen asleep, and even though lightly sleeping I felt someone tapping me on the shoulder, and a voice said "Would you like something to drink Sergeant Major?"

I opened my eyes. Startled, I stared at the hostess. I realized where I was and said, "Yes, I'd like a cup of coffee."

She poured a small cup and handed it to me. I thanked her and slowly drank the coffee. I lit a cigarette and stared out the window at the ocean thirty-nine thousand feet below. I thought about the time back in 1959, when the aircraft load master and I had made a tunnel check out in the wing of an old C-124 high above this same ocean. I smiled at the memory, put out my cigarette, and closing my eyes again, I fell asleep.

My memory book swung wide open, and the memories returned in a vengeful rush, the sounds of the plane, and of my fellow passengers faded away. I seemed to be all by myself, alone somewhere in an undefined, indescribable place. The memories of twenty-four years of military service, all indelible impressions, began a stampede across the vast stage of my mind.

I saw again the frozen paratrooper swaying gently in the wind, as he hung in a tree somewhere in the wilds of Alaska. I recalled my first boat trip across the Atlantic, and my arrival in Germany so many years ago. I felt the blowing snow, the hard wooden train seats, and the novelty of it all. I recalled all my friends from my first unit, and the fun we had shared. I remembered most of the women I had known, and the two that I had loved, and wondered where are they now? I thought about the two boys that I had fathered in Germany. They are both grown men now. I hope they're good men, one is I know for sure, but they will never know me.

Deep into my reveries the numbers of people and events that paraded across the stage from my memory book seemed endless. I tried to reconstruct the years that certain events had occurred, and the people I had met, or places I had visited during a particular time frame. I was unable to do so as the memories surged forward so rapidly.

I pictured once again the multicolored tulip fields in Holland, and in the next second the face of a dead Viet Cong with half his head blown off. I could see my 1937 Mercedes convertible as it sat smoldering totally destroyed, and then the endless snow covered Alp Mountains of Germany. It was as if I had unleashed a torrent of memories, and had lost all control over them.

The battle scarred face of First Sergeant Ironjaws Baker loomed large as he chewed me out for some misstep.

Back from across the years, and countless pages of my memory book they rushed. I saw once more the tear-stained beautiful face of Elona as we said goodbye. Next, the smile of my son Kenny, as he laughed saluted me, and wished me good luck. Then the deep lines of worry on Captain Leadenham's face as he surveyed our jungle camp after we had been almost overrun.

I visualized again the snuff dipping deputy sheriff in Lillington, North Carolina, when I got Art Taylor out of jail.

Once again, I saw the large, ghostly, empty picture window in Hitler's Eagle Nest, the beauty of the Zugspitz in Garmisch, and the squalor in the streets of Colon, Panama.

I heard again the green tracer bullet rounds as they zinged and cracked above my head smashing through our building, and chewing through sandbags. I felt the numbness in my arm, and saw the blood gushing as it poured from my hand, and remembered the confusion in my conscious mind caused by an exploding grenade.

The smiling face of the Texas highway patrolman as he drank from my bottle of scotch whiskey loomed vividly in my memory.

I could feel the bite of leeches as they sucked and feasted on the blood from my feet and legs, and I felt once more the agonizing pain of a punjii stake slicing deeply into my ankle. I shivered again from the frigid cold air in the moonless night sky high above the rice paddies of South Korea waiting to jump from the plane.

I heard someone saying excitedly, "Wake up Sergeant Major, wake up, wake up!"

Groggily, I raced back through a darkened landscape. Vines and thorns tearing at me; dodging native chiefs swinging long sharp swords; screaming Viet Cong banishing AK-47's; jumping over punjii stake pits as large orange and red tiger eyes glowed menacingly at me in the darkness; fat blood-gorged leeches falling freely from my legs saturated and satiated with my blood.

Confused and disoriented, I opened my eyes, and the stewardess' face slowly came into focus. She had a small towel and began wiping my face.

With a look of deep concern on her face she said, "You must have had a nightmare, you were moaning, and talking, and thrashing around, you're wet with sweat."

Taking the small towel from her I said, "Thank you, I'm fine, perhaps just a bad dream. May I have a cup of coffee please?"

I wiped the sweat from my face, my hands were shaking. She brought me a small cup of coffee, and I spilled half of it. Holding the cup with both hands I drank the remainder, and smoked a cigarette. I then walked to the bathroom, washed my face combed my short hair, and returned to my seat. I checked my watch I had been asleep for hours. I was still wet with sweat. I think I must have relived my entire army career. It was all so vivid, so undeniably real. The deeply suppressed memories of so much death, destruction, devastation and desolation may return again someday, but for today the Vietnam War is finally over for me.

CHAPTER 45

My long journey ends

The remainder of the flight was uneventful. We landed in San Francisco, and as usual the troops disappeared as they rushed from one terminal to another, and from one airline to the next. I bought a ticket to Washington National Airport.

About two hours before my flight I called Erin she was at the apartment. The sound of her voice was absolute music to my thirsty ears. I told her how much I loved her and wanted to see her. Then I told her what flight I would be on, and my expected time of arrival in Washington on the early bird flight. I explained that I was going to the Pentagon, and then would catch a bus over to Baltimore.

Before my flight left, I walked into an airport bar and ordered a glass of beer. I lit a cigarette and thought about my old friend Sam Amato, who had reenlisted with me way back in 1953. From his infrequent letters I learned that he had gone to Vietnam for a year, and later had served a couple of tours of duty back in Germany. He had married a German girl, and they now have three children. He's stationed at Fort Polk, Louisiana, a Master Sergeant, and planning to stay for thirty years in the Army. I shook my head in amazement at the turn our lives had taken. I haven't seen him in twenty years, and yet we both were in the Army. Destiny does play some weird tricks on us all.

Finally, I caught my flight and was airborne once again. I had a seat by the window up near the front of the aircraft. I pushed the seat back into a reclining position and just relaxed. I knew that we had about three or more hours ahead of us.

We arrived in Chicago on time, and I changed planes for the final leg into National Airport. The flight wasn't that bad, and we arrived in Washington about seven-thirty in the morning. I caught a taxi over to the Pentagon. After asking several people for directions, I finally found my way into the Combat Arms Branch, and the Enlisted Personnel Assignment Section.

I met and talked to a Master Sergeant who told me flat out he couldn't help me get my orders changed. He denied being the Master Sergeant I had spoken to from Korea.

I then was introduced to a Lieutenant Colonel. I again explained my situation, and why I didn't want to go to Wisconsin. I pleaded my case with all the military dignity, logic and passion I could muster.

He listened patiently, and at the end of my presentation, he said, "Sergeant Major, I understand your position completely, I agree with all your reasons and logic for not going to Wisconsin, but it's no use. I can't change your orders. You know as well as I do that the Army is over strength, and we're looking for positions to place Sergeants Major and Command Sergeants Major. We don't have enough positions to accommodate them all. We're putting them into pigeon holes trying to save them."

I realized that further argument was futile. I had to either eat crap, or fulfill the threat I had made. I opened my briefcase and extracted my request for retirement. I filled in the requested retirement date, and signed the form. I extended it to the Lieutenant Colonel, he accepted it, looked at the form and remarked, "This is most unusual, but I'll make it work for you."

I had requested retirement at Fort Bragg, with a retirement date of November 30, 1973.

He said, "You can go ahead to Baltimore, your orders will be there next week. You'll retire at Fort Bragg the end of this month. I'm sorry that we couldn't make it work out for you, I hope you realize that."

Standing up I said, "Thanks anyway Colonel. It's time I called it a day and retired. I appreciate your interest and your efforts." We shook hands and I walked away.

I had finally made the hard decision, my last official decision as an Army Sergeant Major. I would retire rather than accept an assignment that I didn't want. Refusing to accept and obey official army orders was a completely new and foreign concept for me. A feeling of revulsion swept over me, I felt nauseous.

Even though I understand the army's position, they don't give a damn about mine. The army is an undemocratic world unto itself, and I'm part of that world. I should accept the Army's decision. At my rank, and years of service, if I disagree with the Army's decision, then I only have left the choice of retirement. There is no permissible, acceptable compromise. I completely accept that! First Sergeant Ironjaws Baker was right, as part of the military system I had to make it all work. What a system, help make it work, support it, be a part of it, or get the fuck out! I totally agree with that philosophy.

I left the Pentagon and caught a taxi to the local bus station. I bought a ticket to Baltimore, and then I called Erin and told her the time I would arrive in Baltimore at the bus station.

Arriving at the Baltimore bus station I immediately saw the love of my life Erin, and my daughter Kathy. We rushed into an embrace as I hugged and kissed her with all the pent up passion I had in me. She returned my kiss with equal fervor and emotion.

I then picked up my small daughter, and kissed her as she kept saying, "My daddy's home, my daddy's home!"

I kissed her again and said, "Kathy, your daddy is home to stay, I'll never leave you again."

I then recovered my B-four bag from the baggage section. We walked outside the terminal and I spotted our Pontiac, the car really looked good, and I couldn't wait to drive it again.

I said, "Erin, darling you had best drive the car for now, besides you know the way, and I may be a little rusty driving in the states."

She laughed with that well remembered lilt to her voice and replied, "Darling, I'll drive you anywhere you want just as long as you're with us." I leaned over and kissed her tenderly on the cheek.

Little Kathy sitting on my lap said, "Kiss me daddy." I then kissed her.

I had fifteen days leave, so for the next two weeks we all became reacquainted with each other. Kathy was in the second grade in school, and Erin and I had the entire day to our selves. We took her mom and dad out to lunch and to dinner several times. It was a nice family reunion for all of us.

Erin's mom was happy to keep Kathy as Erin and I planned to drive to Fort Bragg for my retirement. Kathy's school was only two blocks away, so it was no big deal for her mom. I packed only the necessary uniform for myself, and Erin took only what she would need as we loaded up my car for the drive. I wore comfortable civilian clothes. I called down to Fort Bragg and made motel reservations at the small motel that the NCO club operated.

I kissed Kathy goodbye. Then I drove through the Harbor Tunnel, out of Baltimore and onto interstate ninety-five south. It was really an easy drive around Washington, down through Virginia, and then into North Carolina.

The trees in beautiful fall colors were alive, displaying and flaunting their natural beauty. Like native Hawaiian dancers, the trees were swaying and dancing in the light breeze, shimmering in their multicolored costumes.

We had left early, so we arrived at Fort Bragg early in the afternoon. I checked into the motel then I unloaded the car. Erin and I walked up to the club and into the lobby.

The Master of Arms, a tall black Sergeant First Class, asked me for my club card and my ID card. Anticipating this I showed him my military ID card, and my club membership card dated April 1965.

He smiled, handing both cards back to me shook my hand and said, "Welcome back to Fort Bragg, Sergeant Major."

Erin and I had a beer, and then returned to the room. She took a bath and I showered. I put on fresh civilian clothes for the evening. It was chilly, so we both wore warmer clothes than earlier in the day. We walked up to the dining room of the club, and the hostess seated us at a table for dinner. I ordered a scotch and water for myself and a gin and tonic for Erin.

As we sat there having a drink in walked my old friend Billy Bowles with his wife. He immediately came over to my table, and we introduced our wives to each other. Joining us he and I shook hands with a bear hug, what a delight to see him again. He, like me, now had mostly gray hair, and had recently retired as a Sergeant Major.

Shortly thereafter Vince and Harriet came in and joined us. Then Herb and Martha came in, and our table now expanded to two. Little Mac walked in with his wife Susan, joining us as the table grew larger once again. Jim and Emanuell joined us much to my delight. The drinks flowed freely as excited conversations echoed and bounced across and around the tables. Ralph Slaughter and his wife Shirley joined us at the table. I listened and watched my old friends as they conversed, and watched their wives as they participated in animated conversations. Bert, Bob and Doug came by and we exchanged greetings and handshakes.

My old friends Earl, Gene and Steve stopped by and said hello, as we shook hands, and exchanged bear hugs once more. What stories we four could tell, if we were allowed. Art Taylor and his lovely wife joined us. He and I made asses of ourselves as we greeted each other. It was a wonderful evening. We now had three tables filled with many of my oldest friends and their wives.

I thought, *this is the way it's supposed to be. Retire with all your old friends from so many years present to share in the joy and happiness of the moment. Only in Special Forces could this happen.*

We all ordered dinner, and continued to drink and talk as we caught up on the years we had been in different countries, with different missions, at different times around the world. I was drinking scotch and water, and that might have been too strong of a drink for me, but it taste delicious as always, and contributed to my personal warm feelings.

The evening drew to a close, and we gradually began leaving the club, all going our separate ways. Erin had an arm around me as we slowly walked down by the swimming pool, and into our motel room. For the next three days we continued to run into so many of my old friends. Many were still recovering from war wounds suffered earlier in the jungles and rice paddies of Vietnam, Cambodia and Laos.

It was a homecoming for me, and an introduction for Erin into the military brotherhood of the Special Forces soldier. I think at this point in time she fully realized and recognized the undeniable, unexplainable, and unbreakable bond that existed between we who had served together so long, and depended so often on each other for our lives, was one that could neither be denied, diluted, nor dissolved.

Finally, my day of retirement arrived. I woke up early that morning in the motel room. I got up and made a small pot of coffee. As Erin slept I sat in the corner easy chair, smoked a cigarette and sipped a cup of black coffee. I could feel a sense of nervousness creeping over me as I realized that today is my final day in the Army. My plans for the future vague and nebulous, but at the moment such plans weren't of immediate concern.

I kept a tight grip on my book of memories, and just recalled the memory of me as a young farm boy when I first enlisted in 1948.

Fresh from the cotton fields in Alabama, ignorant of the world and its ways, innocent to the temptations of the flesh, impatient to see and experience all this crazy world had to offer.

Had I made a difference in someone's life? I didn't know if I had been a success or a failure in that regard. But one thing for sure I had enjoyed it all. I wouldn't trade one day of my life for any other. I didn't regret any of the things I'd done, only those things that I hadn't done.

I was now almost forty-four-years-old, and my journey had started out at eighteen, a mere teenager. From the cotton fields of Alabama to the Alp Mountains of Europe, across the ridges and rivers of Central America, and through the jungles and rice paddies of Southeast Asia I had traveled, with several other countries mere pit stops along the way.

From a teenager to middle age I had followed the path of the soldier, and now it was all coming to an end. It had started at Fort Jackson, South Carolina, and was now ending just a couple hundred miles to the north at Fort Bragg, North Carolina—fitting perhaps.

I thought of the many friends that I had lost. Many of them will never return home, never know the pleasure of completing a military career. Many of them listed as missing in action, and for too many their bodies never recovered. *But all of them will in my memory book be forever young! For me, they'll never grow old; never get sick, feeble, or diseased. They're always and forever—on a classified mission—somewhere. They'll always remain young and eager Special Forces soldiers pursuing their mission to the end, even though the end is known!*

I had a sip of coffee, and squinting through the spiraling cigarette smoke I thought, what will I take with me from this career? Oddly, I recalled a quotation by Socrates: "The unexamined life is not worth living!"

I grew up in the Army. I achieved a degree of education, and I learned that people are much the same all over the world. I learned to hate prejudice, bigotry and liars, and to love those things that are right and just. I learned that some men are shallow and flimsy, and others deep, reflective, profound.

I'll also take with me the friendship of dozens and dozens of men with whom I've served in both the best and worst of conditions and locations. I served, lived and fought with the best that America has to offer. I thought about all the years, and the many esoteric, arcane things that we did together and separately. They were all unique in their own way.

Billy Walton came to mind. He fought in Korea, and served several years in Nam, and survived the award of multiple purple hearts. My friend Steve who participated in most of the 17 campaigns conducted in Vietnam, and very highly decorated several times over. Art Taylor survived Korea, several tours to Nam and had numerous combat decorations. Joe Marino, survived the D-Day jump into France and then into Holland, Bastogne and the Battle of the Bulge during World War Two, a combat jump into Korea, and numerous tours to Nam, very highly decorated, and universally admired. Major James Larson, with a large family gave his all in defense of freedom. Each of them was unique.

All of us volunteers, and all were united in our desire to serve and protect our country and way of life. Yes, I'll take many more things from this career than I ever brought to the Army at its inception.

The war in Vietnam is over for us; the army is standing down and regrouping. For us in Special Forces it was a long one. Eleven years from 1961 to 1972, longer for us, and the United States than World War One and World War Two combined.

We fought long and hard, and for far too many it was the end of the trail. The end results did not equal the costs. I reached over and pulled my wallet from my pants, extracting a worn card that I carried with me. The little card had typed on it a quotation by John Stuart Mills, the English author and philosopher. In the dim light from the bathroom, I read it quietly, softly, out loud to myself.

"War is an ugly thing, but not the ugliest of things. The decayed and degraded state of moral and patriotic feeling which thinks that nothing is worth war is much worse. The person who has nothing for which he is willing to fight, nothing which is more important that his own personal safety, is a miserable creature and has no chance of being free unless made and kept so by the exertions of better men than himself."

What brilliant logic. All the hippies, Hollywood shit heads, amoral politicians, and media freaks that ranted and railed against the war and the military, all did so while hiding behind our Constitution which gives them the right to debase and defile it. In my opinion, they seem too stupid to realize that if they lived under a communist, fascist or a theocratic society, they would be the first ones—the very first one's—eliminated.

Erin woke up, and I gave her a cup of coffee. She smiled and said, "Thanks sweetheart, are you nervous?"

"No darling, it's a day that had to come, and a day that I've looked forward to. So I have no reason to be nervous."

I lied!

Smiling she replied "Why then are you sitting here in the dark, drinking coffee and smoking cigarettes?"

I laughed and said, "It's because I didn't want to wake you up, and that's the only reason."

I lied again.

The retirement ceremony was scheduled for eleven o'clock in the morning, so we had lots of time to get dressed and have breakfast. My uniform was freshly pressed, and my boots were like a piece of glass. I had always prided myself on my appearance, and today I had to be perfect. I checked and rechecked my uniform. All my combat awards and decorations were in place and in order. My Combat Infantryman's Badge sat on top of it all. My master paratrooper wings, my Korean wings and other badges were perfect. I was ready!

Erin and I walked up to the dining room and had breakfast. We returned to our room and I placed our bags in the trunk of the car. I then checked out of the motel, and slowly drove up to the parade field at Corps Headquarters. I walked out to the parade field and met the officer in charge of the parade and ceremonies. There were five other soldiers retiring on the same day, and a battalion would be marching by in review.

Erin took her place in the seats alongside the parade platform with the guests, other wives, and family members of those retiring. I stepped up on the platform and found my place in the line of soldiers retiring. The band began to play several ever so familiar John Phillips Sousa musical pieces.

The officer in charge began to read the records of the soldiers retiring, and then he began to read out mine. I closed my ears and thought about my old friend Command Sergeant Major "Ironjaws"

Baker, who had retired some thirteen years earlier, and wondered how he felt, and what he thought, as his thirty-two year record of military service was highlighted. Your written record only highlights the major events in your career, it doesn't even begin to relate all the wild, weird, wonderful things that happened in your journey along the way—it really can't.

He finished reading my record and moved on to the next person in line. I had heard very little of what he had said about me. The battalion then began to pass in review. As the national colors passed the reviewing stand, I saluted. I felt a deep sense of personal pride. I knew that for twenty-four years I had tried my best, I had given it my youth, my all. The emotions I felt were ineffable.

As I stood there in the cool, crisp morning air, the sunbeams filtering through the trees danced across the parade field, and onto the band's polished musical instruments reflecting back even more light on this solemn ceremony. I thought, again of my military hero since childhood, General of the Army Douglas MacArthur, when he addressed Congress and told them that: "Old soldiers never die, they just fade away!" Now it's my turn, just another old soldier, I'll just fade away.

The ceremony ended, and I was officially retired. I walked off the platform and into the arms of the love of my life, Erin. She hugged and kissed me, then brushed away the few tears that had silently gathered on my cheeks. We turned and slowly walked away. We reached our car. Stopping, I looked around the area. I loved Fort Bragg. The Fort so vibrant and alive had played such a meaningful and pivotal role in my life.

Back through the Smoke Bomb Hill area, turning left past my old wooden barracks, past the club annex now a Chaplain's office; slowly passing the old parachute shed then reaching Bragg Boulevard, I left Fort Bragg.

My long journey from the cotton fields of Alabama had crossed the world's great oceans, touched several continents, then returned me back safely to my beloved Southland had finally ended.

I closed this Chapter in my memory book!

Back in Baltimore a few weeks later, I sat on the sparkling white marble steps at my in-laws house, watching the kids play in the street, and civilians going about their different ways. I was rather depressed, as I knew that the exciting world of soldiering had ended for me. No more wars to fight, no more classified missions, no parachute jumps, no more excitement; or so I thought.

I heard the phone ring in the house, and then Erin came to the front door.

"Ken, you have a phone call from someone in Washington."

Jim Newton, an old ex-Special Forces friend of mine was on the line.

"Hello Jim, what a nice surprise! What's on your mind?"

I knew that Jim worked in some capacity for the agency. I listened intrigued as he outlined a job. He went into great detail about the position, the pay, the challenges, the dangers, the requirements, and the responsibilities. It was a stateside assignment.

It was an answer to my future, it was an opportunity to use my experience and knowledge in service to my country once again, only in a different role.

I ended the phone call with, "Jim, I'll take the job, when and where do I report?"

THE END